YEARWOOD

'Distinguished by an aptness of style capable of giving the events an aura of mythic, dark importance, this is one of the best high fantasies in some time.'

UNDERSEA

'This has all the weight and mythological resonance missing from most adult fantasy these days.'

WINTERKING

'Dark and intriguing, at once familiar and strange . . .'

Publishers Weekly

The Finnbranch

PAUL HAZEL

SPHERE BOOKS LIMITED

First published in this edition by
Sphere Books Ltd 1986
27 Wrights Lane, London W8 5TZ
Yearwood first published in Great Britain
by Sphere Books Ltd 1983
Undersea first published in Great Britain
by Sphere Books Ltd 1983
Winterking first published in Great Britain
by Sphere Books Ltd 1986
Copyright © 1980, 1982 and 1985 by Paul E. Hazel

Set in 11/12 pt Compugraphic Bem

Printed and bound in Great Britain by
Collins, Glasgow

For Karen, for Sara and for Tom
and for Natalie Greenberg

ACKNOWLEDGMENTS

I would like to express my thanks to Barbara Cizik, who deciphered the manuscript and typed it; to my editor, Natalie Greenberg, for her enthusiasm and guidance; and to my copyeditor, Elisabeth Gleason Humez, for her good counsel. Whatever confusion and error remain are at my insistence.

Ah, it's a long stage, and no inn in sight, and night coming and the body cold.
– Herman Melville
  in a letter to Nathaniel Hawthorne

CONTENTS

Yearwood

PART I

The Winter Brood

CHAPTER ONE

My mother and her women are of the bitter lineage of the Selchie, the spawn of sealmen and shore folk. In their blood the memory of the undersea kingdoms still rages. In their dreams they still lust for the whiskered and webfooted men who mounted their long dead grandmothers on the shores around Hren and at Weeds in the broad days at the world's beginning. Or so it was whispered in kitchens and halls, a song to keep time with the churning, the pitchers upended, the sour loaves rising like summer mold in the pans. The words floated up to the bedlofts. The eager girls listened and gazed remotely at shapes in the straw.

I thought it foolishness. But there were women enough in those years, crones with their crows' looks, maids with wet eyes, who against hope and all reason still set out from our hill kingdoms and made the hard journey to the coast. There they sat on the shore; the black waves rolled in on them. But if the sealmen ever returned, I had not heard of it. Yet Yllvere – my mother as the servants tell it – settled down at first more readily than Urien's other women. Urien – who was not my father – took her to his bed when she had barely begun her courses.

At the start he was pleased with her and her proud looks, her hair yellow as beer. He married her the next year on the Eve of Teimhne, defying the auguries. Teimhne, according to the old Kell reckoning, was the first night of winter and, with the last loss of light, a time of dread. But Urien hated the women's gods. He scoffed at their mysteries. He had spend his youth in the South, where a man's word was foremost and kings held the law. He had only scorn for the Northmen. When even his housethralls complained to him, huddling before the hall fire on his wedding night, sulking and afraid behind their shields, he laughed at them. They begged him to reconsider. He puffed his hairy cheeks and swore. Though a soldier, he was not unlearned. He had kept watch of the stars and understood the progress of seasons. The Kell cannot count, he said. He would have left it at that had they let him.

Yllvere was his third wife and his last. The others had died soon after their weddings though the wise Kell had held those days to be blessed.

The first wife collapsed from fever, the second from a fit which came upon her soon after the birth of the one true heir of the house. The boy was a winter child and sickly, with a birthmark the shape of a horn on his shoulder. The women howled when they saw it and scattered like geese to the hall.

In the evening his mother strangled him. When the servants came to the chamber, her eyes showed only the whites and her mouth foamed. Urien sent the corpse back to her people without guard or ceremony. He had her driven in a plain farmer's cart down to the coast. He refused to pay the price of the burial. Little else was talked of that winter. When Yllvere entered the house, she feared him. She did what he asked and bore him three daughters in as many years. Quickly and silently she bore them, as the aurochs calve in their stalls, her arms folded and nothing in her eyes. But, by all accounts, the wildness in her was merely waiting.

Our house was Morrigan, a seat between the twin peaks of Géar Finn – the highest point in the West. To the east one could look down on a broad plain scattered with river towns and, if one's eyes were keen, to the place where rivers met. There the High King raised Tinkern, the last of godshrines, and Ormkill, the great hall from which, in better days, he ruled. That was a gentle country, worn smooth by its rivers. There the yews grew thick and the furze bloomed golden in April. There, at the river's edge, it was said, every field swelled ripe with barley. On those hillsides the bees were no longer wild but lived, content, in wicker houses set out by men whose dogs, both winter and summer, slept indoors and underfoot. When I was young, such tales seemed strange to me.

Ours was a harder, more ancient land – its rough peaks broken by storms. Our roads, such as they were, had come down from kingdoms now vanished. They were old and narrow. The passes cut through the hills were treacherous, for the stonework was crude and rockslides frequent. Since their making they had never been mended. The guard towers that lined the cliffs had not been manned in the memory of our people. Even Urien's books despaired of true knowledge of them. They spoke of their builders as giants and their fashioning as sorcery. But to my mind such talk was foolishness. Magicians would have built better roads.

To the west were the sea lands which were so often on the tongues of the women. But they were many days' journey from Morrigan. From the battlements, looking out between the teeth of stone or higher up in the house from Urien's walk, where – an old man in the years I knew him – he read in good light and bad from the books of the wars, one could never see the rolling ocean nor the islands off the coast. But from Géar Finn, from the dark wood on the mountainside, Grieve, my sister, said one might truly see them and the ruined towers at the river's mouth and, if the day were clear, the masts of dragon ships that floated in the harbor. I never doubted this, though I knew soon enough that her thin legs had never carried her into the wood, nor that she had ever seen such sights with her own eyes.

'Tell me how you know this?' I asked her. But she would only watch me blankly.

But if I asked, 'What is it like there?' then she would smile, her eyes removed as though they haunted that far place. 'In the broad world,' she would say to me, 'there is nothing to compare with it unless it were the fair realm undersea. There the Selchie first came to land. And, though they are gone, their magic still clings to it. For where they walked, the very sand is emerald and the sea that thunders on the headlands blazes green as fire.' Her voice would quiver then and she would go off into herself. But it was the ships I thought of – the bright ships and the bold men who rode them, free of the land, out in the whirling gulf where only stars watched. There would be silence then, long and unchallenged in the hall.

In those years there were none to argue it. So the years followed, one upon another, much as the Kell had counted them, each one chasing round the next as hawks drive sparrows and are driven forth by eagles in their turn.

I had by then grown tall and could, I judged, compete in matters of strength and cunning with many older than myself. Though I was shy a winter of my fourteenth year, the servants were already wary of me. Lately even my aunts and sisters had begun to treat me with caution.

There are advantages to being born the only son and a bastard in a house of women – but not many. Still, for good or ill, in most things I had my way. By then the housethralls, the bearded men with their battle gear strapped to their horses – they who had come in the years Urien had covered himself with glory – now in his disgrace deserted him. He was too old and plagued with sores. Two servants were needed to lift him from his bed. He could not keep me in rein. The women, being witchfolk, kept their own counsel and left me much to mine.

Nonetheless, I did not tell Yllvere my mind was fixed on climbing to the mountain wood, to the high place where Grieve had promised I could look out on the sea. Yllvere would have forbidden that, if nothing else. She would have set her grim servant to lock me in the stable and kept him there to stand guard by the door. Though I suspected it was little more than a nesting place for crows, the wood was holy to the Kell. For the Kell, who believed their grandfathers were sealmen, swore as well that not a few of their grandmothers had been changed into trees. No matter what I thought of that, I was of no mind to court unneeded trouble and for the sake of prudence determined to go armed.

Before dawn I rose and dressed. Stealthily I crept down the dim backstairs and passed the upper kitchen. Neither the cook nor any of her women was as yet about. If I surprised, as I must have, a gray mouse on the stone, I met with nothing else alive.

The armory ran parallel to the guest hall, along the length of the inner wall. In those years the armory had a gray and empty look. It had had, ever since the thralls rode off. Much of the battle gear was gone, the hooks that held it empty. What little remained was rusted for want of use. Tabak, my mother's servant and the one man under sixty in the house, kept his arms apart, even to the point of sleeping with his ax. But it was none of his I wanted.

The longroom twisted toward the back. In its farthest corner, too removed to be of service if need came suddenly, hung Urien's sword. It was a thick two-handed blade. With it he had killed twelve men. My eyes went to it. Even in the bad light its pommel gleamed. Time had barely touched the metal. But the belt and scabbard were rotted. When I pulled it out, the leather parted, giving off a stench like vile old flesh. My lip curled. I thought, just such a ruin has Urien come to. But I did not much care to dwell on him. The sword settled in my belt, I turned quickly, hastening my steps to get out once more into the air.

In the yard I breathed again. The hens fluttered from my path. I threw a stone at the cook's red dog, who came poking out to bark, and drove him back. I might have used the gate. Instead I climbed the palisade. It was more trouble, but it was nearer the mountain. Perhaps I thought myself a thief and meant to act like one. I found the handholds in the stone with ease. With no great effort I made the ledge. A moment later I was bounding up the mountain.

As I remember, it was April, already two months past the thaw and by chance the sign month of my birth. This was an oddity within the house, for all the women were of the winter brood. But in those days I gave no thought to it. The high fields were green and steamed with morning vapor. As I walked, the mist about me broke. Over the hillside there were flowers, their petals still folded in the raw light before sunrise.

Many I knew – sorrel, mullein root, and asphodel – such as the aunts gathered, bent over and chanting beneath their breaths. Late and early I had seen them, moving speculatively across the fields. Now those fields were empty, and I ran. When, panting, I looked back, the house was still asleep below me. The day dawned cloudless, the air chilled. Even now I cannot remember a time when I felt more alone in all the world nor liked it better.

In my eagerness I went straight for the wood, leaving a darkened track in the grass behind me like a wake. At the border of the upper meadow the ground rose steeply. Out of the grass, I clambered over gray outcroppings of stone. By then, had anyone wished to follow, my destination would have seemed plain enough. I gave no thought to that. I walked west along the rim of the house lands. Tall spires of ash and elm rose like a wall, dividing what was Urien's – the order of orchards, fields and windrows where the sun, like clockwork, rose and set – from the deep wood of the Kell, where daylight dwindled under interwoven boughs, where morning and evening were scarcely set apart and had no meaning.

At the edge of the wood, like gateposts a dozen feet apart, stood two great trees. Their trunks were gray and more massive than pillars. But their branches were thin and spidery, hung thick with moss. In truth they were no gate at all. Nothing entered here. No path penetrated the gloom. In this place woodcutters were forbidden. Even Yllvere and her sisters, though daughters of the Kell, did not visit here but held it in awe, a place apart from men. The wood was old beyond telling. Yet unlike the great forests – Anhornim in the North and Isenveld in the West, whose peoples are numbered in the books of the wars – it had no name. The women, if they spoke of it at all, called it simply the wood upon the mountain.

I was young. What was there to fear, I thought, of a place that is not even worthy of a name? So I brought upon myself the wound that ever since has marked me. But then I did not know it but thought only that presently I would look out on the sea.

I pushed my way in through a screen of brambles. Even as I entered I did not forget the guest prayer. I spoke aloud although it sounded strangely in my ears. When I had done I added, 'Dagda, Lord, I pray you, if this is Anu's wood, keep harm from me.' All else was silent. A gray dusk lay about me. I rubbed my eyes.

I stood within an immense, shaded hall. The floor was carpeted with drifts of leaves, brown and blackened and smelling of mold. The ceiling high above my head was raftered all across with boughs. Between was emptiness. Nothing grew in that bad light. No wind stirred.

I scaled the nearer limbs with both my eyes but found no place to climb. I would have done better with a good rope than a borrowed sword. But I had given no thought to that beforehand, only that the wood was ill rumored and that I had best go armed.

Well, I thought, there is sure to be a good perch farther on. So I lumbered through the drifts of leaves, pleased at least that there was no small bracken to scratch my eyes. Yet, however long I looked, no limb drooped down for me. In all directions there were only the great gray trunks, pale and corpselike, as useless as greased poles. My heart sank. I had come seeking the sea and meant to look on it. Having come this far, I was of no mind to return unsatisfied to Morrigan, to meet, with nothing more to show for it, the questions of my sisters and my aunts. The house rose up again within my thoughts. Angrily, I looked back the way I had come.

He stood there, huge in the tracks that I had made, his broad ax slung upon his shoulder. I gaped at him.

'The boundaries of this place are clear,' he said. 'You have two good eyes. Surely you have seen that none have walked here.'

He could see the anger in my face. The frown he was used to. He knew it at least as well as I knew my own. We were familiar enemies. Though it could not always have been so, it seemed that Tabak had always been about the house. The first of my memories are of him. I was not quite three when a great storm had wrapped itself about the house. Shaken from my bed and blubbering, I had run the dark length of the hall to Yllvere's chamber. He it was who met me outside her door. Each night she would set him there like some tethered animal. His shoulders filled the door frame. He barred the way to her. I remember even his words before he sent me back. 'No, my lordling,' he had said, 'you will find no comfort here.' The house shook in the wind. It was as though the thunder itself had spoken. That memory was with me when I answered him.

'Has she called you from your den to haul me back?' I said. Like a stick thrown to her hound, I thought, and swore. 'You know I will not gladly go with you.'

His eyes were steady. But though his voice was low, yet something of that remembered storm had darkened it.

'It serves little to quarrel with you, lord,' he answered evenly. 'Whether you come or stay, it is on your head, not on mine.'

Still I could not believe that I would be let go so easily.

'Has she not sent you?' I demanded.

He shook his head. 'I saw you climb the wall, bearing a sword that was none of yours. That was enough.' He remained where he was, too far away to take hold of me. I watched him carefully and yet I did not want to meet his eyes.

'And when you do not bring me back?' I said. 'And when she turns her icy stare on you, how will you answer?'

The long, still look of his did not alter. 'Lord, it is no more than you are heir to. She knows it. Like any of the Kell, it is the sea you long for.' His voice was soft but like a curse he uttered it. Of all the household he was the only one who called me lord. I always thought it mockery. But no smile broke his lips. He simply stood and spoke. And yet the words were like a hiss, like a sea wave sucked back upon itself. The sound unnerved me. I would not listen. 'Begone!' I cried and ran myself.

I fled him through the aisles of trees. Panting, I drank the dark air down in gulps. The trees grew thicker. Still I ran. Winded, when at last I turned to see how near he came, I found him gone.

Good riddance to that goblin then, I thought. For so I thought of him – a goblin or some great winter bear, a thing that drags its huge shape through ice caves in the dark. Though, in truth, I was alone in that. To the women he was a handsome man, though it seemed they never liked him better for it. For all their craft there was something deep and old in him they could not manage or outwit.

It troubled me to think that he had followed me, more so if Yllvere had not sent him searching. My mother's servant, he had no leave for actions of his own. He was Yllvere's alone. Whether Urien's sword was gone or not should have made no difference to him. But more it troubled me how easily, for all his dark looks and his warning, he had let me go. Still I could make little of it and, though puzzled, I drove his cold eyes from my mind.

Thereafter I went more slowly. The black leaves whispered above my head, though now I rarely saw them. A grayness smothered everything so that I felt rather than saw the trees' far summits. Yet, it seemed, they frowned on me. Cautiously, I climbed into a ravine and up the rock face at its northern edge. Even above the rock there was no break in the trees. The air felt heavy. I strained my eyes to see. Away to the left the slope mounted up again. I went on. It was the wood then that beckoned me. I wandered. In time I forgot to look for a low branch I might climb. Almost idly I walked beneath the trees. The grayness filled my sight. Like cool deep water it flowed over me.

My feet were well along the road before I noticed it. As long as the road ran straight, the drifting leaves had masked it. But when the slope grew steep, much like a stair, the road climbed and then the heavy blocks of polished stone shone through. It was an ancient road and yet no rents or breaches tore it. The seams, where they were visible beneath the leaves, were fitted with skill and in a manner now long out of use. I knew it was not the broken work of the quarriers of our old kingdoms but a craft far older. The pride and art that fashioned such stone had faded.

Mournfully, I thought of the great age of the world. I was young then and unaccustomed to such thoughts. In the years that came the *filidh* would say of me that I walked deftly in time, at ease in it as man might ford a river. For as the long years passed I came to know its deep currents and its sandy places. In truth, it started there. Much that would befall me, both the blessing and the curse, began in that deep wood as I gazed upon a road shaped in another age, of which neither we nor the Kell had memory nor so much as one whispered name.

Upward the strange road wound. Looping forward and back, it coiled across the land like the spine of a serpent. I wondered how many ages had come and gone since last a man had walked here. I went more quickly then, curious, spurred on by it. After a while the drifted leaves were fewer. Looking back, I found I had left the last of the trees behind. Yet as before the arch of boughs spread black and impenetrable overhead. It puzzled me. Either the leaves did not fall or else an army came, nightly out of the ground, to sweep the debris away. No less than an army could have cleared the vastness of the country along the road. Either way it was foolishness. I went on doggedly. I meant to discover the reason for such a road. Perhaps, I thought, it rises to one pinnacle or the other of Géar Finn. I remembered the sea again. Upon the summit I knew I might look out over all the West, even to holy Hren itself, whose shore, Grieve said, was emerald.

The stair road climbed along steep featureless walls. Well-hidden from the sun, not even moss or lichen grew there. When, for a moment, I leaned my shoulder, slumped, to rest against the wall, the damp cold bit into it. Surprised, I pulled away. With unaccustomed fierceness I remembered the warmth of the house, the hall fire and the oven rooms on the floor beneath. The bright world, Morrigan, its fields and pastures, seemed far away. I wondered if it were still morning there or if the day had passed already into afternoon. Indeed the light, poor as it had been, had faded more. But whether the sun were draining away from the world beyond or whether the tangled canopy had merely thickened I could not guess. No longer seeing where I went, I should have feared to lose my way and circle, unknowing, back upon myself, had I not felt the road, tier on tier, rising steadily through the lake of darkness.

One foot followed another. Only the stair road, it seemed, had gradually altered underfoot. I had been thinking that for some time, weighing the difference, half-unconsciously changing my stride.

Something fled past me on the stair. Although I could not see it, I heard a squeak, felt a small furred body rush by my legs, heard for an instant the scrape of claws on stone trail off below. Startled, I grabbed for the wall to hold my balance. But the cold stone I had expected now was gone. In its place was a dry roughness. I scratched it with my nails. One ragged piece came away in my hand.

I turned it over in my palm. It had the feel of bark. Amazement took me. Then with both hands flat against it, I eased my way along the wall, counting the steps, thirty, then a hundred. Everywhere I touched, the wall was bark, extending immeasurably, ever higher than my reach.

Fearing I knew not what, I edged to the other side. Cautiously, I stretched out my hand. But reaching to my fingers' ends I touched only air. My heart leapt high against my ribs.

I stood at the brink, looking out at a chasm I could not see. One misstep and I would have walked, unknowing, into the gulf of air. A tremor ran through me. I hugged the wall. For the first time in my life I feared the Kell, those subtle women and their spider ways. I had come unbidden to this place, their wood where no men came. For an awful moment, I clung to the bark, afraid to move.

Then indeed I might have fallen. For the darkness filled me and blacker than darkness was my own fear. Yet I had not come courting death. Slowly I raised my head, forcing my eyes to search the great vault overhead. I felt a whirling in my brain. I made myself still.

They were no more than sparks, silver holes torn in the blackness – vague and far away, filtered and recast by the darkness. Yet I saw them, like a sprinkling of stars. I raised myself up and followed them, rung upon rung of the stair road until the darkness turned ashen and shapes appeared as out of a mist.

I had climbed to a high place in a tree whose size was beyond telling. Around me were branches broad as avenues where six men might have walked abreast. About the bole of the tree the stair road curled. Now the ragged bark shone silver. It was evening. The long day I had climbed, tireless, like one under an enchantment. But now the vastness took my breath. I could not close my eyes, for the great sight filled it. I stiffened my limbs and made the last steps to the summit of the stair.

I came out among the ebony leaves at the tree's height. The moonlight fell about me and cast a long shadow at my back.

Then at last my eyes leapt out across the jagged wood, out beyond the mountain wall, across the headlands, tumbling seaward. It was the moment I had come for. Yet even in that moment, the line of the dark-rimmed sea already in my eyes, I shuddered. For in that moment I understood why far below me no leaf fell.

Gwen Gildrun, the name shocked through my blood. It took my breath.

Gwen Gildrun.

From the beginning of the world this tree had grown. I was not unlearned. Though not such a marvel as my aunts would freely speak of, I had looked into the books of lore and taken such instruction as could be found when the *filidh* came riding in in winter, trading their songs for a horn of ale.

Gwen Gildrun they called it, the God-Tree. Its roots, they said, sank far beneath the roots of mountains. Old it was as the land upon whose back it stood, a colossus, age after age adding girth and limb until, formless and ever widening, it spanned many leagues. And from the beginning not one leaf fell nor would until the day of doom when the world cracked and the very moon above me fell and darkness once more swallowed up the mountains and the sea. Yet where it grew the *filidh*, for all their learning, could not tell nor, they said, could any man. In that they erred. In their cold hearts the Kell had kept it.

In that moment I ceased to fear the Kell. This was deeper than any magic of shore folk. Though guardians of the place, they were its servants only. Filled with holy dread, they kept away. Better to crawl among the fields below, searching out rats' teeth and henbane, better to hide indoors boiling cats' bones on the kitchen fires. I was alone in this. I stood at the world's height, alone where none had followed, in a place like unto that where creatures first drew breath. I have done a great thing, I thought. Surely all folk shall talk of this.

I climbed, wondering, through the maze of ancient wood. The undying branches spread in all directions. Indolent they seemed as basking snakes, here smooth and serpentine, but elsewhere curled and knotted, their rough spikes poking up like spears. The tree had no end, no shape. So huge it was that whole great cities might have sunk unseen beneath the humps and swells of shining leaves.

I made a twisted path. In the upper wind the black leaves sighed, the cold air pouring out of the deepest sky. Yet even such a wind could not fill up the quiet. Unmoved and huge, older than the world, the stillness lay beneath the scratch of limbs. The wind sucked at it vainly and was lost. I listened. Something hissed at my back. I turned.

In a nest of vines, still when I looked on them as figures carved in stone, two fledgling crows, their eyes like glittering amber, peered back at me. Frozen and unblinking, they met my gaze.

Suddenly the heart within me laughed. Here was a prize to dazzle even Yllvere and the aunts and proof unchallengeable of my climb. The crows of Gwen Gildrun! The glory of it filled my mind.

I meant to have them. Slowly I slid my hand into the nest and dug among the shards of lizard skulls and cracked fish bones. Their cold still eyes, curious but unmoved, stared back at me. Cautiously I put my hands on them. All bone and down they were. Then all at once afraid, they pecked my thumbs. I cuffed them smartly and wound them in my cloak. They did not cry out. And yet, I should have thought.

Over me the immense dark wings had opened with a crack. For an instant only I saw her, the harsh old head disfigured, ruined with scars. She fell too quickly. When I felt the iron claws rake my shoulder, I had only just lifted my borrowed sword. The blood splashed down along my arm.

That moment we both shrieked, she hot with victory, I with searing pain. I covered myself as best I could with both my arms. Her black shadow passed over me. For a breath's space, I was free of her. I set my teeth, knowing I must find a way to make the stair and make it quickly.

I ducked beneath a limb and ran. The rest happened faster than I thought. I did not see her. She plummeted out of the darkness, from some space invisible between the branches and the moon. Her iron claws grabbed my hair.

With one cruel motion the cold beak thrust itself into my eye. The pain exploded in my skull. I screamed and flailed my arms. Yet I made the opening and plunged back down. The branches caught her. She screeched in anguish, bewailing the loss of her children. Long afterward I heard her, the way barred by the twisted limbs, battering the wood with her vast wings.

Gwen Gildrun covered me. So I escaped the worst of her hatred. But blood poured down my cheek. Weakened, I fell as much as ran. Perhaps the god was with me on the stair. Of the time that followed I have little memory.

CHAPTER TWO

Yllvere and her women found me. I lay at the edge of the wood between the gate trees. She looked into my face. She saw the small life fluttering within my cloak. Sadly, she sent her women back and made them stand across the wall in the next field.

When the women were gone, she knelt beside me. With her own dress linen and a drop from a vial that hung from a silver chain about her waist, she washed my eye, soaking and scouring the rent flesh beneath it where the blood had dried. Her red-gold hair fell before her face and shaded her saucer eyes. Though not quite three-and-thirty, she was mistress of Urien's house and much besides. Because of his sores, his age and shame, she was mistress in truth of the fields and stables and each of the villages about our holding. The pale leaden roof of the forge and the stone walls of the grainery, the houses, sheds and kaleyards and all that was within and without them were in her keeping. The men of the villages, the women and their young, bound to the land, were bound the more to do her bidding. In truth, from the ridge on the high ground wherever it pleased her to look she ruled. And yet those few times in my life that she was gentle with me she seemed shy as a maid.

'I came each day,' she said.

I stared at her uncomprehendingly. 'How long?' I asked.

'Many days.'

I stirred then and moaned. I did not understand. 'It is just this morning at sunrise that I went.' I spoke with difficulty; my thoughts were frayed. I was dizzy and felt that I would faint. She touched my hair and spoke the name she had for me.

'How long?' I pleaded.

She took my head and laid it in her lap. She smiled. 'There is no time within the wood.' Her voice was soft but there was hardness at the edge of it. 'Without we counted, watching the moon pare down and then grow fat again. We did not know when you would return. We waited.' She watched me carefully even as she spoke. So a potter watches, whirling on the wheel the clay beneath his hand, to know that instant when the shape he seeks is made. It gave me pause.

'Why have you sent the women back?' I asked.

She moved and for an instant in the fold of her dress I saw the silver glitter of a knife. She knew that I had seen it and drew back.

'It is a holy place,' she said. 'No man goes there.' There was impatience in her voice but no alarm. 'All that is there is as it was at the world's beginning. The power of fashioning out of fire and air has never gone from it.' She looked at my ruined eyes. 'That which makes may unmake, child,' she said. 'I feared the wood would eat your soul and return to me a man's shape from which the man had gone.'

Whatever thoughts then moved across her face I could not read them. She lifted the knife and fastened it securely within her belt.

She said, 'I was prepared for what might have come here in your stead.' I stared. In those years I lived with her I barely knew the mysteries that claimed her moods. For what child does? But beyond others a strange blood ruled her heart. She was, like all her women, winter born. In her blood seethed memories of the witch kingdoms that were gone. Yet they but gave the outer shape to her grim will. Within their shadow moved another, deeper, more fiercely held, like a knotted fist upon a jewel. I felt its coldness rub against my life. My wits were numb. At the same time her words had shamed me and I burned.

'Mother,' I said, 'it was not death but life I brought back from the wood.' With what strength I had I spread the cloak. The crows in their nesting down began to squawk.

I saw the sharp breath she took then. Her hands slipped back beside her waist. She would not touch them. Presently she said, 'You have gone where no man has gone since the first age and yet you are a child. In this especially. These are not the wild crows of the fields. They are Gwen Gildrun's and in that neither Death's nor Life's. The matter is not fixed. It may be they are both.' I meant to question her, but already she had waved her women near.

Vydd came, Yllvere's sister, wrapped in a blue robe, her face like a withered apple. She walked barefoot, leaning on her staff. Even in those days the sea longing troubled her. She lived not in Morrigan but in a small hut on the mountain. The walls of the great house frightened her, she said – indoors, among so many women, she could not smell the sea. All knew she was mad. But her eyes, if they were wild, were sometimes tender. She smiled at me. They let her come first. Behind her came the attendant women. Of these only a few were from the villages in our

15

holding. Mostly they came from the river towns, out of Laudd and Hwawl, to serve Yllvere, to sit at her feet and learn her craft. Among them were my sisters – Sanngion, Ryth and Grieve, the youngest after me, whom I loved. Only she and mad Vydd smiled on me. When she had seen the crows, Grieve laughed. Then the crows too were comforted and tucked their small heads beneath their stubby wings. The women did not speak to me but bore me on a litter to the house.

This happened in my thirteenth year, in the month of my birth sign, which is April. In the dark of the next moon, when I regained my strength, they held the rite that proclaimed my manhood. I suffered the ceremony silently. All knew I had proved myself beyond their brief mystery on the stable floor. The rite itself was no more than a sham. There were no warriors to share it with me. Urien summoned the millwright out of the village and a few old men from the towns. He offered me neither a sword nor armor. He did not make me his heir. The millwright, who had known him many years, rebuked him for his lack of courtesy. Urien only spat in the dust. 'What good is a one-eyed man?' he said. He was old then and bitter. The dead child was often in his thoughts.

Urien was not a king, nor even a great lord, though the lands he held had grown to rival the most splendid in the North. As a young man in the service of the High King he had killed twelve men that mattered, eleven in the field – enemies, but men like himself, fond of women and hunting and a drink among friends. He knocked them from their horses. Whacking at them long enough to find a hole between the leather and the iron, he drove his thick sword into their flesh. Somewhere, it is written who they were – what wives were widowed, which sons took their place – but little came of it. The eleven earned him many wounds but small fame. The twelfth was Lot, a man in the king's own following, whom Urien slew at the very feet of the king when the court came down on its yearly pilgrimage to the island of Hren. Lot was drunk that day and in a bad temper, which is to say, he was his usual self. He was not beloved, even among his own kindred. Nor do the *filidh* flatter him. He was a man without luck. While drunk near the holy place where the sea narrows between Hren and the mainland, he insulted the king. Nowhere is it written what was said. When in the years that came I heard the words, it was only to me it mattered. But the offense was fresh then. Because of it Urien slit Lot's throat. In the sight of the soldiers he did it and the High King, who had his own reasons, rewarded him with the house and lands of

Morrigan, a gift worthy of kings, ceded to Urien and his descendants forever.

Morrigan was not the first house in the North to be founded on murder. It would not be the last. But like all that is ill gotten, it did him no good. Fate left him only the corpse of a son, his thin neck broken. Such children as Yllvere bore him he could have done without, myself among them. Yet I often wondered whether I would have loved him had I known his company when he was master of Morrigan and his sword arm strong.

There were even times when I wished him my father, since I had none. Sometimes I would wait for hours outside the locked doors of the tower room beneath the mountain, listening to him pace the floor or to the rustle of pages as he read the great books of the wars. Often I heard him curse and call out the names of the house gods or, sadly, remembering the old wars in the South, the names of the dead he knew.

In the winter, when the light was poor, he would summon Grieve to the tower to read to him. I climbed the long stairs after her and she would let me crouch in behind. Hidden in a corner, far from the fire, I would hear the tales of the old wars, of the bold men and burnt towns, or, best of all, of the far green seas where the heathen fleets, dragon-prowed and heavy with gold, rode the foam like serpents themselves. To these tales I owe what knowledge I had of the outer world, of the genealogies of the northern kingdoms, of their histories and statecraft and such practical matters as the mounting of sieges and the marshaling of assaults. They were good teachers, more patient and less trouble than human tutors would have been. If I had no word of praise from them nor any kindness, neither did I suffer the needless cruelty and disapproval for minor and imagined wrongs nor thrashings when I fell into error.

I learned quickly. As Grieve read, her voice thin and plaintive in the cold tower room, I memorized the words. Later, when Urien had gone to his bed, I intoned the lockspell she had shown me and, going in once more, took down the books in their heavy leather sheaths and matched my memory to the words until I had learned to make out the figures on my own. It was a cleric's, not a warrior's, training; yet it served me. It filled the empty places in my longing. It gave me dreams. If it left me unsatisfied with the familiar world of Morrigan, it could not be helped. A youth who has heard of the far sea kingdoms and of their ruin and of the frenzy of dragonkind in their nests of blood at Weeds, he will not willingly content himself with idling before the kitchen fires with only the dark mumbling of his aunts for company. So from the first my mind was fixed on journeying; and, feeling little wanted where I was, I determined early to try my luck in the world. However slow I was in going, the thought was seldom far from me.

One day I had gone out in the fields with Grieve, bearing the crows, one on each shoulder. I meant to teach them to circle above me, scouting the land, and to return at my command.

'Ninguh, go forth,' I cried, lifting my arm and sending the first soaring. 'Ninmir, follow.' She gave me a haughty look over her shoulder. She spread her wings in the bright air and in a moment she was also gone. Then Grieve and I were alone on the hill.

'So I shall go,' I said. 'As easily as a crow soars, so I shall leave this house.'

Her chin dropped down. She would not meet my eye. 'To what place?' she asked.

I answered quickly. 'To Ormkill,' I said, 'to the seat of the High King.' For a moment I closed my one good eye, trying to form a picture of the great oak hall that I had never seen, under whose roofbeams it was said a hundred spearmen might gather and a score of servingwomen at their call.

Grieve frowned. She was but two years older, yet more a mother to me than Yllvere had been. 'Poor boy,' she sighed. 'You live in dreams. It is not as it is written in the books of the wars. The glory of that hall is broken. Fifteen winters are now gone since the High King vanished. The Steward, Thigg, rules in his place, and badly. Once more the riverlands are in arms. The fields are not tended and the farmers starve.'

'Yet I will see it.'

She watched me sadly and did not answer all at once but waited as though she debated with herself. 'And if you should not find him there?' she said at last.

Bitterly I turned aside. I knew she meant my father. A blush crept slowly across my face. Some things are best not spoken.

'Why are you angry?' she asked.

I looked to see if she were mocking me. Her face was still. Yet a shudder went through me. All my life my father had lain beneath a silence in the house. He was a weight upon our tongues that none dared lift. From the servants I understood I was a bastard. They had their ways of seeing that I knew. But though I spied on them and listened unseen to their gossip, beyond this they themselves knew little more. Yllvere never spoke of it. My early questions she met with cold annoyance. I learned quickly to let the matter be. Yet it twisted in me.

Softly, she circled my waist with her thin arm. Then, as through all those first years, Grieve set herself before the void and kept the dark at bay. Already I was taller by four hands. Any who would have seen us walking together across the field would have thought she was the child. Yet her thoughts were deep and as many-channeled as the mines beneath our mountains. At once I regretted my anger.

'I wonder who he is,' I told her simply, 'whether he is a great lord or a man like any other. I have thought of this often and have no answer.' I paused a moment, then went on. 'It is said your father beat her when Yllvere would not give up the name.'

Her lips were parted but she did not speak.

We had reached the huge plate of stone which lay in the eastern meadow. The walls of Morrigan had been quarried here. In places there were still scars from the scoring of the rock. But storms had dulled the lines and left the boulders rounded. A wide track led away from it, along which the heavy blocks that made the palisades had been drawn on sledges. Even this was overgrown. In places it had become indistinguishable from the field. We turned back along it.

My mind still burdened, I had spoken more than I intended. Though, in truth, once started, I had expected no more than the chance to share my mood and so to ease it. A little way on she stopped and took my hand.

'I know the time will come when you will leave,' she said. 'Sorely I will miss you then. But that time is not yet. Deeper than words I know this.' Above us, even as I heard her, the crows were circling, high up in the mountain wind.

'How is it that you know?' I asked.

She made a witch sign in the air between us so I would not continue. Yet I pressed her. She looked at me out of her deep, troubled eyes. Though she was dearer to me than any in the house, something in her look reminded me that she was as much like the others as surely she was apart. In many things their ways were hers. The Kell blood flooded her veins and one might never know for certain whether she or it was master of her thoughts.

'I have watched and counted,' she said thickly. So the Kell have always answered when they meant to keep their secrets to themselves.

I shook my head. She saw then how I hated it.

'Is this all you can say to me?' I shouted.

The sun above the mountain flickered like two mirrored flames within her eyes. She did not blink.

'You must speak with Vydd,' she answered hotly. This told me nothing but I saw how much the words had cost her. I made no more of it. The rest of the way we went in silence. Before the house I called the crows down from the wind.

Ninmir, whose name in the old tongue means Memory, came first. Then Ninguh, whose name means Thought. Fierce with sight, their eyes, like Grieve's, shone red-gold in the sun.

CHAPTER THREE

There were two villages near the House of Morrigan, but the people feared us. Though the times were poor enough, there were no village women willing to nurse a young bastard for a few copper coins. Thus it happened that the first years of my childhood were spent unavoidably in the company of my aunts and sisters. I learned to walk on the hard bakery floor. For toys I had neither a sword nor arrows but a sow's clavicle and ointment jars. It fell to Grieve to teach me to speak. My first words were the names of plants and medicinal herbs. The men's language I had to master on my own, piecing it together from the chronicles of Gedd, the records of wars, which Urien kept under lock in his tower. This also I owe to Grieve. She taught me the lockspells that unsealed the iron doors. With her only I have no quarrel.

The women were foragers, collectors of fungus, foxbane and crows' ankles. Roots and stalks hung from the rafters. Black pots hissed on the open fires. Morning and evening the House of Morrigan smelled of musk, seared oil and burflour cakes baking past midnight in earthen ovens. But their lives, like their bodies, were thin. There was no strength in their food; the wine they made in the press was bitter and the color of water.

Vydd was the oldest. She had come when Yllvere called her, to tutor Sanngion, the first living born, and stayed on for the others, Ryth and Grieve. Yllvere gave them names of her own design, without so much as asking the leave of her lord. Yllvere grew stronger with the birth of each daughter, as Urien grew less. When his liegemen deserted him, she took hold of the house, kept accounts and managed the holding. Yet after their naming she left my sisters to Vydd.

Yllvere had no talent for mothering. She became in its place a mistress of earth magic, which was the legacy of the Kell, and not only the lesser skills of healing but also those more subtle matters of the binding of wills of men and of beasts. With the years she drew into her art. In the day she ordered the planting and spinning and set the hour for the ingathering of the grain. In the evening she withdrew to her cell at the bottom of the house. A long stair went down to it, a place behind the ovens where the floor was so hot it burned the soles of her feet. There she whispered and sang in the old tongue until long after the women had crawled off to their beds. The rest was Vydd's – what my sisters ate and wore, the games played and lore mastered. That much I learned from the servants in the years when they spoke freely before me, a child waddling between their knees. Their eyes filled with mirth at the odd ways of their mistress, before they saw that I understood. Vydd lived in the house then. The walls of Morrigan had not yet begun to fill her with dread nor had she begun to look for the smell of the sea. That time would come.

A month after I had come down from the quarry with Grieve I had still not gone to Vydd's hut on the mountain. Yet the thought deviled me. I sucked on it daily like a sore tooth. When I rolled over in my sleep I saw her withered face in the cracks of the wall. The wind blew under the eaves and I heard the low moan of her voice. Once when I had gone out on the mountain to clear the weeds from the cistern which held the water for the house I saw her against the side of a hill. She was leaning on her stick and looking across to me. She called out the name she had for me. I heard it clearly. I pretended not to notice and went down the long way to the house before I had finished. The truth was, I had been too long alone with my thoughts. But for that day with Grieve and my childhood questions of Yllvere, I had spoken of my father to no living man.

Yet I brooded over him. When I was younger, I had built him into a great lord. In my mind I saw him, wronged by some enemy, rise up in his war gear and full of righteous anger cut an armed man down in his place so that the man twisted like a spider, the cold metal stuck in his chest. In those moments, my own heart racing, we seemed as one. His foes were mine and also his glory. I killed a hundred men in my imagining, all in his service. When I was older I saw the folly of so much gore. Then, though I saw him stern and brave, I hoped there was more to him than a string of murders. Any fool, I reasoned, can poke another man's belly with a knife. I wished him better than that, perhaps because I wished myself more as well. In time I also hated him because he never rode within the walls of Morrigan, his retinue behind him, to acknowledge me. Then I thought, perhaps he is only a tinker or a harper or even a rude farmer from Tyre, a riverman, a maker of fish weirs. But neither lord nor sailor came to claim me. One season rolled on to another. From one month to the next I made ready to set out seeking him, since he had not come. Time passed. Yet I did not go up to Vydd on the mountain. At heart I feared knowing and kept my thoughts to myself.

It was nearly winter when the millwright came up alone from his village. I was in the yard and saw him. He wore a clean longshirt and had brushed his beard. Under his arm he carried a sheaf of tables bound in aurochs' hide. By that I knew he had come on the matter of the service his village owed us. His name was Jjared. Like all men of our mountains he was small, the gray wool of his head barely reaching to the middle of my chest. He grinned when he saw me and came to my side. Despite his holiday dress, he smelled of barley as he had since the months of the harvest.

'Come, lad,' he said cheerfully, 'show me in to Urien. For I have brought the book and come to settle our accounts.' He laughed but there was no mockery in him. Yet between us we both knew he lied. He went to Urien out of their old friendship. In truth, it was Yllvere who had set the service. I knew that when he had finished in the tower, he would follow the long stair down to the oven rooms to meet with my mother and settle the matter in earnest. It has been so as long as I remembered. Still I went with him. That too was for show. He knew the way as well as I.

At the top of the stairs I knocked upon the heavy door. It was cast in one thick slab of iron and drank the sound of my rapping. But Urien had heard it.

'Who comes to me?' he shouted from within, his voice like an echo out of stone.

I started to speak, but Jjared hushed me. Though one of our carls, he was a man well thought of. So I gave him his way in this.

'It is Jjared, my lord,' he answered, 'come to reckon the service.'

'It is well,' Urien said. His voice was softer now. It may be there was even pleasure in it. But before he bade him enter, he added, an old man mumbling to himself, 'See, all is not forgotten. It is the proper day. The winter stars hover at the rim of the horizon. There is a coldness in the ground. I feel it even here.'

A silence followed. I heard the chair scrape and his labored walk across the floor. But on the other side of the door he stopped. Perhaps I moved. There was some uncertainty in his hand upon the latch.

'There is another with you,' he spat accusingly.

My back stiffened. I moved to speak. Once more Jjared placed his hand before his lips and in my stead he answered evenly, 'I met the lad in the yard and bade him bring me to you.'

'Whose lad is that?' he thundered.

Jjared motioned me to silence. But a fire burned in me and I would not have more of it.

'It is Herawd,' I said plainly, using the name Grieve called me. For a moment there was no sound. When he broke the silence, the voice behind the door was cold and stern.

'Send Yllvere's bastard back to her,' he said.

Jjared looked at me. Though it pained me, I was too proud to look away. To this day what interest he had in me I do not know for certain, only that he was a man well schooled in courtesy. It may be that he thought he served us both. Like other men he had no love for the women's gods. It may be he saw in me a hand to strengthen Urien against the Kell. Who is to say? If that were his purpose, it failed him utterly. For in that moment I knew I would go at last to Vydd and soon be done with the house and its lord together.

Halfway down the stair I heard the iron door open. I did not stop to listen. No longer was it a concern of mine.

I went first to the mews at the north end of the stable. No hawks had been cooped there since Lot went off on his unlucky pilgrimage with the High King and Urien came back in his place. But there, tucked back from the narrow windows, on a shelf out of the wind, I kept my crows. I meant to gather what was mine, little as it was. My thoughts on Vydd and what I would say to her, I toyed absently with a mole I had in my pocket. I had found it squeaking by the door, a cat's plaything, and brought it up for them.

'Ninguh,' I called out softly before I had quite reached the place. No voice answered me. I forged into the small passage between the stable and the mews, turned a corner and came before the perch. The shelf was empty. The leather straps with which I had bound the crows were cut. My head swam with astonishment. 'Who would dare this?' I cried aloud. But there were none to answer it. I went out angry, nursing all that wronged me.

The clouds were low over Géar Finn, its twin horns hidden. The wind came down from there, sailing over the walls. Already there were a few brown leaves swirling in the yard, the first carrion of autumn. The air was heavy, gray enough for snow, but there was none.

I went over the wall to avoid the servants and my sisters. I was of no mind for prying eyes and questions. For some time I followed the track north and west, then parted from it. Vydd's hut was away from the land we tilled, in a patch of rubble that barely suited goats. The grass was scarce and the ground littered with mounds of stone. The hut, when I came upon it on the hillside, seemed little more than a slightly larger mound with rough holes scratched into the sides for a door and windows. Flaps of deerhide covered the openings. Rag ends of smoke escaped around the edges. But if Vydd were mad, she was also the eldest witch born. So I had not come this way often. Yet once or twice she had smiled at me, a smile so unlooked-for that it had followed me for days.

I stepped down into the hole and peered inside. Vydd was hunched over a crude table with her back to me, intent on some work of hers I could not see. The hut was dingy with smoke. It was difficult to see much clearly. Yet I recognized at the level of my forehead the herbs of her art, which she had hanging from the roofbeams. The hut smelled of mullein root, dried snakeskin and smoke. The rest seemed to be pots and bowls, loose on the floor or piled one on another along the wall. In one corner I could make out a low bed with just a rag of a blanket. Without turning, she poked at the fire with her stick. Her arm was thin.

I tugged at the flap to let her know someone was there. 'Aunt,' I said, 'I have come to see you.' I ducked inside.

She glanced around without surprise and winked at me. 'Agravaine,' she said, for she had her own name for me, 'I am pleased . . . as they are.' She pulled herself back from her work.

Just above the table a vaporous wing unfolded in the gloom. The dark shape coughed. A second black thing shook its sly head and glared at me. They were my crows and Vydd was the thief. It was in my mouth to rail at her, but something caught my words.

Vydd steadied herself with her crooked stick and stood before me. 'My child,' she said, 'I have had a dream about them. So I went and brought them here to watch them and to see if the dream were true.' This nonsense untied my tongue. I said, 'Had I dreamed of a dragon, I would not stick it in my pocket and run home with it.'

'You may have already,' she answered, laughing. 'Or something very like.' I grew impatient. 'These are mine,' I told her. 'I mean to have them.'

'And so, my fox, you shall. When I am done with them. First I must teach them manspeech. See, already I have cut their tongues. The blood stopped quickly. It is a good sign.' A curl of smoke came from her parted lips. I stared at her angrily. She held in her hand a short pipe, which she put back then between her small mouse teeth. She drew at the stem as though she thought. Then she said, 'You must be patient. It is not such advice as the young take easily. But you will have to make do with it. We old women are like the earth; we give our secrets grudgingly. Still you will learn and we shall give you what is needful as we must.' At that she laughed, a small chirping laugh like a cricket's, and pulled my arm. 'Come, sit with me,' she said. 'Let it rest between us. The crows are only borrowed. Soon enough you will have them back.'

But I stayed by the door so that she was at my arm again. 'Come,' she said in a voice grown softer but with the laughter drained from it. 'An old woman needs company.' I watched her face, a nest of fine wrinkles, her small ragged mouth like a hole in a spider's web. It saddened me. For that I followed her, tucking my head down and stooping my shoulders to keep from bumping the roofbeams. She watched my progress with careful eyes.

'My house was not made for giants,' she said when I had found a place, snug between the table and the wall.

I answered without thinking. 'I am a man like any other.'

She said nothing but made a low murmur in her throat. For some time she appeared to busy herself, shifting bowls of meal and powder without particular purpose between the table and the floor. Perhaps it gave her time to think. I do not know.

'When the liegemen fled the house, you were not born,' she said afterward. 'Such as stayed with him are withered, bent with their years. I doubt that you have seen a proper man.'

'There are men in the villages,' I answered. 'I have talked with the millwright, Jjared, and seen the rest.'

'Then you know what I mean.'

'Truly, they are small,' I said, puzzled. 'They come, it is said, from the folk that tunneled in the mines beneath Géar Finn. They are small as all miners are. I have thought of this, Aunt, and such is my answer. I see nothing more in it.'

She rocked gently as she sat on her stool and listened to me. She was full of tiny movements. She sucked her pipe or bit her thumbs. Yet her eyes were on me like a baited trap. 'Why is it you have turned your mind to this?' she asked when I had done.

I shook my head. 'As I have said, for they are small. Truly, I have seen how the world is.'

'Just so,' she answered chuckling. 'What lad would think himself apart from other men? Yet for this you turn your reason from yourself.' All at once she threw back her small head and gazed at me with dancing eyes. 'Shall I tell you what no others will?'

I had come with questions. So I nodded.

She smiled, but there was sadness in her face as well. She said, 'The village men are as other men, no smaller. Had you been elsewhere you would have known this.'

My skin prickled. 'But you said I had seen no proper man.'

'There are men and there are men,' she said.

I could make nothing of this and glared at her. 'My mother has a servant,' I protested. 'Tabak, the one she keeps to herself to do her bidding.'

'I know of him.'

'Then you have seen there is not an inch between us.'

'He is very like you,' she answered, but I saw she had some other meaning to it.

'I do not follow you,' I said.

She paused a long moment to reprove me. 'Then let it be. I will bring you some broth. Perhaps you will drink a little wisdom down with it. Afterward we will talk about that which brings you.'

I wanted another word, but she was busy muttering among the bowls and ladling water from a crock. When I talked to her, she would not listen, but went on poking the fire. She settled an iron pot on the coals, then lay back to watch it. Rocking gently on her stool, her pipe back between her teeth, she sang. The song was old. Half the words I did not know. There was a part about the lost kingdoms undersea and another meant, I thought, to be the wail of sealmen heard among the rocks. The rest was gibberish, but I felt the longing in it. Ninmir came out of the corner where she had crouched and pranced across the table until she stood before Vydd's knees. The young crow seemed to study my aunt, cocking her black head as though she listened. The song lingered in the air when she had done.

When I found my voice, I said, 'I came to ask about my father.'

She brought me a cup of broth before she spoke. She put it in my hands. 'What have they told you, child?' she asked.

'Nothing, but that I am not Urien's.'

'It is fitting,' she replied gravely. 'For that is all they know.'

'Then you must tell me.'

'First drink what I have given you.'

So that she would go on, I drank. It tasted of brine. 'This is bitter,' I said.

'Truly,' she answered, 'it is that. Now hold your tongue.' Then she drew her stick into her lap and began to measure lengths along it with her thumb until I saw that she was counting. When she came to a certain place, she stopped. When she began to speak, her voice, it seemed, was drawn up from that same far place wherein she had found her song.

'Two winters before your birth,' she said, 'when your mother was just seventeen, she quit Urien's bed at last. Grieve was born then. Thereafter she no longer went to him. The snow was high that year.

When it grew dark and the roofbeams groaned beneath the drifts, the whole house slept on the floor in front of the ovens. Even Urien came down despite his pride. Only Yllvere stayed in the upper house. For she could not bear the sight of the world's men. Agravaine, you know we are the Kell. That at least was never hid from you. And though we have never seen them, still we remember the men of old – how once they came from their fair kingdoms undersea and walked as bold as life upon the shore. In our dreams we feel their breath and see their steaming hair, black as pitch and wet upon their necks. The hollows of our bellies feel the loss. When we awaken in the night, the cold leather of their arms still chills our backs. Whether late or early, in time all yield to it.

'So, child, it came to her as well. Nightly we heard her groaning from her bed. She took to chanting spells and weeping and calling out great oaths. Once a housethrall, who had gone out on the mountain to gather wood, discovered her wandering over the hills without her cloak or even a sheath to cover her. Fearing the worst, I brewed burdock and candle-wick in a broth and set it hot before her. She would not drink. When they had got her to her bed, we stationed guards before the doors. In their boots, to keep themselves awake, the guards placed stones. Yet in spite of vigilance, one morning, yawning and brushing the spellwebs from their eyes, they found her gone.

'Urien shaved his head and wept. He was a man then and she had been his favorite. He forgot his hunting companions. When in the hall they drank and hung on each other's arms, joking about the women in the river towns, he had them beaten. They only sneered at him. Once, when the rage was hottest in his blood, he cut a man with his knife. So one by one they left him, cursing his weakness, his anger and his tears. He did not plead to keep them. But nightly he went to the wall that ringed the yards, each night facing a new direction, first west to the great sea, that being the most likely, then east toward Ormkill. When he saw no sign of her, he turned north to the kingdoms of his own people and when the horizon remained empty, south toward Weeds, where once the dragons came ashore despoiling the godshrine at Reon. What remained of the household waited with him, the women keeping close to the windows, the dog boy on the roof of his kennel, all night under the stars, till all grew weary of the watch.

'One year yielded to the next. It was deep in the second winter when she came back. She rode a fine mare. At her side, leading the horse, was Tabak. He was much larger than Urien or any of the earls, a colossus with a barrel chest and long brown arms. The eyes in his sun-blackened face were deep and strange, the color of almonds. He was dressed, as she was, in embroidered cloth far richer than the hillspun which was then the custom of the house. Yet he was no lord, but her servant only. He wore a huge ax strapped to his back and at his side a stout two-handed sword. Still, for all his weaponry, he was gentle with her. He helped her down from her mount that day with care. The servants crowded into the yard. All saw at once the reason for his gentleness. Neither her robes nor belts of leather and silver could hide the thick swelling she carried beneath. We lowered our eyes so none would see her shame. We thought, having shown herself, she would mount her mare again and ride out through the gates, back to her new-found lord, to the place of his dwelling in some far place. We waited, none daring to speak.

'Your mother stared at us. She called us each by name, her sisters and her daughters and all the servants one by one. Yet there was a majesty in her bearing and we feared her. Grieve hid behind my skirts. She would not go out to her. A fierce glow patched your mother's cheeks. "Tell Urien," she commanded, "that I have brought the house an heir." No one moved. Finally, one old woman, Branwen, the last of Urien's own servants, taking a long glance over her shoulder, disappeared into the house. After a time Urien came to his tower window. His beard was tangled. In two years his hair had gone white. Even the women felt sorry for him. Knowing he was there, Yllvere did not need to look at him. Unclasping her costly cloak and handing it to her servant, she passed calmly over the threshold.

'That spring you were born. A dozen lamps were set by her bedside. There were as many women to attend her. But at the end there was only myself alone with her. The birth was hard. Although she had eased many another into the world before you, you were far larger. Your head and shoulders seemed too broad to pass from her. I took the knife myself. If it were not for the working of the goddess and such skill as I had, you both would have perished. As it was, she lost much blood and kept long to her bed.

'Urien did not come to her. It was I who brought the news. I found him in his tower before the fire. "The thing is done," he said with assurance when he saw me at the door. "It is a manchild," I answered boldly. His look was sullen, but there was craft in his eyes. In his lap he held the book of wars. He closed it quickly. Yet I saw that it was the Red Branch which marks the names and heraldry of the great houses back to the first age. "Well, woman, what is it that she calls him?" he asked me softly. He tried to sweeten his voice, but it did no good. I saw he meant to track it in the book, for all true names follow, root and branch, back to their beginnings. So I was silent.

' "Be not too long, at it," he said.

' "There was no naming," I answered finally and in that I told the truth. Then I said, "At the moment of birth she fainted. I called the women and they took the child."

'At this his breath came from him in a hiss. "See to it that when she gives the name I know it," he warned me harshly. I nodded and went out greatly troubled. But from that time I saw to it that no true name was given you. And this was easier than I had thought.

'I have told you she lost much blood. From the dark of one moon to the dark of another, her mind was addled. She forgot the names of her servingwomen and remained indifferent to her own. All the while you fed at her milk-hard breasts, she took no more note of you than would a viper its young. It was I who held you when you cried. When the weakness left her, she returned to her magic and took up as before. There were the house to manage and the fields. Thereafter you were left to me, and when the fevered dreams burned in my head, it fell to your sisters. They took you as readily as they would take a new doll and tired as easily when you squirmed and vomited. Each named you in her turn. For Sannigon you were Elbrim, for Ryth, Hwyll. They say Grieve calls you Herawd now. She kept you longest, so perhaps that name is best. Yet it is as meaningless as the one I gave you. Still, there was ever someone in the house to do Urien's bidding. I have no doubt that each name was tiptoed up the tower stairs to him nor that he traced them as they came, night after night folding back the pages of the great book in the bad light of the fire until his eyes began to fail. No good it did him.'

Then Vydd laughed and laid her stick against the wall. The pipe was dead in her hand. Once more she filled it and, plucking a live coal from the fire, she puffed her shallow cheeks till it was lit. The blue smoke curled past her forehead and mingled in her hair. Presently she said, 'This much I know of your beginning.' My face fell.

At last I said, 'Some I knew, though much was strange to me. Yet nothing touches on my father, either who he is or where I must go to find him.'

Vydd saw my disappointment. She smiled thinly. 'That hour must come, my child, though it is not yet. Give thanks for that. It is more a blessing than you know. Rather be still and sit with me.'

But I saw only her want of company. So I frowned and stood, crouching beneath the roof. I had my own thoughts and my longing. So

I forgot myself. 'When I open your riddles there is only dust inside,' I told her harshly. Her eyes went queer. She was old and witchborn. It was difficult to remember that she was also a woman. She wept before me. She leaned against the wall, frail as her old stick, and trembled.

'For a time you may keep the crows to teach them,' I said awkwardly, for I sought a way to please her. But truly I knew not how to comfort her.

'The fault is mine that you are cruel,' she said. Her voice was soft as though it came from far off. There was music and sadness in it like a young woman's. 'I feared that Urien would discover what you were and kill you. For that I did not let you have a name. Without a name you have no heart, as no man has until he knows himself. Yet surely your name would give your heart to you and break it all at once.'

I caught her fiercely by the shoulders then. I lifted her. Light as a child she was. 'By the god,' I cried, 'damn hearts and breaking! Just tell me who I am!'

She shivered at my touch. Her eyes burned strangely. For an instant she had laid her head against my chest. A great roar drummed against my ears, a sound so huge I thought it filled the earth. Yet I could not tell what it was. Then, it seemed reluctantly, she pulled herself away. The sound went with her, retreating like a great rain going, like a cloud that drifts far off upon the mountain.

'Put me down, child,' she commanded coldly. Startled, I found an old woman in my arms. She smelled of smoke and salt. My flesh crawled. At once I let her touch the floor. She hobbled back to her stool, then turned to look at me.

She said, 'For years beyond telling, the Kell have watched and counted, child. This only I will tell you. That for which you wait is near. But it goes ever as it must. It will not be hurried. Still, your part will not be hidden longer than you can bear.'

My blood rushed through me and I cried, 'You tell me nothing!'

She turned her face to the wall, drawing her small feet up beneath her like a child. 'Go then to Yllvere,' she murmured thickly. 'Ask her where her servant went the night you were born.'

'You give me but another nut to crack,' I said. 'Better to ask her outright my father's name.'

She hissed at me. Her tongue flickered in her mouth, black like a swan's. A fever took her. Her tangled hair stood out from her head like silver wire. 'You are neither child nor man,' she screamed at me, 'but a fool only. She is greater than all the daughters of the Kell. What was given her has not been given since the world was young. You who share our blood, how is it you are blind to this?'

'I have feared her, but I shall no longer,' I answered when I thought. 'Now I shall not ask, but make her answer.'

Her gray eyes smoldered in her head. She whispered darkly, sucking at her lips. 'She will not answer. The oath that binds her she dares not break. Do only as I bid you. Seek her in her cell when the house sleeps and she is by herself. Then, though it shame you, grab hold of her robe. If you do this, she cannot turn from you. Then she will tell you what she can. Only do not look overlong into her fires. Such was not made for men.'

She ceased. There was a weariness in her face, and pain. Her fury had eaten all my thoughts. I had no word to say to her. So I went out on the hillside. The wind was cold. The bank of clouds had drifted farther down the mountain. In the gray weather a few hard kernels of first snow sped past my eye. Yllvere will be in her cell tonight, I thought. For it was the Eve of Teimhne, when men fear darkness more than other times and stay indoors. Even then I saw how swiftly the light was draining from the world. Already the owls were out hunting. The river lands were dark, the shoulders of the mountain deep in shadow. I went quickly then until at last I saw the walls of Morrigan, its roofs and chimneys pricking into the last light like thorns. For a moment I watched it. There all the years of my life were numbered. But for the villages in our holding and the wood upon the mountain I knew no other place. As I watched, the windows stared back at me, bleak and empty, like the eyes of a man whose soul has left him.

After a time I went down to it. I shunned the back lanes and side doors, that led into the yard, and went instead to the high front gate that opened in the wall. There I entered, much as a stranger would, toiling up the steep road from the east, begging bread and a place indoors before the fire, on this the year's long night.

CHAPTER FOUR

Though I seldom did, I went that night into the hall for company. The meal was done and the servants clearing. By some mischance the dogs got in. Yelping for the smell of meat and snapping at the bones, they toppled a table and had to be driven from the hall. Sanngion, who had put on a new robe only to see a greasy platter overturned upon it, sent word to have the dog boy beaten. She was a woman of middle height, seventeen then, yellow-haired and spare, with the gray eyes of the Kell but with a wide unthinking mouth that was hers only. Like that of all my sisters her skin was fair, almost to whiteness. Yet Yllvere was fairer still, even beyond the race. In the village I had sometimes heard her called the ice witch, though not to my face. But my mother had already gone from the hall, leaving Sanngion to order the women. I saw by the way she sent them scurrying that this pleased her. She held her head tilted slightly, as I had seen my mother do a thousand times, only Sanngion had not her grace. I turned from watching her and stopped a serving girl to take a horn of beer. It may be Sanngion felt my eye had left her. She called out loudly to be certain that I heard, 'Elbrim grows fearless lately. See, sisters, how tardily he came into the hall, the Great Night already fallen.'

'I see not where it is a concern of yours,' I said.

'Our dark brother grows surly too,' she answered without faltering. Yet I saw she glanced sidelong at Ryth to be certain that the other shared her sport. Ryth smiled absently into her cup. Sanngion went on, 'You should not be offended. Indeed it is a pleasure to have you dine with us, so rarely it is you do.'

Ryth giggled. Wiping the wine stain from her upper lip, she said, 'Yes, tell us why you honor us. From what I've seen, you prize the damp mews and nursing wormy crows above our company.'

'No,' said Sanngion. 'It is the dark he prizes, being half in it already.'

Ryth laughed outright then, but nervously. Only Grieve sat silent at her place.

'Truly that is something that I wonder,' Ryth said, joining in. 'As you are, can you both see and dream at once?' She looked around to see what I would say.

Sanngion's smile had widened. She crossed her thin arms upon her breasts. 'Yes, brother, I am curious to hear this also.'

They knew I had no answer for them.

Ryth pouted. 'His love for his crows is more.' Slyly, she began to whine.

'The crows are gone,' I said. Then all at once I rose up from the table. Standing over them, I let them feel my height. 'Today,' I said, 'I gave them to Vydd's keeping.'

Grieve whipped around me. Her breath came sharply. There was wonder in her look, and fear, and, just as I turned to find the door, at the very corner of her lips, a smile.

I went up the stairs that bent around the watchtower. It was opposite to Urien's and smaller, with space for but a single guard. On the stair a lamp was burning. It made a patch of oily soot above the flame. Throughout the house this night the lamps were bright. In the hall and in the kitchen, fires had been built high to last past midnight, when the servants would roll out new logs to keep the fires till morning. Such was the custom on Teimhne. I took the stair lamp down and smothered it.

The guard post was unmanned. Urien had none to watch for him. But Yllvere's fame, her women told each other boldly, had spread among the river lords and kept their spearmen from our mountain. In truth none came. But then Morrigan was always on the edges of the world. I climbed out on the roof, holding to a spike to keep my balance. Here I meant to wait until the housethralls pulled the last logs on the hearths and crawled, weary and relieved, into the safety of their beds. Above the walls I could look out across the night. The smudged light of the nearest village leapt red against the winter clouds. There, alone before the barred doors of his kin, one man would keep a huge fire burning through the night. That also was the custom.

A chill wind drove down from the mountain. I heard the deathless leaves of Gwen Gildrun whisper on it. I closed my mind and would not listen. Instead I thought of Yllvere. Soon, I thought, she will go down the long stair to her cell beneath the house. Yet I knew the rest must sleep before I followed. I pulled the wool of my cloak closer about my shoulders. Still I shivered.

Beyond the wall the world lay silent, hushed but for the wind, and hidden. Only the red light of the village fire was with me. It watched me like an eye. I wished it gone, blinded like my own. I closed the one that saw and sat, waiting for the night to fill my head with darkness, the wind to chill the heart I did not have until it stopped. There are places in the soul a man would hide from, times a man might rather die than see too clearly his own face. I was a long time alone. Then something nudged me. I turned and found Grieve sitting down beside me, the red light of the distant fire curling like a worm in each of her eyes.

'Herawd?' she said.

'It is not my name.'

'She told you, then.'

'Nothing.'

'She spoke with you.'

'She told me a long story which did not have my father's name. For this I was angry with her. So she took away my own.'

'Not then,' she said. 'When you were born.'

'It is the same.'

'No.'

'I do not have it.'

'My father would have killed you had he known.'

'He is too old.'

'Not in the beginning. It was his searching that sucked his life.'

'In the books you read him.'

'Yes.'

'And you knew then what he looked for?'

'Yes.'

'And still you read to him.'

She smiled. 'Only what I pleased, not what he sought.' She looked at me hopefully. 'Come in to the fire,' she said.

It had begun to snow. Huge flakes like wheels of crystal swirled above the roof and filled our sight. I thought of the man upon the mountain whose work it was to feed the fire. I pitied him. The farmers say on Teimhne that even the dead fear this long night, that it will never end. For the dead are the earth's as well and keep her seasons. Drawn, they crawl from their deep shadows. Their faces, the color of iron, hang at the edges of the light. He that keeps the fire must look on them, even on the faces of those he loved.

'Go down to bed,' I told her. She stared at me. Then her face twisted and she broke away. I did not follow her. I heard her footsteps vanish on the stair. A long time after, I went down.

* * *

The fire burned high in the empty hall, throwing the shadows back into corners. A wide passage led past the kitchens. Many doors and openings branched off along the way, the rooms empty but filled with light – here with lamps and there with candles. Everywhere beneath the roof the hot air smelled of wax and oil. The kitchen opened under a broad stone arch. There in the large round chamber the ovens roared with flame. The knives were put away. But on the flat square tables the rising bowls lay abandoned where the cook had left them, unscrubbed and sour. From the scullery there came a sound. I peered in but it was only a pair of eels, still alive and rolling over one another in a pail.

Across the room by the side of the ovens there was a door. It was small and windowless. Its hinges were gray metal. No device marked it. It might have led into the yard or out to the cold pantry where the meat hung in coats of fat and the stone floors were sticky with blood. But it did not. Even in its plainness it was Yllvere's. All the house knew it and let it be.

The latch came easily. It opened with my touch upon the ring. Inside, a narrow stair dropped into the dark. I went a few steps. On one side, cut within the wall, there was a ledge where once, I judged, torches had been kept. Nothing remained but a clay vessel cracked along one side and a black stain where the tar had hardened on the stone. She also is at home in the dark, I thought, and so went on.

At first there was light from above, a wavering glow from the oven fires. Then the narrow stairs turned a corner and the weak light faded. After that I had only the sound of my own breath for company, though once I thought I heard the faint trickle of unseen water dripping on the rock. Gradually the air grew cooler. I felt my way along the wall. The stone was rough and crudely set, older work than the house above. In places there were fissures – some wide enough to hold my fist. I thought of snakes and dared not thrust my hand in them.

It was not the same dark underground. Here daylight never entered. Changeless, with no seasons, the dark had settled ever farther down within itself, bloated yet never satisfied, sucking at the upper world. All my life I had heard whispers, servants' talk, that the stair was deeply delved, cut into the heart of the mountain rock, or that it joined, after twisting through a maze of many tunnels and vaulted rooms, the great mines that lay beneath Géar Finn. I had thought it only women's talk. Now I wondered.

The Kell say that at the beginning, in a place that no man knows, the dark, in the anguish of her labor, waited to devour the sun and moon, her children, as they sprang from her side. Cold she was and hungry, coiled like a serpent about the well from which the waters of time flow into the world. It was the god Duinn, it is said, who tricked her, filling her belly with great stones. I pondered this but could not laugh. Who is to say whether such talk is truth or lies? I knew only that the darkness weighed on me. It stole my sight and blew dust into my mouth. Although I had wished for darkness alone upon the roof, I grew to fear it underground. For a moment I wanted no more of it and wished for light. But then I shook myself, finding courage in my own flesh. Have I not climbed their sacred tree? I thought. Like Duinn, have I not stolen from their dark mother the children of the air?

I went more quickly after that. The passage that had been almost cold grew warmer by degrees. A whisper of parched air blew against my cheek. As suddenly it was gone. But soon it came in scalding waves that buffeted my chest and arms. Deep within the stone something beat and thundered. Then around a corner a red glare leapt up along the wall. I crept down to it. Softly, like a thief, I slipped within my mother's cell.

All at once a sheet of flame took all my sight. Shielding my face, I shuddered and fell back. Intent upon the fire, Yllvere did not notice me. Her arms were raised, her robe dropped to her elbows so that her pale skin took on the color of the fire. The hot wind lifted her long hair, red-gold and gleaming, like a flame itself. Her eyes were fierce, her small mouth twisted, the eldest words of Kell speech in her throat.

'*Si man i yulma nin enquantuva*?' she asked the fire. Then in some sadness of her own she turned away, plucking a bowl from her table. She drew a small claw from it. The nails were red-silver and scattered light. I saw she meant to toss it to the flames. Already she had lifted it. But in that motion, out of the sides of her eyes, she saw me.

'Go back!' she hissed, her clear brows arched, caught up in some half-finished spell. Her look was dangerous. In that moment I took hold of her robe. The thick cloth seemed to sear my hands. This put me in a rage, and I held more tightly till I saw the skin of all my fingers blacken and peel away. The bright blood foamed; stubs of bone poked through my boiling flesh. Then at once the pain and burning passed and I knew it for the spell it was. The cloth was only warm. In anger I let out my breath.

'What am I that you toy with me?' I said. Even as I spoke the firelight darkened a little and the roar of flames grew less.

She studied me out of her deep eyes. 'No man comes here,' she warned and turned again to watch the fire.

I pulled her back.

'None came into your holy wood. And yet I went to it,' I said. She moved fretfully, but I would not let her go.

'I must tend the fire,' she answered quickly, watching it. 'It is my duty. Not even you and your fool's bravery could do it in my place. Not you nor anyone unless I choose.'

I turned my eye to the thing in her hand. 'Surely,' I mocked her, 'you do not feed your fire with lizards' claws. Who is it brings wood down these stairs for you?'

'No one comes here but myself.'

With that I laughed.

She drew her hair back from her face, where it had flown before her eyes. She answered softly, gentle all at once. 'Come to the fire,' she said. 'Gaze into it and see yourself what burns.'

'I have cut enough wood on the mountain to know the look of it,' I answered curtly, for I had not forgotten what Vydd told me and would not look into the flames.

Her pale brows drew together. 'I remember you so small,' she said. 'Your child's hands could not hurt me then.' She shook her head. 'Now let me go.'

'Tell me my father's name,' I said.

A sound came out of her, such as I have heard a hoarpig make when I had cornered it against a rock. A death sound. She could not hide it. She looked at me as one compelled against her will. Then something altered in her face. 'It is not the world's wood I burn,' she said. 'If you would only look at it.'

'I did not come to watch your fire.'

'It is more and greater than you think,' she said. 'Here a root of Gwen Gildrun breaks the earth.' Her bright eyes swept across my face.

'No,' I said. 'It is too far.'

'Hear me,' she whispered. Her eyes were gray and fire-gold as she spoke. 'On the day I came from the bed in which I bore you I found it here, one bent twig growing small up through the stones. I broke it off. I wanted only a little light. And when I had set a flame to it, it passed completely from my thoughts. But on the next night I found it grown again and burned it and so the next. But always there was more than there had been.'

She stopped to draw a breath and loosed it. I saw the weariness in the lines of her throat and wondered. I felt the firelight flicker. She held herself, tightening her fingers on her arms.

'Nightly these fourteen years,' she said, 'I have come to this deep place to clear the maze of wood. Nightly I cast it in the fire. For should I stop, the root of that great tree would drive its hard fingers between the stones that bear the house and it would fall.' Her voice shook slightly and she stopped.

My thoughts came in a swarm, wildly as thoughts had come to me in dreams. I saw the towers tumbled and the walls in ruin. A cold wind whined above the broken stone. Then I thought, what if she lies? Her face was turned back toward the fire. I could not see it.

'Please,' she cried. 'It fades!'

I felt my hand upon her robe. 'Tell me what I ask,' I said.

Her lips had parted but her voice stopped, clenched between her teeth. I had seen Grieve do this and knew at last where she had got it from. She stood a moment, wordless before me.

'Does it require such thought?' I asked harshly.

The tired lines of her mouth drew back. 'Do you think you catch me unprepared in this?' she said. 'I have seen that look in you a thousand times. When you could scarcely talk, your eyes would ask it. When you were older and too proud to ask, then you would hide your face when I would pass and so I knew.'

'Then be done with it!' I shouted. 'Say my father's name and I will let you go.'

'No,' she whispered. 'I will not barter it like a herring wife.' Her voice was shrill. 'I swore it to your father on the day I left him. I swore it by the kingdoms undersea, by all we lost, by our last hope of its return. He made me swear it. It was no choice of mine. But I will live with it and so you must.'

I shook my head from side to side and cursed. I crushed her robe between my hands. 'What sort of man commands so black a promise?'

She drew back a little. 'When you come to him at last, then you must ask him.'

'And will you say where I will find him?'

'No.'

'Or, if ever I saw him, how I would know his face?'

The skin below her eyes was patched with grief. 'I would tell you if I knew,' she answered sadly. 'It was long ago. He will have changed. Men do.'

My hot breath sprang from me. The sharp words tore my throat. 'You leave me nothing, then!' I cried. 'No, less than nothing. Not even my own name to give him.'

Her voice was small, thin as thread of silver. It bound me before I knew. 'This I will give you,' she whispered softly. 'From the beginning I have saved it.' She looked at my long face as one would watch a child. 'You know,' she said, 'that it was given out I fainted before I gave the name. But for the instant I saw you, huge and bawling, my blood still on your face, I knew what it would be. If I fainted, I did so smiling. And I was myself again long before any but Vydd knew. I have kept it since, whispering it in my thoughts.' She paused and smiled at me. She touched my face and smoothed my hair. I felt the robe cloth move, loose, in my lax fingers. Unthinking I let it fall. Even as she saw it she sprang away. At the edge of her low voice was laughter. 'As you were mountain-born,' she said. 'I called you Finn.'

I stared at her in disbelief. 'It is but half a name,' I cried. Already she stood before the fire. Just as she threw it, I saw the silver glitter of the claw as it tumbled toward the hearth. My breath caught. I meant to jerk my head away. Too soon the hot flames reared before my eyes.

'Poor Finn,' she sighed within the roar. 'There was another born that night. I clove the name that you might share it. The other Tabak took away, even before I looked on it or touched its face. Whatever the women thought of Tabak, he was not mine. If he served me, it was service to his lord. And when he took the child, he did his own lord's bidding. I bartered then, one life to ransom one. I paid that price for you, to keep a promise the Kell made when long ago they walked the shores of Hren. There to see the Selchie, their black eyes shining, come walking once more from the sea.'

She finished but I did not look at her. A sickness ate at me and sucked my life. My shoulders slumped. I felt my head fill up with flame.

CHAPTER FIVE

The snow lay deep upon Géar Finn. I saw it one day to the next. When I woke to see the women unfastening the skins from the windows to break the ice and let air in, I saw it. Its two horns stood out white and distant against the winter sky. But in the evening the mountain flung its long arms out at me across the ice fields and the walls. It welled huge and unsatisfied within the yard. Four-handed, it clawed the casement and came in. Restless, it waited in the room, leering from the foot of my bed with both its heads, its mouths unhinged, creaking and moaning like old trees in a gale. Yet it did not frighten me. I knew it for the riddle, unanswered, that raked my mind.

Each night I waited for it, coiled in myself, as cats wait for their prey. But more often, when they remembered and against the cold, the women would rebind the skins. Then if I stirred within the bed, they said it was a fever. Sometimes I tried to speak to them, for I wished the windows clear and open, free to let the mountain in. 'See,' they would whisper among themselves, 'he dreams.' So they would creep out softly, deaf to the mountain, banging with its arms and hands against the wall.

I slept.

Grieve came in the evenings, bearing a lantern and a tray. Without a word she knelt beside the bed. I saw her pale hands take the cup and lift the hot wine to my lips. Perhaps I drank. But it was only her hands that I remembered, her fingers gray with cold. Sometimes there was another, but not in that place. A tree spread over us and the wind was warm. I took hold of her bare arms. Her skin, I remember, was white as ivory. The hair that fell about her shoulders was thick and full, dark as the holes between the stars. Its blackness troubled me. It was like no other I knew except my own. When we kissed, her black eyes did not leave my face. 'Finn,' she murmured once and held me half away. Though I knew it was a dream, it hurt me. I had not dreamed of women so before. I felt an emptiness in the hollow of my palm where her small breast had been. When she was gone, I wept. Perhaps all men know this. Yet it was new to me and I did not understand my grief. In the dream I called after her, a name I could not remember when I awoke.

The sound came softly. Rapping. I sat up in my bed. Blinking, I looked around. A log was sputtering in the grate. I closed my eye and leaned back once more, waiting for sleep to take me and the dream to come. Instead I listened to the wind nuzzling the chimneys like a wolf. The snow hissed on the stones below. In time I nodded and almost slept. Something rapped again. I stirred. My eye went to the door. The servants had left it open. A single torch was flickering in its wall iron, casting a sullen yellow light across the floor. I turned my head, the sound still in my ears, until I knew the place from which it came.

I got up slowly. My knees were stiff and it was hard to stand. To cover my nakedness I dragged the great fur blanket after me. A sharp pain started in my legs and did not stop until it branched all through me like a tree of ice. I hobbled more than walked, dizzy from standing and the cold. When at last I found the window, I tore away the leather strings and pried off the skins where they had frozen to the wood. The snow blew in, a cold gust that stung my face and thatched my brows.

Shaking the dusting of snow from her black wings, the crow hopped quickly from the ledge. She was twice the size she had been and yet I knew her. Her fierce eyes glared at me. She flew up past my face. My wits still wild, I thought she meant to peck my eye. I heard my breath shake faintly from my lips. Instead she perched upon a rafter near my head. She saw me wince.

'I am fed and not on human meat,' she rasped. Her voice was like the rattling of loose stones. Numbly I stared at her. If I had begun to tremble in the cold, I did not feel it.

'What do you want of me?' I said. The sound of my own voice was strange in my ears.

'I am yours and so I came.'

'I did not send for you.'

'No matter; it is time.'

'To what purpose?'

'Twelve days past, the New Year came and went,' she croaked. 'You have slept long enough. I came to wake you.'

I reached for her. My cold fingers scratched the empty air. Then I remember only the coldness where I lay and the hard whine of the wind blowing off the mountain. Later there were voices. The sound of quick feet on the stone. They came and went away. After a while I heard a heavier tread. The door was pulled back wide to let some huge thing pass. Thick arms dug beneath my back. Something pulled, then lifted me. Above my face the dark head loomed, the deep eyes looking down.

For a moment I saw the wolfish grin through the twisted matter of his beard. He knelt and put me gently on the bed.

'Tabak,' I whispered in surprise.

Heedless, the voices went back and forth among themselves.

'– there by the window –'

'– his arms stretched out, the fingers frozen shut –'

'– beating? –'

'– Yes –'

'– the straps. Pulled out, the window –'

'– Why? –'

'To live,' the stern voice said. I saw him go, more like a bear than a man, the great shoulders edging sideways through the door, filling it so that the light from the hall torch faltered and then came back when he had passed. I meant to call to him. It was on my lips.

Her hands were in her lap. Encircled by her gray fingers was a cup of wine. Later I felt the liquid hot within my throat and coughed. Grieve's gray eyes had opened wide.

'Herawd,' she whispered.

'I must teach you my true name,' I said. She did not pay the least attention but flung her thin arms about my shoulders, burying her head against my chest. 'I so feared – ,' she sobbed, her fingers tight in the tangle of my hair.

'You have spilled the wine,' I laughed. I moved to lift her so I might see her face. I found I could. She was startled and pleased at once to see my strength. Her lashes stuck together with her tears. I put her down.

'I had thought – I – ' She tried to speak. She stopped, looking at me suddenly, as though for the first time. 'Mother said – that you – would surely – die,' she said slowly, each word by itself as though she tested every one to see if it were counterfeit. 'You were so cold, she said, that she could barely touch you. When Tabak carried you from the roof –'

'No,' I interrupted her. 'You are mistaken. It was here. I remember it. I had gone to the window.'

'Yes, of course,' she said and smiled, relieved. 'That too, but the first time. That night, on Teimhne, when we had talked and the snow was falling. Then Tabak came into the hall with you.'

But already I had stopped her. 'This you saw?'

'No,' she said, though it made no difference. 'I had not come down. It was Mother, as I told you.'

Again I stopped her. 'Who else saw it?'

'No one. For it was early.'

'But did you touch me?'

She shook her head. 'I came here. I pleaded with her. Still she would not let me in. It was two days before she would unbolt the door. I cried when I saw you. I could not stop. It was my fault I left you in your black mood. But I swear I did not know you meant to stay, the snow already falling.'

'You told her this?'

'Yes.' But she was puzzled then.

Perhaps I smiled. Only she did not like the look of it. I said, 'Then, it was she that told you I was found out on the roof.'

She shifted then, afraid without reason to meet my eye.

'Is this not so?' Perhaps I shouted.

She drew a breath, then let it wither. 'There was a time you came to me,' she said, 'and you would tell me all you thought.' But she saw the cold impatience in my look. 'Yes,' she answered flatly, 'she told me then.'

By the bedside she had left a platter with a few scraps of meat. Each had been cut in strips as one might do to feed a child. Greedily I crammed them in my mouth. The meat was barely warm. She watched me, her head resting on her bent knee. 'You were ever kind to me,' I told her quietly. 'More than I deserved.' But she was used to me. Her eyes by now were dry.

'Tell me what you wish,' she said.

I smiled outright. 'It is unseemly that you should see my nakedness,' I answered. 'If you will, bring up my clothes.'

She retrieved the wine cup without a word, dropped her thin legs to the floor, and stood. 'I will send a servant.' A silence grew between us.

'But should you come yourself,' I said at last and saw her lips pull back tightly from her teeth, 'bring me your father's book.'

Her mouth fell open. 'You went to her!'

I nodded. 'Such as it is, I have a name.'

Behind the curtain of her yellow hair, flying through the door, for one last time I saw her smile.

I had come to myself slowly. In truth I had awakened before Grieve came, and slept again. But I remember how bright the day had seemed when I first woke. I had watched the dust motes dancing in the air. They floated in the glowing light, which slid in at the edges of the window skins. Gaping and bemused, half knowing what I did, I watched them as fish risen from deep water look on air. Perhaps I took them for shining flies. I wonder I did not snap at them. For I remember hunger then, a pain in my belly that twisted like a knife. Truly hunger was always with me in that house. The women ate stingily. One small dove was hearty fare to them. It took six portions to remind me I had eaten, to which I added onions, cheese and bread in larger measures. Still I often went away unsatisfied. The thin aunts, their dinners done, would look up from their dry plates. Perhaps they thought I meant to eat them too. I closed my eyes.

For hours it seemed the wind outside was still. From the house below I heard in snatches the servants talking, a low and intermittent drone too distant to make out the words. It was with that, I think, that I remembered who I was. From the yard there had come the crunch of boots on snow. One of the servants had gone to brush the horses or do some other work. Doubtless in the kitchen the cook had been putting out the loaves. Life is as it was, I had thought, so little note they take of me. But I realized that Yllvere had hid everything from them. Even her own women she kept ignorant.

But for Vydd, I thought. Surely she knew or guessed. Had she not sent Ninmir soaring from the mountain to rap on the window, to wake me from my sleep? But then I thought, perhaps it was a dream. I sat up once more to see the window clearly. The straps that bound the skins had been retied. A few loose pieces lingered on the floor. It proved no more than that I had torn them in my haste. I groaned.

What had I gained from any one of them, I thought, but children's tales and lies? Each answer only left me more to ask. The memory of the fire arched in my head. What Yllvere might have given she did not give. What hope I had had was burned up in the flames. I will have nothing from the Kell, I thought, and turned my mind from them. It was no woman nor any man I waited for, but only the dry pages of a book.

By the third hour, the light already gone upon Géar Finn, Grieve had not come. I paced the cold room. In time I grew bored with my nakedness and wrapped myself once more within a blanket. I sat before the grate and stirred the coals. There were faces in the flames and shadows in the burning wood. Frail and beautiful, they flickered with passing life. Each regarded me with frightened eyes. Almost I thought I knew them. But the fire had changed them before I found the names.

At my back the door squeaked on its hinges.

I did not turn. 'Let me see the book,' I said.

'Give me your name.' The voice was old and edged with care.

I whirled around and saw him. His feet were planted in the doorway. In one hand he held his book, in the other the long sword by which twelve men were dead. I did not mean to be the next.

'I am not armed,' I snarled. 'But even the small hands of a child should be enough for your old throat.'

Silently he stood and watched me. His face was lean, agelined. But it showed no hint of feeling now, only the marks of other sorrow pressed into his mouth. His long thin fingers curled upon the sword hilt. 'You have been too long among the women,' he answered evenly. 'Had I wished you ill, I would have done it when you were still a boy and killing you was no great task.' He was still a moment, his old eyes moving on my face. He lifted the sword. Even then I saw it strained his arm. 'You stole this once when you climbed into the women's wood. Now I mean to give it to you.'

My lips twitched bitterly. I remembered his cold words to me, the millwright watching, the day he did not make me his heir. 'What use is a sword to a one-eyed man?' I said. The blood flared in his face. His own lips parted.

'No better did I expect from you,' he answered angrily. 'Always you were the crooked stick among the straight. Nonetheless, I will keep to what I said.' He went to the bed, then laid the great sword flat across it. 'It saw good service in days that are now gone. And it has kept its fame if I have not.'

I did not know what to make of him. I drew back. But though I hid it, he saw or guessed the question in my look.

'It was my father's sword,' he said, his voice soft as the murmur of the fire. 'And my grandfather's before it came to him. In better days when Meroc ruled, the king's own smith had made it for my kin. My father gave it to me when he died.' He paused as if in thought. 'I have had it since I was a child.'

And still my heart was hard. The struggle between us was only part in words. The firelight brushed his face but brought him no relief. I saw how his mouth had tightened.

He stared, his deep eyes narrowed, cold once more. 'Would you have me hand it now to Sanngion or Ryth?' He gave a bitter laugh. 'A fit thing, do you think, to stir a pot or skewer a chicken?'

I turned to the window so as not to look at him. He could but wonder why I had pulled the strings away and tore the scraped skins down. The night was black and fierce with stars. Beyond the mountain I saw the faint paired lights which mark the north, the travelers' stars. I knew then I would go. And since I did not mean to stay, it mattered little what I said to him.

'There was a time,' I said, 'when I would have taken the smallest gift you gave me. And thanked you for it. There was a time, the night they held the rite for me, when Jjared and the men came up from the towns, I thought that I might even be your heir.'

His old face set hard and cold. 'Heir to what?' he asked, his voice grown soft as though his breath had gone with it. 'To two dead wives and my dead son?'

I started. Perhaps I pitied him. 'It is said,' I answered haltingly, 'that once you were the king's own man, the first of all his soldiers.'

'I killed what he bade me, even among those that followed him.' His eyes clung to my face. At length he said, 'Take the sword. It is better given late than rusting here for want of use.'

I went to the bed and lifted the weapon, hefting the cold metal in my hand. Though I had carried it once before, until that moment I had not felt how deadly a thing it was. I held it up before him. He saw how readily I turned it to my will. I did not forget.

I said, 'I have heard it said you meant to kill me once.'

'Once,' he said. His voice stayed quiet but his eyes had slipped away from mine. I saw them shrink into his head as though he found some memory. 'I loved her once as well,' he answered, his small voice hushed in the stillness of the room. 'You are too young to know how that can drive a man. She was lithe as an eel when I first saw her. I remember how lightly she would spring into my arms. When she came back, fat with you, riding another man's mare two winters after she had gone, I would have killed. There was a dead child in this house before. I knew the look of it. I would not have turned from it, but first I wanted your father's name.'

'So you beat her for it.'

He nodded frankly. 'I have done worse things than strike a whore.'

I was silent. 'She would not tell you,' I said finally, getting past the word.

'I taught myself to wait,' he said. 'You would not be a child forever. I knew one day you would make her tell you.'

I glared at him. 'And I would say what she would not?'

He shook his head and frowned at me. 'I have children of my own within the house.'

A sound came out of me. I had been a fool not to think of it. 'Where is Grieve?' I shouted.

His lips pulled into a smile that blazed across the eyes.

'She did not tell me,' he answered evenly. 'There was no need of it. I found her rummaging among my books. I knew she would not pick through them idly. More, I knew the thought to take from it.'

He kept perfectly still, his deep eyes laughing, even when I grabbed his neck and held the great sword ready to plunge into his throat. 'Where is she now?' I cried.

'I sent her to Yllvere,' he answered, pleased.

'To what place?'

He smiled. 'Where your mother always goes when it grows dark.' He watched me. 'You know that in the kitchen, at the back of it, there is a door.'

I felt the flames shoot up in my head. Before he finished, I was gone.

I took the steps in a dozen leaps, pushed into the hall and passed it. There were still some women squirreling about with lamps and bedding. They screamed to see a naked man run by them with a sword. In the kitchen I faced the cook, who, hearing the noise coming at her from the inner rooms, had a cleaver ready in her hand.

'Keep back,' I warned between my teeth.

She stared at me as one would watch the mad.

I made my way past her to the door. Before I touched it, I saw the latch draw up, heard something move behind the wood. The door came open with a groan. They stood together looking at me, the darkness at their backs, their faces flushed with heat. Grieve had her thin arm about my mother's waist. She leaned on her. The edges of her yellow hair were singed. A patch of blisters had already risen on her cheek.

'Grieve,' I cried to her.

I heard her speak, her voice dry and distant so at first I could not make out the words.

Something moved in my mother's face. She lifted her pale hand. Touching a strand of my sister's hair, she drew it out between her fingers. The ghosts of the fire burned brightly in Grieve's eyes. She whispered but then I heard the words.

'You have gone where no man goes,' she said. 'What you have looked on, no man must see.' She paused, regarding me as I had seen the women look at Urien.

I turned my back on her.

'Finn,' she called out after me.

I let the small voice fade, unanswered. It echoes softly between the walls.

CHAPTER SIX

I had thought myself immune, secure and safe against the worst outrages of my fate. In that, I had been no more than a child. True, I had lived with sorrow and knew that more must come. Yet when I looked ahead at troubles, I expected what I knew. It was gentleness that disarmed me and took me off my guard. I had trusted in that, in Grieve's kind ways. Urien's vengeance was the fruit of old betrayal and his pride. In my anger there was room enough for him and even space for Yllvere's indifference. I knew them both for what they were. Grieve alone escaped from me, she who I had thought was mine – possessed, as one might enfold a dove in the hand, wrapping fingers over its warm body, feeling its small heart flutter against the palm. But when I had gone to look for her – to save her, I had thought – even as she stood before me, I found her gone. I knew then I held but empty air.

The Kell are what they say, the spawn of nevermen and harsh old dreams. The women of the world are one. All their lives are memory. There is no new thing in them. When it came to the test, the Kell blood raged as wild in Grieve as in any of my sisters. In time, the sea longing would surely beat against her brains and she, like the rest of the winter brood, would creep down the mountain wall to the western ocean to wait upon the shore for their impossible lords to come cold and gleaming from the waves. But I was done with that. Before morning I would be gone. Eastward, a direction for which the Kell care nothing.

I had no horse of my own. In the stable I saddled Yllvere's, not a war-horse but nimble-footed and tireless, a gift, the women said, from my father, grown old since its giving yet strangely far from dying.

If I went like a thief, I felt no shame. What was a horse in the balance? My father left me no legacy. Naked I had been born into the house. If I left with little added, it would be enough. What, after all, was a bastard heir to but himself? I took a longshirt, bundled three loaves of travelers' bread and Urien's sword. There was no one to see my going. The women had retired at last to their chambers. My sisters, I imagined, their hair night-snarled and their wide mouths slack and damp, were long in their beds. Grieve, for all I knew, had gone down once more with Yllvere to work at the fire.

Just beyond the gate I turned and gave the house one last salute. In the darkness with all the doors closed and the windows empty, Morrigan had a cold, stupid look like the severed head of an aurochs. It was a house, I was certain, that Death kept – bought with murder, enthralled by a dead boy I could not replace. And were not the Kell dead themselves, I thought, their deep hearts cold as dreams?

Caught up in my thoughts, I did not notice the horseman until he was already close upon me. I had not looked to be followed. Yet he came not from Morrigan but seemingly out of the darkness itself, as though a boulder had been given the shape and form of horse and rider. Without appearing to hurry, he gained on me. The iron shoes of his mount struck blue sparks from the stone. A heavy war helm hid his face and a great cloak covered his shoulders. Yet by his size I knew him well enough.

'Hold, my lord Finn,' he cried as he drew beside me. The flanks of our horses touched lightly. The mare gave a cold shiver.

'Go back to Yllvere,' I ordered.

Tabak shook his dark head. Stolidly he rode beside me. I saw the slits of his eyes through the cleft of his helm but could read nothing in them. He looked straight ahead, surveying the road. If he meant to stop me, he gave no sign of it.

'I am leaving the house,' I said. 'Never shall I return to it.'

'I have heard you,' he replied and rode on as before.

I stared aside awhile to master my anger. Though we were matched in height, I was not his equal.

'What business do you have with me?' I asked at last.

'To follow.'

'I seek no company.'

A brightness had come into his eyes, like the cunning in the eyes of a dog who in all its life has learned one trick and waits to perform it. In the darkness he smiled. In the clefts of the helm, I saw the lips had parted.

'I waited for my lord's birth,' he said. 'Fifteen winters have come and gone since first I heard you cry within the house. Fifteen winters I waited outside your mother's door, my ax at my side, that Urien would not come to her. She is a young woman even now, and you were to be the last of her children. So it was decreed. I did what I was bidden, though it was clear to anyone who watched that Urien had spent his seed. Yet I was faithful to my trust. I waited. Lord, I saw your first steps in the house. I watched you, when you were grown, go off into the fields and saw when they carried you broken, near death, from Gwen Gildrun. Fifteen winters I stood my post. Now my young lord goes forth and the waiting is over.'

It was the longest speech I had heard from him. There was a solemnity about his words and much that made me wonder. But I could not get past the mistake and laughed. 'You have the years wrong,' I said, for I knew my age.

He shook his head. 'Why do you listen to the women?' he asked. 'Surely my lord knows the Kell could never count.'

'I do not know it,' I threw back at him then added, 'but should it be so, what does it matter?'

'You have been too long on this mountain,' Tabak answered gravely. I meant to question him more on it, but a wind sprang up and blew away our voices. I wrapped my cloak across my face and, glad only to be done with it, rode on. For the moment let him come, I thought. The important thing was only to be gone.

Toward morning it rained, a gray cloying drizzle that clung to our eyes and made the stones slick and the footing precarious. We were forced to dismount and lead the horses to keep them from stumbling. By dawn there was no brightening. We went slowly, feeling our way as much as seeing it. There were places where the road, because of its steepness, became rough stairs cut into the track. This the horses found difficult. They fought us and we feared for their legs as much as our own. We cursed them, breathing in the dampness till it hurt our lungs. Beyond the wheeze of our breaths we were as mutes, moving in a world of wet wool. Our sodden boots on the rock made little sound. Except for the occasional whinny of the horses, there was no other, not even the bark of the wild dogs that hunted these mountains. They at least were safe in their dens, tails curled, their muzzles sunk deep in their fur. Not for the first time I thought of my dry bed beneath the eaves. By now the servants were bustling about, the smoking fires brought once more back to flame.

Tabak's absence would be noticed by the servants before mine. More would be made of it. They were used to my wanderings. But the loss of the horses would trouble them. The stableman would be taken before Yllvere and flogged. She would likely do it herself, not trusting the others to beat him soundly. She would not flinch when the skin tore and the welts oozed blood. To her they were lesser creatures. For their part, they expected no more. The idea of cruelty would have surprised both servant and lady.

I put that behind me. Morrigan has lost us both, I thought, and turned my mind instead to Ormkill. Soon I would see for myself if the books were true. I thought of Tinkern, where it was written the presence of the oak god still lingered, where the leaves whispered prophecy, and a man, if he knew how to listen, might hear his destiny. So the hours passed.

A mist held the land in a shroud that stretched from the ground up to heaven. But the track had broadened and we rode again. In the darkness we had come down from the peaks and into the lonely waste of hills the maps call Menhirs. It was a place well named. For here there were no trees or huts but only huge upright stones, man-high but sunken to their knees in the soft earth. It was an ancient place, already old when the road makers were at work in our mountains. The stones themselves were blank, the dark mountain granite worn smooth of runes. If they were god-shrines, time had forgotten them and eaten away their memory like old flesh. Only the acrid smell was left. Indeed, something yet hung in the air and burned my eye. I squinted into the mist, seeking to keep the road. The mare snorted. I had to nudge her belly to drive her on.

Tabak's swollen eyes moved cautiously across the ground. He looked weary, yet he kept to the task. We dared not rest until we had passed the stones. No wind stirred. The horses plodded on. Grown impatient, they sniffed the air. They wanted meadow grass and our weight from off their backs. But throughout the murkbound world there was only the smell of godstones and the damp. I too had grown restless. I had not slept since dawn of the day past and in all that time only tasted a bit of travelers' bread. Beyond all, the darkness wearied me.

At length the horses grew too exhausted to carry us. We dismounted and went on foot. We led them through the weary end of the afternoon. About an hour after sunset the cold deepened and a biting wind sprang up. I began to fear we would not escape this land. The great stones did not diminish. They had become, if anything, more numerous, surrounding us like an army through whose silent ranks we passed as captives.

Once I heard a stream. Lured by its faint slavering, we abandoned the track, thinking the water would lead us downward and away from the hills. But the sound was deceptive. Caught among the stones, it echoed queerly. It was some hours more before the land gave way to the east. We had reached, I judged, the outer buttress of the mountain. Below us was a valley, locked in night. Without forlorn hope I started down, Tabak beside me, his mount's bridle jingling in the stillness.

Partway down the slope a rough figure jutted out of the earth. Its features were gray like the rock and stern as the images carved upon the holy rock at Tinkern. It did not move. At first it seemed no more than a stone itself. But the horses knew it for a man and whinnied.

He was old. A stringy, earth-colored beard lay matted on his chest. His garments were in the olden style, now mostly rags and covered with filth. A feeling of foreboding leapt in me. There was no horse near him. What sort of man, I wondered, would walk these hills in such ill weather? For his part, he studied me from behind his large black eyes. His flesh glinted like slate; the ridges of his features were sharp as broken stone. Slowly, like the action of a man who had not moved in a long time, he raised his hand to us, the gray palm outward in a sign of peace.

'What house are you?' I shouted across to him. Being uneasy, I had kept a distance of some yards between us.

'You are late, Finn,' he called to me, his deep voice hollow.

I glanced back sharply at Tabak. 'You know this man?' I asked. 'For I do not.'

The old man raised his eyebrows. An odd light momentarily softened his hard gaze. 'Do not think, my lord,' he said, 'that your name lies only in your servant's keeping.'

Fearing wizardry, I answered. 'I have a name, it seems, from each that knows me. But the name you give me I had not until I left the one who gave it. At that I tore it from her. Now it seems that it was hidden only from myself, and every beggar on the road has it ready to greet me with.'

'It is known far, my lord, if not as wide as that,' he answered back.

'I do not know you, sir,' I said. The place was strange and the meeting unexpected. Though I bore animosity to no man's kindred, I kept my guard. For there were those who hated Morrigan for the blood that Urien spilled. Others, the threads of whose lives Yllvere had twisted with her sorcery, bore us ill. What power this one had I could not guess. It was enough, I saw, to master my own name even before I myself had grown accustomed to the taste of it.

'Your house, sir,' I demanded.

A flicker of amusement crossed his face. 'These stones,' he said.

'That is no fit answer.'

Once more an icy smile had turned his lips. 'Indeed you are his son,' he answered mildly. 'But you are late in coming. I had looked for you last spring. From what is spoken you were fair-sized then, had climbed Gwen Gildrun and brought down the children of the air. It was then

53

that you were needed. Now you have wasted a full year's turning. Be warned, Finn, the way is long and at the end your father waits.'

The mention of my father, more unlooked-for than my name, took all my breath and wrenched my heart.

I gasped. 'What do you know of him?'

His cold eyes gleamed. 'All that may be known by one who only stands in this one place and listens.'

I had no patience with his riddling. The blood beat at my temples and I no longer thought. 'Answer what I ask!' I cried and pulled my sword. Poor weapon that it was, so long unused, it was weapon enough, I judged, to frighten one old man. I brandished it before him. At my back Tabak had been shouting. In my anger I made no sense of it. Quickly I advanced upon the man. He did not draw back.

I would have struck him. But Tabak was at my side and stayed my hand. Then, before I knew, I saw him kneel, his thick neck bent, and yet he kept his eyes on the man.

The old man smiled. 'Your faithfulness, Tabak, has not escaped me.' The voice, though full of echoes, nonetheless was kind.

'He is a child,' said Tabak, 'and raised by women on the mountain. Sadly, he knows nothing of the world.' I stared at him.

'Teach him quickly, then,' said the man. 'For the world he enters now grows perilous. Since Dagda first set me here to guard the riverlands, to set both Anu and her wood apart and keep the Kell, I have marked the days and watched the seasons turn. Since that first time which no man knows I have seen the darkness creep above the ground and the greater darkness falling from the sky. But I have seen it beaten back. Eight times the oak kings, masters of the lightning, the sun on their shoulders, have ruled it. So much was promised. Now once more I ache from darkness and the dread of it. I feel it cold and biting, gathering before me. But of my company only I remember man-speech. Like the very stone they sleep. And who shall waken them? Who is there who will speak the word? The High King has hidden himself and will not be found. Eight victories were promised. That only. The last was left in doubt. Tabak, you must teach him well. Already it grows late and much is surely lost beyond recall.'

As he spoke I felt, like a vast shadowy river, the huge expanse of years roll over me. Along its current marched the shapes of men and kings. Above their heads fire flashed from the sky. The broad land grumbled. But the swords in their hands were rusted and their eyes were empty. The river took them.

When I saw again, his words had broken off. I heard his grunting breath and came close to him to listen. It hissed away. The cold eyes were no longer on me but on some chaos I could not see. Even in the bad light and the mist I saw the cracked and pitted surface of his face, almost looking like a man. For an instant the hairs on my neck rose up with gooseflesh. Then the blood rushed to my face. I turned my back and would not look at it.

Ignoring me, Tabak went up to the stone and made a sign of reverence before it. There was a hush then.

'What is he?' I whispered, hoarse, amazed, afraid to keep the silence.

Tabak's eyes had narrowed like a lynx's.

'Tabak,' I said, my voice a cry.

The muscles rose on his clenched jaw.

'I command you.'

He bared his teeth, white like stones, the lips pulled back like those of a dog that guards his master's house. 'I am your father's servant,' he said.

'It is his son that bids you speak.'

Tabak paused. 'Do you claim him, then?' he asked. 'Above Vllvere? Denying all the Kell, forsaking them, the house and women?'

I pleaded then. 'I have left the house,' I said. 'Why do you test me?'

'A child may run away and still not leave.'

'No,' I said, for in that moment I understood, 'you shall not bait me. More than I know myself, you know what I am. The women only speak in riddles. You are no better. Answer it yourself, for I cannot.'

When he heard me out, he smiled. It angered me.

'Hear me,' I said. 'Whatever it is I am, I am no farmer's boy that the night wind frightens me. The stone spoke. How, I do not know. Yet I will not close my ears to it. I see only that it touches on my father. Either you will explain it to me or you will not.'

His dark lips twisted into speech. 'Indeed,' he said, 'you are his son.'

I felt my hand close on the pommel of my sword. It gained me nothing. I let it go and swung out my arm and pointed, first east, then north, then west. 'Where do I seek for him?' I asked.

He shook his great sad head. 'I am to follow you,' he said. That only.

I faced the stone again. But the life that flickered about its scornful face had gone. Whether god in fact or druidstone, whatever mystery had made it move and speak had vanished. The chance, such as it had been, was squandered. I frowned to myself, knowing the loss and took the fault, for it was mine.

'It may be that I am yet no more than a child,' I said aloud. But then I remembered my honor, so kept the rest to myself. Without another word to Tabak, I found the mare and mounted her. When I was about to leave, he came.

CHAPTER SEVEN

We went east.

In time the land had softened into undulating hills. The grass, at first no more than stubble sticking out between the stones, by slow progression turned thick and fragrant. We went slowly. The horses grazed. By daylight there was life again. Badgers and hoarpigs rooted in the meadows. As we rode, foxes, barking and flattening their tails, scurried from our path. A host of early flowers sprang up on every side; a light breeze lifted their heads. They were a good sight after the rain. Still I took no joy in them. The dead that are everywhere lay here in shallow graves. I saw their markers in the grass. The fairest lands are boneyards, say the *filidh*; but they make songs of what is sorrow. I did not know these dead nor what battle felled them. Still I grieved for them. The aunts say I had not the stomach for a warrior. Perhaps they were right. The dead have always saddened me, while the hearts of warriors, they say, are glad.

We went on for several miles and by midmorning had found the road again. With good footing we made better progress. The road turned slowly, edging the larger hills and leaving the mountain over my left shoulder. There were no signs of other travelers. Since Urien returned to this mountain, the men of the North rarely came this way. What little trade there was went north by sea along the Bay of Cassiterides and inland from Tywy to Haman and then no farther. Still, the world was a broad place and there were other folk than Urien's kin. Yet from the higher ridges I could mark the road as it ran like a ribbon through dells with grassy sides and stands of birch and hazel. Over the miles I looked, nothing moved on it. The sun shone fitfully. There were still rags of clouds.

'High up, there is a great wind,' said Tabak. 'It drives the last of the storm beyond us.'

'I am glad of it,' I said. 'I have had too much rain. The cold has yet to leave my bones.'

'Be grateful we are down from Géar Finn,' said Tabak. He turned on his mount and looked back the way we came. I followed with my eye. 'This rain is snow there yet. Winter lingers on your mountain.'

I shivered. 'It is its only season,' I answered softly and let the matter be.

We clambered uphill and down. Yet overall the road went lower, running more between the hills than on them. The day wore on. I remembered there was bread within my satchel. Taking some, I passed the rest to Tabak. We ate in silence. Wide grasslands stretched before us.

'Is this not Rasoden?' I asked.

Tabak nodded. 'It is often called that, the plain of horsemen.'

I looked around. 'Are there not towns then where the Undain flows onto this plain?' For from the house I had seen them, a few brave specks of light, their fires at Teimhne. Once when I was small, men came from one of them to speak with Urien, grave men on some errand for their lord. Their stay was brief. For I doubt they found in Urien the man that they remembered or they sought. 'Surely there are such towns,' I said. 'Yet all we see is grass, not even the river.'

'We are south, my lord, of where we should have been.'

I thought aloud, 'I would see the river and the men of towns.'

'The river goes south with us,' he said. 'In three days we shall cross it near the ford at Stephen's Well. There the Steward holds a company of his soldiers, four hundred men, I think, enough at least to satisfy your curiosity. Still, we must be careful if we go among them.'

'Surely a man may pass unnoticed among so many.'

Tabak gazed at me with fine sad eyes. He scratched the back of his broad neck and said, 'Many men might, though they are wary of strangers. Many, but never you or I.'

'Am I so different, then?' I said.

Tabak threw back his head and grinned. 'They are small, these men. Far easier for a wolf to hide among rabbits than for you or me to walk unregarded in their company.'

'They will fear us, then,' I answered quickly. 'So much the better. And I shall go then wherever I please unbothered.'

I saw him laugh, but quietly and to himself. I made no more of it.

The sun sank low behind the mountain's rim. Smooth, bare and endless, with the sky on every side but back of us, the grass, when the wind had touched it, rolled in waves and swells. It seemed, I thought, like what the sea must be. It was strange to me. For I knew only the mountain pastures. There nothing was straight or long, but all things broken by the rock and walls, the very earth heaved up and torn. For the first time in my life, heedless of how great Tabak had said we were, I felt myself small.

The sky was slowly filling with stars. The night breeze blew light and cool. On such nights as a child I had looked out over the mountain wall and to the land that sloped away downward to Rasoden. There was such savor in the sight, it is difficult to describe – to see the world laid out like a silver tapestry, the distant river like a thread of ice.

There was yet no moon.

'I am weary, Tabak,' I said. 'Since I left my bed at Morrigan, I have not slept.'

'Patience, my lord,' he answered almost tenderly. 'One more hill. Beyond it there is a hollow and in the hollow a pool of clear water.'

He was not mistaken. As I leaned against the saddle, I felt the mare come to a halt. I blinked. The road, which had dropped suddenly through a cleft of leering, jagged stones, passed beyond the ridge and entered a small valley. Stands of birch circled the pool, though there were places where the shore was clear. The water stretched before us, black and still. At its soft margins reeds with feathered crowns reached up into the dark like a host of useless spears. I dismounted and let the mare, unfettered, drink. I went down after her, to wash the dust from my face.

Behind me Tabak pushed into the trees and pulled at a branch of twisted wood to be broken for a fire. I wanted only to sleep but would not leave the work for him. At the border of the pool I saw the green spikes of arrowkin. I went into the mud to dig them with my hands. The roots were thick and pulpy, tangled in runners, and almost not worth the effort. But, baked in the coals, they would help us endure the night without discouragement. When I had collected enough to fill my arms, I bundled them in my longshirt and climbed the bank.

The fire crackled warmly. I huddled close to it, my cloak across my shoulders. Tabak came from the horses. He had unstrapped his leather satchel and laid it down between his knees. His helm was off. The lines of his face were drawn. He was, I saw, as weary as I. Yet I knew he would not speak of it. I had spoken once already of my weariness and would not do so again. He said, 'From this place to Stephen's Well the road will be more traveled. I will watch while you sleep. Now always one of us must stay awake.'

I poked at a root with a stick to keep it from burning. 'Then I shall watch first,' I said.

He gave a slight nod. 'As you will,' he said and made a show of yawning.

After he had eaten, he laid his head across his bag, his arms drawn down to either side. I watched over him, keeping the fire. Perhaps he slept, but his face was turned from me where he could see the road. When, as much as the fare permitted, my hunger was appeased, I lay back against a rock. In time the moon rose, a bright crescent clasping a gray rock. A few small clouds scudded by it. The rest of the sky, between the stars, was black. I lay beneath the enormous vault of heaven. It seemed only a moment.

The birds in the thicket announced the morning before it came. The air was still dark. I pulled myself up on my elbows. Tabak squatted on his heels before the fire. In his hands he held the bare carcass of a hoarpig which he had skinned and split along its belly, making one deep cut from its throat down to its balls. He was intent on his butchering. The best meat he tore away in strips, some of which he impaled on wood skewers. The rest was hung to smoke on a rack of green branches laid above the fire. He had been some time at the task before he decided to notice me. His gaze brought the blood into my cheeks and I was of half a mind to offer some excuse. He saw it.

'Finish this,' he said curtly. 'Someone must see to your mare.'

'I slept,' I admitted.

He seemed not to have heard and walked off leaving me with the fire. I stretched the last of the meat above the smoke. The smell was good and took away some of the weariness. Yet I was angry with myself and glad to be alone. The sun came all at once, flooding the horizon from one end to the other. It was not like sunrise on the mountain. It made me uneasy to be so much in the open. But it was a thing past remedy and I would know the world.

In time Tabak came up from the pool leading the horses. He had taken off his longshirt despite the chill. His face and thick shoulders were still wet where he had washed. His flesh shone bright in the sunlight. The sight of him caught in my mind. So the sealmen must have looked to the Kell, I thought, huge and raven-haired, rising out of the foam. But then his fine sad eyes smiled at me and when he spoke it was the voice of a man, like any man.

'I am hungry,' he said.

I turned back to the fire.

Along the way I gathered what I could, the small fruit of tinviel, green, astringent and filled with seeds, and the harsh bulbs of allium, hastily dug. But the meat was good. I carried it wrapped in a cloth on my saddle. We paused at midday under the open sky. The land ahead was empty as the land behind. We ate in silence. Then went on.

The road was now broad and well planned. Nothing put me in mind of dwarves or magicians. It was men's work, solid, earnest and well tended. Grieve had said the riverlands had fallen into ruin, that small lords warred with one another and the farmers starved. If that were so, the ruin lay further on within the Steward's realm; Rasoden was ordered yet. We saw no one. But clearly someone kept the road. Everything seemed quiet, peaceful. It was hard to believe that the High King had fled. A sure hand ruled this place, albeit invisibly.

We passed in time along the edge of fields. In places there were stout gates and hedges. Once in the distance I saw the thatched roof of an outer farm. No smoke came from its chimney. But there was a dog. Yellow-haired, suspicious, it ran from the horses. It was not like our mountain dogs, that took delight in their courage, in bristling and challenging strangers. I thought it odd but soon forgot it.

Toward evening we found shelter by a prodigious wooden gate. It was set alongside the road, its wide posts carved with the figures of men and birds. A path led away from it into an empty field. It served no purpose I could see, but then I did not know the ways of men. Still, in part, it hid us from the road and this seemed to please Tabak. I undid the girths of the mare and tethered her to the gate. Beside it, for the horses, was a wooden trough, which still held some dampness from the rain. I unloaded blankets and took from my sack the tangle of roots and bulbs which I had gathered. I looked forward to the leaping flames in which I meant to roast them. Fire, if it is also the destroyer, still gladdens the heart of the traveler. In those days I thought it walls and a roof against the dark. When I had it crackling, Tabak came in from the field where I had seen him walking by himself.

'See that you do not build it too high,' he said.

Ready for him, I grinned. 'From the road you cannot see it,' I said.

Without blinking Tabak watched the fire. On its fluttering edge, in the play of light and shadow, huge as he was, he seemed no more than an apparition. He said, 'What keeps to the road I have no fear of.'

'This is a tamed land,' I answered. 'In all of Rasoden I have seen nothing more frightening than the sun rising and the sun going down.'

'When you have looked, you have not seen,' said Tabak quietly. I saw the tenseness in his brow. Then all at once he reached into the fire. Taking up a burning brand, he held it so the light fell brightly on the wide posts of the gate. 'What do you see, my lord?' he asked.

I saw a post entwined with the figures of birds and men. The wings were outspread, the great arms straining. Such was the craft that looking, as on my own flesh, I felt the thrashing of those terrible dark wings. The arms, unsubmitting yet weaponless but for one poor stone raised against the onslaught of the air, were like my own. 'I see a gate carved with great skill,' I said.

Tabak did not lower the brand. 'You have not seen,' he said.

I pressed closer. The hosts of figures I saw were in fact one man, one bird, their images repeated and repeated in a coiled battle about the post. Awestruck, I stared into the face of the man. The face, unflinching yet edged with pain, with those deep eyes, that face was mine or one so nearly like it that I cried out.

Tabak watched me. 'It is not you,' he said.

'I thought –'

'In this place,' said Tabak, 'your father fought the crow of Anu. He saw her as she passed overhead, a shadow between the earth and the highest stars. He knew her, and though he was alone and weaponless, he spoke her true name so she could not flee from him. Like an arrow she fell at him. But he took up a stone and pierced her eye. It was a great thing. Until that time no man had marked her. You alone know the cost.' With these last words a sudden gentleness had come into his voice. He saw how it struck me.

'Whatever is bought is paid for, lord,' he added softly. 'It was her due and settled before your birth.'

But I did not like to hear it, for Gwen Gildrun had been my glory. I spat into the dark. The silence was deep and painful. I felt a chill deep as the marrow of my bones.

'Do you swear,' I asked bitterly, 'that it was my father who stood upon this place?'

'He was here if you will see it. He had this gate put up to mark the deed.'

I looked once more upon the gate. Was this indeed my father's face? There was no grandeur in it. The lips came together in pain, a bloodless line, haggard, almost broken. What victory was there in this? It was not, I decided, a fitting memorial. I wondered if the artist mocked him knowingly. He who had known the hidden name and called it, contended with the anger out of the sky and beaten it, in the midst of his glory, did he see only ruin? I could not believe that it was so.

'I trust,' I said arrogantly, 'he had the woodcarver beaten for his work.'

Tabak looked at me as one might look upon a dog boy who had failed a task. 'No, my lord,' he answered. 'Your father praised it as was just. Indeed, the work so pleased him he gave the man the swiftest of his horses and a saddle, such as are made by the men of Bede, a wonder in itself, a king's gift, of carved leather and studded with good silver.'

But I mused. 'There is only pain in my father's face.'

'So there was that day,' said Tabak. 'He was not a fool. The law is one. He knew it. If you cast a stone at heaven, will it not fall to earth? If you steal the eye of the first of Anu's children, will not another of equal prize be taken in return?' His dark eyes fixed on mine.

Through stiffened lips I answered him. 'I am lessened by this. The one thing that was mine, Gwen Gildrun and the crows, is mine no longer. I am made but his reflection. He acted and it befell me. Nothing more.'

Tabak threw the brand back roughly in the fire. I watched the figures on the gate dissolve into the dark. 'He knew what he did,' he said scornfully. 'But what can be said of you? Is it from Yllvere, the winter queen with her pale looks, you get that raven hair or your stature over other men? Did the runty men of Urien's holding give you those bold legs? When you look, what do you see?' His eyes were cold, his features dark with scorn. 'You are your father's son,' he said. 'His seed it was that gave you life, both fair and foul. The great oak makes an oak. Can it be otherwise? Or did you dream that when you found him you might keep your precious bastardy?' In his anger he seized me roughly by the shoulders. Too late he saw what he had done. He had a warrior's pride but he was my father's liegeman first. His oaths held him. Not a nerve, not a muscle of his stirred. His breathing seemed to stop.

Later we lay down to sleep. There were branches near, but I let the fire fade down to coals. In the darkness I saw my father's face. It floated before me. There, within a hand's reach. A doubtful substance, yet I might have touched it. Great dark wings beat about his forehead. It will pass, I thought. Yet inwardly I cursed myself because I feared that it would not. I pressed my palm into my eye. In the rush of pain, the face melted. But in my mind I knew the shape of it; without hearing, I knew it groaned.

'It cannot be,' I said and, although it was barely cold, I trembled. A feeling of loneliness rose in me. I had seen him whom I had never seen. In the wood of the gate I met him face to face. As though I had looked into polished brass – eye, hair and bone, looking back at me, sharing my own flesh. It filled me with horror. I had seen him and yet learned nothing. After all, what comfort is there in a mirror?

Tabak stirred. 'Did I hurt you?' He moved a little. Yet he was like a corpse twitching after an execution – huge upon the ground, his movement thoughtless and unconnected. The poor light of the fire showed none of his features. When he grew still, he might have been a stone. In all things there is both life and death. I thought of the Menhir. Perhaps, I thought, even the great earth grieves.

I looked into the hollow of the fire, into the place where the flame had raged hottest, that was now but scales of ash.

'Did I hurt you?' he said again.

Even in the ashes there is the memory of the fire.

'No,' I said. And then again more gently, 'No.'

Tabak let himself lean back. Once more he became a man. I cast a branch on the fire so we could look at one another. The wood was slow to catch, and we waited for it.

'How old was he then?' I asked after a while.

'As you are, fifteen in the spring.'

But I was not listening. Something came back to me. I said, 'She told me she would not know his face. Men change. I remember it exactly. She would not know the look of him. But when she spoke she looked me in the face.'

Tabak smiled. 'Men change,' he said, repeating her words as though he tested them. For a moment he closed his eyes. If he started to say something, he changed his mind but then went on. 'You must remember she did not know him then, not yet. When she did, he was different. And when she had gone away, back to Urien, he was not the same.'

The fire grew. His features, disheveled from the journey, cinder-red in the firelight, seemed suddenly old. There were hollows under his eyes. 'A man begets himself in a child,' he started, 'but time works on them both. It was not always so. The first men, when at the world's beginning they came upon the land, did not change. Their backs never bent. They loved and fought, but when at last they slipped back to their sea kingdoms they were as they had been. But their magic we have not. Perhaps they no longer have it themselves. Who is to say? Myself, I am not what I was when, at my lord's bidding, I followed Yllvere to her house by Anu's wood.'

I sat with my chin in my hand and looked into the fire. 'But once,' I said, 'he was as I am now.'

'You have your father's youth in you,' he said. 'But his old age you have not.' Something lingered in his face when the words left him. I saw the years on him, like the dust of the road that goes on and on and finds no peace. I said, 'How old would he be now?'

Tabak let his eyes rest on the fire. 'The time that binds him is as your own,' he said. 'He was twice nineteen when he met Yllvere and lay with her. It was the height of summer then. The oaks were full-leaved, the acorns green. I heard his laughter through the grove. It was light on the air, easy at heart, despite his cares. I was his man in that as in other things. That day I held the horses on the far side of the island and watched both the road and the sea. He was hunted then, fearing discovery on all quarters. From the spring which followed when you were born until this time are fifteen more. Together it is three-and-fifty years.'

But I did the sums myself. 'No,' I answered. 'It is fourteen, which makes fifty-two.'

Tabak lifted his black head. 'I will tell you once more and then be done with it,' he answered gravely. 'The Kell cannot count, as I have told you. All Anu's folk mark out their time by the tides. They care nothing how the water lags behind the moon. They are shore folk who never went to sea. They do not track the stars. When winter comes too soon, they say the snow is early. The spring surprises them. Yllvere, inland on Anu's mountain, counted the tides in memory, not what she saw. So did her women. In that a year was lost and more besides.'

He stopped. His rough face drew close to mine. With one hand he had gathered up loose stones from the ground. As though counting, one by one he dropped them to the earth. As they knocked one against the other, the sound of their falling echoed against the darkness. Presently, he said, 'If you would be free of the Kell, you must measure your life as it is.'

I felt the fire on me. I remembered Vydd in her hut marking her stick with her thumb. I did not attempt to reply and turned from him. In time I slept.

During the night I tossed and dreamed, I thought, of the god Duinn who had filled the great belly of the goddess Night with stones. Long into the night I heard the clang of boulders dropped one by one into the dark's wide craw. In my dreams I beheld the darkness, cold, implacable, immune to the cries of men, and yet I knew the god had tricked her. I stood alone at the saw-edged rim, the abyss below me. Death was there. It was our first acquintance. He did not beckon. I slept. The late moon rose.

Toward morning the breeze had freshened. A whisper rose from the grass. In the lingering dark the breeze carried the smell of horses. I stirred, sleep still on me. Without waking I lifted my head. Swords glittered under the moon. I heard the riders call to one another, watched them from a great distance, pointing, trying to decide, brave men but cautious. Slow as dreams they rode down upon us, not knowing what we were. I saw them as through a gauze, like creatures under water, five men and a string of ponies. The ponies had thick haunches; great dark packs were buckled to their backs. I lay as though asleep, scarcely breathing, awaiting them, the first men I would meet abroad in the world.

I did not move. The horses circled.

'Are they men?' asked one gruff voice.

'In form,' said another. The voice was hard but there was reason in it. He brought his mount nearer. 'But see the size of them. They are larger still than the folk we saw two winters past at Tarn. Mark me, they are giant kind or nothing else, such as the *filidh* say live undersea. Though how they came to this place, I know not.'

I saw then they thought us corpses, for Tabak slept like a dead man and I lay still. I rose to meet them.

The four fell back; their little mouths dropped open. But the one, his hair in flaxen braids and a grim sword in his hand, pressed forward. He advanced until he brought his sword within a yard of my chest.

'What manner of thing are you?' he demanded.

'A man.'

The rider looked at me with stern but puzzled eyes. Though I had spoken no more than the truth, the horsemen looked at each other in wonder. Their confusion gave me a moment. Stooping, I shook Tabak till he blinked and yawned.

'Wake,' I said. 'The day has brought us company.'

Laboriously, like a bear just roused from winter sleep, he stirred, turning his sleep-slackened face at first to me and then instantly alert back to the horsemen. Then, without bothering to hurry, in one unbroken motion dwarfing them he stood. Though they rode and we but stood upon the ground, our eyes came level against theirs. The riders watched us with dismay in their faces. At length the one spoke up again.

'Give me your name and tell me whom you serve,' he said. Though the four wavered, I saw that his sword had not once faltered. Spurred by his boldness, the others closed beside him. Strangely, I was disappointed. The men of the outer world, like the men of the villages I knew, were as children. The greatest of their company, he with his ring shirt, battle gear and crested helm together, was scarce four elhws and lean as any of my sisters. The others ranged down to a span shorter, about the size of the servants and the women of our house.

'Your name and liege, sir,' the one repeated.

'Lately it is Finn,' I answered. 'But I am no liegeman.'

The horseman frowned. Behind him one of the others sniggered. They were small men. But armed and mounted they outnumbered us. The one who laughed had a thin nose and hollow cheeks. Tufts of spare yellow hair grew from his chin. A new sword rested in his lap. Boldness, I saw, may set its root in the poorest soil. He laughed again to make a point of it.

'Finn,' he sniggered. 'You were right at the start, Ceorl, we have caught us fishmen.'

But the one hushed him. 'We are men of Bede,' he said. His voice had darkened. It stiffened the men beside him. 'We are smiths and tinkers, but we are soldiers too. We have ridden this land from one sea to the other, wheresoever a fair price may be had for a bright sword or a shirt of twisted rings. But though the High King's gone and the Steward sits in his place, from the one water to the other the law's the same: a man must give his kin and name the lord he serves. Think again, sir. You do us discourtesy at your peril.'

I might have pulled him down with my bare hands. Perhaps he saw that. It did not chasten him. Yet I kept my hands off him and answered mildly, 'I am called Finn, as I have told you. I serve no lord. These last days I came down from the twin-peaked mountain. You see it at my back. If you are strangers to this place, I will tell you it is called Géar Finn, though the women of the mountain call it Anu's paps. There I grew to what I am. But now I go toward Ormkill, where I have never been.'

The horsemen eyed one another. It was a fair answer, but I saw they doubted it. Tabak came forward, keeping the sun at his back so that they squinted at him. His eyes had sparks dancing in them.

'Would you not know me also?' he asked. 'Or is your honor so small a thing it takes offense but one thought at a time?'

The horsemen muttered. But the one looked steadily at Tabak. Unmoved, he answered, 'I know good metal from dross,' he said. 'Nor does it take much wisdom to tell the servant from his master.'

A wolf's grin tore at the hard edges of Tabak's lips. Both anger and irony darted in his deep-set eyes. 'The men of Bede travel back and forth in this country to little purpose,' he said. 'Or else so much journeying has joggled their small brains. Surely, even in these days, memories have not grown so short.' He broke off, laughing coldly. I did not understand his meaning. The horsemen found no words to say but gazed at him.

The one was troubled. I saw him grip his sword more tightly than before. 'Give us your name then, man,' he said. 'I ask it honestly.'

'You know it, Ceorl,' said Tabak. 'As did your father and all the wandering men of Bede from one shore to the other.' He paused. 'I am Tabak ap Ewyn,' he said. He looked around at them and then at last at me.

A stillness fell upon the horsemen. It fell on me also, creeping on my heart. Yet it was their stillness that had taken hold of me. For myself, I drew nothing from the name. From the time I was a child within the house I had heard it. I looked back on my life as far as memory took me. In gentleness and anger Yllvere had used it, calling to him from the locked door of her chamber. Vydd knew it, smiling to herself. But Vydd would smile as secretly at a thrush in a thicket and find grave portents in the colors of the moon. My sisters spoke it, slyly, for they feared him. I waited to understand. But nothing came of it. The horsemen had not shaken off their silence. I turned to Tabak, facing him.

'Your name has taken their speech away,' I said. 'Is it only foolishness in me that I am left unmoved?'

'It is not foolishness,' he answered gently. 'You were mountain born, cut out of a woman in the sight of Anu's wood and reared apart by her own folk. The names men speak you have not heard. So it was kept from you. Even in the book of names you would not have read it. The book holds the majesty of the land. There is no page there for its servants.'

But, thinking I had wounded him, I said, 'It was never hid from me that you were a serving man. Truly, I never thought you less for it.'

'There is nothing to dispute,' he answered. 'You showed as much courtesy as you had learned. No more was looked for.'

'Yet,' I said, 'these men take the name of a servant as a great wonder.'

Tabak smiled then. Looking back I see it was because he knew such words were fated. Something like this must have crossed my mind. For seeing no reason, yet my heart pounded.

'It is not the servant they hold in awe.' Though the men heard him, he spoke only to me. His voice was clear but something gathered at the back of it. He looked pleased and perhaps a little sad. Afterward he added, 'In knowing the servant, they know his lord.'

Around us I felt the horsemen pressing near. The air smelled of horses, of the leather satchels tied to the backs of the ponies, of swords and armor, the acrid smell of iron. To this day I remember it.

'Who is it, then, you serve?' I asked him.

'Ar Elon, Lord of Hren and all the lands between the seas,' he answered.

Though backward and mountain born, I knew the name of the High King.

PART II

Undain

CHAPTER EIGHT

A man's life is not straight. Like a serpent, it turns back upon itself. It sucks the wounded places. In my heart's core I knew it. Nothing is ever forgotten. Under my breath, like a thing still secret, I tasted my father's name. Ar Elon. I thought, there is not a gift given that is not also a curse.

Nothing is forgotten. The name Urien sought, both waking and dreaming, first from the lips of his servants, then last and longest in the chronicles of Gedd, folding back pages till he nearly went blind: that was the only name he knew without looking. Nothing can be cast away. Slowly I went through it all. I thought of the tower room where I had crept in good and bad weather, close behind Grieve, to hear the old tales. Those bold men and faithless ones, all out of the wide Eastlands, those who were but names in my memory, were now my kin. So the serpent turns back upon itself.

With the sword I had stolen to climb Gwen Gildrun, that which I now carried, Urien killed Lot, the High King's man. With that sword he won Morrigan. Little he dreamed when he plunged the blade into the guts of the man, when he saw the man squirm, coughing up blood before the feet of my father, that all the blood would buy him was his ruin. So the serpent turns back upon itself. For a death my father gave Urien Morrigan and the lands upon the mountain, a murderer's fee. But, taking Yllvere, my father cursed the gift.

I thought of Yllvere. Against the wall of flame I saw her face, crimson with the heat of the great fires under the house. Over the long leagues in my mind I sought her. There was blood on my own face, she said, that night when Vydd cut me from her womb. Then it came to me out of the tangle of my thoughts. I heard her words within the roar of burning wood: 'There was another born that night. I clove the name.'

It is written in the Book of Gedd that I wept when I heard the name of my father. So to this day the wise *filidh* tell it. But nowhere it is set down what was in my heart.

* * *

71

'They go toward Stephen's Well, to the Steward's holding,' Tabak said again, for at first I had not been listening. 'If we should go with them, by midday you will drink from the river.'

The horsemen muddled behind Ceorl but were mostly silent, not knowing where to put their eyes. I looked over them. Tabak was still talking. I shook my head at him. I meant to take the place he had raised for me. I said, 'The days we rode together you gave me no answers, only riddles and sawed-off words. Now, before men I have never seen, you unfold my father like a banner.'

But Tabak would not be rebuked. His look fell hard on me. I saw he meant me to keep still. To Ceorl he said, 'You have heard what was said here and you know the claim.'

Ceorl did not look away. 'I have heard it, Tabak ap Ewyn,' he answered. 'You do well to speak openly. Though I am not eager to be part of this, it would be folly to bring a king's heir to the Steward's holding without swordsmen at his back.'

'It is many years since I was elsewhere but the mountain,' Tabak said. 'How is it with Thigg?'

'There is fighting still,' said Ceorl. 'The Steward was never easy with his might. The barons bite at his heels. There are holdings, not many leagues distant, where the inconstant vassals would take up the name of the King's heir whether they believe it or not. Should they master Thigg with him, there would be time enough to judge the claim.'

Tabak looked across at him and smiled. He stood in the fresh sunlight. The mist was all but gone from off the ground. 'And how, Ceorl of Bede, do you judge the claim?'

'I do not judge it.'

'You have but to think on it.'

Ceorl's pale face was solemn. He stared at Tabak a long time from under his helm. 'The lad heard me if you did not,' he answered. 'I took you both for giants.'

'You know the High King stood well above all other men.'

'I have crossed mountains and many rivers,' said the horseman. 'In one place it is spoken that the High King came out of the East, where smoke hangs always before the sun, that at his summoning the crows of battle flock down from the crags of Morg. In another, it is said that he was seaborn, risen on the foam, and that the great whales there did him service. Though here on Rasoden and along the river they say that he was only a red-haired farmer like themselves but that one day Dagda spoke to him and in that moment raised him over other men.'

'And what say the men of Bede?' Tabak asked him.

Ceorl laughed and let his bright sword fall back into his lap. 'In Bede,' he answered, 'if a cat claims he is king, it is thought best to kneel, at least until we have had a chance to see his teeth.'

I glanced quickly at Tabak but discovered nothing in his face. He was looking east, his dark head lifted. The breeze twisted his hair.

'Tell me your name again,' said the horseman.

'Finn ap Ar Elon,' I answered.

The horseman studied me with careful eyes. 'I will ride with you, Lord Finn,' he said. 'At least as far as Stephen's Well. I for one would see the faces of the men of towns when first they looked at you.'

I saw the horsemen mutter. But his word was given.

In the early afternoon we came down near the river. On the uplands there was heather on the sides of the hills, the grass in flower. But the borders of the river were thick pine-wood. We went into the wood along a narrow path. Here, even at midday, there were shadows and in the dampness, flies. The horses went single file. Because of this there was not much said among us and I had my thoughts to myself. Yet even before I saw it, my thoughts were filled with the river.

The Undain flows out of the mountain north of Morrigan. There I imagined it was like the streams I knew, nightmare torrents echoing among the rocks. But on the plain, they say, the river was both broad and still, smooth as a mirror. Here deep-keeled boats came well into the midlands, stopping at towns to trade, the oarsmen sitting at their ease at dockside after a stiff day's work. I longed to see such boats and the masters of water.

The path ran from one turning to another, twisting among boulders and great trees. As we went there were times when I was cut off altogether from the company though I heard the sound of hoofbeats close at hand. It must be that the horsemen lost track of where I was, for in time I heard them speaking openly. The long boughs of the pines drooped over me. In the breeze the needles whispered.

'I had not thought Ceorl so empty-headed,' said a voice. It belonged to the one with the yellow beard, who had called me fishman. I remembered well the sound of it. 'Yet he will pledge his sword to any upstart that comes down from the mountains.'

'Tabak ap Ewyn rides with the lad,' another answered.

The man sniggered. 'If the tales are true, Tabak has ridden with the green mares of Tir-na-n-Og. By that you would have a horse at Ormkill in the King's chair.'

The other laughed. 'Better a green mare than Thigg.'

'Be careful,' said a voice, 'or you will find the doors of this land shut to you.'

'Look to yourself, Wend. If the lad's the King's heir, as they say, there is not a door between this place and hell where they will let you in.'

The yellow beard muttered. 'King's heir or not, he has no allies. When the High King fled, his liegemen scattered. Of those who served him all that are not dead are men too old to lift a sword. Look to yourself. If the barons take him up, they will cast him down soon enough when it pleases them. Think on it. In faith, who is there who will come to him?'

'It may be there are some of Bede who would not fear to serve him,' the other said.

The yellow beard answered. But a fly buzzed in my ear and I missed the words. Later, when we had come into a clearing, I looked to see the man who rode beside him. Our eyes touched for a moment. His corn-colored hair hung from his temples in long plaits like the others', but he sat a head taller and was coarsely made. Strapped to his back was a great broadax. I set it in my mind to remember him. The sun was overhead.

Once more the clearing passed into a shaded wood. But now the ground was steeper, the mare uneasy. I leaned forward and patted her thick neck. She thrashed her tail. Shortly we came down a high ridge. The trees parted. Then nothing hid it from me.

From one stony bank to the other the Undain spread before me like a silver meadow. I was not prepared for its quiet. Its peace sank into the marrow of my bones. Yet beneath its voiceless surface I knew it moved. I felt it, invisible and deep, shifting under the sky, a kingdom of water, black, dark green and silver, all colors and none at once, sliding with none to stop it toward the sea. It enchanted me. At the edge of my mind I was thinking of Grieve. With her tales of the great ocean she had set my heart on traveling. Then I remembered her face as she came up from the fires beneath the house. A chill ran down my neck. I drove the thought from me.

The mare checked at the water's edge and nickered. Sliding from her back, I gave her to herself. She was a gift to Yllvere from my father. Perhaps she knew this bank, or it may be only that she thirsted. Yet she did not drink, but lifted her old head and whinnied. Her cry sounded thin and shrill along the bank. The horsemen, where they knelt on the flat stones, looked up with stupid faces, their small mouths dripping.

High above us a rider broke from the cover of the wood. He stopped on the promontory and held there. He was a stern man with the mark of service on him. On his thick chest he wore a bright ring shirt and yet his head was bare. He did not look at us but spoke over his shoulder, calmly as though scarcely interested in the sight that had greeted him. At his word a mounted column came out of the trees. They took their stations along the ridge. All were clothed in the same fashion, red cloaks on their shoulders and helms with nosepieces jutting down. These were Thigg's men, I judged, or at the least men of his vassals. They knew their number and had not bothered to draw their arms. When their chief saw they were ordered, he pointed down to us.

'Drink deep, men of Bede, then gather your ponies,' he said in a booming voice to carry the distance. 'My captain at Stephen's Well has need of axes and spearheads.'

But Ceorl called up to him, 'In Bede we are free men and come and go as we choose.'

The man spat. 'My captain is not poor,' he cried out sourly. 'He will pay a fair price if the work is good.'

'We will come or not as it pleases us,' Ceorl shouted back. But I saw it was but talk to keep up his spirits. He was quite still.

Tabak stood next to me. 'Rather a poorer price than an honest one, I should guess,' I said lightly. 'Else his captain would not send so many swordsmen to harvest so few smiths.'

'They are a patrol only,' Tabak answered. 'I doubt they rode out seeking either one thing or another but come by chance to shark up whatever they can find.'

Then, for the first time, their chief seemed to notice us. He leaned forward. His red hair was cut close to his head; his mouth was twisted. 'You are not of Bede,' he announced loudly. He made it sound like a great discovery but at the same time one of doubtful interest. 'You had best come with us as well,' he shouted. 'If you are as strong as you are big and can handle a sword without cutting off your knees, my captain may have a place for you.'

When I heard this, I saw he took us for farmers. I thought less of him for that. But the truth was that he was looking down at us from a height and so could not take our full measure. By then several of his company had descended to the bank and come even with us. One pointed me out. I saw they had already begun to mutter among themselves. Exchanging a final word with his companions, the one that had stretched his finger at me set his mount to climb the ridge again. Regaining the promontory, he spoke at his chief's ear. When the man had done, I saw their chief twist his thick neck to sweep his glance along the shore. When he was satisfied as to our number, he spoke.

'I am Eoghan,' he said in a measured voice. 'Behind me are thirty men with swords and lances. My captain at Stephen's Well has four hundred. He is a fair man but quick to take offense. This river and the lands both east and west he holds in Thigg's service.' He made a wide gesture with his hand by which he meant to show the extent of the holding. Then he added, 'It is Thigg's law between the two seas. In this province I am Thigg's eyes and my captain his right arm.'

I glanced aside at Tabak. 'Why does he waste words on this?' I asked, for the speech had puzzled me.

'You have made him unsure of himself,' he answered. 'He knows the folk of Rasoden, and you are not one of them. His man has no doubt told him you and I are twice the size that men should be. He fears now you may be someone of consequence. But not having seen it at the first, he dares not ask you who you are. So he tells you his name, counts his own and his captain's men, and drags in Thigg and the whole countryside to puff himself up. By this he thinks you will respond in kind.'

'And if I do not.'

'They are still thirty and we are seven.'

'We are six at best,' I said darkly, but there was no time to explain it to him.

I walked to the mare and mounted her. With my hand I bade the men of Bede do likewise. I saw Ceorl smile to himself. He threw his leg up over his pony. When his men saw it, they followed him.

Eoghan scratched the beard on his cheek and stared down at us. The few that had come down the bank stood now some distance off. They kept looking up at him yet he would not signal them. At last he roused himself, calling out to me in his great voice.

'What do you do in this place?' he shouted.

'When I have a mare that thirsts, I let her drink,' I called back to him.

He did not know what to make of that.

'I am Thigg's eyes,' he said again. 'I keep watch at this place and at others. What I see I tell my captain. When I tell him of you, he will be curious. And what is the name of the man whose mare thirsts, he will ask me.'

'Then you must tell him that you met a one-eyed man with half a name,' I answered. The men of Bede looked at one another with troubled faces. For their sake I added, 'If you wish you may also say that I have lived my life in Morrigan, which Urien holds, he who was friend to the High King.'

If it surprised him, it seemed as well to suit him better. Eoghan nodded. 'The name is not unknown to me,' he said. 'You are his son, then?'

'I have lived in the house,' I answered. 'If I were his son I would have said it.' Even his own men saw I had answered well. Yet I could see Eoghan was displeased. I doubted he was accustomed to being answered so. His gaze wandered impatiently around our small group of horsemen.

'My captain will have many questions about the North,' he shouted. 'Seldom is it that men come down from the mountain kingdoms.' Into his face there came a kind of smile. 'It would honor my captain,' he continued, 'should one who has lived in the house of the High King's friend stop at his holding.'

Neither Ceorl nor his men nor any of Eoghan's company spoke. It was between us only. But it was a thing I was not used to. For I only had my sisters to match wits with. Yet I knew clearly enough his courtesy was hollow. What was odd was how surely Eoghan, with his twisted smile and pompous bellowing, expected me to see the lie. Seeing no better return, with lies I answered him.

'Your courtesy indeed is welcome,' I called out. I saw that Tabak winked at me. It made me bolder. 'You must tell your captain that when I come to Stephen's Well I shall seek his company. Pleased I will be to tell him that in Eoghan he is well served.' I saw now that among his men some eyed one another, their faces on the edge of laughter. I would have continued in this vein, but Tabak, who had brought his horse near to mine, kicked my knee lightly to hush me. Chastened, I picked up the reins and turned the mare's head to the left along the shore. Over my shoulder I called up to Eoghan. 'I bid you a fair journey,' I shouted. Then slowly I rode from the place, Tabak and the men of Bede beside me.

We rode a little way, just beyond the rocks where the river turned. When we had passed the rocks, I said, 'He let us go. I had not thought he would.'

Tabak shrugged. 'The bank is steep between this place and Stephen's Well. If you will watch the rise, you will see in the spaces between the trees that we are followed.'

But I was angry then and would not consider what he said. 'At least,' I said, 'we will ride into Stephen's Well as men and not as captives.'

'It comes to much the same,' he answered.

Still I would not think of it. I spurred the mare and let her gallop.

*　　*　　*

That night, camped along the shore of the river, with Ceorl and his men on watch by turns, I did not sleep. But when Tabak found a place beside me, I had nothing more to say to him. We had no fire, seeing little need to make it any easier than it was for those who followed us. Now and then we heard their horses. My ears strained, listening for them. I was uneasy. Just before morning it rained – a soft spring rain, the sort that farmers love. I rolled myself in my blanket.

When I woke there was a boat out on the river. My clothes were soaked through, but it was warm and I was in no discomfort. I stood, peering out into the river. In the mist I could see little but the long shadow of its bow. I heard the oars splash, and ran to the river's edge. The water was gray. Already birds were fishing. I looked carefully. For a moment I saw the mast, a naked tree, the sail furled. I wished it closer. But it stayed well into the current and soon had disappeared in the rain. Ceorl saw me staring out at the mist. He came beside me.

'It is a river like any other, lord,' he said grinning.

I said, 'I have seen no other.'

'I see then that I was wrong.'

'In what?'

'When first I saw you, I took you for a sea mage.'

The rain had lessened. A fresh breeze was clearing the mist. I looked down at myself. Steam rose from my arms and my damp clothing. 'My mother is a witch of Anu,' I told him. 'In my blood is mixed the salt blood of the Kell.'

He was thinking but I could not see into it. After a silence he said, 'Whatever else the Kell are, they are as mortal as any that live upon the land.'

'It may be so,' I said but I thought of Vydd and then of Grieve. 'Or it may be they go mad in place of death.'

'I have heard that also,' said Ceorl absently. He held my eye, his thought already gone ahead to something else. 'What runs in your blood from Ar Elon, I wonder?'

I looked out at the river, across the flat sheen of the water, thinking of the tales I had read within the Book of Gedd. 'He was king of the land between the two seas,' I said. 'But whether he drew his strength from the water or the earth it is not written. In my life I have known only the rocks of the mountain. Though I have sought him in the stonefields, he was not there.' I met Ceorl's stare again.

'Then you must seek him here,' he said.

'I do not swim. There was no place to learn.' But already I knew that

I would do it. I sat on the bank and drew off my boots and then my long-shirt. But as I did this, the yellow beard came down on us.

'So it is wash day for the mountain king?' he asked of Ceorl, the smirk still lingering after the question was done. We were still a moment, looking at one another. At Ormkill, I supposed, a king's son would have struck him. But at Ormkill a king's son would have had a troop of house-thralls at his heels. Yet how easy, I thought, to kill a man. Nonetheless, I let the anger drain from me. In the fields above Morrigan I had sometimes seen a small blue snake coiled on a certain stone. Its bite, the women said, would kill. Yet I had gone by it a dozen times and left it whole. Wisely or not, so it was then. Small evils, I judged, were best left to themselves. Otherwise a man would fill his life with nothing else but taking heads. I waded into the river.

The water was cold against my thighs. But since the two watched me I moved quickly out beyond the shallows. Free of the shore, the current tugged at me. The icy ripples rose against my chest and circled my neck like a collar, so that for a moment I felt myself like one of the bodiless heads the great *filidh* sing of, such as guard the gate that leads to Duinn's realm. I lifted my feet from the stones below. For an instant, closing my eye, I felt as though I flew. Still I knew it was not the earth that moved beneath.

It was quiet in the river. I went down and opened my eye. The water was black. I could see nothing. I turned to see the river's roof shining above my head. Its brilliance startled me. I turned from it. The river carried me. I heard it then, whispering among the stones, the water song, the river longing for the sea. An icy lassitude came over me. I passed into dreaming. I thought, there are gods in the river and long-armed demons with bodies like sunken logs and fingers like wet branches. The thought chilled me. I shot out my legs to stand. My feet did not touch the stones.

'Finn,' moaned the river.

I will not drown, I thought.

The voice of the water laughed. 'Stay with me,' it murmured, 'for I will bear you in such state as fits the king's true son, past the little maggot towns and out past rancid Tinkern, out beyond the man-trodden islands at my mouth. Beyond the faint and crawling life on land in the Great Sea, you and I will dive to the oldest of halls, crystal-roofed, limitless and cold. There is a place for you among sea stones where you may hear talk of the first things and the last, such as none before you ever heard.'

'You are a ringing in my ears,' I said. 'No more.'

'I am your blood,' the river sang.

'My blood is not so cold nor yet so pale,' I cried. But my head rang with echoes. The river's laughter drummed against my ears. It mocked me.

'I am the blood of Yllvere and of Grieve,' it sang. 'In you I am the same.'

'No,' I cried out. 'I will be king upon the land.' I knew it, then for the first time. It was a sign to me, like a hot coal found in ashes. I warmed myself before it. The river squealed among the stones. I would not listen.

'Finn,' it sighed but I would not heed the whisper as it fled.

I came up into daylight. I drank the air.

CHAPTER NINE

Fish weirs jutted up a hundred yards from shore. Here the shore flattened and the trees were cut away. On the banks old men sat with nets draped across their withered knees, mending the torn places with wooden shuttles. A few naked children of either sex swam among the rushes. Ceorl rode at our head and was the first seen. The children ran out to him, swarming around his ponies, fingering the packs to see what might be found. The yellow beard, who was called Wend, followed and after him in a knot the others of Bede, their new swords scabbarded. Tabak and I, for we had been talking together, came last, riding out of the trees. The sight of us daunted the children and killed their laughter. Backing away, they hid themselves among the scrub. One red-haired girl I remember, her eyes wide with fear, hugged a bawling infant in her arms. An old woman hobbled out of a hut. Giving me a nasty leer, she claimed them under her apron. A thick-set man in a leather jacket and bearing a broadax stepped out into the light. At his back, ducking under the door frame, came two stout boys with hoisted spears.

Ceorl and his horsemen halted. Tabak and I did likewise. Men continued to emerge from the huts. There were perhaps twenty of fighting age, each armed with a long spear. Still they stayed back from our horses. Ceorl studied them critically, picking out their leader.

'You know us, Cram,' he said. 'Two summers past I traded ax blades with you and hooks of good metal. If it was honest work, you have no cause to turn on me an ax of my own fashioning.'

The man, his eyes narrowed, shook his head. 'I have my worries, smith, as other men. Along the Undain there is little peace. There is no breach of courtesy if my people are vigilant.' Having said that, he advanced toward Ceorl. Ceorl slipped from his mount and met him on the ground. Cram let his anxious eyes rest sharply on Tabak and myself.

'The men of Bede bring more than metal,' he said to him.

Ceorl gave our names. He had met us, he said, on the road that comes out of the north. Cram nodded slowly, without conviction. I could see this did not satisfy him. Behind him an old woman stamped her feet, muttering to all that would listen that we were water trolls. The young men laughed at her. Still, they did not send her away.

Cram called for chairs and a table. 'I would hear of where you have been in two years' roving and of your meeting with such bold men as these,' he said. Then he placed his hand on Ceorl's shoulder and abruptly smiled. 'Such talk, no doubt, will make us thirsty.' He gave another command. The young men dragged a table from his hut. But seeing it was too small for so many, they took down a door and set it upon barrels. Chairs were placed around for us and one for Cram and two old men at his side. The young men stood around. They did not put down their arms.

'What is the danger,' Ceorl asked, 'that your young men bear their weapons and do not sit with us?'

In the meantime a woman had brought forth a pitcher and cups on a platter. Cram poured the beer into the cups himself.

'Young men are not as you and I,' he answered with a sigh. 'They do not always know when they should be afraid and when they should not.'

'Then let them learn,' I said, speaking for the first time.

Ceorl agreed. 'I am not so young,' he said, 'that I would sit with a beer cup between my fingers when boys like these sharpen spear points at my back.'

'Drink, then, and be at ease,' said Cram uncomfortably. Without waiting for us, he lifted his cup to his lips and drank deeply, wiping his mouth with his arm when he had done. Then he called one of the elders of the village and bade him take the spears and pile them in the middle of the clearing. It was done as he commanded, though the young men grumbled. Cram filled his cup once more. 'Now, what news?' he said.

Ceorl looked at the faces of the men and at the children clinging to the women in the doorways. He answered, 'I have never heard there was fear in the eyes of children if men were strong.'

Cram drained the cup.

'Things go ill, friend,' he whispered. He would not meet Ceorl's eyes.

'Has it ever been otherwise?' said Ceorl. But then he added, 'Perhaps Thigg's service lies too hard upon the land.'

'No!' Cram exploded. Then he was excited all at once, shaking his big head and looking up and down the table at us. 'As I am a man who hates evil and villainy, I swear it is not so. Thigg is a fair lord. Let them sink my body in the marshes if it is not so.'

A murmur of astonishment ran through us. There is madness in this man's blood, I thought, and perhaps in his drink as well. Ceorl put down the cup which he had raised. Even the yellow beard, who was seldom without a word, sat quietly, his cup untasted. His squinty eyes, watching Cram, grew harder. There was no sound to be heard save the aspen leaves rustling gently in the wood beyond the village yard. On either side of Cram, the old men trembled. Cram's eyes started stiffly out of his head.

'If you will not drink, then we will trade,' he said. From off his hip he drew a small bag of coins, which he flung clumsily upon the table. They scattered and rolled from one side to the other. Though of no great worth, it was more than I had thought would have been held in the whole of such a village. I took that in and did not miss the warning in it. The trumpets rang.

The horsemen rushed out of the wood. I knew the red cloaks and the helms. I seized my sword. The men of the village rushed toward their spears. Yet I saw well enough that even armed they would stay back. We alone were Eoghan's prey. They knew it. Perhaps Cram had been paid to have his young men take us and, seeing he could not have us addle-headed with his beer, had lost his nerve. Who is to say? Tabak, who had his wits about him still, cast away the chairs to give him room to fight.

The men massed forward, waving spears and swords from upon their mounts. The first of the company drove at me. I hewed the neck of the first horse that reached me. With a scream, it reared its great forelegs, toppling its rider. Before he could crawl away, his arms still in confusion, I caught him in the face. The skull split open under the metal. He was the first man I had killed, but I had no time to think of it. By then the rest were plunging down at us. Ceorl struck one in the side. Tabak drove two back, cutting the knees of the horses and pulling down the startled men with his bare hands. After that they did not press as close but mustered among the huts and before us, cutting off the way to the river. They held their broad shields before them. By ones and twos Cram's men joined the mounted soldiers. It was not long before they had us in a ring.

I saw Cram move among them; his mouth was slack and his gestures uncertain. Eoghan came at last, his mount trotting easily out of the trees. A shout went up from the horsemen. Eoghan surveyed the work of his company, the men in order, the corpses on the ground.

'Better you had come with us at our first meeting,' he called out gravely.

Cram was at his side. 'There was to be no murder,' he whimpered.

Eoghan laughed at him. 'They are my own dead.'

Cram shook his great head and wailed. 'It is in the eyes of the children.'

Eoghan did not answer him. When he rode on, his men gathered quickly at his back.

None of the soldiers' horses would carry me. So they gave me back my own but kept her fettered to two others. The ropes they bound me with cut my wrists. They had needed six men to take me. Yet not one came close enough for sword or ax. Rather they ringed me about and threw stones until I fell, my face bloody and my shoulders bruised with wounds. In this same way they had taken Tabak, even as the men of the mountain towns cripple a stag in its pen. At the feast of the new year I had seen it. The memory came to me as the stones fell. To them we were as monsters. As such, no warrior's honor bound them. Ceorl's men they took in a more manly fashion. Their wounds were deep. Still none of our own were dead.

In that way I stood my first battle and kept my life. We rode the rest of the morning. The soldiers were still, thinking of their comrades. Myself, I thought of the man I killed. In the quiet, with only the footfalls of Eoghan's soldiers, the wind hushed, I remembered the look in his glazed eyes, disbelief more than anguish, before the small face fell apart. There was no glory in it, some farmer's son, no doubt pressed into service by his lord, no quarrel between us but Eoghan's word to him. It was not as the *filidh* tell it. He was a clumsy man. He carried his leather shield too low. His own men left him for the flies.

They had Tabak ride in front of me. Because of his wounds, he kept falling. Later they tied him to the horn of the saddle. He shivered though there was no wind. My heart was in my throat to watch him, once my father's servant, half-slave to Yllvere and waiting fifteen winters, now bidden to be my guardian in the eastern lands. How still he was, grim but strangely without anger. He would take his fate, both good and ill, just as it came. I met his eyes. What must a man bear in service to his lord? I mourned for him more than for myself. My trouble was at least of my own doing.

We rode through meadow lands, close to the river but below the road. I guessed by this that Eoghan meant to take us in secret into Stephen's Well. Twice, when in the distance I saw a string of farm wagons climbing the road along the hill, Eoghan ordered our column halted. He sent two men to pull me roughly from the mare. They pushed my face into the grass. When they let me raise my head, the wagons had gone. The second time I would not mount. The soldiers glared at me.

'I will dress the wounds of my friend,' I said.

'A soldier takes his chances,' mocked the man. 'What is it to me if this one dies?' Then, to prod me, he drew his sword. Still I would not do what he wanted. Eoghan, looking back, saw his man armed and came riding down the line to us. The soldiers drew aside.

'I have ordered that we ride,' Eoghan said harshly.

'He will not,' said the soldier.

Eoghan regarded me distastefully. 'Mount,' he said.

'When I have done,' I answered. 'First, I must wipe the blood from my friend's eyes and close his wounds.'

Eoghan's small eyes turned full to me. 'That he lives at all you owe me. By right the men who took him should have scattered his head and limbs from one end of the village to the other. It would be only just to lay him dead among the death he made.'

I only stared at him.

'Take his arms,' he ordered, 'and lift him.'

Putting up his sword, the one came forward and three more from the ranks of the soldiers.

'If he struggles,' said Eoghan coldly, 'you may beat him. Only leave him enough life's breath that tomorrow he may answer what our captain asks.'

It was not the threat of pain but simply the humiliation that tormented me. It made me reckless. 'By Anu,' I hissed, 'the first that touches me is dead.' The soldiers grinned.

They were men as any other and laughed at the name of the goddess. I do not know what made me invoke her. For I was my father's then and had reasons enough of my own to hate the mysteries of the wood. Yet, once it was spoken, I saw the use of it. With my boot, since I had not the use of my hands, I drew a figure in the twisted grass. The pattern burned in the air as I made it. Poor thing it was, a hearth spell such as any of my sisters used each night to start the kindling. Even the servingwomen knew it. Yet, it frightened the soldiers. They were plainsmen. Among such folk the old religion had been dead a thousand years.

'He is a man witch,' a soldier whispered. The others muttered and made quick signs against the eye.

'Fools,' Eoghan scoffed. 'You wounded him. You bound his hands and made him ride with us.' He turned his horse about. 'Set him on the mare,' he said. He looked at each man when he had finished. A vein beat in his temple. He was accustomed to being obeyed.

The soldiers were silent a moment, uneasy, waiting for one of them to speak. It was a gray-haired man who came forth, a slight man even by their measure. He had a scar across one cheek from the left nostril to his ear. Yet he had a bold voice and made certain that the others heard him. 'Who is to know what a man witch chooses and what he does not?' And then to me, 'Lord, mage, I would have peace with you.'

Eoghan spat. 'If he had power, think you not he would have used it?'

Still the soldiers grumbled. Eoghan stared in anger, without a word.

I saw then that the authority of men is one thing, but the mysteries are greater. A man, if a priest tells him, will plant a rind and throw away the seed. It was not my cunning taught me this. In the faces of the soldiers, still as celebrants, afraid, I saw it. It ordered my mind.

'Take down my friend,' I said. Several soldiers came out of the column, uncertain, unbound the ropes and slid Tabak to the earth. They knew what they risked from Eoghan by that. It was to him I spoke. 'I will go to Stephen's Well,' I said. 'I am eager to see how your captain marshals his four hundred and by that how Thigg is served in this place. For as Thigg is served, so he serves in turn. It marks the stewardship which is his until the true heir comes.'

Then men of Bede looked one to another. Eoghan was watchful of it.

'Untie my hands,' I said.

Out of their number, even in front of Eoghan, a man came forth.

The sun declined toward the horizon. Ocher and huge, it bathed the farthest clouds in copper light. In the east, some leagues before us, rose the walls of Stephen's Well, bright on the one side with the sun's death and on the other, by the river, deep in shadow. Fresh with the spring flood, the water came up to the wall, sucking at the old foundations. Although far off, already I felt small before it. On the landward side the holding jutted a hundred elhws above the trees. Until that time it was the greatest work I had ever seen of man's fashioning, though surely among the most plain. Its steep walls were laid unmortared. Without spires or carvings, bald as a skull, it was a soldier's keep, made to a soldier's rude imagining. Immense it was. Yet it was said that Stephen's Well, for all its height, would huddle in Ormkill's shadow.

From the road broad steps went down to the harbor. Even at a distance I saw it. On either side, backing away from the steps, huge storied buildings loomed above the rock. Each was several times the size of Morrigan. I felt a mountain boy again. But it was the ships that took my thoughts. There were four in the harbor, each of good size. One, whose double sails were bellied full, was setting out downstream to take advantage of the night wind. On the deck as we drew nearer, I saw a man in a blue cloak, hooded, shouting orders to the crew. I could not hear the words. It was still too far and the wind was from the north.

'It is the same ship that passed us in the fog,' said Ceorl.

'Perhaps,' I said, wondering how in the darkness of morning past he had seen anything that marked it. Yet I judged it was not the ship he wished to speak of, though it may have been that it reminded him of something. For he had seen the look on my face when I had come from the river, my hair shining, the steam rolling back from my shoulders. He had heard the claim that Tabak made for me and bound, on the strength of it, his men and honor to my service. Yet I knew well enough it was Tabak that bound him, the fame of Tabak ap Ewyn that gave him certainty. Now Tabak lay limp against his saddle. With the soldier's leave I had bathed his wounds and worked a salve into the cuts. Still I had not Yllvere's or Vydd's skill. Whether he would live I did not know. I saw Ceorl feared that he would not.

'My lord Finn,' Ceorl began unevenly. 'You know that we are few.'

'I know it. And fewer still when we ride inside those walls.' Then watching him, I said, 'You are free, Ceorl, you and those of Bede.'

He flinched and I saw that, without meaning, I had shamed him. 'I have not taken away my word,' he said. 'I meant only to speak plainly.'

'Then speak,' I told him.

Ceorl looked up at me. It strained his neck to do so. The leather of his face was cracked; there were creases about his mouth. Like Tabak, he was older than I had first realized. 'You have humiliated Eoghan, my lord. You knew that. Even now he rides at the back of us, his command broken, as much a captive as if you chained him. Yet if he enters Stephen's Well, he will have his captain's ear.'

'I cannot help that.'

'You might,' he whispered.

I thought of Urien.

'Would you have me slip a knife in him?' I asked. So this is the way it comes to kings, I thought. It angered me. 'Do you think that would gain me better entry or shelter for Tabak or time to heal his wounds?'

He shook his head. 'I would not have you enter here at all.'

'Is your word one thing, then, and mine another?'

He looked perplexed. 'I do not see,' he said.

I answered sharply. 'Twice I have said I meant to come down to this place. Before these men I said it.'

'You are not bound to them.'

'They called me mage and begged my peace.'

Despite his fealty Ceorl laughed. 'For that small fire you scratched in the grass? Forgive me, lord, but in the hills I have seen a farm wife suck a better blaze out of the air to start her supper.'

I knew the truth of that. Perhaps I smiled. 'Fortunately for you and me, these folk are not as widely traveled.'

But Ceorl had dropped his eyes. 'Here they can kill a man as readily as anywhere.'

'I do not doubt it.'

Ceorl made a deep obeisance. 'My lord, I pray you. Only ride past Stephen's Well and I shall go with you wheresoever you require.'

I set my eye on him. 'Do not bind yourself to me more than you must. I do not know myself what drives me or what, in time, I may require of those that follow me.'

We were then within the outer perimeter of the town. Small outbuildings grew up about us. In the lampless doorways I saw the shadows of men – guards, I judged – spears resting in the crooks of their arms. In the poor light it may be that they saw no more, nor maybe wished to see, than a company of their own men passing.

Ceorl rode at my right, on my blind side. 'Truly, I am already bound, Ar Elon's son,' he said. 'I will follow as I can.' I turned to look at him, to fix his face forever in my mind. He was the first man who swore his life to me. Though he thought me wrong, pigheaded, yet he followed me. If I had been able to think then or had foresight, I would have thought, this also is the way of kings. In the years that followed, into the hall that was mine, with the barons like my hounds fighting over the scraps of my table, Ceorl would come in the spring out of the north from the lands I had ceded him. Yearly, the most trusted of my counselors, he would sit at my hearth at Ormkill in the place I kept for him, to drink and remember what we did. Then, before he fell asleep in his beard, he would recall how I disregarded the first advice he gave me. Even now, the god only knows who was right and wrong.

We rode in the middle of the line. At the front, before the tower, I heard a watchman call out.

'Eoghan's company,' said a soldier.

'I do not see him,' said the watchman cautiously.

88

'He comes,' the man answered.

By then we were abreast of the tower and the light of the torches poured over us. When they had a look at me, the guards came to life. Someone lifted a horn to his lips. Its shrill sound called forth other horns within the holding. There was a clank of metal, footfalls and the squeal of hinges. The wall itself was a warren of tunnels, alcoves and small doors. Within I heard men running and orders being passed. Soldiers ducked out of creviced shadows I had thought were stone. In several black lines they wormed out of the rock. I saw little of their faces, small dwarfish men like the rest I had seen in the East, helmeted, clothed in leather studded up and down with iron. Silently they formed in columns about us, pressing in. Out of their number someone bade us dismount.

'Be careful with this man,' I said, gesturing toward Tabak. Without further comment a litter was brought for him. When they had settled him, an immense wooden door, pulled by four men, opened in the holding.

Eoghan, who had come up from behind, now entered at the front. He ran a distrustful eye along his company and, taking the watchman aside, spoke to him privately. The man, staring at me all the while, ran off when Eoghan had finished.

After a moment a burly man without helm or weapon came down the stair along the inner wall. His eyes passed over the line of soldiers, lingering on me in astonishment, then stopped on Eoghan.

'Why would you have your own men put in irons?' he asked sternly.

Eoghan, who had come before him, answered. 'The prisoner,' he said, 'has witched them.'

'What prisoner?'

Eoghan pointed.

The man pulled his beard, stared a time and shook his head. 'It is an odd sort of prisoner who rides into my holding bearing his own sword.'

Shouts rose among Eoghan's company. Eoghan himself cried out above them, his nostrils quivering. No sense could be made from the howling.

'Silence!' the man cried roughly, grasping his beard between his fingers. His eyes gleamed beneath their heavy brows. He extended his hand toward me, pointing. 'Bring this one to my chamber. And the giant on the litter.' Eoghan was about to protest.

'And you, Eoghan,' he grumbled. 'I did not mean to forget you.' Then, turning, 'And you of Bede. Yes, I know you. I mean to have this settled.' He gave a swift glance toward the watchman. 'Now bolt the door,' he ordered, his voice grown heavy. 'I'll have no more marvels at my door this night. If any but Thigg's own messenger come banging, you have my leave to turn them back.'

The watchman nodded. As they had come, the soldiers vanished. Like worms into wood, they were reclaimed by the walls. Then, even before we had left the yard, the torches were put out.

CHAPTER TEN

I waited on the bench. Eoghan had already begun to speak, his loud voice choked with anger. The captain, whose name was ffraw, had dismissed the guards though I guessed he had them stationed outside the door where he could get them quickly enough if he had need of them. He sat on a low stool before the hearthstones. It was his own chamber, and not some prisoners' hall, which I thought odd. There was a bed in one corner and a plain table in another. With his own hands he had pulled the drapery over the window. It was the one luxury in the room, a wide cloth woven with gold and silver threads. Among the folds of the fabric I could pick out the images of an aurochs and a team of horses. The aurochs was crimson, the horses green.

ffraw took no part in the questioning but let Eoghan go on for some time. Once he rose to add another log to the fire. He had a great black kettle boiling on a tripod. He stirred the contents with a stick. With his back to Eoghan he listened, staring into the flames. His brows hung over his eyes; a harsh frown puckered his forehead. When Eoghan had finished, he restrained a sigh and smoothed his matted beard.

'A fire, you say?' he half-asked, half-demanded. 'No more than that?'

Eoghan was adamant. 'Out of the air alone,' he said, his cheeks flushed.

ffraw stared inquisitively at Tabak, laid like a corpse on the litter, before at last he turned to me, his eyebrows raised.

'And did you?' he asked.

I took my finger and tore a livid fragment from the air. The flame, pulled out of emptiness, fell smoldering on the floor, where it expired.

ffraw nodded without surprise. 'You asked his name?' he said to Eoghan, waving his stick at him.

Eoghan bit his upper lip with his yellow teeth. It was not the sort of inquiry he had expected.

'You did ask him?' ffraw repeated.

'He is from the North,' said Eoghan. His voice was bitter. 'From the house which he calls Morrigan, of Urien's line. So he told me. But from the sound of it, my guess is that he means what we call Sléibhte-na-Ban, the mountains of women. In truth he called out the name of the goddess.'

'His *name*, man,' ffraw shouted. There was a commotion at the door. Two guards, hearing the shouting though perhaps missing the words, came in. ffraw did not wave them off but held them at the entrance with a stare.

'His name,' he said again.

'He did not give it.'

'Or to any there?'

'Not that I know.'

ffraw drew himself up, wiping his hands on his longshirt as though to fuss with something. No other reason. The muscles had changed minutely in his jaw. Yet if he were weighing some action, it took only a moment.

'Guards, take this man,' he said.

For an instant the spearmen did not understand. They moved toward me. ffraw's eyebrows arched still higher and he thrust out his stick to make it clear. But Eoghan knew it from the first. A brief spasm twisted his lips. He flung at me a look of feverish hatred. The spearmen grabbed his arms. There was a blade at his back, in the hollow right above his buttocks. When he felt it, his small eyes turned their astonished gaze at ffraw. His shoulders quivered.

The captain watched him quietly. 'Take him to the deepest part of the wall and chain him there,' he said in a low voice. 'Let no one speak to him. If he so much as whispers, you may kill him.'

Eoghan raged and shouted but did not look back when they pushed him through the door.

As though he had forgotten him, ffraw turned once more to poke the fire. Pulling a strip of meat from a rack on the wall, he added it to the kettle. 'Ceorl, you know a soldier's life,' he said, giving him a wink. 'No maid or wife or even an ugly widow to do a man's cooking.' A smile compressed his lips, but his face grew no softer. He found his place on the stool again. I did not know what to think of him. Ceorl, I saw, was uncomfortable. ffraw looked sidelong at Tabak. A secret lay behind his eyes.

'Will he live?' he said to me.

'He is not dead.'

'Not a few of mine are,' he observed. 'And by his hand.' Slowly his expression took on a certain thoughtfulness. 'You have done, I suspect, all you can for him.'

'What could be done,' I said.

In a moment he was up again. 'Come,' he said, 'sit at my table.' Then he pounded the floor with his stick. A new man appeared at the door. He was squat and gray; a dullness sat in his staring eyes. He had not the look of a soldier.

'Beer?' he asked.

ffraw smiled, rubbing his hairy hands. 'A man must drink,' he said. 'And my guests, I judge, have come a long way without much comfort.'

The man hunched his shoulders when ffraw spoke to him. ffraw said no more, and the man went out again. In the next few minutes he went back and forth, bringing knives for the meat and refilling our cups. Lastly he brought a platter piled with soldiers' bread. When he was not needed, the servant stood before the fire. Ceorl kept his eyes on him. We were both uneasy but made the best of it. For some time now I had felt my ignorance. I had not eaten at a table since I left Morrigan. In truth, I little knew what was expected at a man's table. For I was accustomed to my sisters whispering to each other and my aunts holding counsel while the serving-women hovered. I spilled my beer. I had been thinking of Eoghan.

'Ah,' ffraw sighed and put down his heavy cup. His wide bare forehead glistened. He pushed the meat away, having had his fill. 'And are there still barons in the North?' he asked. 'We hear so little news from there.'

'Such barons,' I said, 'as the High King left. We have kept the holdings much the same.'

ffraw bared his great blunt teeth. 'But we are Thigg's now,' he declared. His eyebrows quivered. 'You don't deny it?' I caught the sober glitter of Ceorl's eyes.

'He is Steward,' I acknowledged. Somewhere within the walls I heard muted oaths and men laughing. The soldiers' quarters are to the left, I thought, and set that fact in my memory.

ffraw stirred. 'To be candid,' he said, 'we never did know much about the North. Yours were never friendly folk and held aloof since I remember. It has been a dozen years, I think, since we took a harvest from the hill farms. The *filidh*, I hear, no longer go there.' He looked up. 'Yet now and then,' he said, 'a word comes down to us.' I noticed that his lips were parted slyly. 'It is said, for instance, that now the men are weak and women rule there.' The sneer was not hidden from his voice.

'I am born of such a one,' I said.

'Cu, fill his cup,' ffraw ordered blandly. The servant came from the hearth. 'A witch woman, is she?' ffraw added as though it pricked him just to think of it.

'Of the Kell,' I answered.

'Well, I don't suppose a man would lie about a thing like that,' he said.

'Though it does seem, lad, a queer sort of lineage.' His deliberate black-haired fingers took up his stick again. 'Still, of all that's said of them, I never heard the Kell suckled giants.'

I made no answer.

Ceorl coughed, wanting my notice.

'Damn queer, I think,' said ffraw, the muscles knitting in his jaw.

There was a heaviness in the air, a thickness that the fire could not dispel. ffraw scowled, and I caught in his twisting gestures a piece of the mystery that held his thoughts.

'Like any man,' I said, 'I have a father.'

All at once the room seemed very small. I stood, feeling the floorboards sway beneath my feet and the nearness of the ceiling to my head.

ffraw held himself erect. Without joy, he smiled.

'I know you, Finn, Lord Ar Elonson,' said the captain of Stephen's Well, spreading his black hands on the table. Having spoken, he blew out a great quantity of breath, like a sprinter who has run a race. Then, his duplicity done, he found his voice again. 'Since the last winter storm closed in on your mountain, from that time to this, I knew your coming. All these months in the northwest I sent out my patrols. I did not tell them what they sought. I knew that they would find you. A man eight elhws high cannot pass unseen along the roads. Yet I have thought and taken care. Eoghan, my own right arm, I have cast in irons for you. He is no fool. If he were, I would not have made him what he was. Shortly he would have guessed just what you are. Even half a word is sufficient to a thoughtful man.'

All the while he spoke his eyes were fixed on me. His eyelids were blue and weary. 'My lord,' he said with dignity, 'I have tried my best to think what must be done. I knew that you would come, that, before others, I would receive you in this land. Yet I had no guidance. I could not tell whether you would make your way openly or if you were better served in secret. If anything, I have erred on the side of caution, assuming you meant to keep this to yourself and to me who was given warning. Yet you alone can tell me if I failed.'

I shook my head, for I had yet no words for him. His speech surprised me. I thought of it in silence. Much as well remained unsaid. I knew that too. Beyond the window the night had deepened. There was stillness at last within the walls. The guards, if they yet kept their stations outside the door, could not be heard.

'How came the warning?' I said at last.

ffraw beckoned to his servant. 'It is time, I think,' he said. The man went

When he had settled himself once more, ffraw spoke. 'It was after that last storm, as I have said. I was walking in the practice yard. The day was bright and as I had been long within these walls, looking up, the sun near blinded me. It was, I believe, because I was almost blinded, and so not looking at the world, that first I saw it, a vague hard thing, iron-black and falling from the sky. I knew later that I was meant to see it. Yet perhaps I saw it before its time. High it was and treacherous, I thought. It bolted from the north. I did not take it for a servant. I was about to tell my bowman to shoot it down, when it called my name.'

Cu came through the door. He had his arm outstretched, wrapped all in leather. His face was apprehensive. Before him, its huge claws crooked about his wrist, he bore the crow.

The cruel mouth snapped open. 'Hail, Finn, lord to be of the lands between the seas,' she croaked, her voice a grating whisper.

She tilted her dark head at me. Her eyes shone red-gold in the firelight, distant, beyond all pain, like Grieve's when last I saw her.

'Ninmir!' I exclaimed in wonder.

'So you have named me,' hissed the crow. 'And so I am.'

In that way I began my life at Stephen's Well. For if I were of any mind to hurry on to Ormkill, Tabak's wounds had put an end to it. Morning and evening I climbed the winding stair into the tower in the eastern wall. There they had carried him so that high above the holding, out of its shadow, he might lie day long in the sun for healing. From one day to the next he slept. As he had watched once at my bedside, now I kept the watch at his. Who is the servant now? I wondered. But it was just. Yet, in honesty, I desired as much to stand in that high place. For there above the backs of men I could look out far along the river and the plains.

There, though I told myself my thoughts were all on Ormkill, I often watched the north. I half expected to be followed. Yet I saw nothing but the distant hills and beyond them, gray and hooded, the mountain along whose hard ridges and furrowed glens I had come down. Nightfall often found me there, watching the clouds float southward across the peaks. By midnight the wind would tear them away. Then I would see the belt of stars which men called Undain after the river. A thing of dusty light, it girdled the sky from west to east, as though it alone kept the heavens from falling asunder. I would stare tensely into the velvet dark. Sometimes, despite my cares, I slept. Once in a dream the Menhir, his craggy shoulders thrust into my thoughts like a great gray hill, spoke to me. But on waking I had not the words.

In the mornings white mists shimmered on the water meads. The sun would rise watery from the eastern sea. The green of earth returned. It was spring then. Men called out to one another along the river, their clear strong voices ringing in the morning air. The boats knocked at their moorings. I would look out. Above the fields, descending slowly in wide circles, Ninmir hunted. She would come if I called. Yet I knew I had not tamed her. My eye ached dully. I thought of the tangled lives of both our kindred, the crow's and mine, twisted one about the other like the maze of ivy spiraling about Gwen Gildrun, fastened on each other like the figures on the gate.

Ceorl and those of Bede had taken up their craft again. When I wanted him, I would find Ceorl in the forge, his face flushed with the heat, his chest and arms mired with soot. Hammers rang on anvils. Two men kept the furnace, one to feed the wood, the other at the goatskin bellows. It was hot, brutal work. Yet Ceorl would stay at it both early and late.

'How is Tabak?' he would ask me, shouting above the hammering.

'He grows stronger,' I shouted back at him. 'Soon we shall be on our way.' Yet I felt keenly how the days came and went, how each new morning found us as we were.

In the afternoons I walked into the yard. I had grown accustomed to the slow stares the soldiers gave me. Word of the spellfire had passed quickly among them. A lame horse was brought to me to cure and a ewe from one of the farms with some complaint. I built a mound of green wood and darkened the yard with great quantities of smoke. Not knowing anything beyond that, I mumbled a Kell song I had heard as a child. To my surprise the chestnut mare recovered in a day or two. I never heard what happened to the ewe. But after that I could have filled my days with doctoring. Knowing I wouldn't be twice lucky, I put a stop to it. Nonetheless, it was widely held I was a mage of exceeding power.

Word of my claim, however, seemed to have stopped with ffraw. As things stood, that suited me. For himself ffraw acknowledged the claim but hadn't, I thought, quite made up his mind what he should do. Though I watched, I saw no messenger dispatched to Thigg at Ormkill. Of course, patrols went out each day and the ships pulled away from their moorings to float downstream. It would have been no great matter to have the word sent secretly. Yet it did not seem he did. It was Ninmir, I thought, that restrained him. Like a rope around his neck, she tugged at him. His old thoughts failed. When I went to his table, when the meat was eaten, he would bid me bring her forth. Deep was his silence when he gazed at her.

It was late. The cups were drained. ffraw twisted his fingers in his beard. 'Is there another,' he asked, 'the like of her?'

'He I called Ninguh,' I answered. 'Both in the old tongue. I took them from the tree. It was at the time I came to manhood.'

He was silent, his eyes vague as though he looked into himself. 'Who taught them speech?' he said.

'One of my mother's women, her sister, who lived apart on our mountain.'

'It marks you, lad,' he said. 'Though I am but a soldier and have not walked the way of the mysteries, I have not heard that the children of the air spoke to men since the days of the beginning. Though men forever speak of such things, in my life I have never seen a sign. Yet this is one.'

He laid his hand on mine and leaned forward, as if to tell a secret. 'You know the land is troubled. Thigg sits heavy upon the barons and they grumble. Yet if a new king comes he must master each of them. When you ride to Ormkill, you must send Ninmir before you, as she came to me. She must perch on the High King's chair where Thigg now sits. And when the barons are with him, she must make your claim. In that they will know you are your father's son.'

I nodded, thinking, she is my inheritance. It took me by surprise, for since I was a boy I had thought my father left me no gift but life. Then I told ffraw how I had climbed to the nest, the marvel of Gwen Gildrun, and how, bartered by my father, I had lost my eye. It was a fair tale, he decided. Though he was sorry there was no murder in it and advised me, should the *filidh* make a song of it, to invent three trollish warriors. Then he took pains to tell me the strokes that I must say I gave them and how, though ill matched and a boy, I took their severed heads and set them on the tree.

'I have lived longer and will tell you this,' he said. 'A king must have blood on him if he would make his own men brave. For what man would follow a milky ewe among its enemies? Your father was not squeamish. At the four corners of Ormkill, beneath the posts, he placed the hearts of the barons who betrayed him.'

I was slow to speak, for I had not heard this. 'You saw it?' I asked when I had mastered my feeling.

'I was a lad myself then,' he answered. 'When Ar Elon first came up from Hren, where it is said he walked full-grown out of the sea. Rumor spread from Tywy and Cassiterides and on again to Haman that a giant, as of old, had come once more among men. The people rose to meet him. He gathered them as he rode inland. It was the barons who named him last, when they had no choice, when already he had an army at his back. Even then, some diehards would not swear to him. Those he slew with the people watching. I stood among the many, cheering when he did it. I had left my father's farm to follow him. I was then not yet seventeen.'

He drew a breath. I looked at him. His hair was gray to the root. He had a barrel chest and the thick arms of a warrior, but the strength was old.

'And would you be young again?' I asked him.

He was not a stupid man. He knew what I meant.

'Since Ar Elon fell I have held this place in Thigg's service,' he answered softly. 'Yet I remember that day at Ormkill, the people cheering, your father standing over us. A great figure of a man he was, his black hair shining.' He drew his brows together and laid his fingers flat on his closed eyes. 'I will swear to you,' he said after a little while. 'But what good are my four hundred against all that Thigg can muster?'

He knew I could not answer him. Yet I laughed and made some boast. Lord, Dagda, it was long ago.

In the evening I sat by Tabak's bedside. The sky above the tower and to the north was dark with storm. Curtains of wind-blown rain pummeled the roof stones. The gale sang through the holding. Tabak drew the blanket high upon his chest and coughed.

'Your mind is set on it?' he asked.

I nodded, looking into the storm then southeast along the river. Nothing moved on it. The smaller boats had been dragged onto the bank. 'When you are able,' I told him. 'When the storm is done with us and the river calm.'

Tabak drew himself up, slowly like a man from some great labor. His eyes were bright but his face was pale. He coughed again.

'The light is poor,' he said. 'Let me see your face.'

I turned to him, straightening, trying to look a king.

'I will send Ninmir before me,' I said, 'to perch on the Steward's chair. She will proclaim my coming before the council of the barons. So ffraw advised and it seems good to me.'

Tabak threw back his head, sharply, though it pained him. 'So Thigg shall hear of it and will have his horsemen lie in wait for you.' He laughed. I had not known him so cold.

'ffraw has sworn to me,' I protested. 'I shall ride at the head of his company.'

He answered bitterly. Almost I did not know him. 'It takes but one man to kill a king,' he said. 'Thigg with his armies should safely manage a boy.'

His hard words cut me. 'I *was* a boy in a house of women,' I shouted at him. 'For all I knew my father was a maker of fish weirs. You put it in my head that he was king. What would you have me do? Am I not his heir?' I glared at him.

He made an awkward gesture in the air with his thick hands. Perhaps he tried to grab hold of something that was not there. The pain ate at him. He murmured. But the storm was in my ears and anger filled me.

'It was your word to me,' I cried. 'His blood, you said, came down to me.'

He moved his hand again and I saw then that he was trying to lift himself.

'To you and to the child I took away,' he whispered, his voice haggard, his lips on fire. His hand raked out in front of him. I might have taken hold of it. But a chill ran through me and I cried out.

Even in his pain he watched me. From somewhere behind his eyes where the fever had not reached, a silence waited.

'Where?' I pleaded.

Once more the coughing racked him. There was fresh blood upon the mat. He fell back against the bed, his staring, wild eyes rolling. It was only then I touched him. But he did not know me. That night I stayed close at his bedside till the fit was free of him and he slept.

CHAPTER ELEVEN

The seed is in the flower. The riddle's answer dances about the words that spoke it. Things fall back upon themselves. The prophecy no man could fathom is always plain when the tale is done. So a man carries his death with him all his life, unaware. Had I but listened to the *filidh*, I would have known it. It is the one true song of kings. But I had other things to think of.

All night by his bed I pondered it. When he groaned I turned to him. But when the tendons in his neck would loosen and his forehead cleared, my eye wandered east beyond the tower to the place where rain and river met in one gray line. The Undain, swollen with the storm, swept on before me, toiling toward Ormkill and the sea.

Unlike Urien I did not need to seek the name. I had it before it was given me. 'Géar,' I said to the darkness, tasting it. 'Indeed we two are mountain born.' I thought bitterly of Yllvere, knowing all the while it was not simply a woman's capriciousness but Kell work to the heart. For among the shore folk each well and hill has its own name and the name and its history are one. So it is among their children.

The smell of rain and the wet smell of the stone came to my nostrils. In one tower I thought of another. I remembered Morrigan, its sheer walls cut from the mountain fastness, the blueness of its stone, old beyond imagining. It is the place I know, even to this day, best among the places of the earth. There I came to manhood. Storm-filled, its sky crawled in my dreams; its stony pastures were in the shape of my heels. Yet Géar knew it not, except in the red hour of birth and that is beyond recall. What place, I wondered, was in Géar's memory? What house haunts Géar's dreams? I knew such places, wheresoever they had been, would count for nothing. The name was given. We two were wedded to the mountain, even as the nestlings, though early I had stolen them, were Gwen Gildrun's still.

All night I crouched below the storm, in the wind that racked the tower, muttering the name. The sound was wonder and it was terror. I felt it wash into me like blood. In the shaping darkness I touched it. In the hiss of the rain upon the roof tiles, it beat against my ears. Géar, my father's child and Yllvere's, Géar. It was a god's name but it was a goddess's as well. I do not know which name was older. It was not, I knew, the name of a king. What then need I fear of my father's child?

But Tabak slept and the answer with him. The rain drew away to the south. The morning reddened. I did not wake him. When he stirs, I will have everything from him, I thought. But for the moment I went down the winding stairs and came out by the outer wall and the broad steps that led down to the harbor. The pacing sentries were used to me and let me pass.

I went into the morning. The early light was brilliant as it is after rain. Now I began to hear the din of the docks ahead of me – the sailors' voices, the grunt of men lifting thick barrels, the inland gulls, the rushing river. I walked forward among the ranks of rivermen. In the evening, ahead of the storm, a great ship had sailed into the harbor. It was an odd sight among the lesser craft and I went to have a closer look at it.

It lay at the far end of the wharf, rolling at anchor, the mud-gorged river slapping at its massive sides. Bright oak it was and fitted with iron. Its high bow arched above the deck, even then looking seaward. Its golden wood was cut in the likeness of a salamander, its eyes painted. Someone had hoisted a shield into the rigging. It was meant, I judged, as a sign of peace. I saw the reason. For they were strangers on the river, sea folk by their dress, their yellow hair loose below seal caps, and here by ffraw's leave.

The sound of the sea folk's voices grew less when I came among them. Those who had put their weapons down looked to see they were in reach. So I have always made uneasy those who do not know me. It may be their silence passed to those below the deck. Soon a man came up from below the planking. Seeing him, the sailors touched their brows in deference. He had a great corn-yellow beard and eyes as blue and piercing as the sky on that spring morning. Something stirred in me but I could not place it. By his carriage I took him for the shipmaster. Why are sea folk so far inland? I wondered. Curious, I stepped forward.

'It is a stout ship you have, master,' I called to him.

'Aye, man, it is that,' he answered.

'Nor have I seen the like of it,' I added, 'for it shines like a cup of gold.'

There was pride in the shipmaster's face. 'I saw to the cutting of the boards myself,' he said. 'The trees were of my own choosing. On rocky

Hren I took them, from the high grove that watches on the sea.'

He saw how my breath stopped. 'It is a holy isle,' I said.

He nodded and laughed. 'So I was told by the folk who live along the shore that faces it. We camped the summer there when a storm had left us ruined upon the place, my own ship broken on the rocks. When they saw what I meant, the women came out on the beach to shriek and tear their hair. But when I went over the narrow water and took the trees, their men, though armed against us, would not cross. So I took the trees in peace.'

As I listened, something prompted me. 'I would stand upon those planks,' I said. It was my own doing. In afteryears in the hall I wrested from Thigg, my own wine loosening their tongues, I have heard the *filidh* tell it, their honey words seeking to flatter me. It was a great ax, they said, that the shipmaster had which tempted me, that seeing it I desired it for myself and so went up to take it. In my own hall I never forswore it. This was a thing men could understand. But, in truth, I wished to walk upon godwood.

'I will come up,' I said.

The seamen heard me. They saw my size and, thinking I would swamp them, they murmured, their small eyes darting back and forth like flies. But the shipmaster, as though he had a purpose of his own, did not forbid it.

'Only step lightly, man,' he said.

Gladly I went up and stood upon the deck, in the center, keeping my balance. The planking held. The men who watched me looked relieved. Though I doubted there was much chance of my bursting through, still, men will gawk and I think I must handle all I touch like eggshells.

'Now indeed,' cried the shipmaster, 'I have a ship of wonders.' But for an instant he would not look at me, his blue eyes vacant, as though he took counsel with himself. Then it passed. He laughed again, though grimly, and gave his hand.

'I am Pendyved, Gwynedd's son,' he said.

It was an ancient name but fairly given. It may be he is named after those of old, I thought. So I sought among the names I owned for one to give him in return. Yet a silence held me. Perhaps the god made me cautious. But the day was bright and I threw off the warning, giving him my own. 'I am Finn,' I said and the seamen heard me. Yet in my own ears it sounded clipped, a broken thing, but half a name.

When the names were given, the seamen crept closer to see me, and Pendyved called for wine. His boy brought it in an earthen jar. It was red as currants when he poured it out. As he looked at it, Pendyved shivered and bit his lip. 'So the sap ran when I cut the trees,' he said. 'Red as berries, redder still like blood. The men complained loudly when they saw it, but I held them to the task.' With his own hands he passed me the cup.

I held the cup, small in my fingers, before my face. 'What wine is this?' I asked. 'I do not know the look of it.'

'Rare as druid's breath it is,' said Pendyved surely. 'I found it in a cave on that same island, wrapped in a mantle and behind a wall. Who is to say how old it is? It has the bloom of some ancient summer in it, though. Drink and you will see.'

Truly I thirsted, for I had spent the long night at Tabak's bedside without relief. Its fragrance sprang rich to my nostrils. Full of the scent of the vine it was, of the broad ripened earth at harvest, old but without sourness. Blessed it seemed like a remembered summer.

I took it greedily, pressing the cup against my lips.

'It pleases me,' I said.

Pendyved stared. He had not touched his cup. 'Drink deep,' he urged. But all at once the cup was far too heavy for my arm. An anvil weighed upon my eyelid. I fought it. My heart leapt in me but my veins were thick as stone. Then I saw the sea folk were not men at all but only shadows. The sun shone through their flesh and I knew it was not human flesh but only rags on bones. Pendyved laughed, his parched lips twisting into snakes that fell and hissed on the deck. His yellow hair burned down to ash. The wind swept it smoldering from the naked skull. He had no eyes but dark holes out of which he laughed.

With what strength I had I tore my gaze from him. I felt the great ship shudder. Fleshless arms cast off the mooring ropes. Bony hands ran up the sails. Like webs they were, made of threads and holes, but the wind filled them. Voices that had no sound cried out. The dead crew cheered. Into the white-toothed current the ship turned. On the broad black of the Undain it glided, but not on the sunlit river, rather some dark memory of the river, flowing out from underneath or out of time, I knew not which. Despite my fear and the wine's burning, I made myself still. This is Death's ship, I thought, but Death shall not have me. I did not climb Gwen Gildrun or stare into the fire that burns its root or tear from Yllvere the name she hid that I might perish unsung, before my time. So I boasted to myself. But I felt myself shaking. Still I listened to my thoughts. What harm, I told myself, can the dead hold, being dead? Has not life eaten all their strength and gnawed what force they had, both blood and muscle, down to these pale bones? Else how are they dead? And then I knew it. It was the wine and not the dead that kept me, that drugged my limbs. I will sleep, I thought, and when I wake I shall be free of it.

Then seeing me composed, the eyeless dead nuzzled up to me and huddled near my warmth. Like hounds they were, pawing at my knees, whimpering without breath or sound. It is said that in my sleep I grinned at them, though who among the living saw it I know not.

The stones of Morrigan, spidered with lichen, swung back into my sight. The wave bore me up along the wall and then fell back. Above me the tall elms ringed the yard and the grass was the grass of summer, green as emerald. The cold wave lifted me almost to that high bank before, gently, it drew me back again. It did not seem odd that the sea came high before the walls. The foam danced about my head, stringing out my hair. I floated. In my nakedness the water lifted me, high to the brink of stones where watched the women of the house, their eyes unmoved. Grieve stood among the others, my sisters – Sanngion in white and Ryth in purple. Vydd stood back of them, bent upon her staff. Her head was lifted. Like the very stone of the house she was, gray-eyed as the sea. I lay strengthless before her gaze. The sea wave rose and fell.

A door opened from the oven room. Yllvere came out to walk beneath the trees. She moved in their green shadows, her women at her back – the cook in her apron, the other aunts in robes. She came to rest at the sea edge to watch my bare legs splayed and carried in the heaving tide. From the nameless place that, secret, she kept within her she watched me, her deep eyes distant and chill as stars. But I was used to her. The brine washed in my mouth.

'Tabak I have left at Stephen's Well,' I told her.

Even as she smiled, her long white fingers tightened on her arms. 'Is it only him you think of, Finn?' she asked.

The women raised their faces. There was a dark-haired girl among the rest. The canopy of leaves moved over her. Her face was smooth. It let no feeling out. Her black hair drifted behind her like a cloak. The west wind blew at it. She shivered, her deep eyes moving over the waters where, watching her, I rose and fell.

'Give me your name,' I said.

Motionless, as he waited, Pendyved watched me with no eyes. The night itself was voiceless; the bank, hushed and hidden in the darkness, passed far to either side. The ship, finding wind where there was no wind, sailed on. My breath caught as I woke.

'The wine has passed?' he asked me.

If I do not dream, I thought. But even in my mind he heard me.

'You dream the dream,' he said, 'the living take for life.'

I was silent, watching him. The river was black and solemn, but the ship, disdaining darkness, glittered red as gold.

'What is it the dead wish of me?' I asked.

'To hasten you.' His voice was like a wind from underground. It smelled in the air, the breath of caves. His skullbone gleamed beneath the stars. 'So Ninguh came first to you at Morrigan,' he said, 'and the Menhir after, the very stone, ancient and asleep, awakened to bid you hurry. And when still you lingered, these spare bones from my cold grave, brought back from dust to stand and call you forth again.'

I heard him but thought, what if I am mad? I raised my arm and found the strength of it. I unfolded my fingers and closed them. The nails scratched at my palm. I thought, it is the body of a man I have.

'Such as men are, so you are also,' he sighed.

But I seemed to myself only a burning shell. I blinked and rocked my head to clear it.

'You are a plague of dreams,' I cried, the faces of the women still in my eye. 'I know when I wake and when I sleep. I know the sea does not rise to Morrigan except in dreams.'

'We ride the river,' said Pendyved simply. In the shadows I saw the memory of his yellow hair against the sky. As though I had opened a door to a place that was but was no more, so I found him. The flesh where there was no flesh was lined; the lipless mouth was stern, for care had turned it. I made myself stare at him.

'What are truth and lies in this?' I asked.

'The ship is as I said,' he answered quietly. 'I hewed the wood on Hren, taking back a suit of flesh to do it. Yet even as I was, I stood in wonder of the wood. Dark and old it is, brooding on headlands which face the sea. The trees are tall and terrible to behold – trees that draw breath and listen. Before them the ages of men pass as an hour. It is no wonder the Kell cursed me; but they could not stop the work. Still they screamed their oaths and blistered me with spells. Till he that holds the place, the stony ground and even the trees themselves, took pity on the Kell and veiled the island, piling the darkness up to heaven so the sight was hid from them.' Then he was quiet again. A mist rose from the river and mingled with his flesh.

I shook my head, thinking, what cause is there for such a ship? What purpose worth the price of felling godwood?

'To take you out of Stephen's Well where you had lingered,' Pendyved answered, though I had not asked. 'The ship was fashioned to tempt you upon its decks. So he who rules the island placed in my hands such wine as even the dead may not drink, so that having walked here you would stay.'

Despairing, I looked into those vacant eyes beyond whose emptiness a greater darkness moved. His features twisted. I saw the pain it cost him to keep his man-shape and pitied him.

'What lord would wake the dead?' I wondered.

The skull that had been a man looked grim. 'He has dared greater and done worse. He is not patient, yet he has learned to wait. The strength he has, though it has waned, surpasses the strength of any who still walk upon the land. That which he is able to do he does. You must know it. In you the king's blood drips as well.'

I groaned. 'Am I then his toy?' I asked in anger. 'The mirror of his will? So, if he pushes, I must fall? Say plainly, man, who calls me. Is it his voice in the stone, in the crow's mouth, that seeks my going?'

The skull laughed upon its bony neck. 'Each man is himself,' he said, a thing, no more a man.

I raked the face that was no more.

'Yet I am called,' I cried but found no words to make him answer.

'Speak!' I shouted. But the voice had ceased or else became one with the wind that blew down from another heaven than the one I knew.

The Undain turns east above Ormkill into the face of the sun. I watched its simple round orb rise out of the river. It was the sun I knew. I bathed in its clear light, shedding the darkness like an old skin. Before dawn I had awakened, in the gray hour, cramped and shivering. But now the early mists were gone, the dead with them. Their bones, like ice, had melted in the air. They only serve, I thought. My argument's not with Pendyved but his lord. But the memory left me in a sullen mood. I am called, I thought, but given no counsel. Yet even as I thought it, I knew it lacked for truth. Such words as could perhaps be given Tabak gave me, though often I had received them bitterly.

The ship bore me on, its sails of cloth firm against an earthly wind.

Villages grew out of the soil on the banks. Green walls of sticks now poked above the earth, fresh planting, the defenses of one man against another, the new hatred of the spring. The yellow smoke of cooking fires coiled up from the compounds. I cupped my chin in my hands and gazed at them. There were gardens and cattle here. Hogs snorted at the boles of trees. And there were men, doll-like, distant figures on the bank. They called out in words that could not reach me, pointing to see what seemed a bear, or might have been to them, in man's clothes, larger at least than living men. Alone upon the deck beneath the unmanned sails I watched them. The ship was shining. The air shook with the smell of gold.

So I passed the towns which later I would rule – Arbereth and Elderwyn, Gest and old red Hwawl, upon whose rocks once in the years that came, I dragged the body of the river mage, his hair a nest of moss and snakes, my ax sunk deep in the slime of his oily chest. How the people cheered me then, for the troll had harried them, overturning boats and ripping the hands and feet from the bodies of the men who fished there for as long as anyone of them remembered. Yet then I did not know the names and the towns might have been no more than piles of sticks and fenced-in places for men and beasts, mere scratches in the earth. Yet even then I was not unmindful of my purpose. The name of king was sweet to me, else I would have been more cautious or, alone on Death's ship, more in fear. It was not guile I had but great imagining. I saw my life bent toward kingship as a sapling is bent over in a gale. For surely it sought me first, seeking me out before I turned to look for it. Like the river it bore me – spilling me unthinking as a cataract over the mountain wall to wander across my father's lands toward Ormkill. Long had I dreamed of that great hall before I knew it was my father's court. So I looked with interest on these towns and tried to read the faces of the men who were too far away to see. It did not matter what was hidden or seen. Already they had shaped themselves within my mind. Here is a proper world, I thought. It was a song in my blood. This is the true place of kings. For this I came away from Morrigan. Still, doubts rose in me. Cries went up from the bank. I wondered.

Will they come to me, I thought, as once men came to Ar Elon? For I was yet unschooled in the ways of state. Nor had I the mastery of words to heat the souls of men or hammer them as Ceorl would hammer iron, finding each flaw and hardening the edge. Yet at the last I did not fear the lack. Things came to me. Had I not killed a man? Had not men sworn to me? And if they who had sworn were but a handful, was not the swearing alone the test of it? In this way I talked to myself, puffing myself up, eager for fame. It cannot be called the way of wisdom, yet, I know, it is the way of young men when pride burns fiercely and discretion seems but the infirmity of advancing years. So, it was with me then. And still I sailed.

The wooden towns gave way to towns of stone, the fenced-in yards to broad acres of cultivated land. Now and then there were heralds posted on the shore, holding their stations on walls that snaked along the water's edge. Stairs led up to terraces, roofs piled one upon another. I had not seen the like of it before. My eye was filled with it. People stood thick as bee swarms at the gates. I had not thought the wide earth held so many.

So it was that the baying of the hounds surprised me. The ship had drifted in toward the shore, along the great walls. The town was hidden back of them and only sounds came to me. The hounds yelped wildly. They have scented something, I thought. A horn sounded. I heard it echoing among the houses. What beast, I wondered, is hunted through streets and lanes? Yet I could see nothing, only the high stonework and the roofs above. I heard the clatter of horses racing down stone streets; men called out. I began to wish that I could see the hunt. So I pushed the anchor from the deck.

The howling rang out fiercely. I thought, the hounds are near their quarry. Their baying rose up to heaven, eager, joyous, imagining the kill. I listened. They had turned, I thought, toward the river.

All at once a dark head thrust itself above the wall. The eyes were dazed with fear, the mouth gasping. The shoulders followed, the hands madly seeking hold among the stones. I felt my heart leap. For I knew then what thing was hunted.

By an act more of will than strength the man pulled himself to the top of the wall. He could not have been a man of this place or he would have foreseen the futility of his climb: the hounds behind him but the river too far below, the jump too treacherous. I caught his eye as he saw this. He had his head thrown back. His thin chest heaved for breath. The eyes, empty at first of all but terror, fastened beseechingly on mine.

When first I had seen the shape of the man, I thought, it is a runaway servant or a thief more likely, some grasping beggar surprised with another man's gold. But this man, I saw, was richly dressed. He wore a fur collar, his waist wrapped with two heavy belts of silver. He stood, his eyes opening wide at the sight of my crewless ship, golden in the blue water.

'Hear me, lord,' he cried. 'If the High King's law is still held by any in this land, I claim it.'

'I hear you,' I answered back.

What seemed wildness passed suddenly from his face, surprised, I thought, by courtesy. He lifted his hand, saluting me. He looked grave now and proud, despite his labored breathing. He was a man of middle height, no longer young, and, I saw, weaponless.

'Why do the men here hunt you?' I asked.

He smiled grimly. 'They mean to take the one thing I would not gladly give them.'

'Which is?'

'My life.'

I said nothing. But I had begun to think. Surely this was more than a thief and more than a townsman too.

'For what cause?' I asked. Behind him, out of sight, I could hear men calling out for ladders and the hounds yapping.

'For a song, lord,' he answered, having found his breath again. He looked about himself, carelessly, as though all at once the hunt had become a sport, some lesser matter. It did not seem fool's courage now but somehow cleverness. His eyes were gray; his hair blackened, sleek as a cat's.

'I will tell you, lord, since you have asked me,' he said evenly. 'Last evening I sat at Thigg's table. When the meat was eaten, Thigg asked me for a song. Since that is an art I know, I gave him one, such as had not been heard in that dim hall since Ar Elon ruled, a song of the world's beginning.'

'I see no offense in that.'

'Oh, but there was, lord,' he answered.

I had grown uneasy with his web of words. 'What was the song?' I asked.

'Of Tân,' he said. 'My lord must know it. He was the first man, Tân, whom the gods made out of fire and Rhiain, with him, the first maid, whom they had fashioned out of mist and ice. I sang of the agony of that first love and how Dagda at the last did pity them and gave them shapes of blood and flesh that they might lie down with one another.'

I frowned at him. 'What is the offense?' I asked again.

'None,' he said, 'for any that is a man. But Thigg is a withered tree. His women laugh behind his back. Believe me, lord, my song cut deep.'

'It was a rude song then.'

'Thigg is a rude man. It found him as he was.' The small man straightened, some faint amusement in his eyes. 'But rude or not,' he said, 'it breaches the king's law sorely to kill his bard.'

I thought about this for a moment, recalling the great names that moved through the book of wars, for the king's *filidh* was not unmentioned there, a man so skilled in song that it was as a sword to him.

'Are you Fyris then?' I asked. 'Ar Elon's man?'

We stood facing one another. I felt the ship pitch beneath me. The tide had turned and now was running toward the sea. 'Answer, if it is so,' I cried, 'and if you seek my aid in this.'

But before he spoke I saw a ladder top the wall and then another. A band of men came quickly upon the rampart, no more than a hundred elhws from where the small man stood. There was a chief among them. I knew him by the standard-bearer who went ahead of him and by his linden shield painted with an aurochs. He cried to his men to lift their spears and then, looking across to the man they sought, he shouted, 'Hear me, whoreson, I come to give with point and blade the gift you earned at Thigg's table.'

The *filidh* grinned at them. 'May Thigg's generosity be rewarded in fair kind,' he answered. He threw back his head then and laughed. There was music in it.

The chief cast the first spear. A swarm of spears flew after it. With a yell the men raced to the place where Fyris stood. Yet before the first spear fell, the *filidh*, sinking a moment to his knees, leapt from the high wall, hurling himself out into the river far below. It was a powerful leap, belying the man's slight stature and his age. It carried him beyond the rock just short of the ship's bow, where the water was deep almost to blackness. The soldiers knotted together on the wall. The bubbles broke in the air.

That same instant I jumped. The water lashed my face and shoulders, my belly heaving at the sudden cold. Yet I kept my wits and swam beneath the broad keel of the ship, looking for the place where his body had entered. He was my father's man. If there was nothing else between Thigg and me, now there was this.

The current was swift but I held myself to a rock. The river floor was patched with weed and strewn with cracked stone from the building of the walls. The mud should have been stirred up where he had fallen. But the water, though dark, was clear. I pulled myself deeper. The pressure hardened against my ears. I had taken a good breath before I dove, but I felt my chest grow tight. Dead or living, I thought, I will find him. But there was only rock and river-weed and, after a moment, a pain against my heart. I looked around me one last time and then shot up through the cold emptiness of the water, three body lengths before I broke the air.

Under the river I had turned myself about and so came up in open water facing the other shore. The shouts of men directed me to the bank. I swung my head around, pushing the straight hair from my eye. The men had pulled the ladders up, then dropped them on the river side of the wall. I saw them, man after man, descending. Some had already made the bank, their spears retrieved and lifted with their voices. Yet when I rose, head then shoulders, wading toward the bank, their howls came instead as murmurs, as though they had seen some wonder. Indeed I was not the man they looked for.

It was only then I saw the ship was gone. I swept the river with my eye, twice, astonished, before I truly knew it gone. Not drifted. It was too huge a ship: its bright sides massive, golden in the sunlight, its paired masts tall as forest trees. It had not washed behind the great wharf wall that jutted into the Undain there, but vanished, without whirlpool or ripple, on the calm face of the river, put out like an extinguished star.

So the men of Ormkill found me, staring and open-mouthed as a babe, soaked to the skin, my black hair steaming, a river giant in the place of the man they lost.

As I walked ashore a golden acorn knocked against my thigh. I hid it, shining like a piece of fire, in the darkness beneath my shirt. Then it was that I stepped upon the land.

CHAPTER TWELVE

'You are not Fyris,' said the soldier chief. I saw his anger and his puzzlement. He was tall for a man, coming nearly to my shoulder. He stood poised on the balls of his feet, like a mountain cat about to spring and yet held back by uncertainty. His light brown matted hair stuck out beneath his helmet like a ledge. But his beard was a tangle of dark curls. A scar grew out of it, red and new, branching across his cheek from the jaw to one gray eye. Though the bright sun made him wince, he was no less fierce for it.

His soldiers walked around me, staring at my size. One or two half-held out their hands as though, if they had dared, they would have touched me to see if I were real. But when I shook myself to drive the water off, the soldiers drew away lest the water fall on them. I saw they feared it held some magic to change the shape of things. Only the scarred man stood his ground.

By then, hearing no death cry and grown curious, a crowd of towns-folk, mostly men and boys, had found a way to mount the wall and stood looking down from its height. I heard the buzz of their voices. Further back from windows under the eaves of the near houses, I saw old men and scattered here and there a few women, sleek and groomed, their bare arms hanging on the sills and looking out to see what happened to the hunt. With each moment new faces appeared above the wall. I should have been uneasy among so many, but I thought, these are my father's people. How then can I be stranger among them?

The scarred man blinked and cocked his head. 'I chased a man,' he said, his voice cautious but with an edge to it. 'My hounds were at his heels until he climbed that wall. With my own eyes I watched him jump and saw the river swallow him, even as it spat you forth.' He stopped to watch me. 'Were you not so unlike him, you would be dead.'

It seemed too proud a boast. I said, 'I had not heard they hunted men with dogs in Ar Elon's kingdom, running after them as boys chase hares. I thought the best of men contended here, one with another, as men are made for, one strong arm against another.'

The scarred man frowned. Anger warmed his cheeks. 'This is Thigg's land, not the wizard king's who fled,' he answered. 'Thigg's law was broken. It will be Thigg's price that must be paid.'

I looked down at him. All saw I was not armed. The sword I had I left at Stephen's Well. 'There is but one law for all the land between the seas,' I said. 'The king's *filidh* is sacred. He may not be harmed.' I spoke loudly. Even on the wall the people heard me.

The man's lips whitened. For a while all there were still. I gazed at them with my one eye. Perhaps I did not look wholly human then. The river mud was smeared about my knees. My chest was wreathed with riverweed.

'It is the god Duinn,' someone cried out from the wall. At this the rest stared for none knew whether to believe or not. Yet others took it up and I heard it whispered back and forth.

If he had meant to lunge at me, the scarred man thought better of it then. I watched his eyes. Fear had crept in them, if not belief. I saw he had no mind to quarrel with me more, with the crowd uncertain. For indeed a strangeness hung on me. Like the mists of the water from which I came, I seemed to have risen out of emptiness, cold and veiled. A chill wind blew across their faces.

The scarred man shivered. Yet he could not let the matter go. 'Where is Fyris then?' he said.

I could not answer him. As he fell, the *filidh* had not the look of a man who leaps to death. Still, the best guess was that he was drowned and pulled into the deep channel at the river's heart where it runs most quickly seaward. I saw it would serve me poorly to say as much. Better to let them wonder whether I was some underwater thing or god or Fyris himself transmuted into giant kind.

I said, 'What answer can the hunted give the huntsman?' No more than that and, turning, made my way along the shore.

A great silence full of eyes was all about me. I went a good distance, the soldiers lagging afterward. Farther up the shore, beside the wharf wall, I found the stairs. The steps were crowded with the folk who had come down from the streets above. They were better dressed than the folk I knew. The men wore fur and silver, the women rings and necklaces of blue stones, carved gold and crystal. Beneath their astonishment their eyes were cool. They gave me room as I walked up but did not avert their eyes. Had I been less than I was, I have no doubt I would have amused them, dressed as they found me in a ragged longshirt, the water, if I stopped a moment, making a pool at my feet.

113

I had little time for such musing. I took a pace forward and then another. I had come to the top of the stair and walked into the streets of Ormkill, my father's city. It filled my sight, for I had been only in towns. From the river it had not looked so huge. Now I saw the books were true. The streets were not the crooked lanes that I was used to but broad avenues, paved with washed stone. Nor did the houses lean, rotting and uneven, over streets, crowded in like starved dogs about a bone. Rather they were set back, poised and stately, behind fine mortared walls and gardens, not meant for herbs and cabbages but planted with hedges and flowering trees. Some rose three stories upon the backs of the hills. Above them, on the highest ground, the proud hall of my father shone as though its stones were fire. Its polished ridgebeams seemed the fairest of metals, glittering in vivid sunlight, not the rough oak of which in truth they had been hewn. It took my breath. I longed to stand beneath its arching roof, in the longroom where my father once heard all who came to him, in whose chambers he judged and made the law. But not yet. I knew it. The strangeness that held these folk and gave me space to move as I willed would wear thin. There would be treachery. I was not ready. Tabak lay sick in Stephen's Well. Ceorl and those of Bede, ffraw and his four hundred, when they had found me gone, might guess where I had gone. But they would not ride so openly up these paved streets, unknowing if I walked freely here or rotted in Thigg's prison.

There was a stir behind me. The soldiers, their dogs whimpering and uncertain on their heels, trooped up the street, the scarred man at their head. I saw his eyes, dark and disquieted as those of his hounds. His brow furrowed like that of a man bested in a game whose rules he only half perceived.

'Hold, sir,' he called out after me.

I stopped and waited for him by the gate where two streets met. The pillars of the gate were fashioned of forged iron and hung with heavy rings. A piebald mare and two gray geldings, their muzzles deep in bags of feed, were hitched there. Upon the lintel in broad letters of the Western script was spelled Y Gasgen, or The Cask, which I took for the name of the inn whose wide doors opened into the great guest house beyond the yard. 'Well, what is it?' I asked when he came even with me.

The scarred man rubbed his chin. He leaned forward, his soldiers close behind, clutching their spears. 'Tell me your name and the chief you serve,' he said.

I let the silence drink up his words.

'Are you Thigg's herald?' I asked when I had waited long enough.

'I am a sergeant of his company,' he said as though it were some great thing.

I shook my head.

'Tell Thigg to send his herald,' I answered. 'When I have eaten and rested I will speak to him.'

Once more the silence fell. In the streets the men stood silently and stared. For a moment I did not know whether I had dared too much. A handful I might have killed, but not so many. Had I known the spells that blunt men's wills, I would have murmured them. Instead I made a hard smile play about my lips. Nothing else moved. But I could see in the eyes of the people how they measured me, how the quiet filled their ears.

The scarred man hesitated. He was a year or two older than I and bore himself bravely. Alone, or before his own men only, he would have held. But the hush of the people was too much for him. He himself had watched me walking from the river and heard the voice cry out I was a god. After a long moment, he turned on his heels and was gone. For myself, I turned into the yard, thinking it best to leave the people to themselves, lest some man among them find his voice again.

I met the landlord at the door. He eyed me warily. But if he had seen the commotion in the street, he gave no sign of it. He was a strong-built man with thick brown arms, accustomed I judged to keeping the peace among his guests. The whole of his face, apart from his ears, which were covered with coarse hair, was scarlet. When I told him what I wanted, he shook his red face sadly. He had, he said, no bed to fit me. All the while he kept his gray eyes fixed on my ragged shirt and my wet boots. I found a large coin and dropped it in his hand. The grudging shadow passed slowly from his face.

'Perhaps,' he said, 'perhaps.' And led me down the hall, past the dim common room where three hooded men sat at their cups. It was a large, nearly circular room with a great hearth on either side. Doors ran in and out of it, the largest to the kitchens, the others, I later found, down narrow ill-lit corridors to the guest rooms on the first level. The doors were all of carved oak, dark with age. I heard one creak open. Two of his women peeked in at us. He sent them scurrying for fresh bedding, pillows and a water crock. We had not gone much farther when he knocked at another, calling for his boy. When he found him, a small spindly lad with a worried look, the landlord bid him drag a second bed into a certain room and gave instructions how it was he wished them lashed. The boy, who could not keep his eyes from me, had to be told twice.

'His name is Rapp,' the landlord offered when the boy had gone. 'He's not a bad sort like some his age. But over-curious, if you catch my meaning. Curiosity's no virtue for any that work in a public house. Still,' he added with a wink, 'should you need anything, just bang on the wall and he'll come around.'

He led me, my head and shoulders stooped, along several passages and down a few steps toward the back of the inn. At last he stopped before a door and opened it. 'This should do,' he said. Indeed it was a good-sized room with a high ceiling, but the walls were piled with shelves. It had been, he said, a pantry once that he had made into a spare room for travelers who were none too fussy, some years back when trade was better. 'There's not much need for it nowadays,' he said, 'but, as you see, it might have been made with you in mind.'

I thanked him and waited for him to go.

The landlord's eyes looked at me thoughtfully. 'You've no horse, have you, to be looked after?'

'No.'

'Or,' he asked, 'a pack to be brought in from the street?'

'No.'

The landlord scratched behind his ear. His lips moved, puzzling over some new question. But at that moment there was a faint knock at the door. The women, loaded with bedding, crept in. They were small and dry, their thin faces pinched with nervousness, their dark eyes darting back and forth. Annoyed, the landlord ordered everything dropped in a corner and told them to come back when the second bed had come. The women blushed and turned hastily away. 'After sundown I bring the supper out,' he said. 'But beer is poured both early and late.'

I stood before the room's one window. My shadow fell over him. He stepped backward, then pointed out into the hall. 'Beyond the arch is a door to the stable yard. The well is there, should you wish to wash the river from your hair.' He glanced up as he said it, his small eyes fastened hard upon my face.

'I will sleep,' I told him and put my hand to the door.

Later the boy came dragging the second bed, the women slipping in behind him. The women worked quickly and were shortly gone. But the boy lagged. I saw clearly he was taking longer than was needed.

'What did you see?' I said at last.

His troubled eyes grew round; they burned in his head. Still there was no need to press him. The words spilled out of him. 'I was in a tree by the wall,' he said, the words like a rush of air. 'Truly, sir, I did not mean to look. I was only getting ospreys' eggs. No one was with me. It was by chance only I was there, before I heard the hounds, before the soldiers came chasing the running man who climbed the wall. But they were only looking at the man.' He paused, shy all at once and gazing at his feet. When he spoke again, his voice was low. 'So it must be,' he said, 'in all the city I was the only one who saw it.'

He faltered. His voice trailed off, afraid. I wondered at him. It must have seemed, I knew, that I loomed over him, more like a cliff than a man, a huge crag that might, at a word, drop down to crush him. Yet he had brought it on himself.

'Saw what, lad?' I said.

He turned up his small thin face. 'The ship, sir, the one that you made vanish when you dived.'

I thought a moment. 'Who have you told?'

He shook his head. 'No one. I swear it.' He wiped his nose on the edge of his sleeve. For the first time in many days I smiled.

'You are called Rapp?' I asked.

He nodded.

'And who is it, Rapp, you think I am?'

For all his sniveling he was a smart lad and answered cautiously. 'The old people whisper you are Duinn himself, up from your kingdom undersea.'

I looked at him squarely. 'And do you believe them?'

Despite himself, at the corners of his mouth, he grinned. 'I think, sir,' he answered, bold and yet not daring quite to lift his eyes, 'that the Lord of the Dead would not stink so much of riverweed nor would he come without a servant to clean his boots.'

I laughed outright, the first time since I had left Morrigan. Then kicking off my ungodlike boots, I gave them to him and sent him off. I heard him whistling down the hall.

That day I slept. If Rapp came back, he found me already in my bed. No herald came. There was the sound of horses led along the lane, the whisper of the landlord's women in the hall. In the inn yard, wood was being split for fires. But for the most part, during the day the house was quiet. I slept again. It was not the house sounds that intruded into my dreams.

When I woke the moon was rising. I saw it outside the window, above the houses mounting the steep path of heaven. Like the mouth of a boiling pot it looked, filled with the smoke of clouds. The wind was up. From time to time between my dozings I heard the sparse hard patter of rain. Once for a half hour a rough squall buffeted the house. Outside, on the sloping streets I imagined streamlets building, converging from back lanes and open avenues, falling riverward. It is the Kell blood that makes me think of it, I thought. From the time of my crossing into manhood my sleep had been filled with dreams of water. Since I had come down from Gwen Gildrun the night tides, older than memory, had beaten against my sleep. It was the women's blood. I was sure of it. I thought of Yllvere and Vydd, who counted by remembered tides and counted wrong. They lived in dreams, in the madness of dreams, it seemed to me. In Morrigan, high beneath the mountain wood, the sea forever hidden from them, they waited and did nothing. In the dry cold of mountain rooms they sat, my mother in her chamber, Vydd in her smoky hut along the hillside, spinning idly or working useless charms, excuses of inaction, doing nothing as if waiting was all that mattered. And Grieve, I knew, was like them now. I thought of her, listening to her heart beat, hearing the small sounds of her breath, till she had eaten up the day and nightfall flooded all her sleep with ocean dreams. I lay awake, my eye open, facing the dark window.

I thought, I have come to Ormkill to be king, not dream of it, idle as a woman.

I pulled myself up. Groping, I found my boots where Rapp had left them. Perhaps, I thought, they are still serving in the hall. For all at once I realized that I was hungry. Indeed, it felt as though my belly were an empty sack. I lit the lamp. The light bit into the darkness.

I threw a handful of water on my face and rubbed my fingers into the greasy sockets of my eyes. My flesh felt oddly thin beneath my hands. I thought, I must try to look more lordly, and searched about for a mirror. I meant at last to comb the weed and matter from my hair. After some moments I found a sheet of polished brass tucked upon a shelf and brought it down. Absently, I set it before the lamp. But when I saw myself, my flesh froze.

My beard that I remembered as little more than a swath of down beneath my chin had grown thick and full. Black it was and wild as the great tangle of my hair that fell newly to my shoulders. The skin about my eyes was dark and drawn. It was a man's face, not a boy's. I saw the old roundness of my flesh devoured as a flame melts fat. I stared. I dug my fingers into my face as though it were a mask that I might rip away. The new hard features held. I turned the mirror in the light.

About me I felt the quiet of the night. All things age, I thought. There is not a man who does not at the last shrink down to dust and bones. Yet for what had come upon me there was no accounting. I sat with myself for a long time and listened to the night.

At last I drew a sighing breath. No longer looking at my face, I brushed the weed from my hair and stood erect. My hand found the door and opened it. In the hallway, stooping beneath the low ceiling, I paused and listened. Voices, dulled by the twisting passageway, drifted down from the guest hall. I heard the easy laughter of men at their drink.

The gathering that night was large and mixed. There were perhaps thirty altogether. The loudest sprawled on benches near the smoking fires, telling stories with waving arms or singing half-remembered bursts of songs, the carnage of a *filidh*, just dismembered limbs and fingers of the tales, with nothing whole. The men of cities drank, I saw, like other men, hanging onto one another for dear life or out of friendship or merely to keep their dazed heads off the floor. It put me in mind of what Morrigan must have been, though on a smaller scale, when Urien still had his strength and his company of men in other years before the death of the gray-eyed boy. I hung in the doorway, unnoticed, alone as a ghost that looks down from the wind on the lights of living men. A stranger here, I watched them. Servingwomen and a troop of boys moved with studied care among the revelers. They bore large platters and in their hands were pitchers to refill the cups. The log fire blazed and reddened almost every face. Yet in the shadows a few vague figures, tucked into the deeper corners of the hall, hunched over their tables. Their tankards unlifted, they sucked privately at their pipes. I sought no company. So I made my way among them and found an unused corner far from the fire.

I sat across from three men, the same I thought that I had seen before when the room was nearly empty. Yet I could not be certain. Their faces were well hidden within their hoods and their shoulders obscured in the vague folds of their heavy cloaks. Perhaps they were full of drink. One may have been taller than the rest. But in the bad light I could not make it out. They sat slumped in upon themselves, mute and unmoving. The coals of their pipes glowed faintly in the darkness. The fumes that now and then escaped between their teeth were the only sign that they breathed. I nodded out of courtesy. They let me be.

Still I was thankful when Rapp came and set a platter and a full tankard before me. Perhaps the three watched me as I ate. But while I satisfied myself I took no more note of them. I had put the tankard down for the last time before one spoke.

'You eat, friend, like a man who has just discovered food,' one said quietly around his pipe. He turned a little and I saw the gleam of his dark eyes. But the mouth was hidden.

I did not answer.

'Sir,' he said accusingly, 'I spoke to you.'

'Hold your noise,' said another. 'He will not speak to the likes of us. He is the one we saw come up from the river, scaring Thigg's poor soldiers. Best let him be. He is too grand despite his rags.'

The first looked at me suspiciously. 'He is the size of that one, sure enough,' he said. 'He has but one eye, too.' I saw in the shadow the thin lips twist into a smile. All at once he straightened, pushing his leg boots out against the floor. As he did he seemed to grow. I saw his bearded head, unexpectedly huge, now only half-concealed within his hood. The cheeks were swarthy; a wolf's grin tore at the edges of his lips. Yet it was not until he threw off his hood that I knew him.

'Tabak,' I gasped.

'Be still,' he whispered and put his great hand before my mouth.

Slowly the others pulled back their hoods. So I knew them, Ceorl with his yellow braids and ffraw, his mad bright old eyes shining. But it was to Tabak I spoke first, in disbelief and then in joy.

'I left you in your bed at Stephen's Well,' I cried. 'Two days ago you seemed near death.'

He shook his great head. 'It is a year, my lord,' he said. 'ffraw will tell you. For all that time he kept us, even against the grumbling of his men.'

ffraw gazed at me and then over his wide shoulder like a child who cannot help himself, frightened and yet knowing he is too old to be afraid. 'It is so, my lord,' he muttered thickly. 'We have lived. For the world does not stand still. But long, my lord, we searched the shore for you. Far along the river's rock we went to see what the flood would wash there.' He hesitated. 'Even now, though here I see you, that sight still freezes me when I looked out and saw you step upon the planks of that great ship that rested in my harbor. With these tired eyes I saw it fade.' His mouth turned, awkward and confused, only then remembering the point that Tabak wished him to make. 'From that day unto this,' he said with sudden sureness, 'it is one year.'

By his eyes I saw how deep this went. For I knew what he must see, what Tabak saw and Ceorl as well, they who were the first to swear to me, though then it was a boy they swore to. Green I was then, new as mountain wood, no man that ruled. I saw how they studied the changes in my face. But already my mind had turned from them.

Instead Pendyved's face rose smoking in my thoughts, the peeled lips cracking backward to the skull. I heard once more his ice-cold breath and felt his pain. One year. The thought came at me like a knife.

I thought, truly Duinn must pity the dead he keeps, for he makes their time pass quickly. Else how could it be borne? Then only did I see the thing the god had placed on me. The night had worn upon the Undain but not as the earth's night wanes. On the earth the long spring had lingered, turned summer and waited until at last it tightened into seed. One season passed onto the next. The red sun rose and fell. But where I rode the river, morning and evening, it seemed one day. If Pendyved's lord had meant to hurry me, it was by his own strange measure. So ever the Kell had counted, my aunt upon her staff, my mother dreaming at her fire. I groaned.

Yllvere's shape rose out of my memory. I saw her as she looked that night I had taken my name though I had come seeking my father's. 'How shall I know his face?' I said. Behind her the root of Gwen Gildrun hissed upon the hearth. Her small voice was deep when she answered, but it was sharper than the tongue of the flame. 'He will have changed,' she said. The words caught in her throat. 'Men do.' I set my teeth. This night at Ormkill, had she looked into the shadow of my face, she would have found a stranger there, like him she lost, no man she knew.

PART III

The Girl in the Oak

CHAPTER THIRTEEN

Time creeps as slow blood drips from sores or spurts like heart's blood from new wounds. Either way, life goes with it. It is the way of things. Yet, looking back, it seems time laid hold of me more roughly than it did other men. For like a wolf, it watched me and where I went it followed at my heels. Three times before I ruled I felt its horned tongue lapping at my veins. The first was that spring I crossed the manhood, stumbling stupid with dizziness down from Gwen Gildrun with the crows. Then it took a month. And when I looked on Yllvere's fire, it drank a winter dry. I remember the sheet of flame and how my mind sank into emptiness like a stone thrown in the sea. But the Undain was a gaping wound. A year fled out of me. I felt the dryness at my heart. To fight it, I took the hand of each of them and pressed it. But to ffraw I said, 'Where are your soldiers?'

We had gone from the hall and down to the high room the landlord had given me. Though I had pinned my eye on him for the space of several breaths, old ffraw was silent.

'Lord, they left me and I left them,' he said at last, his gruff voice dark with anger. 'At first I led them as I always had. We went along the river, seeking the ship that took you. We marched as far as Hwawl for news of you. But summer came. The flies got in their mouths and they were sick of tramping through wet bogs and mire. Though they would not speak to me, I heard them grumble. You were a river troll, they said, no true man, and so worth no more chasing than the mist. Their eyes grew hard. When I pushed them, I saw their necks stiffen. Then word came down to me that Eoghan was released, freed by the guard I put on him. The men I had left went over to him. The message that he sent was for the rest to join him. My soldiers heard it. They were like children. With little thought, they went, forswearing me.' He snorted. 'The wise look forward. All they knew was the weather and the flies.'

Tabak shook his head. 'They knew Eoghan was a man much like themselves.'

But ffraw said bitterly, 'Finn walked among them. Though we kept among ourselves the secret of his claim, they knew him as a man set apart. They begged his peace and called him mage.'

'You expect too much,' said Tabak quietly. 'They are only men. And men forget what they no longer see.'

They were silent.

'And what of those of Bede?' I asked.

'Lord,' said Ceorl sadly, 'with them it was the same.' His blue eyes opened and looked in mine. I saw the grief there.

But I forced my voice to steadiness. 'Those whom I needed most held true.' I made myself smile on them. Then in earnest we traded tales. Late into the night we talked. So I learned how those of Bede, whose spokesman came to be the yellow beard, had argued openly with Ceorl. For they were traveling smiths and hated any place that kept them long though there was work enough at Stephen's Well among so many soldiers. In that company, Ceorl said, were his own kin, his sister's sons. Yet they broke with him. As he related it, he nodded sorrowfully and passed his fire-blackened hand over his tired eyes.

'They have gone their own way now,' he said, 'west of the river, down to the great sea towns.'

So I heard him out and more besides from ffraw. But Tabak said little, only that the year had healed his wounds. Yet he pressed me about the ship. I said what I thought prudent. I told them of Pendyved and how I drank the ancient wine and slept. ffraw pulled at his beard, his dark eyes wide. Yet for my part there was less to tell, for it had not seemed a year. But always Tabak came back to the ship and what I knew of it. I told him what Pendyved said, where the wood was cut and how the Kell women screamed at him. Tabak listened. The moon shone down on him through the room's high window. Its faint glow lay cold on the furrows of his face. His eyes were sad. I saw some thought was stirring up behind them.

He said aloud, 'Where is that ship now?' His voice was stern. I remembered then how we had fought when last I saw him, the thunder booming about the tower room. In the hollow of my shirt, against my flesh, the acorn burned. Its fire ran through me. I set my teeth. Though I felt no mirth, I laughed. 'We grow like two old women, you and I, hoarding our secrets as though we thought them gold.'

His hard look did not soften. His teeth shone like a wolf's. He said, 'Gold is as rust compared to that ship's worth.' But I did not answer him. I thought, this one thing I hold of my own.

A stillness hung in the air. 'The night wears away,' said Ceorl. He of all of us preserved some gentleness. I owe it to his craft. He would rather fashion arms than bear them. 'Let us sleep,' he said. 'We are a year delayed. We can surely wait till morning to decide what must be done.'

All saw the sense of that. Once more we embraced and spoke our gladness. Slowly, one after another, they slipped out to their rooms.

I awoke to find a small figure bending over me. I turned upon the bed, half out of a dream. Still her face and those remote dark eyes, resigned, without hope or fear, looked back at me. It seemed a damp leaf brushed my arm. It faded. I was in the room again. Rapp shook my arm. The gray bad light was back of him. I yawned.

'Surely,' I said, 'it is not already morning.'

Rapp shook his head. 'I am sorry, sir, to rouse you. But even at this hour a man comes seeking you.' I sat up sharply. 'Do you know him?' I asked.

'He is dressed like Thigg's soldiers but grander.'

I thought, it is the herald. 'Where is he?' I asked.

'If you will follow, I will bring you where he is.'

It did not suit me. I said, 'Do you know the rooms of the three who sat with me last evening?'

He nodded loyally.

'Wake them,' I said. 'But see that they come quickly and come armed.'

I got up when he had gone. Standing before the window I ran my fingers through my tangled hair, thinking once more to straighten it. In the dark street I could just make out a tethered horse searching for weeds in the cracks of the paving stones. The herald has come alone, I thought, and knew that Thigg was careless of who I was. Doubtless word had reached him quickly of how I had come into his city. It could not have been hidden. It was likely he would have heard it before his sergeant brought the news himself. Yet all that day had passed and the night besides before he sent his man. I made myself look at it.

Tabak came first with Ceorl after him, then ffraw, old and panting, still buckling his sword.

'Thigg has sent his herald to me,' I said.

ffraw squinted and blurted out before he could stop himself. 'It comes too soon,' he said. 'When your father came to this place, the countryside had risen up with him. He met the barons with a host.'

But even Tabak, who disapproved, knew better. He lifted his ax to me. 'We argued this when you left Stephen's Well. Yet I swore to serve you, even in foolishness. But have you thought what you would say to him?'

'I must look at him,' I said. 'When I have seen Thigg, I will best decide what follows.'

Day came over the edge of the world. The new sun rising through the clouds seemed like a ghost. The herald rode slowly through the streets before us. Tabak bade me take his mare, but I would not. So I walked among the horses. The streets were nearly empty. I saw then that Thigg had given some thought to when he would call me, setting a time before men stirred from their houses. Still, it was the time that I had waited for. If I were unprepared for it, I had no one else to blame.

Not far along the road we came upon a mage, a spindly man, old, his hair uncut, clothed in a worn brown robe. Little he seemed to profit by his craft. But that he was a mage was clear enough. His face bore the look that such men have, still, drawn in upon himself, secretive as stars. He carried a bundle of branches on his back. Though not much to speak of, perhaps a dozen branches bound with cord, it seemed a cruel weight for one so old.

'Old man,' I said, 'I am climbing the hill to Ormkill. If you go there as well, I will take your load for you.'

He shook his head, running his palm over one of the branches. 'It is the last of winter wood,' he said. 'I saved it, setting it apart from the rest, for the first fire of summer. With great care I hoarded it, a holy thing. But for the High King himself, none but old men may carry it.' His breath wheezed as he spoke.

I knew the custom. It made me think. 'Indeed, a year has gone,' I said, 'with Beltane almost on us.'

The old man rubbed his chin. 'Not almost. As any child knows, this is its eve. The very hills will seem to burn this night, that the summer may come without fault.' Though there was fierceness in his voice, he coughed. I pitied him.

'That precious wood of yours will not burn at all,' I said, 'unless you get it to the hill.'

'You see that I have started early.'

'You are too proud, old man,' I said. 'And much too old to carry your burden far.' With that I took the branches from his back and put them on my own. Yet at once the bundle weighed on me, not as a few dry sticks, but thick and huge as a great tree itself. I staggered.

The old man opened his narrow eyes a little wider. I saw, wondering, a swift softening spasm cross his withered face. 'Dagda reward you,

Lord Ar Elon's son,' he said. 'By this I know you. For surely in the world of living men there is no other who could lift that wood or bear it.' He wiped his face and sighed. 'Truly, lord, I am glad to be free of it myself.'

The herald who rode ahead of us, not looking back, had yet to notice we had stopped. But my companions looked from one to another. At last their eyes had settled on the mage, amazed. The old man felt their gaze but passed it off. He stood very still, his head tilted. There was something unearthly about the hush that fell. He seemed to be listening to the quiet earth about him, to the folk still sleeping in their houses, to a far song of a bird, perhaps, from among the rest, to even the sun's hushed rising. He tightened the dirty rag that held his robe.

'You must bear these sticks to Thigg,' he said, 'and lay them at his feet in that great hall. It is a gift men will remember.' He spoke in a half-whisper, grim and still, but on Tabak, just for a moment, he smiled.

I breathed again but my head was spinning. I meant, when I had caught my breath, to question him. But he turned and strode on up the hill, quick as a young man.

It was Tabak's eye I sought. 'He knew you.'

My liegeman nodded. 'There are some yet, even in this place, who served your father.'

I took a step and lurched under the burden of the wood. I spat. 'He is no man at all,' I grumbled. Sweat broke out on my brow. 'There is no muscle and bone made that long would carry this.'

Tabak eyed me. When he had thought some time, he answered. 'Your father, when he left his land and people, forswearing rule of them, kept hold of his right. He yet rules and in his fashion keeps his court, though it has dwindled. Still, if no men will do his bidding, under earth and sea are things that will.'

I glanced at him and then away. I might have pursued it. But it seemed, always, my thoughts halted at some edge. After that all were silent. The herald went on as before and we, at last, went after him.

How I made the hill I do not know. The wood tore at every muscle. The pains shot down my back and into my knees. But even then I was angered more because I could not understand all that Tabak said. I knew he tested me. It had been his way since his first words to me, hinting that I was more to be thought of than some mountain brat but always leaving more unanswered than I had started with. Always he had led me to some dark river in my thoughts. Again he had left me at its edge. But he would never show the way to cross it. I knew I would have to find the way myself. My thoughts were heavy and would not move.

When we made the hill, the city was already stirring. Children came out of doors and stood about, round-eyed, as I passed. Men of some importance pushed out of doorways. Gathered at the wells that ringed the outer perimeters of the royal yard, they drank the water and, rebuckling their arms, talked among themselves. By their bearing I took them for lords, the great barons of the land. Their sons attended them. The rest, passing the pitchers or bringing up swords for their masters to buckle, were servants, each dressed in the special livery of his house. These, when they had done their service, drew back, lest they seem to listen.

The servants saw us before their lords would look at us and yet their eyes were blank. It may have been, with my poor clothes and bundle of sticks, they thought me a man of their own station. If the barons looked up, it was to acknowledge the Steward's herald. But when at last they saw us, the barons stopped their talk and stared, not caring to hide their curiosity. A large man with a round face and rounder eyes spoke something to the rest. Though I did not hear the words, I saw them laugh. These were the men who would either fight or follow me when I came to rule. I meant to set their faces in my mind.

Their shrewd, impatient eyes stared back in turn, studying my size with interest as in a market men might judge the worth of an aurochs, but more thoughtful and abstracted. Doubtless they had had as boys, like any others, the run of stables and cattle barns. But now with me as much as cattle they left such day-to-day affairs to those of lesser rank. Their concerns, to look at them, had grown both wider and less exact. On their own lands, looking out they saw, I imagined, neither woods nor fields nor even the bent necks of their grazing herds but only the great curve of the earth. Perhaps they found it a more fitting sight. Their dress was heavy with silver and embroidered cloth. The ridges of their faces were hard, their small eyes without sympathy. Their word, in the land they held, was law.

The large man thrust himself out from the rest. With slow great strides he came up to me.

'Woodsman,' he called out loudly, 'do you not know the custom? It is old man's work to bear the last of winter wood to Thigg's fire.'

Because of his height, his forehead was nearly level with my chest. He gave a short laugh. He was accustomed, I saw, to ordering men and thought nothing that I stood over him. His small round eyes were hard with mockery.

'Woodsman,' he shouted, 'are you deaf? I spoke to you.'

I saw my chance.

'Lord,' I answered humbly, bowing my head to his, 'it is a fair thing to remind me of what is due. Indeed it is old man's work and, seeing you, it does me no honor I did not think of it. But as you have corrected me, I will not neglect what is right.'

Without another word I drew a branch of the charmed wood from my back and with one motion placed it on his shoulders. At once, beneath its strange great weight, he fell.

The man groaned. His servant ran to him. But, struggle as he might, he could not pull the branch from him. Other servants followed. But though they pulled together, they could not lift it. From under his burden the man glared up at me.

I smiled at him. 'You have nothing to complain of, lord,' I said. 'You reminded me that it was old man's work, and you, I swear it, were the first old man I saw.' Then still smiling, though it pained me, I bent down and, drawing off the branch, returned it to my back. I waited.

Before more came of it, the keeper of Thigg's door opened the thing he was charged with. The old wood whined on its hinges. The man peered out, squinting in the sunlight. In a glance he took in old ffraw, Tabak and Ceorl on their horses. If he saw me at all it was as one among the servants clustered about the man in rich dress just lifting himself from the ground.

'Which is the man Thigg sent for?' he asked.

The herald pointed. 'He with the wood,' he said.

The keeper of the door screwed up his eyes. He seemed more goat than man. His fungus-colored cheeks were sunken and his beard a wisp of pale gray fur on his bony chin. He slid between a niggardly crack he had made between the door and its frame. He stared at me and scratched his head.

'That is the one, you say, that came out of the river and set foolish folk to whispering?' he asked, questioning the herald as though he were a child. 'The one, you say, who wouldn't talk with soldiers but wanted Thigg's own herald sent to him?'

The herald shook his head. 'I didn't say any of that,' he said reproachfully. 'But he is that same man or I would not have brought him.'

'You are certain, then?'

'There are fools enough in the land between the seas,' the herald growled. 'Add not your piece to it.'

'Be quiet,' snapped the other. 'It is with Thigg's own voice I speak in this.'

The herald was still. The old man chuckled to have won. Then stroking his goat's whiskers, he motioned me nearer. With the load of wood still on my back, I came to him.

Arching his gray brows, he looked me up and down. 'You say that you are mountain born?' he asked.

That sobered me. 'I am that,' I answered, uncertain, but thinking, it was no more than a guess.

'Of Urien's house?'

I stopped. I saw the quickness in his deep old eyes, his gray lips smiling, and knew it could not be blind luck that led him. 'What need have you to question what, it seems, you know?' I asked.

He looked around. His sharp glance slid across the faces of the barons. 'No need, I warrant, lad, as far as it matters to you and me. But not without interest to some men here.'

I looked back at the barons, wondering what Urien's name might mean to them. Doubtless in the old days they had known him. But I could make nothing of the game the doorkeeper played with me.

'Their interest is none of my own,' I said. 'I have walked up a great hill this morning, early as it was that the herald came for me. Now that I am here, I will see Thigg.'

'And so you shall,' said the doorkeeper, nodding slyly. 'This evening perhaps, or, if not then, tomorrow.' And he closed the door abruptly and was gone.

There was a deep quiet. ffraw broke it.

'Lord, if you but ask, I will break down the door myself,' he said hotly. 'For I have never seen such lack of courtesy.'

But I shook my head. I remembered what Fyris said was rumored and knew the use that I might make of it. 'No,' I said. 'It is early and it must be that Thigg still lies abed with his women. Why else would a man act as he has done, a guest at his door? No,' I said so that the others heard me. 'It would be deeper discourtesy to interrupt a man at his pleasure.'

I saw the barons grin. It was what I looked for.

'I will wait by his door,' I said loudly. 'Perhaps he will beget a son. I have heard he lacks one and it is said that morning on the Summer's Eve is the best time for making boys.'

So I set down the wood – the barons laughing – and sat beside it on the ground.

CHAPTER FOURTEEN

All morning men drifted into the yard. Like wrecked lumber in a pond when the spillway's closed, they gathered, turning in slow eddies, barred, the hall doors shut even to those who thought they did the Steward's business. No little grumbling was heard among them – a pair of barons with matters of land rights to be settled, a merchant with a retinue of servants bearing sacks and scales, a horsemaster, the sheriff with a dozen men-at-arms – proud men all, weighing the wrongs they thought were done them. And to each, word of my slander was passed. Each man, some behind their beards and others openly, grinned. But in time they wearied of it. The day wore on. All at once a stout red-faced man rose unsteadily from the chair his thralls had carried up for him. He had on a blue robe of rich new cloth. But he had been drinking to pass the time, and the robe was stained where he had spilled the cup. Around his neck he wore a greasy silver chain. His thick fingers were knotted with rings. With his left hand he knuckled loudly on the door. When no one answered, he lumbered across the yard to where I sat. The red of his face had deepened.

'Say if you are not the cause of this,' he rasped. But his thralls came after him and, after some discussion, led him back. Yet I saw that when he had settled his flesh once more into his chair and had drawn another cup, he called to him the man that earlier I had shamed. Looking straight across at me, they talked.

ffraw winced.

'What are their names?' I asked.

'The drunkard is Hring,' he said. 'He is Lord of Redd-march in the East. The other, Anhils, third cousin some say to Thigg. At least he claims it. Together they hold great lands, though not the greatest here. Still, there is little to be gained in forcing such men to lie under one blanket.' But I only nodded, knowing well enough what I had won and lost.

'They will fall of their own deeds,' I said. But Tabak, who heard the boast, sat apart, keeping his eyes fixed on the ground.

'You are sullen, friend,' I said to him.

'With reason, lord.'

I shook my head. 'I do not see it. Something guides me. Did you not hear how the people whisper of me? Something moves in this.' Then I told them how I had met my father's *filidh*, or a being that took his shape, upon the river wall. 'And then this morning that old man, if man he was, gave me such a gift of wood that giving it to Thigg would cause great wonder in the court.' I was filled with a sense of the inevitable. 'Nothing in this moves by chance,' I said.

'It never did,' said Tabak sadly and then he looked at me. 'But there is more than one hand in the turning. From the first the only question was whose strength would prevail.'

'I have put my own hand in at last,' I said.

From under his old brows he stared. 'Thigg knows you.'

'That I am of Urien's house. That matters little.'

'What matters,' said Tabak, 'is how he knew.'

But then the great doors opened. The eyes of every man were turned to it and all were silenced. The keeper of the door appeared. 'Thigg bids you come,' he said. Then he leaned back against the door frame, scratching his chin bristles, watching the barons stir and rise, their servants, sobered, fumbling with their gear, gathering weapons and satchels, ready to move from one place to another. The butcher called his boy, who, because of some old fear between them, whimpered, his legs stiffening before the same fear drove him on. Then like one creature, the barons, loaded down with silver, wrapped in blue wool and prickly with knives, moved toward the door.

Inside, its shutters closed, the great room was dense with smoke. Worse, it smelled of sweat and old spilled beer, more the den of a wintering bear than some king's hall. A dozen pillars of thick trees held up the roof. But in the bad light I could not see if they were carved or painted. I saw only that the house was long and wide. Shadows filled it. Benches were scattered over the floor stone. The barons milled among them finding seats and, stopping the thralls that passed, demanding drink, already arguing whose rights took precedent. The sound of them beat against the walls. It was not the quiet of a court where one man ruled.

I looked for Thigg. But already there was a cluster of barons crowded before the platform at the far end of the house. Immense fires roared in the hearths at either side as though so near to summer the Steward still could find no warmth. I could not see him. I pushed my way in. The bundle of wood poked out from my shoulder. Because of it men stared angrily but cleared the way.

My three companions followed in my wake – Tabak with his cloak drawn back and dressed more bravely than a lord; ffraw in his soldier's garb and polished helm; and Ceorl, though a smith, clothed by his own craft in a wondrous shirt of rings, such as would have gladdened the heart of any who ruled the houses of the South. I only looked a beggar in my ragged cloak, my beard and hair, defying all my efforts, still rank with the river. But it was the god, I thought, that shaped it thus. I was content to trust in that. And so I laughed.

All heard me. Thigg looked up; his barons startled, parting before his chair. He saw me then for the first time, standing in the middle of the hall like a thirteenth tree among the pillars that held the house, the wood on my shoulder. The sun was nearer setting then. The small light that entered through the louver in the roof reddened suddenly like a wound reopened. It fell crimson on my face and shoulders. Like a flame I burned before men's eyes. It is said that beside me all else seemed smoke and shadows, the barons shrunken and darkened, fumbling in their finery.

At last there was silence. Thigg did not move in his chair. Small and old he looked in it, a chair fashioned for my father, its feet carved with great claws, its massive back spread with aurochs hide. He seemed to sense how ill it suited him. For when the barons pulled back he raised his hand and held them close to him, comforted, it seemed, by their small-ness, warmed by the vague warmth of creatures like himself. His gray eyes stared out at me. Yet though I felt that they would waver they did not. His hair was iron gray, pulled down into braids; his beard of the same color. On his forehead he wore a crown, new-made of beaten metal, too small to have fitted my father. We watched one another across the open space of floor. At length I spoke.

'I greet you, Thigg, Steward here, lord by grace of the High King till his heir comes. Morning and evening I have waited in the yard you keep, one day since your herald called for me. Yet I did not grow impatient. Pleasures, it is said, are few enough among men who bear the cares of the land. I would not cut yours short nor in them do I find a breach of courtesy.'

Hearing me, all the court watched him with dark, wondering faces. Smiles pulled secretly at the lips of the barons who had waited with me in the yard. Remembering the jest, their eyes laughed. Thigg saw it, his eyes cold yet puzzled under the gray knit of his brows. The man nearest him leaned down and whispered in his ear. Thigg bent his head as he listened. When he lifted it again, his lips had whitened. The gray brows hardened. Still, it was not to me he spoke.

'By this deceit he only harms himself,' he said. His voice was low, his anger well hidden at the back of it. Yet all heard him. It is said that in those years Thigg's rule was strained, that the barons grumbled and that he rode their backs as cautiously as if he rode on eggshells. If that were true yet, he had learned the trick of balance. It was not as I expected. I heard ffraw breathing at my back and knew he was uneasy.

'Well,' Thigg said, fixing his stare on me at last, 'what service have you come to offer?'

ffraw glanced at me and then away again. Ceorl muttered to himself. Only Tabak, now at my side, was still. They saw what now must come.

'Lord, it is the King's Wood I bear you,' and saying it, I cast the great burden from my shoulders to the floor. It fell as a boulder might, with a crashing sound that shook the walls. So great a sound had not been heard within the house since first my father laid its corners. Even the men-at-arms fell back, gaping. Yet they were mindful of their swords. At the light's edge I marked the faces of the men who drew.

Still Thigg showed no alarm. He reached out with his thin hand, motioning the housethralls from their corners, bidding them come down and drag the wood up to the hearths. The servingmen crept forward. Several together, they tugged at the heavy limbs. All heard their groans. But when they could not move the wood, the thralls drew back with frightened eyes, none daring to look at his lord. It is now, I thought. Slowly, I turned from Thigg to face the hall.

'Hear me, men of this place,' I cried, my voice light and high, soaring above the heads of men like a sword that is lifted on a hill, the harbinger of battle. 'I am Finn, Lord Ar Elon's son.' My bright words stung the air. I saw their brightness. Men stopped their breath. 'This is the hall my father raised, the hall that I am heir to.' I heard them murmur. Yet I felt how I stood over them. Their murmuring dissolved like sea waves on the shore. I felt it fade. In that quiet it was to Thigg I spoke, my voice grown full and booming. 'Tabak ap Ewyn is my witness, my father's man. This wood my proof. Any who would gainsay it, let him lift one branch to feed the fire.' So my words, grown huge, filled the room and the minds of all men there. I waited.

Thigg did not move. Nothing altered in his face. At last he spoke, his voice so small that almost I did not listen. 'You have made your claim,' he said, seemingly not in anger but only weariness. 'Having done it, as you must, now go home to your mountain.' His head was lifted then, erect and cold. His eyes were iron right to their centers. 'Take up goatherding or whatever Urien's folk have come to now. But leave the rule of men to those more fit for it.'

I twisted. Tabak stirred beside me but I cried out, 'Have you not heard?'

'Heard!' Thigg shouted then. 'You do not know how many times. Not a summer comes but some green lad stumbles down from a mountain or drags himself up from the old sea towns, filled with his glory and sandfleas, too eager even to wash the salt from his hair. One by one they come to stand before me, claiming kingship. If all the tales were true, Ar Elon planted sons as readily and in such numbers as any of my vassals sows his fields. Every hillside grows an heir.' He stopped. His thin lips curled. 'Go back to your mountain. It is enough to be king of goats and stones.'

I felt myself grow pale. He had made his moment well. The barons muttered. Though I had stirred them, now I saw a cold doubt touch them. Indeed for that one moment I felt a stranger to myself. In truth, there was one other born with me. Who knew where Ar Elon went and what he did when he fled Ormkill? Though I had not thought of it, it was not impossible that there were other sons. My heart sank. My skin crawled cold upon my flesh. I would have railed at him but I had no words. Had I spoken, I knew I would have stammered. Sickened, I sought out Tabak with my eye.

He that shared my height drew himself up, rising from the hidden places in himself until he seemed nearly alone in the hall and even I his lesser shadow. The features of his face were stern.

'How lightly, my Lord Steward, you speak of getting sons. Where are the round bellies of your women?' He paused and looked around the hall, meeting the eyes of all the barons, each in turn. 'Where is the line of sons to follow him? When breath goes out of him, who stands in his place? Or does he mean to send his armies out to pluck heirs like apples from the wood?'

In the firelight his ax showed back the flame. For a time there were none who would answer him. It was a baron, the oldest there, who broke the quiet, one I had not seen, with thin bent knees. He kept two thralls close by his side to help him stand.

'It is little joy you bring to us, Tabak ap Ewyn,' he said sadly. 'Yes, I know you if these men do not. For most were boys then and the others here who should have welcomed you are either blind or fools, hatching their own designs. But what proof is there even if you name him? Thigg is just in this. We have had enough of bastards and their claims. And I will tell you, if it is too long you have been away, each claim, if any take to it, means war among us. Nor is there any certainty in marvels. You know yourself that there are women in my house who can throw a spell on wood.'

For a breath's space there was silence. Then Tabak spoke again, his voice quiet. 'There is one who knows,' he said. I saw how his eyes caught Thigg's and pinned them. And it seemed to some that the Steward's flesh grew pale. In the glow before the fire Tabak laughed.

'Indeed, Thigg, you have grown overproud since we both served our lord,' he said, 'or else more careless than is fitting for a man who rules.' Something passed between them that no man knew. Tabak's smile was grim. He took a step closer to the fire. 'This long day you have heard her counsel, but having heard it you should have driven her out where none would see or question her.' He turned then, gazing toward the hearth. He stretched forth his long arm to her.

'Lady,' he called aloud, 'what welcome is this for your son?'

Her figure bent above the flames, I had thought her but a crone, old in Thigg's service, slumped behind her cloak and scratching stupidly in the coals. Since I had entered, she had walked up and down before the hearth, her back to us. So I had watched her without seeing. But at Tabak's word she turned. I saw too plainly then.

The eyes that looked into mine were cold. No warmth they took from the fire she watched nor any joy, it seemed, in seeing me. Cold they were and kept their secrets. The chill in them froze my heart. After a long moment she looked away.

'He is the size of him I bore,' she said.

Tabak frowned. 'No more than this?'

'The hair's as black but he had not a man's whiskers.' She seemed to think. 'It is a year and more since last I saw him.' The barons muttered. But again Tabak spoke, his deep voice thick with scorn. 'And are there so many men, my lady, who have had an eye torn from their heads?'

She seemed not to have heard but came down to where Thigg sat, resting her light arm upon my father's chair. What brought her here I could not guess. Yet I knew well that, whatever for the moment bound her, she served herself, not Thigg. Her face was calm, white-masked like the moon's. She let her cloak fall to her feet; the gown beneath took light like alabaster. Boldly she threw back her head, shaking her hair from the coif that kept it. She was young yet and tall for a woman. Very like a queen she looked. The barons knew it. I saw it in their eyes.

'Long ago,' she said, her soft voice pitched for all to hear, 'I bore your king a son. Though Ar Elon was outlawed then, he was king enough and I only a woman. He knew whose wife I was and what we did. So with great oaths he bound me, that if ever a child should come of it the king's shame would not pass to him, nor his glory either. By all that is holy I took the oaths.' She sighed, keeping her eyes down as though afraid. Then in a small voice that kept them still she said, 'Now these oaths I break.'

But then I could not bear it. My face, it is said, was wild. Fury twisted it. I lifted my arms. Men told me afterward they feared I would strangle her. The old pain boiled in my veins.

'Break now?' I cried. For bitterly I remembered how long those oaths had held, year upon year unbroken, when it was only a private thing between us. Her face before the fire held in my mind.

Yet even then I knew I spoke against myself. It was a king's secret, not a man's. I let the child's hurt die. 'Speak, then,' I said. 'By Anu, lady, say as you never would my father's name and mine together in one breath.'

I watched her, the mountain witch who bore me and ever after hid her heart. 'He is changed,' she said softly, quietly to all assembled, not to me. Her voice was so like a maid's I only saw the complexities piled up behind it. She had gathered her gown in both her hands and knotted it between her fingers till the blood ran out of them. All who saw it pitied her. The men pressed close, their faces clouded. She allowed them to see how much she trembled. 'I do not know,' she said and shook her pretty head. 'Men are like the sea that rings the earth, the same but every day they wear a different face.'

Then Thigg spoke, his voice grown smooth. 'Lady, that is no answer.'

Between them I caught the half-curves of their smiles.

'There is a test,' she said. She paused, waiting for understanding to come to them. Thigg nodded, his sly thin smile no longer hidden.

The old baron stood out from his brothers, free even of his servants. 'It is his death if he is false,' he said. 'No kings while I have lived have done it, nor any in my father's time.' Then he paused, the wrinkles of his face for one small moment smooth as though for that one moment he were young again. 'But once,' he said, 'when men were not so far removed from gods, it was the one true mark of kingship to wrestle Life from Death upon the Mound.'

Thigg smiled broadly, his gray eyes fixed on mine. 'If indeed it is your right, you are free to claim it.'

I flashed a look at Tabak, seeking an explanation for the trial they set, for I knew not what was wanted. Something stirred behind his eyes but I could not read it.

'What is the deed?' I asked aloud.

'Tinkern is the godshrine your father built,' said Tabak slowly. 'It shares its name with the island upon which he set it and with the oak grove, though both are older than the thing he made. At the grove's heart there is a great earth mound.' He waited. I saw how he picked each word with care. 'It is not your father's work,' he said. 'No man raised it and none but kings have stood upon its height. But few, having climbed there, walked down again. Most left their flesh for birds. There the god still lingers. Even the greatest warriors dared not go to bring the royal corpses back for burial.'

'But what is found there?' I said, my voice too loud.

He looked at Yllvere. A servant, he had followed her fifteen winters, abandoned to the western mountains, far from his lord. In silence she returned his stare. Whatever their separate thoughts, they wove this one thread between them. She did not fear him now. Before the two of them I felt a child.

'Will you not tell me, then?' I said.

'What was broken will be mended,' she answered calmly. Something hovered about her eyes and on her lips. 'The old promise will be kept.' She looked up. Her eyes under her white lashes were fixed on the servant she had lost, alone among the rest, a man the like of me but not myself.

'Lady,' he said gently, 'in this no oath is broken. What was taken now comes back. You know it or you would not send him to the isle.'

She faced him, her forehead, set off against her hair, like a stone wrapped in wool. 'Who is it that you serve?' she said.

'The son,' he answered simply. 'And you, my lady?'

Her face did not change. But she looked away.

No one spoke.

The old baron broke the quiet as he had before. 'And will you claim it, lad?' he said.

'Claim what?' I cried. 'No man will tell me.'

'A fool's death,' he answered gently, 'or else the praise of all the folk between the seas, the king's lands whole again.'

It burned in me, the quiet and the smiles, Tabak and my mother, the riddle my life inevitably came round to. 'What is the deed?' I said once more, despairing, expecting no answer.

He shook his old tired head. 'Why, what we spoke of. Will you meet, like kings of old, the witch that waits upon the Mound?'

It was a child's answer I gave him, being unschooled in the craft that I was heir to. Only looking back did I come to know it was the only answer I might have given.

I thought of the Kell, the women of the mountain. They hung in my memory, thin and sour, pale as flowers drying in rafters – Vydd, a pipe between her mouse teeth, spelling words from crows; Yllvere, as much smoke as blood and bones, invoking ashes, whispering to flames; my sisters Ryth and Sanngion, their lips wrinkled and red with wine, whose laughter was like a curse to me. I thought of Grieve.

'I have,' I said, 'some familiarity with witches.'

If he heard my bitterness, he did not remark on it.

'You will do it, then?' he asked.

I nodded.

Out of the darkness Tabak grinned and Yllvere with him. Thigg rose from my father's chair and laughed. Had that moment been cut loose from all that was before and what came after, they would have seemed, as in that instant they appeared to me, creatures of one mind, not what they were, travelers met at a crossroad and bound the next moment on their separate ways. But, looking, I saw only together how they smiled.

CHAPTER FIFTEEN

So once more she had left him. This time, I thought, Urien will not have torn his hair nor climbed the battlements seeking her shape upon the roads. He was long past love of her. Yet, with what he hated gone, I wondered where he turned his mind. Perhaps, for a time, he would try to master his own house again. The village men would come to him. It was summer, after all, and time to set the service. With Yllvere gone, they would no longer smile behind their hands. Yet I doubted that the women would obey him. My sisters were accustomed to their own ways. The aunts had never done his will. Perhaps, his books and anger useless, he would come down to take his chair within the hall or walk his own broad lands again, barking to the thralls what should be set out and planted, which aurochs butchered and which let fatten for another year.

Grieve would not minister to him. The firelight leaping in her eyes, she would mind the burning beneath the house. He would need to scratch his own coals in the grate, pour his own thin wine, master of a house where no men lived. I feared that not even his own hounds would follow him.

Why had she come? It was not Thigg. She had no awe of men. Biting back false tears, she ruled the barons. Whether by a woman's or a witch's wiles, she had her way.

Tabak knew. I turned to ask him, but the doors of my father's hall flew open with a bang. The great host of men swarmed through it, bearing me along.

The night was cool and bright. We had no need of torches, for it was Beltane. The lower sky was red behind the houses, lit up with fires as though each hillside burned. Red shadows danced before the blazing logs, lithe and pale as Duinn's dead come back from their gray land. But these were not the ghosts of men but men themselves. Seeing the crowd that spilled from the hall, they followed, filling the alleys and the street. In their number I found myself cut off from Tabak and our company. I was pushed against a kitchen thrall.

'Lord,' he said, 'I saw you climb up from the river. For the peace of the land, this night I wish you well.' He stammered something more but I did not hear it. I bent down, waiting, till he added, 'My dad said once it was a sea king that would save us.'

His voice was thin and reedy but it was edged with wonder. I doubted he had ever spoken unbidden to a lord. I did not tell him I was mountain-born and not the lord he looked for. For some moments the crowd pushed us along together.

'Have you seen the witch?' I asked.

He flushed. 'No,' he said, 'I've naught to do with that.'

'But others have?'

Feebly he shook his head. 'Who is to say?' Horror rode his voice. I saw that he had only meant to wish me well, never thinking that a high-born man would answer back. But still I pressed him.

'Yet there are some,' I said, 'who've seen her.'

'No, lord,' he answered bitterly. 'I cannot tell. It is said there always was a witch upon the Mound. But some say she is young and others that she is old, old even as the Mound itself. My dad, to tell the truth, never said either.'

'But did he say what she did to the kings she met?'

His small eyes darted. 'Aye, that he said,' he whispered hoarsely. 'Not that I would be forgetting it. Tore out their very hearts, he said. Tore them out with her own teeth.' His nervous glance fell on me once more. But the crush of men pulled him away. I looked after him till he was lost.

By now, as word of my claim spread, the women of the city came rushing out of doors. Daughters of the houses, both proud and surly, their gowns heavy with rings, pushed out ahead, their servingwomen puffing at their heels. Churls, slaves and freemen scrambled across the stones. Before me I saw the banner of the Steward furling. At my back I heard the tread of his soldiers. Men shouted. Horsemen clattered up behind. In the cool, damp night, still but for the crackling fires, it was as though the people of the city had become a storm. The earth itself held only quiet. The wood smoke floated up, placid, drifting, the only cloud there was. On such a night the stars seem sharp and close.

If I feared this thing, yet my heart was gladdened by the sight of so many. I saw the faces of the people as one sees faces in a dream: smiles, teeth, noses and eyebrows, the backs of heads and helmets. I could not tell who was cunning and who dim-witted. Leather armor squeaked beside me. Arms, swords and banners flashed in and out of view. The space between the houses swirled. Caught up in the noise and stirring, I could not tell whether I was at its center or its edge. But when we reached the lower streets, the crowd drew back and gave me room.

Thigg waited up ahead, standing on the earthworks that rimmed the river, down from the wall where first I entered the city. Yllvere was beside him. Close at hand Tabak waited, ffraw and Ceorl in his shadow. The rest were barons.

The river murmured. For a moment I thought I heard Pendyved's laugh. But when I turned my ear to it, it was only the sound of the water. I took no comfort in that sound. The mindless ripples sucked the shore. No life moved upon it. In the darkness I could not see the farther side nor was there any island visible. For all I knew the river ran empty forever. Yet it was the same. Undain I had seen in daylight. We are not unalike, I thought. Somewhere in the distant hills were springs from which this river also took its life. I wondered at it. The river's darkness was mirrored in my mother's eyes.

'Is this,' I asked, 'the legacy you give me?' I meant the river and the dark, the witch that awaited me, and never a gentle word from her that bore me.

Her hair in the firelight was red as torches. Her face was quiet, her bold eyes aloof and still. 'I owed my children only life,' she answered. 'The rest was Anu's.'

But I would not be so easily dismissed. I caught her gown and railed at her. 'Why do you shame me before my people? It needs no test. Only a word from you, no more. But you would never have it so. Quick as you could, you left Urien to his shame. And now, having seen your chance again, you turn that shame to me.'

She did not falter. With stern sorrow she met my eye. 'What is your complaint?' she asked. 'If you are that child, but for that shame, you never were.'

I shivered. 'It is the king's shame too,' I stammered. 'My father, his people no longer serving him . . .' But I had not the words.

Thigg gave me a look past all his men. His thin lips turned, his long face unbelieving. The muscles rose on his spare jaw. 'Why do we suffer such a fool?' he raged. 'Does he think one bastard more or less made any difference, one ill-got child could turn the people from their king?' He looked from face to face. 'Where has he been that he speaks so readily of the king's shame, of which the broad world knows, and he, it seems, knows nothing?' A scowl covered his brow. His anger shook him. 'Dare he think the people turned from Ar Elon and set me, Steward, in his place because in his dotage Ar Elon fiddled with a woman and the woman bore?'

He cast his angry look once more across the barons. 'Where has he been that he knows so little, not the king's shame nor the land's ailing?'

Alone I should have answered him. But Tabak took my place. In his eyes was sorrow.

'That too was kept from him,' he said, 'and much besides. So I hid him on the mountain, hidden in the old Kell ways and among its women, away from men lest he hear how lightly a child is fathered, lest in ignorance, blind to what he was, he give his seed.' Then he looked long into the faces of the men about him. When he had spoken his voice was like the darkness itself. Those who had been stirred by Thigg's anger grew still again. Now Tabak's silence made them uneasy. They felt lessened. Beyond Ar Elon and myself, in all their lives they had not seen so tall a man nor heard words that came so hot from the heart's core. Then he laughed at them, a great laugh that blew away the night.

'You that know the High King's shame must know also why I kept it from his heir,' he said. 'The world's not changed.' He paused. His black hair shone; his face was vast. In his huge hands they saw he held an ax. They wanted desperately to look away, their small necks like twisted ropes above their shoulders.

'Death comes after life,' he said. 'You know that. The best kings have one season.' Yllvere frowned, but he would not look at her. Her white hands dropped from her gown. 'Like breeds like,' he said. 'Our kings are yearwood, their lives a summer. We cut them down to feed the fire. They warm our winter and keep the dark at bay. That is their gift.' He laughed again, the wolf's grin that I knew. But then he seemed to tire, his fury spent.

He looked off into the darkness of the river. 'You are wise as well as foolish, Finn,' he said. 'I trust one or the other will save you. Sure enough it is that a little of both you owe to me. But what service I had to give I gave you. I can do no more. Others, more than you know, conspired to bring you to this place. They, not I, will have to see you through it.' He smiled, yet before I found my voice, he walked away along a path that went among the river stones. Living, I never saw him more, though it was years, long after I rode east and in the way of things came back to rule, before I stopped half-expecting him. Even then, the men who knew me best, the barons who shared my table, were never fools enough to ask of it when they saw me start, the roast uncut before me, my great jaw slack and listening to a laugh that boomed outside the door. It was always someone else. Still, on dreary winter evenings, the snow piled high outside the door, the hounds about my feet and nodding by the hearth, my thoughts would often turn and fill with memories and doubt.

For all I loved him I never knew with surety whether his service, woven of all its threads, did me at the last more good than ill. The good I knew, or did when I stopped hating him. That too was long ago. Dazed and burned, my mother's curses ringing in my ears, I knew the thick brown arms that bore me up the winding stair, out of the oven fires that roared beneath the house. He kept my life then. But it was he as well who brought me to the river and there delivered me to the greater fire, hotter than ovens though it had no flame.

But he, who had been my voice when I had none, was gone. My good eye raked the empty space where he had been. The white faces of the barons stared, waiting to see what I would do. My heart drove fast against my ribs.

For a moment I mourned him. But his words, grown huge, broke in my mind and blasted all the rest. I felt them move there, fierce, secret, invading the places I never looked.

I had been kept, he said, lest I spill my seed. It was not, he said, what I had thought. The mountain and the women were meant to hide my manhood, not my name. When I thought of it, I gasped. The color rose about my eyes. But the people of the city, crowded close, saw only the shudder of my breath. I wheeled around.

Truly, too long I had been a child, looking backward, puzzling over roots and stones, old books and older names, seeking only what came before. I thought of Ar Elon and pitied him. He had never known his son.

Startled, Yllvere looked away. The blood beat in her face. I felt its warmth. I saw the muscles moving soundlessly within her throat.

I raised my head, ignoring her. Out of my own flesh would come an heir. Kings make kings. Tabak had said it a hundred times before I heard. Like breeds like, both oaks and kings. I had to lose him before I heard.

It was Thigg I turned to, waiting behind his eyes.

'Where is the island?' I said. 'For I shall meet the witch and, mastering whatever death she offers, come back to rule.'

The old Steward was still a moment, his gray eyes flickering back and forth among the faces of his men.

'A true king need only enter the river,' he answered softly. 'For it is said the waters of the earth will bear him safe enough and he will find its shore.' He stopped, restless and unsure, a smaller shadow against the shadows of his soldiers.

Ceorl came silently beside me and, at his shoulder, ffraw. Their brows were drawn.

'If it is your wish, I will go with you,' said Ceorl. He was the only one of Bede who had not deserted me. But for his deep voice and the murmur, deeper than any man sound, of the river all was quiet.

I found that I could smile. I looked at him. I knew he feared to go with me.

'Who is it that you serve?' I asked.

'You, my lord.'

'And you, my brave ffraw?'

His mouth twisted, stilled. 'As I was your father's man, so I am yours.'

'That is enough,' I said and did not wait to see if they would answer more but turned from them and went down among the stones that made the shore.

A thin breeze blew off the water. The cold had gone from it. Above me, without looking, I could feel the people looking down. I saw no island, only the black water like a rimless floor beneath the stars. It was not a floor a man could walk upon. I knew that I would sink beneath it, the black water sucking at my life.

The people wondered what I would do as much as I. Over my shoulder I saw them nudging and whispering. Some had come down and perched on the nearer stones. Thigg followed, his retinue about him. I saw their armor glittering and the flash of their swords beneath the stars. Thigg was of no mind to see me turn from this. I saw clearly enough why he had laughed when in the high hall I had claimed the test.

'The water is deep here, Finn,' he said. 'Even for such as you.' He shifted his darting eyes and smiled. 'Or did you think you would wade out to find the isle?'

'How deep?' I asked.

His old brows flickered a little, drawing together, pleased. 'Too deep for giant kind,' he said. 'So deep that even the greatest ship might moor here.'

It was then I saw my way.

I drew a breath and pulled my longshirt from my neck and shoulders. Even as I lifted it I felt the weight of the thing I kept there. My fingers touched it. It warmed my palm. I cried out.

'Even you, Thigg, shall see now what I am.' Then I cast the thing before me. At once the dark air shook; the water boiled. Out of the foam the bright hull rose, the wood of its sides golden, its sails like sheets of flame.

147

It is the one marvel the *filidh* always sing of, the one that marked me because it happened in the people's eyes. They could not speak. Awe held them even as I climbed upon its deck.

Like a crown it rested on the water, trembling in the buzzing air as though it lived. Yet to the dead I owed it, to Pendyved, who, called from the earth where his bones were scattered, rose and dared to cut godwood.

Only for a moment it seemed to rest. Then a great wind where there was no wind sprang up. The charmed wood creaked. The ghost sails filled, and, tugging at their stays, the great ship moved. The people of the city, all of Ormkill down from my father's hall, watched it from the bank. An apparition of crystal light, it filled their eyes when it was near them like the sun itself at midday. But it dwindled quickly as it moved, free of them, out into the blackened river. Until, in the farthest darkness, it seemed but a distant star, glittering, faint, removed. It vanished when they blinked.

Then, like Tabak, I was gone.

CHAPTER SIXTEEN

I did not sail the ship. With its own eyes it found its way past towns and villages, the lights of men. Then there was only wilderness. Some hours before I heard the wind waves break on its rough shore, I smelled the salt and felt the sea tide fight the river's current. The island, I decided, if I had not missed it in the dark, lay close to the river's mouth. Little I knew in those years how far inland the vast sea reaches with its briny tongue, bearing the whirling gulls above its flood, stiff ocean gales blowing at its head.

But at dawn I came to it and in the fresh light saw that it was many leagues farther to the headlands and the sea. The island, when I saw it, was greater than any of the river islands I had seen. A massive tract of forest, its roots and stones together, torn from the bank where it had grown, it floated until long after in the south it snagged and held. The bald rocks at its northern edge parted the water, which boiled on to either side. But for the rest the tall old trees came close to the shore, their black thick roots splayed and dug into the bank like fingers trying to hold on, as though they feared the island, never belonging where it was, might yet move on and find some other place.

The wood itself was wild, thick almost to choking. Woven among themselves, only the highest branches held a few bare patches on which the circling crows could perch. They were the first crows I had seen since the ship I rode had taken me from Stephen's Well. I thought of Ninmir. But these were fish crows and too small. Yet their hollow coughs reminded me of how I had thought to send her, black, forbidding, speaking human speech, to sit upon Thigg's chair and name me king. I saw once more, though often I had fought it, how seldom the world moved as I willed but as it must.

As I sailed nearer, I looked for a place to put ashore. There were no easy moorings. No hand, it seemed, had delved among those rocks. If ever there had been a wooden pier it had rotted long ago. Indeed, though those of Ormkill knew it, it seemed unlikely that they had walked here or that their fathers had. It was a place they held in memory, passed down in *filidhes'* songs from a time so long before only the kings' names were kept and the memory of the witch upon the Mound, a few bright stones, the treasure lost. Or so it seemed. And yet I knew that here my father raised the god-shrine. I doubted that, whatever he was, with his own hands he had laid the stone.

The great ship rolled along the island's western side. Close in toward the shore, the high trees stole the wind. I heard the deep keel scrape on gravel. The wide hull shook and turned until at last it came to rest, stuck fast on a bar. It was safe here near the bank. I might leave it and come back, though how I would float it once more I could not tell. Yet I knew the fell ship saw to itself.

With no more thought to it, I let myself down into the river. There I hung, waiting for the voices. Deep among its stones the river moaned. I listened, but there were no words. I had feared the river mage. Though once already I had beaten him, the memory of his whispers still hissed in my ears promising the cool green dark and palaces undersea. I would have rather then that his slippery arm reached out to pull me down. That was a better fight. For words weigh heavier than the press of arms, and the memory of words, more bitter still. I took a breath. There was no sound but the water and the crows.

After a time I ceased to listen. With some struggling I found my feet among the stones. The bar was piled up high beneath, though not so high that any of Ormkill's small folk might walk, their heads above water. I did, but to my neck in places, ill-footed, poking out for buried logs and holes, mindful still of anything that lurked. Yet nothing came snorting up or slipped between my legs.

A dozen elhws from the shore the bar gave out. As best I could I swam, my heart quaking until I touched the sand. I drew myself up, shivering, in the dim light beneath the trees. There I sprawled among the stones, not caring where they stuck me. Thus in daylight and good weather I came to Tinkern. And there, since I had not dared to sleep an hour of the night upon the river and as the wood was hushed, I laid my head in the crook of my arm and closed my eye.

A bird kept calling. Its low song drifted through the wood, a gentle song rising and falling softly as smoke in air. I thought it kept me awake. Yet when I raised my head, no longer hearing it, it was already evening. The river, swollen with the tide, lapped gently near my feet. Farther off, where I had left it, the great ship waited, immobile on the bar. The dying sun behind it, its masts and rigging etched a fretwork of shadows across the river's back. Even as I watched, the shadows deepened. I felt the evening come. From pools among the roots the gray fine mist curled high to meet it. There was no wind to tear at it. I yawned.

Not a few elhws from the bank the wood was thick and dark. The dripping branches, deep with the richness of new leaves, rose like a wall. I felt better where I was, only needing a few dry sticks to scratch a fire. I would wait, I thought, till morning, pleased still to linger. For I was not eager to try the wood at night, less eager to find the sacred place or what it held. Not yet. Oh, I did not run from it. Whatever wills that breathed in the world and those other things, unbreathing – Pendyved and the speaking stone, whatever else that bent me to this – for myself I claimed it. I would feel them sometimes, edging near, invisible, eager as hounds for the hunt. Yet I would keep them back and would often go for days on end without their notice. But at other times, when I would feel them most, their buzz about my ears like the sea-hum of a shell, even then my own need would run ahead of theirs. For was I not the king's true son and they, bloodless and unreal, his servants only?

I built a fire. I made it from the scattered roots of a windfall and banked it high against the dark. I have no love of fires. Yet then my skin did not blister before the fire's warmth as it does now. These last years I have kept one for the men who serve me. For, being men, they do not know the dark and they fear it, thinking the cold is bitter. And when the *filidh* sing, as I have taught them, of the crystal halls on the deep sea floor and of the sea-green silver horses that I rode beneath the foam, they only mutter in the dry hair of their beards and stare. But on Tinkern that night long ago I built a fire. High against the trees I made it, that though I did not seek her yet, the witch of the Mound would know that I had come.

Under the arch of leaves the air was gentle. It was summer and I was farther south and west than I had ever been. Deep and still as they stood, here the trees grew broad as well as high, not spare and spidery like the mountain oaks I knew. Godwood they were, wheresoever they were rooted. Yet I felt that the god of this place must be an easier, wiser lord, more like his trees. He gave them fuller life.

Later, east of the island, the summer moon rose yellow in the sky. Its pale light drifted through the branches. I walked to the river's edge where I could look out. The moon's eye floated in the ripples. You and I, I told it, are pulled from the same dark womb. For a long time I stood watching. The river scrubbed at the moon like a smooth white-yellow stone lodged in its throat. The river could not wash it from its place. But it was no company. I wandered back and lay beside the dying fire, scraping ashes over the red coals until, but for the moon, the world was dark again.

There were owls in the wood. I heard one screech just before the kill. Toward midnight the bird whose song I had listened to the day I landed began its call again. I thought it odd. I knew no creature with both a morning and a midnight song. It was likely, I thought, that the moon had wakened it. But with nothing else to keep my mind, I listened. Mostly it came from far back in the tract. Then it seemed lost and trembling, high as a child's wail but not as shrill. It touched me. I knew not why. I must find words for it, I thought, and give it to the *filidh*. But on my tongue it sounded thick and cold. Thereafter I let it be.

For some time it was still. I dozed. When it came again, the song was from the nearer wood. Then I could almost hear the words. But, lulled by its gentle music as a feather is lifted by the wind, I climbed toward sleep.

It was morning when I woke. By my right hand, when I moved, I found a broad new leaf. Wrapped within it lay a dozen blue mussels. They were still wet where they had been cut from the river stones. I had been left an offering. I smiled. There were people here. I looked out. But I saw only my own deep marks upon the bank. It would wait. I cracked the mussels on a stone and ate each one. Perhaps, I thought, there is a village on the island or at least a priest to keep the shrine. The day was clear again. I felt lucky and full of the god. Whether priest or bogie, the wood had welcomed me. I went to the river and washed, knowing I must do then the thing for which I had come.

When I entered under the trees, I remembered Anu's wood and the great gore crow that ruled it. I thought, have I not stolen the children of the air? Surely then, I can take a thing that's mine.

There was no path. Yet I found my way, keeping the sound of the river at my back until its murmur faded like a breath of air. I was in the deep wood then, green with ferns and black with the great boles of old trees. But it was not like Anu's wood. Here no sad quiet lay like stone upon the earth. Rather, wood doves bickered continually overhead. Squirrels trooped through the branches squeaking with a sound like rubbing sticks. Once, when I had crossed a deer track, a gray old boar with yellow tusks came blundering out to charge me till I raised my hand and laughed. All around I could feel the wood swarming and crowding. And in those few tight places where a slim ray of sun slid through, faint starry flowers grew. Still there were no gaping holes, rising tier on tier within the canopy of leaves, where one could truly see the sky. What light there was seemed green and pale, though here no gloom was mixed with it.

After several hours I knew I was lost. On an island, I thought, you need only walk to come to water. But I could not make a straight path through the trees. No streams crossed my wanderings. I waded some time through a low black marsh and found a lightning-blasted oak uprooted. But other trees had shouldered in its place. I tramped the margins of the swamp. No brook fed it. After that I kept to higher ground. Still the way grew no easier.

There is no village here, I thought, no priest, no god-shrine. To raise monuments one needs first to break a road on which to drag the stone. Even if it were now overgrown, there would be signs. But, looking down, I should have watched the trees. Heedless, I lumbered through the undergrowth. Roped with wild grape and bound with creepers, the branches above me let in no more light. Yet I should have noticed that lately I had no need to swerve to pass the knees and roots of trees. No longer did they stand within my path but off to either side. Angry and unseeing, I called on the names of power that I knew. As if to challenge heaven, I threw back my head, my voice already lifted. But then my hot breath caught within my throat.

Before my swimming eye a blaze of whiteness flashed. Ahead of me at the end of a narrow avenue of trees the old wood opened like a door. I saw a wide green glade. About its rim in a mighty circle stood a ring of stones, each massive, twice the height and more of a man. At its center, piled higher even than the towers of Morrigan, there rose a grassy mound. I stopped.

I had wandered, I knew, much of the island. Surely, I thought, I have already tramped through this place and did not find it. Then, slowly, as I looked, I came to see the wonder of the place, that a man might not come to it until the god was willing.

The sun's full light poured through the opening in the trees. For a hundred elhws it fell straight to the earth. It seemed a golden pillar set upon the ground. Crows were rising and falling in its light. I watched them. But when they dropped, I saw, they never touched the Mound, though more than once they lit on the ring of stones. Yet I did not feel any dread in that bright air and wondered. The glade was green, the sweet air gentle.

This place is blessed, I thought. Why then do the birds so fear it? I looked some time and thought. The Mound was old, so Tabak said, compounded of the ancient earth when men had not yet walked upon the land. Perhaps, I mused, the world as it was then cannot mix with what came after. Yet how then should a king of later days find grace to walk upon its back? So I debated with myself. It may be that I said my thoughts aloud.

The voice fell out of the air. Soft as the rain it was, but there was laughter at the back of it. 'The blood of kings comes down from those first things,' it said. 'There is no wonder when like will mix with like.'

I looked up sharply. There were only trees above. One, an oak, was unmatched among the rest. Its great branches twisted in a maze of wood. Its green-black leaves lay thick as birds upon a new-sown hill. I stood beneath it rubbing the chin beneath my beard.

'Never before this have I talked with trees,' I said.

'Nor have you yet,' it answered back, even more like laughter than before. 'Their voices are gruff and deep and hard to hear. Nor do they lightly speak with kings who ride in ships cut from their kin.'

I stopped and thought before I spoke. I said, 'You know then what I am?'

'None but kings and giants ever come,' it said. 'And you, my lord, I see are both.'

I cast my eye once more through all the branches. Only the oak itself looked back at me. 'Have you seen so many kings,' I asked, 'that you are certain of the look of them?'

I heard it laugh again. 'You are the first, my lord,' it said. 'But the old woman who has sat upon that hill since first the sun looked down on it has marked each one. At night, when she and I grow weary looking at each other and the dark, she takes the shapes they had and speaks the lovely words they spoke to her. So I have learned the look of kings and all their talk from the first that ever walked upon the land, the salt still wet upon his arms.'

I heard but puzzled at the words. The grim heights of the mountain rose, troubling my thought. Huddled beneath its double crag, I saw once more the house where I was born. It takes me for what I am not, I thought. 'I am no sea king,' I answered, almost sad it was not so.

'Your hair's as black,' it laughed. 'Near black as mine. The old woman says that I am water-spawn. It cannot be that you are other than you seem.'

My eye wide open, I stared hard as I might at nothing I could see. 'Come down,' I said, 'and let me look at you.'

It did not answer.

'Perhaps you fear me.'

The laugh came quickly then, but it had darkened before it stilled. 'Do not yet go upon the Mound,' it said.

It made me angry. I turned as if I meant to walk away, then changed my mind, more angry than before. 'Come down if you would have me do your bidding,' I shouted up to it. My voice rang cold beneath the tree. But its echo brought back only silence. No leaf moved. It is a bogie, I decided. I thought, it is a foolish thing to quarrel with what can't be seen. I turned once more.

'Do not go,' it pleaded softly.

'Then will you come to me?'

I waited. The silence went on as though I had not spoken. Whether a bogie or the witch's drab, it would not give me what I asked. As I listened more I thought I heard a cry, blade-sharp then muffled, sobbed back with straining breath. Something wept within the twisted wood, quietly as though it hated to be heard. I could not give a reason. Yet it stung me. I thought, I have my own grief. Still, I could not get free of it.

Perplexed, I laid my back against the oak. I let my shoulder dig into the bark, something nagging in my memory, something – though I reached for it – I could not touch. Casting my thoughts as nets to catch at it, I forgot to move.

The day wore on. I watched the lordling crows rising and falling above the Mound. They wait as well, I thought, hungry for king's flesh.

The evening came. The trees reached up and caught the sun. I watched it die. I saw the darkness come swarming up from underground and the mists come stalking through the aisles of trees, long-fingered, stooped, like heavy headless men, their beating hearts ripped from their chests.

Perhaps, I thought, it cries because it dare not show itself. And I imagined it, both furred and scaled, misshaped, ugly, drooling foam. Or else, I thought, the witch has swallowed what it was and left but a scrap of voice unchewed. It made no difference. Knowing there was another, whatever shape it had, I longed for company. The night wore on. Yet no sleep came.

I saw her early, walking slowly among the trees. Her shift was green and shining as the oak. The new sun at her back, I saw the lithe long shadow of her calves within the cloth. She laughed to see that I had noticed her.

I had no need to question who she was. Her hair, as she had said, was black as mine. She wore it parted from her face, then loose upon her shoulders. She looked younger than my sisters but to my eye more fair. In her white hands she bore a fresh-killed hare, its bloody legs twitching with remembered life.

'You brought me mussels when I came,' I said, 'and now a hare.'

The eyes that looked in mine were large, brown-black as the aurochs', flecked with gold. I could not read them.

'This is the old woman's wood,' she said. 'You dare eat only what I bring you.'

She held the hare out like an offering. Reaching, I took it. My clutching hands slid vainly over fur.

Its blood was black and dried upon my hands when I awoke. Scattered at my feet I saw its bones, cracked through, the marrow gone. A gray light welled up from the ground. It was not yet morning. I did not remember if I slept.

'Drink,' she said, already near me. The word quivered in the air like a plucked string of a harp. I felt her breath. Prodding, she nestled the bowl within my hands. I felt the weight of it, unable to decide.

'Drink deep, my lord. From the well beneath the Mound I drew it, the world's own blood. It never fell as rain.'

Uncertain, I pushed my fevered lips to touch the rim. Cool as the earth it seemed, cold as the old stones underground. I drank. But in my throat the water turned to ash.

I woke again. I did not hunger. In the red and seeming dawn I stood out from the tree. Among the roots I found a broken bowl. I did not thirst.

In the red light I heard her laughter.

'Will you come to me?' I asked.

Her laughter answered, gentle and amused. 'Lord, you are slow to learn,' she whispered. 'Twice I came to you and twice you let me go.'

I heard the rustle of her shift behind me and did not turn. 'Three times,' I said. 'Each a dream.'

'But I am here, my lord. You need only turn to look at me.'

Still I was afraid.

'My lord?'

I set my teeth. 'I will not watch you shrink to dust and bone.'

I heard her move, her shoulders at my back. I felt the softness of her breasts against me. But I had no word for her. Her laugh was bitter then.

'Go without my help,' she said, her voice already cold. 'Meet the old woman on the Mound. And may you live. But surely then, even as now I breathe, I shall turn to dust and bone and all the nights I waited for you be for nothing.' Her breath caught and she stopped.

Morning came. The red light paled, turned white against the trees.

Green and empty in the meadow the high Mound shone. Bright even as the sun it seemed. Yet I knew it was a tomb. She is the same, I thought, and yet I heard her weep. She laid her trembling head against my back.

'You are the only king who came to me,' she said. 'For the old woman there were others. For me you were the only one who was to come.'

But the taste of ashes was in my mouth. I thought of the broken bowl and scattered bones. My memories came down like hail upon my head. I thought of Grieve and all the women of the Kell waiting for what never came. I pitied her, half-knowing she was my imagining and in that same moment certain she was not. The *filidh* say that I was steadfast then. But they only repeat the lies I told them. I was young and had never had a woman. The sound of her breath flamed in my lungs, the shape of her small hands seared like coals against my back. With brown-black hungry eyes I knew she watched me.

'You are the witch,' I cried. But the shout I gave came out a moan.

'No,' she said. 'I would have told you.'

I did not answer. There was no more I could do. I turned, expecting emptiness. I touched her face. The flesh beneath my hand was warm.

She stared at me as though she cast out all her soul through her dark eyes. She said, 'So at the end you find me, lord.'

'As I have dreamed you.'

She shook her head. 'No, as I am.'

I reached for her with both my hands. At once her flesh went up like husks in flames. In her place I felt the fissured oak, its old bark split and cold against my face. A great wind rocked the branches overhead and drove the swirling leaves that filled the wood and fell on me like cataracts of fire until, at last, they closed my eye.

The storm, if that it was, had vanished when I woke. I found her seated near me on the ground. The line of her neck was tilted like a swan's. Her lips were parted, amused but not surprised. In her tangled hair she wore a crown of braided twigs and leaves. The sun, now truly risen, rode at her back. In her lap she cradled a small hare, its dead eyes blank, and in her white hands a bowl. She smiled at me.

'You are the first man I have served,' she said.

The memory of the night came back. A lightness filled my head. She is a tree in woman's shape, I thought. The soles of her feet are black and splayed beneath her gown. If I lifted it I would find her legs were rooted in the earth. But her face was rapt and tranquil. A patch of sunlight fell against her cheek.

Taking up a silver knife, she skinned the hare. To keep from watching her I set a flame. When I had done, she laid the hare's white body in the hottest part and after it had roasted, cut the joint.

A great emptiness hung around me. The wood, the fire, the bowl were mere pictures painted in the air. I did not know what time had passed. Yet because I hungered I took the flesh and tore it with my teeth. Her deep eyes smiled.

She held the bowl out to me. It was in my mind to dash it to the ground. Yet, thirsting, I put it to my lips. The breath of the water felt cool against my face. I drank it to the bottom. Her black eyes danced.

'The old woman does not eat or drink,' she said. 'All that I have made for her she turns away.'

I raised my brows. I had not meant to speak, but I remembered what was said of her, how the witch tore out and ate the hearts of kings. It rose unbidden to my lips. 'I have heard she dines on other fare,' I said.

Her small mouth twisted at the edge. 'Who is to say? Since I lived, you are the first who came.'

'And yet you speak to her.'

'My lord, we are two women by ourselves. The nights are long. I have heard her say a thousand times what each king said and all she answered, word by word. Only I do not know the end.'

But I meant to have the truth of it and said, 'But you have surely guessed, and still you stay with her.'

She dropped her eyes. 'This is an island, lord. Nowhere does it touch the land.'

'Ships pass.'

'And do not stop.' Her crow-black hair hung at her cheek. She lifted it as if it were a wing till her deep sad eyes had found my face. 'I have stood upon the rocks myself and called to them. But they are little men and much afraid. I have watched them screw up their little faces and stick their little trembling fingers in their ears.' Her mouth was set. 'You may keep such men as that,' she said. 'Myself, I would not lick their bones.'

I tried to read her countenance, but it was closed.

'Ar Elon came,' I cried, 'and by the stones he left I judge he did not fear the witch.'

She laughed. 'Like you he was no little man.'

My backbone shivered. 'You saw him, then?' I asked.

'I have watched the old woman walk the meadow's rim, changed, like his own shadow, chanting, as she remembered them, the holy words that raised the stones. I have watched her pull down branches of the deepest wood, whispering to herself, to make his arms and whole great trees to compound his legs.' Her mouth worked oddly yet she smiled. 'Lord, I have stood as close to his shape as I stand to you.' She took a breath. 'And seeing him, I knew what you must be.'

I tried the meaning of her words and did not like them. I was not my father's mirror. Suddenly it became important that she not find me so. I turned so she could see me fully, my hair still wild, my blasted eye, my clothes that would have shamed a beggar, never mind a king.

It was my bitterness that spoke. 'He was two-eyed like any man,' I said. 'And king already when he came.'

She had bitten the inside of her lip. I saw the blood. 'What do I care of that?' she asked. It troubled me.

'Was it not a king you sought?'

At once the sight went from her eyes. 'There are kings enough,' she said defiantly.

I did not follow her.

She wheeled around. 'Can you not see that I have guessed? Have I not seen you walk up from the river's edge, taller than ever were the men who lived on land? In truth, whatever you say to me, I saw it. Your black hair, sea-made, was shining in the air.'

Her bright eyes shone beneath her tears. She shivered though the wind was warm. Mute before her, I touched her hair, then took her small white shoulders inside my hands.

'Long have I watched and counted, lord,' she said. 'Now you have come again as ever it was promised.' She wept. Yet even as she spoke her voice was not one but many. Within each word a thousand voices rose, each old and sharp with longing. I turned aside. Too well I knew the words and cursed them. Even in this I could not be parted from the Kell. I felt my face grow white and still.

For a breath's space she looked up at me. I felt her push her hands to find my back.

'Who is it that you say I am?' I asked.

She made no sound but drew me to herself. She did not fade. Meeting those still, dark eyes, I knew only that she wanted me. I found the strings that held her gown. When I had seen her nakedness, she laughed outright. Somewhere within the oak a bird began its song.

CHAPTER SEVENTEEN

When we were still, she kept her arms around my neck. Her breasts were warm against my skin, her thick hair spread upon my shoulder like a fan. She touched my face.

I never knew the ease of love as on that morning. When in my bed in the empty place far back in the hall – the candles guttered, the barons gone – I have lain against the body of my queen and heard the wind wail as it willed along the hill, her bold eyes would catch the candles' fire and, watching me, she would know some other face had disturbed my sleep. I was blessed that she was wise. She never spoke of it. She had her sons and my ear when it was needed. As much as man and woman may, we had made our peace. But on that morning I could not see so far ahead. The bird, perhaps dreaming itself, had quit its song.

She sat up at last, the leaves still clinging to her hair.

'You cannot meet the old woman as you are,' she said.

I smiled, looking down at my own nakedness. 'Will I too greatly frighten her as I am?' I asked, but got up afterward and pulled my longshirt over me.

The small lines of her mouth drew back. 'Nor is that enough, I think,' she said. 'You will need both arms and armor, lord.'

I looked her up and down. She had not bothered yet to cover herself. My heart was light. But I caught the solemnity within her eyes.

'The sword that I had I left at Stephen's Well,' I said. 'And even that was borrowed. As to armor, there was never a ring shirt made that I could wear.'

She drew her shift over her head, then raked out her long hair with her fingers. 'I have not wasted the years I awaited you,' she answered. At once she turned toward the path that ran deep into the wood. 'Come,' she said, not looking back. 'Such as will be needed I have made.'

I followed her into the greenwood. But the path had known only her feet. Scarcely a leaf was turned and nowhere was it worn. I trailed her around ivy-covered trunks, through hedges that brushed and scraped my thighs and soaked my skin with dew. When I was slow, she called to me. But as quickly as I went, she kept ahead. The sun slowly faded, then disappeared, though in a moment it showed in another place.

The way descended into a valley of grim oaks. Their enormous branches erupted close to the ground. Their leaves were thick and green and blocked my going. Heedless, I lumbered into them. But there were times I lost sight of her. Then all at once I would see her hair, like something winged, darting among the trees. Already short of breath, I followed after. The black shadow kept a girl's height as it fled. But suddenly it rose like smoke into the trees. I stopped before it. Formless, just at the edge of sight, a broad black wing unfolded from a branch.

The great crow shivered. It cracked its dry red mouth and hissed. 'You delay,' it said, its old voice harsh as wind on stones. 'Already ships have moored off this island's shore. Thigg comes, his barons with him, to see with his own eyes if you are a corpse.'

The eye it had was gray with age.

'You are neither crow of mine,' I said. I did not breathe.

Its great eye glittered. 'Mine they were till you stole them. My life's last children, though you took them early.'

I felt a ghostly run of fire branch through my skull. 'It was not without cost to me,' I murmured. 'Since you took the other, I have looked out on but half the world.'

The old eye blinked.

'We shall be even, you and I,' it rasped.

In the upper branches a sad wind moaned. Moving, it tore a hole through which a single shaft of sunlight fell like a sword. For a moment I saw her as she was. Her bony neck was bare and eaten, the immense wings spare and thick with lice. She turned her mangled head that I might see it. A gray hole swam before me where her eye had been. Horror crept over me. There was a feel of sickness in my head. But I felt my anger more.

'I never bartered eyes with you,' I cried. 'How shall we be even, then? It was Ar Elon who cast the stone at you. I was not asked. When he did it, I was not born.'

Her glazed eye, fixed on mine, seemed indifferent.

'Nor did you ask when you took from me the last children of the air,' she rasped. 'No more than shall be asked of you when the final price is paid.'

I stared, knowing it was Anu's crow. But suddenly it was Yllvere's face that rose before me, both bird and woman. Huge wings outspread, no longer bare but bright as gold, outreached till they had filled the wood.

A brightness fell from them. They stunned my sight. But though I stared in wonder, my heart was cold.

'I do not serve the Crow of Death,' I said.

Her smooth white face showed no surprise, no hurt. 'Anu has many daughters,' she answered softly. 'But each one is Herself. It has not changed. She only takes what I have given. Life for life.'

I felt her arms as though she held me, white, enfolding, warm as wool, her peace I had never known. My own arms ached for it. Still, I stiffened.

'Lady,' I asked her roughly, 'why have you sent me here to die upon the Mound?'

The shining head was bowed. Black feathers sprouted from her throat. The brightness went. In its place I felt the rotting dark.

'How shall you die,' it hissed, 'when I can see but half of you?' Opening wide its fleshless beak, it jeered, 'Fool, half-blind, how shall you live?' The old head sank back into the gloom and grinned. 'Deceived, this night already you have eaten bones for flesh and taken dust for drink. Bitter will that be to you. More bitter still the bride you took.'

It laughed a laugh that made no sound.

I closed my ears. But the stench of death blew in my nostrils, pushed into my skull and crushed my thought. Already the trees were gone, sunk down to choking dust. The bare sloping hills beneath were crumbling. I caught the last rough glimpse of stones that fell, shrunken into flaming cinders, lost as sparks, snuffed out. A blind wind nosed across the waste that was the earth, till ragged, mortal, even that was gone. For an awful moment I was alone.

Lady, in that darkness it was your face I met. Where nothing else was, your soft eyes followed me, held me, frightened and amazed, as if we touched. If bitterness would come of you, it was not yet. If you were false, I would not know of it before I must. Your warm breath moved beneath my heart. It was your smile that turned my lips. Then, before you had a name, I was at peace. Your eyes were shining. In that darkness they leapt like fires.

I felt my legs again. I stood once more at the border of the wood, the treeless glade in front of me. Where her eyes had been, the light still was, paired stars glittering in the evening sky, the Mound beneath. In time I went toward it.

Grief comes soon enough to men. Yet whatever else would come, I knew that I had met the dark, Death's worst, and was not betrayed. Now the shadows lay where they belonged. I smiled.

Presently I came within the ring of upright stones. The tall gray rock was almost even with my head. Marked with lichen, scarred with runes and carvings, the stones seemed older than my father's time. Yet I knew that it was he who had set them there. Perhaps even then he was condemned, shamed though I did not know the cause, abandoned by the folk he ruled. But this was his work; his word had lifted them.

Even as men are, so each stone was different – some long or burly, others smooth or grizzled, though all were huge. They were not quarried here, I thought, nor any two in one place. But where they had been dug I could not guess. Silently, I went among them, squinting at the shapes. The gray rock shone beneath the stars. Proud as kings they were, but their sides were cold as winter earth.

I stopped. Among them one stood taller than the rest. Yet even though the rock was worn, I read among the scoured lines the faded glory of a lordlike face. A strangeness came over me. I spoke to it. It took no notice but kept its narrowed eyes fixed on the Mound.

At its knees, where the stone had sunk into the ground, I found a ring shirt of a size that I might wear and at its side a sword so huge that I alone might carry it. The blade was one clear piece of metal, but the hilt was carved. Wrought amid the twisted gold I saw a man shape, naked, the face in pain. In his arms, contending with him, Death's crow outspread her terrible wings. Their warring hung in balance, the victory in doubt. By that I knew the sword was mine, new-made, with no history but the one that I would write with it. I took it in my hand. Feeling the weight of it, I smiled.

Surely, I thought, she would not arm me against herself. She is no witch, then, but what she seems.

Comforted, I took the ring shirt and put it on. The links were burnished gold, yet there was no softness in the metal. Pleased, I thought, never has a king gone so richly armed as this. And still I knew this was no maiden craft. But in truth, I thought, neither is this any black art but only what it seems. Gladdened, I lifted the sword once more. The starlight glittered on the blade. Each link of the heavy mail shone back the light in turn. I thought, now I will do what I have promised.

The glade was empty. Because I was too young to try so great a thing unnoticed, I cried out to the stone, 'This I swear and you are witness. I shall not leave this place until I have wrung from her who rules it the right of kings.'

When I had spoken, I went out from the stones. The way was short. It was not long before I stood within the shadow of the Mound. I scaled its far height with my eye. There was no mark or stone upon its back, only one great hill grown thick with grass. Since the world was new, it is said, men never built so near to heaven.

Yet it was a hill like other hills, not crystal, as the harpers tell it. Once before the meat I heard a *filidh*, whose song men swore went lighter to their heads than wine, plucking at the strings and calling out how I had seen the starlight shining through the Mound. Before my chair where all could see it, I had him whipped. My smallest son sat blubbering from his mother's lap that I was cruel. But the man knew what I meant. When the people will hear foolishness, no king can give the law.

The edges of the Mound rose gently. At first I climbed as easily as I walked the high meadows above Morrigan. The grass was deep, but not so that it mattered. A light wind came ruffling from the east, caught the grass and set it rolling like the sea. So easeful did it seem that had I kept my eye to it my thoughts would have deepened and I might have slept. But mostly I listened. The wind sighed. Soft it was as the breath of a man who dreams.

I climbed a long time. Though I was wary, my hand gripped the great sword lightly. On the stair road before Gwen Gildrun I had clutched fast the sword I borrowed, like my own life, fearing that should I let one go I would surely lose the other. I was bolder now. In truth, perhaps, the dark was not so thick as it had seemed beneath the Tree, though it was queerer. The sky was deep and high. In the vault of heaven two stars shone. The heavens were but one more hill above the one I climbed.

At that same moment a long, low roll of thunder broke above the Mound. I heard it echo back against the wood. Dully, I went on. I yearned then only to be done with it, to meet the witch and, if I lived, to rule. I sought no truth, no reasons. I longed only for a night's peace, for sleep and, when I woke, the girl beside me in my bed. The air was soft, the long grass whispering. What did I care, I thought, to argue with the dark. It struck without pain, was gentle, gave no lasting dreams. It is said the gods do not love a quiet man, yet I knew they let him be. There is some good in that, I thought. The Mound was empty. The wind blew softly over the edges of the hill and then was lost.

It seemed that all I did was climb. I gave my thoughts to nothing else. My knees bent and one foot came down after another. I was no longer certain where I went. There were moments when I thought I climbed the rough tower to Urien's chamber and others when I was as certain I descended the narrow steps to Yllvere's cell. Only there was no end.

The mail shirt grew heavy; the great sword weighed upon my hand. I was of half a mind to cast them off. No dark shapes rose snarling in my path. No serpents pressed about my legs. I thought of what I did. Was this the test that made the men of Ormkill tremble? Made Thigg, imagining it, smile? I shivered. Though for a time I had forgotten everything, I remembered then I would be king. In a sudden great revulsion I felt my whole life clamoring through my veins, bitter and unused. Despairing, I remembered what ffraw had said the night he swore his life to me: A king must have blood on him if he would make his own men brave. When I go down to them, I thought, what will I say? Shamed, I cried out to the dark.

'Dagda,' I shouted, 'was I given arms to walk an empty hill?'

'Come, my lord,' she answered even as I saw her. 'Do not be angry. You will find use enough for your sword when you go down again.'

She was all in green and shining. A pale light came out of the ground on which she stood. At first I did not see the trouble in her look. It was the Mound I saw. The grass was parted and in its place a bed of scented fern, woven with the living leaves of oak and hazel. The pillows were of twisted grass, shaped into the form but growing still. I watched but could not hold her eyes. It seemed that I had stepped outside the earth. In some lost part of me I knew it was high summer then. But without the stars I had no sure sense of the season. The air was flecked with light and shadow, nor was one marked from the other. It seemed I stood within some holy place before time ran.

I rubbed my eye. For a brief moment I felt her gaze and then it fled.

'Where is the witch you serve?' I asked.

She trembled. Her lips moved before she had her voice. 'She was old, as I have told you.' I saw she meant to look at me, but her eyes kept slipping past. She sighed, her fingers twisting through her hair. Her face seemed paler than it was. 'She would have met you as she met the others,' she said, looking off. 'She would have found some shape to come at you. You know, she could be anything she pleased, an ox with iron horns so wide the moon might fall between; or, if she wished, small and unnoticed as a wasp. Barely would you have heard its buzzing. But the poison in its sting would have made your king's blood boil, even your great shoulders slump and tear.' Her body stiffened. 'Lord,' she whispered, 'can you not see I feared for you?' Seeing her anguish, I moved beside her. She leaned against me, nestling in the shadow beneath my arm. She looked up, seeming smaller than she was.

'Where is she gone?' I said.

There was a sadness in her eyes I could not read. 'Lord – ,' she answered faintly, 'it is already done.'

I drew back, not knowing what she meant. To hold me she put her hands up to my chest.

'We were two women by ourselves,' she said. 'Ever she knew my thoughts. And when she looked into them she saw what I must do to save you. Knowing it, she fled. But more I knew her wiles.' She was silent then, staring at the bed of fern and hazel growing at her feet. She gripped her hands as often I had seen Yllvere do, twisting each finger. Even then a smile played at her lips. So her mood swung back and forth from grief to pride and back to grief again. She said, 'In a barrow on the Mound I found her hiding. By her long ears I pulled her out. She it was I brought to you. She it was, when you had roasted it, you ate.'

She watched me, helpless, pleased. Tall as a spear she was, upright and about to fall.

'But even as you took the flesh, she turned herself to hare's blood. But then I ran and found a bowl and caught each drop.' She lay back her head to watch me. 'And that,' she said, 'you drank.'

Something broke in me. I stared. But still I would not believe.

'It was a dream,' I choked.

'Lord,' she answered, 'so first it was. So are all great spells at first.' A flush had deepened around her eyes. 'But not at the end. Nor was it all my dreaming by itself. Standing beneath the oak you joined it. Our dreams together whispered in her mind. Always she was drawn to power. How then could she help it? Our dreaming called to her. And it was a king who dreamed with me, striding through the dark. What could she do? Her soul slipped out beyond her reach. Already dreaming, she closed her night-black eyes. Then she was a black-eyed hare running on the hill. I ran behind her. I saw where she had dug beneath the ground.'

She smiled slowly, letting her strong voice fade. Once more she put her arms around my neck.

'So it is done, my lord,' she murmured. 'Now is the end of it and you are king.'

I felt my face grow white and still.

'If this is so,' I stammered, my small voice sharp with fear. 'If this,' I halted, knowing the thought and hating it. I felt the witch's blood grow thick and sticky in my throat. She saw my thoughts. A fool might have seen them. Yet she smiled.

'You won,' she cried. 'What does it matter how? Always it was one life against another. So even among the gods it is. Need we be other than they are? She would have taken your own flesh within her mouth. She meant to. There were, you know, so many kings that came before.'

Sweat thick as blood poured from my forehead. 'No!' I raged. 'They met her as she met them. She won or they did.' I stopped, my hands clenched, my thick arms lifted. Before all of Ormkill I had claimed this thing; more, I had sworn it to myself. 'It was you,' I shouted. 'I came to face her. But you have done it in my place.'

She stood, unafraid, but swaying, her hands clasped tightly to my side. She raised her head. It tilted like a crow's. 'Lord,' she whispered, 'was it not promised from the start that I should help you? In truth, you know it. I at least have not forgotten it.' She sighed. Turning a rueful look at me she sang:

> 'Sea-made, the last of giants
> Shall meet the maid on Tinkern Hill
> There what was broken shall be mended
>   On Tinkern, above the bones of kings.

The old woman sang it. I learned it on her lap. I had scarcely walked before she saw I knew the words.'

There was a blankness in her eyes. The wind blew harder. A wing of her raven hair was lifted across her face. I pulled it back and laid my great hands over hers. They burned.

'Who is it that you say I am?'

'A giant, lord.' Her pale chin trembled. 'He that the old woman said would come once more, bearing a likeness of Ar Elon, but not him.' She paused. In the light that came out of the ground I saw her blush. 'He that first carried me to this place,' she said, 'that left me here a babe with that old woman.' Her dark brows were knit and troubled. Yet she laughed. 'So ever as I dreamed you, so you are.'

I turned my head. So she had laughed and wept when I had lain with her. I felt my heart grow still.

'How old do you say I am?'

'Lord, I have watched and counted – ,' she began. But I knew it. For so the Kell have always counted, careless of the stars. Her deep black eyes, so like my own, gazed at me shamelessly.

'Lord,' she asked, as though the thought had only come to her, 'when I was delivered to your care, was not my true name given you? For the old woman, though she had many names for me, had not the one that I was born with.'

I looked into her yearning face, a child's face, wild as it was grave.

Her passions, both fears and smiles together, changed her features as the weather changes, both bright and shadow. I knew then why men lie, even the best of men. In that at least I might have been the old dark man she dreamed I was. I thought, what good will knowing do her? But the name I would not keep. From the first it had only half been mine.

'Géar,' I whispered though the name was blood and ashes in my mouth.

'Géar' she whispered back. Then in joy she shouted it. It was the wind that found it and blew it round the hill.

Away in the east among the gray shapes of the wood I saw a ruddy glow. For a moment I confused it with the rising sun. But as I watched, it broke and spread into a hundred tiny flames. Slowly the lights crept out beyond the trees. Twisting in ragged lines, they climbed among the stones. The lights grew stronger until, as they drew nearer, they had become flaming branches lifted in men's hands. Mail-clad with painted shields I saw them, a host of soldiers, red cloaks on their shoulders, proud men with burnished helms. At the head of each cohort walked a herald, a stave in his hand and on each pole a banner, bright in the torchlight with Thigg's colors.

A smile spread nimbly on her lips. 'See, my lord,' she cried, 'the men of Ormkill come to claim their king.'

And, High King of all the lands between the seas, I watched them come, bitterly, for then I knew the cost. Seeing me, that I was whole, not slaughtered, they raised a cry. But I saw as clearly that there were many, rising at their backs, who were not men at all, though those of Ormkill, their faces on me, saw them not. Yet for a moment I put it by.

When I had come down she was beside me, close at my heels, inside my shadow. Yet when I stepped upon the level ground, before the soldiers, she would not follow. Without a word or cry she halted. Her gown was shining. I saw the wonder that filled men's eyes. Seeing it, I turned. I thought, no man need know that I have slept with her nor who she is.

'Come,' I said so all men heard it. 'Among my people you shall be an honored guest. With your hand you gave them to me. Where I rule, no hand shall be raised except to give you welcome.'

There was silence, for suddenly all the torches gave little light. The wood beyond had crowded closer to their backs. The Mound rose brooding over them. Uneasy, the soldiers would not look at one another. I looked and saw Thigg standing by himself, his barons far from him. His eyes were hollow. Where once there had been cleverness, now there was only fear.

'Will you not welcome her?' I said aloud to him.

I did not wait to hear him answer but turned once more to Géar, my sister. 'Why do you wait?' I asked.

Keeping my eye between her and the soldiers, I saw too late that Thigg was not alone. A woman stepped out from behind his back. I knew her. Her gray eyes looked straight into mine.

'Where is the old woman, lord?' she asked. She had not used the word before. By her look I saw that she acknowledged me, flesh of her flesh, now lord of all these lands. But what else she saw in me I could not tell.

'Dead,' I answered.

She watched me with her gray-green silent eyes. There were no tears on her lashes, yet it seemed she pitied me and perhaps herself as well. If fate had been my master, it was hers. Bound with oaths to him that fathered me, she had severed her last children. Unmoved, even then, she sent one child away to keep the other, though both were crying in her ears. So she had cast lots and bartered with her gods. When the lots fell, she did what they decreed. And now we met. Tabak had said it. What was taken away now came back. Though when he spoke, it had not seemed a curse.

'Dead,' I answered back once more.

Her face was quiet. She said, 'Then she is bound to stay on this same hill.'

I would not have it so. 'What is the cause?' I shouted.

It was Géar that answered, dry-eyed, one woman like another. 'There has always been a witch upon the Mound. It cannot change.' Her face was fixed and proud, red where the sun's first rays had touched it. The dawn wind played in her raven hair.

'Lord,' she added softly, 'when I took her life I knew I traded mine. To keep your life I bartered it, one life for another. I knew when it was done I would wait upon the Mound. I do not fear it now.' Looking down at me she smiled. 'Nor will be alone. Autumn will turn this island's wood to flame when you are gone. Yet though I burn with it, I know the winter comes. It is a sea wind that blows the snow. So I shall think of you. And when the winter's over, I shall have a son. Only you must not come for him. But I shall send him to you when he is grown. In all things save only one he will be your equal. So among all men you will know him.'

She turned her head, her crow's hair drifting behind her like a cloak. A red line traced the rim of the wood. The new sun, lifted above the trees, fell red upon the great stones that ringed the Mound. Her head raised, her eyes unblinking, she saw what I alone had seen and beyond that something more. Her face changed then.

'One thing you must promise me,' she said, her voice made cold. 'You must tell him that he may never rule upon the land. It is only you I love, even to the world's end. For should our son, seeking to be king, come here to meet the witch upon the Mound, in truth, my fair lord, our son will find her.'

Her shoulders, strained taut, fell suddenly. She closed her eyes. Already there were feathers sprouting in her hair.

'Even in the sun,' she murmured, 'this day is cold.' Her head dropped to her knees. When once more she lifted it, I saw the flashing beak, the eyes that were no longer woman's eyes. The Mound was still. The soldiers sank away, afraid to move.

'Géar,' I whispered.

It was a crow's fierce cry that answered me. For one brief moment I caught her mind, felt before I lost her the sudden sweep of earth beneath her wings.

From the host of men there came a roar. Now that she who frightened them was gone, they surged forward, terrible and brave. I would not look at them.

'Woman,' I cried above their shouting, 'from the first you knew, even as Tabak did. Together, knowing, you sent me here to lie with her.'

Even above the noise she heard me. Though the men shrieked I heard her sigh. 'Who would you be mated with?' she cried. 'Never since the world was young were any born upon the land as both you are, sea-made and of the ancient blood. Would you have squandered your seed on some land wife, made more brats whose only life was scratching ground and breaking stone?'

She stared up at my sun-racked face. She drew a long, slow breath and loosed it. 'On land, my lord, there was no other fit to bear your son.'

I spat, angered again to hear the lie. 'I was born upon the land,' I cried. 'On a mountain, the land about me everywhere I looked.'

Yllvere unlaced her knotted hands, quietly as though some old worry had been put aside. 'You are your father's son,' she said. There was a kind of triumph in her sea-gray eyes, a look that only women have, holy, deeper than her single life, as though a patience, old before her birth but passed to her, had borne its fruit at last. 'And he the last great Selchie of the Western Sea, found when we had thought that all were lost. Found though he was dying even then and may be dying still. (For the wild old seamen went ever slow to death.) But it was I that found him while life he had. I bore him children, the old blood in me yet. Though lessened, it had come down from my mother, when it was stronger, and from my mother's mother, when it was whole, unmixed with the coarse blood of the little men who live on land. Now our children will bear a son, the old blood new in him. Now the sea road that was closed shall open and my son's son shall walk the green halls undersea.'

Amazed, my eye fixed on her slender hands hanging free outside her gown. Long I had wished those hands had held me. I would not wish it more. I lifted my eye to meet her own.

'Your son's son,' I murmured, the sound of my voice grown bitter in my ears. 'Not who I was, nor what I did, nor whether I'd be king.'

'King?' she echoed as though the word had caught her by surprise. She stared beyond me to the summit of the Mound, as though she struggled to recall what happened there. 'Are there not kings enough?' she asked. Her voice was low.

'He you treasured above all else was king,' I said. 'High King over all these lands.'

She broke in, puzzled, uncertain, it seemed, of what I guessed or knew. Doubtless she had thought I should have taken more from what she said. 'He was only king a little while,' she said. 'Soon enough they drove him from the hall he raised, contemptuous little men not knowing what they saw. An army he had never sought to gather traveled at his back. Though he never looked for them, they followed him, an immense black-whiskered mighty man, the sea mist still steaming from his hair. All spring and summer they tramped behind him. They were gleeful when he murdered barons, thankful when he made the laws. Though he barely gave a thought to them.

'But winter came. Indoors they saw he would not sit before the heat of their bright fires nor eat their cooking. Instead he would have black eels and pale white squid brought up from far sea towns. When they saw his jaw had swollen and his dark eyes, wanting salt, turn yellow in the air, their welcome changed to grins of fear. Then they muttered in their dirty holes, huddled close beside their fires and thought again of the oaths they'd made. Then, in secret, the barons he had not killed plotted how to drive him forth.

'King? My lord, your father did not come ashore to rule. The last of what he was, he came ashore to breed and die. He looked for nothing else. He ruled because he found it there to do. In that only perhaps he was as other men, needful of some work to fill his days. And so he ruled, careless, but wiser than any lord that went before. But when he had fathered you, he was done with little men and done, I knew as well, with women too. He dragged himself to some high place where he could watch the ocean and the sky. There he waits, keeping to one place, that death may find him at the last.'

She shook her head. 'King,' she cried out one last time. 'My lord, do you think that such a father would leave his son so miserly an inheritance?'

And there it was.

The words that she would never say, now freely spoken, said before all the hosts of Ormkill, my father's people, though if she were to be believed, they were not his folk at all and the kingship was nothing.

The sun poured down emptily upon the world. I looked. On every side there stretched away the land, first the meadow, then the wood, an island broad enough so that I had wandered it and lost my way. Yet one bright river bounded it all. If that were so, the vast realm I sought to rule, its ranging swamps and rampart mountains, its men and cities and circling birds, what more was it but another scrap of earth between the seas? I groaned with the ache of my own smallness. I felt bereft. I had dreamed of sitting in my father's chair in a hall he raised upon a hill, a girl with raven hair at my right hand. For all its worth I might have stayed within my room at Morrigan, walking the little space between my bed and fire. From the beginning the Kell had no patience with such little dreams. They wanted oceans and the rough wet touch of wild seamen, huge when they came to land, great-whiskered, webbed in feet and hands, large as the old gods, men whose salt blood festered in the air, whose flesh, brown and glistening beneath the waves, swelled and rotted in the sun. Such a man my father was, and I, if Yllvere at last were to be believed, the same.

Too late I knew the High King's shame and why the landsmen rose against him. Yet, I knew, these very men, their sons with them, flesh of their small flesh, would follow me unquestioningly. When I had walked from the river, new and huge upon their streets, there had been many, even then, ready to name me king. Now down from the Mound, seeing the wonder in their faces, I was king to them indeed. King at least for as long as the land shape held. Until, if I were to believe her, my smooth skin blistered, crusted over with dull scales, or sprouted tusks or whatever bogie shape fell to me. King, though it was nothing in her eyes. I sucked my wound and lifted up my arms.

All at once I was aware of the hosts of Ormkill standing at my feet. Their bodies tense, sword bright in each small hand, they waited to see what I would do. It was clear that they made nothing of what I asked

Yllvere or what she answered. To them it was all wonder and gibberish and women changing into birds. I stared out among their faces. Only two stared boldly back at me or saw my pain.

'You are faithful yet, old ffraw,' I said. And to the second, 'It is not yet finished, man of Bede. Though you came to me early, still you must go on waiting.'

'I do not understand you, lord,' Ceorl answered. His face was sad. Like ffraw he was no longer young. Together, having sworn to me, they had tramped the wilds of the realm between the seas seeking where I would be found. But when they found me, I had gone off again. A thin wind blew over the field, from behind the host where no man looked. Ceorl sniffed the air. There was something in it he did not like.

I strode forward, coming away from the Mound. The soldiers parted. I reached out my long arm to Ceorl.

'It is not yet time for me to rule,' I said. 'There is one thing more that I must know, one place more that I must go.'

His gray lips tried to smile. But I saw he felt himself unjustly used. He had left his own folk to serve a king. So in truth had most men there, journeying from Ormkill, eager either to see my corpse or, if my claim were honest, deliver up a crown. Then seeing me whole and walking from the Mound, the kingship won, it had been in their mouths to cheer. In their hearts were great oaths ready to be sworn. Since first light they had waited. Now filled, they were about to burst. But the business with the women got in the way. Their eyes narrowed. For Ceorl it went deeper. He had waited longer, given up more. I saw him shiver. The blood drained from his face.

Once more I broke the quiet.

'Hear me, each of you,' I shouted to the host. 'Hear me and bring back my words to Ormkill, to Stephen's Well, to old red Hwawl, wheresoever men dwell in the land, to the greatest and the least of towns. I name my Stewards, ffraw and Ceorl of Bede, jointly in my place. Serve them. They will keep the peace. Lest any man among you grumble, know it is their word I shall hear and none beside when I come back to rule.'

The soldiers stirred. There were questions in their eyes, in some bewilderment, in others fear. And none were more bewildered or afraid than the two that I put over them. Yet the eyes of the barons were empty, even as mirrors are, casting back the world they saw and nothing of themselves. But I could guess what thoughts were smoldering in their skulls.

'Two I name to hold the land,' I cried. 'And the third to hold the two and give them counsel, her word first, even over theirs.' Then I named her, Yllvere, my mother, she who had set the order of Morrigan, its orchards and its fields, whose word in the wild North among her women was as near the law as any, whose cunning, I doubted not, was sharper than that of even the most thoughtful of the barons. The soldiers heard me. The name took all their sight. Blind and mute they stood like men who have seen the sun, bright overhead, devoured by the moon, amazed, as if a moth, instead of burning, ate the flame. Only she looked up at me.

'You dare much,' she said softly, though the sound was in all men's ears.

'You care so little for the land that it is safe from you,' I answered.

She drew a breath. 'You go to him?'

'When you will say the place.'

She smiled, though even then her mouth was frowning at the edge. I saw her longing, old and unassuageable. Much of what my father was I would never know. Yet, before the rest, it came to my mind, whether in glory or in folly, he was her lover and had lain with her. Once his heart had cried her name. And she, whatever now she had become, had answered him.

Her eyes had a strange glitter. 'He has gone to Hren,' she said. 'Back to that high place where first he came to land.' She made some motion with her slender hand, tentatively as if she meant almost to take it back. 'Lord, you know it. It is the place where Urien slew Lot and won our house for thanks. Still, you dare not go there lightly or alone.'

'I do not go alone,' I said.

She shook her head. 'There no men will follow you.'

'They are not men I call,' I answered. 'Or do you forget, lady, what it is you made me?' She gave no answer.

I had in my hand the sword that Géar had given me. New-made, it had never gone through the belly of a man. Yet it shone red as copper when I lifted it, as though the very air could bleed.

The wind blew. And on it suddenly, when the sword was flashed, the thunder of heavy feet came to the host. The soldiers shivered when they heard the sound. Those who turned saw them first, the tall shapes black against the wood. But those too frightened to move their head, their faces frozen, the next moment saw them nonetheless. Huge and moving from all sides, like an avalanche that walks on level ground, the stones of Ar Elon's ring tramped toward the Mound.

Gray old faces were carved and pitted in the rock. Though they were men no longer, yet they had the look of kings. Their rumbling voices were borne across the field, roaring, tongueless, without words – an empty soulless noise like gravel drawn by tides along a beach. The true men caught at their ears with the pain of it. Yllvere only did not shudder at the sound.

'These will be my companions,' I said to her. Perhaps she heard me above the sound. She smiled. Years later, when I came east, inland from where I put to shore along the coast, they told me she was dead. Nine years she had ruled the folk of Ormkill then and all the lands between the seas.

PART IV

Hren

CHAPTER EIGHTEEN

They were not like the stones of Menhir. Those stones were thrust out of the earth like crusted fingers, raised out of the grass like dead men's hands. Those stones were soldiers, but soldiers who had grown unmindful of their guard. So long had they been rooted in their place that some had fallen and all but one had forgotten speech. They were the ruin of ages already passed. If they once had had names, those were forgotten. Men had lost track of who they were. Save for the one who waited, their eyes were closed. The stones of Ar Elon's ring were not the same. Their hard eyes bright as garnets, they had kept their watch upon the Mound, tireless, one year to the next since Ar Elon set them there.

No weeds grew at their feet. The thyme and thorn grass, which throughout the field lay thick and deep, here curled back before them, the young runners trampled in the earth. Once each moon the great stones breathed. So R'gnir told me, he that was foremost of the nine who came with me. We walked beneath the oak shade, the men of Ormkill already at our backs. His voice was gentle, like a mist escaping from the ground.

'Long we had been dead when Ar Elon called us forth,' he said. 'Even our bones were cracked and gone. Still we remembered our own names, for the earth remembers when even men forget. But he, though ocean born, had heard them. Night after night he called to us until we could not keep from listening. For, know this, lord, the dead are sad and long to be remembered. Hearing our own names again, his voice insistent, still warm with life, though there was nothing left of us, we came. He remade us then of what we had become, with arms of granite, nails of slate. From the mountain's core he cut our hearts. Speaking to the stone, he quickened it.'

Remembering, he sighed. He was old. He set down his broad rough furrowed feet, one after the other, sluggishly. He compelled each to move. The land shook under him like the beat of his slow heart. Yet in all this neither pain nor bitterness rose to his thick face. Anger leaches from the oldest dead, I thought, till they are free.

Behind us I heard the men of Ormkill shouting, a storm of anger broken out among them. Already several of the barons were barking orders of their own. I heard Thigg call his name, then Yllvere's voice lifted over it. My heart was too full of other things. I was glad I could not hear her words. The tumult rose. It would be no easy thing to master those of Ormkill. Yet at the start, the sight of walking stones would linger in their eyes. I trusted to their fear, that with the strands of it she might weave her rule.

This time I did not lose my way within the wood. The road I had come to last through wandering I followed now. The nine, advancing slowly with their heavy gait, swept the low scrub before them and trampled the smaller trees. Nine came. The rest, many times that number – for among them were all the generations of kings since men first walked on land – still kept their watch upon the Mound. The old witch was gone, but they knew another had taken her place. I thought of the black-eyed girl who had walked beside me through the wood. Her neck was white as the inside of a shell. What filled her head, I wondered, when she saw me go?

The sun stood fully overhead when we came out from beneath the trees. We found the shore and there the great ship as I had left it, rocking in the current. A crowd of lesser boats were drawn up on the stony edge of land. So the soldiers and their barons had come to the place. Scarcely a dozen men had been left behind to guard the craft. They fell back groaning when they saw what moved among them, their mouths gaping, drooling in their beards with fear. I forgot them as soon as they had slunk from sight. The river knocked at the great ship's hull.

'Great as that ship is,' I said, 'it will not carry you.'

R'gnir turned his gray face from the water. 'You are still thinking like a man,' he said. With a long unwinking stare he watched me. It may be that he laughed, but it was hard to tell. 'We shall walk beneath the river, lord. And when we have made the other bank we shall walk beside you as you sail. Though we are slow of step, we do not tire. When you must sleep, we shall not stop to rest.' He stood a moment. 'Together we shall come to rocky Hren. That much was promised. It cannot be forsworn.'

Too many oaths had been sworn this day, I thought. Some must break or, if not, their keeping was beyond my understanding. 'Men lie,' I answered him. 'I have seen great oaths melt before a moment's anger.'

R'gnir grumbled. 'The oaths men make have only a man's strength in them. He that swore we would go down to Hren was not a man. His oath will hold.'

That was the last speech I had with him before he set his feet within the river. The water lapped about his knees. He walked. The river leapt up to his chest. The other kings went after; their going lashed the water into foam. Then I was left alone upon the bank.

Shortly, I knew that I must go myself. For a moment, unhurriedly, I stood gazing out across the world. The wind was blowing upriver, from the south. There was a breath of salt upon it. Behind me the greenwood was still. Beyond the trees, hidden at the island's heart, I knew the little men of Ormkill still argued about the stewards I had put over them. In my mind's eye I saw Yllvere, her hair like white gold lifted in the wind, her gray eyes terrible and deep. ffraw and Ceorl were with her, the last of the men I knew. I feared for them and for the promises I had made. More I feared the child, growing in the belly of a woman I barely knew, my sister. Her dark eyes stared at me, her lips moved faintly with words I could not hear. The women of the world are one, I thought, all born of the same dark womb. How then, I wondered, are all their children strangers? I had come to the river's edge, alone.

The Undain groaned. Feeling the sandy bottom with my feet, I waded into the black water. I walked as the kings had walked before me. The cold rose through my loins and clamped a ring around my heart. The bottom fell away. Nor shall I touch the land again, I thought, until I rest on rocky Hren. To no man I swore it, but to myself. I floated from the land, a disembodied head. The river murmured. A tender, agitating scent rose to my nostrils. Shivering with the cold, I knew it, crow-black and steaming, the scent of sea hair shining on my shoulders. I dropped my head beneath the waves. Huge before me, the hull of that great ship rocked overhead.

She bore me.

The river wound through the glad green heart of the land. The hedgerows at the river's edge were rife with birds. Deer drank in the shallows. The soft wind rippled the face of the water, then, unthinking, lost its breath, stilled by the long green summer's peace. The sails hung slack. I drifted south, my only work as steersman at the oar. One day yielded to the next. Each nightfall was pierced with brilliant stars, each morning fair, the great sun golden at its height.

When I hungered, I moored the ship north of some neck of land or cast the anchor in the stillness of a wooded cove, a green bluff over me. There in cold pools I dove for eels and dug blue mussels with my fingers from the rock. At night I stared hard across the shadows to the beach.

Before dawn the old kings passed, their shields and armor of rough stone, glittering dully in the moon's eye. Stealthfully they went, keeping to the thick, dripping grayness of the trees lest they raise alarm among the farms. Yet men could not help but hear the terror of their passing – the shaking earth, the thunder of old trees uprooted on their way. Afraid, none ventured forth. But in the day they went and found the tall hills beaten down. Along the river the deep old wood was tossed to either side and splintered, the very earth stones crushed. So a way was cleared between Tinkern and the sea. The King's Road, it was named in later days when I sent my *filidh* out to spread the tale. But the hearts of the farmers could not be moved. To them and to their children it was the Witch's Walk, for the marvel fell in the first year when Yllvere was mistress of the land. So even to this day the wrong name is better known, though I have taken care to mention it before the court. Even there I have seen the younger barons smile behind their hands. The king grows old, they say among themselves. You little men, I whisper in my beard, you would have crawled back screaming to your mothers' wombs rather than see what I have seen. The young men and I watch each other uneasily across the floor stones of my hall. Yet when rain drums hard against the roof and thunder growls outside the doors, they are quick enough to look and see whether it is the gods or else their king whose anger shakes the earth.

If there is weather for sails, it is not over far from Tinkern to the sea. But there was no wind. The great ship, that which was sent, Pendyved boasted, so as to hurry me, lagged in the south's damp bottom lands where the banks are leagues to either side. The moon pared down. I grew uneasy with hunting eels or sitting the sun-long on the golden deck with only the phantoms of my thoughts for company. Yet each day I felt the tide's tug more. I learned to count the hours till it turned and marked how it advanced. All day the water sucked at the hollow weeds along the shore. Then there was nothing but myself and the lonely piping of white birds. Seeming incorporeal and bleached of life, like nothing I had seen before, they wheeled and cried above the marshes at the river's edge. I thought them souls of drowned men come up-river from their deaths, drifting back from the immense oceans of the South and West, the seas too huge to ease their pain. At night my dreams were haunted by the bark of seals.

With each day I thought of Ar Elon more. I am the seed, I thought, that he left growing in a woman while he wandered. I winced, a coldness creeping toward my heart. Even so I abandoned Géar, my sister, and the child she carried. A bastard and a bastard's son. So the threads of the weave are drawn together on the loom. In my anger I clawed a sign in the empty air. The sickly yellow flame rained down upon the deck. It reminded me only that I was as much Kell as I was his. I swore, crying out to Duinn, he that rules the dead. My words fled out across the water's waste. The smudge of far hills did not send them back. The river kept them. Together we fell toward the gulf.

One night there was a squall. In the morning the river had turned more green and salt than I had seen. The tide ran fuller at the flood. Now the banks rose boldly in the west. There old towers leered from promontories, a line along the rock like broken teeth. At the mouths of creeks that fed the wash I saw small boats pulled up along the stones. But no men came. If the villages had dogs, the men killed them or drove them to safety in the wood. At night there were no fires. That year the herring tax went unpaid, for the sailors let their pitched keels dry upon the banks and stayed at home, idle and afraid to follow in my path. The sea was cursed, they said, wheresoever I had passed. It may have been so. Either way their children starved for it.

When next I woke I heard the sea waves crashing on the shore. Sitting up, I saw the brave wide ocean fill my sight. I rubbed my eye. It was not a thing I knew. Huge, it rolled in from the world's end or beyond. Panting with exhausted breath, it heaved its thousand torpid arms against the coast, went slack and, groaning, heaved itself again. Yet away from the land it seemed unmoved. My eye sought its farthest boundary. With nothing to contain it, I wondered why it did not drain away. Resting on nothing, yet it held – vast and unsupported, the heaven's mirror. Before it I felt poor and fugitive, no better than those small men who fled from me, leaving their houses in order to hide among the stones. When I breathed again, my breath rasped in my ears like something tearing.

In the afternoon the sky turned heavy, battered by the wind. I kept the great ship moored in the lee of an island at the river's mouth. There all day I sat and watched the harbor town, empty of its folk. Hren was north along the coast, no river journey. In truth, I feared the passage on the open sea, feared it as any man will fear a great thing which he has never done. Then I cursed the river folk. Had they not fled, I would have walked among them and bidden the bravest come with me and man the sails. It was many days since I had seen the shapes of R'gnir and the kings tramping the hills west of the river. By then, I judged, they had turned north themselves. No counsel would I have from them, nor comfort either.

Unsettled, I saw to some small matters on the ship, for I had taught myself to keep the sail lines free and the great ropes coiled. The day wore on. I looked up when I had done. A line of thunderheads had massed above the town, casting purple shadows on the rock. Lightning leapt among the clouds; thunder bellowed but there was no rain. Still the water foamed, churned white as milk within a pail. It was while I was watching, impatient to be setting out, afraid to go, that I saw the webbed brown fingers reach out of the spray, become whole hands with shining nails, reaching because they did not need to grope, knowing from the first where they would find the mooring line. The head came after, old and ugly, pointed, as if pressing against the tide had narrowed it. Its rough blunt teeth were bared. Its harsh breath sucked the air. Sea hair, black and green, clung to its shoulders. Fixed on where I stood, it gave me as deep a glance as I have ever had from beast or man. Then, throwing back its head, it climbed the rope effortlessly and in a moment flung itself upon the deck. I saw then what it was.

He smiled.

'Well met again, my lord,' he said.

But it was not that the beast knew manspeech that astounded me. Crows talk and even boulders grumble. It was that he had smiled. Black leather lips pulled back from yellow teeth. The fierce lips turned. So now and then, when I most hated her, Yllvere had smiled. It was nothing I understood. I would not have been more amazed if at the earth's deep core, beneath the bones of mountains, I had found a stone that bore my name.

The arms were short. Still I took care to stay beyond their reach. The mad wild eyes, like the teeth, were yellow.

'If we have met,' I said, 'I do not know it.'

'Lord, the moon long I swam beneath the river's roof, and now at the sea edge the salt has tangled all my hair. For, lord, until I spied your ship I had not tasted the sweet air since I leapt the wall that rings that city where Ar Elon ruled.' He turned his whiskered head. Where the hair was pulled back and plastered wet against his neck, I saw no ear but only a knob of darkened flesh, much like a seal's. He scratched the place with his shining nails.

'You are . . .,' I started, 'or were,' I stammered, 'Fyris, whose song brought the Steward's anger. Once a man . . . ' But seeing it was so, I stopped.

His sly mouth crooked. 'Who drowned?' The clever undead eyes looked deep into mine. 'The sea knows what shape best suits the things that dwell in it,' he said. 'For myself, as the sea willed, I am what pleases me.'

I shook my head. My pulse beat strangely and my long face burned. I said, 'I have not found that a man might be what he desires.'

Absently he found another place to scratch along his flank. 'Lord,' he barked, the words whistling through his teeth, 'you have forgotten how the gods first pitied Tân and changed him. He was fire and the maid he wanted mist and ice. You know they did not leave him as he was for all men now alive come down from him. We are not pitied less because we are his sons. There is a vessel for all that burns. Out of Dagda's pity. Else the world long since we would have gone up in flames.' An old gentle laugh came from his lips. 'Even the heart of Ar Elon's son, cursed as it was blessed, was not made too small to beat.'

Out of the cramped space in the clouded sky a rain-washed moon gazed down.

'Mark,' he said. 'The moon long I have waited undersea, the wide ocean rotting the shape I wore till I had found another. For I meant to be here when you came, to sail this ship, as you could not, that at the last you should come to Hren.'

From off his shoulder he drew a satchel. With care he opened the flap that sealed it from the sea. I saw the carved neck of a harp. He drew it out and laid it on his knees.

A shadow gathered in his face. The lips, that at first had been open as he thought, now came together in a line, haggard, bloodless. I had seen that look before but could not place it. He shifted restlessly. When he had drawn a breath, he ran a thumb softly across the strings. And then he played, the harp notes wheeling into the night like birds.

Listening, I drew the anchor. He played the song again. Unslackened, persistent, its music filled the bay. The song was as wind to the sails. Like cool air out of the north it filled them. The bow nosed out beyond the skerry, free of the harbor and the empty town. Beyond the headlands the moon rode to our left, silver in the heaven's darkness, green silver in the darkness of the sea.

My life was still. It was the sea that held it, not myself. I had known such times before, when Pendyved took me, when I had looked into the fire. Surely, I felt some piece of my life was coming to a close. I felt it gathering at my back, ready to be cast behind. Yet I was helpless to send it on its way. I studied the *filidh's* face, a man's no longer, trying to guess where his mind was when he played. But he had little time for me. His song consumed him. When he stopped, the great ship floundered. So morning and evening he played upon the strings.

The second day we went beyond the sight of land. I had slept beneath an awning on the deck. When I woke and looked there was nothing but low clouds far off to show where land had been. The third day the sea was all around.

'Why do we come out so far?' I asked. 'Hren lies north and close upon the shore.'

The *filidh* stared out to things I could not see. For a moment he ceased his song. 'If you would live, you must come on it from the west, even as Ar Elon did,' he said.

'The stone kings come by land,' I answered.

'They are already dead,' he replied and went back to his song.

The fourth day he did not play at all. The wind that was not heaven's wind died out. He took my place beneath the awning. Long into the day he slept. Asleep, I grew less certain of the shape of him. A mist had risen about the ship and mantled his features. He was not so small as he had seemed, I thought. From behind the blankness of the mist I heard the droning labor of his breath. Once, when he had turned, an arm fell long across the deck. But of his head, laid back against the mast, whether it too was changed, I could see nothing. The mist withheld it. It was as though I looked into a wall of vaporous wool.

For a long time there was silence. The sea lay sleek and flat as any mountain pond. I ranged the ship. The fifth day dawned without the sun. I leaned, exhausted, against the rail. The eye that I had lost was sick with pain.

Soft drops, thickened from the fog, fell from the rigging. It was so still I heard them splash into the sea. I heard them sink, one drop among the million, one lucid sound in the huge monotonous quiet of the deep.

I was never certain when I slept. Waking, I would pretend that I was backing into sleep once more. The sky held the same gray emptiness whenever I awoke. I prayed for rain, for sun, for darkness, for the whales that lived beneath to rise and batter the great hull with their looming heads.

I reckoned it was three days more.

The first sound cracked the stillness like a goblet broken by a stone. It was distant, yet it seemed to roar. In time it grew still louder in my ears, until I knew it was the crash of waves upon a beach.

The great wave bore me up along the wall and then fell back. The ship ran down into the dip between the water hills. I cried out. For when it rose again – the great mist shredded like a cloth – I saw the rough blue stones of Morrigan. Tall elms ringed the yard. Grieve stood among the others, my sisters, aunts, Vydd bent upon her staff. Yllvere came walking from among the trees, her deep eyes distant and chill as stars. The red gates of morning opened. I looked upon the women of the house.

'Where is Géar?' I asked them.

But when I had said her name she came. Her black hair drifted behind her like a cloak. I held my hands to her but, the sea between us, we could not touch. All I had known of her came back and so I yearned for her. She would not meet my eye. Cradled in her arms she carried a dark-haired quiet child. For a moment, the silence between us hung like a wave.

No, I thought, there is yet no child. It is not long since I left her.

'The water brings me dreams,' I said aloud.

From behind, the brown hand with its black nails had clasped my shoulders, and I turned. The ambiguity of his shape and features had gone, had settled back into the form I had seen on him when first he sprang out of the sea.

'Not dreams, lord,' he said. 'The sea is too big to care about your life or mine. You cannot scar it like the land. Your dreams are lost in it.'

Still I looked straight across to the women, cool under the trees, standing on the emerald grass and looking back. The child woke. I heard him cry.

'Do you not see?' I asked.

He answered bluntly. 'Each man licks the wounds he has,' he said. 'So the tongue comes back to what it cannot cure.'

I waited till the wave had borne me up once more along the wall. The house was so near to me I might have knocked upon the doors. For a moment I came level with her eyes. For that instant I looked into their depths.

'What will you name the child?' I said.

Behind her, small beside my sisters, Vydd, old and bent and leaning on her stick, had parted her dry lips. But only the gray smoke of her pipe came through her teeth. I knew then I would have no answer. She had kept such a secret once before. The deep fevered current of her blood she shared with Géar. I felt my own shared blood grow cold. For if the women of the house were one, so were the men. I had begun to shiver. I knew, like Urien, that now for long years I must seek a name that would not be given. For all it changes, the wise *filidh* only know one song. All men must sing it. I thought of Ar Elon then, for that once without bitterness, knowing at the last that the fathers are as much cursed as their sons.

Beside me the seaman hunched his shoulders, coughed. I pulled my eye away from her I watched. He waited. The wind was fitful between the rough sea hills.

'We have stayed too long,' I said. 'Take up your harp.' He had it waiting.

So out of the west, the open sea, where nothing is but mist and water hills, I came to Hren. So Ar Elon came to shore, over the long blank sea to that same place, though no ship carried him.

CHAPTER NINETEEN

The air was still. The gray sea was quiet as an old woman. Softly, it muttered half-remembered grudges to itself, grudges so old that no man has heard of them.

In the light of morning the walls of the island rose above the sea, a hundred elhws of blue-gray stone. At its crown the oak wood, lifted high from the sea edge, blazed red with autumn. I stared at it with a half-lidded, exhausted eye. The tide was sliding in. I had not slept. The long way in, I had stayed awake listening to the ocean's old complaint and with it, in even measure, the *filidh's* song till they rose and fell together and I scarcely parted them. Yet I knew that gaunt old seaman sang his own deep grief and not the sea's. Drab he seemed and sullen as his song was sad, like some cross and jilted lover. Yet at the last I knew all grief was one. It is the same bare cup whether it has been spilled or never held the wine.

He paused in his thumbing. His forehead wrinkled. He seemed to examine the wedge of land thrust up from the sea. 'That island stood before the land beyond it rose,' he said. 'The trees that grow there grew in the world's first light. Their roots reach down to the oldest darkness that was before.'

The crease in his eyelids pulled as though with some subtle pain. 'Under those old trees, knowing that the darkness gnaws them both, Ar Elon waits and listens.'

The west wind rose as though it meant to drive us on the shore. It stung my cheek. It angered me.

'What does he think to hear?' I scoffed. He felt it in my look. I had heard too many tales and was tired of riddling. Inside each shell was always another shell, no kernel. I had come myself. I meant no more to listen to what any man or bogie guessed or thought. I spat into the sea.

The seaman grunted and looked up at the sky.

'I will put you ashore beneath the wood,' he said. 'There a path leads from the beach. If you can follow it, in time you will find a wall. Within the wall there is a gate such as a man might pass through, though I never heard that any man came back again. If you pass it, you will find a beast your father keeps but which, in his keeping it, keeps him. It is this beast that you must come to, if ever you will look on him or see Ar Elon as he is.'

The seaman hesitated, peering into my face as if only then a thought had come to him. 'Lord,' he said, 'you have lost an eye.'

The old itch welled up in my throat. 'It was my father bartered it,' I said, the old anger new again. 'What was never his he gave to buy his glory.'

There were white birds above the island, crying out. If he answered, the words were lost beneath their cries.

The swells were heavy. Rushing in, they roared when we came near the rocks. A great wave broke above the bow. It swung the ship. The seaman put his hand behind my back.

'Jump,' he shouted and with one motion pushed me. Too startled to take a breath, I fell. The green-black water hissed about my head. Yet my first thought was not for air. Frenzied, I clutched my belt to feel the new-made sword that Géar had given me. At last I felt the pommel in my hand. Smiling then, I gave a mighty kick and rose through spray and bubbled foam.

All was quiet but for the water and the wind. The great ship rested idle beyond the breakers; light as a cork it took the swells. Already its sails were down upon the deck. But the seaman whose work that was had gone. I called to him. No answer came.

Wet and steaming, I walked out on the beach. Sitting on the stony shore where once Urien slew Lot and won his house and all that followed, I emptied my boots. It was not a triumphant coming. Yet there were none to see how the king of the lands between the seas stripped the tangled waterweed out of the greater tangle of his hair. I dug a little yellow crab out of my beard. Sharp as the crab's pinch, a thought came back to me. Even as I came to Hren, so I had entered my father's city, looking more like a drowned sailor than his heir. But then I thought, my rightful inheritance never was the land but rather the whale's deep, weed and yellow crabs. I laughed.

Above the cliff edge, sharp against the heavens, the island's ancient wood reared over me. From those trees, I knew, the charmed wood of the ship was cut. There Lord Ar Elon waited, he that had waked Pendyved from the dead, that had set the stone kings around the Mound at Tinkern, slaughtered barons and built a hall greater than any in the land, its corners posted with the hearts of those that hated him. Among the deeds, remembered and forgotten, both great and small, he found a woman, already wife of a man who followed him, and lay with her. When he had done with her, he never saw her more. I wondered. She herself had said his kingdom on the land was nothing in his mind. Had she been more? By what they were, the Kell would take such matters seriously. Yet I could not think what pressed his thoughts that night he took what gladly she had given him. My heart beat thickly. I wondered if, when I had seen him, I would know his mind. I rose. Standing by the sea edge, I looked toward the wood.

A path ran clearly from the upper beach, winding back and forth into the rock. Well worn it seemed, great boulders cast aside, the sand scraped down to the rock beneath. I thought, they were not men who passed here. For I knew the track of R'gnir and the kings. I did not wait for the sun to dry me, but went then as I was and with some effort came up at last upon the headlands.

Beyond the rock, the air was filled with the whisper of the leaves. Yet this was but the lesser wood, where saplings grew beside great oaks. Whatever grew here, from the first green shoot, was gnarled in the sea wind as the slow years turned. In time each rotted through and fell. Here as in the towns of men were birth and ruin, both gathered in one place. Had I stayed at Morrigan, I would have lived just such a life and gone to death at last like any man. One day I would have dug a pit for Urien's bones. In turn, others, my sons if I had had them there, would have opened up the earth for me. There is no small comfort in that, men say, old men who have learned to smile on Death as women smile at infants in their arms. So I might have been, content to watch my short life measured out. Perhaps it might have suited me had I not, so early, stood above the heads of other men or had there never been in Anu's wood above the house a tree whose black leaves whispered, though never one leaf, not in the world's time, fell.

I left the little mortal wood behind.

Now the bodies of the trees grew thick. Their gray unchanging trunks were hung with tendrils, roped with vines. The path I followed twisted as though it meant to keep out of their reach. No small things grew up beneath their shade. What sunlight filtered through was soft as moonlight, changed. The shifting colors of the earth were muted, silvered, hid. Then even they were gone. I sensed, more than I saw, the steep land rise ahead of me.

When at last I came to it, the wall loomed up like a piece of the dark itself. It gathered there as evening gathers, not built stone by stone; but, rising, it was everywhere at once. Even as I watched it seemed to grow, a high shadow without cleft or stairs, running over the back of the earth to either side. I had no doubt it was the wall the seaman spoke of. Yet he had said a man might find his way beyond it. But everywhere its outward face was sheer, too high to scale. Alone I had no hope to cross it. My eye ran over it but found no end. A man might as well assault the night. For some time I walked along its length. The more I walked, the higher still it reached.

'Though I have sworn it, I see no way to enter here,' I said aloud.

'You have done well enough to come,' a voice beside me said.

R'gnir pulled his rough shape from the wall. The bare earth buckled as he moved. The stone kings followed at his back. Even in the darkness their shadows fell upon my face. Yet little comfort I took from seeing them.

'What good to come at all if it is closed to me?' I said.

R'gnir answered. 'You need only look,' he said and pointed.

In truth at that same moment I made out the two great pillars of a gate. A massive lintel lay above. I skirted the shoulders of the wall and went to it. The gate was ancient, black as iron. It shone as of itself. But some strange cunning had fitted it to the wall. There was no handle nor was there any way I could see to enter it. I turned away.

'It has no latch,' I said. 'Nor are there hinges.'

'Nor need it have,' he said. 'It is Death's gate and so not hard to pass. Since men first lived, more skill was needed to keep this side of it.'

I saw the watchful silence of the kings and was not satisfied. Close by me they muttered to themselves, softly, in a language of their own. 'How may I know?' I said.

R'gnir answered. 'All this day we waited for you,' he said. 'From the morning, as we stood our watch, a thousand passed. You traveled your own way or you would have met them in the wood, lame men and whole, mere girls limping from their beds. Out of Tyre and Imradis they came. From all the broad lands of the earth they found their way. Not an hour gone, the folk of one great town went on before us. The battle at their gates had passed inside. Their blood had not yet dried upon their necks.' His thick old face was sad. 'Fear not, lord,' he said, 'if a man bleeds, he will find a way to enter here.'

'And live?' I said. 'And still come back?'

He dropped his eyes. 'You are in peril. Who is to say that you are not? And yet the one you seek there lives.'

His eyes flashed open. I saw the anger gathered at their backs. 'There is the gate before you, lord,' he said.

Across the space between us I felt his sudden anger move, unchecked and howling. 'Go,' he said. 'But you must swear to kill me when you are done. Swear it or I shall stalk you through the living world. Nor shall I rest until I eat you whole. Nor shall I stop until I've found your heart's deep stem.'

He finished. But there was no stillness. The creatures of his flesh peered out at me. I could not guess the cause. I knew only that it was not just. What was the good of killing him? Had I not seen it? Death never gave back life.

I cried at him, 'How can you give and take away at once?'

His gaze fell hard against my face.

'Who shall ever answer you?' he said. 'There were never answers to the things you ask. At least no answers that a man will listen to.'

'Not everything,' I shouted. 'Just this thing between us: why should I swear to take your life?'

'What would you hear?' he shouted back. 'You take from me that only which I gave.'

But I heard him dimly. There was a roaring in my head. I knew only that I must see my father, that R'gnir, whether dead or living, said he was the way to him. Beyond that little, I could work nothing out.

'Swear,' he cried.

The faces in the stone king's flesh were screaming in my ears. Still R'gnir's voice roared over them.

'I have not promised to go mildly to my death. Your life, like mine, hangs in the balance. Though I am slow to move, my flesh is stone and you will have to sweat to cut my heart.' He laughed. 'What after all is the quickness of a boy to me, a boy but scarcely bloodied and half blind? I at least shall fight with two good eyes.'

Thus Urien had mocked me.

It was his face I saw among the hundred that haunted R'gnir's flesh. His twisted beard was laid like yellow snow upon his knees. Still his eyes were bright. Their hard gaze had not softened. They mocked me yet.

My anger filled me and I swore.

The stone king moved.

In an instant he had placed himself between the posts. The dread dark gate split wide. Then one last time old R'gnir looked on me. The thin, haggard line of his cold lips was parted. Perhaps he smiled. I took no notice. There was a land beyond the darkness of the wall.

CHAPTER TWENTY

The great oaks stood apart. Their trunks were huge, but their height, crowned with many boughs, could not be judged. If the wind rocked their summits, I could not see it from the ground. It may be that in the upper air they whispered, but the words, whether senseless or deep with cunning, could not be heard. Old beyond the world, what they were men little knew. Such wood had Pendyved cut to build my ship. So old they were, men said, that they had learned to listen to the thoughts of men. Who is to say? It may be that they heard the Kell when the shore folk cursed Pendyved for his work. I did not doubt the Kell had seen the huge trees falling.

The land was high. To the east across the strait, the small towns of the Kell lay huddled on the shore. Beyond them, like an outstretched arm, the cloven mountains that I knew fled north as far as sight could reach. Set somewhere among their piled blue stones was Morrigan; above the house another wood. There I had climbed to see the place where now I stood, not knowing then what place this was, nor the long way I would come to it.

I felt the wind upon my face. Sharp as the world's wind, it brought no peace. I waited. If the dead had walked here, as R'gnir said, their dragging feet should have trampled the heather black and cracked the stone. Yet they left no sign. If they had come, they had walked off in the air. I thought, the dead are so many their kingdom must be broader than the lands of earth. It may be that each man has his own place and this is mine.

I walked beneath the trees. No leaf had fallen, but what had not turned gold was red. Late flowers bloomed in the deep spaces between the trees, a few blue spikes, the rest gray bracken. Already the thistles had had their heads blown off.

It is written that I found the oak wood red as blood as though the island were a corpse I had come to hack. The *filidh* make much of that. They would have it that my thoughts were bloody when I first walked beneath the trees.

The *filidh* never thought ill of a man for murder. In truth, death was their trade and murder what they bartered most. Whether in the narrow gloom of a crofter's hut or in a wide king's hall, it earned their ale. Yet, so often told, it may be that mere death grew tame to them, that the old lord slept and the women went about their work unless the tale was warmed with wonders and the cold moon spouted gore.

But that was not the way of it. The corpse I made there was not for the sake of the year's cold turning, nor the color of the oaks. No unexpected frenzy stirred my blood. I killed for the sake of what I was, had always been. No more. We knew it, he and I. The marvels were a part of it, not added on. It is said the oldest wounds lie nearest the heart. I knew the truth of it. The blood I spilled had been running from my birth.

Where the hill rose steeply I found a path. Old work it was, like the roads that crossed our mountain. It ran due west. Although here and there thick roots had broken through the plates of stone, I made my way. It is not for nothing this is made, I thought. The wind trod with me.

Soon, to either side huge chimneys of blue stone rose up. Close to the track the trees were less, but beyond the stone, dark with ivy on their sides, the ridges rose again, and there the oaks held on against the wind.

I listened. There were birds within the rock. In great ragged flocks they had settled there, clambering in each other's way, squawking and fighting for a place to stand. Their rusty voices scraped the air. Indignant, bitter, their cries were filled with old complaints, old oaths against the wind and rock. Their pale beaks shone, quarrelsome and sharp as knives. I bowed my head, meaning not to look at them. Still I could not keep my eye away. The rock was like the rock that made the walls of Morrigan, its harsh stone blue as the very stone that made the stable wall beside the mews. Leather reins were hanging from the wall, saddles piled up in orderly fashion on the floor. I could not think.

'Do you not know us, brother?' the birds called out to me.

My eye turned back to them. Their feathers were grim and black as holes between the stars. Brokenly they rose and beat the air. I knew them not.

'Brother,' they called to me.

I set my teeth and answered stubbornly. 'The crows I knew were women and the women crows. Each one was Anu's and none of mine.'

Two laughed together, set apart. They flew and hissed about my head.

'You named me Ninguh,' the first crow rasped. 'When the snow lay deep upon Géar Finn, I tapped the window till you woke. Cruel the winter was, yet crueler the spell fire was that filled your head.'

I knew him then and stiffened. The other flew up by my ear.

'Ninmir you named me. Before you came to Stephen's Well, I went to it, that ffraw would hear your name. For Ar Elon's sake, he swore to you.'

Once more I stiffened, for my sight had cleared. The shafts of chimneys grew up with the trees so, when I looked, I saw that the towers and the wood were one. Already doors had opened in the oaks. It would not be strange, I thought, to see the cook, her red cheeks puffing, wrapped against the cold, come ambling into the frozen yard to scatter crumbs, the great birds falling to her feet. I sniffed the air. It seemed dark as the deep kitchens beneath the house, thick with the smell of onions, dried cod and oil. Like salt in wounds the memories of Morrigan washed back on me. I turned away.

'Long has it been since last you came to me,' I said.

'Brother, we are dead,' they answered.

The air itself was darkening, closing without a flaw upon itself until the oaks, the towers and the sky that held them all were one. I looked into the dark.

'This is not the place I sought,' I told them. 'Where are the holy wood of Hren and he that rules it?'

The crows came out of the air and sat upon my shoulders. I felt their careful talons on my flesh. Ninmir nuzzled her old beak beside my ear.

'Brother, you have forgotten all you knew,' she hissed. 'Death walks only where the living went. From the hour of your birth His hounds have licked your heels. How could they follow except where you had gone? It is not otherwise. There is but one earth under heaven, whether the sun has risen or the light has gone from it.'

I did not answer. The uselessness of remembering held my tongue. I sought a stranger, Ar Elon, whom I had never seen, not someone I had lost. But this wood was not his wood but Morrigan. These trees were not his trees but towers, their blue stone barren but for the excrement of birds.

'Only tell me where he is,' I said.

Her faint breath rattled. 'You have had my counsel. The dead have no wisdom for a living man.'

I ground my teeth. Like all the Kell, they gave no finished answers but only half-said things that were worse for knowing.

The old anger filled my heart. 'Where!' I cried.

She drew a final breath. 'Upon the hill there is a mere,' she rasped.

'There is a beast that waits you there, that beast he keeps. It has not changed. It may be you can make him answer. Yet, brother, how shall you find what you have sought unless, before you looked, you knew what it could be?'

I swore, but she was done. Her drab wing she had folded across her eyes. She shrank away. So I left her, her scaly head tucked deep beneath her wing so that I would not see the look in her sad eyes nor what they held.

Above the island a huge moon rose. Its rim was broken at the edge, horned and shining. Its light fell cold upon the wood until, the uplands ashen, near white as though with early snow, I could not tell what was moon-silvered and what was frost. The track wound slowly. Comfortless, in my cold hand I grasped the untried sword that Géar had given me.

Sometimes in the silence I fancied I heard a moaning at my back. But when I stopped to listen, it was only the night wind prowling the island from the west. It was gentle but enough, I thought, to fill a sail. I remembered the golden ship that waited on the shore. Tomorrow I would feel that same wind on my neck. Tomorrow, if that is given me, I thought.

In time the trees came to an end. Gaunt and bitten by the wind, but a few bare stumps were left to straggle into the open field. A gray waste stretched before my sight. Scarred and weathered, it hung above the sea. Yet I was relieved. From its borders I saw the shores of all the western lands, the mountains and the mouths of rivers where they poured into the gulf. If the wood below were Morrigan, these at least were not the fields above the house. Truly, I thought, I have not seen such lands before. I did not wait to see if they would change but stretched out my legs as far as they would go.

The land still rose. I climbed the hill until I thought I would come out on the stars, until in the great open places I grew afraid and walked with caution, looking for shadows where I might be hidden. There was a sullen feeling in the air. I shuddered. The hill seemed long as the night itself.

Long after, when the quiet and the blackness lay heaviest upon the hill, I came at last to the high mere's edge. Alone I stood on the stones that ringed its banks. The wind was still. No breath stirred on its waters and yet it shone, pale with its own grim light, as though foul candles burned beneath its depths. The *filidh* say it is no proper mere but a fragment of the ancient sea, left rotting in that place. So it had been, they judged, and would be long after I had gone, the home of churning sea worms and krakens tangled in their silver hair. But when I looked, I saw only that the mere was shining, pitiless and cold beneath the moon.

I was alone. Men I might have brought with me. Yet knowing them, I did not hold them to their promises. Those oaths were hollow. It was my father's blood they swore to. I had my own. Ar Elon. My heart cried out to him, not as a lost child cries for home but as a man, weary with the day, will snuff the candle, daring the darkness, ready at any cost for dreams. But cursed by my half-blindness, so destined always to be surprised, I found its eyes already set upon my face.

It waited in the mere, quiet as the stone that bore it or like a snake upon a stone, scaled, huge, like a thing already dead. And yet it lived, arrogant to hold to life where death had taken all the rest. Slime dripped from its night-black hair. Its flesh was blistered, the thick arms rotting where they sank into the mere, the hands long-fingered, bent, unlike a man's. It had a fish half-eaten in its jaws.

'So we are met,' it called out thickly, my father's beast but not my father. The crows spoke gibberish. The thing that was not a man stared back at me. There was weariness in its old face, and pain. But its mockery was more.

'Fool,' it wailed, 'none passes me. These years I waited, I met the little men that came. One last game they had with me. Now their heads rot separate from the rest.' Then it laughed, its rank head lifted, grinning at the moon. 'Can you tell me you are different from them?'

I did not answer. The hands of all the men I knew had blood on them. I might have said it, but I felt my silence like a nut between my jaws.

'Fool!' it whined and, though it laughed again, it saw my longing. With all my might I pushed the knowledge back. My heart pounded. But my thoughts were lead. Yet even then I must have known. For that brief space it looked at me, something more than hatred or even laughter in its swollen eyes. Then darkness filled them and it sprang.

Like a striking snake it flashed across the mere, its black hands flying to my throat. I felt the hot blood on my neck. In the tail of my eye I saw the white bone sticking out. But when it lunged again I caught the thrust against my sword. Where I hacked it, the old flesh burned, red flames licking out from the wounds. The black flesh fell away like burning rags. There was stone beneath. Then, as I watched, the great black fingers hardened, thickened with its chest and arms until it rose, one thick pillar out of rock. My breath lay in-drawn in my mouth. It was

Lord R'gnir's face it wore. It was the old king's eyes that glittered, cold and red as garnets in its head.

'An oath you swore to kill me, Finn,' it cried and swung its heavy sword across my knees. But, falling, I pulled its craglike shoulder after me. I wrenched it down and slammed my own blade hard against its ribs. The sword recoiled. I heard it fall among the stones. The old king laughed.

'There was never a sword fashioned that would cut cold stone,' it roared. My face white as my knuckles, I turned away.

But it was there.

It edged around, moving like a cat before it springs. It had no ears. Sea hair, black and green, clung to its shoulders. Its rough blunt yellow teeth were bared. He snarled, my father's harper. He smelled of weed and crabs. It seared my thoughts. Amazed, unthinking, I circled with him until against my foot, unlooked-for, I felt the heavy metal of my blade. I stooped to lift it. He seemed surprised.

'What man has given you a sword to murder me?' he barked.

I felt the burning metal that was no gift from him that fathered me. It was a flame that ran beneath my skin, into the roots of my hair, and filled my brain. I sucked the air.

'No man,' I cried, and all at once I felt the darkness, a hardness in me melt. 'She gave it who had no gift from him nor saw his face. No more she had from him than I did.'

My anger, remembered, was like a flame. I would have done with this and all the changing shapes he flung at me, both men and beasts, things already dead, not him I sought.

The seaman sneered. 'Ever there were too many women in this, Finn. The first death was for that. The others followed.'

I meant to speak no more but only to stick my blade in him. Yet I found the words already in my mouth. 'What death?' I said.

'Lot's, whom Urien slew, because his tongue was loose within his head.'

It was one door I had not opened. But it was Urien's, no use to me. He never was my father. When I left the mountain, I was free of him. And yet I raised my head. 'I never heard,' I said, 'the words that got his dying.'

'That thing is done.'

'Yet I would hear them.'

The seaman's eyes were strange and restless in his head. 'Lot swore Lord Ar Elon never came ashore to rule, that he cared nothing for the lives of men.'

My heart was still. 'What made him come?'

'That which brought the ancient Selchie, though the stones of the land are dry and the sun is cruel.'

I shook my head. 'That does not answer what Lot said nor why Urien slew him.'

'He said the truth.'

'What cause is that?'

'Urien did not know that it was so.'

I saw him smile. 'What were the words?' I said.

His eyes were quiet. 'Lot was a little man and often drunk. For three days as they rode toward Hren he had been muttering in his cup. He was of Twyw, his folk the Kell. His wife had left him. That last day, when they reached the island, his cup was filled and so he emptied it. He told the king to crawl back to the rotting sea, to rut with squid and whales or whatever godless thing would have him, only he must leave the women of the land to such as were true men. Himself, he was a little man. But his voice was loud. The people heard him. It was to this that Urien took offense and so – his head.'

The seaman laughed, yet his eyes were cold and sad as the darkness undersea. A blackness twisted in their depths. I do not think he knew me when he sprang. His eyes had yet to find me when he leapt, fixed as they were on the murderous edges of the thing he flung at me. With one great stroke I drove my sword up through his throat and on, deep into the dreadful head. It passed his eyes. But when he fell, I caught him in my arms.

His head, which needed no jaws to speak or eyes to look at me, turned at last to meet my face. The wisps of Pendyved's hair were blowing from his skull. Like leaves before a wind they fell away. My strange thoughts raced. But already the skull had changed, grown flesh again. Wondering, I saw the old bent head of the mage who bore the wood up Ormkill's hill. I felt his gaze. A spasm ran across his lips. Gray and haggard, they pulled back in a smile. So enemy and friend had smiled at me. His breath blew out of him. And still he spoke.

'Now, a little while you shall be free of it,' he sighed. 'Yet you must know the wood grows year by year. When you have grown too huge and black for what springs up beneath, a woodsman . . .'

But after that he did not move. It may be that his life was already gone from him, though it seemed he barely noticed it.

I dragged the corpse up from the mere. The flesh, no mind to rule it, squirmed upon its rack of bones. A new face gathered on the skull, peered out, curious and troubled to be awake, then, vague, slid sideways, fell.

But then another took its place. Men I saw, great kings with distant burning looks, and squinting fools, and sometimes, roused within the graying flesh, the heads of beasts, a sadness in them, gazing out with desperate, cunning eyes. They shifted as I watched them, fretfully, as clouds change in a gale. A few, before their dying took them, I had known.

In death he had my size, the same black hair. I lugged the corpse, the soles of his great feet scoring the ground we crossed, until I had him on a stone. On the high place of the island, the sea at every side, I built a cairn. From the legs I built it, setting each stone with care. Before I placed the last, I looked once more at what lay dead. The flesh was still. I saw at last the years on him, the creases of his neck, the cold gray cheeks. The wind blew from the west and tore his hair, tormenting it as though unsatisfied. Uncertain, it blew into his eyes. But if it found one last spark there, it blew it out.

The dawn came quietly, red above the land. Soon, I thought, I shall go down and close the gate the stone kings watch. But I did not go, and long I sat with quiet, bloody hands. At last, in the stillness, I lifted the ax where he had dropped it and, grieving, set it down upon the face I knew.

Thus ends the first book of the Finnbranch, which is called *Yearwood*. The second is called *Undersea*.

Undersea

PROLOGUE

This is the second book of the Finnbranch. The first book, *Yearwood*, told of the early manhood of Finn, who, when Yllvere gave birth to him, was given no name. His mother and her women were the Kell, of the lineage of the Selchie, the spawn of sealmen and shorefolk. They were witch women, living apart and in dreams in a house called Morrigan on the side of the highest mountain in the North or West. Long after the whiskered and webfooted men left them and went back to the sea the women still pined for them. Finn was the son of the last of the sealmen to come up on the land, but this his mother hid from him along with his name – for the boy was not the child of her husband.

In the month of his birth, in April, Finn went walking in the forbidden wood on the mountain. There he found and climbed the god-tree, Gwen Gildrun, whose vast branches spanned many miles. At the tree's summit a crow pecked out his eye. Though half-blinded, he brought two fledgling crows away with him. Vydd, his mother's sister, stole them and taught them man-speech. From her Finn learned a part of the mystery of his birth. From his mother, in her deep cell under the house, where nightly she kept great fires burning the root of the god-tree, he learned that another child had been born with him, that his mother's dark servant, Tabak, had taken the child. But no more than that would she tell him.

Unsatisfied, Finn set out from Morrigan seeking his birthright. Tabak rode with him. On their journey it was revealed that Finn's father was Ar Elon, once High King of the land. But the old king had abandoned his rule and, in disgrace, gone into hiding. Convinced of his destiny, Finn decided to claim the kingship. Before he could reach his father's court at Ormkill he was taken aboard a ghost ship and swept away out of the world. Finn passed a year among the dead. When at last he returned, he went to his father's hall intending to announce his birthright and claim the rule. There he performed marvels. To many he seemed the very image of the vanished king. Nonetheless, he was not believed. Even his mother, who had come to the hall, would not acknowledge him. Plotting with Thigg, Ar Elon's steward, she tricked Finn into accepting a test of his claim: he must scale the sacred mound on the island of Tinkern and battle the witch who waited there. No man would go with him. Even Tabak, seemingly, left him.

Finn journeyed alone to Tinkern. There he met a girl hiding in an oak; and, not knowing she was the child Tabak had taken, he slept with her. She was Géar, his own sister; and she, thinking he was Tabak and seeking to preserve his life, murdered the witch in his place. Neither knew the fault. But from the first Yllvere had planned it. Now her children would have a son, a sealman like the great men of old, his wild blood unmixed with the coarse blood of the little men who lived on land. He would open the sea road and rule once more the lands beneath the sea.

The first part closed on Hren, an island off the western coast of Finn's kingdom where the dead went to begin their journey to the Other World. Here, Ar Elon, his huge shape swollen and ghastly from too many years on the land, had taken himself to die. He forced Finn to fight with him and, wanting death, permitted himself to be slain. In dying his flesh passed through many changes. New faces, one after another, gathered on his skull, peered out and changed again. A few, before the changes took them, Finn had known. The last face, when death was done with it, was Tabak's.

PART I

Tywy

CHAPTER ONE

The light rose south of the island. The wind, nosing at the rim of the world, uncovered it like the brow of a skull the peat had buried. The grave, great weight of all my lands could not withhold it. Beyond meadow and moor, the blue wall of mountains, it pulled itself free. So stones in winter are thrust above ground; even so the sun rises.

'May your bones lie longer in the earth,' I cried to the corpse of my father. Beneath the cairn of stones that kept him, my father held his tongue.

Along the great hill of the island the dying grasses trembled. Their dry heads, humbled by the wind, leaned toward the mainland and whispered. It had not changed. The grass withers; men die. Gray birds gather over the wood and look southward. Cold-eyed ghosts, their bleak lives snatched too soon, walk out once more onto the windy hills. In the emptiness of their hearts they remember the hail fires and laughter.

'May you stay dead!' I shouted. The gale took the curse and blew it back in my teeth. I did not need to look – the blood was still on the blade with which I had struck him.

Once he was High King, Ar Elon, the lord out of nowhere. From the marshes of the moon he had come to them, from the mists beyond Mhor – the god alone knew – perhaps fallen nine nights from a star. In the beginning there was no accounting. But though a stranger, soon enough he sat at the councils. From his chair he gave judgments, his chair that was so huge that all who came after to sit in his place seemed as children. It little mattered that his voice was stern; the land prospered under his hand; that much, in wonder, men said of him. Like a summer, sang the *filidh*, he had come among men.

But one summer, like any other, soon passes. Sea hair, both black and green, grew again from his shoulders. Thick webs reappeared between his blunt fingers. Too late they saw what he was – his dark flesh ugly in men's eyes, his foul breath smelling of fish. Too late the old men remembered. Once before, the sealmen had come to shore. Still wet from the western ocean, they had walked up on the beaches; naked, they had invaded the towns. There they had taken themselves wives from the lesser folk on the land. Their wise eyes were shining; they had crabs in their hair. But the women, it is said, their heads filled with old tales and longing, went with them eagerly.

One night the young men broke into my father's chamber. With axes they splintered the door at the back of the hall. For the shame of their manhood they meant to butcher him, to pull him panting from the white trembling arms of the girl. He had already gone. So, with no accounting, Ar Elon went from my mother's bed.

So in winter the rains beat down on the roofpeaks; the gale blows incessantly. Then one day the light, without notice, pours out of heaven; the sky, once sweet with disorder, is empty.

I examined the blood on my fingers. My hands would wash clean of his blood. The webs that one day would stretch between knuckles I could cut away. Yet beneath the knife I knew the blood would spurt again, his blood that gave me life and shared my veins, his blood splashing on my wrists and soaking my long arms. I swore, feeling my heart beat hotly, like a stranger I had shut within.

The bracken was trampled where we fought, the merestone littered with matted hair and bone. A few late flies had come out of the air and settled. Soon enough death would have them. Without pity, even the least of things is taken. How then, I thought, shall a man be free of it?

Sadly I handled the sword that Géar, my sister, had given me. The god knows she had not guessed the use I had for it. Her skin was ivory, her hair in shadow as I stood over her, as I drew on my cloak to cover my nakedness. She knew not who I was. Seeing her, what man would have told her?

I went down to the pool where I had slaughtered him. Though I was weary, I saw to my wounds. The dust I washed from my hair and the blood from my arms. The wind waves lapped the bank. They came without ceasing, cold as any of their immense gray sisters in the sea. This did not seem strange to me. When, before the first age, the ocean rolled back from the land, this one fragment of itself was left behind. Here through long ages its bright deep waters lingered, fed of nothing but itself, immune to the drying wind, unwarmed in summer. But though men spoke of it, until I climbed the hill, its place had been hidden.

I knelt at its hard margins, bent from my shoulders, my good eye open. The water flooded over me. For a time my pulse, which had been booming, slowed. Beneath the wind the great soft quiet seeped into my veins. I thought, If a man could but breathe this, would he not forsake the land? So almost, I would myself and let my stewards, whatever their failings, whatever the loss of my own glory, rule in my place. But all at once my chest felt tight.

Gasping, I lay back on the ground. Ar Elon would have been less troubled. But he was ocean born. I had not his magic or his skill. Instead I took the horn flask I carried in my cloak, unstoppered it and dipped it in the pool. Whatever charm the water had to soothe my wounds I meant to take with me. I stood then looking out.

The island lay at the limit of the land, just off the coast. From that high place all the West was ocean. Once, across its vastness Ar Elon rode to shore. I would not look at it. To the east the headlands of my kingdom fell away, retreating league on league toward Ormkill and the hall that in the years which had followed my father raised with his thick hands. Whichever way I looked I found his memory. I strained my neck to watch the heavens. But even there the sun, grown huge, had scorched the sky. Behind it like a length of bloody hair it dragged the clouds, the harsh hills under them smeared red with gore. My wits were frayed and it may be that I ran.

Long after, I came down to the island's eastern side, the beach in front of me. Across the salt grass and the dunes I saw the walls and roofs of Tywy, my mother's holding. The ramparts that closed the yard were set with fires. Smoke poured from the rock. In pale old-ivory wraiths it wrapped the walls, rolled out in angry plumes along the shore. From the sea edge inland, north beyond the dike, it seemed the broad earth burned. But Tywy was at its heart. A hot breath raked my face. It blew upon my rage as wind on coals.

'By Dagda, Lord,' I shouted, 'what right have such men to their lives?'

In truth I hated them who kept the fires, not any one I knew but strangers, my mother's kin. The smoke they made lay heavy as a corpse upon the land. I wished them dead.

Because I had no curragh with which to cross the water, I fastened the sword to my belt and ran out on the lip of land. The grave black water fell on me. But if the sea were cold, I did not feel it. I leapt through the waves with beating arms. Around me I heard the hollow thunder of the sea. Softly, slapping at my sides, it sighed his name.

At every side the water streamed with sand. I pulled myself up once more upon the land I ruled, which was Ar Elon's before it passed to me. The water moaned. The tall waves, sliding back, hissed along the beach like his lost breath. Hearing them sob and gag among the stones, I lifted up my arms and screamed. Gray birds reeled above the land.

Out on the hills three men were walking. Hearing me, they turned aside. With awful sureness they lumbered through the gloom until the smoke curled back from them, I saw their splayed, enormous feet and their heads like barrels and knew I wished no more to look at them. Hair like marsh weeds clung to their skulls; they dragged their arms. At sight of them, my long face blanched with pain.

They did not turn aside. As they came they passed a branch of alder from one to the other reluctantly. The last to hold the branch, when he had come abreast of me, lifted his head and gazed at me beseechingly. A sound like wind on leaves came from his throat; his breath was cold.

'Lord,' he said, 'I know not who you are. But we are brothers. The Mughain, our foster mother, plucked us from the wood and set us here to guard the coast, for none of her own kin would do it. In truth, we do not much care for it ourselves. But, lord, we cannot let you pass.'

I knew that tears were streaming down my face. I drew my sword.

The second gray man took the branch. The smoke behind him blotted out the land. Now it blew around his knees and shoulders and tangled in his hair.

'Though barely we have life ourselves,' he said, 'for the Mughain when she found us had but one breath to blow our souls to life, yet the land we guard was made for living men. Into his kingdom, lord, we may not let you come.'

In my eye, the *filidh* say, was sorrow beyond telling. The third man saw it. Desolately he took the branch. He held it trembling.

'Lord,' he said, 'the Mughain's house is poor. Her cattle all are barren and every woman is with child. No man would have them as they are. Her beer is sour. Even the benches in her hall are rotted through. Lord, we pray you, go back to the sea. Among the living there is no welcome for the dead.'

I meant to think of something else. But Ar Elon came into my mind. I saw his face as it was when life had left him, the flesh already cold, the flat eyes still. 'I am the king of this land that you would keep me from,' I cried.

'Ar Elon, lord,' he whispered and fell down humbly to his knees. He did not know the fault. It was enough I knew it. My anger opened like a wound, poured out; and reason fled with it. Already I had raised my hand.

With one quick stroke I took the head. Dully it bounced among the stones. The second I gave no time to howl. Before he found his strength my sword cracked through his shoulder, rent the woody flesh and came out stainless in the air. He crumpled, a pool of water dripping from his side. The last man scrambled, ducked among the rocks and ran. I lunged for him and grabbed his hair. I threw back the shapeless head so that the throat was bared. He saw the bright sword come at him. When it tore into his chest, he clutched the blade and wept. Again I thrust the metal in. He fell, his raw lips black with pain.

I turned to look elsewhere, to clear my head, and saw at my back the first man, his neck a foaming stalk, the second, trailing one grim arm behind him, rise from their haunches. They stood upright, the sea in back of them. Unwearied, wailing as they came, they ran at me and caught me in their arms, pulled at my legs and gouged my eye. Once more I brought my sword against a skull, high and upward from the shoulders. With ease I flicked it from its neck. But when I stepped too near the head, it set its teeth, undaunted, in my heel.

From one hour to the next I kept at that work. Their blunt black fingers snapped; before my fury their chest split, their long arms opening to piny, resinous veins. But whatever I hacked and tore shook itself and twisted back to life. My nostrils quivered and my eye grew wild. Yet I gave myself to the madness willingly. Then like cordwood they were cut apart, fell into pieces; but on the ground they healed. Among the stones, inexplicably they gathered root and fingers, pulled up their black old heavy arms, mounted to their brown strong knees and stood. I flailed at them, but Death, though it had dispatched Ar Elon and would take me when it could, would not have them. Wherever I turned it seemed only that I drew more dreadfully within their grasp. At every step they blocked the way, massed tall in front of me. Overshadowed, I could no longer see the sky. And yet my anger raged.

Evening was near; a dull mist crossed the ground. Still we fought. But now, more surely, I saw the sorrow in their darkened eyes, eyes set like thick brown amber in their mossy heads, a thatch of leaves and broken twigs bent over them. A second time that day, now at the close of it, my pain unspent, I raised a cry. Then for one clear moment my sight, which had been sunk in the gloom of carcasses and severed limbs, was lifted over it.

On a hill outside the town I saw the women of Tywy assembled, their hair unbraided, their garments dropped about their feet. Their rosy breasts they lifted in their palms. Out of the midst of the women one of middle years walked down to me. Like the rest she was naked. The copper hair that fell to her shoulders was streaked with gray. Her own full breasts she had thrust out, white in both her hands. She called out something. Staring, I did not hear the words but turned aside, confused, my anger withered.

I dropped my sword. Still the women murmured fearfully. From their backs a company of men crept forth with ropes. But I had shut my eye and did not see them until I felt their panicked fingers on my arms. Thick ropes crossed my shoulders, pulled up sharply through my legs. I groaned and when they yanked the line, I fell. The ground came up at me.

When I saw again, twisting my neck around, I looked out on the broad dark plain that rimmed the town. As far as I could see the land was one vast ruin of splintered wood, the branches smashed and scattered, whole great trees uprooted and strewn upon the ground.

I shifted and saw her copper hair as she stood over me. She had raised a sheath so that her breasts were covered. I saw the shrewdness in her proud gray eyes. Her hand brought quiet. The people waited.

'From this time and forever this place is holy,' she called out clearly. 'For in one day he cleared a grove one league on every side. Nor has any man done such work since our mothers' mothers embraced the seal-lords here on this same shore. Then this wood was planted. Since then it stood. But in one day this new lord cut it down.'

I meant to stand and answer; the words were in my mouth. Straining, I had crawled up to my knees. Though since the morning I had labored, I had not lost my strength. But when I found my legs, a sudden weariness sucked at my heart. I felt it rising to my head, glowing until the earth was all one whiteness and there was nothing I could do but close my eye.

Slow blood was weeping from my wounds. I tried to move but, stiffened after sleep, I found that I could barely lift my head. My shoulders knotted, I lay in the darkness, my broad back deep in a rug of skins someone had spread along the floor.

Below the grate the fire breathed fitfully; now mostly coals, it gave no light. I listened. As far as I could tell, the room was empty and the household slept. The guards, if any had been called to keep the watch, waited beyond the doors, careless or themselves asleep. My mind wandered. Grown restless, I felt the stillness more sharply than my wounds.

I was alone. Even when I left Morrigan, when I sought no man's company, it had been with Tabak riding at my back. Then, though all the rest of Bede deserted me, I gathered Ceorl and kept him. In time even ffraw, despite his older loyalties and his fears, came into my service. Their rough hands they gave in friendship as much as fealty. Now I had neither. In Ormkill, across the land, they shared the king's chair in my place, so far away it seemed no use to me. A king needs his companions by him; they give him balance and, if it comes to that, there is always someone there to bind his wounds.

I bit my lip and thought. The pink coals blackened. Through the louver in the roof a single dazzling star peered down at me.

It was some time before I noticed the carving on the wall. By then, though I could not distinguish faces, I saw clearly enough that they were figures of women, slender but of a size and roundness that, if cold rock could breathe, they might have lived. With aching pain I moved my head.

They stood, as in a procession, posed along the wall. In their arms they carried baskets but in the hand of one there was a scythe. Each face was turned; the profile cut in deep relief. With my eye I followed where they looked. Set back in the farthest wall, the image of stone rising out of stone itself, I saw the ragged cliffs of Hren, tall above a thrashing sea. From that bleak shore I had come to Tywy, my mother's holding. Here where I was, among the women, she had lived before Urien, in the years that came, brought her as a bride north to Morrigan.

I thought, I am in a shrine. The thought rose blackly in my mind. I knew it was a holy place, that some women's rite was mirrored on the wall. Once more I tried to read the faces in the dark; but the carvers had put no thoughts into the stone. I moved my good eye over them. One shadow, rounder and taller by some inches than the rest, blinked. She turned her slender neck to look at me. I heard the warm sigh of her breath.

'My lord,' she said, 'are you at peace?'

I stared. It was all I could do to move my head. She waited. 'Tell me who you are,' I said.

She smiled back tolerantly. 'I am the Mughain. They were my liegemen who brought you here.'

I looked more closely at the dark to see what other shapes it hid.

She shook her head. 'I sent them out. It was not fitting that you should find armed men when you woke. Nor was it safe. Myself, I took your sword.'

She stood out from the wall. During her long watch it seemed the very dark had melted with her flesh; she shivered now to drive it off. Even then it clung to her – huge, opaque, stirring up behind her gown. Thickening and reaching out, it was like nothing else except the churning fumes that smothered Tywy. Through such smoke, her foster sons had come to me. Until that moment I had forgotten. But now I saw again the havoc on the shore, the terrible moving wood, the stark black-fingered arms, frenzied and grasping for my life.

'I saw no wood,' I cried out suddenly. 'Not at first, not at any rate from Hren nor even on the beach when I had crossed the strait.'

The Mughain smiled. Her pale lips parted slyly. 'This is the cause of it,' she said. 'We built our fires with wet green logs. And when we had no more of them, with the linen of our beds and at the last with the beds themselves, all soaked in brine. Had there been need of them, we would have burned the houses and the barns or, with all else lacking, the stout ships resting at our wharves. So the smoke we made lay heavy on the ground, rolled out into the wood and covered it. When you came to shore, you knew not what it was and in your anger battled with the trees. This we did so that you would spend your wrath before you came to us.'

My brow had furrowed. Her strange sad gentleness puzzled me. I said, 'Yet you did not stop at that but met me there with all your women, your robes undone, your garments at your feet.'

As though reminded, she pulled her gown more tightly around her breasts. She said, 'So enormous was your rage, though the wood was broken, that I saw your anger had not cooled. I called my women. Those whose shame was too great we held. The boldest stripped the others until, young and old, as the goddess made women, we stood in front of you.'

I listened but it made me wonder. 'Lady,' I said, bewildered, 'how was it that you knew my rage and set all this before me?'

'Be patient with us, lord,' she said. 'It is your peace we crave.' Once more she shivered. Had it not been for the darkness I was certain I would have seen a patch of color flame her cheeks. Surely it was in her voice. 'Once,' she answered softly, 'there was a man the like of you, taller than our men ever were, walking up alone out of the sea . . .'

I knew the name but would not say it. I felt her watching.

'Woman,' I cried out fiercely, 'such men are dead!'

But already she had crossed the floor. I felt her round arms suddenly, warm against my neck. I dug my head between her breasts. My great hands raked her hair, pulled at it until she sighed. I knew it hurt her. Yet through the night, as a mother rocks a child, she held me gently as I wept.

CHAPTER TWO

I did not hear the endless long winter roaring of the sea nor did the shock of morning sunlight awaken me. When, late in the afternoon, I stirred, I was alone. For some hours more I kept to that place. Outside the window the sky had turned a brownish black. Hail rattled the thatch. No one came. In time the storm drifted away to the south. I rose and looked out. The long vista of the beach was a dull, cold silver; the sea was still.

I knew little of maps, not in those years. I thought only, I am here at the sea edge; all that is land and east is mine. To this day that thought comes back to me. I gazed across the shadows lengthening on the floor. By then any stableboy in Ormkill knew better than I what I was heir to.

The wide pillared hall was empty of furnishings. The hangings had been taken from the walls, gone, they let me know soon enough, to feed the fires that had saved them from my wrath. I did not doubt that there were some whose thin old fingers had dyed the threads nor that others there had stitched the winding colors to the cloth. They knew the loss but did not grumble. What fare they had they put in front of me. The Mughain had filled my cup herself. It lay neglected now where I had pushed it, unmindful of courtesy, beyond my reach. Her proud mouth straightened.

'No,' I answered stubbornly. 'Fifteen winters she kept him by her, tethered at her door, bound there like any of her hounds – no more than that. Surely not a king, not even a man, just a brachlet that did her bidding.' I looked around. 'Yet can any tell me that in all that time she had not guessed?'

The Mughain's chair was set up on a dais at the far end of the house, beyond the hearth. Her mouth was pinched. Sometimes, it seemed, she found it hard to look at me. Once more her face, uncomprehending, drew taut beneath her brows. The lame hag, Cerridwen, stood at her back. She mumbled to herself or to the Mughain. Strands of her iron-gray hair lay wet against her mouth; her old woman's arms were blackened from the fires. At their feet, holding the Mughain's footstool, a young girl lifted her pretty head. Her yellow hair fell forward. Puzzled, she shook it back.

'The seal-lords take whatever shape pleases them,' she said impatiently.

The Mughain bent above the girl. She touched the girl's long yellow hair and smoothed it. 'He is young yet for a king,' she answered her.

But the girl stirred, unsatisfied. 'He is tall as those old lords. He swam the strait from Hren. Nor has any man done that.' Her look grew thoughtful. 'It must be that a man learns something being dead.'

Cerridwen laughed. 'Child,' she said, 'he is all the younger for it then. For how can any man find life again except as a babe?'

So for some minutes the talk went swiftly back and forth, ignoring me. Listening, I felt my anger drive within my veins. 'I was not dead!' I shouted.

In the back of the hall the men of the holding, not wanted at the hearth, gave up their muttering. One or two were fussing with their arms. I heard the metal slip out from the sheaths, the buckles rattling. Among the Kell the women keep the mysteries and the rule. But even to those without authority some truths are never welcome. The Mughain saw it. Her bold eyes slapped a warning on the faces of her kin.

'Of my own will I brought him to my house,' she told them sharply.

But a man had risen from his bench. He got up slowly, letting all who cared watch him see the knife that he was dragging from his belt. Still, he knew what he did. Beads of sweat had broken out on his old brow. 'Lady,' he said to her, 'we are not children that you can disregard us.'

The Mughain cast him an evil look but it did not dissuade him.

'Myself,' he said, 'when Mabon died, my sister's son, I laid him in the coracle. I rigged the sail myself and pushed the small boat into the sea. Then swiftly as a tern it sped away to Hren. Nor was it long before its ribs lay broken on the rocks. So Duinn gathered what was his.' The man looked down. 'These nine years I have mourned the boy. Yet I am not a fool. If I saw him now, even if he cried to me, I would not rush to take the rotted flesh back in my arms.' He glanced at the Mughain, then at his brothers. 'Let the dead stay dead,' he added loudly. His old hands were trembling.

I ground my teeth. 'There was a man I left there. He was dead. But as I am I came away.'

From the dais Cerridwen grinned. 'What does a man know?' she asked the air above her head. She waited until some shape that seemed to have gathered there had gone. When at last she found my face, she grunted softly. 'Three deaths you shall have, my lord,' she said. Her eyes, watching me, grew hard with cunning. 'A day is coming when you will be given to the fire. But that is not enough. Another day is coming, worse than the other, when the sea that cradled you will suck out your last breath. Then all the waters of the earth will fall on you.' She stood upright, no longer leaning against the queen's chair. The blood had pushed up into her white face. 'So much will come,' she whispered darkly, 'as surely as you are born of woman. But the sword that waited from your birth to strike at you has done its work.'

If she had more to say, I did not care to listen. So I laughed. 'Is this the best wisdom of the Kell?' I asked. 'Is this a corpse you see in front of you?' It was to Cerridwen I had spoken. The Mughain answered. Her face was gentle, amusement bright in her eyes.

'Has any man, even a king, brought one life from the womb?' She shook her head to show that this was foolishness. The women smiled. 'How then can any man know what is taken when life vanishes?' Her lips, turning at their edges, smiled. A woman's smile. 'You are not different. What you left on Hren you will not have again.'

I stood rigid, my every muscle fixed on her. So it was I did not hear the quick hard scrape of boots along the floor. The knife, unlooked for, sank into the thickness of my back. I swung around. The man, his face twisted, had stumbled to his knees.

Clumsily I groped for the handle of the blade. Without thinking I found the grip and pulled it out. The bright cold metal glittered of itself, dry, unbloodied, as though the knife had been driven into sand.

Cerridwen stamped her small lame feet. 'That death,' she cried, 'you have had already. Twice you cannot die of it.' I turned away.

The men of the holding had scrambled back against the doors. Fear sucking at their throats, they made no sound. But the Mughain had lifted her white arms and screamed at them. All watched her. Only the girl at her feet had turned to stare at me. Her thin breasts rose and fell beneath her gown. If she had meant to speak, there was no need of it. Her heart was shining in her eyes.

The next morning the man was taken to the yard. There, after they had strapped his legs, they strung him headlong from a post; but it was the women, standing back a score of paces, who cast the spears. He was not young. His hair was grizzled, his beard hoary and untrimmed. What little strength he held to left him quickly and he died. They left him hanging for the birds – a sign to the men of the holding – but no birds came. When, late in the day, the clouds massed above the land, they cut him down. Sadly, his brothers bore him to the shore. Huddled over him, muttering to themselves, they laid him in the boat. For a time I watched them. Out of the southeast a stiff breeze prowled the coast; still I do not know whether it carried him across to Hren. Long before he would have reached the rocks, I walked away.

South of the island the headlands tumbled back, fallen into mounds of starved brown grass, mussel shells and stone. Here through detritus and broken hills the river from which the holding drew its name had chiseled a deep channel in the rock. Gathered from the scarps and scarred, steep shoulders of the nearby peaks, its current never slid through low soft bottomlands but rushed with ceaseless fury toward the gulf. No desolate islands stood in the river's path. Each spring the wharves that lined the banks were washed away; the men rebuilt them wearily, with curses, I thought, as much as timber. But I did not know this then and only saw how the piers were dragged out on the beach.

Brooding I went along the bank. In the brisk wind the ships were tugging at their lines. I saw how small they were; only one had more than a single mast. I did not wonder that Pendyved had laughed at the men of Tywy. Their small ships never sailed beyond the sight of land. Their service, had the Mughain offered it, would have proved of no great worth. The rivermen of Abereth and Elderwyn, knowing little, would have known as much about deep water. They at least were accustomed to having kings over them and would have followed me more readily. But I put the thought away. From where I was, even hell, I knew, was closer at hand than Abereth.

As I walked on and had gone beyond a spur of land where the shore was hidden, cut off by the hills, I saw the girl who had held the Mughain's footstool. She was sitting high up on a boulder, her knees drawn up, and looking down at me. Though against the cold she had wrapped a worn brown shawl about her shoulders, the rag did not keep her from trembling. Her gray eyes flickered, shifting as though uncertain whether I would stop and speak with her. She need not have been troubled; I had had enough of my own company.

I climbed up among the boulders, out onto the bare rock where she sat like a gannet. 'Why do you wait here?' I asked. 'The Kell are gathered on the beach to watch Lord Duinn take back the dead.' But her thoughts like burrs had stuck to something else. Her chin lifted.

'There will be another,' she said soberly. 'And if he cannot drive you from the hall, another after him. I know them, lord. They will not tire of it.'

She watched me silently. In her nearness I felt a deep uneasy strength, slighter, I thought, than the Mughain's but real nonetheless and, in a way, more disturbing. Something dragged at my memory, my skin prickled and, though I did not know what to make of it, at first I did not answer.

She was no longer quite a child, yet her skin was smooth and white as beach stones, in places nearly transparent. The fine small veins were blue as bruises underneath. Her brows, yellow like her hair, had knitted together. But when I did not rise to go, she smiled.

'I am their king,' I said. 'In time, perhaps, they will learn to swear to me.' She heard me out but answered proudly.

'Here the Mughain rules as her mother's sister ruled before.' Slowly she let her gaze run over me. 'As I shall rule when she is dead.'

I was surprised but mastered it. 'May you have a strong hand then,' I said not unkindly, knowing it made no difference, that whatever their custom I was king. 'And more luck,' I added, 'than I have had.'

'It was never luck the seal-lords had,' she said, 'but the great old power forged beneath the sea.' Her eyes were fixed on me with quiet certainty. 'You cannot hide it. We were not sleeping when you cleared the wood.'

My patience went. 'Some were sleeping,' I said, 'or else gone off somewhere sharpening their knives.' With cold anger I took hold of her arms. 'What power is it that no men fear?' I asked, 'that cannot keep even old men from meaning harm?'

She murmured thickly and looked away. 'You cannot rule what is not yours,' she said.

Whose she thought, it was plain enough. But then, I thought, she is the Mughain's; it is best she deal with it. I let my breath go out of me. She dropped her head.

'And what is mine?' I asked her finally. The color mounted in her face. Still, she did not need to think.

'The land that is not land.'

I laughed. 'So you would have me king of whales and fishes?'

Her face, unprepared, seemed honestly surprised. 'Is that not the world's first kingdom? Cerridwen says it is, the first and perhaps the last that there will be. No little thing. More certainty than the few poor acres of stone the women hold at Tywy.'

It may be that I saw the truth in that. I said, 'But I have never been there.'

'Lord?'

'Not to the deepest halls,' I said. 'And all I know of them I have only heard the *filidh* whisper after wine.'

Some thought of hers had deepened in her eyes. 'Then you must go yourself and see.' Her brows flickered upward. 'You mean to go.'

Perhaps it was a question. I was not listening. I felt my hands spread on the rock, its surface cold as the waste of water hills, felt it moving, cold and dark, endless beneath the shifting sky. Once more out of memory the vague insistent waves leapt against the shore of the island. In the blue, still shadows of the trees, Géar, my sister, lifted up for me the child that was still waiting to be born. I heard his cry. A strange, sweet urgency plucked at my thoughts. Almost I would go. But then I thought, when I saw the island, the harper manned the sails. In Tywy I had no crew nor, in truth, any man to do me service. The stone bit into my palm. Suddenly my heart grew bitter. I said, 'Will eagles fly down from your hills to carry me?'

Her mouth, I saw, had crooked into a smile.

'We have seen the ship,' she said triumphantly. 'Three days before you came to us we saw it, riding the western ocean, shining in the darkness like a star.' Her eyes were bright and held me. 'By that, as of old, we knew a seal-lord had come again.'

But I had had a stomach full of the awe these women felt because a man stood over them. I stiffened, facing her.

'You waited here for me,' I said, to speak of something else, 'knowing I would come.'

She stopped. Her jaw dropped. 'I saw the look you had when the women threw their spears,' she said. 'When you turned away, I saw the path you followed and I ran ahead.'

'What do you want?'

'To look at you.'

We stood. Uncertain of what should then be said, I left the rock and turned back toward the river. Along the way she kept close to me, within my shadow so that as we walked my left hand for a moment brushed her yellow hair. It was a moment before I found my voice.

'Forgive me,' I said, 'but I do not know your name.'

'Yllvere,' she answered simply.

No man is born hating the gods; in time it comes to him. But I was young and slow to learn. Hearing her, I smiled. 'I had not thought that name was much in use among the Kell,' I said. But the wind was cold; it blew between us. 'My mother –' I began but the wind went on grumbling and I let it go. When we reached the river, she ran, not looking back.

*   *   *

The hall was set on high ground and reached by steps. None of the works of men is measureless; and as such things are counted this work was only passing old. Still, I doubted whether among the women there were any living who had watched these gray stones lifted into place, surf stones and channel boulders hauled out slippery from the bay in summer, then strapped to sledges of winter cartage up the snow-smoothed hills. Little had been quarried on the land. The masons wanted searock. In places a delicate crust of bleached white shells still patched the stone; on others, vague impressions skittered mysteriously as though webbed small feet or fins had somehow briefly touched there and gone. In all, nine towers, like bluffs above high water, held the walls. Three jutted black and bare along the northern face; another three, their rough sides hidden by creeping stems and leafless ivy, rose from the cart road in the south. The last, as beautiful as they were precarious, coiled with their outer stairs about the threshold up to uneasy heights. I gawked at them.

It must be that the Kell thought they had built grandly – perhaps a seal-lord's keep, the memory of something once glimpsed shining undersea. But for all its splendor, the work was crude, the rock porous and pitted with sea worms. It ill fitted a stormy coast. Two of the towers I saw plainly were already crumbling. Huge, sliding gaps had opened between the stones. Trusting to night whispers and sailors' mutterings, the Kell were not revered for their skill as masons. Still, it may be they did not see this as a failing. The women, at least, believing the old tales, had never looked for permanence upon the land.

I mounted the cracked stairs warily. The doors stood open. The wind, tugging at my cloak, swirled around my legs and went on before me. It almost seemed as if the pillars, groaning, edged apart. The wind rubbed by them. One of us, I thought, will one day bring this hall to ruin.

The hag Cerridwen waited by the door, soot in her hair, her arms still blackened from the fires. She looked up when I passed.

'Lord,' she said, 'it is time I bathed your wound.'

But my mind was on the girl and I answered sharply, 'You have said yourself it would not harm me.'

'I have said you cannot die of it.'

With her small hand she took hold of my sleeve and, leading me, she hobbled toward the hearth. A high oak table had been pulled before the fire; on its back a wide basin had been set. Two housewomen waited at the side, one with a white water crock, the other with a pile of fresh linen neatly folded in her arms. When I came near them, they curtsied but their eager faces never left off watching me. Without a word to either, Cerridwen took the crock.

'You will have to sit,' she said to me, 'or I shall never reach your back.'

She looked over her own bent shoulder, then called out brusquely. Before the wall where the spears were kept two men were huddling by themselves. They shrank back hearing her. Yet after a moment, mulishly, they found a bench and brought it out. The scabbards hanging at their belts were empty. They did not speak but dragged the bench before the fire and went off quickly.

'It would seem,' I said, 'the Mughain no longer trusts her word to keep the peace.'

Cerridwen's hair was thin as the trails of smoke that coiled from the fire. As always she was frowning. 'What peace can there be among such men?' she said.

'I have not wronged them.'

'It is enough they have to look at you.'

My lips drew back. 'I see no fault in being who I am.'

She laughed and shook her head. 'You have faults enough. Yet they have not seen them. When they stare at you, it is only their own smallness that fills their eyes.' She laughed again grimly and poked at the cinders dying in the grate. 'But once, my lord, it was only women's tales they lived with.'

'And now?' I said.

'They see more clearly what they are not.'

Such talk, I knew, gained nothing. I ignored her. But since the bench was low, there was no easy place to rest my legs. I pushed them out and, settling myself as well as I could, I pulled the longshirt up from my shoulders. Where the knife had entered the flesh was tender; the touch of the cloth inflamed it more. Cerridwen saw me wince; but when she had filled the basin and gathered a swath of linen in her hands, she gave no thought to it and scoured the wound with all her might. I bore it while I could but then cried out.

'Your years have taught you little skill,' I snapped. 'I would rather take the wound again than have you heal it.'

She dropped the linen. 'Yet it must be done,' she answered spitefully.

'Then find a maid with gentler hands.'

She stepped back where she could watch me. Her sour look gave way to something like a smile. 'I shall call her, lord,' she said. Then swiftly, despite her limp, she scurried off across the stones.

I waited with the housewomen. By then a dozen more had swarmed into the hall, their white arms laden with cups and trenchers. Red sides of meat were hauled in to be hoisted onto racks above the fire. Stirring and chattering, the women might have been a band of soldiers, weighed down with spoil, home from wars. But I had lingered by the hearth and they hung back, uncertain, and began instead to whisper back and forth among themselves. The two beside me hovered, waiting.

'What is the name,' I asked, 'of the girl Cerridwen went for?'

'Which, my lord?' said the woman nearest me. For something to do, she scratched her neck.

'The one,' I said, 'fairer than all the Mughain's women, who held her footstool.'

She turned indignantly. 'Yllvere,' she pouted but added nothing. Indeed such a heavy silence fell on her I almost doubted that she spoke. Still, I pressed her.

'And were there others?'

'Lord?'

'With that same name?'

'Now?'

'At any time,' I said and swore, 'in all your memory, back twenty, thirty years.'

She smoothed her own fair hair; her eyes were blank. 'Lord,' she said, 'I would have been no more than a child.'

'It is not,' I said, 'so large a holding.' My voice was cold. It slighted her. I said, 'You would remember.'

Yet she would not and shook her head and glared at me.

'Once,' I went on bitterly, 'there was another child, here in this same holding, a girl with yellow hair. . . .'

She looked away.

Along the wall, where only now the lamps were being lit, a door pushed open. With strange relief I met her eyes. Her feet made no sound on the floor. She came quietly, nervously refastening the brooch that held her gown. Sensing her urgency, the housewoman stepped aside. The rest were quiet; but at the hearth the gray-lipped servant, not wanting to seem idle, gathered a load of wood and, muttering beneath her breath, tossed it at the coals.

The dry wood, long kept indoors, caught at once. A bank of flames roared red against the walls. Then all at once the faces of the women, that had looked pinched and drawn with winter, bloomed. They stirred and twittered; startled by the flames, one or two cried out. But Yllvere seemed to draw some strength from it. She looked unblinking at the coals. Her arms and throat took on their color; her flesh turned crimson until it seemed her heart, grown suddenly too large, would burst. She looked at me. High against my chest I might have lifted her.

'Child,' I said, 'what year is this?'

She did not answer. Her nearness burned. I shut it out.

I said, 'Who rules in Ormkill?'

She looked perplexed. 'Surely, lord,' she said, 'you know him. The *filidh* say yourself you named him steward, Thigg, your own man. . . .'

I waited. So I have seen a man gored by an aurochs walk away. Only later his friends went after him and found him dead outside the wall, the flies already settling on his eyes. For a time she hesitated. Then, not knowing what was wrong, she took the linen. I felt her hands on me, fevered, awkward, slipping down. She was surprised when it offended me.

'Send the women back,' I ordered.

Thoughtless of any shame, she protested. 'It is near the time for serving, lord,' she said. 'Shortly the men will come and all the women.'

But she saw my anger. Reluctantly she gave the word and one by one the women went. I saw then how she steadied herself, how despite her confusion and doubt, her quick gray eyes had fixed on me. Even so, we were alone before she took a breath. She shifted nearer, one hand resting lightly on my shoulder, ready to be snatched away. But with the other she found the wound and worked at it. It stung. When I swore, her fingers stiffened.

'Lord,' she said, 'I do not understand. Cerridwen said you asked for me.'

In the fire-warmed air her hair clung damply to her neck. Straightening unhappily, she pulled it back. I grieved to look at her.

'It is not the wound,' I said.

The small muscles of her throat moved soundlessly. 'Just tell me what you want,' she said when she found the words.

I shook my head.

A pang of sorrow caught her throat. 'Lord,' she murmured but her breath went out of her. I held her eyes.

'I do not understand,' she said once more, her dry voice quiet, hurt. 'I have watched you since you came,' she said. 'First when you walked out of the bay and later in this hall when Cerridwen spoke and then once more when we were talking by the river and you asked my name. All the while I tried to think just what you wanted. Each time I looked at you.

But still, my lord, I do not know. How can I?' Her head moved jerkily. 'Your face so changes when I look.'

I knew the words. Reaching out, I touched her sadly, gently, on the corner of her mouth.

On Géar Finn, I thought, the first snow has already fallen. The nights grow long. Soon the boy, never meant for life, will be laid squalling in his mother's icy bed. By morning he would have been strangled. Remembering, though I had not seen it, for it was only servant's talk, I thought: Now it cannot be more than a few months longer – perhaps in the spring when the great rains stab the ground. Then Urien – not the man I knew, not even the man I remembered but Urien nonetheless – will ride down from his mountain, from the house and lands that Ar Elon had ceded him. It was six days' journey to the coast but at last, prancing and impatient, his war-horse would canter lightly across the sand. The sea air would be still and heavy. Ahead of him, out of the fog, he would see the nine uneven towers of Tywy, the women's holding. The horse, the servants had told me, was a gelding. But Urien, his hair still black, his beard like wet dark wool, was still a man.

Her lips were soft. Under my hand I felt them harden.

'Child,' I said, 'though at first I did not know you, you are the same.'

The doors were bronze and fitted with iron. When the Mughain threw them back, they rang. The air stirred back of her, fluttering the rich embroidery of her winter gown. Her fine red-copper hair fell in a disheveled mass about her shoulders. Away from the fire her face was white. The cold still clung from her crossing the outer yard. Seeing us, she stopped. I saw her anger.

'Why have you sent the women out?' she cried.

Yllvere glared at her.

Let in once more to jar the pillars, the night wind swept on by us and pounced upon the flames. The sparks flew to the ceiling. But in the grate the fire blazed red as women's blood, terrible and triumphant as the open womb. Cerridwen had not been mistaken. As far as the women saw, it was a corpse that stood in front of them. I thought: she never once asked the name of the man I killed. I clenched my teeth. The fire ate at my memory as rust eats iron.

'Lady,' I said to the Mughain, 'tell me who you say I am.'

Her hard small eyes found no comfort in my face. 'Why do you play with me?' she asked suspiciously. 'From the first I welcomed you. Against the warning of the men of my own house I brought you in, though in your rage you would have slaughtered us.'

229

The worm of smoke that covered Tywy woke in my thoughts. White as death it reached out from the holding. I said, 'It was the fires I hated. Those who made them, I wanted dead.'

It made no sense to her. 'But, lord,' she said, 'it was the fires that saved us.'

Yet I could look ahead as she could not. 'Who is to say? It may be death would have served them better.' My long shadow lay across her gown. Her head was tilted back to look at me. A sudden flush had risen near her eyes; it left her puzzled.

'Why,' she asked, 'should it seem strange to name you to yourself?'

I took her hand. I had known its touch when she was old. I said. 'You have not answered.' Because she was afraid, I drew her nearer.

Abruptly as a girl she smiled. If Yllvere stared at her, she did not notice.

'You are Ar Elon, lord,' she whispered.

'Dear Vydd,' I said to the Mughain, 'it is only you who must bathe my wounds.'

CHAPTER THREE

In my old age I made a list of all I lost. In the Book of Gedd I made it, eighteen vellum pages, jeweled and painted. Whatever I had misplaced or abandoned I put there – the sword that too late Urien had given me, the head of Tabak bloodied and hidden beneath the stone on Hren, a girl's dark hair, spread on my thick shoulders like a fan. I was three years at the work; for I had my scribes, hunched above the pages as I bent over them, change all the great names into ornamented beasts and the lesser names into a wood. Now clawed and branched, the script, the *filidh* tell me, cannot be read. 'You have not looked!' I shout at them. Behind their white old hands they smile at me. But when the winter comes and great storms howl outside the doors I take the huge book from the shelf and run my fingers across the straggling sentences, looping forward and back as though following the spine of a serpent. They are old men but I am older. They do not remember the years before their births.

'How do you know my name?' she insisted.

My mind turned on the question awkwardly. 'In the vast halls under-sea,' I lied, knowing that Yllvere saw it. 'Among the great lords there,' I said, uncaring, 'I heard it whispered.'

The Mughain took up the linen. When she had soaked it in the basin, she applied it gently to my back.

'Ho!' I cried. Startled, I clutched at my sides with pain.

Quickly I fumbled in my cloak. Out of a fold I lifted the flask that I had filled with the soothing waters I had taken from the mere on the island. The basin I tipped unceremoniously onto the floor. But before she spoke I had restored it and into the wide mouth I emptied the flask of what it held.

'There is little enough,' I said, 'yet once this brought me peace.'

In the brittle silence the Mughain once more lifted her arm; but above the basin, gazing into it, she stopped. A stillness held her. Unmoving, she lingered; a faint luminescence reflected back into her eyes.

'I have ruled as it was given me,' she said slowly. Her voice was flat, the words coming from far away. 'Here among my women I kept where I was – year after year – but no king came to me. And yet I was never such a fool as to take to my bed a man of my own holding. I bore no sons. My foster sons I pulled like alders from the marsh. But even the stiff life I gave them you took back.' She blinked. 'Now once again I am childless.'

She turned her head then, wearily, forcing it until I felt myself the reluctance of its turning. 'Now a king has come,' she said softly, 'out of the wide ocean as it was promised. From the walls of my holding I watched him walk up on the shore. Taller he stood than other men; his dark hair was shining.' Suddenly the sound of her own voice seemed to trouble her; something pulled at her throat, yet she would not stop the words. 'I have ruled alone in Tywy,' she said, 'a queen and yet a woman like any other. And what a woman could do I did, even with the people watching. Though he smelled of battle and blood still covered his arms, when he came before me, I threw off my gown.' She paused. 'But the lord, I think, was not looking. Or if he watched, it was only to see how my small sister smiled at him.'

I bent my head. It had been in my mind to go east toward Ormkill, to sit at last in the king's chair that was mine and give the law. But I knew then that the doors of my own land would be closed to me. If any lord was meant to stand before her it was still Ar Elon. 'I have no business on the land,' I said harshly, more to myself than to the women. On Hren, beyond the dark gate on the hill, where I had taken the life of him the women longed for, I had lost my way. I said, 'To me it does not matter. Whoever rules or is born here is not my concern.'

My aunt looked up. 'Lord,' she said, 'I am not asking what you think. I have seen my gray hairs and I live with them.'

'Then tell me plainly.'

To my surprise, she laughed. 'I do not know it plainly. If I did, there would be no need to speak of it.' For a moment, familiar and unhurried, she held my eye.

'I shall have a son,' she said quietly, 'not of alder branches but of flesh. How can I tell you? Yet I have seen him standing over me in a place that I have never been, a place heavy with peat smoke and small light. It is hard to see and yet, if I reach out my hand, each pot and vessel is where I put it. On the fire a fine old kettle is boiling. I smell the broth.'

I did not wish to think. 'What would you have me answer?'

'If this is so.'

I started. 'How would I know?'

'It was yourself who poured it out,' she said and tugged at me. 'Come. Look into it before it fades.'

But when I stood over the basin I saw only the clear water and the dark old metal shining underneath. I heard only the shifting of her gown and thought, it is nothing. But all at once the water blurred, grew fathomless. The smoke that poured from the basin, which all of a sudden was everywhere, engulfed me. I battled it vainly. Angered, I waded into it and bumped my head.

Thick stalks and herbs, mountain flowers, dry and brittle, gathered in bunches, hung low from the rafters. I hunched my shoulders. Cramped beneath the ceiling, I stood as best I could, as I had once before when I was a boy and had no name of my own that men would listen to. I squinted but there was no need of it. Well enough I knew the hut and the old woman, thin as the stick with which she poked the fire. Her face was a nest of wrinkles. Seeing me, she looked up. Without wonder or surprise, knowing that in time I would come to her, she smiled.

'Agravaine,' she said, using her old name for me, 'I am pleased.'

Out of the curling smoke, just above the table, a vaporous wing unfolded with a crack. The crow's black eyes stared back at me. My head throbbing, I turned away.

In the basin the water shimmered. Rag ends of smoke drifted through the hall. Forgetting where I was, I had stumbled. Had Vydd not held me I would have walked into the fire.

'Lord?' she asked, afraid.

Despite the pain in my skull I made myself look at her, Vydd, my mother's sister, to whom I owed and would owe wonder and longing, the gifts not given in my begetting. In the years that were already gone but were yet to come she sat and would sit beside me by the fire in her poor hut on the mountain. There, though I was a child and impatient, she told and would tell me tales of my birth. In that I might have been a son to her. Almost I would have told her, but the wind blew through the doors of the holding – the bitter wind from Hren. I felt its damp breath on my shoulders and shivered. In the shape of my palms I felt the cold stone of that place where, amazed and desperate, I had crawled from the cyclic and uncounted waves, out of the waste of ocean where the long years rolled without turning. I thought, Whatever happens is not finished. Like serpents our lives turn back upon themselves.

'Lady,' I lied to her, 'I do not know the mysteries of birth. Yourself you have said it. Such matters are for women.' Grimly I sat at the table, then after a moment I reached for the basin, tipping it sideways, draining the queer bright water back into the flask.

'Lord,' she said helplessly. One last time she reached out to touch my shoulder, to hold it. The fire gleamed in the gray and copper of her hair, on the small weary lines of her face.

She said, 'I have no skill, it seems, in greeting kings. But as I could I welcomed you.' She went then without another word, out through the doors of the holding, her gown drifting behind her, to summon the women.

Yllvere watched me. She heard the slow indrawing of my breath.

'What have you hid from her?' she said.

It was my shape you saw, I thought, that first you remembered when Ar Elon came to you. So you went and will go to him, gladly, not knowing the fault, thinking how once you had met in the years that are already gone but not faded, thinking, Already I have bathed his wounds.

I did not answer. At my back, grumbling among themselves, the men of the holding came into the hall.

There was no peace that night but after the death of the man there was quiet. The men found their places somberly and sat staring at their hands or plucking at their boots. The housewomen, uncertain why they had been ordered out and then as quickly brought back again, hurried through their work with a discontented stillness but with care. Straightaway the meat was put onto the racks and lifted over the fires. But if their hands were busy, their faces were drawn. I saw how they watched me, pausing when they thought I was not looking. A few were pretty, but with the onset of winter their sun-whitened hair had begun to darken. Against drabness they had smeared goose fat into their pallid flesh until it shone. Their braids, freshly plaited, hung over gowns that had been left all morning to air in the yard. As they jostled back and forth their arm-rings glittered. But I asked nothing of them and they went on with their labors sullenly.

By the time the trenchers had been brought out and the bread loaded onto the table the wind had died. The smoke holes were not drawing; a blue haze fell like webs from the ceiling. The men coughed and, remembering the dead, ate sparingly. I could not see into their faces, but I knew the shame in them and did not fault it. All men, seeing death, must die a little. Still the man was none of mine and after the second keg had been broached, I pulled my chair aside. The unfriendliness of the lower hall, where at last the men had begun to stir at their cups, had not improved; I saw nothing to be gained in waiting for the beer to warm them. Already some tongues were loosening.

As I went by one of the benches a man stood up unsteadily. I saw him swallow.

'Every fool thing we have done,' he said.

I looked at him blankly.

'Every fool thing they have told us,' he said bitterly.

The Mughain had risen but I laughed and pushed on by him.

The light from the hall stabbed in yellow spikes through the shutters. Gleaming, it poked into the yard. But under the wall, beneath the low-sweeping eaves, the darkness closed in upon itself. Groping, I caught my boot on the edge of a flagstone and stumbled. Even at that, it was a relief to get out into the air. Behind me in the hall someone shouted. The sound seemed far away.

The yard sloped to the south, turned crookedly along a lane that wandered through a cluster of squalid sheds, then lost itself utterly among the byres and forges, the lesser outbuildings of the holding. Somewhere ahead of me I could smell horses and the damp strong odor of winter hay. To the left, I thought, was the shrine where I had slept after I had cleared the wood. I remembered the rug of skins that had covered me and hoped no one had gone off with it. In truth, I longed for sleep. I went, following my memory, under a low arch and up a short run of stairs until I came before a rough door in the rock. But when I gave a shove to it, I found it bolted.

In the nearer darkness a curlew shrilled. The air, I noticed, was heavy with the scent of kelp. I could hear the water and knew I had gone too far. Bewildered, I turned back once more, trudging up the slope and counting the houses. That is the wellshed, I thought, for I had passed it in the morning. But when I had come up nearer to it and mounted the blunt worn steps, I found that it was not. For a moment I stood puzzled, looking out into the yard. Too tired to think, I leaned my shoulder heavily against the door. With a groan the thick boards pushed inward, spilling me into a narrow room.

A single lantern swung from a wallspike, dangerously, rocking back and forth. Its light was poor, but after the darkness I had to shade my eye. I blinked. At the center of the room, her head uncovered and powdered with the dust of grain, Cerridwen was working a quern. Her thin fingers were wrapped about the shaft that moved the upper stone. Gritting her teeth, she pulled at it. The floor stone growled, sending a shiver through the walls.

'Latch the door,' she said, not looking up, 'or they will find you.'

Before I thought, I had put my hand to the metal.

She snorted gently. 'It is a wise man,' she whispered, 'who, uncomplaining, does a woman's bidding.'

'I did not leave the hall to hide from them.'

She did not answer. Instead, her frail hands closed more tightly on the shaft. Grunting, she swung the stone. The thick floor rumbled; the dust flew up and rimed her hair. Something tugged at me, making me dizzy. For what seemed a long while she kept at it, but at last, out of breath, she stopped. Then for the first time, her meager chest heaving, she looked up. 'Now open the door,' she said.

'You bade me close it.' Yet, unthinking, stiffly, I found I had put my hand to the latch. The door squealed open. But when I stared out, my eye grew wide.

The dark long walls and the towers had somehow slid over to the left. The mountain behind the hall was fixed and still, the same bright stars frozen over it. Everything was as it should have been except the houses, sheds and barns, and even the flagged yard under them, had seemed to turn like pieces on a potter's wheel. In all things they were unchanged and perfect, only they had come to rest facing another way. Doubting, I shook my head.

'How have you done this? Why?'

Her eyes looked off. 'To save your life,' she said, and pointed.

Across the yard, where before I had missed it, I saw the shrine. On the seaward side, crawling along its length, two men scraped low against the ground. Between them they dragged a heavy bar. Making the steps, they straightened, hefting the bar up after them. Hurriedly they set it in the doormounts. Then as one stood back, the other, wielding a hammer, beat the ringing metal into place.

At once, as though the sound had been a signal, the doors of the holding burst open. A stream of men came blundering from the hall. The smoking torches in their hands waved drunkenly. Their short arms and small red faces jerking in and out of light, they ran across the yard. Swarming among the sheds and shouting, they bunched up at last before the dark walls. There, they crawled up on each other's backs, scrambling nearer the roof. The flames on the torchheads, unsteady in their hands, paused and wobbled. Then someone shouted, once clearly above the rest. The men who had got into the eaves tossed up the brands.

The wall were stone, but the roof was thatch, dry straw and wattle. Small gulping fires caught at the edges. But quickly, finding the seams of pitch, they ran a dozen courses toward the peak, flaring until, just at the summit, the fires raised one glowing head, like a yellow crown, golden, shining on the night's black shoulders. The burning seared the air. Heat pounding their faces, the men fell back. Within the hiss of flames a roofbeam moaned, cracked inward suddenly and fell crashing with a roar. About the burning shell of the building the small men cheered.

But I was quiet. It was my death that made them howl.

'Very well,' Cerridwen said. 'You have seen it. Now close the door.'

Turning, I saw her face, red, like her gown, in the light of the burning. Her fingers loosened, then stretched out again about the shaft. I closed the door.

'Cerridwen,' I began.

'Hush,' she whispered and took a firmer hold of the shaft. A deep unending pulse rumbled through the floor, knocking the loose stones from the wall. The chamber held for a moment, then, groaning, pulled beyond its strength, it twisted. I waited for the blow. But nothing touched me, only a wave of blackness dark against my eye. Then as suddenly something clicked, slipped softly into place and stopped. The walls that had seemed to tremble found their old hard shapes again. I stared. Cerridwen dropped her hands.

'It is done,' she said wearily. 'You have your life. Though it is little wonder the men at our holding hate you. Yet the debt we owed is paid.'

I felt the muscles in my jaw grow hard. I had bargained enough with women. 'There is nothing owed,' I said.

She raised her head. 'Too well we loved you, lord.' She almost smiled. 'More than our husbands, loved when we should have hated you, you with your stench of blackness, the salt still in your hair. More than our own fair sons we loved you. That is fault enough.'

Her gray loose hair had drifted across her face. She pushed it back. So Yllvere might have done. So might any of my sisters.

'Still, I took away the death they planned,' she said. Watching me, she sighed. 'Yet you might have smiled on one of us. If not out of love at least from pity. Here among my women you might have got a child.'

I flinched. 'It is done,' I whispered. 'On Tinkern through a woman's trickery I left my seed.'

Her lips pulled tight. 'That time has yet to come.'

'It will.'

'I know it.'

'And me?'

'Yes,' she nodded wearily. Then sadly, 'Yes.'

'Not what your women think but who I am.'

'Yes.'

The flame of the lamp flickered on the dry lines of her face. She leaned forward, resting her thin arms on the quern. 'But you are the one who came,' she said, 'the one we saw walking from the sea.' She straightened, her gray eyes waiting, still. 'How can it matter then whether you are Ar Elon or his heir?'

'To me it matters.'

'No,' she spat, angry all at once. As suddenly the life that was in her seemed to shrink and fade, the life that clings to flesh and marks it, man or woman, from the pale, uncaring earth. Only her eyes were left. Blank and empty as the winter sun, they watched me out of their ragged holes. 'Here you might have ended it,' she said, 'cut short your branching lives and stilled your blood.'

But I knew only my anger. 'No,' I cried. 'You are no judge over me,' and swore.

She made no answer. From beneath her cloak she drew a sword. Its deep-carved hilt shone with the warring images of men and birds. It was my own. She saw the deadly thing it was and winced when she gave it into my hand. 'Take this plaything then,' she said. 'Now surely you will have need of it. For you are Duinn's now and none of mine.'

My fingers closed on the bright hilt greedily. But it was not for myself alone I took it. 'Witch!' I cried. 'It was a woman who first put this in my hand.'

She drew a breath and I saw once more it was a woman breathing, tired and old, the strangeness gone from her. 'Dear Finn,' she murmured, 'you were ever slow to learn.' I would have answered, but sadly she hobbled to the door and opened it. One last time I saw how the house had turned and the darkness with it. The empty light of morning lay on the shore. The wind, nosing among the sheds and houses, blew over the threshold. In the roots of my hair and in the creases of my lips I felt it, grave and uneasy and tasting of salt.

So I fled my kingdom without one man to do me service, leaving the hut of Cerridwen, though the land she lived in was my own. They thought me dead. Still I did not follow the clear path down to the shore but prowled the brown lands and the fens by the river. There, I judged, I could not be seen, not from the hall nor higher up from the towers. No one gave chase. And yet I did not doubt there were some who picked through the stones, turning the smoking timbers for proof of my bones. The mired ground sucked at my boots. I listened. No shouts shook the air.

Gradually the bog gave way and I waded through water up to my knees. Even then the tide was going. In time I had worked my way into the cuts of streams, following the tide out until the water ran only at my ankles. On the banks small brown troops of crabs, all remnants and stragglers, the last of the season, moved through the grass. The birds were gone. The great birds never came ashore in winter. Solitary, far over the ocean, they lived and fed. The cold moon silvered their feathers. So they kept apart through the dark half of the year – watchful, unsleeping, far from their kind.

Had I been other than I was, I would have had a troop of my own to keep me company. But another man, his cup well filled, resigned to the women's fire, would have had no need of them. Despite the bright air, the sharpness of morning, he would have stayed ashore. Better he would have been for it. It needed no witch to know the weather. The wind came ruffling out of the northwest. In a week there would be ice in the marshes and in another, on the hay fields, on the dunes, nests of snow bending and crippling the stalks of grass.

Out on the windy flats I looked over the water. The tide ebbed, draining the marsh. Yet beyond the land the sea was not made greater by its going. So the ocean will take me to itself, I thought – quietly, without notice, with only the cold and wind for company.

I paced the shore. In the cover of the grass I found an old curragh held to a sunken post with snarls of rope. My sword, I knew, would have made shorter work, but such use demeaned its worth. Slowly, with my fingers, I unplaited the knots. When I had done, I dragged the black hulk from its place and hauled it through acres of stinking mud down to the channel.

The craft was heavy, the old skins sodden, needing restretching and rubbing with wool grease. But I did not much care how well it would last in the sea. I wanted it only to carry me across the strait, then around to the far side of the island where my ship lay at mooring. Though I had done it once, I was now of no mind to swim the distance. To keep clear of the holding I had gone farther south and so more than doubled the length of water I would have to cross.

I stopped for a breath and looked seaward. The air was filled with the strident hissing of waves. As they crashed on the shore I counted them, and when I knew the lull would come, I pushed into the slack. The sea rose suddenly. A plume of water drenched my back.

Still I am away, I thought, though, in truth, I had yet to escape the land. The peat-black waves, muddied by the Tywy, thrummed on the

239

leather sides. I could still smell the land, the scent of marsh grass, the weed smell of the shoals, the close, fetid stink of miles of mud.

Low in the water the curragh, despite the current, dragged. Without stirring, before I had put my back to the oar, for a moment the great sloping line of a wave lifted me. I looked up. High on the bluff, above the nest-strewn crevices and empty ledges in the rock, I saw a pair of figures running, racing ahead until the land ended and they stood at the edge, their long hair streaming back. A third dim figure limped up behind. Then three together they stood, one no different from the others now, distant, no more than shadows. I heard a cry. Scattered by the gale, only a thin sound lingered. Like the sad, sweet crying of birds it drifted over the strait.

So it was that I abandoned them and not only the lands and women but all that was mine: the first spring calving of the aurochs; the ripe, swollen fruit of the trees; even the salmon, red as oakwood, unwearied, climbing the falls – mine by right whether bear or man caught him. I took only the sword that Cerridwen gave back. So the sea would not rust it, I had wrapped it in my cloak.

PART II

Tech Duinn

CHAPTER FOUR

This only I set down, myself, in my own hand. I see the letters, slight and cramped. I have to squint to look at them.

Even Grieve, who taught me, whose kindness held out longest, would have laughed to see this thin scraping of my outsized hands. Bears, she would have said, if taught their letters, must write like bears. In massive strokes, she would have said – like the bloody swiping of their paws. Had they known of it, my scribes would have nodded solemnly. But kings, they would have added – knowing their place and knowing mine – kings ought never to write at all.

Indeed these books are scribework, taken down as I paced the hall, my robe neglected, forgetful even of the winter and the cold, while they, wrapped and bundled, pressed near the fire and, listening, made their bold marks dutifully or because I fed them. More likely that. For who in this fool's age would give work to scholars if the king will not?

But this they did not do.

The rest I knew. After I had rehearsed the words, I spoke and they wrote down. But when I had told them how I took the curragh and left the land, how the wailing women watched me go, I sat down glumly.

They waited, thinking, He is weary. Only let him call for wine and he will start again. Or, because I had kept them long in the house, He is only thinking. Some cold thought out of his memory, breathing freshly upon him, has made him quiet. Only wait and he will find the words. So they waited, alert and grave. So they would have waited – thinking, It is only a moment – until morning.

I sent them out.

The young men went eagerly, went to relieve themselves in the yard, went unconcerned to climb into the lofts, to find, if they looked for it, the uncritical warmth of a girl. Only the old men lingered. They stood in the cold and dark. They made much of watching the wood smoke, the last sparks of the coals, thinking because they had no women who wanted them, had as I had only sleep in front of them, that I would call them back, thinking, It is only some old man's secret, some matter of love or pride he will not let the young men hear.

I banged the floor with my stick until they went.

It was not, I am certain, forgetfulness. The thoughts of some men molder, grow soft as age takes hold of them. But even now I can recall a bent face by the loom, a white arm lifted, the smell of wool . . . even fifty years after, a smile I saw just once and never saw again. It was not shame. That I had groped and fondled my own sister, had mated her, by now men knew. They knew its issue. How can a war be hid from those who fought it? For myself, I had made too many corpses to suppose I might bind the wounds of living men with lies. It was not pride. As I knew the tale I told it. But of the leaving of Tywy, except for the wailing of the women, I have no memory. But neither, the god knows, have I forgotten anything.

It snowed, the white storm pouring silently out of a darkened sky, the close sky lowering until the space between the waves and heavens was no more than the length of the second mast. The foremast, from the sprit onward, belonged already to the upper world. Life narrowed. Pressed between sea and air, the far-off roar of breakers echoed dimly like faint sounds heard in caves.

Fearful of the rocks, I had come on deck. The air was cold. Snow, swirling over the bow, danced in the rigging like damp white moths. Except for the distant surf, the sea was calm. The darkness sucked my heart.

It was that I remember – before all other things – awakening without any sense of sleep to a world somehow diminished, moving cramped against a smallness made more terrible because it hovered just out of reach.

I could not see the land ahead, but through the quiet storm I heard it, the long waves rolling onto the rocks. I broke the ice and, when I had freed the line, cast out the anchor. I felt it drag, groping, the bottom near. After one false catch, it held. Swung back from its ruin, as though begrudging safety, the great ship groaned.

The woman will not hear of it. 'It is twelve days' journey out from Hren to far Tech Duinn,' she interrupts. 'No less than that. You who had no skill with ships, nor men to follow you or work the sails, no provisions even for a man alone, how did you live to see that place?' She does not smile.

Her father, before I made a lord of him, was a linen merchant down in Harl. A steady, strapping ugly man with bright corn whiskers, he was good company and in my court or on the field my surest judge of men. Sadly, he had no head for figures. From the day I met him until I put a stop to it, his daughter, knowing his worth as she knew her own, kept his ledgers and accounts.

The hall is quiet. She holds my eye, weighing my look as I stare back at her. To this day she will have me to the penny.

'Who marked the distance then?' I growled at her.

'Husband,' she answers quietly, 'it was Meth Clêr, your own shipmaster.'

I frown. 'He is a brave man and I find no fault in him. Yet, lady, he himself never sailed from Hren.'

Her small white hands are folded in her lap. She has no need to lift them now. Yet in her father's house, where we had been left alone the night I told her I would have her as my queen, she had hurled herself down and clasped my knees. Then, until I took an oath I meant it, she had not let me go. Now she looks past me, across the hall.

'Has any man?' she asks.

I summon a girl to fill my cup.

'No man,' I answer evenly, 'only a king.'

All day beneath the planking I sat brooding, walled by the ship's ribs, keeping what warmth I could with a small round pot of coals. Even in the thickening cold, when numbness invades the limbs and reason fades, there is a kind of peace. I slept. It was evening once again when I awoke. The storm was gone.

I hugged my shoulders and, jogging on my toes to bring back feeling, climbed upon the deck. I looked out through the linked ropes in the bow. A gritty light still slanted through the clouds. Low and squalling, they rolled on westward. I gave no thought to them. A huge white island reared up on my left. Southward the coast was steep, piled high with snow-patched stone and hanging crags. But northward the tall peaks halted, leaving abandoned towers in the rock as though here where air and water met, the elements, seeking once to fashion a common measure of their might, had somehow gone beyond their strengths and let it be, not overthrown or ruined, but just unfinished. The desolate, uneven dunes swept again into the sea. The shore was rubble. Pounded by the surf, the cold stones rang.

I knew nothing of this island. But it had no harbors, no place to land. No herring boats, whirled out by gales, their crews half-starved, had thought it safe to try its beaches. No men at least had come wide-eyed back with tales of it. Better a slow death tightening belts than certain slaughter on the rocks. Pushing on, they either starved or drowned. And yet I hungered.

With no better claim on me, I kept my vigil and thought of

cormorants and gulls and snares to catch them. I remembered, oddly, how when I was a child, out in the pantry Grieve had left, against ill-luck, offerings of milk for elves. Great saucers filled to the rim they were. For a quarter-hour, until the last light drowned, I thought of little else.

The ship, unminded – pulled at its anchor by the tide – drifted shoreward in the dark. It scissored back and forth before the land. Too late I felt it slide. Across the outer bar the black sea rolled and staggered on the stones.

There was no chance to wait for morning. The sunrise would have found me pinned beneath the mast or slivered through with twisted wood. The keel struck ground. An arm of water slashed across the deck, shook loose the planking and hooked me at the knees. With no more time to think I leapt down from the rail, swung for a moment from the ledge above the tumbling sea and dropped. My head snapped back and water rushed into my lungs. I gagged. Yet I did not seek the air but, lulled by darkness, dreaded it. Far beneath the rushing sheets of foam I closed my eye.

The Kell say each wave has its own soul. In truth, the roar when long waves shake the beach, heard in the darkness, will seem the cries of people in the sea. The hosts of drowned men call out in their sleep. Nor have I found fault with that. For when I moved within the galleries of the dark, borne down by black cold arms, the hair along my neck hard-laced with ice, I felt the wayward, longing sighs of other life. In the grinding undertone of stones, the hiss of sand along the shoals, I heard their guarded whispers and their screams.

Somewhere out ahead of me an avalanche of water jarred the world. So I would find my death, Cerridwen had said.

But in the darkness I remembered that I wanted air. Wildly, knowing that to live I must make the land, I stretched out my arms. My head was turned, my one eye open.

From underneath I saw the monstrous gray corpse rocking in the harsh waves over me. The uncurled, huge fingers spread; they reached down helplessly. I looked into the tangle of his hair. His sad, blank eyes were staring. Then, though the sea was full enough, I would have wept. But the hand was swift against my throat.

I seized the wrists. Flinching in the grip, I broke it. The arms had softened. The gray old flesh that he had molded by his will had weakened, changed. The sea itself was not the same, the mutinous dark waves that once had seemed to struggle with the sky fell silent. Lapsed back into foam, they lapped his sides. He did not speak. Yet the old fear welled in me. He cannot have my place, I thought. Nor would I ever let him wash to shore.

Reaching up, I grabbed his heels. With only a touch, like a bladder poked with a knife, he fell. His legs closed around and over me. I pulled him down.

On the cold sea floor I set him on a stone. As I had on Hren, I rolled up rocks to make his cairn. But when I went to put the last stone down, to close his eyes, the head moved sadly on his neck. Already rotted, the face gave way and one last shape was roused up from his flesh. I stared and yet I did not need to look.

On Hren in my anger I had not thought. But now, remembering, I saw how with his murder he had baited me. It was not his death I made. I never took his life; he gave it freely, knowing it was not lost. Better then I knew myself, the women saw what thing I was. With my own hand I had piled the rocks on every side. On my own face, unbelieving, looking up, I had laid the stone.

Up from deep water the huge old sealman hauled himself into the air. His nostrils twitched. His dripping skin lay furrowed on his back; his hair was matted. As though uncertain, he tried the air. But when he felt it rush back biting to his lungs, he raked his snarled long graying beard and smiled. Curled under the light of stars, the waves grinned up at him. Only then, like a lord who had received his due, he turned to watch the land.

Tall crags, barred to him by walls of surf, loomed overhead. His deep eyes narrowed, studying each thick shadow in the rock, every star's thin glimmer on the ice. It was a cheerless place to come to land, he thought, and yet he knew a hundred other isles, each colder, each ringed about with vaster walls of surf. In the clearness of his memory, bright as dreams just out of sleep, the old lord named them to himself.

The Island of the Wind, he thought, for wind was first; the Island of the Shouting Wind, for that came next, and an island each for its four quarters; the six ice islands the six winds hardened out of foam; the Island of Virgins whom the gods made cold; the Island of Maidens who three times rebuff the men who come to them . . . and so he named them quietly, remembering. With each name he drew an icy breath until his cold flesh that never wanted warmth began to shiver and his blunt teeth chattered in his mouth. By then, swept free of clouds, the sky had become both high and deep. But his eyes, once clear, were rheumed with thought. Yet he could not name the land he saw.

Then I must go to it, he thought.

League-long waves had massed in rows beyond the shore. Unconcerned, he let them pull him from the edge. A mass of water thrust up slow and thick. At its swollen crest it rippled. Then all at once, tripped by the cutting rocks beneath, with a resounding roar it fell apart. The boiling rush rebounded from the beach. Fountains, spewing foam, shot up and battered him. The water caught him round the chest. Yet, hardly marking it, he moved against the surf as he had moved in battle against a crowd of men. His broad back took the blows. Row on row, the long black waves hurled down on him. He waded in.

A grizzled, burly man stood in his way. The waves swarmed over him, broke on the ledges of his shoulders. Yet he might have grown there like a stone, brown kelp clinging to his six long arms. His head was bare, his hair curled tightly to his scalp. The sealman saw his eyes. In the poor light of stars, they shone back brightly. He did not stir. Though he had left off his mail and had brought neither sword nor ax with him, by his bearing it was clear he meant no man to pass at either side.

'How are you here?' he shouted. In between the cataracts of surf, before the next wave fell, there was a silence and the sealman heard him.

'I have come upon a hundred isles,' he answered back. But then he had to shout himself above the thunder and the drag of stones. 'Nor,' he bellowed, 'has any man long stood in my way.'

As thought the other spoke to it, the next wave held. 'Longer will I stand in front of you,' he said and motioned at the land with one of several arms. 'For here,' he added, 'no man who ever was has come.'

The sealman looked at him, took the measure of the other's reach, assessed his quickness. He listened to his lagging breath. Then joyously the sealman straightened. 'How should this shore be different from the rest?' he boasted. 'On twelve islands I met the heralds on the shoals. Bold men they were, who did not leave their swords at home. Bold men, they met me bravely. Still the eels had bones to suck when I was done.'

Another wave had left its place and fell. The sealman felt the whip of white surf, the cold weight of the sea as it poured over him. 'Twelve times,' he roared above the noise, 'horsemen drove at me from stations in the rock. They were not clumsy. Carefully they aimed and hurled their spears. Yet their mares did not go hungry but had manflesh for fodder when evening came.'

A flood of marbly foam engulfed his knees. The sealman felt it thrust between his legs but did not move. 'Nor can it be otherwise with us,' he said. 'For I have never raised my arm against a man and missed my mark.'

A great wave fell to ruin. The baffled water ran downhill against the sea. Then there was silence. He waited.

'Yet you are dead,' the other said.

The sealman's mouth grew taut. For a breath's space he wavered, grew anxious. For a moment, distracted, he looked beyond the man. He saw the white worn winter hills, the grim gray stones along the beach. Over half-seen shapes the dust of snow had thickened. It seemed to him that he had never seen such lack of glory. 'Has there ever been a more unwanted land?' he said.

The other nodded, 'It is bleak work making mountains.'

The sealman only gritted his teeth and swore. 'You rant,' he said, 'and it is empty.'

The other gave a sigh. He stretched his six brown-knuckled hands before him. The churning waves wrenched from their patterned fall. They melted into one black crest that, screaming, reared. Out of the awful cold and mist there came a woeful keening. Unyielding, the sealman pressed against the noise. Four hands reached out and took his thighs and bent his arms. Blunt fingers stabbed about his throat and squeezed.

The sealman gave a short, incredulous cough. The buzz of glowing sparks surprised him. His chest was tight. Never before had his cold lungs wanted breath. He was Ar Elon. Could he not dive whole days beneath the pounding seas, his thick hair weaving into darkness, down countless fathoms to the shining floor? Had he not raced with dolphins through strange deep halls, unhurried when even they, his brothers, rose for air? But now his fierce lungs ached for breath. He fought but could not free the arms that held him. Because he could not stand, he crawled, bewildered, sick with rage, and scraped a trough to hide among the stones.

Far off he heard the ocean's roar. But nearer, swollen up inside his ribs, a shapeless darkness turned like something in a sack. It wiggled. He did not weep. So it is only death, he thought, and felt, for an instant, as through a shell, a naked beak peck through his flesh.

A cold rain of spray fell on the rocks. From rents and smoking pools blasts of icy vapor blew into the air. I was tired, too tired and hurt to stand, and when I tried, I crumpled. The slow dark river of the tide, its fury broken, rolled gasping at my knees. There, sunk into crevices, diverted into rifts and faults, it hissed away among the broken slate and stones. I wished that it would carry me. I wanted only to lie down with it, to slide, uncaring, back into the sea.

'I will bear you,' a voice spoke softly at my side. Thick arms covered with woolly hair embraced my shoulders; long arms crooked high around my chest. With easy strength they lifted me.

I squirmed but dared not meet his face. Four great arms shifted, found a better hold; another arm, unneeded, pointed ahead. My tired eyes followed, north, along a narrow valley cut back by a snaking river into the hills. At its far end, strangely clear in the distance, I saw an immense stone house raised up beyond a gate. It was shaped like a crofter's hut, save that it was higher and wider and had a great many windows. Its sprawling roof of heather thatch seemed broad enough to shelter not only the hall at Tywy but all its sheds and byres together. I looked back and then looked up again, amazed. Its doors stood open. The shifting light of fires poured out from it. My heart leapt and I clutched his hair.

'It is not far,' he spoke up reassuringly. 'Before morning I will have you there.'

Then quickly, as though my weight were no more than a pack of wool, he left the beach and, mounting the stone, in a moment he was bounding along a rocky trail beneath the hills. Soon on either side tall cliffs rose up like towers. Their grim shadows lay across the track. He ran ahead.

We did not speak. On my left I heard the moan of water stumbling seaward under plates of ice. Though I could not see the river, now and then, a hundred elhws below, I caught a glint of silver; but then the night closed in once more; the cliffs grew higher and the wind blew cold.

Braced to his back, I felt his heavy shoulders sway as stride by stride he climbed beneath deep-fissured walls, angling among the stones and drifted domes of snow. In places he had to burrow. Armfuls of damp, slick wetness clung and melted on my neck. The man went on. The house was not half so near as he had said. There was a time I thought I had a glimpse of it; a vague light blinked and faded. Through a cleft within the rock I saw a star.

At last I drowsed. Neither sleeping nor awake, I felt the floating vastness of the night but, jostled over the high places of the earth, whether the night was above or under me I could not tell. Little pleased to lurch among the crags, the wind blew fitfully. I felt the cold and pulled myself awake. Near me everything seemed clear, but in the distance the blackness wavered like shapes in dreams. It was hard to look. Wearied, perhaps I slept again though it may be I had forgotten to close my eye. Though I had not sought him, Ar Elon's face slipped into my mind. Thrown on its side, the bloodstained head was halved and bubbling. In a pool of its own blood, it fell away in sticky clumps. The sea, I thought, has eaten him. And someone else. I tried to think. But who the other was I did not know.

More often I heard the sharp, thin clack of hooves; heard, though now I was full of sleep, the bleating cries of crowding phantoms that leapt and butted near his legs. He walked among them easily. He showed no fear. Softly, humming to himself, he called out names.

The trail seemed endless, the night as long. Worst of all, the bad air reeked of wool. Oily, soaking into flesh and hair, it filled my pores, took form and weight against my itching back. I yawned and, turning, threw out my arm. I felt it sink within a mound that spread and sagged like the prickly softness of a myrtle bog. Startled, I opened my eye. From a dozen windows the light of morning, glimmering yellow on the sills, poured down on me and lit the golden fuzz of piles of wool where for uncounted hours I had sprawled asleep.

I was in the house, though because of its unbroken height from floor to ceiling, it seemed more like a barn. From a fire pit in the center a blue coil of smoke curled upward, crossing the great blank space between until it was sucked into the morning through a deep hole in the thatch. A quarter of the floor was cut away, sunk into a stone-paved stell below, wide itself as a paddock and reached by a ramp, where huge sheep milled sedately or worried in the wooden cribs for hay. The remainder of the floor was divided roughly into thirds, the largest given over to a sort of kitchen, strewn with old iron cauldrons, ladles, mugs and knives. In the center was a thick worm-eaten table. Laddered between the windows were racks of shelves lined with brown large bowls, a score of ram skulls and, near the bottom, a great many moldy books in cracked leather bindings. The rest was fairly evenly halved between a bedroom study where the white limewashed walls were hung with what seemed maps, though of no lands I knew, and pushed into a wide corner and behind a row of all-purpose chests, a woolroom. It was there among the rugs of fleece that I looked out. The dry wool, far from the fire, was cold. I shivered.

'You might come and warm yourself,' the old man said. Dressed in a simple longshirt rolled to his elbows, he crouched near the fire, adding one log and then another and another, each with different hands. He was the equal of my height and though his strength, it seemed, was greater, it was the strength of a mortal man. Age had seared his looks and bent his back. His large face was plain, his thin smile dogged as an old hill farmer's. In one hand he had a shank of mutton which, when spitted, he laid carefully across the flames.

'I am a cotter,' he said afterward.

'Whose man?' I asked.

He grinned. 'None I know of.'

He did not seem to understand. 'To whom,' I said, 'do you owe wool and service?'

His mild brown eyes, large under wiry brows, seemed suddenly annoyed. He scratched his ear. 'No man,' he said at last and turned and then turned back. 'I do hope you like mutton,' he began but just as quickly paused. 'Though,' he said, 'as that is all there is, no doubt you will have it anyway.'

I stood up so he could look at me, thinking my dark looks might drive some sense into him.

'I am Finn,' I said, 'Ar Elon's heir.'

But he only gave me a worried stare and shook his head.

'No, lord,' he called out firmly. 'He is the one man clearly you are not.'

CHAPTER FIVE

There was no sweet smell of roasting meat. After many minutes in the fire the flesh was neither singed nor blistered. The shy smoke shrank from it. The cotter pulled himself up slowly and, unconcerned, he ambled off, returning some time later with a greater load of split dry wood. When he had replenished the fire, he sat cross-legged before the pit. Puffing up his cheeks, he blew into the ash. Soon a new fire peeped out of the coals and found its voice. Like a red bird it flapped and sang. With gathered strength, great wings of flame rose up again and beat the air. Sweating against the heat, the man slid back. And yet not one drop of grease fell on the wood. The cotter gazed at the cold mass of uncooked meat. Showing no particular interest, he chewed his thumb.

I watched him carefully. Yet nothing happened. So I rose and seeing no other course but to share his company, I made a place beside him on the floor. My clothes were stiff. Hardened overnight, they smelled of salt and rubbed my wounds. Though I tried to give no sign of it, he heard me sigh.

'It is no little thing,' he said, 'to reach this island.'

'What choice has a drowning man?' I said. 'My ship foundered. The land was near.'

He grinned. 'No choice at all. He drowns.'

'I lived.'

He nodded slightly. 'Your death, my lord, was always fire.'

'And the sword,' I said bitterly, 'and drowning after.' He did not answer. I set my chin in my palm. I stroked the place where my rough hair had always been. He saw the sudden strangeness in my eyes. Shifting, he laid two great hands on me. They fumbled, meaning comfort, on my back. With tar and broom he had salved the sores of all his flocks. It may be he knew no poultice for a man. Quietly, as though he had no wish for the sheep to hear, he said, 'It was a bearded man I stopped, that I left tangling in his hair and rolling backward in the surf.'

I stared.

'In truth,' he said, 'he was one like that.' He cleared his throat. 'And a corpse already, though we fought.' He looked at me. 'Still,' he said, 'I never let the groaning dead come on the shore. In the night with the wild wind rising from the south and west they crawl up on the stones and scare poor sheep. Then it is a wonder I get them back to feed.'

Somewhere beneath the floor an old ram stamped his hooves. 'Aye,' the cotter went on softly and clutched my hands, 'that one was bearded, his black hair twisted with the white, all snarled with salt, a corpse already. Not a sheared, fair lad the like of you.'

He stopped and in the silence I could hear the useless breathing of the fire, the mutton cold. I looked down and saw my own pale flesh, white as any of the children of Kell, saw it out of two clear eyes, as I had not seen anything since I climbed the windy stair about Gwen Gildrun, before the crow. Now with both eyes I drank in the brightness of the morning, the licking fire, the crouched six-handed man, his old neck twisted round to look at me. He saw my fear.

'Twice,' he said quietly, 'the men you are no longer tried to reach the shore. They could not come to it. This was no place for them. Here no living man may walk, nor, until all is ready, can the dead.'

In the sheath of flesh that was not mine I shivered. 'You live,' I said, 'here where by your words . . . ' Reeling, I stopped and shut my eyes. Yet beneath the lids I saw him. He drew a breath. The fire so newly lit had dwindled to a single flame. Gazing into it, he raised his hand, but touching nothing, let it fall.

'For ages I have sat upon the rocks,' he said, 'and watched the corpses floating in. So long in the sea, they have no strength to harm a man but they kill with grief. So Finn pitied the corpse and failed. As for Ar Elon, he had only forgotten he was dead. Myself, I did no more than hold him back till he remembered.'

'Then what am I?' I whispered helplessly.

'The son.'

'Whose?'

'Ar Elon's,' he said and scratched his ear. 'Finn's.'

'Surely . . . '

He shook his head. His long sad face was pained. 'I swore to serve you, lord,' he said. 'But there are mornings in the world I rue it.' Within him something snapped. He stood up suddenly. 'By your leave, I'll fetch the third damn load of wood,' he said, 'burn the mutton one last time and have my breakfast.'

After he had eaten he was gone, calling the sheep out of the stell and driving them through the broad doors into the air. I knew nothing of sheep. Yet it did not seem the dumb beasts, impatient and nudging each other's sides, had sensed his anger. He chanted over them, singing a strange discordant insolent melody. The ill sound scraped their backs, scattering and rebounding like pebbles thrown against a wall. Then as suddenly he fell silent. But the sheep kept on with the noise he started, the tuneless chant returning to him, tranquil and with a fullness he had not given it as though nothing pleased sheep more than wandering out to pasture on cold rock and crusted snow. The last ewe tossed her halfwit's head. With a haughty look she passed the threshold.

When the house was still, I tried the meat. The third time in the fire indeed had roasted it; but the flesh was stringy and I put it aside before I had my fill. I remembered the carcasses the old men of the towns beneath our holding, too lame to hunt, had sometimes brought in for the pot. Though stewed all day, such meat had never truly softened. He did not butcher this, I thought; he found it dead. Yet, bewildered, I remembered he had said no dead could come upon this land.

He is a fool, I thought. At the same time I tried not to think, for the talk of other selves had frightened me. Yet, though I would not, I remembered the quiet corpse that I had buried in the sea, remembered though it was not my memory, the other, his full lips black as a mare's, his long hair wet upon his back. Though I did not want to look, I saw him mount the beach again on splayed webbed feet, saw, as a man sees himself, out of his own eyes, the six-armed giant standing up ahead. I waved the thing away and clenched my teeth.

At that moment I saw the basin.

It was round and deep, the match of the one the Mughain's women had set out for me. It had been left on the table, the knives and crockery placed aside. Warily, I lifted it. A faint sweat broke out on my brow.

Out of my cloak I took the flask. I did not hurry. There were no eyes on me to make me awkward. When I had settled the basin in my lap, I hunched my shoulders over it. Then slowly, I poured the clear Hren water into its depths. The surface shimmered. The white light from the windows reflected in my face. I waited, expecting the beaded light to dance, the bands of brightness to twist and snake, to burst like small choked veins, a swollen world of mist and smoke beneath. So on Tywy it happened. I did not move. Yet it was only the same quiet room I saw and at its center a man, his pale hands tightening on the edges of a metal bowl. His white hair hung at his shoulders. Out of deep gray startled eyes I watched him blink.

* * *

I stood outside the door looking over the hard, dormant fields that edged the house. Against the snow the sky was brilliant. But in the yard the drifts were trampled, muddied and turned to slop by hooves. The rutted track ran west below the walls, turned through an ancient gate and disappeared. I wondered if there was any good in running after him. Though at first he had seemed gentle, even cheerful, it had not seemed much like friendship at the end. Yet he had sworn, he had said, to serve me. But sworn to whom? He had not sworn, I knew, to me.

I moved off the step and into the yard, not yet following him, only moving. Beyond the gate the path plunged toward the sea. An immense wall ran along the hill, its great height sloping back until I was not certain that I saw its summit. Its shaping must have been outside memory, for everywhere I looked the old foundations were breached and crumbled. Here and there boulders the size of oxen had fallen out of place and filled the path. The wall itself had been dug away behind them. But even in these delvings I never saw bare earth but only layered stones of inner walls as though not only the spurs and ridges of the hills were stonework but the whole prodigious island one great fortress made with hands. Despite my cares, I smiled to think of it, imagining so vast a holding that mountains were its towers or that the barren fields that checkered out of sight across the hills were no more in fact than tiles laid thick along its roof. I wondered where I got such thoughts. It did not matter they were foolishness. They warmed my heart, settled for a moment the wild strange shapes into things I knew.

The path twisted. I wedged myself around the stones, marveling how the old man had carried me through such narrowness, how in the morning he drove his flocks back through them. Loose stones scuffled at my feet, rolled over the edge, and hurtled soundlessly into the pit below. It was the space of several breaths before I heard the thin, far sound when finally they struck the ice. Thereafter I kept more closely to the wall.

I walked until the sun was high above the island, until the shadows that had shriveled began to grow again. The path dropped dangerously. Still, I was high up when the wall fell back, leaving open country straight ahead. Down a mile, to either side of a short bent crag, I saw the shingled beach where I had come ashore. The tide was out. White specks of sheep were straggling across the stones, their small heads browsing in the pools for weed. The sea was well beyond them, stretching gray and definite toward a far clear edge. If there were other isles and kingdoms in the West, even from this place, with two good eyes, I could not see them. I plodded on.

256

The river that all day I had followed at a distance now was near. Because I thirsted, I left the track. I slithered down the slope, fumbling over sliding stones, and came at last with several bruises to the bank. Out of a drift I worked a stone. When I had freed it, I cast it at the ice. After several tries the hard ice splintered but the water was so cold it stung. Then for several minutes, catching my breath, I waited.

The day had been still, with no air moving. Now as evening came, a cold mist drifted inland from the sea. Though I was weary, I found I had to hurry on to keep from freezing. I went along the bank, my hands shoved deep inside my shirt for warmth. I dug my fingers against the skin and felt the strange hair prickling, the thick nubs of nipples. I went on, but an odd uneasiness went with me. Whosesoever flesh this was, it was not my own.

I thought, I am the son. The word was meaningless.

When I had come out onto the beach, the flocks were moving in. The tide had turned and followed them. The surf was building. I heard the dim air boom against the cliffs. I stared. Yet, however long I looked, it still seemed monstrous, each wave like a wall of headless men, their torsos fused, flinging their bound flesh in endless rage against the stone. The great rocks tore them to shreds. At their backs the sun was setting. The sea was red.

In some other life, now done with, or some life yet to come, I heard or would hear old women lisping tales across the looms. Their dry tongues move like shuttles clicking back and forth, telling the daughters of the house how it was on such nights in winter, the old sun dying, the new moon hooked and dangling in the heaven's ear, that the young brown sealmen rose out of the freezing bay and taking manshapes danced and warmed themselves upon the shore. Their manes and shoulders would, they said, have glittered like the foam. Hidden in the rocks, the lonely landwives, watching, ached with joy.

Alone, I waited, restless and staring at the wastes of stone, feeling the evening creep in. A grim moon edged above the hills but brought no light. In the lowering dark the cold sheep stirred and bleated. Once more, uncertain, I ran my eyes along the beach, across its desolate faults and muddy terraces, but no youths danced. The sea was blank, a lake of old dead men. It flung up corpses. I found no joy in it and muttered to myself. Better should I have been had I stayed in Tywy, I thought. There at least I might have fought the death they offered me.

The cotter was nowhere to be seen. Indeed, with darkness falling, it grew ever harder to see anything at all. One gets used to light, to the coming and going of servants with brands and candles. At Morrigan my mother always set some women by the fire to rake and poke it. In that house there were always whispers; even down the darkest corridor, a cough, the sound of footsteps hurrying.

He will not be far away, I thought, nor gone beyond the hearing of his flocks. So I went to stand where the sheep were huddled in the damp. They watched me, each black head lifted, the round eyes searching and afraid. The cold night deepened. The surf crashed endlessly.

Then all at once the crests of waves were wrinkling with the radiance of stars. The beach turned silver and the moon seemed bright. From the cliff behind me the sound of laughter boomed. I whirled around.

A gate rose shining up against the rock. Between the posts the shadow of a cave sank back from sight. Laughing, holding his sides with one great pair of hands, the cotter strode out briskly from the hill. Despite the cold, his face was sleek with sweat. He had a long-handled mallet in his arms and in his hands a spike and several shovels. A length of straw rope was trailing loose about his neck. Relieved, my heart leapt when I looked at him. Yet I had my pride.

'Why do you laugh?' I said.

He turned, bewildered for a moment, to see me there. The mirth went out of him. 'You have no cause to spy on me,' he said. 'When the work is done, I'll see you hear of it.' His voice was harsh, yet I had not expected the resentment in his eyes.

'I did not come to spy,' I said.

'You came.'

'The house was empty. I gave no thought to what you did.'

His old head tilted, stiffened, the anger suddenly going from his stare. Yet for the look he gave me I might have struck him with a whip. I did not understand the change in him. 'Perhaps I am too old,' he said, 'too old and too feeble for your will.' His grim mouth closed, then opened awkwardly. 'Yet I have done the best I could. The work is dreary. Long, you know, I've been at it.' He stopped but went on staring. 'And what harm is there if, when I am free of it, I laugh?' His face was set. Still, it was the face of a man who grieves.

I shook my head. 'I was alone.'

He frowned.

'So you have always been,' he answered gloomily. 'And so you shall be until I've done.'

He turned and called out roughly to his flocks. Though I tried to think of words to say to him, I did not find them.

*   *   *

I could not climb the hills again. I stood still, unwilling out of anger to say as much, but knowing that if on the way I stumbled I would never let him take me on his back. The cotter shambled up and down, his old sides heaving. Wistfully he looked off at the distant peaks. Yet he did not go. Finally, whistling sharply through his teeth, he drove the sheep against the cliff, turned them – whistling louder – until they pressed into the wide mouth of the cave. They went in gladly, untroubled by the dark. Muttering, he stood by the post until the last had passed him. 'Come on, then,' he said to me. Still I lagged and by the time I followed, having fumbled with something in his cloak, he had a taper lit. With that small light he set fire to several torches he had gathered up with a spare hand and, moving methodically about the room, had put them into brackets on the wall.

I stopped at the entrance, a great bare hall opening in front of me, and gawked. It was no sea-cave but manwork, delved and cut back deeply in the hill. Thick columns, naked, without paint or carving, rose at either side to support the ceiling. The span between was empty. At the back a broad archway led away again into the dark. I stood and looked. The old man, knowing the place, stared back at me. He drew no nearer.

'This portal will be last,' he said. 'It is not finished.' There was a tone in the cotter's voice that might have been annoyance, or might have been the mask of it.

'Within,' he said, 'are nine times ninety halls.'

'And at its heart?'

His brown eye flashed. 'A maze of tunnels, lord,' he said, 'long twisting passages, vaults and rooms.'

'And under them?'

'The dark.'

I saw, I imagined nothing. Yet, far from its beginning or its end, I found a thread. 'But in the deepest place?' I asked.

He smiled. 'A throne.'

Like rain upon parched land a joy washed over me. It had no cause, no reason. No form or color crossed my mind, no glimmering of stones, no fine gold glittering. A coolness only touched my memory. And yet I felt a vastness risen underneath the hill: cold, invisible, too huge for any man, and yet a throne. Not knowing why, I laughed.

There was a man beside me in the hall. He laid the mallet and the spike aside, left them leaning with his shovels on the wall.

'Then you are pleased?' he said.

I looked about once more, uncertain, remembering there was light, and saw that there before me were two plain chairs, cut from the rock, not shadows, and a fire pit with wood already stacked and waiting on the floor. A small square table had been dragged before it. On its back were two deep cups and at the edge a jar. 'You knew that I would come,' I said.

'Surely there would be one of you.'

I felt the blood rise in my neck. 'Which one am I?'

'Llugh,' he answered softly, 'the shining one, the white.'

I shook my head.

He heard my halting breath and sighed. 'How should you remember? When the shapes that once had held you walked the land, Géar had not her son.' He scratched his ear. 'Truly, lord, what child has heard his name before his birth?' He turned and, going to the fire pit, lit the wood. The flames danced up between the stones. I watched him silently.

When he had heated the wine, he brought a cup and put it roughly in my hands. I did not feel it. For a heartbeat in the shadow of an oak I had seen her dark eyes laughing. I knew it was another place. It was only a moment, but I spilled the wine. One red drop slid gently between my fingers. 'Is it for Llugh,' I said, 'you cut into the hill?'

He reached out for the cup. 'No.' The word was bitter. Hard as a stone it flew against the wall.

'You serve me.'

'I serve the three who came.'

'Two are dead.'

He shrugged. 'I am too stupid to argue with you, lord. Who am I to know your ways? Build the hall, you say. I built it.' His sad old peasant's face had darkened. He looked away.

The silence, that had lain always at our backs, crept forth and sat between us.

Later, propped against a chair, he slept. Outside the slow pulse of the breakers filled the night. For a moment I stood over him, considering the old head, the square mass of his shoulders. His hands were open. Stretched across his belly, the long scarred fingers twitched. Even dreaming, without hope, now without thought, he kept at his work.

I stepped across the fire. The flames stirred briefly with my passing, then settled back. They gave no light to the room beyond. Out of the bracket on the wall I took a torch.

CHAPTER SIX

The cotter sat before his table, his arms sprawled over the parchment, working with three hands. He held his head cocked to one side, intent, unhearing. The quills moved back and forth from the inkwells. He did not turn until I had closed the door, until I had mounted the well-worn steps and stood unsteady at his back.

'Are you satisfied?' he asked quietly.

I unclasped my wet cloak and let it sink beside me to the floor. A smear of dampness spread along the stones, grew into puddles. He did not notice. Over his shoulders I could see the small black marks he had been making on the parchment. They were clustered all in one corner, near the edge, like a dozen irregular chips of glass. He did not wait to hear my answer but turned again to stare at them himself. He had been drawing islands.

'I was lost,' I said.

A hard rain whitened the windows. When I had climbed the hill from the shore it had been snow, a thick suffocating snow blown in gusts and mixed with thunder. Against the winter sky the outline of mountains had melted into a fog, a cold miasmic damp that clung to my eyes and webbed my lungs. Before me and behind the drifted path had tumbled off in mist. I was in the air again. But I had not been less afraid. It had been no different underground, my hands fumbling on the rock, feeling the darkness slip away invisibly.

'The first room,' I said unevenly, 'branched into three others, those three each to three again. And so it went on endlessly.' He sat staring at his parchment. 'The torch,' I said, 'burned out.'

He moved his eyes back to my face. 'And the throne?'

But then I could not bear to look at him. I held on fiercely to his chair, feeling the thin chill roots of fear drive through my blood. The corner of my lip caught on my teeth. 'I was lost,' I said, 'I told you. There was only darkness.'

He got up slowly, easing himself away from the table. 'Come to the fire,' he said, his old hands moving firmly under my arms to steady me. His face was drawn.

'Tell me who you are,' I said.

'Why?'

'Because I ask.'

He frowned. 'My lord, you are weary.'

Stiffening, I looked back at him. 'I would hear your answer.'

He was silent awhile, his head lifted, like one who sees what he had thought was gone. The deep haggard line of his mouth pulled thinly at the edge. 'Fir Dhearga,' he said. I saw him smile. 'So the first kings called me when they walked on land. But they who called me so are gone. That name went with them.' His lips closed for a moment while he thought. 'Thereafter I had many names, though there was none but myself to hear them. Now, if you will listen, you will hear it is Mug Dafad the bold sheep name me. In their pride, my lord, they take me for their servant.' His red brows arched. I meant to press him but he sat me down beside the fire, so close the flames licked near my legs. 'Aye,' he said, 'perhaps that name is best.'

The stench of burning blew into my face. I scowled. 'If you know me, you know I find no warmth in this!'

He laughed outright. 'Lord,' he said, 'though I have tried to think, it is hard to know what you remember.'

I did not like the sound but the fire was hot. It took my breath. Sweating, with what strength I had I fumbled with my shirt. I had tugged it half off my back when a tear in the damp cloth tangled in my hair and caught. Silently, needing his help, I said his name. He sat unmoving.

'You' – I said aloud – 'you I have forgotten utterly.'

'I know,' he said, 'Yet I have not.' The words came whispered through his teeth. I felt his hand.

Freed from the shirt, I stared up at him.

A dark wind buffeted the house, hurling rain like spearheads against the windows. So the winter storms had beat against the ledges, drumming on the panes at Morrigan. I strove not to think of it and yet I remembered how at Morrigan it was more often snow. There even in full summer the wind blew cold, coming from the west, from the landless reaches of the sea. I remembered standing on the landing outside Urien's door, before the mullioned windows and looking over the ridge, out over the sloping shoulders of our mountain. Sweeping across the summit, the storms had draped the fields with tatters of linen, with long and prickly cloaks of deep, white wool. I had not moved. A voice was murmuring. Through the locked door of his chamber Urien cried out as he read from the books of the wars. I heard it clearly.

Mug Dafad turned his head.

The voice melted, the fire sprang up again, blistering my face.

'Llugh?' he asked but I was done with madness.

'I am myself!' I panted. 'From Géar Finn, from the rough peaks of the mountain I have my name.' The flames shone glittering through the white mane of my hair. I pushed the strands aside and swore.

Mug Dafad leaned back on two long arms. 'And?'

'Nor shall I lose it.'

He looked out past me, across the emptiness of his house, out through the streaming windows toward the sea. The storm had not given up its hammering.

'It is too soon,' he said above the noise. 'Though why, being unready, you chose to come I do not understand.' He shrugged. 'Yet who,' he said, 'has ever known just what you wanted?' He stood for a moment wordlessly. It seemed to me he grieved.

'Come, lord,' he said at last. 'I have saved your sword. The night you came I fished it from the deep. Nor have I let your great ship come to ruin. Even now it lies waiting outside the reef.'

Unbelieving I stared at him. 'The storm still rages.'

'Lord,' he interrupted me, 'who would stop you if you meant to stay?' He smiled. 'Tomorrow, surely, will be soon enough. But while the storm lasts I must teach you how to cross the sea again. It is long since you came out of the west and the way is hard.' He paused. 'The more so,' he added, 'since you will not remember what you know.'

He left the fire. 'Come,' he said, 'all this night I have been working on charts and drawing islands.'

They have dragged the chair out into the air where I can watch the beach. The armorers hover at my right hand, fondling my weapons like children with new toys. They are afraid, and yet I see their eagerness. Long they have heard of my victories, how I humiliated the barons at Dineiden, how like a bull in battle I have warded the land. Still, it is only weird airs and old man's talk to them. They are too young to have seen it.

The place where we have gathered rustles with new-budded leaves. Slowly the wood has crept back, the shattered limbs cleared and saplings grown tall in their place. I remember the women, their naked breasts red in the last light of evening; many are now in their graves.

The shadow of the leaves speckles the arms of the boys. There are patches in the growth where I can see ahead. It will be a long day, I think. All around me I hear the clink of weapons, the men swearing softly because of the flies.

Njal, my youngest, lifts my sword. It is the first time he has carried it. His fingers linger on the hilt. 'Who now can doubt your strength?' he says proudly. 'Never have I heard that so many came at a king's summoning. There is not a hall that doesn't stand empty, not a field where the men haven't left off their plowing.'

Grown trees stand over us. I look down at my hands. 'I was alone when first I came here,' I answer quietly. 'Then this place was a deep old wood.' I smile. 'I had none to help me then and yet above I made a field of it. Mag Finn, they named it.'

There is no need to say more to him. He is Unn's child; his hair has the same gold color hers had once. Alike he has her cunning. He sees this aged scarred face, these heavy bones jutting under yellowed flesh.

'The years have not been unkind,' he murmurs softly. 'Each season has brought increase of glory. Never, I swear it, have I seen such a force.' He is looking out over the crouching backs of the soldiers. 'Now you have only to raise your hand.'

The young men near us draw themselves up trying to make their ghost-white faces look less frightened, to seem as brave as Njal's word would have them. With new oaths they have promised to protect at any cost the body of their king.

'It is an army of boys I have,' I tell him. 'Better I would have liked it if I had Ceorl with me.'

He is looking over the water. 'Who am I to remind you, lord?' he says. 'Yet all men die. Only the king goes on and on.'

'Still, I would have wished him here.'

Something in his face pleads quiet, but he laughs. 'It is only a boy,' he says, 'who comes over the waves to fight with you.'

He has not yet given me the sword. I lay my hand beside his on the hilt. I say, 'He is my son.'

Njal's tanned, large face is streaked with dust. He does not move. Along the western horizon the faint bland shadow of a cloud seems hardly to advance. Its distant lightning forks noiselessly. Somehow the cloud is nearer.

'He is my heir,' I say, 'the first child of my loins.'

His fingers stick against the hilt. His breath is harsh.

But already the sentinels have seen the first bright sails. 'Llugh comes!' they cry out in warning and alarm. On the strand and back into the trees the landsmen take up the cry. The wood is filled with unsurpassed, unbelievable roaring.

'You must strive to look more kingly,' Mug Dafad said.

He had given me a new longshirt embroidered with vines, bright green leaves and berries. Though snug across the shoulders, it fitted well enough, I thought. The useless armholes could always be resewn. The white long cloak was trimmed with ermine and clasped with bronze. Three buckles of silver he had fastened to my waist. Into one hand he put a gaudy shield and under my left arm the rolled parchment, bound in a sheath of kid and secured with seven gold coils of chain. Almost I felt like the barons who stood at Thigg's call at Ormkill. Surely a man could not fight so dressed. I wriggled.

Mug Dafad's deep eyes looked hard at mine. 'The Penandrun are old,' he said. 'Pray their sight is not so keen as once it was.' He took his old hand from my back and winked. 'Fear nothing. A stiff wind will blow away the smell of sheep.'

Wavelets clucked against the hull, the rigging creaked. He took, I saw, some joy in that. He said, 'You have only to go as I taught you, westward where the sea and sky make one gray line. Yet if all else fails, as each day closes, sail at the sun.'

I strain to tell it – even now, though six score times I've said the words and, after a dozen tellings, more or less the same. Though not in the hall. Not among such men as earn their drink with tales, men who have whole histories in their heads, though they speak cold-heartedly, who know not only what last Urien said to me but where he spoke and what it meant and the name, god knows, of the first star shining that night when evening came. To them I dare not tell anything, not that didn't happen one, two, three toward death or with a leap into the bed of a woman. I told a red-haired farmer down in Harl, told it twice, in fact, because I bought the wine. He thought there should be more about the sheep. Say what you will.

In a crofter's hut, the houseman twisting twigs of heather, his fat wife spinning, I told it backward. In truth, it made no sense to him. Still we laughed and the houseman, seeing the poverty of his table, pushed his daughter at me in place of ale. Afterward, while she pinched fleas against her thighs, I told it straight. She did her best to seem polite but knew, she said, a livelier tale about a wheelwright who met a female bogey on the road to Tyre.

Say what you will. The world is wide and if death is wider, yet eternity has but a narrow door.

White the island was and barren. So even in the books of the wars it is written. It rose from the gray ocean like a floating town, half-made, like a citadel whose roofs were mountain rock, whose deepest heart was darkness. Old it was as the rocking sea and hollowed like a hall. Three times I tried to climb upon the shore. Twice, staggering against the surf, against shapes I might have dreamt, I fell back witless. The third time an immense old man found the thing I was, alone and shaking on the stones. Like senseless mutton he strapped me to his back, hauled me up to the drifted hills and set me in his house. Some days I spent there. No man was witness to what we said. But when I left, my hair was white and I had both my eyes. Under my arm I bore a rolled-up map of islands in the West.

The old men cough. The young men smile behind their hands.

'You mites! You flies!' I scream at them. 'When you come knocking, if I will not have you, who is there to let you in?'

CHAPTER SEVEN

It is no great matter getting used to other flesh. Ever boys shoot up, thickening what once was lean. So youths turn men and old men, sleeping by the wall, grow fat. Yet no arm remembers that its reach was less. The flesh scarce knows the thoughts of men. With me it was no different. In three days I have forgotten I had all my sight and saw, without regarding it, like other men. The gray clouds drifted west across the bow. I lived; the blood worked in my veins. Though they were not my legs, such as they were, they held me when I stood. It was only in the evenings I remembered Llugh.

In dreams, on the island that rose only in sleep, Géar held him out to me, her white arms lifted above the waves. I saw the child, wrapped in a dirty rag and crying for the sea. He inspired no terror. In truth such dreaming convinced me I had little yet to fear from him. Only Géar bewildered me. I saw her walking on the shore, her white face radiant as she watched the boy. For that I grieved. Bitterly, I considered the faithlessness of women, who will be made happy by a squealing babe in dirty linen.

But in the days I had no time to think of her. I was alone. It needed twenty men, I thought, to keep the sails.

The first rigging Mug Dafad set, and while that served well enough when the wind was at my back, out of the smell of land, the breeze turned around. The ocean heaved up sliding hills, the sleek sails tore and there was nothing I could do but drop the lines. Those I could not free, for the deck pitched under me, I cut through with my sword. But even then the broad ship rolled. To keep from falling I crawled back to sit on the bench beneath the awning. A far-off grayness wrapped the sun. I folded my arms and watched the rolling ocean cover it.

A child of the land imagines there is an infinite horizon out at sea, a vastness proclaiming immortality. Yet how small the world seems from the deck. With no height greater than the mast to climb, the bravest sailor looks at best a few short leagues ahead. Far better then is a house on a blowing hill. When night and storm come prowling, a man can always bar the door.

The ship rocked fretfully. In time I slept. When I awoke the wind was running through my flesh. Unrested still, I leaned against the rail. The tail of some dream lashing in my head, I was not listening. Yet the air, it seemed, was filled with belling cries. I turned my head.

From the north and east the water all about was black with seals. Barking with grief, they crowded near the ship. Thrusting up their chiseled heads, they gasped for air. Their bleak eyes found me on the deck, stared with such mad fright when they saw me that I looked away, looked past them to where the sea was blank.

Yet there was something.

Black, two fathoms deep, a wrinkling shadow moved beneath the waves. It had no form, no more than night has, yet it advanced unceasingly as night advances. With awful certainty the shadow passed beneath their outer ranks.

The mobbed seals wailed. I caught their fear – not of the dark itself but of the stillness out ahead of it, the uneasy quiet before the blackness slithered up to sight. I tugged my cloak. Straining with my neck, I felt the vast head rising with my own.

Hill-like, mossed and scaled, horribly it cut the air. The head split wide. I saw the rows of dagger teeth. Already reddened, a seal corpse lay mangled in its mouth. There was a grim, brief silence. Chunks of lifeless meat bobbed in the sea.

The huge tail slapped. With bleeding jaws it lumbered in once more. Ten thousand flippers scratched; ten thousand scrambled. Black, splattered bodies rolled down headless in the waves. I heard its roar. As though in answer, a cry out of my own chest coursed through the ship. The long boards shuddered, pulled against their ribs, and squealed. Clamping shut my eyes, I jerked away. But, even blind, I felt my clawed great fingers rake on flesh. Against my teeth a throbbing belly came apart.

I forced my eyelids open.

The sea had fallen. I did not understand, nor did I want to understand it, now. I shook my head.

Beyond the bow, sculling with his webbed black hands, a seal was watching me. His coat was bright beneath the stars, without a wound. About him were the corpses of his kin. 'Lord,' he called up solemnly, 'why do you let us die?'

Unknowing what I had done or not done, my voice was cold. 'How have I wronged you?' I called to him. 'Myself, I never sought your life.'

His clear eyes, black as currants, shone with grief. 'What does it matter what you sought? Over the sea we saw a great ship shining and we came. But what seemed light welled into darkness and night devoured us.'

I looked away. 'Surely, there is safety somewhere. The sea is wide.'

'Not wide enough.'

I clutched the rail. I said, 'What is it that you want?'

He grunted bitterly. 'Only tell us, lord, where you are not.'

There was a dryness at my heart. I strove to touch it. But out of my own flesh, even as I roared, the Darkness that had been only waiting came.

'White he is – like some ice hill,' the voice said stubbornly.

The other swore. 'As are some seals,' he said.

The faces I could barely see looked down at me.

'Yet he is a man.'

'So we were once.'

'And yet, lord, he is a man and white.'

The other spat. 'Then you must ask him what he is.'

The smaller paused. His long nose whiskers twitched. 'He sleeps,' he said.

But I sat up, to look at them. The greater snorted. Begrudgingly he moved a ponderous flipper just out of reach. Thereafter he did not stir. His head was large, not quite a seal's nor yet a man's. In the dampness, though the wind had roughened it, his coat was silver; his dark eyes shone, brighter than mortal eyes. I set my teeth.

'Where is the Dark?' I said.

The smaller swallowed twice before he spoke. 'Man,' he answered, 'already it is night.'

I looked across the rail. The sea and sky were all one dimness, with no clear line between. But if it were night, it was a night without stars. The ship moved softly through a mist.

'There were seals,' I said.

The smaller stared uneasily. 'There are always seals.'

'No,' I said, 'the sea was black with them.'

The other, who had not spoken at all to me, was quiet, his remote eyes turned back to watch the waves. 'Twelve days we swam alone,' he said, his deep voice low, 'and there was nothing before us or behind and nothing on either side.'

I looked at him and past him. Indeed the sea was empty, the corpses gone. 'Then it was only a dream,' I said, relieved. 'I am glad of that. Had it been otherwise I would have owed you whatever blood-price is due your rank.'

His bull neck straightened. 'Then, man, you would have owed me much. In my own country I was king.'

He shambled nearer, his blunt nails scraping on the deck. His great bulk overhung me like a ledge. Yet, looking up, I smiled. 'That is an odd thing surely,' I answered him, 'for I was king myself of the only land I know.' So that I would have my height again, I stood. He took no notice.

'What land?' he said.

'Tir rhwng Moroedd, the land between the seas.'

'Just one more island.' His proud lip curled. 'What claim is that to grandness? There is no lack of islands.'

I smiled again. 'It is not from the land my kingship comes.'

The sealman scowled. 'Say then who you are,' he said.

He saw me pause.

'By Dagda,' he said dryly, 'either you are someone or you are not.'

I waited, though there was no cause for it. Since I had gone into the world, so men had challenged me. And freely I had answered, taking good care that all should hear, a name that I had shouted before the Menhir, before swordsmen and tinkers, before Thigg himself and all his hosts and heralds in my father's hall. Even to Mug Dafad, though he had muttered, I has sworn it. Yet now I stood looking down at my white hands. The mist blew cold and damp across my nostrils. It had the smell of darkness on it, the urine smell of fear. I bent my head. The air rushed by me. It smelled, I knew, of the blood of seals.

'I am Finn,' I told him.

The sealman nodded.

'I am Llugh, the son of Finn.'

His dark stare hardened; his face became a stone.

'I am Ar Elon,' I whispered, 'though he is dead.' My voice trailed off.

I stopped, for already I had said more than I knew. Yet the words, having found shape in my mouth, seemed hard as fact. Three deaths I would have, Cerridwen said. Three lives, then, were mine as well. Yet there was something more. Fragments, pieces making nothing whole, jerked in my head. It was as when from the door at Cerridwen's hut I had looked north and south at once, on darkness and morning, as the old stone turned, except surely it was the stone that was still, the great earth wheeling around instead. I could not find my place. My head was spinning.

The sealman grunted. I lifted my neck.

As far as his bulk would let him I saw him kneel. The smaller followed, his webbed short fingers spread in homage, his weak unseeing eyes bent toward the deck. But the eyes of the other were hard and still. He watched me carefully.

'It is little enough joy I have had since I took this shape,' he said. 'No more will this bring me. There is no help for it. The world goes as it must.' He straightened awkwardly. 'Lord,' he whispered, his low voice certain as it was dismayed, 'you have my service and, as far as I may give it, that of my servant.'

I thought of all the men who once had sworn to me, to me as to Ar Elon they had sworn.

'What name did you know?' I said.

He frowned: a king himself though bound in a beast's rank flesh, half one thing and half another, even as I was, shared among my lives.

'The one name,' he answered evenly, 'you would not say.'

The men are gone, frightened like dogs of thunder, slinking from the hall, not looking back. Even he who must attend the king has gotten himself safe beyond the doors. In the grim light of the little fires I give them I see he has gone off without his pike. He hasn't, I know, the stomach to come back for it. I think, how will there be courage in the land when the heart of the king is mad? It is a good thought worth repeating, worth telling the *filidh* when, their bellies empty, they creep back with light . . . like hounds, I think, whose only bravery is their bellies' growl. Poor hounds, I think, frightened by an old king telling tales.

'Do you fear me as well?' I ask her.

Half-listening, she brushes her old woman's hair off her face. 'What are your lies to me?' she answer quietly. 'I who bore your children?' Her voice is tired, the shrillness muted by a yawn. It is an old argument, more habit now than anger. 'Was there a night,' she sighs, 'I didn't hear your whisperings?'

Her thin arms folded, she passes among the deserted benches. 'Your ravings,' she runs on softly, 'and shouting to old dead men.' She stoops, resting her cheek against the cool stones of the hearth. 'The guests gone from my house – men who came out of kindness, out of faith to honor us.' She touches, wearily, the hilt of my sword where it hangs from its brace by the logs and kettles. She turns her head.

'My lord, are you certain it is Llugh who comes against us?'

'Yes.'

She rises stiffly, her flat eyes moving among the benches, seeing each place where the men are not. 'How do you know?' she asks me.

'Woman, I have always known.'

Her hands are clenched against her flesh. 'You?' she says, her small voice dry, a whisper in the cold. But for the sentries the yards below are empty. I hear them shifting on frozen boots, watching the distance, uneasy in the chill black air. Inside, the fires at last are dead, the darkness greater than the night without. Only her eyes are bright.

'You – who were never certain? – who were always asking but never, though you walked with marvels, never asked them outright what they meant?'

'Yes.'

'You knew?'

'Yes.'

'What Mug Dafad built beneath the hill?' She pauses. 'The name . . .,' she begins.

I lean forward, looking across the floor stones from the chair that was always mine, from which in the years before her birth I ruled this folk. There are voices in the hall, but only I can hear them. In the darkness I can almost distinguish the figures of the barons, bold men in their finery, the lean hounds sucking bones at their feet. Like brown leaves are the faces of the men who are gone. There is stiffness in my neck. I turn. Against my shoulders the seahair bristles.

In the morning it rained. Listening, I blinked awake beneath the awning. Silver curtains shunted off from the canvas but within it was almost dry. During the night the wind had come around to the south, casting a storm before it. Still, it was unlike any rain I knew. The air was filled with a vague, weightless light. The soft rain fell without touching it, as though in one place worlds of air and water passed without meeting. I drew a breath.

At my left hand was a fish, green-scaled and silver-bellied. A trickle of blood was clotted at its mouth. The hand that had placed it there pulled away.

'I have left that,' he said in a boy's cracked voice. Naked and shivering, he sat outside the awning, the rain matting his dark hair. He was small and so scrawny I might have added up his ribs. About his bare knees was a mound of heads and fishbones.

'It is poor fare,' I said, staring, 'that leaves you thin.'

His teeth were rattling but he grinned. 'Lord,' he said, 'I was a seal when I ate them. What good they did me that shape has.' He poked his own frail arms. 'Truly,' he said, 'I was better off with fur but the spell is hard. I keep forgetting.'

I saw how pitifully he hugged himself. Drawing off my cloak, I threw it out to him. He snatched it gratefully and tugging the embroidered cloth about his shoulders he cried out gaily. 'Lord,' he shouted, 'I swear if ever men or seals come at you, it is Wyck you shall have at your hand.'

I felt a smile half crease my mouth. 'That is your name?'

He nodded.

'Then, Wyck, you have my thanks,' I said and laughed for the wind was not as cold as it had been and the rain was outside the awning. With no more thought I took the fish. The meat was odd and, although I did not much like the taste of it, it made short work. 'And where is your master?' I asked with my last mouthful.

Wyck's eyes which had been darting happily rested on his feet. He prodded them. 'He feeds in the sea,' he said, wistful all at once. 'He was a mage before he was a king. There is wizardry in his marrow and salt in his veins.' Still digging at his toes, he sighed. 'He never forgets the words.'

I had been a boy myself and heard at their spellfires the aunts, smelling at crow's rumps and muttering, quoting the old speech learned by heart, wild words I have never mastered. I frowned. Wise and sad were the women of the Kell, but one by one death took them.

'They are only words,' I said.

The boy cocked his head.

The rain had darkened and a man came forth from it. Tall he was and naked as the boy. But it was the sea that ran from his shoulders. He paused at the awning, his wide nostrils sniffing the air. He looked down at the fisbones.

'I trust he left a scrap for you.'

'As much as he was able.'

The tall man laughed. His head was long and horselike but it had a king's steadiness. His big hands were motionless by his side. Without my leave he came under the awning.

I had not forgotten our meeting.

'What name did you swear to?' I asked. For in the night, even as he knelt, I had gone off to sleep.

Under his upper lip his horse teeth showed in a grin. 'What, lord,' he answered back, 'accepts such an oath unknowing?'

I saw the truth of that, but thought, knowing less, brave men have sworn to me. Need comes, as unlooked for as oaths. Only a fool neglects help when it is offered. But I saw he was just. 'It is as you say. It was only rudeness I gave you.'

'That is a fair answer,' he said. 'As fair will I give you. But a tale comes with it.' His eyes that were strange in a seal were stranger in a man. He did not blink as I watched them.

I said: 'I will hear it.'

273

He found a place for himself and sat, putting his big hands on his knees. 'I was a king myself,' he said, 'of Tir na Trí Oilean, which, although they are called that, are no lands at all but only islands. The islands themselves hardly deserve to be called so. The greatest is no more than a coppice of brushwood sticking high out of the sea and the lesser but two hills off the coast. Yet I was king over them as my father was. Though, in truth, we were both kings for show. The women rule there, the king's only business hunting boars in the wood and watching the ocean.'

I knew the feeling and liked him better for it. I said: 'So it was when I was a boy at Morrigan.'

He smiled. 'Yet even that came to less. There have been many kings since the world was young, and few pigs. When I took the kingship I had only the sea to look at.'

'That would be a most unkingly business,' I said.

'Surely there was not much luck in it,' he answered. 'Still, morning and evening I walked on the shore. For as the days went, the air itself of the uplands seemed to sour in my lungs and the stone of my wife-sister's house was without glory. Far better, I thought, were the salt wind and the stones that rolled in the surf. It came even that I slept at the shore's edge. And since he was as unneeded as I, for then there was little work for his hounds, I brought my dog boy for company.'

He glanced at the boy. 'Even as he is now,' he said, 'so he was then: eager and sad by turns, small help and great trouble. Yet he would be ruled by me. So together we sat on the banks that faced westward, upon the great ocean, watching the dolphins leap and the small fish scurry under the birds. I taught him the few spells my sisters had taught me. He would sit open-mouthed, eyes staring. But he never remembered. Or as storms broke the stillness, we would watch the white skies darken, the squalls coming in with a hiss like the waves. Such was my rule. In the gray cold mornings, when it would have seemed easier to have stayed in the hall, we would walk on the strand, throwing stones at the empty sea.

'Only one day we looked out and saw that all the wide sea was thick with sails, thicker than ever it had been with storm clouds or birds. The prows of the great ships pointed straight at the land. Men swarmed on the decks, shouted and lifted their spears. Like thunder their howls rolled across to us.

'The boy jumped up, his legs dancing with fear. We must flee, he cried to me. But, I thought, I have stood too long looking at nothing to be frightened when there is something to see. So I kept where I was; and the boy, though I had no power to help him, stood with me.

'We looked; and all at once up the slope of the beach a woman came toward us, out of the sea. The sheath she wore clung to her breasts and waist, nor did she free it for modesty but clambered up swiftly on the stones. A boy she had with her, scarcely more than a babe, his hair white with the morning as hers was black. But his shoulders were already big and in his hands he bore armor for two men. Never had I seen such armor. The new helms shone like twisting suns, the mail-coats gleamed. Yet, the god knows, the light in her gray black eyes was brighter still. She touched her brow.

'*Lady*, I called out joyously, *it is no great love I have for women, for my house is burdened with many, yet you I would gladly welcome.*

'Those deep eyes looked in mine. If I saw the warning there, the pride beyond all hope such as the *filidh* say the best men have when death is sure, yet I would not be warned. Her small breasts trembled in the cold. I longed to warm them.

'*Tell me what you wish*, I said, *for I see you have come in haste and not for nothing. Yet, though there is a fleet of fierce men at your back, if there is a thing that I might do and keep my honor, I will do it.*

'Her face was tilted up. Above the breakers I could hear the knock of warriors throwing down their oars.

'*Lord,*' she pleaded, *if the mother of men put good in you, put on this armor.*

'Already the warriors were leaping onto the shore. Close at my heels the dog boy wept.

'Surely this is my death, I thought. Yet I would not die naked. *Only dress my boy as well*, I said, *for he stood with me when he might have run.*

'So she helped me, and her white-haired lad moved with equal grace about poor Wyck so that we rose together, the shining metal braced and tight. It was the lad who put the helmet in my hand.

'*Stand off*, I said, *perhaps I may buy their mercy on you with my death.*

'But then he spoke, his voice colder and stranger than a child's. *It is against myself I've seen you armed*, he said. His eyes that were dark and unwinking looked in mine. *But not for this day. You must grow a little in wisdom and I in brawn before we meet.* As though to drive off the cold, he shook himself. He laughed then, deep as a man.

'*Far safer were you by your sister's fire*, he said. *There you would have had a lot more suited you; in your own bed you might have fathered kings. But you would watch the rolling deep.* His stern smile faded. I heard his breath. *It takes its price.* But before I found a word to answer he had turned.

'Slowly he went down among the stones to where the warriors waited. Seeing him, they cheered. A man came forward, a war chief by his crest and colors. He met the boy and, lifting him ceremoniously, carried him to the bow of the longboat pulled up farthest on the shore. At this there was a buzzing. Crowding around him, the warriors went into their boats.

'I rubbed my eyes. I said, *This will be my shame forever, that I stood staring while a boy came out of the sea and wished my death.*

'The woman watched me sidelong. But when she moved to back away, I took her arm. The flesh was cold but it was flesh, the small bones thin beneath. There was no glory. Like any of my sister's brats, she wriggled in my hand.

'*Woman*, I said, *what ill gift have you given me?* Her child's lip jutted out. I thought, For all her shining looks, she is no goddess but a maid. I held her tighter. She turned in anger and in one haughty glance took in the shore, the few bare fields, the pinched and cheerless town above. On the highest place my sister's hall lay cramped against the rock. Her eyes smiled spitefully. *Who will remember the landkings of this place?* she said. *It is the sea I give you.*

'*You gave me armor* – I scowled – *and my death, I think, though it was a boy who challenged me.*

'*He is my son,* she whispered. Then all at once her child's hurt face seemed changed again, burnt white against the sea. She was as she had been, a woman with a woman's loveliness. A patch of color climbed her throat. She moved against me. *My husband's gods reward you, lord,* she cried, *as I have gained only the hate of mine.* Her voice died in her. Her eyes had lifted to my face. I let her go. There was a silence.

'*It was because I am a woman that you took the armor,* she said at last. *We are not different. Because he was a man I took my own lord to my bed. Even as you, he knew not what he bought with that. For he has bound himself with oaths and will not remember what was always plain. And yet, though he will wreck the world, I gave a sword to him.* Her lips pulled back. *So I have armed you, lord, to stand beside him in his need, though he takes from me the one other thing that I have loved.* Her head was bent. I saw the tears that fell between her breasts. I might have spoken.

'Her mouth twitched a little, steadied. *He goes to kill my son.* She turned, looking up again. *And though he has arts and skills such as no man ever had, yet you must help him if you can.*

'I watched her blankly. I said, not understanding, *I am just a man.*

'*No man was given less than will be asked of him.* She smiled. From under the nightfall of her hair I saw, despite her sorrow, a kind of triumph in her eyes. She touched my neck. It was then she spoke the words that my poor dog boy will not remember, words fair and gentle as the summer dusk, as soft as sleep, yet warm they were as a woman's breath, the breath that wakes a tired man in his bed. I heard them and it seemed in answer my own blood burned. My head was dizzy. I seemed to fade. The firm flesh melted, steamed, and became a fog that, drifting, spread and swelled. My mouth grew long, my pale skin darkened, and my nails turned black. Unhinged from joints, my long legs widened and my back grew thick. I felt as though every part of me were moving until, against the armor, the metal split along its seams, splintered and, rooting in my flesh, rayed out as hair. So that when I had a shape once more to stand in front of her, it was a seal's.

'The boy was crouching at my feet. His face was twisted, the old lines gone and new ones rutted in their place. The wind came rushing coldly from the sea. Despite his silver coat, the new fat on his hams and thighs, he shivered.

'She smiled again. *The sea will never harm him, lord*, she said and laughed, *though I fear it will not warm him either*. She stretched herself and looked out at the waves.

'But my heart was filled with dread. *And what do you wish me?*

'*May you have peace, Glas Awyddn. I have no strength to send you out or call you back. It was yourself who promised me your aid. I did not ask it. Even now, if fear is greater than your pride, go back to your sister's house. By her fire you will find your man's flesh whole again.*'

His face, that was a man's face now, looked up. In the depths of his strange eyes I saw the memory of that cold shore, the memory of longing and pity: the man's longing for a maid, the pity, beyond all longing, that would not see her pain.

'So you swore the oath.'

His chin rose proudly.

'Yet how did she know where I would be?'

Forcing his voice to steadiness, he said, 'Lord, how could she know? She saw you only once. And, though she lay with you, she never knew your heart.'

I stared.

Glas Awyddn's breath went out of him. His big hands shifted on his knees. 'Lord,' he said slowly, 'how shall any living man come into being except a woman bring him from the womb? I cannot tell you what she did. It was not my plan or my contriving. Yet it was she who made me as I am.'

His eyes met mine. 'She sent me west,' he said. 'Twelve days across the slate-gray sea, west where nothing is but only fog and wind and rolling waves. Twelve days and we saw no men, no islands, heard no sound but the gull's cry, lost as we were, far from land. On the last day, when the sky was low and churning overhead, we saw your ship. Yet by the way it leaned and drifted, its sails unstrung, we did not think to find it manned. The day was closing. Weary, wanting only to ease the stiffness of our arms, we climbed onto the deck. Myself, I thought you were a corpse. It was my boy who rolled your head and touched your shoulder. Even then I did not wonder who you were. The thought of her so stirred me I could not think the lord that she would send me to would seem a man.'

'Until I said my name.'

'Lord, there were three you gave me.'

'And none you knew.'

'Let it be as you please,' Glas Awyddn said.

But I shook my head. 'Yet one you knew, though I would not say it.'

His breath grew short and for a moment I could hear only the rain, the harsh pounding rain such as fell when with Tabak I left Morrigan. It hammered the deck and roiled the sea. So it falls, I thought, over the fields and the forests of earth, on the houses of men, the deafening rain that keeps away silence. So it may be that it fell on the gray roof stones of Tech Duinn, upon the House of the Dead. Glas Awyddn stood. 'A sword she said she had given you with which to wreck the world.'

We looked at one another.

'The name,' I whispered. But though bravely he answered, I already knew.

PART III

Old Men's Songs

CHAPTER EIGHT

They have reason to love me in Hwawl, red Hwawl where in the blue of late evening the waters washed red on the shore. Upward from fish weirs the blood smell crept into the air, climbed out of the river like a mist. It stank in my nostrils. Still, I was king three years before I went to them. If they begrudged me this, I did not hear of it. Well enough they knew of my war with the barons. But when I had settled the matter at Dineiden, before the first snow, I went home. There I rebuilt the tomb they had raised up quickly to cover Yllvere. I had the rock quarried at Bheur and floated on barges. Because of the weight of the stone and the fear of ice, I had the barges refitted. The tax was heavy that year. Nonetheless, men thought, let him honor his dead. My strength was still new to them and the land once again was at peace.

The envoy from Hwawl came in the spring. I met him on the wharves, for his sail had been seen a mile upriver and word sent down to me. He was a big red-haired man of about my years. Already he had three sons, he told me, each the like of himself. Though none, he feared, would reach an age to have sons of his own. He looked down at his boots. The spring sunlight cooked his white face like a sausage. He sweated. So one after another men came to me out of the towns. From the cities it was always matters of land rights and trade, and the bribes matched their purses in horses and gold. Always I took what was offered, then did what I pleased. But from the towns, from towns that were too small for streets, from fishermen's cottages lost and untraceable along the creeks of the saltmarsh, from huts on the moorlands and the spare, scraped-up villages, stony and comfortless under the white chalk hills, from the least and the most forgotten of these came tales: hounds that howled at noon and ate manflesh, boars with tusks long as pikes, harts with two heads, giants with none, green mists and leopards, demons, dead men and dreams. In Hwawl, it was the Fuathan. Though whether it was six or seven or only one who ranged by himself up and down the rough banks, overturning boats and grabbing with icy fingers at the legs of men, he could not say.

The man had brought a girl with him, clear-skinned and round-breasted, with hair red and disordered as the flame on a torchhead. She was nearer fourteen than twenty but had been well schooled and laughed when she saw I was watching. How little, I thought, they remember Ar Elon. Yet all things will be as they must. He should have had me go with him without the gift of the girl, myself and Glas Awyddn for company, though a few soldiers with nets would have handled the matter more swiftly and with less chance of harm.

Somewhere it is written what I did there, how I hauled the river mage out on the rock, my ax sunk deep in the slime of his chest. His hairsnakes tightened around my neck; the coils spilled over my shoulders. But against the puffed silver heads, pressed near my mouth, I whispered my name. In terror they fled me, sank back into the rushes and were no longer seen. More than that I barely remember. For the space of a few breaths there must have been silence, the silence of wonder, and afterward cheers. The sun winked in the branches, the water was spotted with shadows and flies. In the late, still afternoon I washed the gore from my arms. In the evening I was made a guest of the village.

Because they had no hall to hold us, the fires were built in the open. Under the boughs of a great rambling oak they piled up the wood, in the high solemn place closed off from the town where time out of mind their old men settled quarrels and the women told tales.

We climbed a steep embankment to reach it, away from the river, though the current's cool murmur kept in my hearing all the way through the trees. Above the wood, the land was scraped and cleared, the ground flattened by the long years the villagers had tramped there. Only the oak thrust upward, undiminished, indifferent to the stirrings of men. Undisturbed by their passing, by the bandy-legged priest, the dogs and the women, it breathed without bitterness. The sky, where only the tree reached, was quiet. No cloud hid the stars.

I had been the last to enter the circle. Before I had settled, an old woman hobbled in front of the fires. She was gap-toothed and ugly, her short arms greased to the elbows from skimming fat from the kettles. Some restlessness possessed her and she tugged at her rags, stamping her small feet impatiently until the last man looked up. The girl they had given me saw her and slipped her smooth hand in mine. The old woman chuckled.

'Well you have done for us this day,' she cried, 'though as well we have served you. For in Hwawl there never was a girl more likely to please. She is not so cold as Yllvere nor as fated as Géar, but will keep your side warm in the evening and in the cold of the morning deliver up sons.'

I heard the men grumble. Whatever they knew of this, the name of the witch queen had filled them with dread. My eye opened wide. 'Woman,' I said, 'where have you learned this?' I was thinking of Géar. But then the tables were being laid under the tree and the cooks came carrying platters and the boys bearing wine. We ate and the men laughed again. Their mouths crammed with meat, they recounted the terrors of the river mage, which grew in the telling. The young widows looked wistful and wept. Still they took the cups when the wine came around; with gulping sighs they drank their revenge. Some smiled after that. One, who had kept the boy coming, hiked her skirts to her belly and danced, her round legs red and stumbling in the light of the fires. The old wives scolded and howled, but the boys peered out from the branches and grinned. Once more the wine was passed. The priest hummed to himself; men put away sorrow. Warm talk and laughter filled the air. When the old woman stood, not a man shouted her down. The embers were dying and they were ready for tales.

She stood in the clearing, staring at where I sat on the high seat under the oak. She looked like a gray gnome of wood. Such figures the old ones placed at the feet of the dead – shrunken and quiet, watching with unwinking eyes the brief journeys of the living, the endless wearying voyages of the men who were gone.

'My lord,' she said and held out her arms.

The feasting had ceased. The boys had climbed down from the branches and sat on the ground. A child had been wailing. Calmly, unhurried, his mother gave him her breast.

The old woman looked over the ranks of men, over the blank fields beyond them to the west. It may be, even before she spoke, that the listeners felt a vastness stirring, bodiless and invisible, over the farthest hills, the merest edge of a darkness, blacker than night. No breeze turned the leaves.

'In the West there is a tree . . .,' she said and stopped, listening to her own small voice floating out on the silence. 'A tree so huge that this great oak is but a stalk of grass beside it – so wide that in itself it is a wood. Yet never in the world's time had any man seen it. In secret, from one age to another, it grew. In its branches the great birds found refuge. Not the least of them was Badb, the crow that was Anu's. She made her nest at the summit, in the high place looking over the earth. And as vast as that tree was, so was the body of Badb. When she lifted her wings, a shadow covered the world, and the hills and the valleys fell into darkness all the way to the sea. In the harbors, thinking it was a storm in the mountains, the sailors hid under the decks, cursing the air. Only one man did not curse it or shake his fists at the darkness. He was a boy then and lived in the North, in a great house that women kept, keeping it and the boy to themselves. For they knew who he was, if he did not. They saw that if ever he lifted his eyes he would go out from their rooms, from their fires and their spinning, and the thing that he was, that they had kept and shielded out of longing and fear, that which they loved and had hated, would be free in the world. Yet one day, because it could not be otherwise, one day he left them, going up in the hills. And the wood that had always been closed opened up for him. In the darkness, under the roof of its branches, he found a stair . . .'

I lay back, hearing the voice of the woman, the tale moving in and out of my thoughts with my breath. My eye looked into the darkness. I remembered the climb and the fight I had with the crow. And every word the woman spoke was as I knew it. But a shadow crossed my face and I sighed. 'Woman,' I said, 'surely you are first among the tellers of tales. For although none came with me, yet so clear is the telling you might have climbed at my side. But long I have lived with this. Tonight I would hear something new.'

The men of Hwawl looked puzzled. *What tales are more pleasing*, they wondered, *than tales of his youth? What talk would he hear that is sweeter than praise?* But the old woman smiled.

'If there were anything new, a king would have heard it,' she answered. But then she thought again and her little eyes sank into her white withered face like knots in wood. 'Yet there are tales so old they are remembered only in sleep and never on waking. Such might come new to your ears.'

But Glas Awyddn glanced at her doubtfully. 'Lord,' he said boldly, 'what is forgotten is best left where it is.' But I saw the men watching and stretched out my hand.

'Would you have thought that,' I whispered, 'when you gave me my name. Beyond that, where is there harm? It is certain I never learned anything quickly. Yet one thing is more certain: I never listened except I was ready to hear.'

He wore a man's face then as I did, the seal's features wiped away, as though the years in the West were but dreams that had troubled our sleep. It was a man's bare face that stiffened. But I laughed and, drawing a ring from my finger, I tossed it at the old woman's feet.

Slowly she bent forward to grasp it. 'Aye,' she said softly, both mocking and greedy, as a cat will take hold of its prey, 'as small even as this was the gift the Dagda gave once to Ar Elon . . .'

'An acorn?'

'A ship,' I repeated, 'for both were the same. The long boards sprouted cold in the harbor. The walls by the river blanched white with its shining and men hid their eyes. So under the very spears of Thigg's soldiers I left them, and the ship, though I had no skill with it, brought me south to Tinkern and then onto Hren. But when I saw the waves of the sea I despaired.'

'My master can sail it,' Wyck piped up bravely from under my cloak.

Glas Awyddn sat quietly listening, his hand bent; I could not see his face. The rain had been drawn up like a garment gathered one fold after another to itself. The water lay naked beneath it. I looked out. Over the bow a few late stars glittered brightly. So the same stars shone at the beginning, unfaded and close to the earth, before men chased them away with their wondering.

'What is it you want?' said Glas Awyddn.

'What has any man wanted?'

The tall man looked up. 'I should fear you, then,' he said.

'Fear a man?'

The wind made him squint. 'Him more than the Other.'

Something scratched at the keel. Through the boards I could feel it, though there was nothing to see. A long, easy swell rolled under the ship, lifting it gently and steadily, then setting it down.

'If there is land,' I said, 'I must find it.'

'And if there is not?' said Glas Awyddn.

Wyck's mouth crooked up suddenly. He had been waiting for morning. As he watched, the ship lurched once more.

'We're aground,' the boy whispered.

But there was no ground.

Behind, in the east, day crept above the edge of the world. Glas Awyddn went aft in the new light to watch it. Out of the shadows the sun lit his flesh like a torch.

'Lord,' he said softly, 'they have taken the sea.'

I shifted under the awning. 'Come quickly,' he said. I went down to him slowly, watching the sky lighten, the sun grown huge and white off the stern. I stared out intently, glancing around and behind. But all I saw was ocean. The new sun poured over it, as pure and as clear as a spring.

Glas Awyddn shuddered. 'Look into its depths,' he said, softly.

I looked down.

At first I saw nothing; and then, dawning on my eyes at no definite moment, I knew there were shapes, blurred shapes growing sharp in the dimness, shapes too massive and high for what should have been there. Crouching close to the rail, my mouth on the wood, I stared.

The face of the water was thinning. Soon there were mountains, their rough peaks thrust up and gleaming under the waves. Like a crow the ship slipped over ridges and walls, over heels of harsh stone half veiled in the flood, over bare slopes and hunched broken stone. Like the shadow of a cloud, the hull cast its long darkness over their backs.

Glas Awyddn caught hold of my arm. Leaning forward, he pointed.

Tugged by the wind, the ship drifted over a ledge. The rock ended suddenly on the brink of a cliff. On the far side, fallen steeply away, lay a broad open plain, a great bay cut out of the mountains and stretching west, league on league to the edge of sight. Clearing the peaks, the sunlight floated down to it, spreading out with its fingers. But the plain, when the sun reached it, was green, green with slow swaying boughs, green with bracken and sedge. There were meads and bogs and, though it was fathoms deep, the white shimmering thread of a stream, which passed out from the ledge and wound under gentle hills and out onto the plain. On the banks of the stream a house lifted its square bulk against the green, jagged mass of trees. The smoke from its chimney rose curling through the pale, shining sea.

'There are men in this place,' said Glas Awyddn.

'Not men,' I said, 'though, perhaps, if fires burn, there is something to breathe.'

'Indeed,' said Glas Awyddn, 'there is a way of proving it.' He moved up the deck. 'Wyck,' he said sharply. The boy nodded. His small face looked calm, but his eyes were glassy and his forehead was damp. He backed off slowly, then turned, disappearing behind the mast.

The ship scraped among reeds floating loose in the sea. Squinting in the brightness, I saw low upon the water a maze of tiny islets, hummocks choking with marsh grass and the tangle of wet dwarf trees. The isles glided past, following a spur of the mountain, curving north and west at the edge of the plain. The waves came in gently, sucking the weed. Glas Awyddn took the steering oar, turning the ship in the current until it slowed, nosing into a channel that skirted the margins of a shallow hill. The breeze dropped in back of the island. The ship, with barely a sound, drifted close to the bank. The air was still. When the bow touched the ground, Glas Awyddn went forward to see to the mooring.

He came back with Wyck at his heels. Between them they carried their armor, the boy struggling under the weight of brigandine, the sleeve of the bright mail caught firmly between his teeth to keep it from dragging. He marched along dutifully, steady and serious; but now and again he glanced at Glas Awyddn, his child's face red as fire. Glas Awyddn saw it. He laid down his arms, searching out from the bundle a coarse gray shirt to go under the rings and a belt set with silver.

The boy held his breath.

'You must stand by the rail,' Glas Awyddn said lightly. 'It is enough that one of us tries this.'

Wyck made no answer, but took hold of the mail, lifting it high to the tall man's shoulders. The armholes were stiff; Glas Awyddn grunted. Even magic, I thought, has its flaws. I could not help thinking of Géar. Foreknowing, she had fashioned him armor; in whatever place she kept she had waited and watched, knowing the shape of the man she must meet, thinking, *This will be the girth of his waist, this the span of his shoulders* – though the man never stood in his flesh by her chair, never bowed his neck the least jot, never guided her hands. So, by small measures, she misjudged him; and the mail pulled tight and fell short at the wrists, and under the arms it was open.

His face was ablaze from the sun on the metal. The boy tugged the last buckle into its place. The man turned from him to look at the island.

A line of old alders grew close to the bank. Some of the cones, already fallen, bobbed swollen and black in the wash. Beyond, the hill and the trees were green, but it was the wild, late green of summer's end. It was winter, I knew, when I had taken my leave of Tech Duinn.

'You are a fool to come with me,' I said.

Glas Awyddn smiled. 'It cannot be helped.' He passed his hand slowly along the finely wrought rings of his shirt. 'Least of all can I help it. I was there when a woman came out of the sea.'

He walked ahead quickly. At the bow he lifted himself over the gunwales and jumped to the beach.

All I saw for a moment was the hot sunlight glittering white on the shore. Presently he crossed into a shadow. He lingered awhile, catching his breath in the coolness, then began to walk once more, moving away over the sharp gray stones. Just inside the point a great bare rock ran into the water. He leapt onto its back. By then he was well out of hearing. His hand came up slowly to his face. I could see he was whispering.

The change began at his feet. His head drew back once; a short, quivering wave passed over his neck. For a moment again he was motionless. The sun baked his fur.

A light breeze blew over the blazing mirror of the sea. I stretched myself out on the deck, listening to the water. The boy nodded sleepily. There was a bird in the alders. I could hear its sharp, bitter song. It kept me awake.

It was not a crow. Crows haunted the inland meadows, prancing on turf and walls, pecking in the stacks of dry hay, finding next to the byre the corpse of a badger left prickly and dead. A few, smaller but no less glossy and black, scavenged the channel islands. But there were none out at sea, none to perch on my shoulder or whisper a name.

Wyck woke and turned over, laying his dark head near my knee.

'She was a crow when it pleased her,' I said.

The boy looked perplexed.

'The woman,' I said, 'who came out of the sea.'

It was almost midday; the sky was empty and clear. The boy yawned and sat up, my cloak slipping off his shoulders.

'It must be soon,' I said. 'Get up and dress yourself in your armor.'

He poked at his feet.

'Twelve days you lived in the sea,' I reminded him.

He shivered and had to clench his teeth to keep them from rattling. His eyes found my face. 'It was Glas Awyddn who spoke to her,' he said stiffly. Yet he stood. 'Lord,' he said over his shoulder, 'I have lived on the sea, never under it.' His lower lip trembled. Shamed, he looked out at the west.

All at once he shouted.

Even as I lurched to my feet Wyck ran to the rail. With a bound he was over it.

In the wide quiet bay I caught a glimpse of Glas Awyddn's head – his cheek gashed and swollen, his muzzle smeared with blood. He struggled to rise, but his strength went out of him, and he fell. Gentle waves scudded over his chest. He snarled, then flung out his hands, grabbing hold of the weed. The birds shrilled from the bluff. He turned his head, listening. His wide nostrils twitched. By then the boy had reached him, but the man waved him back. Glas Awyddn stood. When he waded ashore, grimy with blood and with weed, he was grinning.

'There are men,' said Glas Awyddn, resting close to the fire Wyck had made for him. Stars frosted the blackness. Already the wind blew cold, but so near the fire my clothes reeked with sweat. I pulled myself back and sat under the trees. 'At least there was one,' Glas Awyddn said. He slumped back and sighed. 'It was not long after I set out that I came to a river. Nonetheless, I was a good while walking beside it, for the current was swift and I saw no way to cross.'

Wyck's eye were wide. 'Lord,' he said softly, 'how can there be rivers under the sea? Or, if there are – for you have gone there and seen one – how can there be any great trouble in crossing them?' He stared at the man, his face flushed in the light. 'I' – he said swallowing – 'I – I would have swum over its back, for the sea would be everywhere.'

Glas Awyddn laughed. 'There the water is thin. A man walks through it much as a man walks in the air. The wind blows, or what seems like wind, for the grass moves and whispers. And when I took my breath, what I breathed was both bitter and sweet, smelling of hay and pitch, the sharp smell of dung blowing down from the hills.' He waited.

From the darkness outside the fire I watched him. 'Go on,' I said.

Glas Awyddn smiled wanly. 'At first,' he said, 'where I walked, the land to either side of the river was open. But as the river slunk forward the grassy slopes gave way to bracken and then to a wood. Grim old trees hunched over the track. The long boughs were twisted; they scratched at the sun. Between the black roots the water rushed on over terraces, rank and slippery with weed, plunged thundering into pools, then fell away again in the dimness until even that great roaring was lost and quiet under the trees. I went on warily, keeping close to the bank. Now and again a chill light flickered between the boughs. For a moment it would speckle the mist and the stone. Then all at once something flashed in the river.

'Turning my head, I saw there was a man standing alone in the flood. He was leaning hard on his spear. At his waist a long sword was buckled. As I saw him he was lifting it free.

'His head was uncovered. For the rest he was well warded with ring mail and iron. But his sword and his armor were as red as his hair. Before I could speak he bowed low to me.

'*You are in dear straits, Glas Awyddn*, he said. I looked and I saw him; and yet I felt a loneliness, deeper even than the loneliness of the wood, sucking close to my heart.

'The Redd Man watched me. *Unless I carry you*, he said, *you cannot cross*. He was silent a little, then added: *Nor will I carry you unless you first give me the thing that I ask. For here is the only way into Tir fo Thuinn. Since the beginning no lord has ever gone in or gone out of it except with my leave.*

'For another space there was silence. Then I said quietly, *It will not be a small thing that you want.*

'*To some it is little.*

'*And to you?*

'*Have you loved?* said the Redd Man.

'I stood stiff on the bank. *Once*, I said softly, but the dread of that answer caught fast in my throat.

'The river was heaving. For a moment I could hear no sound but the water swirling against him. I stared but there was nothing to see.

'Yet, looking down from the ship, I had seen the green land that must lie beyond, a land brighter and greener than any land above the sea. I longed to run forward across the cold water, through the dark wood and out onto the green bright plain, under a sky like no other. It was such a place she had promised. For nothing less had she given me armor.

'*Tell me the price*, I said hotly.

'*No more than one drop of your heart's blood*, he answered, his voice just a whisper. I was not certain he spoke it aloud. Yet his lips moved. I saw the sweat of his brow. *Come then*, I murmured. *If you will have it, you will not have it idly.*

'*Nor did I mean to*, he said. And as he spoke he cast his great spear.

'The shaft whistled past me, with such force that the point halved the tough bole of an oak. The deep wood lay open and bled. When he saw where it struck, he sprang forward. I leapt down to meet him.

'The water hissed cold at my knees, came clawing and shouldering until it seemed bodies and arms. Heedless, the Redd Man plunged through them. He was waving his sword. By a hair's breadth I ducked him, my own blade coming up, flickering close to his head. Grunting, he knocked it aside.

'So for some minutes we drove at each other. Many cuts I had from him then, many rends and slashes, but nothing went deep. For as fiercely as he hurled himself at me, I hurled myself back. Yet as the day wore my lunges grew wilder. My head rang, dizzy and racing with blood. I felt my arm stiffen.

'Panting, I struggled out to the slab of a stone sticking out of the river, scrambled up on its sides to get my height over him. I was still but the shadows were running. The trees ran and the river was shrinking away. Even the darkness grew small. It quivered and shrank. And yet in that smallness I seemed even less. I turned my head sharply. He was waiting. His red hair lay wet on his neck.

'*You are a brave man, Glas Awyddn*, he said, *but a man's breath grows short.*

'With the last of my strength I struck out at his face. The metal beat only on emptiness.

'He was smiling. I saw, though I saw nothing clearly, the flash of his sword leaping high to my chest.

'I shook when it touched me as though a sliver of ice had been laid at my heart. The smooth flesh parted, just under the arm where the ring mail was short. A single drop slipped from the cut like a tear. On the hard edge of his thumb the man caught it.

'*It is little enough*, said the Redd Man, *yet it is all that I bargained*.

'But as suddenly my wits had come back.

'*What thing have you taken?* I said. *It is not my life, for I have it.*

'His gray eyes were gentle and sad. *There is*, he said, *another thing that is gone with it. But come, for I owe you in turn.*

'*You are bound to it?*

'*Yes.*

'*Though I were twice what I am?*

'He nodded.

'*Or twice that again?*

'*Though you were a mountain*, he said, *I would carry you.*

'*Now?*

'*At your will. This bargain will keep.*'

Glas Awyddn grinned but his long face was pale.

'So I left him,' he said, 'climbed up toward the air, though then I was weary. On the shores of the high world I could scarcely make myself stand.'

He shifted, drawing himself nearer the fire. 'So I have earned our passage into the land. For if I grab hold of you and take Wyck as well to my side, he has sworn he must carry us.'

'He has sworn,' he said, staring in front of him. His gray lips were set in a smile. He was trembling.

'Lord,' he said softly, 'it is cold in the air.'

I looked past him. Nor did I tell him then the thing he had lost.

CHAPTER NINE

Of course it felt like going home; but then there never was a footpath that led wet to a hollow, a dry lane into Abereth or a paved street in Tyre I did not feel somehow was bringing me homeward. How then could it matter this flesh had not been there, never gone to those distant and invisible halls? Even the birds of one season, April spawn and untraveled, feel the same sweet longing in the blood. In the cool, shortening nights thickening into blackness, when the sand is quiet, before the storms pour eastward and the winds whirl loud across the dunes, the birds gather. Asleep, their short necks curled under their wings, they dream of countries that, waking, they have never crossed.

Not this meat. Little did Llugh know of that land, not his pale flesh that I wore, wore in truth before he had use of it. Yet the blood, born over and over, saw it clearly, saw without needing to look the morning lying flushed on the back of the sea, heard without listening the cool murmur, the cold endless rush of the tide as it fled over great bedded stones. Sharp as the sword of the Redd Man the memory went through me. I did not turn my head. In the cheerless halls of *Tir fo Thuinn* the old men waited and sang.

Glas Awyddn shivered.

He was sitting on a small ledge of stone next to the fire, drinking from a cup of hot wine Wyck had given him. His lesser wounds had closed; the great wound had not. During the night the boy, who at last had struggled into his armor, had cleansed the broken flesh. With care he had dressed it. Before dawn I had watched him tearing strips from my cloak. Now he shook his hands above the wound to drive off the flies.

He said, 'You must wait until it heals.'

'No,' Glas Awyddn said shortly and fell silent, gazing out with flat, vacant eyes. The water no longer reflected the land. The strong sunlight cut straight through the surface. Beneath the faint ripples he could see the green hillsides dropping away and beyond them, the deep vale of the wood.

The boy only looked at his feet. He had grown very red in the face.

I was not part of this and waited.

At last Glas Awyddn spoke, his voice roughened and grainy with weariness. But though weary, his breath was a rising wind. It blew over the body of the boy, bearing the words Wyck would never remember, words that tasted like blood, that slid like oil into the creases of his flesh and yet had no permanence. Shaming him, they slipped from his mind though already he had heard them, once on another shore, the woman rising cold from the sea, making no effort to hide her disdain for the land or to cover her nakedness. Her little dark nipples had pressed close to his chest. The boy's flesh moved. His ears ringing, he no longer heard.

The small, dark eyes never left Glas Awyddn's face. The young seal said nothing.

It was like walking out of a warm, hushed room into rain. We went single file, descending through a monotonous and persistent mist along the edge of an escarpment, then down a deep cleft in the rock. Stones we idly kicked aside tumbled slowly in the current and tangled in weed. The narrow ravine turned and plummeted. Carefully, edging our way, we climbed down from the sky.

At the bottom the deep grass flourished and the sorrel burst into damp purple bloom. The waves crawled above us, casting long shadows below. At first we could hear the dull thunder dragging over our heads. But soon even that came to nothing. To the south there were patches of brightness. Glas Awyddn walked ahead. Some steps behind, we followed him. The mist died away of itself. The ground seemed almost dry again.

Not a soul was to be seen; even the grass seemed untrampled where earlier Glas Awyddn had walked to the wood. The hillside was silent. I listened, hearing only the stony noise of the river as we approached the trees. The air was full of the scent of thistle and leaves. The boy dawdled, dragging his heels, his thick feet – not truly a man's nor a seal's – scratching tufts from the grass. The late sun fell straight in his face. On his short neck the fur stood out stiffly.

'You did not change,' he complained to me in a low voice.

A strand of my white hair had come loose from its binding and covered my cheek. Without answering I thrust it back.

The boy pushed out his lip resentfully 'I kept his hounds,' he said. 'It was not so much. But he kept me because there were hounds to keep – though there were no more pigs in the wood to keep them for. But the memory of the pigs was something.' He glanced sideways, avoiding my eyes. 'He had no more than that, only the memory of kings in a land where women ruled.'

'He has left that place,' I said.

He dug at the grass. 'Aye,' he whispered. 'He is something now.' His breath came fiercely.

I turned his head. Above the bristling snout the eyes were dazed with grief. I looked down at them and into his face that was a boy's face still, from which the reshaping had neither altered nor worn the hunger or loneliness or the longing for glory. So ever it is that boys, before they are fit to stand, would be off, though the road never led elsewhere but to dying.

I raised my hand.

In the hall it brings no quiet.

'Had I another day,' the old man pleads, dry-lipped, remembering the lost weight of his loins that for thirty years had been cold and lifeless, 'had I another hour, lord, I would have kissed her.'

I am not listening.

'I would also serve you, lord,' he whispered. Softly, sorely, the boy had begun to weep. I too had been like him. I remembered that.

Small figures detach themselves from the throng and come across the floor to stand at my chair. The sweet, nauseating smell of burning flesh blows through the hall. A screaming woman wriggles at my feet. 'It cannot be!' she rails, her hair in flames. 'I sprinkled blood on the step, left milk for elves. Whenever I baked the bread, I blessed it, twice.'

I look away.

'Lord?'

Because he dared no longer hope, I pitied him.

'Until the end of all things come,' I said, 'you will not serve me. Be what you will be, your heart will not lose its strength or your flesh fail. Only never let it be said I have no mercy. This one I have saved.'

The boy watched me, uncomprehendingly, as though across a great space he watched the moon.

With my lifted hand I struck him. The seal shape came apart, blew into a mist that wavered and became a shape again. Startled, he looked down at his hands and feet, running his eyes across his flesh. He drew a breath. And then another as though he were not yet certain the chest that filled was his. His head came up. His eyes burned.

Glas Awyddn's back was twisted; he favored his arm. Nonetheless, now and again, he stooped painfully, studying the ground. After several minutes he halted. Kneeling, he caught something between his webbed fingers, rubbed it twice, then brought it under his nostrils.

'There were soldiers here,' he said, not looking around. 'Not an hour past. Here they waited. Here one lay, though I fear he took but fitful rest. See, his wounds were many and he bled.'

'Then they will not be far,' Wyck said, a strangeness in his voice.

Glas Awyddn wheeled back toward him as he spoke. A boy's shape crowded suddenly into his sight. He made himself still. The field was silent. 'We shall overtake them in the wood,' Wyck said quietly. 'Still, we shall make no haste ourselves, for your wound is deep.'

Something changed in Glas Awyddn's jaw. 'How came this?' he said.

But already Wyck was looking past him, his keen eyes following the path of the river. The light was dying. In the place where the river turned and vanished under the trees its icy waters glistened queerly.

'I will have an answer,' Glas Awyddn said.

Wyck cocked his head. The air was darker. A thin wind stirred the grass and set it trembling. It carried the screams of a man.

'They will have met him,' Wyck said grimly. Harsh as crows the clang of weapons climbed the ashen sky above the wood.

The banks were fissured and eaten away by the current – a warren of holes and awkward overhanging rock. The water swirled invisibly beneath, ripping the low twigs from the bank and bearing them off with it. The air hung close. Rank and heavy, smelling of earth and sedge, it distorted the scrape of metal, the grunting of breath. His eyes glazed, Glas Awyddn stumbled ahead distrustfully. He shook his head, trying to clear it of weariness. He seemed uncertain of the way, though it was clear enough that all that was needed was to follow the river. The few stars that shone like cold sparks through the branches only deepened the gloom.

Glas Awyddn cursed. 'I have not the wit to find it, lord,' he said miserably. 'In the day it seemed like night. But the night is blacker.'

But the blackness blew cool on my neck. A joy washed over me. Such was the darkness underneath the hill, in the hall that was nearly finished. I looked around, remembering the endless room where no true fire ever reached. *Behold my court*, I thought. Though I saw nothing, its beauty was before me, there as it had been, remembered and dreamed, through all the years that were and those that would be. I smiled. The dead hosts murmured. Like the tremor of the sea against the stone their changing, intermingled voices melted into a roar. I lifted my own. Its greater sound swept forward over them, more splendid and terrible, like the voice of the storm.

Glas Awyddn was swearing.

I woke.

His shrill cries rose higher, drowning out the sound of the sea. He was lost.

Yet I knew the place well enough when I reached it. The huddled shapes of the sealmen lay powerless, crouched in the shadows, in the ruin of the wood. Except for the fear in their faces they might have been stones. But the old man, leaning hard on his spear, stood out plainly.

'Good evening, Mug Dafad,' I said to him.

'You have my welcome, lord,' the Redd Man answered.

Glas Awyddn stared. His breath hissed painfully. 'You knew him,' he whispered. Fist clenched, betrayed, he was pressing near me.

'Be still,' I ordered. 'You did as you wished.' In the grumbling echo of my voice I could hear the storm. The mist rose up from the river in curling threads.

His ring mail rusted and fouled, Mug Dafad waded toward the bank. Even in the darkness I could see the gore and weed that clung to him. Six-handed, like an ungainly spider, he crawled across the stones. His large bare feet were swollen. His horse teeth chattered. He made a face.

'I would have stood at a gate,' he said glumly. 'A gatesman at least has some dignity, a dry place to stand. You might have seen to it, in respect for my years. Not a gift, mind you. What I ask I have paid for. Earned, I should think, by those years underground, long years, though in truth I do not mourn them. . . .' He stopped. A moment's strange recognition wavered, passed over his eyes. 'I have good cause to remember,' he muttered, 'for I had all my strength and outshone all men.'

Grunting loudly, he made the last leap to the bank. Muck trailed from his armor.

'A gatesman would have been just,' he scowled, glaring down at his thumbs, at the spots of blood on them. 'I am no butcher.'

From the tangled brush, hurt, the sealmen stared at him. Nicked and blunted, their swords lay out of reach.

'Who are they?' I said.

'Kings. Like you, Ar Elon's spawn.' He met my eyes. 'The god knows how many of the hundred isles Ar Elon bred on, how many women, clasping him, he left with sons. I doubt he counted.'

My heart came to my throat. 'You know this?'

But I saw he mocked me. Under his shaggy brows, his gray eyes smiled again. 'Who is to say?' he answered. 'Myself, I have given little thought to it. The work you set me lies the other side of birth. But surely as their toes are webbed, some sea thing got them and none but kings or those that follow them would brave this land.'

'Or you,' I answered him.

He laughed. 'Lord, they gave me what I asked. At least I took it. So if they wish it still, with what is left, they are free to follow you.'

The three lay motionless, one upon the other as though their wounds had stuck them there. I walked around them. Though the darkness smothered their faces, I could just make out the spikes of seahair, dark and light, uncoiled on their shoulders. The wind blew over them; but, if it gnawed their flesh, they were afraid to shiver. I pulled my sword and struck the nearest with the flat of it. The man looked up. His round eyes focused some distance to the left of where I stood.

'Can you stand?' I said.

He drew a breath but gave no greeting.

I turned my neck. 'It is better,' I said, 'their land were left to women than to have such ill kings over them.'

The man sat up. His face was vague as a web of shadows. He looked at the river.

He is *gone*, the man said wonderingly. The voice was distant, like the buzzing of a fly. I strained to hear it. Another shifted, kneeling, reaching with both hands for his sword. He moved without noise, his garments blurred. The blade, half as long as himself, he jerked up suddenly before his face. The point, touching nothing, flicked past my knees.

Did you see him?

No. A darkness.

The third man rose, his long white hair unbound, brushing his tired face.

There are others, he said. *I have heard them whispering.*

The youngest looked very hard at the trees, at the partings between the gray branches where, in the sky that was under the sky of heaven, a darkness gathered. *Perhaps a storm is coming*, he said.

I would know thunder.

The youngest bent his head slightly. He could see the mist, tarnished, the color of smoke, lagging over the back of the river. *It is ghosts, then*, he said. Wyck was standing in front of him. Gently, as though he were touching a wound, he reached out his fingers.

'He has my own face,' Wyck said steadily. But his voice stopped and he let his arm fall.

Through his white lashes the eyes of the pale king smiled. *Be at peace*, he said to the youngest. *Many heads would have rolled at his feet had he wished it, for from all the world's islands men come to him. Yet, had it been so, when we ourselves came to the ford, there would have been only their picked bones to walk on.* He turned his head silently. For a moment he met my gaze. For an instant he held it. As men watch the small stars flare cold in the dusk, so we watched one another. One by one the stars melted. He took the boy's arm. *No*, he said slowly, *there are corpses enough. What need has he to add to them?*

Glas Awyddn groaned, his eyes brooding on what could not be seen in the darkness. Men he saw, warlike and tall, and heard their hard voices: two black and grumbling as seals; two pale as the wave's crest, guileful and whispering; one red – even as night flooded over him – as blood. Among them he saw his own face but joyless he turned from it. Once he had seen her; in awe he had watched her climbing wet from the sea. But now, when he tried to remember her, he could not. Even then he could not imagine a world with her gone from it. Yet it seemed, so violent was the pain he had, that there was only wind and emptiness in the place where he had kept her memory.

'He knows,' Mug Dafad said softly.

My own face, white as one star in the darkness, was still. 'We shall cross then,' I said. 'In truth he has paid for it.'

The hard, ageless strength of his arms locked hold of my flesh. I felt his great hand on me, unexpectedly gentle – his old hand, sticky with blood. With five other hands he groped for the rest. Then, unfaltering, though the storm screamed over us, he bore us into the flood.

The darkness on the other side was full of trees, thrashing in the wind and rain. The downpour brawled. Leaning forward, Mug Dafad set me at last in the shallows. Men splashed around him, skidded and swore, getting their legs in his way. A thing swerved past me, as dreams pass – a thrust of air, flashed across my sight and gone. Unmindful, I slogged up the bank, turned, and glanced behind to make certain that the others followed. The ground was rutted. It fell away in soggy clumps. Sunk to his knees, Wyck tried to stand. Pitching forward, he scrambled, seized a slippery root, and hauled himself exhausted on a stone. Glas Awyddn labored after him, his teeth bared in a wretched grin. His limbs were shaking. I caught him by the shoulders; and, his weight against me, led him up the bank. I propped his sagging back as best I could against a tree. He moved to raise himself.

'Lie still,' I ordered.

He looked down dolefully.

The three were gone. For the space of several breaths I listened. I could not be certain. It was, I knew, no loss to me if they had vanished.

For, seeing his other lives, what man would follow me? Surely a man would think on it. Not Glas Awyddn perhaps. What had he to think on for the moment but his pain? I waited for Wyck to speak. But he only sat, his rank clothes sodden, a stream of water dripping from his hair.

Thunder cracked above the trees. Mug Dafad, his back to me, waded again into the river. In the murk it was hard to see, and yet I watched him go, unbidden, already out of hearing, to the place I had set for him. For all his mockery, alone he served me faithfully.

There is a scent – like bristling smoke – of wool. I smell them before they cross the threshold. I have ordered the doors of the winter hall left open despite the cold. They will see they are expected, know whatever lies are whispered, that they have not caught me unprepared in this. Great-shouldered, weighted with silver, they walk unhurried along the line of empty tables and the sprawl of stools. The old woman, rising from her corner, stands forth to announce them. With a glance at one another, to test me, they wave her back. They think my heart will stop before their stares. But I know each one of them and could, if they would ask it, name the man who dyed the wool of their rich mantles – for I know the color – and even the village, east of Tyre, above the seawall where the loom was kept, and – the god knows – the woman, her white arms lifted, who did the work.

The hangings to either side of me flap in the wind. In the yard I hear their soldiers. For the rest, with all my housethralls fled, the hall is quiet.

'You are early,' I say to them, 'and in the wrong place.'

The barons scowl. Inside the wool their flesh is lathered with sweat. They had ridden the best part of a week to stand here, whipping their horses, driving them and beasts over the icy hills from Reddmarch, so great is their eagerness.

The seahair has fallen loose from my shoulders; the green ragged edge of it covers the twisted gold of the hilt. The sword is spread on my knees. I will not move to touch it. I say, 'Not until spring shall I summon your armies. And then I shall lead them myself, at Tywy.' Hring breathes something inaudible. He thinks I should tremble. He is a man without luck. At Dineiden, when I slaughtered the barons, he groveled and squealed. It was on that wide field with all his men pushing up from behind, staring, when with red, sweating hands he grabbed hold of my cloak. Since I spared him he has never forgiven me.

'He comes from the sea,' I say to him, picking him out from the rest. 'Out of *Tir fo Thuinn* with a thousand ships And not a man with him has ever stood on the land.' I look around calmly. 'They have webs for toes. In their clawed hands they wield tridents instead of spears.' I pause. 'If we let them,' I say, 'they will fight in the surf.' There is no anger in my eye, only false weariness at their misreckoning. 'Did you think that on the dry streets of Ormkill I would have need of you?'

Hring's face is swollen with rage. 'In the god's name,' he shouts at me, 'why do you think we have come?'

Unn has stood so quietly by my chair they have not guessed she is weeping. Her hand slips from her mouth.

'Who will meet those fell ships if you murder him?' she wails.

'It is only the king he wants,' say Anhils stubbornly. He is second to Hring, keeping a step back in his shadow. One of his hands is hidden in the thick of his mantle.

They are only men and cannot imagine how I long for death.

'Let your men come to me,' I say. 'Lest there be any lies said of this, let it be in their sight.'

At the doors the captains have watched. When Hring nods his assent, they come forward, passing through the portal, blinking and uncertain, out of the cold sunlight, into the vast, darkened cold of the hall. A host of men push in after them, men who have been called forth from the warmth of their houses for winter soldiering. Their boots filled with straw, they have marched numbly over the frosted moors. Cursing the cold that comes down from heaven, they have come to see the death of the king. Through the dimness comes the scrape of their swords.

My flesh is yellowed and blistered and rots in the air. It accepts the knife blandly. It is done so quickly not even the queen cries out. Anhils is the first to see there is no wound. He holds the long knife stupidly. For a moment I think he will drive it in once more, not out of hate, but, like a child, in wonder. He cannot have listened when my harpers sang of my meeting with the men of Tywy. It may be it was only lies to him. Who is to say? That other time the men of the holding scrambled, breathless, back against the doors. They crowd me now.

I stand.

Despite the sea tusks and the stench of flesh, the shape of my young manhood warms my face. I think of the shining beach where I first came to land. The western shore is lovely in April. Landward there are clear green hills that mount, free of the sea's confusion, as though by counted, separate steps toward heaven. A girl is sitting on the sand. Through the bright austerity of air I see her plainly.

'At Tywy,' I say to them, 'in the spring.'

It is with one voice they answer.

The midmorning sun was cool, the light half-shaded though we had left the wood and wandered the deep grassland west of the river. The plain stretched off into a haze, blue-green like the grass and purple at its farthest edge. Wyck ran before us, his gloom cast off, eager to see what this world held. I was left to tramp beside Glas Awyddn. Because of his wound I was afraid to urge him on. His fingers lingered near his side, exploring the air above it. Yet something had hardened in his stare. He craned his neck to look ahead.

Nearly invisible against the hillside, a great horse tossed its head and whinnied. Another answered. But it was only when it had trotted to the crest, its vigorous strong shoulders and pale mane streaming against the open sky, that I saw it.

Wyck halted, pointed toward the hill, and yelled. 'The green mares!' he cried, astonished. At once he started off again, clicking his tongue and whistling as though the beasts were nothing stranger than his hounds or that, hearing his commotion, they might come to him.

Glas Awyddn gave me a look across his shoulder. 'In this place how are there mares?' he said.

'You took the wound.' I felt the creases deepen between my brows. I said, 'He will see the difference if he gets near enough.'

Glas Awyddn followed Wyck's progress up the slope. 'They will kick his head in for his pains,' he said.

'No doubt that will be near enough.'

I think he smiled. His heavy eyelids flickered. For a moment.

'Listen,' he whispered.

The two green stallions grazed the hilltop, pulling the clumps of weed noisily. Wyck was already halfway up, whistling and slapping at his thighs.

Instantly there came the din of furious galloping. A wave of fur caps and faces broke at once above the hill, reared in a prodigious rush, and, braying, fell upon the startled horses. A dozen ropes uncoiled, flew. They struck like snakes, catching the bare green necks, tangling the kicking legs, and held. Even then one stallion stood straight up, shrieking like a man, wrenching the ropes that bound him. He thrust his head, turned, and sprang away. But as suddenly the sealmen were in front of him. On the eastern spur of the hill, hobbled, trying to catch the snares between his teeth, he fell. With a howl of victory the sealmen slid from their mounts and met him on the ground. The stallion snorted, trying to evade the rough touch of the man who stroked his neck.

'That was too easy,' the sealman said. He grasped the long mane disappointedly. 'I'll wager he's been caught before and tamed.' His voice was loud. I heard it clearly, booming over the beaten grass. He straightened himself, wiping the horse sweat from his palms. The pale sun shone on the brown of his cheeks, the blackness of his eyes. The damp length of his seal-hair clung to his neck.

There were twenty sealmen with him, none quite so tall, but like him, webbed and shining-haired, men lean and brown as oak leaves, well muscled and vigorous. They milled about the hill, walking around the stallions, examining the horseflesh with steady, piercing eyes. There were no grooms. All seemed of equal age and rank, young lords like those in the old tale whom Ossary, King of Sciath, once took in fosterage, requiring as a pledge of loyalty the sons of one year from each *tuath*, from the defiant vassals who long had warred with him. Indeed, the sealmen looked and moved as though they had come to manhood in one house and shared its purpose. In the tale – if I have not forgotten it – when they had learned the use of arms, they killed Sciath's king and burned the hall he had reared them in. Who is to say? The old tales always closed with death.

Glas Awyddn plucked at my arm. 'They come to meet us, lord,' he said.

Already Wyck was deep in the press of men, but if he were aware of them he gave no sign of it. He strode forward, his body anticipating and sidestepping each knot of men and yet not meeting any face. They saw, as he passed them, the fevered expectancy in his eyes. He went straight for the stallions. The sealmen let him go. It was a sight worth seeing.

'He has always lived with beasts,' Glas Awyddn said.

The first line of sealmen closed with us. At their head the man who had been first to reach the stallion unbelted his long sword and swept it up to touch his forehead.

'The White!' he cried. His huge face broke out in a wide grin. The men jostling up behind him cheered. I saw the faces turned to me. So, thinking I had won a great victory, the men of Ormkill had turned to me when I had come from the Mound, small men standing with their swords unbloodied, thinking I had slaughtered the hag, had spread the vile old wreckage of her flesh across the hill. The pale sun glowed on their brown faces. Someone shouted. But the memory, lying cold across my thoughts, remained.

The first stepped up to me. 'Lord,' he announced in a loud voice, 'you are a better sight than all the sea's horses. Truly, we had wearied of listening to the Penandrun tell of your coming. Too long they have been here. They can never remember whether it was once you came or whether you were yet to come.' He clapped his webbed hand on my shoulder. 'But that you are here is clear enough.' He gave a great laugh.

'Llugh!' a man cried. And the host of sealmen answered: 'Llugh-Llugh-Llugh.'

The grass was thick on the hillside. The sealmen had come down from the place where the stallions were roped and hobbled, leaving Wyck alone with them. Leaning over a broad green back, he twisted its mane in his fingers. Vague transparent clouds drifted across the wide sky. His thin chest swelled with a breath. For no reason, merely for the stillness of the morning and the strength of the powerful beast under him, Wyck smiled.

'I shall walk,' I said. The sealman who had brought me the harnessed stallion gave it instead into Wyck's hands. Very small Wyck looked beside it. Yet he patted its flank and though they had no horses in Tír na Trí Oileán, he threw his narrow legs over its back. He clicked his tongue loudly. The stallion took two quick strides, then halted, twisting its head to look at him. Wyck laughed and drove his fingers beneath the mane.

'You will make a good horseman,' the sealman said.

'Who would not, upon such a beast?' Wyck answered. He was still smiling, his eyes spellbound with cheerfulness.

Two men were needed to lift Glas Awyddn up behind a rider. Because he had little strength in his arms, he was bound with three bands of leather. Nonetheless, he held himself straight and, when it seemed to him no one was watching, out of pride he loosened the straps.

Once more the sealman brought me the reins. His eyes were alive with curiosity tinged with uneasiness. All the rest had mounted. I shook my head.

'Lord, as you will,' he said and, bowing under my gaze, went off to find his own place in the troop. I knew I would slow their going, but there were few beasts that could bear me, even the brawny green stallions of the Penandrun's plain. I recalled the great bay I had ridden from Morrigan, thieving it from the stables while the women slept. I was still a boy then, though none could have told me that. Already I had twice the height of the men I knew.

For the first time I spoke to them:

'Your horses are for children.'

The sealmen were quiet. They went slowly so I could keep their pace.

High in the upper air, where the sky seemed sea again, there were dolphins. Like shuttles they wove their dark bodies before the sun's diminished face, crossing and recrossing above the horizon. The light met no other obstacle. It flooded the endless grassland with a glorious enrapturing green, richer and more luminous than any that grew on land. However, it seems, I thought, it is grass. Still I did not look down often.

The track they followed was no clear road but rather a chain of landmarks: a hill with a certain slant, a forking stream; a grove of slight, green alders spied for a moment far up against the valley wall. It went mostly south. After two hours' walk, the sun moved at my back. Because they rode, we went without stopping. Beneath their fur caps the faces of the sealmen wore a chastened silence, the ruin of that eagerness which had brightened them when they had shouted the name they thought was mine.

The lead man brooded. The seal blood showed in him, in the tangle of his sea-black hair and blunt black eyes. His mouth was wide and grim beneath his bristles, not a mouth that was apt to stay quiet. His brown cheeks reddened. No longer able to contain himself, he threw aside his reins and dropped down beside me, letting the stallion trot along at his heels.

'I'd not tell you what to think,' he said. 'You are here to be lord of us. Yet what joy do we have but our horses?'

Though the narrow slits of their eyes were turned elsewhere, the sealmen listened. A murmur went through them, like a sigh.

He studied my face, staring longest at the ash-white hair that fell away from my forehead and covered my neck. 'Since we came to this land,' he said, 'whenever the Penandrun give us leave from their chambers, we ride. They would teach us war, but it is only old tales they care for. It is better to ride – better to cast a lance at full gallop, to take a head leaning down from a proud stallion's back. That is study enough.' He swore, his mouth turning sourly. The burn on his face seemed to deepen. 'By the god,' he snapped, 'what are the tales of dead kings to us?'

'It was dead kings who made this war,' I said.

He scowled. 'Such kings, however royal, will not fight it.'

I let a moment pass, long enough so that he felt the silence.

'It will be fought,' I said, 'by men who swear to me.'

He shifted. 'I have sworn,' he answered. His voice was guarded. Yet, like the sound of stones struck in the sea, it carried.

The wind roused. Smelling of horses, it blew southward over our backs. The sealmen pressed nearer, looking elsewhere, and listening. Now and again one turned his head. Something seemed to hover, moth-like, on the edge of sight. Men stared. There was nothing.

'When strangers come,' I said, 'who meets them?'

'No one. Or, by chance, as you are met, by men out riding. More often they find their own way in. It is a broad land, but there is nothing in it but the old one's court and the town around it. If any will brave the Redd Man, they will not be frightened by a little walk. They find us.'

'And were you met?' I said.

'I wandered.'

'How long?'

He gave a thought to it. 'A week,' he said, 'or a season.' He paused, glancing distractedly at the sun that was close to setting. 'There is only day and night. And the days are like all other days and each night is the same.' He looked, lifting his head, as though he had suddenly discovered a thing of worth was gone. 'On land,' he said, 'I had twelve captains under me and knew each one and the year and the season each had sworn to me and the number of men he brought, even to the count of arrows their quivers held.' He moved abruptly, a new thought breaking through the odd, pre-occupied expression in his eyes. 'I am Eachanhagen. Lord, I tell you that you may remember it. Almost I had forgotten. Hearing the old tales over and over, sometimes I mistake the old names for my own.' His voice sounded husky. 'We grow like them, those old men, forgetting our own names or how the days go or the season.'

'So a man may cross,' I said, 'and wander some time before he is found?'

'Yes,' Eachanhagen said softly. 'So I have myself.'

'Some days.'

'Many days. Yes, or a season. It may have been a summer I walked this land.'

'But in the end he is found.'

He nodded. 'Or he comes in himself.'

'The Penandrun will not come out for him?' I said.

He spat. 'They are where they are. As the sea is where it is.'

Something swayed against me. I moved away from it. The sealman behind me wrenched his reins, avoiding the further touch of nothing he could see. The lines of horses broke into a strange confusion. I did not share it.

'Lend me the horse, Eachanhagen,' I said. 'Though it is small and unworthy, I've a mind to ride into the old men's town.'

We rode, but the tracks of the horses were obliterated. They vanished with our passing as though the hooves were weightless, the deep marks worn away at once like muddy scrapings in the wellhead of a spring. Within a breath of our passing the *liobhagnach*, the sweet-scented weed that abounded in the valleys and on the low sides of the ridges, grew over the tracks. As swiftly as a stallion could gallop, so swiftly the *liobhagnach* healed. And when we were gone there was nothing to see but a featureless carpet of grass. And nothing for a man, though he looked with care, to follow.

The sky showed the first hint of twilight. The stallion bearing Glas Awyddn had to be kicked repeatedly to keep its head up and away from the weed. Yet the rider showed no resentment and the stallion paid him no heed. The troop moved slowly. Gradually Eachanhagen's gaze turned southward, traveling over the graying plain as a sailor looks over water, its deep reflection darkening the flesh under his eyes. A slip of a moon had risen above the horizon. The horses passed along the ridge. Soon they were only shadows, stubborn and black against the sky's gentleness. Had there been watchers, they could not have been certain whether they saw any breathing thing but rather a grove of distant trees that wavered a little and fluttered in the wind. Indeed they must have been trees, for at last they rooted, and were still in the darkness. Then, no watcher, even one who looked with more than mortal sight, would have thought it worth his while to pause on his journey or to climb the steep bank to look at them.

The sealmen sat on the ground, resting against their saddles, as though the smooth hard leather were the softest of chairs, as fine as any Sciath's king set before his fosterlings. The men had drawn off their caps and sat waiting. Not a man among them had forgotten courtesy. When we had eaten, without urging, they gave me their names.

'Gywn I was, Nudd's heir though I had no father,' said a youth, his face high in the cheekbones, a thatch of raven hair hanging down to his shoulders. 'We had a farm at Blaensawde. But early Nudd sent me away, up the long valley to the shores of a lake to graze his cattle. I went because he bade me but more I went, because by the fire I had heard the women whisper that I was the son of the lakeman. And, truly, I had not been there long when I saw a tall old man sitting on the surface of the lake. *Come then, Black One,* I cried in a great voice. *Arise and own me.* As I shouted, the man came walking across the smooth water. And when he came to the shore he gave me three smart blows, and not one of them was pleasant. With the first I laughed bitterly and with the second I wept. But with the third my thoughts clouded. Then it was a seal's head I threw back and it was with a seal's clumsiness I lumbered into the lake to cool the itching of my skin. Thereafter I no longer walked on the land but hunted eels off the bank in the fogs of the morning. When autumn came, I found the river and went down to the sea.'

I heard his breath, labored and puffing.

'You were Gywn,' I said.

'Himself,' said the youth. He set his two long-fingered hands on his knees, hands not only large but of extraordinary strength, with harsh round knuckles and blunt nails. Between the long fingers stretched a hairless oily web. In the little light the moon gave, the dark flesh glittered.

Another raised his voice. 'I was Dwfen,' he said, 'but though I lived below Cefyn Clun Tyno, on the sides of the mountain, with me it was much the same. For I left the house where I was fostered and went seeking my father. Still, I had not gone farther than the stream at the foot of the mountain when three men met me. And each one gave me a blow. When they had finished, the first went away with my sword and the second with my cloak and kirtle. But the third, pitying my nakedness, gave me a ragged brown skin to wrap around me. But when he saw me put it on, he wept. *My child! O My child!* he cried to me. *How shall you live on the land?* Hearing him, I looked down and saw the oily leather, my great feet splayed and widened like a seal's. So I hid myself, slipping away into the stream. Shamed, I sank beneath the curling weed into the cool darkness, out of the light, down where the current ran deepest, ran cold to the sea.'

Lost in the memory, his fingers twisted in the lengths of his hair.

'And as well you were a fosterling?' I asked.

'I have said it.'

'And each man here?'

Eachanhagen leaned hard on his saddle, his thick brows crooked up anxiously. Such ignorance was beyond his imagining. Unbelieving, he pushed close to my ear. 'Lord,' he whispered, 'what he says is true. More, it is his honor. So he traces his blood to the seafolk and to such as would claim kin with you.' He shook his head. His face was scarred with wounds. I could see the old hurts in it. 'Why do you question them?' he murmured. 'They are men and mean to follow you.'

Beyond him, above the thrusts and folds of hills, the few stars blurred. The sea's chill breath eased nearer the ground, spilling its coldness over us. I held his eye. 'It was yourself who said I could not trust your memory.'

'Only the names,' he said darkly, keeping a check on his anger. 'In the years that have come and gone, many a man has had use of them. What lasting good, then, are our names to us? It is our deeds that matter.' His voice was low; the sound of another rode over it, the gruff voice loud as it was filled with tenderness.

'South of the point at Fawkes,' another youth began. 'A furlong or so from land, the bay being still . . .'

Remembering, he covered his eyes with his blunt fingers. His voice rose and fell.

'Lord, my name was Annwn. I had a wife, although I can no longer see her face. . . .'

I looked into the dark, into the night shaping and reshaping itself as he spoke. His long memory ran before me. In the wet darkness, the few stars blazed and dwindled and blazed again.

I sat up on the ground. The rim of the sun had floated above the steep valley wall. The high sea crawled against the peaks. Its far sound came down to me. A dull thunder rolled over the plain. I pulled myself up. A knot of sealmen, already mounted, sat on their horses, gazing impatiently over the ground. Eachanhagen came to me, leading a stallion.

'Will you ride again?' he said.

I tried to remember whether I had heard his voice among the rest. There had been many tales. In the end I had lost track of the faces.

'Well?' he asked again.

I found the stirrup.

We left the place. Later, glancing back, I could not tell that hill from any other. To the west and south lay other hills, fair and green, waist-high with *liobhagnach*, and no different from the ones behind. Like men going watchful into the surf, the horses waded deep into the weed. They moved at a slow trot, no distance between them, as though they feared the grass had hidden faults. Indeed, the horses sometimes veered at what seemed nothing. Wheeling in one adhering mass, their strides unbroken, they pulled suddenly to the left or right and then plunged on.

A shiver of terror would run the length of my stallion. With ignorant reassurance I scratched his coat. He tossed his head, whickering gently as though I had earned his trust. But for myself, I was quiet, listening to fragments of the sealmen's talk, their laughter sharp against the hollow booming of the upper sea. They spoke only of horses. I did not think. The mountains' ragged rim fell far behind.

We went more quickly then, riding over the backs of the hills where the ground was harder. Yet now and then I heard the noise of water. Small streams washed the slopes. Springs with hovering clouds of fog lurked in the glens. Beside them dwarf trees bloomed, their brief white flowers pale and small. In time I felt the wind again. Grown cool and restless, its long breath muttered.

Once in a sheltering valley, open to the south, I saw what seemed to be a gleaming pillar looming tall in front of us. Its sides were crystal, flashing like the dew beneath the morning sun. But when we came nearer and could hear its roar, I saw it was a vast fountain, filling up the space between the land and sky. The ground shook under it. The air above was heavy and bent the light. It almost seemed the hills had broken loose, that they slid and floated over us. Blobs of weed, shining like bubbles, drifted upward. A cold rain drenched my hair.

'Even here,' Eachanhagen shouted, 'there are places where the land still wars against the sea.'

'And which will be master?' I asked him.

He stared. A glistening runnel washed the side of his nose. But then he laughed. 'One thing is sure,' he boomed, 'it will be fought in earnest now that you are home again.'

We rode six days or seven. I am not certain. Far away to the south the land was rising. Wyck sniffed the air. He had taken to riding with a whip between his teeth. During the long hours of daylight he seldom paused. He cantered across the green meadows, moving easily in and out of ranks of the sealmen or standing, his full weight on the stirrups, he raced the clouds southward until we barely had sight of him. In the cool sunlight of the late afternoon, his pace slackened but, still without weariness, he leaned over the neck of the stallion, whispering. He had plaited his own thick hair into braids. He had done the same with the mane of his stallion. In the evenings he slept apart, the beast tethered near him where, if he woke, he could look at it.

Glas Awyddn stayed at my left hand. His face set, wasted by sickness, he did not seem to hear the hooves that pounded under him. His movements grew heavier and more blundering. Yet he would take no help. One morning he would no longer let them strap him to his mount. Exhaustion lay like weights on both his eyelids. Cursing, his features disfigured, he tried to throw the leather bands into the face of the man who had come to assist him. The bands fell short. When he turned, I saw the red stain wetting the rings of his armor. He wavered.

I caught him under the ribs.

'I can count his bones,' I said wonderingly. Eachanhagen came trotting back along the line to look at us. 'How long before we find the old one's court?' I said.

'For what purpose?' he asked. 'They have no healing.'

'There must be somewhere.'

He looked discomfited. 'I will take you,' he said grudgingly. The sealmen behind him examined the ground. Not a man looked up.

'How far?' I asked.

It was on the fourth day, at the close of it, that we reached the house.

The dusk was already falling when we saw the first trees. A pale glow lingered over the west, like airy mountains – the faint double image of the more solid peaks beneath. The land climbed steeply, rose, and was broken into rough, uneven hills, their deep, grass-clad backs turned gray in the twilight. Knots of low, spreading junipers clung to the banks. Farther off, dark, columnar cedars huddled together on a hill, still as tall old men. Eachanhagen slackened his pace. We had descended into the fold of a valley and begun to mount the ridge that climbed from it. Here the trees stood nearer, like an army that had taken the land by stealth, drawn up silently rank by rank across the valley's rim. The sealmen looked up at the huge old branches doubtfully and rode closer together. In the cold air I could hear the neighing of horses.

Beneath the tangled roots there were paving stones. Sometimes I heard the nervous click of hooves against them. Yet, if there were a road, in time we wandered from it. Even then, in the gloom and darkness, I felt I knew the place – though in truth it was not much like the mountain wood at Morrigan or the trees on Hren. Still, there was the same queer sad feeling of oldness, like the air in a closed-up room where a man is dying, where out of deference not a chair is moved. There was no wind. If the moon sailed over the trees, not a flicker of light slipped through the branches. So I had no way of knowing how we found the house. Only suddenly there was a wall that barred our way. We dismounted. With fumbling hands I chanced upon a pair of iron rings and fastened the reins. Someone had discovered the door and knocked upon it. As the door was opened, a shaft of yellow light flashed over us. Wyck stood in the midst of it, his proud head bent beneath the low stone lintel, his sword drawn and catching the light.

'Begone,' a clear voice said. 'Little enough peace I have had from the sealmen. Little more will I get from them.'

'Whatever you grieve for was none of my doing,' Wyck answered. He had lifted his blade and returned it again to its sheath. At the edge of the light the sealmen stared at him wonderingly. Quickly he spoke, but his voice was soft and secret. Not a man heard what he said. But neither did any man lean forward to listen for each had turned from the door. So Eachanhagen turned, his broad back to the house, gazing away from its brightness.

'May he find healing,' he whispered tonelessly.

With none to help me I took Glas Awyddn down from the stallion. His eyes were clamped shut; in the gleam of dusty light they seemed hollow. His dark head sagged forward, his jaw coming to rest on my shoulder. He was light as a child when I lifted him.

'Come,' a voice said, '*he* is welcome.'

I stepped over the threshold, tilting my head, turning sideways, pulling the thin legs of Glas Awyddn after me.

The room was large. In the hearthwall a great fire reached and shifted. But though I looked, I could not see into the corners. I turned. Even shut behind walls I made out the scent of grass, of bark and water, each vivid as though I had never entered a house. My nostrils quivered. From further off another scent came wafting toward me, slighter, masked beneath the cool smell of the evening, a scent so parched and wizened at first I barely noticed it. I let Glas Awyddn slip down by my waist and then down to the wide floor strewn with rushes.

'Leave him now,' a voice behind me said.

A shadow came away from the door, walked slowly on the edge of the light, paying no heed to me. It stopped by the shape of Glas Awyddn, gazing down at him. A loose gown, falling straight from the shoulders and sweeping the floor, hid the tall figure. But with the cowl drawn back I saw the withered majesty of the face. Against the moving flames the straight long hair shone with a flinty gleam. The woman was old but with that strength that once in a great while time yields to age, as the fairest of metals is made pure by the fire. Unhurried, she removed a small knife from her gown. Spreading her slender fingers, she knelt above the body of the man.

Even in his swoon Glas Awyddn felt it. His eyelids fluttered, and for a moment his bewilderment was stronger than his pain. He had groaned.

'How . . . in this place,' he murmured, '. . . are there women?'

A frown half troubled her face. 'It is because I am old,' she answered, mocking him gently. 'The old are not women. So I am permitted. As well, when I can be persuaded, I do the sealmen some service.' She leaned over him, her gray hair straying over the rims of her direct, unchanging eyes. Watching her, he was slow to see the knife. She rubbed it absently against a leather strap to sharpen the edge.

His brows flickered up.

The old woman smiled. 'Be at peace, woman's child,' she said softly. 'No man can change what must come. The first wound you have had already. Her memory, the intimate still beauty you yearned to look upon, that went with it, gone with the first drop of your heart's blood. Be at peace. What is the face of a woman? It will have faded. Beauty is the first of the things that vanish. Lie quiet, then. I have not lost the skill of my fingers. Though the blade is sharp, I wield it quickly. Cold it is, colder than anything in the world but it will ease the fire her warm words left with you. So the second drop takes away bitterness.' She paused. 'It cannot be called healing. Yet a man can live with it.'

'And the third?' Wyck said.

She heard the awe in his voice and looked up at him curiously. Measuring the thinness of his chest and shoulders, her old face hardened. 'You have no wound,' she said almost silently, something taking her breath.

'He is a boy,' I said in his place. 'He has never loved.'

For the first time she raised her eyes to me. The white length of my hair hung down the sides of my cheeks. Watching how she stared, my hand rose to smooth it. But she was still, her stillness, deep and unbroken as a stone's, spreading through the great room until only the twisting fire fought it, struggling to keep its breath. The sleeves of her gown lay heavily over her wrists, concealing the small tip of the knife. Her voice was low when she spoke.

'Daughters I have had,' she whispered, 'white as the pebbles that wash on the shore, daughters black as blood and as many as apples. And sons with them, sons like the foam of the seawaves that raid the coast, sons dark as the seeds of the fruit left rotting in autumn. White and dark are my children.' Her hard eyes remained fixed on me. 'Yet you are none of them.'

I was silent.

'Many I have welcomed to my bed. With the onset of winter, when the sea was clamped with ice and land lay hard as any stone, then they began to think of my hearth and longing. So they came to my door. And though they were webbed or scaled, husbands I made of them. Though they slid or flew, though their breath froze my neck, yet I welcomed them.' Her deep eyes shone. 'Yet, lord, you are none of them.'

My scribe is nodding.

'Which are the daughters?' I ask him.

His fingers are blue with the cold. It is almost morning but the guards are still asleep on the benches. I have ordered the doors left open. Through the gaping hole I will watch the sun rising. Invisible, beyond the gray mountains, its feeble light trembles. Nor will it soon rise high enough to warm the souls or even the bones of the men who lie at the hall's end, breathing and tangled in dreams.

'Which?' I say again to prompt him.

A dreaming man offers a groan.

The little scribe straightens. He gives me a false and shining smile to prove he is awake. His pages lie scattered about on the floor. He plucks one up, discards it, finds another. Finally, with a kind of shame, he asks, 'Lord, would it be on the land, you mean?' His head is rigid.

'Yes.'

'And the sea?' He is hoping for light. Surely the cook will come soon, he thinks, and set the dogs barking and the men crawling up backward out of their sleep, stretching, cursing their joints' stiffness and demanding drink, men swollen-eyed and sick of dreaming, men little eager for tales.

'Yes,' I remind him.

'There was Ryth,' he says slowly, 'Sanngion. And Grieve.'

'And with the seablood?'

'Géar'

'And before her?'

'Yllvere, who ruled us, and the Mughain, who ruled only women.'

'And before?'

He stammers, but no words come out of him. Perhaps he can hear them, panting and whistling; or buried in darkness, perhaps he is listening to the whisper of fins. Like a frightened child's, his eyes have rolled back in his head.

'And there were men,' the old woman said softly, 'hairy and naked, coming out of the sea.' For a moment the great room seemed empty except for the strangled breath of the fire and the strange scent that came to my nostrils. Tears ran along the cheeks of the woman.

Her eyes half closed. 'You should be one of them. Yet it is hard to tell just what you are – you who bear the third and cruelest wound, that which takes away most, yet is kindest, for it takes away memory.' She lifted her hands. The sleeve of her gown fell back along the white length of her arms. 'Yet you hold fast to it.'

Her eyes were open.

From far off I heard my own voice whispering. 'Lady, I have put on flesh again.'

For a little while she was silent. Yet all at once, though she held her back to it, I saw the firelight dance in her eyes. 'Long we have looked across the world at one another,' she said. 'Before the first men came up on the shore, before the beasts walked there or the iron-shouldered fishes crawled in the waves, across the deep – when not even the first timid stars were there to light it – I saw you watching me. No liegemen had you then or underkings. They were my gift to you. But the sea was between us. So out of myself I made a son to warm me, licking open his eyes so he could look on me. Pale as the dawn he was, as red as the evening, but his face was like nothing but myself. Because you were not in him, I sent him away from me, out into the whirling darkness, far from the world. Then I could see your face again. But because I was still alone, I called him back. So between his coming and going I have lived. So I have grown old . . . Now you are in my house.' She waited. There was no fear in her. 'Lord,' she said, 'I have thought you were too proud.'

'It was not pride.'

She smiled. 'It cannot be you meant it humbly.'

'What is done is done,' I said. 'It is hard to change that.'

'Still, for my sake, he will war with you.'

'I shall bear it.'

The old woman laughed. 'Then there is no help for it. It cannot be otherwise than I must bear it also. Yet I would know why you would have it so.'

'There was a woman once,' I said. 'White as the stone she was, dark . . .' I hesitated, watching as she sat above the body of the man. Her strength was fire, the fire that comes out of stone, that cracks its own heart out of gentleness. Her eyes were shining. I said, 'I have not forgotten. Lady, I would not forget.'

When he saw us, Eachanhagen hurried out from under the trees. 'Now we shall ride!' he shouted. It was not yet dawn. A vague light, broken by the countless faults in the leaves and branches, spread over the grassy yard like rain. Impatient, he splashed through the gloom, bearing a heavy saddle on the ledge of his shoulder, a bit in his hand. But until we had come away from the house, he would not greet us. His eyes wandered in every direction except the one that would have him look at it.

'We shall ride,' he shouted again.

He had begun to bridle the stallion and kept his head close to its neck, gazing off through the trees. He moved quickly.

'You have my thanks,' Glas Awyddn said.

Eachanhagen stroked the stallion's muzzle. He did not look up, would not gaze at the pale, emaciated face that, if it were not healed, was at least a face again. 'It was cold,' he said hoarsely.

'Truly,' Glas Awyddn answered him, 'it was that.'

'Though her fire warmed the air,' Eachanhagen whispered, 'though the sparks danced and the logs of her trees roared in the hearth . . .'

Glas Awyddn winced. 'Still I could not keep from shivering.' But he stopped, for he saw well enough that Eachanhagen knew what it was: to become an emptiness beyond measure, a void that nothing filled, that no fire, however hot, could warm. Indeed, each man knew it, but the boy did not. Rather it seemed to him that the fire had wrapped all about him, had held him blessed, safe in its ease, in its soft, inexhaustible warmth – like a child.

'It was only the smell,' Wyck said, 'that troubled me.' Even in memory his nostrils wrinkled with disgust. He breathed again deeply, to drive it away with the smell of the day.

'She is old,' I told him, 'and dying.'

Wyck looked at me strangely. His jaw hardened. 'No,' he said. 'How shall death have her? It was the smell of the corpses.'

One of the stallions whickered. The sealmen were leading the excited horses into the yard. The bridles, studded with silver, gleamed in the murk. The horses pawed at the ground.

'In the corners,' Wyck said, 'where the fire scarcely reached, in the high rafters, three corpses, hanged as from the gallows . . .' He rubbed the back of his neck. '. . . Three heads dangling, vile and rotting, but not asleep. Lord,' he said, his voice surprised, 'were you not listening? Through the night she spoke with them.'

Glas Awyddn cast a glance at me. The wolf's grin that once he had lost pulled again at his lips.

The scribe mutters gravely.

'Which are the dead?' I asked him.

'There are many,' he answers. 'How shall a man remember them? Even I cannot, though you have filled me with names.'

I sit and wait.

There is only silence. The sun has yet to climb above the gray mountains. He looks around and behind him. He would like to hear a noise, but there is only the sound of his breath.

'The boy not yet come to manhood,' he says at last to keep away silence, 'the husband, the . . .'

'They were ourselves,' said Glas Awyddn.

Wyck shook his head. He was only a boy. When they brought up the horses he smiled.

*   *   *

'Where came this horse?' I asked them. I did not add, Where should such men find him, a horse like winter and white snow, a horse without blemish or peer, walking easily out of the morning? He came slowly, treading the soft green turf, his eight legs moving regally, his matched gait stately as mourners shouldering a bier. He dropped his broad fore-head, meeting my own.

'Where?' I repeated.

'You shall judge that yourself,' a man at my side said thickly. He was afraid to look at the stallion and did not move his head.

Yet another man whispered, 'Lord, he came from the wood.'

The sealmen were quiet. They stared back toward the trees, toward the deep wood through which they had passed in the evening, through which they must go again, though soon the sun would fill it. A light breeze wafted into the yard, bearing the sweet scent of leaves. Eager they were to be going, yet the gladness had gone from them, and they shivered. But whatever the sealmen thought, Wyck beamed.

He said in wonder, 'Never have I seen such a horse.'

'Nor will you ever see the like of him,' Eachanhagen answered, his face thoughtful and still when he turned to me, 'Yet he has come to you,' he said. 'For surely there is not one among all of us, only yourself, who would ride him.'

Even then Wyck would have reached for his mane. 'Just for a moment,' he pleaded. I met his eyes.

'Indeed, lord,' he said quietly, 'he is yours.' He turned aside quickly, finding his own. The dust from the prancing horses hid his face. He jerked at the reins.

Glas Awyddn took hold of the mount I had ridden. One by one, the sealmen climbed onto the backs of their horses until no man was stand-ing. They lifted their necks and swung their wide shoulders. Impatient, a man called out. But though the horses stamped, not one sprang forward.

Eachanhagen's brows came together meditatively. 'The horses know him,' he said, 'if men do not. Swift and tireless these horses are, and great-hearted as kings. More sense they have than men. They will not walk ahead of him.'

I pulled myself up. Beneath my legs I felt the great strength of the stallion, the width of his hard, thickened spine, the muscles rippling effortlessly under his flesh. 'If he leads,' I said, 'they must follow him.'

Eachanhagen smiled. 'Even such a horse,' he said, 'has a master.'

I lifted my arm and went, with the horses trotting behind me, under the trees. If a woman stood by the door, I did not look back. So a man does not look twice at a stone. I did not grieve. It is so simple a truth that any child knows it. However masked and hidden, the wide earth is everywhere the same. It cannot be otherwise. Whatever a man passes waits ahead of him. Else which of her sons would be bold enough to poke his nose out of doors?

By the time we were well under the branches the breeze had softened, bringing a mist. Not the great mist such as rolls in for weeks together upon the coast at Brehnum-Sawle. This did not come by force. Rather it crept between roots and slunk around hooves. Here and there, thickened, it cloistered in hollows, pale as the froth in discarded caldrons. A chill came with it.

Eachanhagen, his sharp breath fogged, rode with his fur cap pulled down over his ears. He had hidden the fingers of one hand under his arm. But for myself I was not discontented. In truth, I found a strange comfort in the mists' gentle drifting, gentler than the coming of the tides, sweeping as softly into the morning as the first cool rains in autumn.

Some miles from the house the land sloped down. The ground turned soggy and wet. Emboldened, the mist climbed from the horses' knees to their withers; it dripped in their hair. The shapes of the trees grew dim, and their branches came at me suddenly out of the air. I picked my way carefully so that the horses could follow. A wind sprang up, but it was sullen and wet and blew nothing away. Through the dampness I heard the men cursing. They had their right. We were longer leaving the wood than going into it. More often I gave the great horse his head. He took me gladly then, his hoof-beats quickening; as though he judged my height, I was less troubled by the switch of branches and the tearing of brambles against my legs. No longer bending double, the riders edged up closer. The great horse stepped lightly in front of them. Nevertheless, it was a long slow business. Though we had little to look at, the day was wearing. The mist grew raw. On the edges of its whiteness there were shadows.

'They are but trees we pass,' said a flat voice from back in the line.

'This is still her wood.'

A man snorted. 'And they are still trees.'

'No.' It was Eachanhagen then, his tired voice rumbling deep in his chest. 'They are taller and older. Much taller and a great deal older, I think, and less likely to stay where she put them.'

A man laughed recklessly.

I looked behind, but there was only the cloud of mist, the jingle of bridles. I rubbed my smarting eyes and listened. There was a noise like wind ruffling leaves. A gentle wind or very far off. They are not small trees certainly, I thought. For, if I saw nothing, I felt their hugeness. The horses lumbered blind beneath their shadows. Somewhere, in the highest branches, an evening lark sang. The same man coughed.

'I would ride the plain again,' he said.

'He must find what he seeks here.'

'I pray he finds it quickly then,' the man grumbled. He said little else and yet the words stung me. I knew what was fitting and what was not. Truly, we had come a long way and gone nowhere. Nonetheless, I needed no man's groaning.

The ears of my stallion were bent in the damp. Watching them, I gave vent to my anger. 'See that it is my own business that takes you,' I scolded. The stallion neighed blissfully and went on as before.

If there were ground under us, it went upward.

When I cared to look, I saw nothing. But the trees were there, unseen and unquiet. Their strange leaves were tossing. The stallion lifted his head. A frost seemd to creep through his shoulders. I plucked at his mane.

As I straightened, he veered all at once. His long neck lunged forward. His hooves barely struck at the stones. I heard the oaths of the sealmen as they straggled behind. Bolted awake, they drove their heels into the flanks of the horses. Fearful, they hurled themselves upward. Yet as suddenly the way had grown clear. Mists that had clung uncoiled their fingers. Mists that had blotted out hills slunk down around stones. Then it was, though the air itself was darkening, I first saw the trees, trees ageless and black, trees towering over the gray earth as only the One Tree rose above Morrigan.

We had climbed a steep bank. To the west, beyond the ridge, the wood dropped away to the plain. Already fallen, the sun gave no light to it. Yet so great was their height that the topmost branches yet watched it and kindled with flame. I rode looking up.

The stallion jerked his head nervously.

Heedless, I was urging him onward. At the raw edge a stone loosened and fell. In that moment I saw the pit under me.

Slipping down from their mounts, the sealmen stood about staring, their faces turned grave and quiet in the hush of the evening. It was Wyck who broke it. Pointing out with a hand that trembled, he touched ever so gently the flank of my stallion, brushing a clod of earth from his hair.

'Lord?' he said softly.

'I have eyes of my own to watch with,' I said.

The bank was pulled wide, wrenched open like jaws. Tendrils were snarled at its brink. Farther down the carnage of old twisted roots poked out through the walls, the nest of wood sundered and split as though cracked and torn upward when the thing that long had stood there had awakened and climbed from the earth.

'There are black trees over us,' Eachanhagen said.

The sealmen drew back and looked at the stallion. As they watched him, his great chest heaved deeply and they saw the pale shine of his throat and the width of his shoulders. The eight thick legs under him stood monstrous in the dusk. Forcing themselves to believe, the sealmen kept their eyes open. But the darkness muffled their voices. I did not need to hear.

'Surely,' I told them, 'there was one that was white.'

'A horse?'

'A ship,' I repeat. 'It is the breaking waves that are called the horses of the sealmen, but the ninth is Gwen Gildrun. It was myself long ago who planted it, in the wood above Morrigan. But it was a ship before and after, and a horse only when I had need of it.'

The boy looks at his hands. He came from the kitchen because a boy must come when a king calls him though the grown men laugh and the women, back by the ovens, shake their old heads. He would prefer, I know, the work in the stables or in the high barn, where from the windows, facing the north and east, he can watch my grim soldiers riding out to the wars. But it takes half a morning for the thralls to find him there, and the kitchen is closer to hand.

He has but lately come and his fingers are coated with grease. He rubs their sides in his hair to clean them. Because I will not long suffer his silence, at last he looks up.

He answers me quietly. 'The *filidh* say they are sheep. That ninth is a ram.' His voice is low.

Out in the dawn there are crows. I can hear them flocking down from the roofpeaks. They prance on the cobbles, their black feet tapping lightly like blind men with sticks. Before the last bright star faded, they were awake, seeking the vermin that nest in the thatch. But not even their hunger can keep them. Before the cook rises or the first soldier, muttering, reaches out for his boots, the crows will have gone. The blue morning beckons them. Like boys and old kings, they can make do without sleep.

I rest my long arms on the chair. 'That is not different. Whether horses or sheep, they must come as I call them. If you would have

319

listened, you would have heard. They were the Redd Man's once. But now they are mine again.'

His dark eyes look out from under their shadows. 'Must a thing be what a man calls it?'

I see the trap. '*Things* must be.'

'And men?'

I press my great hands against his smooth shoulders. Under the narrow flesh the bone is as thin as a crow's. Soon enough it will thicken. Already in his eyes there is too much cleverness. I think, *I have had my peace. Even a king cannot keep the seed in the ground or a god, the new sun from pulling free of earth.* And yet I would hold him. I say, 'There was a woman once.'

'A goddess?' he asks dutifully.

'Yes.' My voice breaks. 'It was Anu. . . . In the dark of one evening I rode through her wood. A company of men I had with me, trotting behind. . . .'

He is not listening.

The soldiers have come in at the door, taking his sight. Not a man of them is mighty or tall, but their legs are well girded and their broad backs heavy with iron. Beyond the wall of the mountain the sun has already lifted its head. The yellow light burns on the metal. The boy stops his breath.

'Llugh.'

I turned, but it was only a sealman muttering, jolted awake in his saddle, the sun in his face.

Silently, during the night, we had come down through the trees, the sealmen no more awake than their horses, passing quietly westward down the slopes of the hills. The trees had grown smaller, more like the trees men knew, chestnut and maple and oak. They stood farther back – until now and then in the ragged holes between branches there had been stars, winking and bright in the evening. But gradually the darkness behind them had faded. Then at last we had come to the edge of a stream. Upon its smooth surface I had caught the first glint of dawn. There had been deep prints of hooves at the ford, there before us and gone. He has found horses, I thought. I had touched the cold flank of my stallion. He had lengthened his stride. So we had passed quickly over the water and come out on the far side from under the eaves of the wood and onto the green plain, turned gold in the morning.

My stallion snorted and sniffed at the air.

'He has scented an animal,' Eachanhagen said. But I knew he had not.

My eyes went back to the road. It came out of the north, cutting beneath the shoulder of a hill, then wound away southward and eastward. It skirted the edge of the wood, which marched along beside it, just out of reach. Gleams of sunlight struck the stones, turning the road tawny and brown, the colors of autumn. I gazed over it thoughtfully. At the farthest edge of sight there was a mountain. Vague and colorless, it floated on the world's rim as though neither land nor sea were certain where it stood or which would claim it.

'Should a man find this road,' I said, 'would he come at last among the Penandrun?'

'Lord, it is traveled,' Eachanhagen said. 'There would be men to find him now.'

'And if he would not be found?'

'Lord, it is a road. It goes where it goes. A man would follow it.'

Glas Awyddn stroked his raven beard and laughed. 'What way is there left to you, my king, but into trouble? I never heard a man went looking for a war and never found it.'

'Men may do as they please,' I said impatiently. Giving a nudge to the stallion, I sent him out along the stones.

The great road widened as we went, as the slightest stream widens, until as it spread it seemed an army might have moved along it, rank by rank. Indeed, the plates of stone were worn with use, and some were cracked. In places, where after rains the mud had seeped down from the banks, there were ruts and holes. Here once, by the look of them, enormous wagons must have mired before the soldiers, swearing at their teams, had pushed the thick wheels out and on again. Elsewhere the grass itself, like an arm of the tide, had washed across it. But whether mud or grass had covered it, there were stones beneath. Well set and solid, laid with a careful eye, they remained the lasting proof that men had made the road and that, however the sea had changed them, those men were landsmen once. Hurt by the harsh, incisive brightness of the stones, my tired eyes left them and blinked.

Eachanhagen rode just behind me. I did not need to look at him.

'As easily I might have looked north,' I said. 'Myself, I chose to ride southward, to the mountain and the old ones' court.'

I heard his silence.

'Not a man of us came unknowing his fate,' he said at last. 'If you go to the Penandrun, we must follow you. If you linger there, in the sea-girt hall, trading tales with men grown too old and stretched for death, what shall we do but sit with you and listen? How are you different? Soon enough you will long to see the North again, to climb beyond the place where this road is broken and walk on the shore.' He sighed. 'Even the tide goes back and forth. How then shall the heart of a king keep from turning?'

'It would depend,' I said, 'on what he was lord of.'

His stallion lurched forward. 'You are the Promised One!' he cried.

'Llugh,' a man whispered from back in the line. As though the word were an echo it rose from the plain, gathered a strength from the trampling of horses and a will from their breath. 'Llugh,' the host whispered. 'Llugh.'

Glas Awyddn laughed.

Below me to the left the road ran down into a hollow. Bent sharply eastward, beyond the tongue of the wood, it seemed to vanish. Trees and wild bracken encroached on the stones. Away to the south the road swept back again, but close at hand the signs of stonework faded under deepening shadows. The sealmen knew this place. Giving no thought to it, they rode contentedly, talking among themselves. Wyck rode in the midst of the troop, his face open, his mount trotting easily. At the front I was alone with Glas Awyddn.

A smoky light lit up the branches. One or two of the trees were red, with the sun's death or with autumn.

'He has horses now,' I said, 'and has gone ahead of us.'

'The three of them?'

'They are as we are. Bound as we are bound.'

'Even the boy?'

I looked at him gloomily. 'He – alone of all the earth – is free of me. That was my right, though never before have I used it. Yet when the battle comes, perhaps at the end of it, when hope is least, he will serve me. I cannot tell. It was fate that trapped me into pitying. Fate must see what comes of it. How shall I weigh the chance? Though once again I have shouldered my memory, one mystery I have kept, even from myself.'

I was silent after that. But Glas Awyddn went rushing on, leaping swiftly from what was to what might be, holding his balance by fierceness, as a man crosses a torrent, stone by stone.

'But for Wyck,' he said, 'you know the end.'

'Yes.'

'And the Penandrun?'

'They are the first of singers. As it is their song, they know its

His eyes watched me, eyes that could pierce a man though they
in my service. 'Then they will see the fault,' he said.

'See and then forget it too. Too often they have sung the tale. Too
well they know it. For in every deed they see the broad tale stretching
out, all that was its cause and all as well that springs up after, until there
is nothing left that is itself, that does not bear the shape of all the rest.
How then does it matter if it is Llugh, in fact, who comes to them? From
their great halls, looking out, they shall see a bold man riding down the
sea's bright plain. They are not gulled or cheated. A man comes riding.
They know the rest. At whatever point I enter, the tale runs on from it.'

His hand was still in his beard. He said, 'Llugh rides before us. He
will be first in the halls.'

'Which is first?' I asked.

'Lord?'

'Was it darkness or light?'

His face grew long and he looked with greater interest at his knees.
'Lord,' he said sullenly, 'I am only a man.'

I smiled. 'Then be at peace,' I said, 'for it is not for you to manage it.'

There was silence again, except for the clop of hooves and the horses'
breathing, and after a little while – somewhere out ahead, beyond
where the road turned and was hidden – a whisper. The sky was still
light, but the light trembled and grew thin. The horses were beginning
to shake their heads. I listened. Halfway along the curve of the road,
where it sank farther down into the hollow and the trees that crowded
its eastern edge pulled back like a hedge, there was a barley field.
Unswerving, the road ran straight through it. The seed had not been
sown to either side but had grown up between the stones, ignoring
them, as though the great old road were an inconvenience that would
pass. At the corner of the field a tall old man, his wide shoulders covered
by a coat, was cutting the barley. The last slanting sunlight dappled his
back. As he mowed, the blade rang out softly.

'Reaper,' I called out to him, 'have you seen a man riding ahead
of us?'

Toward the end of each stroke the old man leaned forward. He did
not look up. 'I have been mowing since daybreak, lord,' he grumbled.
'Still the work is not finished. What time do I have to look at the road?'

'It is but a little field.'

The barley fell in neat rows to his left, one after another unceasingly.
'Truly,' he said, 'it is no greater than that. Yet it is great enough. For

whatever I cut keeps on growing. Still, I mean to finish. This is my field. I plowed it when it was only salt, and when it grew I watched over it.' He groaned faintly. 'That was not the work of a moment. Nor is this. So, lord, by your leave, I will wish good day to you.' .

My smile only deepened. The last light faded red from the blade of the scythe. It was dark then. The sealmen, who could no longer see one another, stumbled up from behind, leading their horses. They kept their feet on the stones, inching forward. Eachanhagen groped with his hands. 'Lord,' he called out. Several times he had shouted.

'I am here,' I said, 'but come no farther. There is a field in front of me but it would be a grisly thing to come into it. Tie your horses where they are and do not let them feed in the stubble.'

'Lord,' Eachanhagen said crossly, 'this will not be the first time we have been here.' I had touched his pride. 'What is a field?' he said. 'Along the road there are many.'

'This,' I said, 'has a man in it.'

'So there was when we rode out, an old reaper in a long red coat taking the barley. What do I care of that?' Though he knew the rest heard him, he had made his voice loud. 'There have always been reapers,' he added.

'Indeed,' I said, 'but then I have not always been with you.'

He was a brave man, but he had only the darkness to look at. Though he had been coming forward, he took a step back.

They did not strain their eyes when the late moon rose, peering down at the plain. For each man there was only breath and snoring. Even the horses, huddled together, were asleep. Hunched, sunk down on a stone, I had begun my watch. The field was shining. The sky above it, though it had never yielded its blackness, shone with a steady, unbroken light. I sat and waited.

'It is getting late,' the reaper said.

I looked around and saw him standing alone in the silver stubble. He looked old, older than I remembered him. Wearily, he lifted his coat. Out of an inside pocket he extracted a grease jar and from another a hone. When the coat was open, I saw the rest of his arms.

'He will come.'

'He but lately walked,' the reaper said. 'Though already he thinks himself grand, his mother's lap still seems wide to him. In the quiet, when night comes and the mists that climb the Mound take shape against him, he hides himself in her hair.'

'Glas Awyddn has seen him,' I said. 'He has given him armor.'

The reaper made no answer.

My voice grew stern. 'Yourself,' I said, 'have carried him across the river.'

He had set the jar down and the hone with it. 'I do not deny it, lord,' he said. 'Here I carried him. And never have I felt such lightness for he was as nothing in my arms.' Reaching out, he took the hone. When it had dripped, he rolled it over the sand. 'But you,' he groaned, 'were a torment in my knees and on my back a bitterness.'

His eyes narrowed and he began to sharpen the scythe. 'But the men I bore here were never living men – only men who were or those who yet would be.' He shook his head. 'On land, at least, he is a boy. Nine years will she keep him with her on the Mound. Twice nine again must follow before at Tywy he comes to you.'

'There is a man riding,' I said.

And though before there had been nothing but a field and the moon gently gilding the stubble, of a sudden a man was riding, handsome and tall, on a horse pale as dawn. He came, passing out of the field's emptiness and into the light, as day comes, out of itself, not from shadows. I saw his brow then, white as a stone against darkness, unwrinkled as stone – for as yet no grief had come to him, his new life unsung and untroubled. He came to the top of the field where the barley was cut. There he let the stallion drop his pale head to graze on the stubble.

'Good evening, little one,' I said to him.

He smiled, his deep eyes searching over the field. When he found where I was, he went on smiling. 'As well my greeting, lord, though I doubt that I am less than you.'

Indeed he was taller than any man had been except myself. But I said, 'Who is there to judge between us here? Let it be. What comes, comes soon enough. At Tywy we will settle it and not before. Now I am only glad to look at you.' Still, I saw how, smiling, he watched me, taking the measure of my legs and shoulders.

'This is my realm,' he said.

I laughed. 'Child, I got you born in it.'

The lips like my own pulled back. 'I was not certain, lord, that you would say it.' It seemed that for a moment I saw a flash of redness on his cheeks. But then it was autumn and he was but partway in this place, and there were blazing oaks in back of him. He said, 'On land you will not claim me.'

'There she will have you to herself.'

'Lord,' he answered simply, 'she never knew a man but once. She never had a woman's life but that one day she took you to the Mound.'

'It was her choosing.'

He went on smiling. 'She never looked for any other. But because of it she will fill all the days that now must come with memory – your shape, your words . . . your hand upon her in the dark.' For a moment silence crept into his mouth.

'Lord,' he said slowly, 'though now I am too young to know the grief of that, in time I must. And when that sorrow comes, it will be always with me, a pain that never sleeps or lets me rest. The god knows I will hate you then.'

I watched him quietly. 'Child, I know it.' But I saw as well that it was only a tale to him and laughed. He looked relieved.

And yet his fingers closed about his reins. 'I am going south to the halls,' he said. It was nothing idle. The words were judged.

'In time,' I said, 'when it is fitting and the turning comes to it.'

'I am here,' he answered. 'By whatever cause, even your own. I have a horse and men to go with me.'

In the deep field, farther off, I saw the shapes that sometimes were Glas Awyddn and sometimes Wyck. And sometimes not. My long jaw set a little. 'It is their everlasting deaths to go with you,' I said, 'now, before their time. Your choice, and the price for it, to take them.'

He smiled but the smile was grander then. 'How shall you strike at me?' he said. The great smile deepened. 'This realm is mine. And they are mine who come with me. I mean no insult to your strength. Yet, lord, how shall you raise the least hand here when even the flesh you are clothed in is my own?'

'I will not.'

'Lord?'

'Child, this is not your field, or mine.' I turned my neck and with the turning he saw the old one standing out ahead of me. His hands were warty from his trades, his coat too big so it could hold his arms. The moon rose higher. Even then its cold lights was lost in the wool of his hair, slid down the sides of his huge shoulders. But on the long curve of the scythe it was burning.

'I have my work,' the reaper said.

The boy's smile was frozen. 'I do not stand in the way of it,' he said softly. But he contrived to look some other way. A breath of air, imperceptible to his flesh, reached out for the barley. The small heads murmured. He would not listen. But something in the shape and color of the night made him aware of what his eyes would see, what his ears would hear, if he would make use of them. He plucked at the reins, then took hold of them deliberately, pulling the head of his great horse away from the stubble. There was something dripping from the stallion's mouth. Between his jaws a thing cracked.

He said, 'I have no part in this.'

'When I gave you life, you took it gladly.'

He did not move. The night was cold and, though his hands were colder, I saw how he steadied them. I saw as well how his eyes looked out from under their shadows. In the south, low and black on the horizon, under the cold stars, in the halls of the Penandrun there were men and armies, waiting.

'Why have you brought me here?' he said.

'Once, child, before I murder you, to see your face.'

The field, the center of the field where the barley and the sea road met, was empty. In the hush toward dawn, the sealmen stirred. Beneath their labored breath, in the fields and halls, in the sweeping seas and windy beaches at the ends of sleep, they heard thinly, if at all, the echo of hooves retreating, going north along the road. Though if they heard, they did not think to follow. In some other place they were lords and kings. But here they were soldiers, and soldiers follow what is nearest them. They slept again.

Because I did not sleep, I had been walking on the margins of the road, walking slowly, stopping now and then to stir with my foot whatever I could find – a piece of straw rope, a broken drag dropped from the back of a brewer's wagon and abandoned on the stone. The dew, if it can be called dew undersea, was heavy. My hair was wet. I touched it, fingering its strangeness, knowing it was not my own. I was alone – for the first time since I had seen Glas Awyddn swimming in the sea.

Off in the chilly wood a bird was squealing.

'Has he gone?'

I spun around. Wyck was standing in the road. Wrapped in what was left of my cloak, he grinned.

'I heard you talking – I was asleep and it woke me.' He yawned and pulled the cloak more tightly around his neck.

'You choose your time ill,' I said harshly. 'You were better off sleeping.'

He shrugged. 'It was better I was Glas Awyddn's dog boy, but you have seen to it that I am not.'

He walked beside me. A breeze, passing through the wood, blew the first dried leaves across our path. In the south, before the lesser darkness, the nine peaks began to shape themselves against the sky.

'Lord,' he said, 'I was content. I did not need to see my life stretched out. Like any man, I would have had my strength grow less and less.'

'Why do you not sleep?'

His head came up. 'Why, lord, have you taken death from me?'

'Have you finished?'

'If you will answer that.' He paused, his dark eyes watching.

I touched his hair, a boy's fine hair that year by year would never coarsen. But even then my eyes strayed past him, following the road's faint ribbon north between the hills. No figure turned.

'He would not take the gift,' I said.

The peaks grew brighter as day came. In time, drawing up behind, the sealmen brought our horses.

A day more and in the distance there were wagons – small, odd wagons of uncertain cargo, pressing purposefully toward the south. From the back of my stallion I counted twenty and twenty more and could have kept on counting but for the dust raised by wheels and the sudden knots where some by mischance halted and the line backed up. There were men on horses and men trotting along beside the jolting wagons, men with flocks and men with herds, men striding alone in the midst of their beasts and darting with them when they turned. But all went south-ward, returning to the winter pasturage at summer's end.

Wyck gazed silently across the endless stream, as a child gazes at a river and wonders at its source.

'Where do their numbers come?' he said at last.

'From the North.'

'No,' he said. 'I did not mean that.' I saw him square his shoulders and take his grip more firmly on the reins. 'In this place,' he said quietly, 'how are there more of them?'

So any child must ask the one great question whose answer he has already guessed.

'Being what they are,' he said, 'what this place is.'

'Being men.'

'And stallions, bulls, and rams.'

I did not answer. My eyes went back along the road.

'How do they increase?' he said again, unashamed at last to show his impatience.

I could hear their voices now, the noise and jostling, the braying and bleating, the oaths of men.

Glas Awyddn laughed. Still his eyes held little mirth.

'The Redd Man keeps at his work,' he said.

We passed the stragglers first, men in indifferent, neglected dress, advancing sideways, their necks craned back, not intent on us but on the land behind, the all-consuming brightness of the autumn sky, the fields they had left. Their nostrils flared, trying to keep the last scent of the grass.

'Is there still some summer in the North?' a man asked sulkily. He had only felt my horse beside him and did not look up. As though he hardly noticed that he spoke aloud, he said, 'I warned them we had gone too soon. There were yet fish in the pools. There were stalks we had not gathered. Nor was the wind so harsh. I would have borne it.' His little restless eyes fixed on nothing I could see, he gave a drawnout sigh. I did not answer it. There is no use in speaking to the newly dead. Their heads are filled only with memory.

Though dead as well, the sheep moved skittishly. Bounding among their brothers, leaping on their backs, they went on breathing the damp close odors of wool and hide, indifferently. So they had always moved, in vast, distrustful flocks, ignorant of all misfortunes but their own. Death little changed that. But the herdsmen, accustomed to keeping watch, turned their quick, harsh eyes upon us. Not a man spoke to me. Still, they dipped their heads. I felt the name they whispered, changed to eagerness. Smiles came out of their faces.

'Come along, Dinas. Come along, Vawr. Come along, you black-faced devils,' they shouted. 'In the Penandrun's halls there are barns to shut you in, warm cribs and hay to keep your bellies warm when the hail comes biting.'

The road was better then, built with smooth gray stones and more often tended. Even the sprawling grass had been swept back on the banks, and the larches that had grown too close cut down to keep their spreading fingers from poking off the caps of the wagoners. The banks were steep, for here, as well, in wet weather the mud moved down from the fields and had to be flung up on either side. The sun, in the middle of its height, threw a brightness without warmth at the sweating horses. Men shouted out to them across their rumps. Rocking back and forth on the stones, the wagons thundered.

As our line passed them the sharp faces of the wagoners turned toward me. Their eyes, that were used to wonders, that had been left dull and blank with death and then reborn, those same eyes burned. They were not soldiers. They would not fight or meet again the monstrous dread. Llugh would not marshal them nor make corpses of them twice; yet they were his folk and knew the promise. Like any soldier, they stood to gain the land. Their eyelids flickered, their tongues came out indecently.

A man without a cap to hide his ragged hair stared up at me from his wagon. He had set his hand before his lips, afraid to speak.

'What do you wish?' I said.

'Shall we be whole again?' he stammered, but I saw that it was only part of what he meant.

'You have legs and arms.'

He shook his head and the rest of him shook with it. He blinked with fear and cunning. Like a worn old cloth his mouth split wide. 'Lord,' he grinned, 'are there women still?'

I stopped to wait for Eachanhagen to catch up with me. He came slowly, for from every wagon questions came at him: Was I in truth the Promised One? If I were meant to come in glory, why was it the small one wore my cloak? Why was it torn? When would I gather the armies? If not by winter, would it be by spring? When could they expect to see their towns again, their farms at Brehnum-Sawle, at Tyre, the marsh at Mhor? Did sweet william grow in gardens still? Would I remember that, but lately come? Did housewives yet dry hops against the chimneys? Were vines still planted deep? Did it rain on the Eve of Teimhne last? Or was it snow as always? Would all, for certain, come with me when I went to Tywy?

He answered what he could, though that was little, and shouted that surely I would make plain as much as I wanted when we made the halls, that for himself he was content with that and they should ask no more.

'They fill the road,' I said to him when his stallion had drawn abreast of mine.

'They are many. But year by year there are more.'

'There were few,' I said, 'by the river when we crossed.'

Eachanhagen stiffened his back. 'Only kings and armed men cross there. For that is the grandest place. But there are a thousand streams. Truly, not a trickle runs seaward but somewhere along it a redd man is waiting. Men find them, men like any other but unlike soldiers, not looking for death but only running down to fetch rushes or, their minds elsewhere, driving the red oxen to drink in the shallows. It does not matter, so long as there is water to cross. You would not know this. The highborn never do. Those with their forged swords and armor, who courted death, give little thought to men who blunder into it, whom death takes just as surely but unaware.'

'Their lords are no less dead.'

His brown cheeks reddened. 'It is not the same.'

'Yourself, you were a soldier.'

'Was,' he said. 'Am,' he went on in a disgusted voice; 'will ever be.' He paused. 'Yet once I was a diker, as low a man as these men are. Ten years I drained the fens, awash in slop, making fields with a wooden shovel for them who were lords and owned marshes but wanted land. I was but two years a soldier. War came and they took my shovel and put a spear in its place. So I made death instead.'

'And came, when death took you, by the grandest way into *Tir fo Thuinn*. And were put ahead of other men.'

'So I might fight again.'

'Would you change it?'

He was not old. There was not so much as a single gray hair on his head. He had a sword in his belt and in his left hand a lance with three sharp points. Along beside him the wagons pitched and rolled. The faces of the wagoners, like burning masks, looked out at us with fear and envy. He did not turn his head.

He said, 'I know the work.' A deep, heartbroken pride showed in his face. Ahead, in the shadow of the banks, an old man with a wooden shovel was clearing black mud from the stone.

Farther on there were other bands of wagons but the same smell of men and the turf smell of horses on the thick evening air. There were horse-men as well, gathered in from the plain, riding in through the heather and the waist-deep weed. The tireless green horses climbed over the embankments with care. The long shadows of lances grew like a brown thicket at my left hand. No man cried out. Yet one by one their chiefs rode up the line to look at me. Perhaps Eachanhagen spoke to them. I heard only the quick hoofbeats trotting back. The sound washed soft then hard, then soft then hard again, like waves against stone. So, alone on my great ship, I had heard the gray sea lapping the hull. The waves had seemed like hoofbeats then. It made no difference. The waves were armies, the horsemen fierce as any cursing sea. And should I walk upon the land, even the boulders there, I knew, would take new life and follow me. Had not the gaunt old stones risen up behind Ar Elon when I had his shape? I had not called them. No more did I call these men.

In darkness, hours I never counted passed. The moon was late; the stars, their dim lights shifted by the upper sea, were unreliable. The sea road rolled away beneath. I no longer listened, not even to the wind, though now it blew with a keener edge. I let my mind drift into darkness, into the soundless holes that worm through sleep, and for a space, between midnight and morning, remembered nothing. So even the least wave cast at heaven hangs for a moment at its height. However cursed, some strength, however fleeting, holds its fall.

I drew an icy breath. It was nearly dawn.

Gray streaks showed for a moment in the east, then with a strange deep quiet the endless rushing cloud poured over us. A hail of grass and tiny broken twigs blew in front of the horses. The rain came after, headlong, pounding the stones. There was no riding into it. Wiping a stream of water from my eyes, I gazed at the size of the army straggling at my back. The long lines of mail-clad men checked their steeds and sent them leaping away from the swollen torrents that gorged on the hills. I sent my own horse up, climbing the fissured and crumbling walls.

A roaring confusion rose and buried what was left of the line. The harnessed horses screamed. At once the road was crammed with wagoners, swimming, scrambling, when they could reach them, to the tops of the wains. Boxes sprang from their stays. Barrels raced off in the current, knocking into the horses. Rolling and tumbling savagely, they piled up like a dam where the road angled sharply until, in a rush, they broke again in one thick mass, like a piece of the bank itself, sliding away out of sight.

A moment passed.

The wind blew wickedly but the rain no longer beat down with any force. A ray of chilly light cut through the cloud. The road, where the tide was draining, seemed suddenly shabby and cold. The horses walked about shivering. On the banks, above the high-water marks, the enterprising sheep stood out with startling clarity. The sky grew paler. Already I could see a few men climbing down, wading out through the mud. Squeezing their caps, they had begun to think how to upend a wagon that had been deposited on its back.

With astonishing speed the soldiers picked up their lances. Once more they slung their painted shields across their shoulders. Soon one or two rode forward. I was quiet watching them. I could hear the air again, moving in the grass. The herdsmen walked slowly down the southward slope. The horsemen gathered, talking among themselves or mending their gear, leaving the wagoners to salvage what they could. There were no hard glances. In the years undersea they had grown used to floods. By midmorning they had made a great pile of sodden hay and barrels, boxes, bound flax and coopered tubs, of jars and bladders and sacks, all that had spilled and floated or had not been too deeply buried and could be dug out and left to dry.

Eachanhagen hesitated. He smiled to himself then took a few steps closer to where I stood, dismounted, staring out at the road.

'Lord, it is time we went,' he said.

Silhouetted against the chalky light, I saw the lines of horsemen winding toward us up the brow of the hill. Wyck was with them, near the front, his nose and his chin thrust out proudly. A fur cap he had got hold of somewhere was pulled down snug on his head. For the last time I saw him grinning. He looked as though he had just been in a fight and won. I supposed it was the sea he had fought with.

'And the wagoners?'

'They will take what they can with the wagons left. What they cannot will be come back for.'

I grunted, as if unconvinced. 'And the drowned men?' I said.

He laughed. It was a good laugh. Truly, though I would have his head on the stones of Tywy, the first wave in, for he was Llugh's and served him, yet I sometimes thought that I would sooner lose myself the service of all the faithless devils with me on the land than never hear the sound of it. He took up the reins of his stallion lightly and found its back. He smiled, his forehead wrinkling.

'They will dig themselves out.' He was about to turn, then added, 'And those who will not, the next wave will wash free or else the dikers will.' He paused, looking down at his own thick arms. 'I told you I was one myself. We'll not let them sleep.'

I walked on a few paces.

'It will be a bitter war,' I said.

For a moment he watched me strangely, then he laughed. 'How is it, lord,' he asked, 'that they will slaughter us?'

Over the days the nine small towers had grown ever larger in the south. By now they took a quarter of the sky, huge as the new dark moon, each looming up so tall it seemed it made its own black night on the climbing hills that rose before us. Along the road there were stands of birch and a few stiff vines. The wood that long had followed us had trailed off to the east, leaving the black hills open. In the fields the grass was thin. I felt the soldiers watching me. I pushed them on. In the evening we came upon houses. Low against the ground, their roofs staved in, they had been abandoned when the wells turned brackish with the rains. The ground still smelled of flood. The men were grumbling. I did not let them rest. The miles went by.

Now some of the hills were walled at their summits but the sentries had been called in; the platforms were empty, the stables cleared. The road bent around beneath their shadows.

Glas Awyddn gazed ahead. The clouds had parted and, though the sky was darkening, the air was clear. 'There is something shining underneath the peaks,' he said. He rose up in his stirrups. 'I have seen it twice between the hills, though the darkness of the towers sometimes blots it out.'

'It is the lake that circles about their halls,' Eachanhagen said. 'Beyond these hills the road lies straight. By morning you will see it plainly.'

'And the ships,' a soldier close by him said.

Eachanhagen nodded. 'And the ships that wait to take us to the land.'

Wyck woke after sunrise. Sunk down in his saddle, he had slept for several hours as the last stars faded. His eyes were red. After he woke he sat a long time rocking gently as the stallion, close packed with the other horses, ambled across the long causeway that connected the shore of the lake with the ramparts – still a mile off – of the nine-towered mountain. His thick shoulders rose and fell. He did not look at the ships or the mountain. While the road had run down swiftly on the other side of the hills, turning a wide curve by the harbor, stretching away south again past pens and building yards, he had been dreaming. A cold gooseflesh stood up on his arms. The soldiers nearest him nudged one another and grinned.

At the end of the causeway the nine stone towers rose without preface from the lake. The old stonework glittered, gleaming with a brilliance reflected from the lake. Ancient and tall those towers were: a mountain built on water, the blue rock dragged up from the deepest ocean and set on piles, spread across ledges and islands, a city and a mountain threaded with channels and spanned with bridges, arched and high themselves as hills. Men who knew of it said that in the oldest days the seal-lords who built here built as the god built the world's fastness, with the same sureness, with thought and not with hands. As they neared, the eyes of the sealmen sparkled.

'In all the world there are no halls like these,' a sealman said to Wyck.

He winked with silent laughter at the boy's long face. Wyck stared at the water gloomily, laced and unlaced his brooding fingers on the reins.

'You smile,' Wyck said, 'but before many days the winter comes.'

The line of the sealman's mouth stretched wide with laughter. 'We have the sun,' he cried. 'How shall it be winter when Llugh dwells with us?' His deep voice boomed, the sound of it carrying across the lake with a strength and joy that reached the farthest walls and echoed back.

Along the line the sealmen looked in each other's eyes. The tales at last were true. Even the shame of dying at a stranger's hands, the hideous quiver in the flesh when the bones were parted, the spray of blood and pain, now seemed as nothing. It was the trade of soldiering. What else could be expected when a man took arms? But all would be paid for now. The faces of the sealmen, looking up, listening with wonder, were lit with the same conviction and delight.

The glimmering colors of the harbor danced on the stone. In the first of the towers, high up where the gulls were soaring, a window was open. A shadow moved against the light, passed, and then, distracted, came back again.

The head of a very ancient man thrust itself outside the casement. The light made him blink. The ridges of his forehead were shrouded with dismal patches of hair. Blown in the wind, they lent a kind of uncertainty and shapelessness to the skull. The sealmen found it hard to remember what they saw.

'Grandfather!' a sealman shouted. 'Have you not seen? It is Llugh who rides with us!'

The old man straightened. Looking nowhere in particular, he uttered a word. But what it was there was no telling.

The flank of Wyck's stallion brushed against mine. I saw the look of desolation in his face.

'What do you fear so much?' I said quietly.

'In the dark,' he whispered, 'coming down from the hills . . .' He stopped.

'Child?'

'I dreamed.' His eyes went suddenly to my face. 'There is another hall,' he said, his voice just a whisper above the footfall of horses. 'A hall both vaster and deeper than these halls are. Since the world was, no light ever came there.'

'That was not hid from you.'

'Lord, I did not know it.'

I answered thoughtlessly, 'Glas Awyddn knew, before I knew myself. Truly, I remember little what I was until he came.' I saw the hurt. 'Until I saw you both,' I said.

His stallion leapt forward.

The horses thundered along the worn stones of the causeway. The men rode four abreast, their long black lances outlined against the rock. But for all their number they might have been shadows. Though I knew it gave him no company, I urged my own mount again to his side. Without a word I reached across for his reins. He paid no heed to it. His eyes were empty. To the depth of his being there was loneliness. After a moment he turned to watch the old man leaning out of the tower. Something drew his eyes more fiercely to the ancient head.

'His mouth is cruel,' Wyck said, 'as cruel and sharp as an old cock salmon.'

'Child, you have learned to look,' I said gently. Before my own eyes the causeway was a blur of horses. I lifted my head. 'That is more than can be said for these brave men. For they have never looked.'

Free of the reins, the boy's hands trembled. He pressed them strengthlessly against the stallion's withers. If there were some warmth in that flesh, it passed to him. He said, 'When I came to this place, I thought of nothing more than to ride with them, mounted on a horse such as I had never seen in dreams or racing the tide across the whole width of the bright sea floor, preparing for war.'

'That war will come.'

His head was lowered. 'The Penandrun are very old,' he said.

'I too am old.'

For the first time he stared at me. 'It is a child they look for.'

'A boy,' I said, 'with the glamour of fire in him, fair as good weather.' I laughed. 'Bright as the glow of gold.'

Then sun, safe on its own high path, covered the lake with blazing light. On every side, as though the boundless sky were mirrored in the rock, the stones of the towers stretched away. In the brightness, in the heart of the burning, he saw, at the very last clearly, I was not there.

'Lord,' he stammered, his voice so fragile I knew that it would break. 'They will see . . .'

'Nothing,' I answered him firmly, '. . . unless you mention it.'

She reaches out to touch my arm and, not finding it, wakes instantly. The cool air of autumn drifts in through the window. A capricious breeze, but not unkind, it swirls over the risen flesh of her nipples. She has been dreaming and, turning her thin shoulders at the edge of sleep, has driven off the coverlet. For a moment she draws it back then sits up sharply. From that high place, through the oblong hole where the wind comes and goes as it pleases, immune to her governance, she can see the river licked up white under the stars. The room itself is dark. Even against her tongue I have had my will in that.

'Husband?' she says softly.

The chair by the doors is half in shadow, but now she sees no one is in it. Still, she is not frightened. Ever since our sons were nine-month born, came howling out of her like any other, with mannish hands and mannish feet, she seldom gives a thought to signs and portents. 'This is a king's house,' she is fond of saying. 'A king's peace I shall have in it.'

When I do not answer she climbs from the bed and irritably, without her covering, walks to the window. At first there is no sound, then quite close someone is talking. In the yard a guard is pacing. The breeze flutters past her, taking some of her resentment with it. She is nearly thirty-eight. The starlight silhouettes her figure. A bit of light slants across each breast as she turns back again. They are still full. In seventeen years she has not forgotten how to bargain with the dark.

'I have been dreaming,' she says ruminatively.

'A stranger?' I ask from the chair, the face she cannot see mischievous.

'No stranger, husband,' she answers. 'It is your own sons I am thinking of.' She heaves her thin shoulders, walking boldly toward where she has decided I must be.

'Woman, I warn you. I have lain with a hundred queens.'

She laughs. 'With their bones, to hear you talk of it.'

I feel her breath. She is resolved, as much and in as many ways as her grand strapping father was, though through all the sorrowing days he marched with me across the cantreds, treading the muddy reaches of the Tywy and back to the valley's narrow end, he marshaled hosts. A girl, a woman now, as resolved and earnest as her father, neither discomfited nor shamed, she holds in front of me the breasts and belly that got our sons, as she has held them before the passing guard, though as yet, because I will not move, she does not know for certain I am here.

'Woman, I have dreamed myself.'

Thinking surely now I must take hold of her, she does not reach out.

'Lord?'

'Before the sea was cold,' I say, 'before there was any land for it to roll against, across the stillness that was then, we faced each other, her face that was not a woman's yet – for there were no women until she decided she would be the first – that face intent and white on mine, and mine that I myself had made so I could stare at her, mine dark with shame, afraid now that I had fashioned it that she would see its longing, our two faces looked out and all we knew was fear.'

Had she a gown to cover her, she would have had some use for her small fingers, a seam to straighten, some little fold to fasten back. Yet, knowing her worth, she keeps them quiet on her thighs.

'Lord,' she sighs, resentful and yet, perhaps, because she is used to this as well, amused. 'Lord,' in a voice made almost tender, 'what should you fear? Already I have made you sons.'

The deeds of my youth are not now remembered. Nor has any woman cared how once the darkness moved or how I plucked the worlds from it. It is only because I have not touched her, she reaches down.

'Not your sons,' I whisper hoarsely. 'It was myself I meant to get reborn.'

She does not listen. It is only because she has felt the chair is empty that she screams.

The Penandrun were at work in their towers when the sealmen came. The one who saw them did not think to tell the rest. It was too great a labor to descend the stairs, to cross the yards and mount again the endless steps that circled up the inner walls. At the city's bright enneadic heights there were too many cocklofts and chambers. He did not move at all. Every now and then his distant, little-seeing eyes would open. The sun warmed his face. He felt only the creeping of his ancient blood. Like all his brothers, he longed for the days he had lost. The new thunder of horses on the causeway brought nothing that had not already left him discontented.

He knew exactly how the sealmen would look, their lances discarded, locked away from them for the winter while he taught them tales they saw no use to learn. He knew how they would whisper when he turned his back, how they would mutter when, in the midst of the song, his own deep boredom for the moment replaced with wonder, he saw the slopes and beaches swarm with men, saw the white bay filled with sails, the sealmen climbing naked from the sea.

Tywy, he thought.

But in this place the harbor was blue and tranquil, the only sound the commotion of horses. That was no more strange today than it had ever been nor any more worth his notice. He glanced down, the lines of his face unchanging. The same lances waved; the same green stallions trotted on the stones. Yet, just once, above the usual shouting a man called out to him.

'Grandfather!'

The old one cocked his head. He rubbed his eyes and cocked his head again.

The sealmen and their horses were gone, the causeway silent. He stared back at the room absently. Now, for some hours, the sun had left it. Without moving, he noticed his thin wrinkled fingers were white with frost, white as the morning, white, he recalled suddenly, as an eight-legged stallion. He raised his head. Though he had not moved for a very long time, he went to the stairs.

The tunnels were fair-sized but the sealmen were many. Yet as they rode, men turned aside, driving the horses under wide galleries of dark, polished stone, urging them to the left and right in the darkness under the walls. Wyck caught glimpses of their armor. He could not have found the way himself. On the plain the road had gone on before him, the mountain growing larger, drawing him onto it. Here there were too many passages, twisting, opening suddenly and blankly, and no ray of light marking one from the next. The men around him were nearly as indistinguishable. But he did not move his head. He was trying to remember the exact look on his face – the sun burning above him on the causeway – as it faded.

'There are deeper ways under this,' Eachanhagen said. There were stairs and doorways now, below the arched ceiling, hollowed out in the deep mountain rock. He saw them dimly. A breath of chill air, escaping from the delvings, blew over his back. Eachanhagen's voice echoed. 'The stells and the stables are below us,' he said, 'the grooms' halls and forges. There are others farther down.'

Had he stopped to think, Wyck would have noticed that already they had descended well beneath the level of the lake. The passage plunged steeply. The cold air thickened and dripped. But he had felt no dread of the tunnels, had given no thought to them. Still, his hands trembled. He ran them cold on his forehead and into his hair.

'Someone must tell them,' he said. His unhappy eyes found the unchanging eyes of the tall man beside him.

'Tell them what?'

'That their dreams are nothing.'

Eachanhagen looked down at him. In his left hand, the sealman carried a high, smooth lance, its butt resting against the flank of his stallion. Its points were deadly. At a gallop he could drive them into a yard of wood. He was a fearsome man. And yet he had not forgotten the first morning he had ridden here, into a darkness unearthly and filled with the pounding of hooves. The boy was small. What chance has he, the man thought, against the things of his imagining?

The sealman smiled. 'The tunnels open up to the yards beyond,' he said. 'In a moment you will see the sun again.'

But the ceilings lowered and the sealmen bent down, tipping their lances. The last gleamings faded. The horses tramped across darkness; the echoes fell farther back. The horsemen swept on and took no heed of them. Wyck heard their pace quickening. If the man heard him sobbing, he did not remark on it.

In time there was light again, a vague, dusty light softening the edges of the stone far ahead of them, then a slender crack that yawned, that grew wider until the advancing mouth of the tunnel filled with daylight. Then at last Wyck saw the hosts of men, the grooms and the scavengers, the fetchers and hardwaremen, streaming out of the holes and warrens, slamming the doors on their forges, shouting and pouring over the walls. A sealman raised his horn and blew. The sound rose above the thunder of feet on the gangways. Under the cavernous roof of tunnels the air rang with shouts. 'Llugh!' the men yelled. They ran alongside the horses, their eyes darting from one man to the next.

The passage climbed swiftly. The first of the horsemen passed under the archway, into a yard opened up to the morning. The shouts of a greater host greeted them. The sound grew to a roaring. Another sound waited behind it, unused and impatient. Rank by rank the horsemen entered the yard, the sound growing restless, swelling when each new man came into the light, but lapsing back when the shadows had left him. Glas Awyddn passed beneath the stone's edge, Eachanhagen behind him. Just beyond the portal they halted. Above them, along the curving terraces carved into the rock, ten thousand figures stood, their shoulders rigid, their dark eyes flickering. Now, like the horseman, the host of men waited. Moved by the hush, a stallion whickered. A sealman patted his neck.

They saw the great horse as he broke from the portal. His white head was lifted, his head turning coldly. But the sound they had waited to make had died in their throats. It was so still they might have heard, even from far off, the flutter of the wind through the cloaks of the old ones looking down from their towers. The old ones themselves were silent: the horse was riderless.

Eachanhagen was the first to speak. No amazement rooted his tongue. He stood high in his stirrups. 'He had come!' he shouted, shaking his fists at the ramparts and terraces. 'The men with me rode with him. Here before you is the horse he rode. Have any seen the like of him?' He spat. 'Who are you to question if in the tunnels he went his own way? Which of you would choose for him? Even now he speaks with the old ones.'

Necks craned upward. And indeed in each tower the tall windows were empty, the old ones gone from them. The many faces of the hosts moved again, uneasily.

Eachanhagen put aside his lance. 'Come then,' he boomed. 'Where are the grooms? Our horses have ridden long and are weary.' He looked around him into the faces of the hosts. The silence made him shout again. But at last the captains called out. The stretch of waiting loosened. Once more a sealman lifted his horn. Before the high note ended a man leapt free of the walls. Another man followed. To the left a ramp of rough planking slid down into the yard. The grooms came running along it. 'He is here,' the grooms whispered. 'These men have seen him. Soon enough, when he pleases, he will show himself.' Discontented but knowing now what must surely come, the grooms went forth, spreading out among the horses, hailing the men they knew. All the way up to the high open windows, if there was not laughter, once again there was shouting.

The riders closest to Eachanhagen did not climb from their mounts. They looked up at the towers. But even to them the grooms came at last, albeit more slowly, for the great stallion, his head tossing, paced the ground in front of them. The sharp white sunlight danced on his back. The light dazzled the grooms.

But there was one who did not fear him. He came away from the wall, and the younger grooms made a path for him. Though one leg was lame, he walked quickly. He seemed nearer a hundred than fifty, but his brows were pointed and stiff and his beard was as red as a coal in a grate. He was groom master and dressed for his office, in a thick cloak of mixed wools, rachan-shaded and stained at the edge. A strange benevolence shone in his owlish round eyes as he came up to the stallion. Cooing, he reached for his muzzle.

The stallion drew back.

'Eachanhagen?' Glas Awyddn said.

'It is only fitting,' the sealman answered. 'Now he will be stabled apart, in a place that long has been kept for him.'

The old man edged nearer. 'May the god be my witness!' he cried. 'In a hall to himself. And myself I will curry him. Alone I will do it. Though the old ones set me a hundred tasks, I will neglect them.' His trembling fingers reached for the mane.

'It is your life if he is lamed,' Glas Awyddn said.

'Truly,' the old man said, 'what is the life of a dead man?'

The boy came up, last, leading his stallion. Glas Awyddn saw he was watching.

'Go yourself,' Glas Awyddn said to him. 'See that all that is done is done with care.' He had meant it as a gift. Yet, because he had dared not look at him further, he turned away. Only Eachanhagen watched after them, the old man and the boy, the great horse between them, going back through the portal. The long face of the sealman had hardened.

'The blame is not on us,' he said, 'but on yourself.'

'There was always risk.'

'Still, you tempt it.'

The sun poured its fire on the center of the yard. Directly overhead, it filled the cracks of the earth, warming the cramped, exhausted sinews of the stallions. Under their mail the sealmen sweated. Only one man felt the edge of the wind or remembered its coldness. Glas Awyddn pulled his mantle over his neck.

'How will I keep the salmon from the falls?' he said. 'No more than that may I keep him, though once he was dear to me.'

Eachanhagen frowned. A groom was taking his stallion. 'It was for Llugh to decide,' he said.

Glas Awyddn sucked his breath through his teeth.

The great hall faced north and east. When he walked into it Glas Awyddn saw the wide leaded windows looking over the lake and, on the far side, under the hills, the masts of the ships, like a forest of brown, leafless trees sticking up in the harbor. The windows went straight to the roofbeam, the ceiling arched and tall, so that the ships themselves might have fitted beneath it. The space between was swimming with light.

He had come in at the front of company, Eachanhagen beside him. Despite the press of men, Glas Awyddn stopped at the doors. His back straightened. Under the casements he saw a high platform, carved from the rock. Broad stairs went up to it. On either side of the steps were chairs, their arms studded with bronze and inlaid with horn. He did not need to count them. The nine were empty. But the floor was crowded. At first, seeing so many, he did not understand why there was quiet. The leather in his armor creaked. The hilt of his sword flashed gold in the sunlight.

A guard came forward. He was a big man. His seahair was russet; his eyes, in their anger, nearly as red. It was to Eachanhagen he spoke.

'I greet you,' he said, 'but it is a stranger's welcome you have from me. Well enough you know the law. Never before have you brought your weapons into the hall.' He was not armed but, as though his size were all the shield and arms he needed, he stepped in front of them. The listeners leaned nearer.

'Why are you speaking law to me?' Eachanhagen said. 'We learned war here. Now war has come to it.' He smiled, a wolf's mile. Out of courtesy the guard smiled back. But the smile was thin, the smile of a man remembering pain. His voice sounded weary. He said, 'Since I crossed the blood river, this law has stood.'

'I do not fault it,' Eachanhagen said. The sun on his armor brought out the scents of hair and sweat. The soldiers shifted. A heaviness clung to them. But then he laughed. 'Truly,' Eachanhagen said, 'who would trust such men – crowded in one hall – with arms? Men without love, without mercy.' He stared at them, looked hard into faces that neither looked away nor looked back.

The guard waited. He said, 'Even as you said it, it was the law.'

'It was made and now it is broken.' Eachanhagen walked sharply past him. But before he beckoned his soldiers he turned. 'This was their house and their law while they ruled it. We have no quarrel. Old men bring advice, sad tales, and laws.' He had lifted his hand; they saw the length of the shining sword he had drawn with it. 'The new king brings war.'

The guard moved abruptly, but the tautness in his face had changed to astonishment. 'We are doing this,' he said.

Eachanhagen's lips twisted back. 'It is the tales.'

'Sir?'

'They are happening.'

Glas Awyddn shrugged. Without meaning, the words buzzed around him. He was staring across the guard's shoulder toward the gray windows, feeling how the brightness had gone from them. He was much too high, he decided, to hear voices. The wind whimpered on the ledges, scraping the stones. Only the thunder of wheels drifted up to him.

He made his way to the stairs and climbed the steep platform. The darkening clouds were piling up behind the hills. He looked down at the lake. Along the causeway he saw the line of wagons moving across from the harbor. With his good eye he tried to count the herds and flocks that were swept along with them, going in through the walls. He could not tally them. The seaglass was thick. Still his nostrils flared. Catching the bitter scent of sheep, he remembered that the dead were numberless. Seized with impatience, he turned his back.

Even unwatched, the flocks and the herdsmen came without pausing, swelling the city, filling the yards and stells with the damp, oily bodies of beasts and men. He could not deny their numbers, yet their coming had left him with a feeling of unbearable emptiness.

It was the waiting, he told himself. But he was thinking of the woman he had seen just once – now slid beyond recognition or imagining – coming out of the sea. It seemed a lifetime ago, yet she whose face he could not now remember remained with him. Neither young nor old, now without flesh, without even substance, she bound him. Without her, he realized, his heart sinking, he was not, not himself surely but only the Un-Man's shadow – Duinn, Lord of Tricks and Lies.

He ground his teeth. Even then, though he was lost and nothing, he found a piece of a thing to chew on. He held it in his jaws. Thin, it was like a thread of a woman's hair.

The grooms were running about in confusion. The tunnels were filled with wagons and sheep. On the gangways the hostlers chattered like starlings. The gray darkness, like a wind swollen and bristling with the sounds of hooves and murmuring, rolled against him. But when the light from the open yard had dimmed and vanished, when the last thralls and housemen, gone their own ways, had wormed again into the rock, Wyck could still hear the stallion beside him. The passage dipped lower. The floor was slippery and smelled. Cobwebs tickled his face. Through the walls he could hear the deep, muffled groaning of the lake. The stallion whickered, but now the sound comforted him, easing his pain. The boy swallowed bravely.

He no longer tried to believe he would not ride him. From the morning he had seen the great horse trotting out from the old woman's wood he had known this. Yet for the days and nights they had ridden through the realm, through the strange quiet wood and out again onto the plain, he had kept his heart closed to it. From that morning, his hands – as though they knew him better than his blood – had ached to touch him. His eyes, by themselves, had slid across his coat, had watched in sly wonder how at every stride each prodigious white hoof judged the ground. And yet all the while he had dared not tell himself.

Unwanted now, the lord's ungentle face slipped into his mind. He knew – had known before the boy, looking elsewhere, had even attempted not to think. One shoulder shrugged. Glas Awyddn gave me leave, Wyck thought. The floor was paved with harsh old stones. The boy was almost running when the man, panting behind him, caught his arm.

Beyond a black arch a faint light shone, a new light, gentle as the light of dawn. The stallion walked into it. Wyck would have followed, but the old man lunged ahead. Boldly, though he was short of breath, he barred the way.

'Hold boy,' he panted. 'It is his hall. He must be the first to enter it.'

'I was told to go with you.'

The old man grunted. He wheezed despairingly and shook his head. 'Your lord was no more pleased than I to have you come.'

The boy was silent. The hooves of the stallion did not seem to clatter on the stones. They caught each other's eyes just once, then Wyck edged by him.

It was as though a veil had parted, a veil he had never known was there. He saw the shining walls, rising clear and bright, but, though he ran his eyes over them, he could find no breach or opening. His legs shifted restlessly. There were no torches, and yet a light that had no source was slowly filling the hall, flowing steadily into it as though from emptiness. He did not see the stallion.

The groom master moved behind him. 'For a thousand years,' he said, 'this hall stood waiting. As patient as I could be, though seldom in this place, I waited with it.'

Wyck turned. The man was bearing a bundle of loose straw away from the wall.

'In all that time I have not learned myself,' he said glumly, not looking up, 'what He will have need of. I can only do what I have done and hope.' He let the straw drop to the floor and scattered it. Without straightening, he mopped his forehead. His robe was open; Wyck saw the number of his arms. 'Come,' the man said, 'if I must have you, I'll have as well your hand with this.'

'You have hands enough.'

'The work takes many.'

The boy shrank back from him. 'Lord,' he said slowly, 'twice already I have seen you, at the blood river and in the field, yet I do not know that work.'

'How would a boy hear of it?' he said coldly. He lifted his head, plain as a farmer's and ruined with scars. 'Yet it was no riddle. It is the first work that was ever done, though it is never finished. So I have kept at it.' He reached again for the straw. A brightness filled the air in front of him. Wyck followed after.

'Still, I do not know it,' he said.

'Dividing.'

'What?'

'The wind in its quarters, the darkness from morning, a man –'

The boy was not listening. He was staring. Once more the eight white hooves of the stallion were trotting on the stones.

'He is here,' the boy whispered, 'but for a moment he was not.' The man looked across at him, gauging the wonder in his bony face. Something changed in him.

'He rides with the sun,' the old man said carefully. 'So at least it is said.' His lips parted, then closed again firmly as though he debated with himself. The straw was still in his hand. He straightened wearily. 'Surely,' he said, 'he comes and goes as he pleases. And so he might. For he is free of everything except his will.'

The boy cocked his head. 'Yet if a man rode him,' Wyck said softly, 'could he be ridden there?'

'To what place?'

'Across the bright heavens –'

'He would have his death,' the man said quickly. The cleft between the old red brows deepened. 'And not the little death we know, but that beyond rebirth, which Duinn gives.' Himself, he thought of the monstrous dark, the cold beyond bearing. For a moment, even in the light, he found he was shivering.

'But if there were a man – or even a boy –' Wyck went on eagerly, 'who could not die?' He drew a swift, silent breath. His unlined, long face was beaming.

In the first hour of morning, when there was still darkness, the Penandrun sent a herald to Eachanhagen and to all of the chiefs of the sealmen in their scattered barracks under the walls. Eachanhagen was already wide awake. In truth he had been unable to sleep and had kept the watch himself, trying to wear out his impatience by pacing the stones. Toward morning he had gone out onto the dark platform overhanging the lake. Alone in the shadows he had waited, staring up at the towers. The chill water under him no longer seemed to knock at the walls. A less stubborn man might have noticed. He had been too filled with waiting to hear sounds that were not. But he saw the herald before the other man saw him.

'Has he been seen, man?' he yelled. 'Has he called for us?'

'No,' the herald answered him darkly. 'It is the Penandrun who want you.'

'Myself?'

The man's face hardened. 'When have they ever wanted one of you?' he said. 'Call your hosts and go to them.'

Eachanhagen's lips were a savage line. 'He has come,' he said grimly and walked past him.

There were no lights in the yards, none in the passages winding cold in the darkness, or in the deep stone cellars, none in the rooms without number that made up the holding. What light is there where no fires burn? There was only a sound, like the sea wind scraping the rock, only a whisper, like the seal's crying, filling the chambers where the lonely men slept. The herald's eyes flickered. They banged open the doors.

'You brag a great deal about your skill in a battle you have never fought,' the heralds called out loudly, making the sleeping men jump, their slack faces turn purple with rage. 'To your feet, lads, and quickly,' they shouted. 'These old men do not lack wisdom. They will have you shame them when you come to land.'

Nowhere is it different.

Cups and stools were thrown at the backs of the heralds, who, expecting little else, had, by a whisker, gotten themselves safely beyond the thick doors. The sealmen grumbled. But they reached for their boots. And in the end they went – for so the heralds had always summoned them – even eagerly, stretching their legs in the cold, striding off in the darkness. Over his shoulder a man with a piercing and lively eye grinned at his comrades. He had a sharp, ugly face but the harsh timbre of his voice had turned to wonder. 'It is all right, then,' he laughed. 'We are not rousted for nothing.'

Not that any, now within the walls, had seen him. But on the sea road they had passed him. The memory still haunted them. They stared at one another and in their death-filled faces each saw the same grave longing and delight. He was the Promised One.

In him the flame of life still burned, charmed and undiminished. Himself he knew no death, had never known it. His sea-black eyes, they had seen, had pride in them but no deeper shadow. Like no other king he had come to this place gladly, down to these brooding halls, unshaped as any child, without a wound.

He was a flame.

They looked at one another and in their eyes that neither fell nor grew strained they saw the chance the fire might catch with nearness. They were not men; they were eyes that tore holes in the darkness, waiting. So on the shrouded hill at Hwawl and Abereth the living men waited.

Huddled near the piles of wood, no longer watching the great sparks fly against the winter's dark, they waited for dawn. On the beaches of Tywy, the cliffs behind them red with burning, the women looked at the sea.

The passage was narrow, the movement back and forth considerable. Glas Awyddn pressed himself along, then in through the doors. Many more were lumbering in in back of him. He allowed himself to be pushed onto one of the benches. He could hear the voice of Eachanhagen booming loudly out in the passage, reprimanding a groom. When he came in himself, climbing over the backs and shoulders of his men, a gust of laughter greeted him. Sullenly, awkward in front of their grinning, he ordered a man elsewhere and sat down at last, as inconspicuously as his size and his anger would let him, beside Glas Awyddn.

'You must hurry yourself hereafter,' a man in front shouted back at him.

There was another gust of laughter.

Eachanhagen scowled but did not answer. His mouth tightened.

'It is ill done,' he said to Glas Awyddn quietly. 'He may have my share of this, if he wants it.' His head bent forward. He sucked one of his blunt fingers.

'What is it?' Glas Awyddn asked.

'I do not know.'

The wind brushed on the window glass. The sealmen waited. Gradually, as darkness was replaced with morning, they saw in disbelief it was snowing. They looked beyond the tall windows. Snow came swirling out of the sky like frosted breath. Deep as twilight it was filling the harbor. Against the storm the ships' naked rigging seemed draped with sails.

Glas Awyddn turned his back from the windows. He rubbed his cold arms.

'I have not seen Wyck,' he said. He stopped abruptly. He felt a stiff wind moving over him.

As though on its own a wide panel swung out from the casement. But it was a man, without question, his shoulders bent beneath his cloak, who pushed it shut. He was old and hobbled. Wet flakes clung to his brows. He did not brush them out, did not notice them. He shook his damp cloak when he was only half out of it. When he had gotten himself free of it, he hung it from a carved peg on the wall.

'I had thought,' he began. He paused, nodding to Eachanhagen and to one or two of the others formally, to Gwyn and to Annwn, who nodded back. 'I had thought,' he went on quietly, 'you must have come.'

Without his cloak his thinness showed painfully. He looked out sadly over the rows of men. His bloodless lips narrowed. 'This year there are more of you,' he said softly, in a voice that could scarcely be heard and yet needed to be no louder.

Because he had no hope of keeping silent, Eachanhagen turned his broad shoulders. 'Old one,' he murmured, 'there were three that I found.'

The sightless eyes did not appear to look.

In the hall there was a crowd of men and not one from whom the thing was hidden. But the men were quiet.

Eachanhagen frowned. His great voice, filling the hall as the old one's had not, barely trembled. 'He has come,' he said.

The sealmen grinned. Already a few more standing.

'So they have always come,' the old one whispered.

'No.'

The old one turned to watch the snow make heavy curtains on the glass. His hand drifted upward, touching for a moment the lines of his mouth. 'There is a boy,' he said, 'and in the deepest hall an eight-legged stallion.' His face held a look of more than human weariness. 'Even in the towers such things are heard.' His deep old eyes looked back at Eachanhagen.

'I will tell you this,' he said. 'Before first light I went myself. Though in a thousand years I had not left these halls, I went out walking. In the darkness I stood on the quay.' He stared, as though in wonder at himself. A strange, astonished anger moved his breath. 'You have not been alone in waiting. Long we sought the river's mouth, the memory of the lost way back. Before the cold moon flew into the dark or the day star burned, we yearned to walk the stronger, clearer world again.'

They saw the awful stillness in his face. He was looking past them as though their staring were as blank as all the years, as empty as the glass through which they saw the harbor fill with snow instead of light.

'Before there were dreams,' he said, 'or men to dream them, when there were yet no women growing pale with pain, no hot small arms reaching out in joy or grief for sons, alone, prowling the icy coast, we waited.'

Eachanhagen faced him squarely. One of his hands was hidden in the thick of his mantle. His hot rage burned. 'That waiting's done,' he said.

'It is too soon.'

'Lord, I rode with him.'

The old one's breath hissed irritably between his teeth. 'In the spring,' he said, 'when the wind blows east across the waves.' He stopped to moisten his lips. He paused as though, in thinking only, he could taste the foam, could feel at his back the east wind filling the sails. 'Ships without number he will send against the land.' He raised his head. 'Bright ships, white as gulls, and as many as the birds in April.' He stared, his chilled voice lowering until it seemed no voice at all, only a sound the wind made. 'I went to look myself,' he said. 'Those ships lay frozen in the ice.'

Eachanhagen leaned forward. The years and the longing had not lessened his strength.

'Here in this hall!' Eachanhagen shouted.

'No. You have not listened.' The old one stood quietly. 'Once at Tywy,' he said, 'there was a man, gray-haired and grieving the death of a boy.' His flesh was blistered and yellow. But though he saw poorly, he saw the huge man running, the bold legs leaping onto the dais. He was not surprised. With deep certainty, by heart, he knew the blade's sharpness.

When he had drawn it out, Eachanhagen lifted the stainless sword in the air in front of him. The taut muscles of his face broke into wonder. 'I have done this,' he whispered. 'Once –'

'No,' the old one said gently. 'In the years that must come there is another – at Ormkill, before the king's chair. As well, it will be a boy they are fearing then.' He smiled. 'A boy on a stallion coming out of the sea.'

In the hall there is silence. The old one does not falter. For a thousand years, alive in his memory, he has carried the wound.

He climbed into the tower alone. Through the little glassless windows he saw the roofs of the holding gleaming silver with starlight, saw the hushed yards standing dark and empty below him. The storm had blown off to the east. But the air was bitter. He drew the borrowed cloak about his thin shoulders.

'I cannot go,' he had told them.

'Then whom shall we send?' they had asked helplessly. 'Each of us has sworn already. Whole companies have trooped before them, swearing – all who saw him, on the sea road and the plain. Still they only whisper on about the spring.'

The boy had straightened, his dark eyes distant as he met their own. 'I would have sworn myself,' he had told them softly. 'With all I was, I would have sworn to him, not to some old men that I had seen him, that he was here with us, but to himself, to give my service.' They had heard the stallion, disturbed by their pleading, moving in the hall beyond. They had wished themselves elsewhere. The boy's voice had caught. He had raised his prideful eyes to look at them. 'Yet,' he had said, 'he would not have me.'

They had sought him last, when there had been no man left who had not sworn, when all, though they had been grave and honest, had been met with mockery. They had not come gladly. They had no love for these deep halls. Better the upper yards and the winter winds that howled along the lake than the brooding depths, far under the walls, where the stallion laired, hidden in its gloom though himself he was a thing of light.

'Child,' they had murmured, 'there is no deceit in us. We have seen him though we are not believed.'

'I know what you have seen,' he had answered them. 'It is well for you I will not go and swear to it.'

But he had gone.

The worn steps climbed beyond his sight. On the stallion's back, he thought, already I would have sailed beyond the sea. He imagined the sprawling city growing small beneath. Like a fistful of crags, he thought, the harsh tides rushing over it until it seemed one speck lost in the waves, until even the earth itself seemed but one more darkness in between the stars.

He had begun to think.

He had not seen himself the sealmen climbing the tower to the old one's court. But he knew they went, knew they swore great oaths that they had seen him, though in the rooms and halls they searched he was not found. Word spread among the grooms, went as quickly as to any other to the groom master's ear. So Wyck had heard it though he had not left the stallion's hall. He sat and waited.

The old man dragged a score of fingers through his hair. 'They had dreamed of the day that he would come,' he said. 'But in their dreams he led them from the hall.'

The boy smiled grimly. 'Then it was only dreams.'

'No.'

'And lies.'

'No.'

'But he is Duinn.'

'He is a man – though he was the first who died, the first who ever found darkness. Though he opened the sea road that the dead might follow him – still he is a man.'

The boy only half listened. Glas Awyddn's words came back to him. 'Then we have all the more to fear,' he said, repeating them, not yet guessing what they meant. He felt the breath of the stallion, felt the warmth of the muzzle searching his back. *Horse, Great Horse*, he thought, *I will come for you*.

He left the hall.

After a while it seemed the endless stairs might reach themselves to the winds above the sea. But there was a door at the end of them. Wyck reached out his hand for the latchring and pulled it back. A stench blew in his face.

He remembered the smell of the corpses. But there had been a fire in the old woman's hut, a flame that had flared in the darkness, a warmth that had held him. Here there was only cold. His nostrils wrinkled.

Night curled around him, night's blackness, windy and porous and filled with empty space. Beyond the doomed roof there was nothing but darkness. He pulled the cloak about his thin shoulders.

'You are the last,' the voices out of the air said quietly. 'Come then and swear.'

Wyck craned his neck until he saw where the nine were sitting in the dark and silence, their faces motionless as faces stitched in tapestries. Each face was turned aside, showing a single edge, as though the mischance and confusion of all their years had been compressed and sharpened. Like figures in a tale, he thought, men of whom it was remembered only that they burned or drowned and nothing else. A smile he had never smiled came to his lips. 'Come,' they said again.

Wyck shook his head. 'You have not believed them.'

The nine looked across at him. They did not raise an eyelid.

'They are men,' Wyck said, 'who dwelt with you and listened, men who only gave you back what you had promised them.'

Nothing moved but his own quick breath. He felt their stillness and knew it gave him power over them. He grinned more broadly. Because there was strength in his neck, he lifted it.

'What do you want?' he said boldly.

'To hear you swear.'

He drew another breath and loosed it. He watched its warmth, white for a moment, turn into darkness. Yet he could breathe again.

'You would not believe,' he said.

'Does that matter?'

That once he did not answer. The silence became deeper. The corpse smell ate at his thoughts, and yet he knew the darkness and emptiness were outside of him. Shut within his flesh, where they could not reach it, there was a warmth, a flame that spread and mingled with his blood, a flame that came of itself, with no accounting. He turned, his startled eyes seeking beyond them.

'You are here,' he said.

His voice drifted, unanswered, into the night.

'May I see you?'

'No.'

'Yet you are one of them.'

Unmoved, I watched him.

'I was before they were,' I said.

He looked away. 'Lord, they are only shadows.'

'Less perhaps. Yet why should you be surprised at that?'

'You let me think that they were real.'

'You might have guessed. I barely gave them shapes or names, but set them in an outlandish court, beyond the world's edge, where the sea was dry.'

I saw he wept.

'Child, it was never different. From the first the tale was mine. What voice had I to have them speak with but my own?'

He shook his head. Though he had no answer, I could feel the flames that licked at him.

'I would have sworn to you,' he whispered.

'That was before you knew.'

'Glas Awyddn swore.'

'Child, I have many names. His was always one of them. From the beginning we were bound. Once he had loved her. Once, when he had no thought of loving, had turned his heart from it, in the emptiness of the morning he looked out at the sea.'

His fingers tightened on the edges of the cloak. So Yllvere had held the fabric of her gown, knotting it, when at Ormkill before the barons she had withheld my name. Even in the darkness the cloak was shining. He let it drop. 'Lord,' he said softly, 'I would have loved.'

I was silent. Though I had held the worlds between my jaws and crushed them, even from my mouth no words would come.

* * *

The black waves break on the headlands at Tywy. The cold rain blows in gusts through the hall; the standing walls echo. Across the backs of the corpses the nine have come walking, treading on what lies stiffening as men will cross a river on stones. They are weighed down with grief. The earth, for its thinness, will not hold them.

From my place in the rock I look down at them. There are no longer doors or a roof to keep them out.

'We bear our own witness,' they murmur. 'We are more than shadows.'

'You are what you have always been,' I say, 'as I am.'

They are not content. The wind wanders through them, lifting their hair.

'Brother,' they whisper, 'you might have welcomed him. Until you stiffened your neck, there never was a companion truer than Death, nor a lord more willing to take men to his service. Yet you met him with silence.'

But my jaw is set. 'How,' I ask them, 'through all the long years have you failed to know my heart?'

The rain shocks the earth, the icy rain filling up silence. The wind blows from sea, across from the island where over and over I have murdered and am slain. I climb down from the rock.

But when I have come at last to Ormkill, to the brow of the hill overlooking the river, the nine are ahead of me, waiting. Already in the darkness the women are burning the dead. So the nine must stand in the air, finding their shapes in the smoke and the cinders that leap from the fires. I hear them grumble.

'Lord,' they say in one voice, 'let us not go from one place to another, unknowing. Now, if it is your will, we will listen.'

His own poor shadow, shaped by the starlight, fled ragged before him, ran down the worn steps, turning the circuits of the stairs just ahead of him, turning over and over until he knew – though his shame gave him strength – he would not overtake it. A sob rose from his throat. His swimming eyes blurred on the rock.

It had seemed so little.

Indeed it could not have been much, not to him to whom all must be given. Still the boy wept.

Caught by its brooch, the cloak flapped desperately over his shoulders. Though his flesh burned, he pulled the gilded cloth more securely about him. This only he gave me, he thought, gave me freely, with no other reason than the rain fell and I shivered. He remembered the rain splashing down on the deck of the ship. He remembered the shape of the man, gleaming and white, like a vast snow mountain set adrift in the sea. But the heart of the man, like the heart of a mountain, was silent. The boy turned his head.

When he made the last circuit, he came out into the yard opened up in the darkness. Men who had crowded onto platforms and walls moved their stiff faces. Their eyes were impatient with waiting. Their lips trembled.

Last they had sent him. Little he had seemed to them, not enough to do their bidding, a child while they were men. But they had sent him, despite their bafflement, though even as they had sworn the nine had mocked them. He was their one hope and their last.

But his eyes strained over their backs, looking past them to the post of a gate where the stairs sank away again under the walls. He lifted his neck. Despite the cold, his face was bathed with sweat.

Only Glas Awyddn moved. Meaning comfort, he put out his hand.

The boy shifted.

He had begun to think again and yet it was no different from the thought that had come to him over and over since the day he first walked from the old woman's hut and saw a stallion, without blemish, trotting out of the morning.

Horse, Great Horse, he thought.

He left them and went to the stairs.

The stallion was waiting.

Ahead of him the rock seemed to open. The harsh old walls parted. The brilliant hooves flew over them, spurning their hardness and bitterness, the cold beyond hope. Under his legs the great stallion climbed as the sun climbs, setting his hooves above the small, rotted towers. The dark rim of the sea was below him.

He was free. Yet he had found no comfort. He was free and therefore knew he was unwanted. Beyond the little darkened world, high over it where the darkness holds no human shape, in the silence that wears neither likeness nor majesty, the breath of flame filled him and he burned.

Thus ends the second book of the Finnbranch, which is called *Undersea*. The last is called *Winterking*.

Winterking

PART I

The River

CHAPTER ONE

The photographs of that time, printed from glass plate negatives, reveal a landscape at once more barren and roomy, a world puzzlingly larger (not merely less cluttered) than the word bequeathed to us. The pastures to either side of the House-tenuc, the sixty river miles between Devon and New Awanux, had then only lately begun to close again with trees. But the trees are small, all second growth; the men do not as yet seem uncomfortable beside them. Their expressions reflect no amazement at the huge bald earth nor any knowledge of their little place in it. Their reputation for being perceptive, while not entirely undeserved, did not truly encompass the land. To them it was Eden though the fires of workshops and mills made a twilight by midday over the rutted hills. The lie which their fathers had carried across the Atlantic persisted with the sons. But the land had never been Eden, not even when a wilderness of gloomy wood had covered the valley. The last naked men living along the upper reaches where the river was narrow and stands of sycamore still crowded out the sun knew all the while it was Hobbamocko, not Jehovah, who ruled there. The English, however, who had covered their genitals for longer than they had been a nation or gone over the sea, never asked them.

So it happened that Jehovah's white clapboard houses, like a species of mechanical mushroom, sprang up inexhaustibly. There were four on the Stratford flats. In New Awanux itself there were twenty. Old Okanuck, son of Ansantawae, the wind of memory blowing across his mind, sat laughing merrily in the corner of the longhouse and struck his hams. Alone, he had burned seven of Jehovah's houses, had walked up to them boldly across the green commons, bearing a torch in each hand. The ghosts of those burnings still flamed in his eyes. The warriors saw it and were cheered.

'The land did not want them,' old Okanuck said. 'If it had, those houses would have grown back, like the madarch, drawing their substance from the bones of the buried wood. So our longhouses grew then, year after year in the same place, nested in the damp, in the oak-shade, taking their strength from the ground.'

A smile sank in his toothless mouth. Like the earth he had darkness inside of him. And foxcubs and black birds, he maintained, shaking with laughter. And a thousand oak trees, wind-storms and the seeds of spiders. 'Only see that I am planted deep,' he howled gleefully, 'and I will grow a world again. A better world.' Old Okanuck winked. 'No Awanux.'

They gave him his pipe.

When the silence had lasted for many heartbeats, a boy with thunderous brows reached across to touch the old one's shoulder. The faces of the men turned on him disapprovingly. But Okanuck, setting the pipe aside, gave him an encouraging nod.

'The Awanux are many,' the boy said angrily.

Okanuck did not take the boy any less seriously but grinned. 'We are more,' he said kindly. With a sweep of his outsized hands he motioned the boy to sit nearer and to share the pipe. Okanuck watched as the boy parted his lips and sucked in great quantities of maggoty smoke. But, though the smoke filled the boy's chest, inside there was emptiness. The smoke was drawn in and lost.

'Once,' the boy said, uncomforted. 'Perhaps it was different then. But now it is they who increase.'

Okanuck leaned forward. 'They are only a frost,' he said slyly, 'a frost on Cupheag, on Metichanwon, a chilly smear on Ohomowauke. . . .' His brows were lifted. Despite his age his hair was black as oak-shade. 'Who, knowing the frost,' he asked, 'fears it?'

Outside the longhouse the valley was sealed by cloud. Okanuck felt no resentment. He laughed.

'The earth is under it,' Okanuck said. 'Deep down. Undying.' Gingerly, with the clawed edge of his toes, he dug for lice, scratching in the mat of dense feathers on the underside of his black and cobalt wings.

'Crows?'

'Surely not,' was the immediate answer. 'Dark, nameless birds. The type doesn't matter. But water birds of some sort, I should think – though, of course, the shapes are drawn from the earth, not the river.' He smiled. '. . . Pulled aloft from the fields and then transformed, one pattern to the next, until they soar.' Turning in his desk chair, the speaker pointed. 'The white birds, on the other hand, emerge directly from the sky.'

He paused, appearing to search for a phrase which, in fact, he knew quite precisely. 'As though,' he began again, 'some quality in the white horizon . . . in the whiteness itself . . . exactly matches the whiteness of the birds.' He let that sink in. 'See, near the top – to the left of the center line – how the birds begin all at once, sky and birds in one tessellation – simultaneously. You do see it?'

The younger man nodded but continued to examine the woodcut of white and black birds silently.

Pleased with his explanation, the speaker went on smiling. He was perhaps a decade older than the younger man, just a shade past thirty and already balding. The woodcut hung on the south wall of the study. It had taken him the better part of six months to save for the print. Now as his gaze traveled appreciatively over the repeated images of birds, his sense of uneasiness in the younger man grew a bit sharper. Yet for another moment he chose to ignore it. He tipped a little farther back in his chair.

His name was George Harwood. He was an assistant professor of Awanux. He had a blonde wife and a five-year-old daughter, neither of whom he could quite afford. He lived with both in three cramped rooms in the basement of West Bridge Hall, where individual scholars before him had lived since the time of its founding. His duties, for which he was paid only slightly more than the wage of an instructor, included tutoring a dozen or so of the more promising young men. And this young man, with his long, odd, unboyish face, was accounted to be the most promising.

Indeed, Harwood had long since been aware of a twinge of jealousy whenever he considered Will Wykeham. Harwood himself had once been thought of as something of a prodigy, a man to be watched. This was not boasting. When he was barely nineteen he had produced a thousand-page study of the myths of the Flying Dutchman, a study of such scope and interest that, he had been assured, with a very little tightening it might well have found a berth at the college press. But there had been interruptions. He had been burdened with other matters and the work had dragged on without completion.

Wykeham, of course, had yet to accomplish anything of equal breadth of learning, a paper on Chaucer, a few brief articles on Milton, jewel-like, it was said, nearly perfect but on a small scale. The younger man had a talent for appearing to inhabit the author's world, an instinct for the nuances of language now fallen out of use, an instinct which permitted him to suggest a number of rather clever interpretations, wonderfully clear once he mentioned them but previously escaping the attention of more seasoned scholars. The senior faculty noticed him. On one occasion hearing Wykeham deliver a paper on *Paradise Lost* the Dean himself had whispered discreetly to Harwood, 'One might well suppose the boy had lived in the Garden and had spoken personally with the Snake.' Harwood's mouth had twitched up at the corners. The Dean, who was a kindly man and inclined to like undergraduates indiscriminately, promptly forgot the remark. It was envy that caused Harwood to remember it nearly half a year until at Greenchurch, on the edge of panic, the words came back to him.

Beyond the window the river was blurred with cloud.

Having turned away from the woodcut, Harwood found the younger man looking at him intently. For an instant Harwood had the curious feeling he was staring directly into the blank March weather. The eyes, while not large, conveyed an almost overwhelming bleakness, as though through their slight openings Harwood glimpsed the cold mist and the hills beyond them, fading north in the rain. But it was the long square face that had most shaken him. The strong features, gathered close to the center, left an expanse of unexpected whiteness. It was a face with room in it. Whatever trouble had momentarily set its mark there, the face itself, with a surprising sense of quiet, remained essentially free of concern. Harwood found himself suddenly ill at ease.

'You said they reminded you of crows,' he said unevenly.

'I'm sorry. Not really.' Wykeham's voice came from miles off. 'I was just thinking of crows.' For a time the younger man looked past him, staring through the window at a clump of elms set off at the edge of the broad college lawn. 'I saw one this morning. A great scruffy-looking fellow. Too big for a shore crow. It was waiting for me by the post office gate when I went for the mail.'

'Waiting?'

Wykeham's frown vanished. 'I think so,' he said. His eyes turned abruptly toward Harwood. 'You might say a prophet of doom.' Wykeham reached across his chest and into the inner pocket of his jacket and drew forth an envelope. He dropped it on the desk in front of Harwood.

'You may read it,' Wykeham said. 'But the short of it is, I shall be leaving New Awanux by Saturday.'

With one pink hand Harwood reached halfway to the letter. Both men shared a love of light holiday literature. Harwood lifted an eyebrow. 'Oughtn't you have said,' he bantered, ' "I must be gone before morning"?'

Wykeham managed to smile and sigh all at once. 'Really, George, this is serious. You might at least have a look.'

The envelope was addressed: William Wykeham, Esq., College Station, New Awanux-on-Housetenuc. The address, set down in yellowish-brown ink, was large and florid, with much embellishment and too many capitals. Harwood glanced at it dubiously before pulling out four sheets of white paper. He laid the letter on the desk in front of him and began to read.

'My Dear Mr. Wykeham, Undoubtedly the lawyers have informed you of the untimely demise of Michael Morag. Clearly your guardian was a just man and died peacefully (as his service deserved), leaving your affairs in good order and myself, as I believe those same lawyers must dutifully have written you, to manage and discharge them in his place. I regret I had not the pleasure of meeting him. Indeed he must have been a most pleasant man as is well evidenced by the comforts of the parsonage wherein for so many years he resided, where I (by terms and covenants of the Will and by my appointment lately to this parish) consider myself now fortunate to have established my own household.

'I am told that yourself you never met the Reverend Mr. Morag, although it cannot be more, at least not greatly more (if it is not too discourteous to remind you), than sixty miles from New Awanux to your properties here in Devon. AND THE TRAINS RUN WITH SOME FREQUENCY! But then, of course, you have been traveling and had only come to these shores, as it were, and at that for the first time, when you matriculated and have since been much involved with your studies.

'So, as it happened, we both missed knowing the good Morag. More's the pity. Such a thoughtful man! Did you know that even on his deathbed, seeing his end and seeing as well, I might say, that another would soon come after him, he had four hundred bottles of the finest porter laid freshly aside in the pantry. . . .'

Harwood began to fidget in his chair.

'Yes, I know,' said Wykeham, shaking his head. 'It would appear he is something of an ass.'

Harwood looked incredulous. 'He says he's now your guardian.'

Wykeham nodded. 'Yes of course,' he put in quickly, making as little as possible of the other's surprise. 'My father and mother died when I was quite young. A shipping accident I am told, although it hasn't prevented the lawyers from. . . . Not that I minded.' He paused. 'You might skip the second page. It's the third that matters.'

Harwood shuffled the papers. His forehead wrinkled. Damned if he could think of Wykeham at the mercy of lawyers and guardians. Frankly, now that he put his mind to it, he could not think of anyone less likely to be intimidated by men of any stripe. But guardians. That was new. He hadn't suspected Wykeham was an orphan. Without really thinking what he was saying, he blurted out: 'This Morag fellow left some property, is it?'

'No.'

'It says – let me find it – a will. . . .'

Harwood became aware of Wykeham's eyes again.

'Morag was the executor,' Wykeham said quietly. 'It's my grandfather's will. The property has been in my family for years. The executor, who is always a minister of some sort, gets the use of the parsonage. Now that Morag is dead there is a new man.'

'Y-yes. Quite,' said Harwood, annoyed at getting it wrong and almost stammering. It's those damn eyes, he thought. He was still holding the letter. 'But what is this business about leaving school?'

'It begins on the third page,' said Wykeham.

Harwood glanced hurriedly at the second sheet but realizing Wykeham was watching, he put it aside for the next.

The first paragraph consisted mainly of accounts: so much for tailors, for booksellers, for a wine-merchant. Harwood added them mentally and was shocked by the sum. The man's robbing him, Harwood thought, but then he noticed that the bills were in every case Wykeham's. Paid, all paid, Harwood thought gloomily. He moved in his chair and settled down again to read. There was mention of builders and gardeners and a particularly old man, a gamekeeper, who for no reason was being especially difficult and then:

'So I would be obliged, Mr. Wykeham, if you might spare a day to come and talk with him.'

Harwood went back to read it once more.

'. . . "South Wood" is cleared. Morag, to do him credit, saw to that last autumn before his decline. He was wonderfully thorough and found twenty new men for the work, each under fifty. Nonetheless, you may be certain, I rechecked the Register myself. Not a man born before '96 and most thirtyish or younger. I mean them to start fencing "Black Wood" as soon as the ground warms. So there is progress! All the same there is rather a hitch up at "Black Wood," in the Keeper's Cottage, to put it exactly.

'John Chance he calls himself. The man's nearly eighty and hunched over like a tree in a gale. Still he fairly howled when we tried to evict him. He says we "daren't" move him, says he has a paper that gives him rights there, though of course he wouldn't show it. But the police won't touch him. They were boys on the place when Chance was younger. He taught them to snare rabbits or some such!!? In any event, they're no help nor want to be. So Chance stays where he is. And I am powerless.

'It's you he wants. He told me himself, twice. "Send me the Heir," he shouted (shouted, mind you). "He'll speak with me." Naturally, I said it was quite out of the question. But I really don't know what else to do – what with the ground almost ready. And the delay will cost! So I would be obliged . . .'

Harwood skimmed the rest, down to the name, Timothy Longford, and a postscript, scribbled precariously close to the bottom, inquiring whether Wykeham would be kind enough to secure two volumes, already purchased by Longford and only waiting delivery, at a bookseller on Abbey Street.

Harwood turned the last page over.

'Is that it?' he asked rather defensively, afraid he had missed something else. 'You're leaving school in order to fire a game-keeper?'

Wykeham seemed to concentrate very hard. 'In a way I suppose I am,' he said carefully. 'Except, of course, I very much doubt I shall end up firing him.' He stood. 'I just wanted to say good-bye.' Wykeham held out his hand.

'You are serious.'

As he squeezed Harwood's fingers Wykeham smiled.

'It would seem that I must be.'

CHAPTER TWO

Harwood met with two more students after lunch but was not, he realized, very helpful. When the latter had gone, he spent another half an hour looking through his notes for a Saturday morning class on Blake, trying to decipher, without quite remembering how it went, the line of an argument he had made at least a dozen times. At last, seeing no improvement in his wits, he closed the book resentfully, rose and, taking his coat from his chair, hurried out onto the common without thinking to fasten the door. The afternoon was still bitter with the hard breath of sleet in the wind. The cold went straight through him and he pulled the coat tighter.

The coat was nearly twelve years old and had a frayed collar; little strips of torn lining trailed beneath the hem. He could well imagine how he looked in it. For the price of the woodcut he might have purchased a better than adequate replacement. But the chill wouldn't last, he was certain, for it was nearly April and with the good weather he could get by in his shirtsleeves. Damn, he thought, remembering the door.

In the middle of the common he turned. There were puddles all around him; his shoes squelched as he zigzagged over the huge brown lawn until he was brought up short under the clump of elms. In the shade of vanished summers troops of young men had worn away the grass, leaving a patch of bare earth. In the drizzle the patch had become a shallow pond. Harwood looked about dismally. He was just turning his neck when something stirred in the branches: a black smear. But when he faced it squarely, he saw it was a crow. Its raffish head crooked sideways, absurdly, like a thief caught in the act.

It's the money, Harwood thought with a start. He remembered the extraordinary sums he had seen in the letter and knew, in a moment of utterly useless honesty, he would have chucked school himself, would have chucked it, in fact, a damn sight faster than Wykeham.

His Grace the Duke of West Redding pulled out his watch and, scanning the face, made a mental note to remind Maintenance to adjust the wall clock by a minute. He was sharply aware of the quiet. As he waited he listened. He heard the faint patter of rain on the windows, the distant clank of his private elevator as it climbed the two hundred eleven feet from the public corridor in the bank's main lobby. The ledger which had been in his personal care for thirty-eight of his sixty years lay closed on the desk in front of him. Precious little leisure he had had in those years; although, truthfully, he had not sought it. He had been eager and clever, capable of prodigious work and infinite care. The young men of his own generation, who by station and training might have seemed more worthy of the chance, had professed to be horrified by his diligence, his eighteen-hour days, his independent and consuming studies of asset depreciation, exclusions and trusts. To be perfectly honest, if by some miracle he could have been given a second crack at it, he doubted he could have managed it again himself. A miracle indeed! The Duke touched the closed ledger with his manicured fingers. He did not choose to open it for one last look.

This morning, as he dressed, he had found himself whistling. He had stood at the window of his town house overlooking the Park. Gazing across at the shadowy towers of the College, he had seen a quizzical smile reflected back at him in the glass. Certainly he had no immediate plans, but it was agreeable and stimulating to think of what he still might do. On his doorstep he had waved aside his driver and, unmindful of the rain, had instead set off walking. He had taken a roundabout route, following the High Street down to the river and only then turning, nearly reversing his tracks, before heading north again along Chapel Street. Even so, the public doors had not yet been opened when he marched into the office of the senior clerk.

'Send me Houseman,' the Duke had said.

Caught between duty and surprise, the senior clerk had sputtered.

'He's quite bright, I believe,' the Duke had said reassuringly.

The clerk had small black eyes and a dry mouth like a lizard's. He had shaken his head slightly. 'Your Grace,' he had said unhappily, 'he's no more than a boy.'

'He's twenty-two,' the Duke had said, half to himself, '. . . as I was.'

From behind his desk the Duke rose, large and unbent despite his age, and came out into the center of the room just as the young man slid the brass cage to his left and stepped from the elevator. Houseman himself was tall, only casually erect, with thick, long arms and huge square hands which at first glance seemed ill suited for quiet tasks with ink and paper. Now although he had been watching for months, the Duke found himself studying the young man with renewed curiosity.

He saw clearly what had made the senior clerk nervous. Although they met you straight on, Houseman's alert dark eyes, having made their judgment, were inclined to look about on their own. For a moment the young man's face had turned, gazing down over the city through the rain. The dull sound of thunder rolled on the air. It was not a face, the Duke decided, made content by waiting.

'Thank you for coming,' the Duke greeted him.

Houseman nodded.

'You would do me an added favor,' the Duke said, 'if you would sit in my chair.' His voice was quiet, his own face still.

Houseman's gaze lingered there a moment, then unhesitatingly he walked behind the desk. But he stood, his back to the room, as though transfixed. On the window, one drop edged toward another. When the wind joined them, they fell.

'They were all betting you would pick Roger Henshaw,' the younger man said.

'He's not gone without notice. Remember that. You will have need of him.'

'I know,' Houseman answered, without irony. 'I would have picked him if it had been my choice.'

The Duke smiled.

'Then you will remember.' The Duke pulled a second chair up to the desk so that at last Houseman sat in the first, the great chair, his hands to either side of the ledger.

Houseman felt at once that the chair suited him as it would not a smaller man.

'What is expected?' he asked.

'In a very few minutes,' the Duke said, 'a young man will come here. A summary record of the affairs of his family is before you. He does not manage them and will not, even in part, for several years more. For the moment you will deal almost exclusively with a man named Longford. There are letters concerning him in the vault. From what I have seen he is a fool, as the two others I have known in his position have been. That does not matter. For thirty-eight years it was one of my responsibilities to make certain that the trustees and guardians were of no significance. Now it is yours. It is entirely legal. Longford holds but a limited copy of the will. He cannot begin to imagine its true scope or complexity. The full will is here. Its authority, duly granted and affirmed, rests – as long as you have the confidence of the heir – with you. In time the young man will doubtlessly wish to share some little part of it himself but only by way of amusement. You will find he really has no interest in day-to-day business. It's the long view you must take with him. If you do, he will be generous.'

The Duke flicked his watch open.

'He will want to speak with you at some length,' he said, 'to see what you are like. You must be entirely candid. He will make a point of that and yet I shouldn't worry. It will not be a test. If he hadn't faith in my judgment, I should not have been here to greet you.'

'Shall I see him often?' Houseman asked.

There was such a long silence that Houseman, who under other circumstances would have been immune, became embarrassed.

'Only once,' the Duke said finally. He took a deep breath. 'That is the reason for this talk. Generally you will confer by letter.'

One side of the older man's face twitched ever so slightly. It would have been kinder, Houseman knew, to ignore it. But at the very last moment, when he might have let pity rule him, it struck him that there was something important here and he would not let it pass.

'Yet, Your Grace, you know him. And rather well, by your description.'

The Duke did not look up. 'I knew the grandfather. Met him here in this room.' His head straightened. 'Just once.'

Both men heard the clank of the elevator.

The Duke was already standing. By the time the brass cage slid back he had slipped from the room. Nevertheless the door to the outer office remained slightly ajar. There was another long silence.

When the dark young man stepped onto the carpet, Houseman found himself listening to the rain rather than staring. For a moment the room seemed dwarfed by the sound of rain. The young man came no closer and Houseman realized that he too was listening. Then the wind changed, taking the rain away from the glass. The young man went on listening. Small creases turned up at the corner of his mouth.

'You have my thanks, Your Grace,' Wykeham said fondly.

With a deep satisfied click the door pulled shut.

A bell on a hook jingled when he entered the shop. The wind had reversed his umbrella, cracking two of its ribs. Wykeham abandoned it by the door. A pool of water collected under his feet. Trying to get his coat unbuttoned with numb fingers, at first he did not notice the woman sitting by the warming stove and peering up at him angrily. He dug about in his inside pocket for a handkerchief.

'Is it books you're wanting?' the woman said impatiently.

Her voice was foreign. The sound of distant streets rang at the back of it, the old faded music of crowded twilight streets where as a girl she had walked boldly under the eyes of sailors. She had not known then that those same streets stretched over the sea nor had she known the dream of the man with his black whiskers, a parcel of books in his duffel, when he smiled from the doorway.

'Bodø?' Wykeham asked. The woman's face, which once may have been as haughty and brave as the pictures of heroines in her husband's books, was no longer pretty, but when she laughed with surprise he was nearly certain it had been so.

'Do you know it?'

'I have stopped there,' he said, coming across the floor to stand by her, warming his hands at the stove. Her eyes shone like gold in the dusk of the shop. 'My ship lay over in the harbor,' he said, 'buying herring. Too soon we were gone.'

Wanting to keep him she said, 'It is so far away. You could not have been more than a boy.'

Someone was shuffling along the dark aisle lined with books or rather the shadow of books, brown and sour as leaf-mold, piled high to the ceiling. 'Nora,' a man's voice called out sharply.

A gray head ending with a grizzled beard thrust itelf into view. It belonged to a short, wiry man of about fifty. He had on an old sailor's cap worn to the same indefinite color as his hair. He glanced about suspiciously. Grown apprehensive under his gaze, the woman turned from him.

'I will make tea,' she said. 'You would like that.'

'Yes,' Wykeham said softly. 'That would be kind.'

Wykeham sat in an armchair watching the empty street fill with rain. In silence they drank the tea from delicate china cups whose touch made the shopkeeper moody and uncomfortable. He finished while the tea was still too hot and put the cup down.

'Well and good,' the man said. He made a point of not looking at his wife, 'This is, after all, a business.'

Wykeham put aside his cup.

'Is there much of a market for antique books?' he inquired mildly.

'Ah!' the shopkeeper cried. 'Not just old books. I have everything!'

He pointed down at the floor. 'Underneath,' he said, 'I have two great rooms. And above.' He raised his arm, lifting it dramatically. 'Six floors, groaning under the burden.' He smiled inwardly, his impatience forgotten. 'One must try to have everything.'

'Will you have a cake?' asked the woman.

'Yes, thank you,' said Wykeham.

The shopkeeper did not blink.

'There is not a book so awful,' he said, 'that it will not have its adherents. Or a book, however marvelous, that doesn't for a time fall out of fashion. Sooner or later, then, I have them: old books, yes. But new ones as well, picked up for a song and waiting discovery.'

'You have, I believe,' Wykeham said, 'two volumes on order for the Reverend Mr. Longford.'

The woman stopped. She knew she had no more to offer him.

'You are not . . .,' she said.

'Hardly.' Wykeham smiled. 'I am merely doing a favor.'

'Perhaps there is something.' She looked around desperately. 'Carl, where is that nice picture book on Norway?'

It was not what she meant to say. She had not wanted to involve her husband, but she was frightened and the words fell from her mouth.

Wykeham looked across at her. 'I regret,' he began.

The shopkeeper had risen. He walked to the front of the shop, where he rummaged under the counter. He kept his back to them but she knew he was listening.

When he stood again before them, two small books under his arm, she still had not spoken. Yet she reached out impulsively. Digging between her husband's shirt and the dry leather bindings, she took the books into her own fragile hands. The shopkeeper grunted with surprise.

Ignoring him, she turned back the front cover of the largest volume, finding a bill resting on a lithograph of a huge, naked Indian. The bill was marked in her husband's clear black letters. Timothy Longford, Greenchurch Parsonage, it read, £8, Paid. She was quite certain Wykeham had seen it.

'That will be ten pounds,' she whispered, looking straight up at him in terror.

Wykeham paid without protest. When he had gone, she went upstairs immediately and got into bed, where she lay on her pillow, listening to the storm. But it was the sound of the crowded streets she heard and the knock of the herring boats, rocking in the great distant harbor. Later, when her husband came into the room, his eyes were watchful. Nevertheless, thinking of his wife's cleverness, how with a cup of tea and a half-eaten cake she had earned him more than double the price, he gave her a grin.

A strand of her light brown hair lay wet on her cheek. The years in a different country had made her timid and she would not look at him. It had been another woman altogether, a girl of seventeen who in another place and without encouragement dared talk with strangers. She had not meant to remember her. She had put her away. It was for her awakening, into a world that had no place for her, that something was owed; for that she had demanded payment.

Wykeham sat at his desk past midnight, under the yellow light of the one lamp that had not been packed away. But for a few clothes and a suitcase the room was nearly as bare as on the day he had first seen it. The furniture had gone to storage, the odds and ends put into boxes to be carted off. He loved the feel of the small empty room, blank as the cell of an Irish hermit, loved it more because he so seldom chose to live plainly. Wykeham had always been fascinated and excited by things. As a result the rooms where he had lived had often had the thick and complicated air of thirdhand shops where everything is treasured and nothing is thrown away: bicycle parts had rested in the bath, books in the foyer. Pots, pictures, and embroideries, the enameled tooth of an extinct elephant (preserved in the jaw), a chimney brush without bristles, a shepherd's crook, several fish scalers, a pair of surgical scissors and a Chinese lacquer screen, among many more such notable items, he had only lately picked from the clutter, labeled and set out for the movers.

Deep in the evening, before he had finally sunk back into the desk chair, turning at last to the letters, he had swept the floor. Under the single electric light the plain, tea-colored boards, now dull and grim, had reminded him of the thin brown layers of hardened silt he had sometimes seen in the exposed rock in the hills above Ohonowauke. There were millions of years in the stone but almost none of it barren. In the dry beds of ancient streams he had found the remnants of the changing but never ending abundance of life, bred generation upon generation, out-dated and puzzling but seemingly imperishable. Only now and then there had been a brief gritty band, a patch empty of bone and shell, as though for a season even the gods, wearied of their hosts and retainers and with a momentary sigh of relief, had ordered them gone.

The open window looked out onto the common. The storm had gone and with it the last smoke-like rags of clouds, blowing eastward over the sea. The air that crept under the sash, stirring the sheets of white paper, was no longer bitter.

He finished printing the address on a thick package tied with cord, then set it aside. On a fresh sheet he wrote the name of a girl. He had been careful. There had been nothing promised between them but he felt he owed her an explanation. They had said good-bye rather formally at the entrance of the library where she worked behind the order desk on the main floor. She had stood quietly watching him descend the stairs. When he had turned, she had waved.

'It doesn't make sense,' she had told him.

'I know that.' But he knew that it did.

She spoke Latin and German, had studied Greek, but had never been out of the city. They met in the evenings, after her work, in a room in the King's Hotel. He had talked to her of ships and of all the places they had taken him.

'How have you gone so far?' she had asked.

'I started early.'

But she had never been content with that. 'I will make a covenant between you and me,' she had laughed, baiting him. 'You will tell me everything about all the great, sweet places that ever were and I will show you the mysteries sailors dream of when they are far from land.'

She was nearly thirty, ten years older than she guessed he was. Some mornings there were puffy circles under her brown eyes. Often, as though troubled, she said his name with her lips only. Now she had turned on her side, her slender legs curled up and rubbing his. He had told her of Antioch and Alexandria, the Canaries and the westward bulge of Africa, of camels and the Greenland ice, the Shoulders of Jupiter, the docks at Spithead and Madeira and the channel towers at Dover burning lime. But he had never promised.

He sealed the letter and took another sheet. Across the way a few cold lights glittered. After a long time even these winked out. Two more letters lay carefully folded at his left hand. It was very late but he did not move from the chair. He felt no weariness. Once again the world stood before him. He looked out over the common, its darkness made blacker by the fissured shadow of a grove of elms.

The crow alighted on the window ledge. Its sly head twisted around on its neck.

'Why are you not asleep?' Wykeham asked it.

'Like you,' the crow answered, 'I am waiting for dawn.'

CHAPTER THREE

In those years the mails, delivered throughout the city by postman on foot, moved more rapidly than is now the custom. On Saturdays the first delivery was completed by eight-thirty. In the outer districts, where the houses were spread apart, and on a few of the larger plots, where there were barns though there was no livestock, the second occasionally dragged on toward evening. But along the congested streets of the center city the second post arrived no later than noon. At twelve-thirty Harwood's blonde wife brought the package in from the porch and left it on the kitchen table. When she came in once more from the back for the wash and found the package still there, she called out to her husband.

Harwood emerged from his study where despite the howls of his daughter he had been trying to rearrange his notes on the Dutchman. His skin was white and dull and he was wearing suspenders over yesterday's shirt.

'No one sends me things,' she said in that tone that told him she was making no special claim, only speaking the truth.

A streak of sunlight fell across her faded skirt. Her knuckles were red and her forearms were wet to the elbows.

He sat down at the table and began fumbling with the taut cord fastened with sailors' knots. She stood at his back, looking over his shoulder in silence. Inside the heavy paper there was a coat of new, thick bog-smelling tweed. He made a vague gesture, as though apologizing because his good fortune excluded her.

'You had better go thank him,' she said.

At one o'clock a dozen letters lay unopened on the counter of the empty shop on Abbey Street. Out of idleness Nora took them up. Her husband, mumbling to himself, was unpacking cartons. His voice rumbled loudly but without meaning. Her thoughts took no notice. With skillful indifference she sorted the letters, bills into one pile, orders into the next, a third for the private correspondence that went back and forth between dealers with rumors of acquisitions, estate sales not listed in the papers, quiet inquiries and lies. She spread the unopened letters in front of her like a gypsy woman, alone in a booth, reading the cards out of habit.

During the night she had dreamt she had fallen asleep in a tower. When she awoke, still knowing it was a dream, that she had only dreamt of waking, she had found that an immense hedge of thorns had grown up around her. She had gone to the window and opened it. The cold, raw morning air streamed in. But the din she had expected, the sounds from her father's stables, the clatter of carriages in the yard below her, had gone. In the hallway outside her door she discovered her little maid, her smock, and her flesh as well, turned to a fibrous dust. The tiny gold ring that had been her own gift to the girl was hanging loose on the narrow bone of her finger.

Toward morning Nora had awakened in her bed, next to her husband. The delicate pink color of the sky had told her that the rain was over. Something was within my reach, she thought, but I have not touched it. She placed the last letter down on the counter. In a small, spidery old-fashioned script she read her name. Within the envelope there were several folded pages and a steamer ticket on the *Konge Harald* for Bodø.

The Duke, who had known Wykeham rather better than the others, anticipated the letter and had directed his butler to bring the post in to him as soon as it came. There was a single, deferential knock on the door of the solarium. The man entered briskly, bearing a square silver tray on which the creamy white envelope rested. When he had set it down, the man stepped aside and waited discreetly.

'There will be no answer,' the Duke said. The man prepared to go but the Duke leaned back his head. It was a smooth, dark, aristocratic head, not the sort of a head of a man of business. Nonetheless His Grace had had his start in business and had given his life to it. The title had come late and had seemed to him both unnecessary and humorous. Yet he had never protested. He suspected, though nothing had been said directly, that Wykeham was somehow behind it. Fortunately, the title was not hereditary. He had never married and had no children to be disappointed. Nevertheless, the prospect of its eventual mortality pleased him. While, over these last months particularly, he had felt his days shortening, he had never cast a covetous eye on more of life than God, in whose affective agency in human affairs he maintained a guarded disbelief, had allotted him. Unlike most men, unlike Wykeham himself, he was certain, the Duke wished no more of the world when he died than it bury him.

'Your Grace,' the man said.

'If you will, John,' said the Duke, 'have my driver ready at six.'

When the man departed the Duke unsealed the letter and found exactly the blunt, authoritative expression of gratitude he had expected. He had been single-minded in his devotion to Wykeham. That their relationship consisted almost exclusively of the contents of the letters between them, his own, of which he still preserved copies, all bearing the same postmark, Wykeham's sporting stamps of almost infinite color and variety, stamps of green mangoes and Spanish kings, cathedrals and gardens in Burma, coming to him from every longitude and meridian on the face of the globe, that his devotion was the product not of smiles and handshakes but of written words did not matter to him. Letters, if one took the time, could be made clear and definite and might, with appropriate care, escape the imprecision which so characterized the shifting, haphazard life he saw about him. Of course the relationship would have gained no footing at all had Wykeham not responded in kind. The Duke remembered his pleasant shock of surprise when he had read Wykeham's first letter, now thirteen years ago, when Wykeham ought to have been a boy of seven.

The letter had come by steamer from Egypt. The Duke had expected some childish babble about pyramids or perhaps, because children so rarely notice what adults take for granted, nothing about pyramids and in its place a great deal more than he cared to hear about the ship's monkey. Instead Wykeham had written about women – and not the women of the bazaar, leaning over their boxes of figs and shouting to buyers, but rather the wave of young English women who had come out with their engineer husbands, women in heavy skirts despite the climate who spoke tirelessly of their Queen's setting a formidable example and sent home for dogs.

He writes as if he were a Roman emperor, the Duke remembered he had thought, as though the boredom of the long voyage had sharpened the boy's perceptions and given him a double set of ears and eyes, the second detached and sardonic, gazing with amused interest over the dark plowed earth of the delta, over the sky's illimitable whiteness, watching, listening to the hobnob of women as though he were watching and listening to the strutting and hooting of birds.

What he had not expected was the invitation, dated six months in advance – for October – to a dinner at Wykeham's Devon estate. Puzzled, the Duke laid the letter aside on the table. The butler had long since gone beyond hearing.

'What do you make of that?' His Grace asked no one in particular.

* * *

It was not chance that brought them. Yet it must have seemed like chance to the two young women arriving separately but within a few moments of one another at the information desk in the waiting room at Water Street Station. The Duke lifted his eyes from the timetable to look across at the dark-haired woman asking the track number of the evening train to Devon and at the woman behind her, listening closely to the clerk's answer. The answer given, he watched them turn quickly away, in both faces the same apprehension and seriousness. He recognized at once that in some fashion they were Wykeham's and that each had come alone, unaware of the other. His eyes followed their long legs and slender hips into the crowd. In his imagination younger women were always slender, and he congratulated himself on sharing Wykeham's admiration for the clear bold grace of slender women. He wondered whether Wykeham had managed to sleep with both of them.

The waiting room was dim. The air, pulled in from the platform, was full of the smell of steam. When he looked around again, he had lost them. He stood off to the side, watching quietly, for he knew there was plenty of time. A man pushed hurriedly past him, inquiring anxiously at the desk. He was tall and balding. He had on a new gray overcoat of such elegance that for a moment the Duke was certain he must have met him. Then suddenly he got a glimpse of the man's wet shoes. He has walked here through puddles, the Duke reflected, disappointed. The discovery remained on the Duke's face, mingled with bewilderment, until he overheard the clerk answer: 'Devon? Certainly, sir. Track nine.' His Grace smiled. Wykeham, he thought, still enchanted but wiser.

Harwood turned his eyes doubtfully and began to hunt for the gate.

'I beg your pardon,' the Duke said, moving nearer. 'Nine is out by the river. If you will permit me . . .'

'I'd be obliged,' Harwood said. He fell in beside the older man gratefully.

Neither was carrying luggage.

'I'm not actually catching the train,' Harwood said.

'Like yourself,' said the Duke mildly, 'I have been planning to miss it.'

It was Harwood's dinnertime and except for the coat he would not have come. But the obligation nagged at him. Late in the afternoon he had gone to Wykeham's room in the college, thinking he still might find him. When he had knocked, no one had answered. He had tried the next door and met a sullen-looking boy who barely knew Wykeham and was of no help. He had intended then to return to his rooms but walking across the courtyard, he had encountered a groundsman counting a few crisp bills with his blackened fingers.

'Paid me right well,' the man had answered him breezily. 'Not many like him. Though I'll admit I had a bit of trouble with all them boxes.' He folded the bills twice and thrust them into his pocket. The man grinned. 'Engaged me for three hours and paid me for six, its being Saturday and all and my own time. Though I'd have settled for four. But me and Jake got him off.'

'Where?'

'Down to Water Street.'

'I-I'm sorry I don't –' Harwood stammered.

'To the trains.'

Watching Harwood turn and rush into the street, the groundsman shook his head. But then it had been his experience that education, if it did anything, made it harder for those who had it to find their way around.

An hour before closing Carolyn simply walked away from her desk. The woman who worked with her had to admit she hadn't been of much use anyway. She had arrived late and kept going to the bathroom. When, looking owlish and tired, she managed to stay at the desk she uncrinkled a piece of paper, read it again then crushed it only to repeat the process a few minutes later. The circles under her eyes seemed to darken like bruises. 'Why don't you just go home,' the woman had whispered to her kindly. But as a matter of pride, she stayed. Gradually the students marshaled behind her desk drifted to other lines. Carolyn no longer looked up. The clock behind her started the little whirring sound it made before it announced the hour. She closed her eyes tightly. Then she collected the paper, slipped the strap of her bag over her narrow shoulder and went toward the stairs. He had never made a secret of how and when he was going. He had simply taken for granted, she thought, hating for a moment his arrogance, that because he had not specifically requested it she would not come to watch him go.

Before she expected it, Nora was through the doors of the station and out on the platform. The woman walked stiffly in front of her. Because it was already dark and she did not know the way, Nora hurried after, climbing when the woman climbed a steep metal bridge which crossed the track bed nearest the station. A heavy puffing engine passed sluggishly under her. The steam came up from below.

380

He will have forgotten me, Nora said to herself, though she clutched in her hand the ticket that only he, although his letter had been unsigned, could have sent her.

Half believing it was a college prank, she had left the shop and gone out into the streets she seldom walked and barely knew even after a dozen years in this land of strangers. On her way she had stopped and looked into store windows, gazing at female mannequins of frozen elegance, wearing clothes she had never dreamed of. In the end, standing before a slovenly red-faced agent in the office of the steamship line, she waited as he searched through the records. Yes, of course, the ticket was valid. She saw his sly, conspiratorial smile. He leaned forward over the desk on his fat arms. He remembered now, he said, the man who had made the purchase. He had no doubt, he told her, that the young man had ample reason to be grateful.

Her head throbbing, she retreated into the darkening street just at the moment when Wykeham stepped out of his cab. A second cab had drawn up behind. Two men began unloading trunks and boxes onto the sidewalk. The streetlamps were coming on and lit her pale tense face. She hadn't meant to stay out so late. She couldn't think of what after their brief, odd encounter in the shop she might actually say to him.

Feeling foolish and yet determined, she drifted into the street. When she had crossed over, the young man, who had kept his back toward her, had already disappeared into the monstrous old station. A breath of night air swirled around her legs. She stood among the trunks and boxes holding herself so still it almost seemed to the men easing boxes down beside her that she was waiting to be lifted onto the loading cart.

'Your pardon, miss,' one of the men said to her. 'Is there something?'

Nora hadn't noticed the man and so did not hear what he was saying. The boxes were growing around her like the wild black hedge that had surrounded her in her dream. Indeed she felt like the girl in the dream: beset on all sides by great dangers and yet somehow made larger to meet them. She was frightened. But because she was frightened she also felt she carried inside her a braver destiny.

The man jabbed at her with his finger. 'Miss,' he repeated.

She saw him then. At the same time she saw the tag on the box he had set at her feet. She gave a startled laugh. It is fate, she thought recklessly, not certain it was so. In the tiny old-fashioned letters that had been on the envelope she had read his destination.

Selecting a door at random, she walked past the man and into the immense dimness of the waiting room.

* * *

The train loomed in the blackness, hissing to itself.

'There,' the Duke said.

Harwood walked ahead but the Duke lingered. Hearing the other's footsteps stop, Harwood turned and looked over his shoulder.

'Are you coming?' he asked.

The Duke shook his head. He smiled. 'I can see from here.'

Harwood nodded and went on.

His Grace held back in the shadows. Perhaps no great harm would be done if Wykeham should see him. After all, he had been invited to Greenchurch and so presumably Wykeham, ignoring the prohibition or perhaps rewriting it, intended that at last he should meet him face-to-face. But for thirty-eight years he had been the Will's most faithful servant and the Will was clear on that point, as it was on so many others. His Grace would be granted one audience with but one member of the family. Thereafter, while he was free to maintain an active correspondence with its male heirs whether in residence at Greenchurch or scattered over the globe, he must never seek another meeting. And he had met (and therefore should have been satisfied) the grandfather, Joseph Wykeham, a grave young man when he stepped into the Duke's office, tall and well spoken and, according to the records, slightly younger than himself. But of course that had been long ago. Joseph had died or at least had been declared missing, then dead. Then, from time to time, His Grace had written the improbably named Sebastian, the father, who had been born abroad, married early and who with all hands had gone to the bottom in the Gulf of Iskanderun without once writing back. It was young William, for reasons which even now remained largely obscure to His Grace, who had been set alone on the Turkish coast and, thereby surviving the disaster, began seven years later to send letters addressed starkly to West Redding, Leeds Bank, New Awanux, the Americas.

It was for William only that the Duke maintained a lasting affection. And yet when the boy, finally a young man, had come in from his wanderings to begin his studies, His Grace had kept his distance as the Will required. The letters still flew back and forth, crossing a few narrow streets where once they had crossed the oceans. But the Duke had come no nearer. Faithful to his trust, even when the latest Wykeham (for there never seemed more than one at a time) announced that the Duke's term would be ended or later when it was learned that Wykeham (the first Wykeham to enter the bank in more than a generation) had come himself to meet the new man, even then, faithfully, His Grace had left the room as Wykeham had come in.

The younger men were left to each other's company. That was as it should have been. The Duke had been the servant of the Will for thirty-eight years but for thirty-eight years he had been its master as well. His hand went into his pocket, touching the letter. Well, the whole bloody tangle is Houseman's now, he thought. How then was he still bound?

The Duke lifted his head.

The realization came to him, almost as a physical shock, that he was looking directly across the platform at Wykeham.

CHAPTER FOUR

It was simply that there was no time (both too little and none at all). It seemed to happen all at once. In an instant there were men and women of no consequence, milling about the platform, preparing to mount the steps as soon as the conductors had opened the doors. While Carolyn was herself preparing, although for what she was not yet certain, Wykeham was suddenly walking ahead of her. She had no idea from where he had come. His dark head was turned, staring upward into the cars as he passed them. Carolyn opened her mouth. Then she saw the woman beside her, a woman she had not before seen, suddenly rush ahead. In the same instant the conductor swung open the door.

Wykeham stopped, waiting for the thin metal door to be hooked back. From beneath the engine there still came a clattering and the laughing curse of steam. And yet, as if by stopping, he brought her to a stop as well. She waited, feeling, just for the moment, as though the world itself had stopped. She did not move. The woman went by her. Carolyn saw only her profile, sick with longing, and knew beyond dispute or reason that this woman too had followed him.

It happened all too quickly. The conductor came down the steps. Wykeham climbed up. He turned left into the car and was gone. Other people moved into the car, finding their seats, lifting bags and huge bundles onto the racks. He was surely one of them. The woman's lips moved but, as though trapped by the glass, they made no sound.

It was George Harwood who first noticed her. She was not especially pretty although he guessed that once she might have been. Such things are hard to judge but he suspected that she was several years his senior. He had not meant to look at her. He had caught a glimpse of Wykeham just as he stepped onto the train. He had run forward to meet him but a crowd of passengers blocked his way. Harwood turned, walking slowly back in the direction he had come, looking up into the windows. It was, he thought later, simply because she looked so surprised and in his experience people on trains, their destinations and perhaps even their lives clearly in mind, never did.

The edge of her cider-colored hair fell across her shoulders. Her eyes were wide open, grown round. She looked, he decided, like a woman in a tale for children. Caught by a gust of adventure, he wondered not who she was but where she was going. For a moment, with the extravagance of one who has read too many books, he fancied that her journey might take her in and out of sorrow to the ends of the earth. Harwood shrugged, aware suddenly that he was being foolish. In the cars the passengers had settled. He still had not seen Wykeham.

The conductors reboarded the train, leaned out and looked down the tracks. The engine uttered a scream.

The last porters scattered. The Duke listened to the pad of their feet as the platform emptied. Only he had seen them all, the dark-haired woman wandering aimlessly under the windows, the man a few paces behind, his hands thrust clumsily into the pockets of a coat that was too grand for him. He had not thought about them, nor about the other woman although he had watched her as well. Even Houseman, though he should not have been there, had gone from his mind.

The wind came in off the river, catching the edge of a sign above his head. The sign creaked and groaned. The Duke listened without hearing. But all the while he had watched. He had seen Wykeham's assured steady gait as he walked between seats, striding with the same unhurried ease with which he had once stepped from the elevator into the room with its great windows. It had seemed a long time ago and yet the Duke hadn't needed to explore his memory. It had been the same long face. The Duke had watched him stop at the front of the car, reach up with his hand to place a small package, the one thing he had carried, onto the rack. And His Grace had kept on watching although, from the first, he had been certain.

Wykeham dropped his hand. Showing no consternation, though the other had no right to be where he was, he slid into the seat beside Houseman.

The Duke shook his head. He would see Houseman fired. He could do that much. It's a different world, the Duke thought sadly. Nothing will make it the same. But all at once he felt that he had got it wrong.

He cocked his head with a slightly puzzled air.

The pale light fell on Joseph's dark face.

It hadn't even occurred to the Duke to confuse the matter with family resemblance. He had looked and he knew. In that he had not been mistaken. His Grace was nearly invisible in the darkness but he stepped deeper into the shadow. I must be getting old, he thought. And yet, he was almost smiling as he saw the two young men in the window, William with Joseph's face, Houseman with a face that once might have been his own.

How then is the world different, the Duke wondered, if the years are nothing and there is no time?

CHAPTER FIVE

At first the train moved slowly, crawling past docks and shipyards. Twenty minutes from Water Street Station Wykeham could still see the outer reaches of New Awanux, the slums gone, but the buildings no less slovenly. For a time the tracks left the river, and the train, now rocking gently, clattered past derelict houses. It depressed him to think of the men who must live there, men he imagined who rose early, starting out along the edges of the roads in darkness to walk to the mills at the city's heart. The great trains sped by them but there was never enough for the fare.

His thoughts made him restless and he was pleased when at last the river swung back into view. Far out in the channel he saw by the lamps hung from their cabins the small black shapes of trawlermen returning late from the bay. He found as always a sort of reassurance in the fact that there were yet some men who steered their own lives. They would ride down into the bay again in the morning, just as fishermen had done for thousands of years and would do for thousands more.

The thought comforted him. Perhaps they were not entirely free, for the sea bound them, but they were as free as men needed to be. He understood such men for he had spent the greatest part of his life in crossing the oceans.

Helped by the memory, he stared once more into the dark. Because he was thinking, he did not hear at first the words of the man sitting next to him.

'Barnum,' Houseman repeated, 'Phineas T. Barnum, to set it out whole.'

Wykeham looked perplexed.

Houseman allowed himself the satisfaction of a grin. Even by his own harsh standards he had to admit, given the little time there had been to manage things, he had performed a miracle. But now that he had secured Wykeham's notice, Houseman waited. There was a great deal to be discovered about Wykeham and it was best to be careful.

Wykeham recognized that look. The first months with a new man were always dangerous. At the start, as good a man as His Grace had made foolish errors. His strength was that he learned from them. Toward the end, in some few matters Wykeham had even begun to trust his judgment, although it was backed by less experience, as much as his own.

But in this the Duke had failed. Already the prohibition had been violated.

He will be disappointed, Wykeham thought, that his last decision did not do him credit. Still, Wykeham hoped for the best. He even smiled, lightly, because Houseman, who had smiled once, was now trying very hard not to.

'Barnum?' he asked.

'Surely you've heard of him – the man with the circuses,' Houseman answered. 'I rented the stable car from his agent in Bridgeport. Where else was I to find one large enough?' Then despite the best of his intentions he broke into a grin. 'They use it, he told me, for shipping elephants.'

Wykeham turned. 'Painted red I would gather.'

Houseman nodded. 'With large yellow letters.' Hearing himself, his smile vanished. ' "The Greatest Show on Earth," ' he said softly. He could imagine what Wykeham was thinking. 'But –' he began.

'But?'

'It's dark,' Houseman filled in quietly. 'We loaded in the dark as well. It was after midnight, yesterday. Or this morning really. Too dark to see the hand in front of your face. The car went right into the barn. The tracks were there just as you said they would be. Apparently had been for years although you could see they served no purpose. Hadn't any, until that is –'

Wykeham watched the sudden change in his expression. At least he isn't stupid, Wykeham thought, not very much relieved.

Houseman was no longer quite looking at him. 'Well, whatever it is went in by itself and no one's the wiser. I closed the doors myself.' He managed to turn toward Wykeham. 'I was there,' he said without apology. 'Someone responsible had to be. And I saw to it.' He waited. 'But even I couldn't tell you what was in there.' He waited again. 'In any event,' he said, 'now it's done. And it will be with you in Devon.'

'It's a horse,' Wykeham said although the question had not been asked directly. 'A rather peculiar and rather unusually large horse,' he said in answer to the unasked question that followed.

Houseman kept his hands in his lap and nodded.

'You realize,' Wykeham said without a trace of awkwardness, 'that you should not have come.'

'His Grace said,' Houseman started but he saw that led nowhere. 'There are things that will need doing at the other end. Arrangements . . .'

'Which I shall see to. Or others will. I am not without resources. Letters were written. I already have at Greenchurch, I believe, several dozen men in my employ. New men, I will grant you. Like yourself, untested –'

Houseman looked pale.

'Of course, I recognize you acted out of the best of intentions,' Wykeham added. 'And I have always appreciated a certain zeal. I expect that His Grace saw that in you. Perhaps, when you return, you will have another talk with him. I shall write you. You may trust to that. But for the time being –'

Houseman knew enough to stand.

'Make certain you look up His Grace,' Wykeham said by way of good-bye.

The evil rumblings in Houseman's stomach told him all too clearly he was going to be ill. He lurched down the aisle heading for the next car, only stopping a moment outside the lavatory. He rattled the handle desperately but the door was locked.

There are pieces which belong in the puzzle, their curious irregularity perfectly matching the oddly shaped hole in the left corner, their unexpected shading the exact color of sunlight on dark foliage, pieces which nevertheless are set aside at the outset and only rediscovered after searching and anguish. So Nora, who had begun looking for portents in dreams, had taken the ten-pound note from the drawer in anticipation of nothing, simply because she felt she had earned it.

She had never intended to follow him. When the letter had come, she had set out merely to discover whether the ticket was real and not a joke in cranky repayment for having asked him to pay once more for what had already been paid for. For if in fact their meeting had been destined, she had not recognized the first stirrings of the thought until, fleeing from the vulgar insinuations of the ticket agent, she had come upon the young man once again at the station. Without looking I have seen him twice, she had thought, as though twice was lucky and a sign. And so, even as near as she was to beginning, she had missed the start. She had taken the ten-pound note not knowing she would or that she would have need of it, but remembering perhaps that it was more than she had ever taken into the streets of Bodø. It was not until she had mounted the steps of the train that she realized that while ten pounds would more than cover the fare, it would leave her less for all the uncertainty that must surely come after.

The first time the conductor came through he collected no tickets. Nora stared out the window waiting to be certain he had gone, keeping her face turned so he would not remember it. But it was that face, before her journey had ever started, that Harwood had seen from the platform and would remember though the year was nearly over when he next saw her, running across the snow-covered lawn, down from the great house at Greenchurch, though her hair would then be golden.

Before the conductor returned she had locked herself in the lavatory. Later, someone had stood outside and rattled the handle frantically. She could hear little gulping sounds. But eventually whoever it was had gone away.

The train made its first stop at Stratford, which the Indians had called Cupheag, and the next at Metichanwun, whose name, for no more reason than they had rejected the other, the English had kept. They were small towns and few passengers either left the train or joined it. The conductor hadn't bothered to come through punching tickets until just before Bristol. Four miles out, when the train came onto the flats by the river, one could sometimes see the tall smokestacks of the factories. But the furnaces no longer burned at night. They made clocks in Bristol and the demand for clocks had diminished. Even at this hour there would be men on the platform waiting to board the train, workmen with their families, their few belongings packed. From up the river, from Devon, there had come rumours of work.

The conductor paused before Wykeham and asked for his ticket.

'You're the gentleman with the circus car,' the conductor said, not quite making it a question for he had seen how the young man was dressed and now that he had been through the cars he had found no one else who looked likely to have been able to afford the expense.

Wykeham turned slightly.

'You wouldn't mind saying what it is you have in there,' the conductor said carefully, not certain as yet whether the young man was being rude or whether he had been dozing.

The conductor rested his arm on the back of the seat.

'You're too young a fella to remember perhaps,' he said. 'But the circuses used to come through here quite often. Years back, when times were better. And, of course, they would stop at Bristol. Then on up the line to Ohomawauke. Queer name, Ohomawauke – Indian.' He seemed to think of something else. 'But then the circuses brought queer folk too. You're not, by the way – I mean you're not dressed like . . .'

Wykeham looked disinterested. 'Horses,' he said matter-of-factly.

'Rather a large car for horses,' the conductor said testily, beginning to take offense.

'Large horses,' Wykeham answered.

'The windows all boarded up.'

'– And blind.'

The conductor took Wykeham's ticket, punched several small holes in it, and, muttering, went hurriedly on. He had no intention of coming back to speak to the young man. Certainly he would not have except for the second young man in the car after who when he tried to wake him he found was dead. There was no need to go through his pockets. Unfolded in his lap was the rental agreement for the circus car. There were three names on the paper, one clearly that of the business agent for the circus and two others.

The train was held in Bristol for a little under an hour. Two policemen, who arrived at once, stared defiantly at the corpse rather as if it deserved most of the blame, turned its head, felt for a pulse and asked questions of the nearest passengers. A woman said that she had thought the man was drunk. She said:

'He kept on making little coughing noises. And mumbling. Not that it made sense, you understand. I could tell he wasn't right.' She shook her head with knowing sadness. 'But don't his eyes look odd,' she said.

The policemen were not distracted.

'Do you remember the words exactly?' the sergeant asked.

'Just foolishness.'

The sergeant tugged at his belt importantly. 'We shall be the judge of that,' he told her.

'The world's coming apart,' the woman answered softly. She was a small tense woman. She seemed about to blubber.

The sergeant stood in front of the corpse so she would not have to stare at it. 'Yes,' he said in a calming tone, not looking at her but at the other policeman. 'These things can be difficult. If you would just –'

'No!' the woman said with a sudden fierceness. 'It's what the poor man said. The world's coming apart, coming apart. Over and over.'

It was the doctor who asked if anyone knew the man. So it was not until then that the conductor, who had already thought of it but who had not been asked, went into the other car and came back with Wykeham. A shadow of stern regret passed over his features.

'This is Mr. Houseman,' the conductor said, guessing from the names he had read on the paper and introducing the young man to the policemen.

The policemen shook hands with Wykeham. They had not thought of that before either. They had sons who were older, but somehow, looking at the young man, you did.

'That, I am sorry to say, is Houseman,' Wykeham corrected them. Something caught the corner of his eye. Wykeham stopped, fished under the seat and, retrieving a piece of paper, presented it to the sergeant. 'We were traveling together from New Awanux,' he told them. 'He was only newly in my employ.' Wykeham looked down at the collar buttoned firmly around the throat of the dead man. A fragment of straw clung to the starched white cloth. He brushed it off. 'Understandably we rode separately.' Only his eyes betrayed his grief. 'I wish he had told me he was ill,' he said.

The passengers kept edging nearer and had to be shooed away. The doctor had closed the dead man's shirt and was wiping his fingers on his handkerchief. Death, he told them, was the result of heart failure or shock, or perhaps both. Unusual in a young man but it happened.

There was not much else to be done. The body was taken off. Shortly afterward Wykeham himself left the train to telegraph the bank. He left instructions for someone to travel out on the next train and ride back with the body. At the funeral there would be a lavish array of flowers and a card signed in his own hand. Houseman, it would be discovered, to the surprise of his family, had purchased a generous insurance policy for which his parents, because there had been no wife, were beneficiaries. Death always leaves loose ends. But those which could be tidied up would be.

In something short of an hour the new passengers were permitted onto the train. In the confusion Nora came out of the lavatory. The window in the cubicle had been painted over and she had sat in the little space, her knees drawn up, unable to look out. Over the course of the journey persons unknown had banged at the door and wrenched the handle. To make matters worse she had begun to hear whispers about policemen. She had been frightened and she was now more than willing to pay the fare from wherever she now was. But though she sat in the open, no one thought to ask for it.

PART II

The Hill and the Tower

CHAPTER ONE

The error in the maps of that time seemed to arise both from the limitations in the knowledge of the world of the men who made them and from the limitations inherent in maps themselves. That man's knowledge of his world continues to be imperfect is perhaps widely enough accepted as to need no defense. The problem with mapping is, as it has always been, that each map is the surrogate of space and not the space itself. It is a problem familiar to poets: It is the heart, before a line is written, that takes the wound. . . .

At Ohomawauke the river bends, following the nearly perfect figure of an 'S' tipped on its side. Along this broadly cursive pattern Devon lies both west and south. The figure is too huge to be seen from the hill at Ohomawauke which gave the town its name. The name itself meant owl's nest (or literally owl-place) once but owls stay deep in the wood where they can sit all night among the boughs. Crows fly higher but never high enough. Coming in from the moon you would have seen it, shining with the moon's reflected light. Even a thousand years before the English came to make their marks on the land, amid the illiterate vegetable scrawl of the naked continent, there would have seemed a sign, as if a vanished race had left a message for a god. Certainly it would not have surprised the Reverend Mr. Longford if this were so. He had devoted many months to the attempt to reduce just this possibility to a few clear lines of proof.

He settled back easily atop the cart in the stationyard. He was gazing over the empty tracks to the place where the train, although he would hear it long before, would come into view. After forty years his whiskers were still the rich chestnut color they had been at twenty. His eyes were deep and with the years had seemed to grow deeper still. To the dismay of a score of women in a half dozen churches he had married young and fully expected to have his helpmate with him through eternity. It was a quarter of twelve already; the train was late.

Longford had come north from Maryland, from a little country church in Mt. Airy where at the request of his bishop he had spent three years.

Longford had left in November and gone to stay with a sister in New York. In January, right after Christmas, he had been installed in the parsonage at Greenchurch. Before he had ever heard of Wykeham or the Will, he had asked for the appointment. While in divinity school, one of the numberless tiny colleges named after Wesley, he had been looking through an atlas and discovered, like a piece of ancient mischief, the figure of an 'S' lying on its side. During the years that followed he had never quite forgotten it. When at last the bishop had offered Devon, although he was quick to point out that the post included certain added and unusual responsibilities, Longford had agreed at once.

There were three cars in the carriage house, two model A's and the Pope-Hartford, but all were up on blocks. In the first months, with so many more pressing matters to contend with, Longford had never had Charon Hunt, blacksmith, mechanic, drive his equally primitive Ford pickup along the dark wooded road which led to Greenchurch. The pickup itself was so old and so often fell into disrepair it needed both Hunt's skills to keep the relic just bolting along within the village. Then too, the cars were probably not worth the trouble. Longford imagined that with Wykeham coming the time was not far off when they would be replaced with a fleet of sleek new ones. Longford had no illusions on that point. Wykeham after all was a boy of twenty and could afford to do what he pleased. Longford, however, having no other choice, had backed the cart from the hay barn, settled the horse and hitched him, then set off down the long avenue toward the village. At the top of the green, behind the feed store and the church, he had passed by the rambling building that served as Hunt's garage. Parked to the side was the dark green Dodge Longford had driven from Maryland and then nursed patiently up from New York. It had waited since January for a missing part. For three months Longford had wandered past it several times a day, going on foot around the village on pastoral visits. This evening, after dinner, he had walked the two miles to the big house at Greenchurch to fetch the cart and later, after Wykeham had been settled, whatever luggage he had brought with him lifted to the porch and the lights switched on, Longford would walk back. But when he saw the car, the corners of his deep blue eyes rose in a smile. It was much the same smile he would have given on this or any night to shut-ins and invalid members of his congregation. The pains of this world are temporary, it seemed to say, wait.

As the Reverend Mr. Longford turned the cart into the stationyard he was content. Wykeham, he hoped, would soon settle the odd business with John Chance. There was more to the old gamekeeper, he suspected, than met the eye but it was a matter between the old man and the boy. What he really wanted from Wykeham was permission to fell a few trees on the crown of East Wood, above the house. The trees were giants and even now, before the April bloom they blocked the view of the river. If he could have them down, he was convinced it would open up the clear line of sight he needed to make the final measurements. He was not unprepared. After months of planning he now had ample chains and flags and while in New York, scraping together the last of his savings, he had purchased a new brass surveying compass. He hoped Wykeham had remembered to drop by the booksellers before he left New Awanux. One of the volumes was particularly necessary. Longford smiled again as he thought of it: *Geodaesia, or the Art of Measuring Land Made Easie.*

The darkness by the river was lit suddenly by the one glaring lamp at the front of the train. As if smelling other horses, the cart horse tossed its head.

The Bristol men and their women, carrying all they had, climbed down first and looked around bleakly at the small station and the one empty street: city people in a country town. The stationmaster greeted them easily. There was a boarding-house, he told them, not far, just opposite Hunt's garage. And yes, there was work, for those who didn't mind long hours and were good with their hands. But, of course, it was already Sunday; they would have to wait over. The man in the cart, the Reverend Mr. Longford, was the man to see but not until Monday. Though it wouldn't hurt, the stationmaster added with a wink, if the good Mr. Longford happened to get a glimpse of them in the back pews of Greenchurch in the morning. The stationmaster studied their faces, then shook his head. Perhaps one or two would do, he thought; the rest would be gone in a fortnight.

No one remembered a slender straight-haired woman with no luggage. The surprise had long since passed from her face. She hurried across the platform only pausing a moment to stare at the horse cart. If she felt a blush rising against her neck and checks, in the darkness it attracted no notice. She looked back all at once and saw Wykeham step down from the train, saw him raise a hand in greeting to the man in the cart. The hand holding the reins lifted in turn, the greeting of strangers. For a moment she felt the same dark knot of fear she had felt as a child when she had dared herself over the edge of sleep. But she continued on into the stationyard and across the gravel and the darkness of the one long street received her.

Wykeham counted out a few shillings for the stationmaster. The man looked disappointed.

'For your boy,' Wykeham said, 'when he has unloaded the boxes.'

The man brightened. 'And the stable car?' he asked, a hint of authority restored to his voice.

'It's all in the shipping orders,' Wykeham answered. 'Though you might check them yourself to see if there is any added expense. The car stays here the night and goes back empty the first of the week.'

The man dug his hands into his pockets where he kept a string of keys. 'And the contents?' he asked.

'Quite safe,' Wykeham said, 'by itself. You needn't bother. Longford will have a gang of men by tomorrow evening to handle everything. I am sure we shall manage.'

'You wouldn't know when?'

'Late, I should think.'

The stationmaster watched Wykeham turn. 'Mr. Wykeham,' he called out suddenly.

The young man glanced over his shoulder. The stationmaster looked almost embarrassed.

'My grandfather knew yours,' the man said. It seemed like a compliment and for a moment it silenced him. But then the man grinned. 'Welcome home, sir,' he said.

'There's something wrong with the mails,' Longford complained when, the boxes loaded and Wykeham settled on the seat beside him, they turned up the empty street toward Greenchurch. 'I had hoped you would have found me further along but I'm afraid the letter didn't come until this morning.' Longford gave the reins a shake as though to hurry both the horse and his preparations at once. 'I did carry up some fresh linen from the parsonage,' he said. 'Monday I'll see there is someone out there to begin airing your own.'

'Tomorrow, if you wouldn't mind,' Wykeham said, as though he had already given some thought of it, 'after breakfast. A woman, just on trial, for the kitchen and a maid. Just to start. I shall be needing several. And in the afternoon, say at four-thirty, a half dozen men.'

Longford pulled at his handsome whiskers. 'William,' he began, not yet insisting. 'It has perhaps escaped your attention. But after all there can be no question . . .'

The cart moved against the shadows of the trees. Away from the last scattered lights of the village the stars burned fiercely. Longford hadn't noticed when Wykeham withdrew the package from his coat.

'You see I have brought your books,' Wykeham interrupted him. It seemed such an artless and generous gesture, so meant to please that for the moment Longford let the abrogation die on his lips. He could afford to wait. The horse stepped lightly ahead of them. But as the young man chatted on about boats and his schooling, the right moment seemed continually pushed beyond reach. It was not until the cart had actually stopped before the porch of the great house and they were helping each other down with the boxes, that Longford, with the return of resolve, placed his fatherly hand on Wykeham's shoulder.

'About tomorrow,' he said firmly.

It was dark under the eaves. Hedges that had not been trimmed for years grew up over the sagging porch railings. In the daylight Longford had seen the work that was needed here, like the Lord's work, a never-ending task of pruning and rebuilding, a labor before which, unless refreshed in Christ, even a man of persevering conscience must despair.

'One day in seven,' Longford said. 'Not in His honor only but because of the spirit of man . . .'

Wykeham walked away from him. Out of the shadow of the house, Wykeham turned abruptly. Longford saw the tears streaming down his face.

'I am sorry,' Wykeham whispered. 'There was a man of my acquaintance. . . . He died this evening on the train.' Slowly he straightened himself. Longford came down beside him.

'No,' Wykeham said softly, rejecting his arm. 'You go on home. I shall be fine.'

'I hardly . . .,' Longford protested.

'No, honestly. I am sure to manage.'

Nevertheless Longford lingered on for a quarter hour, ready if anything were needed. Under the circumstances he was not so ill mannered as to mention the Sabbath.

The doctor puzzled over the corpse. He had pulled back the sheet to examine its eyes and was surprised again at their helpless wonder. He had gone to his house and, without waking his wife, had returned through the quiet streets with his camera. His own dark eyes screwed up at the corners as he focused the lens. He had a theory that the eyes of dead men held, even some hours after death, the slowly fading image of whatever last they looked on. It was a phenomenon he suspected without the least sliver of proof. He arranged the lamps to throw a greater flood of light against the pale, almost spectral head. The irises were a brownish green, roughly the color of the earth at the edge of the wood near the fine gambrel-roofed house in Cambridge where he had been born.

The undertaker already knew all he wanted to know about corpses. 'You'll lock up, Oliver?' he wondered.

'Yes – yes,' Dr. Holmes said defensively. 'I shouldn't be but a few minutes.' He repositioned the lamp, for it seemed to him that the wide dead eyes kept on drinking the light. He hesitated, then pushed the lamp nearer.

CHAPTER TWO

In the same darkness, on a hill overlooking the river, old Okanuck knocked out his pipe. A few strings of tobacco curled with a moment's redness but, unsustained by his breath, they blackened the ground. Only the fierce stars and the hearts of the Pequods, with equal fierceness, kept their brightness.

Outwardly he was nearly invisible, his wings held perfectly still, guarded and immune to the wind. It was the best sort of vanishing trick: turning the darkness within him inside out. Not even the owls had seen a movement or sensed a presence. And yet there were mornings in the world, the blackness running inward back through his veins, when he would have seemed as clear as a shaft of sunshine slanting down through the trees. In neither case would a man have seen him. But Okanuck was old and skilled. The boy was only a boy and he was gone.

In the towns along the river the English slept; the lights of their houses that earlier had been gorged with light were darkened now, the warmth gone without a fading spark or a memory. Walking on, he followed the path where the English road had been. But it was not the road he was following. The hilltop regions where the English first took hold were the first to lose them. The roots of trees overgrasped the pasture walls; the cleared meadows closed with shade. Now to either side the big cellar holes of the once great houses were filled with elderberry and cedar. The scratches left on the rotting wood were made by thorns. Watching and remembering, Okanuck climbed among the moss-backed stones. 'Oohoomau-auke,' he whispered, giving back to the place the name it had never lost.

From across the river valley a glint of firelight caught his eye. Despite his uneasiness, Okanuck smiled. John Chance is awake, he thought. Even among the English there were a few very old men who, seeing all too clearly the rest that awaited them, neglected sleep. Okanuck went down to the bottom of the wood where the track became an English road again. If, as he feared, the boy had set out in anger to begin his own grim war against the English, Chance more than any other would have heard of it. Though in these last years he seldom went from the falling-down steps of his cottage in Black Wood, the young men of the towns still tramped out to talk with him. The young, not yet content to sit in their shops and houses, knew far better than their elders the back lanes and abandoned barns, the remote discarded edges of the towns where among the rusted implements and broken machinery of his enemy the boy might go to brood and plan their further ruin.

Okanuck skirted Paper Birch Farm though for a moment he had been tempted to peer in at the bedroom window of the old widow Birch and the three hounds which she now slept with and had since the night sixty years ago when after rather more thorn wine than he was used to Okanuck had floated down to the third-story window and waved at her.

Of course they were not the same hounds. Sometimes, in the long summer darkness, he had slipped into the side yard where they were buried, one generation after another, still keeping watch. Through the trampled earth he had renewed his acquaintance with their bones. At first, thinking he was a hound himself, come nosing and pawing, eager to disinter them, they had only whined mournfully. But in time they had grown fond of him and looked forward to his coming. Like Okanuck they had thought themselves well rid of the skinny young man their mistress had married and who had to be buried himself soon after, ten miles to the west and south in the cemetery at Greenchurch. The hounds, although they had no sense of human beauty, suspected nonetheless it was her physical attractiveness that drew Okanuck again and again to the grass-covered mound a hundred yards from the house. She is old now, they had told him. Unsurprised, he had nodded. Better than most he knew how these English perished. He had never gone back to her window. And yet sometimes he saw her face in the airy darkness, her red hair disordered on her pillow.

But though he skirted the farm, Okanuck came in sight of it. It took him only a quarter of a mile out of his way but then it brought him nearer the far end of the village than was absolutely necessary. Even at this hour there were likely to be men on the road. With a kind of wondering sadness Okanuck turned. He unfolded his wings. Their broad edges caught the air with a thump. Reaching out in a series of sharp, increasingly distant handholds, Okanuck pulled himself into the sky. Woods and fields wheeled away under him, their particular land-marks diminishing, even as the land itself swung more fully into his sight. In the deep evening air the little darkened farm slid far behind.

*　　*　　*

John Chance leaned back in his chair and regarded the cluttered yard beyond the rough front steps of his cottage. Because of his years he was not always certain where he was in time. It was far easier and, to his thinking, more to the point to keep watch of the seasons than to weigh his mind with the useless addition of dates. The years kept piling up no matter if he wished them to or not but between one and another there was never much to tell them apart. On the other hand, the seasons and the weathers that rushed along with them meandered and changed: gales howled in Black Wood, yellow leaves fell like showers of gold and under the crusts of rotted snow the green spikes of deer grass lifted their heads. Great things and small pressed themselves on his attention but the only firm conclusion he was willing to come to was that the winter advanced and receded and that the summer followed spring.

John Chance glanced out at the evening. He knew more or less it was April but he remained uncommitted as to whether it was precisely this April or some other come blowing from his memory. He had the impression, however, because he needed a blanket wrapped about his shoulders, that he was old. Very old, he thought with a deep, clear pride. For a second time the awakened breeze brushed his face and he looked up.

Okanuck grinned at him.

'Now it's the end of the world, is it?' Chance said, smiling back. 'The impatient dead coming in from the hills, eyes filled with murder.'

Okanuck went on grinning. They liked one another well enough to joke at each other's expense and gladly traded wounds, unharmed by an honesty that would have parted lesser friends. Though not the sort of thing he would have denied if pressed, Okanuck never cared to be reminded he was dead and so the old man never failed to find a way to mention it.

'I thought I'd find you dead as well,' Okanuck answered.

'No. Not yet.' A sly triumph showed in Chance's eyes. 'I've made April and still hope to make one more.'

Okanuck looked with gentle disapproval at the old man's crippled legs. 'It's not the life I'd dream of,' he said kindly.

'Hell, it's life,' Chance said. Enjoying himself, he leaned farther back in his chair. 'Besides, Wyck's come back again and I've a mind to see one last time what he's up to.'

Okanuck grunted. 'Which one is he now?'

'William – or so Morag thought, poor man. And he had, for he showed me them, a bundle of letters all signed with a great scrawl of a

W, which might have been for William as much as Wykeham.' Beside him on the steps was a half empty bottle. Chance reached down for it and when he had had a taste of the whisky he passed the bottle sociably into one of Okanuck's large clawed hands. 'And the man, Longford, called him that,' Chance said, 'coming around not a month ago when there were still patches of snow in Black Wood, saying Master William this and Master William that, as though he knew him already. Wanted me off the property, he said, in William's name. It took me a moment or two at first to figure out just who he meant. But it's likely it's William.'

'It would be,' Okanuck said. 'Leastways he's been a handful of Williams since the English came, since Bradford anyway.' He drank the whisky. His eyes narrowed and he stared into the web of the branches. He was trying to remember the names that had been before. 'They were usually Welsh,' he said.

'Wyck?'

Okanuck nodded. 'Names like Kyfarwydd or Gwalstawd. Hard to say unless you were used to them but then he kept hold of them longer, there being no need to pretend he was anyone but himself.'

While Okanuck was speaking, Chance began to notice he was colder. The whisky warmed his throat and belly so at first he paid no attention. But gradually he felt a damp cold nosing about his feet. He kicked at it lamely. He was not yet frightened. But from now on, he realised, he would have to be vigilant.

They both heard the crack of a rifle shot and they both started. The sound echoed between the cleft of hills. Chance jabbed the side of his shoe at the dark. What had been there had gone elsewhere, ignoring him.

'There are poachers in East Wood,' he said.

Okanuck's eyes were wide open. He could see only the sky and the nearer trees. Somewhere in the dark men were running, their sides heaving, stumbling because they had not dared to carry a lantern. The paths were grown over or blocked with timber. They heard a man swearing, far across the wood.

'That would be Fred Norfolk for the mouth of him,' Chance said. 'And Charon Hunt with him.' The wind backed off, taking the sound of the men away with it.

In the stillness Okanuck let himself breathe again.

'You were worried,' Chance said.

'For a moment.' Okanuck gave him a sideways grin. 'But Fred Norfolk never did hit anything.' He spotted the whisky and sat down with the bottle between his knees. His toes dragged in the dirt. After that there was no moving him and he began to explain why he had come.

Longford looked up from the text of the sermon he was still writing and found his wife staring at him from their bed. It was early and the lamp at his desk gave a warmer glow of light than the little that came in the south window. Longford had begun the work alone, beneath the stairs, on the dining room table. But as soon as he had heard Plum stirring he had gone up, seeking her help with one phrase or another. He had just finished reading aloud a particularly complicated passage which she had already corrected twice.

'I shall go if I must,' she said on another matter altogether.

'Dear Plum,' he sighed, relieved, aware that he could not really have expected anyone else to do it and that even if he had, she would have gone anyway. 'You will tell him,' he said, 'that this is a special case and not how things will be handled ordinarily.' She looked preoccupied. He cleared his throat. 'I'll admit I might have been more forceful. It is best to begin with a clear understanding. I've always said that.' He looked back guiltily at his sermon, adjusting the spectacles he only wore indoors and away from his flock. He said: 'It was just that I was caught unprepared when he told me about the death of his friend.'

She waited to be quite certain he had finished. She knew he meant well but it was one of his greatest faults that he never knew when to stop.

'He won't think, do you suppose, you actually are the kitchen help?'

She met his eyes. 'I shall be certain to tell him,' she said.

Later he went down the walk with her and opened the gate. He had put his spectacles in his inside pocket. His arm wrapped around her, warming her in the morning's chill.

'You don't mind?' he asked again, assured now, needing no answer.

Beside her he seemed to grow taller, his shoulders a full foot higher than her own. Her chin was tucked down and he could not see her smile. At a point where the street climbed the first hill she looked back and found him watching. She waved, already missing him.

At the entrance to the estate, there were two broad oaks, already coming into leaf, one to either side of the drive. There was no sign. Its lack had never puzzled her for she had seen at once that the trees announced plainly, to anyone who cared to look, that this was Greenchurch. The church on the other hand – back in the village – though it shared the name and was in fact a church and had been painted a shadowed and peculiarly ancient shade of green, had a placard importantly out on the lawn. It was not hard to imagine which had held the name longer. The steeple in the village would have been dwarfed by these trees. She squinted up into their leafy branches, losing her sight among the clouds and countries, the acres and deep green seas of the mounting oak-wood. A kind of old-fashioned awe filled her. Going up the drive, her face dropped to a human height again, she saw another face, pale against the gray bark of the oak, and got a bewildered stare in return.

The woman, who had been reclining, stood quickly. There was a stain on the sleeve of her coat; her disheveled hair, darkened by the shade, half covered her neck.

'My girl,' Plum Longford said breezily, though the other was no child, 'you look as though you slept in the wood.' To Plum's surprise, the woman nodded.

'I'm not from this place,' the woman said quietly, in a way that made Plum wonder if truly she had come from anywhere. The woman blushed. 'I wasn't sure just where to go,' she said, turning abruptly, taking a nervous glance up the long slope of the drive. 'It doesn't feel right going up there.'

'You mean it didn't' – Plum helped her – 'last night in the dark?'

'Then too,' she answered.

Plum noticed that the woman's small hands were clutching a paper. Plum had met most of the village women but there were always some, she knew, who hung back and now with the reopening of the estate there were strangers coming every day. Mostly they were men. But eventually, Plum decided, there had to be women as well, hired for the kitchen and housekeeping, though, under the circumstances, she knew Tim would have preferred them older and, well, more matronly. She found herself inspecting the woman's slender legs and laughed at herself.

'You'll be wanting to see my husband,' Plum said, 'for he is in charge of the hiring.'

'I haven't —' the woman began.

'May I see that?' Plum interrrupted her, for she was accustomed to being in charge. She reached out for the paper, expecting an employment notice.

'He gave that to me,' the woman said but she let Plum take hold of it. Plum turned the paper over in her fingers. It was the steamer ticket to Bodø.

'I mean to exchange it,' Nora said, smiling. 'I will rent a box at the post office so I will have a place when they send the money back. I have it all figured out. I was going to go down to post it this morning but then I remembered it was Sunday. But I will go tomorrow.'

'Who gave it to you?' Plum asked, astonished and trying to find the beginning.

'The young man who was come to live here.'

'Why?'

Nora closed her eyes as though she were looking for something but wasn't altogether certain it could be found outside of her. 'I am hoping,' she said, 'it is fate.'

'And if it isn't?'

Nora ran her fingers into her cider-colored hair, trying vaguely to restore it to order. Among the brown strands, Plum noticed, there were little flecks of gold. Nora opened her eyes and Plum became conscious again of their remarkable innocence. Somehow it touched her.

'I don't suppose he knows you have come,' she said, in a voice that seemed unlike her, almost embarrassed. While she had mistaken practically everything at first, very quickly Plum was beginning to readjust her thinking. Tim, she knew, would have ben scandalized. But her own view of life had always been kinder and more tolerant for she knew the world better. The truth was, she was eight years older than her husband. 'Look,' she said gently, 'it is really none of my business.'

'No,' Nora said. 'He doesn't know.'

They had begun to walk up the drive. Beyond the sentinel oaks the light was brighter. Plum looked about. The broad trimmed lawns had long ago turned into meadows. The plantings of exotic trees, brought from Europe and the Orient, had been left to grow wild. Only an experienced eye would have marked them apart from the elms and maples. Yet Plum half sensed their oddity. Who can say she doesn't belong here? she thought. Though if she were wanted, Plum guessed, he would not have given her a steamer ticket. Bodø was in Norway, wasn't it? Almost the other side of the earth.

'I am Hannah Longford,' she said, 'though my friends call me Plum.'

'Like the heavy thing —' Nora screwed up her face in wonder. 'You know, the weight sailors use to tell how deep the sea is. Like that?'

Plum laughed. 'That too! Yes,' Plum answered, deciding she liked her without reservation. 'And your own?' she asked, still smiling.

'Nora.'

Plum waited for her to finish.

'Only Nora,' she said after a moment. 'Now at any rate. You see, I've run away from the rest of it.'

'You have a husband?'

Nora looked blank.

No, Plum thought, I shall not let it matter – I have decided to be a friend to her. Plum began to walk a little more briskly, trusting her body to keep her mind from thinking. There was the good feel of gravel under her feet. Out in the morning, rising over the trees, a crow circled, eyeing them. It opened its black throat and cursed. Or perhaps it was only the cough of the battered Ford pickup, bounding around a turn in the drive up ahead of them. Nora climbed up the embankment and hid in the trees. But though she stepped into the grass Plum more or less held her ground. It was Charon Hunt, of course, driving and another man, his head averted, refusing to acknowledge he saw her or not wanting to be seen. Plum waved at them. The truck barreled past. There was a large canvas sack in the back. Whatever was in it was heavy. The truck bounced and swayed but the sack did not budge. The truck took the turn by the oaks widely, edging precariously near one of the trunks, rattling over the snarl of roots and, with a roar of its old engine, vanished.

'You needn't worry,' Plum called out to Nora. 'They didn't care to be looked at anymore than you. So I doubt they will be saying they've seen us.'

Nora peered out from the brush. Her white skin was reddened down to her throat.

'It's just that I'm not ready yet,' she said.

'Well, you had best hurry, my girl,' Plum laughed, 'the house is not much more of a walk.'

Nora shook her head and stayed where she was.

'What will you do, then?' Plum wondered.

'When I have my money,' Nora said, knowing that part, having begun her thinking somewhere in the middle, 'then I will rent some place. I will live in the town he lives in. I will wait till he notices.'

'Until then?'

Nora brightened. 'Couldn't you,' she began. 'I mean, already you've been so kind.'

But Plum knew she could not, not with Tim. Though she could get him around most things, she knew with a pang of hard feminine regret, this would not be one of them, knew, despite his tenderness for her. She remembered the warmth of his arm about her waist. No, she thought, until it was all sorted out it was best perhaps Tim did not learn she was here. But clearly something had to be done and, as she looked around, it was equally clear to her that it would have to be herself who would have to do it. She studied the paper, which with the sudden appearance of the truck she had neglected to hand back to Nora.

'I shall keep this,' Plum said firmly. 'It has the address right here on the top. I'll send it off myself tomorrow. You needn't go into town. In the meantime . . .' It really was a fine muddle, she thought. Who knew what had gone on between them? Or was likely to? Not yet anyway, she decided, not if she could help it. Certainly the woman could not go up to the house but neither could she be permitted to sleep under the trees.

Nora stepped out on the grass.

'No you don't,' Plum said with the sudden fierceness of inspiration.

'Plum?'

But a small smile was shaping itself into the corners of Plum's mouth and she mounted the embankment with a sturdy, determined tread. 'Turn around,' she directed, coming under the edge of the wood. 'Now walk straight ahead,' she said, driving Nora before her into the limb-tangled darkness that even in the bold light of morning always made Black Wood seem like one of the straggling, spectral provinces of night.

An hour later Plum let herself into the Great House without knocking. The hall was empty. Nonetheless she made her way carefully, trying the doors at random, until far in the back of the house and down a half level of stairs she discovered the kitchen. It was the largest kitchen she had ever been in. There were a great many copper-covered tables and at least five black stoves. Off to the side there was a separate room for a pantry, another for the table service and a third, quite a bit smaller, with drying racks and sinks. A month ago the first of the groundsmen and the chief hostler and his boy had been let in to make their suppers. They had left, she saw, exactly the sort of disorder she had expected whenever men were let alone in a kitchen. Plum poked about impatiently. Now that Wykeham was here, of course, this would all have to stop. She begn to collect the scattered plates and saucers.

The young man, in his gray tweeds, came in quietly behind her. Plum's first impression as she turned and found him smiling at her was that he was dressed like an old man. She had an armful of dishes and, becoming increasingly irritated, had just discovered a new hoard of messy platters wrapped in a tablecloth and hidden under a chair. Her breath came quickly through her teeth.

'I don't suppose you know you have a woman waiting for you in the wood?' she asked him angrily.

Wykeham held open the kitchen door. A crow hopped across the threshold. Its rakish black head was tilted up so it could look at him.

'The other one . . .,' Wykeham asked, seeming only mildly interested. He returned the crow's black stare. 'Did you think she was pretty?'

CHAPTER THREE

'You should not have asked.'

'Would you have answered?'

'No.'

'Then there could have been no harm.'

'It is harm enough if she thinks you are heartless.'

'She may think what she likes.'

'She will in any event. That proves nothing.'

'Then it little matters if I ask you questions.'

'It was never the asking.'

'Then what?'

'It was the thing you asked'

'Whether a shop girl was pretty?'

'Yes.'

'And was she?'

'I am no judge. You all have fat legs and hair.'

Wykeham grinned. 'There! I have you,' he shouted happily. With both hands he hauled himself up the last rungs of the ladder. His large dark face pressed against the small attic window, he stared, smiling, down at the lawn. 'And on two counts,' he said. 'The first being that you are incapable of speech. And the second that, speechless or not, you are no fit judge. In neither case could she have thought I took my question seriously. Therefore there is no harm.' Wykeham scratched the glossy feathers along the crow's neck but the crow turned away sulkily.

'You are wrong in both,' it rasped. It hopped to the sill, holding its place with a sudden spasm of its heavy wings. It brought its head level. It blinked in the daylight. 'For if,' it continued, 'I could not answer, then she could only have thought it was herself you meant to ask.'

'And the second?'

'She was fit to judge.'

Wykeham looked annoyed. 'What can that matter? She is just an old woman.'

'And therefore you are heartless,' the crow answered. 'And she knows it. Accordingly there is harm.'

Wykeham reached for its neck. But the wary crow flew up into the rafters.

'Open the window and let me out,' it said. 'I have spent the whole night watching and now I am hungry.' The crow looked Wykeham straight in the face. Wykeham knew he would not be able to catch it.

'There is a new-killed rat in the pantry,' he said.

The crow turned its back on him resentfully. 'In the drive there is a hare,' it said, 'run over by a truck.' The crow picked at the underside of one of its long feathers with its beak. A little gust of wind rattled the window pane. It was already some hours since the woman had deserted the kitchen and the house was quiet.

'I had been meaning to mention it earlier,' the crow said. 'It appears, lord, that they have shot an Indian.'

The wind had freshened all morning, tearing off small branches and throwing them to the lawn. In the afternoon Wykeham heard the wind prowling under the eaves and muttering among the loose bricks of the chimneys. He sat at his desk making drafts of a long letter to His Grace which, with each rewriting, grew shorter and shorter. The truth was he was agonizing over a verb in the very first sentence, struggling over meanings as a man will only struggle over a love letter, which, in a limited sense, this was.

Dear Callaghan, the letter began but his letters always started so and the salutation was essentially without content. *I regret that I must request* was what he had written first and the letter ran on to two pages. They both lay crumpled in a basket at his feet. He dug his pen into the inkwell, starting over. *I need your help once more,* the second announced bluntly. The rest came a word at a time, grudgingly. He folded the single page over and set it aside. The deepening afternoon sunlight came in through the window behind him and lit the edges of a fresh sheet. The shadow of his right hand lay across its middle. He wondered what thoughts would come into Callaghan's mind when he unsealed the envelope and began to read. Wykeham was desperately sorry about the death of Houseman. But there had been no choice. It was not the killing, though in fact he had never relished it.

He had killed before, both with his own hands and by proxy. He had never pretended, as men often did, that both cases were not very much the same, but he had been at it longer and had less reason to lie to himself. The wars in which he had taken his first heads and left the bubbling necks empty were no longer remembered; the lands over which he had fought were no longer lands, but ocean. Yet he had never failed to understand what it meant or what a powerful thing it was to take a life or to be less frightened by it.

He did not expect to be understood. He knew that not even the most rugged men now living could have lived as he had lived, gone where he had gone, or done what, to the horror of his soul, he had had to do. Nevertheless, for Callaghan's sake as much as for the young man himself, he wished that Houseman had continued.

I must call you again into service, he wrote at last. *Houseman, failing, is dead and I shall trust no one else in this enterprise. I have no other reward to offer you except my affection;* he stopped, then added, *everlastingly.*

Beneath the tiny printed letters he set a large cursive 'W.' For a moment he looked at it oddly. His hand must have been unsteady. He had just about decided to make a second copy when he heard the men tramping onto the porch.

He sealed up the letter in the envelope he had already addressed. Still, it was curious, he thought as he walked into the hall. Tipped on its side, rather as if he had been falling as he had written it, the one bold letter of his signature almost seemed an 'S.'

He put it out of his mind. Walking toward the door, he pulled on his coat.

The men looked shy when they came for work. It was the first time they had ever seen such a big, queer house. Silently, collecting on the porch, they waited for the last straggler to remove his cap.

'Is there a man among you who has ever handled a horse?' Wykeham asked them.

When he had come out, they had stepped back, crowding against the railing, and looked puzzled. The wind, which had been building up all day, tugged at their collars.

'There's work here he told us,' George Tennison answered, who for twenty-seven years had been a tool and die maker at the Bristol clock-works. 'Maybe we never asked what kind, but Longford never said it was horses.' George Tennison winced, thinking he had walked a good long way for nothing. He was about to put on his cap again, there being no further need for deference, when his eye ran into an unexpected piece of mischief in the young man's face. He smiled himself. 'Though I could,' he said, grinning, 'manage to pick up after a horse.' He contrived to wink at the man next to him. 'And Sam here, he'd be right good at it.'

Sam snorted but after that they all seemed a little less miserable. One by one Wykeham asked them their names and in turn each man came forth to shake hands with him.

'I'm Jakey.'

'I am pleased to have you, Jakey.'

'Adam France, sir.'

'Adam.'

The others came forward. Despite the formality, as if their shared amusement at the thought of horse manure were bond enough, the curse lifted from the air.

'Mostly it is your backs I'll be wanting,' Wykeham told them, leading them off the porch and up the slope by the side of the house. 'Though one of you, George I think, will have to ride with me when the rest are finished.' He paused and there was a moment's dead silence. George Tennison seemed dubious. 'It's the horse,' Wykeham said, 'that does the work. All you do is hold on to him.' Wykeham smiled. 'And of course, it pays double.'

'I'm your man, then,' George said.

Wykeham laughed. 'That was just what I was hoping.'

There were birds in the wood, blown along by the wind from branch to branch or simply fleeing ahead of them, it was difficult to tell which. But because it was East Wood there were breaks where the evening light yet lingered, coppery and brown-yellow. They could still see one another clearly. Nonetheless Wykeham had brought along lanterns. Although he was not used to looking at the sky, George Tennison thought that they had at least another hour of daylight. He clambered up on a stone and looked out through a dusky thicket of sumac. They were, he judged, a half mile or so from the house and climbing along the high uneven edge of a hill but Wykeham had yet to mention what they were doing there. With long, unbroken strides he kept on going and they tramped behind, dodging the ragged limbs, their arms already welted and their perplexed sweating faces smeared with the blood of small scratches.

Far below him George Tennison heard what he guessed was the river. We're high up, he thought and wondered whether he'd break his neck scrambling around in the darkness when evening came for good or they walked, as Wykeham showed every intention of doing, straight up at the stars. 'Even then more likely than not,' he mumbled under his breath, 'he'll just keep on going.' But at the top they came to a clearing. Wykeham waited at its edge.

414

'There,' he said, pointing, though there was nothing in particular to see.

The wood merely came to a halt, leaving a rough circle nearly a hundred feet across. The undergrowth had stopped with the trees. There were a few blue flowers, of the sort without many roots that grow anywhere, and a crop of leprous white toadstools that grow only from decaying timbers. Otherwise the clearing was empty and flat. A tunnel of glowing light opened above it.

'Set the lanterns alight,' Wykeham told them, 'and later we needn't be bothered.' He took a lantern himself, turned a knob at its base until the wick swelled with vapor. When it began to flicker, he put the lantern aside, his face looking curiously pleased in the fog of yellow light, and walking beyond the edge, began scraping the side of his boot in the rags of weed. Underneath there were boards.

'Pull up the planking,' he said. 'But be careful.'

None of the planks was nailed and the wood, long out in the weather, was soft. It shifted easily and though it creaked, nothing staved in. Gradually the sky darkened. The last hour they laboured on in the shine of the lanterns. We must look like a crew of devils, George Tennison thought, opening a pit. He could see the immense hollowness growing under him, the steep earthen sides falling into a blackness too dark to be reached by the lanterns.

'This a barn cellar?' he asked the man working next to him.

Adam France shrugged his shoulders. 'Christ if I know. But it's deep.'

'Why would any one put a barn so far from the house?' George Tennison wondered. Not that it mattered. Almost despite himself, he was beginning to enjoy the work. It was actually quite an adventure, he decided. He imagined coming back in the small hours to the boarding-house where Mrs. Tennison would be waiting for him. She would badger him with questions. 'Woman,' he saw himself answering, 'he's a mad-man certain.' Then he would count out the pile of guineas, letting each clink in the darkness on the dresser. He was astonished and disappointed when the last board came up.

'That will do,' Wykeham said, in a voice which seemed to say, Now off with you, the rest is my business only. But the Bristol men lingered about at the edge. Adam France was reaching down with a lantern.

'It smells like an open grave,' Sam said.

'Much you would know of that,' George Tennison answered.

'Take the lanterns,' Wykeham said. And they did that.

*   *   *

George Tennison stood in the doorway of the stable watching his fellows walking away down the drive. He waved and got a wave back but the darkness took them and the wind muttered and he lost the sounds of their shoes on the gravel. He ambled around out in front and peered in at the door. A light had been clicked on and he could make out a large center room.

The stables had been divided. The left side, beyond the tackroom, disappeared down an aisle of wooden half doors behind which the beasts paced warily. To the right the stalls had been dismantled and the flooring replaced with paving stones. At the far end the huge black shapes of several very elegant, very old automobiles, now dull with dust, waited uselessly on blocks. It had been nearly forty years since George Tennison had seen the like of them.

With a stab of memory he recalled the busy streets of Bristol. Sitting on the curb in the heart of the market, his eyes filled with envy, he had watched the great cars pass. He had discovered then, for the first time, how bitter the part was he had been given to play in the world. As if no time had passed, with the same deep humiliation, he felt again his smallness and swore.

At last there was a click of a latch, a clop of hooves. For an instant the light behind him was blotted out by a shadow. Through the dim opening Wykeham came forth leading a mare.

'Hold the reins,' he said.

'And mine?' George Tennison wondered, stepping aside awkwardly, for the mare was huge. 'Surely for myself, a gentler . . .'

Already the mare was beginning to dance. Wykeham grinned. 'Going out you will sit up beside me,' he said. 'But watch me carefully, for you will be riding her back.' He laid his hand on the horn of the saddle, then finding the stirrup, hauled himself up. 'I will have your hand,' he said.

George Tennison made a tentative protest; but strong fingers closed on his wrist. All at once his thin legs were straddling the mare's wide back.

'You do remember the way out by the roads?'

'I expect so,' George Tennison answered. 'I walked them.'

For a moment or two the mare trotted agreeably along the dark drive. But then Wykeham prodded her side and with alarming speed she bolted into the wood.

For all George Tennison knew the mare might have leapt into pure darkness. A menace of shadows surged past his head. He could hear the thudding hooves, each jolting step shaking him clear to the bone. He grabbed hold of Wykeham's waist. The young man laughed.

When George Tennison opened his eyes again, the mare was trotting easily under the trees; the old trunks were distinct and separate against the sky's shining blackness. The metal of the bridle, even the leaves of the trees seemed as lustrous as mirrors. The older man drew a breath. Between the branches, halfway out to the stars a flight of swans rose like an arrow aimed at the moon.

'This is South Wood,' Wykeham told him solemnly but the man heard the note of eagerness beneath. Wykeham shook the reins gently. 'The tree-cutters have been busy here,' he said. 'Yet their work comes to nothing.'

They rode through the wood. Although he could only see the back of the younger man's head, George Tennison imagined he was smiling. The mare lifted her neck.

A long time after, or perhaps a short time, he never knew which, George Tennison realized that they were close to the village. Soon he saw the houses, snug behind their fences, and the top of the green and he remembered that he had not asked where they were going.

'It is not far to the station,' Wykeham announced all at once. 'You will leave me there. You might,' he added, 'tie the mare up for the night wherever it is you are staying. You could ride her out to the house, if you wished, after breakfast.'

George Tennison hesitated but then in his mind's eye he saw Mrs. Tennison peering out from the window into the morning, watching him climb like a jockey onto the back of the mare. 'I would like that,' he said, suddenly grinning himself.

'Where are the men?' the stationmaster asked him.

'I have sent them to their beds. Well you might go yourself.'

'I have stayed to help.'

'You look tired,' Wykeham said. But the stationmaster insisted on walking with him into the yard where the stable car waited on the siding. Nevertheless he found he needed to lean on a post or a gate, if only for a moment, holding his weary head nearly upright in the cradle of his arms.

The stationmaster awoke as the two A.M. train was pulling out of the station. The wind had dropped. An odd scent filled his nostrils. When he tried the doors of the car he found they were unbolted. He swung them open and poked in with his lamp. Its yellow beam ran along the floor and over the sides of the huge empty stall. His nostrils twitched, smelling the thick, unmistakable scent of oak-wood.

CHAPTER FOUR

'A tree?'

'At the crown of East Wood,' Longford continued, pushing his cup away from him and into the assortment of abandoned luncheon dishes. 'Up from the house,' he said, 'in the direct line of sight to the river.'

Plum saw his disappointment. 'Are you certain?' she asked.

'I have made the measurements a good half dozen times,' he snapped, unaccustomedly cross with her for having doubted him. Plum folded her napkin. Her instincts told her to let it be. There had been no talk yet. She reached for the cup, seeking to touch what he had touched and restore whatever connection had broken. The mild brown liquid slopped unexpectedly over the rim. She watched the stain spread through the tablecloth and thought with gathering irritation, He might at least have drunk a little.

'But if it wasn't there yesterday,' she complained.

'But it was,' he persisted, 'this morning.' Indeed it had very much been there. He had come up the drive, having started out early to have his little chat with Wykeham, to invite him to dinner (after all, the young man was his ward and there were things to be settled), to mention, in passing, the matter of a few old trees he wanted cleared from the wood. As he had let his gaze drift over the familiar line of the foliage, he had seen the shocking new growth, brash in the sunlight, like an enemy standard raised overnight on the hill. He had still not gotten over his surprise or his anguish. Only yesterday there had been nothing but gaunt, dying trees. He had banged on the door. No one answered and he had tacked up a scribbled note on an envelope letting Wykeham know in the firmest possible way that he was expected at the parsonage at seven. On the way back toward the village he had met a man leading a mare. It was his habit to smile even at strangers, but he had trudged on past George Tennison sullenly, without looking up.

The box was surprisingly heavy yet the old man continued to lift it. For much the same reason once a week he limped into the village for whisky. To do less, even by the smallest measure, would be to admit finally that he had grown too old. He removed the box from the corner, sliding it first with the combined efforts of his feet and hands. It was a pretty box, he had always thought, compounded of a great many layers of lacquered wood and fitted with a pair of heavy brass hinges. For several minutes it rested on the seat of the chair. When his heart had stopped pounding and the whiteness had gone from before his eyes, he lifted the box onto the table. He would not let the woman help him. Not yet, he thought with sly cunning. The woman squeezed next to him; he could see her bosom rise and fall with expectation. He was not altogether certain he approved. Angels, he had been taught, were, or at least ought to be, sexless.

Nora reached for the lid.

'There is a lock,' Chance said. He began to fumble in his pockets. Though it was difficult with her standing so close to him, he avoided her touch. He was still not frightened. But with Death's Angel come into the house, he would have to be careful.

Nora was happily unaware of his mistrust. Since Plum had brought her to his cottage, she had simply been waiting for whatever would happen next. She had not bothered to listen when the two had spoken. She may have wondered where she was but the sound of the wind, filling the tree-tops, reminded her of the great tidal race at Bodø, and the sound had dis-tracted her. Nora had not followed when Plum made her way to the door. No other words had been spoken. The old man spent the night sitting out on his step; she had slept, without dreaming, in his bed. When she awoke she had made him breakfast which, since he refused it, she had eaten cheer-fully. She hadn't the slightest idea what to do afterward. She had been sitting on the stool and humming when Chance came in the door.

'You'll not find me any easier prey than you've found him,' Chance warned her.

Nora caught a glimpse of her face in the window glass and wondered at the wicked flush on her cheeks. The morning was warm. Breathing in the tingly scent of her own damp skin, she unbuttoned her blouse.

'Found who?' she asked, watching her reflection. The fabric of the blouse still clung to her. She wriggled and dug behind her back. Because he was only an old man and it scarcely mattered, she unfastened her brassiere.

'He you have chased forever,' he said. 'Though you ain't got him.' He began to feel braver. 'Nor is it likely you would.'

She looked at him doubtfully.

'Could you tell me what you mean?' she said.

His gnomish smile widened; for he saw this as proof of his toughness. 'Oh, better than that. I can show you!'

It was then he had gone for the box.

'Sixty – seventy years ago I made the drawing,' he was saying as he placed the key in the lock. He pulled the lid open. 'I was a lad myself then, running where he ran and near as fast if I'm not mistaken. Galloping off after hares in the wood. Chasing foxes in and out of barns . . . and houses that ain't houses anymore, weren't houses then to tell the truth, just big old cellar holes.' He put in his hand, touching the paper deep inside.

Watching his face, Nora had a sudden premonition. With that part of her mind that had always taken the pieces of her life and rearranged them until, however wayward, they seemed to fit into a single urgent tale, she thought: So my father would have mourned his youth. It did not matter that she had never known her father; she found the old man comforting. She glanced about the tiny cottage that was bedroom and kitchen and remembered the little room in Bodø and the ghost of the father who was not dead but gone. She would be glad of this old man's company. She would not let it matter that he did not care for her own. So Eve smiled, discovering her will was stronger, that it could change the face of paradise. With just such a smile, Nora took the faded paper from the old man's fingers.

'He wasn't pleased,' Chance said. He crouched in front of her, trembling and holding himself upright with the butt of his stick. 'Not one bit pleased when I told him I had done it. Hated the idea of anyone making pictures of him.' Chance looked at her craftily. 'But I kept it anyway. And he knows I have it. Told the same to Longford when he came around trying to chase me off. He won't send me packing, I told him.'

There was a little twitch of a smile, a pause while he stretched out his arm excitedly and pointed. 'See for yourself,' he said. 'Not a line changed!' He waited but she did not answer. 'You do see?' he had cried at her.

But Nora kept her mouth shut. It was already too late to cover her breasts with the paper. She had simply stepped back. Wykeham stood in the doorway. He did not move but then he did not have to to make her heart beat faster. Not that she minded. But she wondered how long he had been standing there, dressed in his old man's coat, watching her nakedness.

It was fairly late, past eight-thirty, when Wykeham knocked on the door of the parsonage. Longford, who had fallen asleep in his reading chair, now stood bewildered in the middle of the front room. It was

Plum who had gone to the door. Wykeham waited on the step. He was holding an envelope in his large fingers. Plum glared at him suspiciously.

'Forgive me,' Wykeham said. 'I do hope the dinner is not ruined.' Before she had found the courage to answer, he walked past her into the hall. She hurried after, pausing to relight a lamp on a table outside the kitchen. At last he turned so that she could see the side of his face. The features were strong and roughly handsome. Except for the way the wind had tousled his dark hair, he did not look like a boy.

'It was only that I just found the note,' he said in a voice blameless and contrite by turns. She was aware of his slow smile. She was not deceived. She thought, Something has happened.

Longford put aside the book and came forward.

Wykeham waved the note in front of him. 'I am sorry if there has been any inconvenience.'

'Quite all right,' Longford said. 'My mistake probably.' He showed Wykeham into the parlor. There was a brief silence. 'You have already met Mrs. Longford, I believe,' he said formally.

Wykeham smiled. 'Yes. Yesterday, very early.'

Longford's lower lip turned ever so slightly as Wykeham took a seat in the upholstered chair where Longford himself had been reading. There was a longer silence. Longford blundered about the room. Settling at last on the edge of a sofa he had never liked, he crossed his legs uncomfortably. Plum remained standing.

'It was kind of you,' Wykeham said to her, 'to make a start on the kitchen. It needed a woman. The workmen, I am afraid, left quite a shambles.'

'Men do,' she said, watching him. So far she had told her husband nothing of her visit to Greenchurch. Tim had not even remarked on it, when after the service he had come back to the parsonage and found her already home and furiously cleaning her own kitchen. He had merely welcomed the sight of her in her apron.

'But as you say,' Plum continued, 'it was only a start.'

'But a beginning has been made,' Wykeham said cheerfully. 'And I am grateful.'

Longford uncrossed his long legs. He had completely forgotten to look for a housekeeper. It was this awful business about the trees. He thought, At least he's come and we can get that settled. But he was impatient with himself because he had not remembered.

'Tomorrow,' Longford said apologetically, a little taken aback by the petulance in his voice. 'There are women in the village who would be glad of the work.' He turned to his wife. 'What would you say, dear,' he asked her, 'to Mrs. Hunt?' Strangely he could not read her face. 'Or Mrs. Norfolk?' he suggested more tentatively.

'That will not be necessary,' Wykeham interrupted.

Plum's eyes were suddenly on his. Her color deepened.

'But I insist,' Longford rumbled. 'After all, I had promised.'

'You needn't have,' Wykeham said. 'Quite by chance I have managed to find someone myself.' .

After dinner, while the men were still seated and Plum was out of the room, Longford put the question directly.

'What exactly do you know about this woman?' he asked.

'Do either of you want tea?' Plum inquired from the kitchen where she had seemed for a time unusually quiet. Longford murmured noncommittally.

'Yes,' Wykeham said. 'Thank you.'

They both heard the water spilling from the tap. With noisy efficiency Plum seemed to be clearing away, washing up and brewing the tea all at once. What's got into her? Longford wondered. He glanced at the open doorway as her shadow passed. After several minutes Plum came in with a tray.

'Nearly forty,' Longford was saying. 'I daresay that seems a safe age in a woman.' But noticing the look on Plum's face, he added charitably: 'Of course age is merely a state of mind.'

Rewarded with a smile, he turned again to Wykeham. 'Certainly,' he said, 'you wouldn't object if Mrs. Longford were to call on her.' He looked to see Wykeham's reaction and added, although nothing more was needed: 'Certain little formalities. You can well understand.' Well satisfied with himself, he stood for a long moment in the middle of the room, smiling. Out of the corner of his eye Wykeham saw Plum look hastily away.

They carried their tea into the parlor.

The furniture, in large measure, had come with the parsonage. Except for a chair or two and a photograph of Longford's father, looking very much like Longford himself, the furnishings were in fact Wykeham's, having come down with the estate and passed along with the pulpit, for temporary use, from one minister to the next. There were pieces from a half dozen periods, English and Dutch, pieces elegant and droll, austere and operatic. Wykeham sank willingly into the stiff, horsehair sofa Longford loathed and seemed, Plum thought, almost immediately pleased with it. He balanced his cup on his knees in a way that made her think of an Oxford dandy. Yet, with his big hands and square shoulders, he would not have appeared out of place among the laborers her husband had hired on his behalf. Indeed, she imagined he was skillful at things that they were and her husband was not.

Plum glanced across the room at her husband. The questions about Wykeham's schooling and travels had been exhausted insofar as Longford had patience to ask or to listen. Wykeham had already promised twice to vist Black Wood and pay a call on John Chance. Tim ran his blunt fingers along the spine of his book. She saw he was preparing himself and wished somehow she were sitting next to him and could slip her hand into his. Then he could ask what he liked. Yet she blamed herself for having argued with him earlier. Nevertheless she dreaded the question. Only the strength of her deep affection kept her quiet.

Longford arched his wide brows. 'I have the distinct impression,' he said, beginning already well into his argument, 'that there is a new tree in East Wood.'

Wykeham waited.

'Undoubtedly it isn't the sort of thing you would likely have noticed?'

Slowly Wykeham finished his tea. He glanced at Plum before he set his cup aside. Finally, he shook his head.

'I didn't think you would,' said Longford, disappointed. 'Though I can assure you it is there now and wasn't yesterday.'

There was a pause. Plum had such a strong sense of impending disaster she nearly stood. She was looking for an excuse to mention the hour, to remind Wykeham that he ought to be going. She was even willing, somewhat contradictorily, to offer more tea though she knew perfectly well none was wanted.

'You can imagine, I hope, my astonishment,' Longford was saying. 'I have paid extraordinary attention to the trees in East Wood. There are one or two matters about them I had planned to discuss with you. Trivial, some might think. But from my own point of view I should say they were most important.' His handsome face tightened with seriousness. Plum saw him about to plunge once again along a path the young man, not knowing him, could not have expected to follow. She wished Wykeham were the gentleman she was now fairly certain he was not. Then he might have succeeded, where she admitted only failure, in diverting him.

'A tree?' Wykeham showed no expression but Plum knew very well he goaded him.

Longford nodded. 'Precisely,' he said. 'A tree where no tree had been.'

His voice made an eager, quivering sound, not at all like a clergyman's.

The curtains stirred dully in back of him. Plum could hear the whisper of the cloth as clearly as if it were the sly whisper of women in the parish hall. A half dozen churches in a dozen years. A sadness fell on her. During their last months in Maryland, as elsewhere, there had been talk. She was prepared as well for silence. But Wykeham turned his head.

'How did you first come to notice it?' he asked, without a trace of irony.

Longford thought the question over. 'It is easy enough to see,' he said at last. 'But the reason I saw it, I believe, was that I so thoroughly hadn't expected it to be there.' He drew a breath and eased himself up in the chair. 'For a week,' he said, 'whenever I went out to Greenchurch, I had watched that little bit of wood. I was waiting to see, when the trees came to leaf, which wouldn't bloom and were dead timber. You see I wanted your permission, a favor to some studies I am pursuing, to cut a few branches, maybe a tree or two, so I could get a clearer view from the house to the river.'

Longford leaned a little nearer. 'You, William, would not have minded. It was old wood and scarcely a leaf . . .' He remembered the top of the hill. There had been a view over great stretches of bare limbs and, in patches, the pearly mist of the river. 'It would not have done much damage,' he said. 'Dead wood and dying. I know, I am pleased to think, every inch of the timber. I had picked out the trees.' Though he had just got himself going, he made himself stop. The night air moved the curtain. He was trying not to think of his wife, who was sitting very still, watching him.

'It's in this book,' Longford said because suddenly he was beginning to discover that he had not the words for the turning of his own thought. 'One of the two books,' he said after a moment, 'you were kind enough to bring up from New Awanux. You didn't by any chance happen to look through it?'

'No.'

'Well, it's in here,' Longford said. 'Not the whole thing of course. I've seen the clues myself, followed them in fact for some time, until, quite independently, they led me here. Really the book is no more than the confirmation of my own work.' He leaned farther out and gave the small volume to Wykeham. He waited while Wykeham folded back the front cover. There was the same plate of a naked Indian Wykeham had seen in the shop on Abbey Street. On an inside page he found the title: *The Celt and the Red Man: A Preliminary Discourse on the Old Welsh*

Origins of the Algonquin Language. The book had been published in Boston in the middle of the last century. Wykeham turned past the table of contents. 'Proofs,' the author began, 'must not be arguments, but testimonies.'

Longford cleared his throat.

'I believe,' he said rapidly, 'that the first Indians, the true Indians, were Welsh.' He forced himself to smile. 'If you know how to look, everything points to it. Though I do sometimes wish I were an etymologist.' Indeed it annoyed him that he could pronounce a mere fraction of the words whose embedded sources and branching histories he had followed in his reading. He suspected, because he had not mastered the sounds, that some meaning always eluded him. 'Yet I haven't done badly,' he said. 'I have made astounding progress, especially in the relationship between topography and language. And yet,' he said, 'if only one had other lives. Time to pursue things thoroughly. Haven't you wished that yourself?'

'I thought they were Chinamen,' Wykeham said.

'Oh they were,' Longford answered. 'Yes. Very definitely. Beyond dispute. But later.' Suddenly he looked very grave. 'It all sounds, I know, William, quite foolish. But it fits. Not perfectly by any means; but a sight better than any other explanation I've heard of. For one thing there are dolmens. Right here in the village. In Devon. Huge upright stones and root cellars. Though of course they aren't root cellars at all. And writing on the bare rock! Not simple pictographs but whole stanzas: battles and eulogies, clear facts of history. In deep-cut Ogham letters!' An effervescence of spirit had filled him. He leaned forward as though catching the breeze from the window. Plum, for once, gazed at him without pity.

'I know,' Longford said. 'Certainly, I know what you think.' But his look implored Wykeham not to judge him too quickly. 'I can show you the proof,' he admonished him. 'And not only in the stones and cellars of the village.'

Looking away, Wykeham began to explore the pages of the book. There were drawings of boulders cradled on smaller stones and drawings of Indian sachems, spear-armed, alone by a pool in a wood or surrounded by archers, Indians kneeling before altars or standing under the open sky on the bluffs at Ohomowauke. But for the most part there were drawings of letters, plate after plate of Ogham nicks and scratches, cut on squared stone or wooden billets, the English translations marching sensibly along underneath.

'Stones can be forgeries,' Longford said. 'I'm the first to admit that. The farmers who first settled here were learned men, university men not a few of them, reading Phoenician and writing Greek.'

Plum was looking out the window. On the far side, across the darkened green, the lights were burning in Charon Hunt's garage. She could make out a knot of men standing there. It was difficult to see their faces but their figures, in the illumination of the garage lamps, had a dramatic and furtive quality. Hunt himself had seldom been anything but polite to her. But Plum had always had the impression, even when he wasn't, that he was scowling. He was a large man, strong and angular, of no certain age. He had masses of deep red hair crowding low on his forehead. It was not exactly that she objected to the man's coloring. Yet neither was it entirely unrelated, she reflected, to the brashness and anger she sensed was inside him. He had as well, she knew, a habit of appearing where he was least expected, like the morning she had watched him speeding recklessly down the winding drive from Greenchurch, too preoccupied or too guilty to wave. The breeze touched her face and she sighed, wondering for the moment less about her husband than what Charon Hunt and his cronies were up to. She was all but certain they were up to no good.

Wykeham's gray-black eyes held no hint of amusement.

Longford was explaining how the river, along the stretch that included both Ohomowauke and Devon, described, as though by a conscious act of will, an almost perfect letter 'S.' 'Except,' he said, 'to my mind it isn't properly an "S" at all. At least not any longer. You see I'm rather persuaded that over the last half century or so it's been changing.'

He stood up. 'I have,' he said, 'if you care to have a look, some drawings of my own.' He went to his desk and pulled open the drawer. He was glad that Plum was there. He hadn't, so far, explained this to anyone, not in any great detail. It was time she heard it fully. He spread a large wrinkled paper on the desk top.

'Come along, William,' he said. He looked back at his wife. Wykeham and Plum joined him silently.

Longford smoothed the paper with the side of his hand.

The map, to Plum's embarrassment, looked like a drawing for children. Devon and Ohomowauke were marked clearly enough, as were the greater towns and cities to the south, but not with the orthodox cartographer's symbols. For Bristol Longford had sketched a ridiculous frowning clockface and for Ohomowauke an owl made of flowers.

Devon itself was a ring on nine towers, black on the land, and quite a bit larger than the size of the village seemed to warrant. Presumably the wavy lines meandering among them represented the river. There were too many lines, however, and they wandered confusedly. Longford traced a set of lines with his finger.

'This is the old river,' he said, 'the river one can still see on the government maps of the region. Oddly, the surveyors weren't that far off. Quite surprising given their equipment. Less than a few meters error at any one point.' He traced the lines again, his finger following a gentler curve which tracked north from Bristol, bent around Ohomowauke, then south until in a sinuous line, leaving Devon, it swung north once more along the far western edge. 'But you would expect,' he added significantly, 'at least I did, a common error.' He paused. 'Well, there isn't.' He gave a furtive glance at Wykeham, then turned again to the map. 'Actually,' he said, 'the error changes rather wildly.'

Wykeham examined the lines carefully. 'So you assumed,' Wykeham said, 'that the error was common – because it should have been – and figured the difference.'

'Yes.' Longford looked startled. 'Yes, of course.' For the first time he broke into a grin. 'Though, to tell the truth, I had some sleepless nights before it occurred to me.'

'And the true measurement?'

Longford went on grinning. Indeed he couldn't help feeling flattered by the way Wykeham put it. 'Yes,' he said, pleased, 'I have made, I think, a number of rather exact measurements.'

Conscious of disloyalty, Plum turned again to the paper and found, even against her better judgment, her attention attracted to the largest of the nine towers scratched on the hillsides of Devon.

'The channel is straightening,' her husband was saying. 'The bends, I believe, have sharpened.'

She bent over to examine the drawings more closely. At the base of the tower there was a sort of absurd scribble which she suspected must have been meant to be thorns. What an odd thing, she thought.

'All I need,' Longford continued, 'is the final measurement.'

'Which is from Greenchurch?' Wykeham asked. 'From my hilltop?'
Longford nodded.

'For which you wish my permission to cut down not only the old trees but the inconvenient new one.'

'Tim,' Plum said, not listening, her eyes riveted on a small dark square hidden among the crosshatch of lines which suggested the stonework at the top of the tower. It was hardly more than a blot, with just a fleck or two of white highlights. Yet there was a feeling of delicate roundness and a suggestion . . . though it was silly. 'Tim,' she asked, not aware she was interrupting him, her voice raised more than was necessary.

'What's this square?' she asked, pointing down at the tower.

He did not look. 'Tell you later,' he said for he was eager to hear Wykeham's answer.

She pressed her thumb on the undecipherable blur of lines. 'Tell me *now*.'

He looked straight at her and then at the paper. Half in anger, he smiled.

'Just a window,' he said quickly, solicitously, already looking back at Wykeham.

'I guessed that. But who is inside looking out?'

'Who?'

'Obviously there is someone. A face.' But she saw all at once that he did not see it, that she was being foolish. It was only a blot. It was astonishing how much she read into things. She lifted her head. In a moment she was able to laugh at herself. She was thankful at least she hadn't actually mentioned she had thought that the face was Nora's.

Wykeham, who had pretended not to hear, studied the paper. He kept his square shoulders turned, excluding Plum. But even from the back she thought he looked preoccupied and ill at ease.

'This figure,' he said, addressing himself to Longford, 'the one the river is changing to.'

Longford pointed to the lines again, ran his hands sharply in the air just above them. 'Of course I cannot be positive,' he said. 'Not without the last measurement. But I believe it's a "W" or will be when the banks have all straightened. And here.' He pulled the map edgewise so that Wykeham might have a clearer view of it. 'I don't suppose it means much of anything. Though it is curious. Having found one letter, as it were, staring out of the earth. Perhaps your eye just plays tricks.' His finger rested on a little slip of a lake, south of East Wood. The lake, probably no more than a large pond, was curved like the paring of a fingernail. 'Of course the scale is different,' he said. 'But they're both water and from a certain distance, seen from the air, or on a map . . .'

Wykeham shook his head, either in disapproval or annoyance. There was a silence.

'It's a "C," isn't it?' Plum asked. Longford beamed.

'It is pronounced "ku," ' Wykeham told her softly. He had

straightened his back. His face, now that Plum saw it, looked odd. She had noticed it before, a hardness in him which showed itself only now and then, but which somehow seemed more like him than his smile.

'I didn't quite . . .,' Longford began.

' "Cw",' Wykeham said quietly. 'Pronounced "ku." It is the question asked by cuckoos and owls in the old Triads; the first question that poets must master since there is no definite answer. It means "where?" ' He took his outsized hands from his pockets. 'I am surprised you did not come across it in your reading,' he said, 'for it is Welsh.'

Plum could tell from his voice he was leaving. 'I shall think about the tree,' he said in a way that ended the conversation. He shook hands with Longford, who, because he did not quite know what to think said nothing. Wykeham left him standing awkwardly by the desk. 'Thank you again,' Wykeham called back. Plum went beside him to the door and opened it.

The lamps of Hunt's garage had been switched off. The green and the surrounding houses seemed strangely malevolent. She was still holding onto the latch. She hadn't realized, until then, she was shivering.

Wykeham tilted his head.

'She wished me to ask,' he said in a voice serious and not unkind, 'whether you had managed to send her letter.'

Plum wanted to cry out. But he had taken her hand. Her fingers which were not dainty or small seemed lost in the strength of his grasp and, although she had promised herself she would not answer, she nodded.

CHAPTER FIVE

Like Luther, His Grace thought, consoling himself, remembering that even the mighty theologian had suffered from the same disorder of the bowels. Humbled, he had endured the ailment more or less stoically. He refused to see his physician. He had his port and ate normally. Work generally set him to rights. With the beginning of each new week, within an hour after he had returned to his desk he felt a pressure building in his lower intestine. Then, with a gratifying urgency, he would head for the lavatory. This arrangement worked perfectly well. His Grace saw nothing greatly amiss. He had not fully considered, however, until it was already too late the effect of retirement on his bowels.

The corners of the Duke's mouth pulled down sullenly. In his house across from the park he had been sitting for a quarter of an hour, counting the diamond-shaped tiles on the lavatory floor. He had been trying to determine, without actually looking, the exact number of tiles hidden beneath a Chinese vanity. He had no particular reason for wanting to know this yet he had brought a small collapsible desk in with him. Already he had covered half a page with figures. Down below a young man from the bank began to knock on the thick, paneled door. The Duke, his head filled with calculations, took no notice.

The telegram announcing Houseman's death arrived at the bank some hours before dawn on Sunday morning. It had been received by the watchman, who, because there was no one to relieve him, had waited until the next man came on duty before taking a cab to the apartment of the senior clerk. By then it was nearly seven-thirty. The old clerk, although he had opposed Houseman's appointment, had been honestly shocked. He had seen to many of the arrangements himself and met the train bearing the body. He had even, after he had informed the chief partners, gone to visit the young man's family. Gently he had broken the news to the disbelieving parents. Houseman had always been neatly if somewhat inexpensively dressed so the senior clerk had been wholly unprepared for the deep poverty of the parents' quarters. The mother, a large, nervous woman, wept profoundly and had held onto his arm as though she had feared that he too, a stranger, might be taken from her. Putting aside his reservations, he had told her how fond everyone had been of her son.

It was left to the partners to inform His Grace. They conferred in the middle of the day. It had been scarcely two days since they had been lifted unto the top rung of power and not, they were uncomfortably aware, by any skill of their own but by the Duke's climbing down. Nevertheless they considered for several hours the consequences of withholding the news from him. They were not without certain grievances. By rights, a young man from one of their own departments should have been appointed master of the Will instead of Houseman. They had had, of course, their own schemes for getting around him, by taking a subtle control of the Wykeham trusts until for practical purposes they would rule them. Accordingly, although it had dramatically cleared the way, they had little enthusiasm for Houseman's death. They could not be certain who would be appointed next. Unsettled, they debated for some time the merits of installing, temporarily, a man of their own.

'It isn't a question of one being better than another,' the first partner said, 'I daresay, the issue is who Wykeham is most likely to accept.'

'Which leaves us,' the second partner said, 'with His Grace.'

'The Duke has taken his retirement.'

'Nor would I have him. I was thinking of him simply as an intermediary.'

'Yet surely, as soon as he had one foot in the door again . . .'

'We could see to it that the door was shut.'

'And if Wykeham wanted him?'

The second partner grinned. 'It was Wykeham who sacked him. Too old, that's my guess. I think you will find, gentlemen, that we shall be fairly safe on that quarter.'

The talk turned to other matters. On Monday, two hours after the bank had opened, a junior clerk, because this business should not be made to appear too important, rapped apprehensively on the door of the Duke's house. The butler left him on the landing where he waited, blinking unfamiliarly at prints of old-fashioned gentlemen dressed for hunting. The Duke emerged presently, engulfed in a roseate dressing gown. His face appeared similarly colored as though he had been engaged in some strenuous and, seemingly, unsuccessful labor.

'Your Grace,' the clerk squeaked, 'I bring dreadful news.'

The ponderous brass gate opened. Within, the Duke pressed the elevator car's single button and heard, as though he had never been gone, the magical whine of its motors. Deus ex machina, the Duke thought mockingly but without embarrassment. The gentle lights fluttered, reflected on the walls of rubbed mahogany. It was then, reminded of opulence, that His Grace first realized that the world had been unfair to Arthur Houseman.

It was not the sort of thing which would ordinarily have troubled him. The death of a man, particularly a young man without accomplishments, while saddening, was not an event likely to be much remembered. Yet he had picked this one man out, though few had seen the worth in him. With disturbing clarity the Duke remembered the look on Houseman's face just as Wykeham sat down beside him. Houseman's face had had a look of extraordinary anticipation, a look which the Duke had resented bitterly until something of its eagerness had reminded him of himself. The lines of his own lips hardened. As well I had violated the prohibition, the Duke thought, had gone to the station, although the Will required there be no second meeting. He was acutely aware that he had entered by chance a world whose dangers he did not and, despite his skills, might never understand. After two days' absence the Duke stepped again into his office. Through the huge windows he looked out once more on the great tangled city of New Awanux.

It pleased him to stand again at the center, with the accumulating wealth of the Wykeham trusts passing through his fingers. In this place he had been a lord in fact as well as title, able at his word to send from the docks of Cardiff a fleet of colliers into the Severn fogs or by the mere scratch of his name to swell or shrink, as the times demanded, the crews of men who worked the forges and the precision shops in Bristol.

The brash sunlight glinted on the steeple of the center church. Without quite being able to chart the progress of his thoughts the Duke found himself wondering how it was that Wykeham, who might have ruled all this and more beyond imagining had with no agitation, no perceptible reluctance or doubt, left these matters in his charge instead. With an amazement which over the last days had only heightened, he wondered what Wykeham, his one life stretching out, might do if he wished. Or what he might have done!

There was a rattle of the gate behind him.

The partners walked in briskly. As they came into the room they saw the tall old lord by the window. They stood still and waited. From their places they had an almost equal view of New Awanux yet they failed to notice either the color of the sky or the pillars of smoke rising starkly from the mills. They looked instead at each other.

'Your Grace,' the chief partner said, 'it is a bitter day for all of us.'

'Please have a seat,' the Duke said, his tone gracious, as though the office were still his own.

They sat opposite him, saying what is always said of sorrow and disrupted lives. Leisurely, and yet sooner than perhaps was fitting, the talk turned from death. They began to explain what they had planned for him, its temporary nature, its obvious usefulness to the bank. The Duke settled himself in his chair. His head was tilted ever so slightly so that he could keep watch out the window. Only half listening, he gazed across the rows of buildings as though face to face with a mystery. Even from this height, he could see no definite pattern. Grumbling, he put on his glasses. To the younger men he looked suddenly older.

'It need only be for a day or two,' the second partner said. 'Time enough for an exchange of letters. We have a list of candidates. You might, nonetheless, suggest whomever you like. Wykeham trusts you. And certainly the board would find any suggestion you would care to make acceptable.'

His Grace was silent. He was trying to imagine the city from the air, to see it whole, but he found his eye dwelling on one detail after another. The partners were staring at him.

He knew an answer was expected; he was trying to think of one when once more the elevator gave a groan. The gate parted and the senior clerk came into the room.

'I beg your pardon,' he said. He nodded to the others. 'Gentlemen.' He had an envelope between his thin fingers. 'It was sent around from your house, Your Grace, and looked important. Of course I recognized the hand.' The clerk set the letter on the desktop. Without waiting the Duke broke open the seal.

The letter was set down in the same small, precise hand he had expected. *I must call you again into service*, it began. For a second or two more His Grace turned in his chair. He seemed somehow heavier. Suddenly he gave a sly glance at the clerk, rose and went from the room.

The partners looked at one another in disbelief.

'I don't suppose you understand any of this,' one said to the clerk.

The clerk was barely a month younger than the Duke and had worked for him for twenty years. He did not quite dare a grin.

Soon after, in a cubicle off the landing, the ancient plumbing roared.

'This will be your room,' Wykeham had told her, pausing outside the door.

'And your own?'

'Above,' he had said, not even smiling. When he had told her she must come with him up to the Great House and stay there, he had already been half out the door of the old man's cottage. She had gone after him, hastening through Black Wood, dazed but untroubled by the ease with which he meant to take her in.

'I have left my husband,' she had said.

He had plunged through the trees. 'It is time you were somewhere,' he had answered.

In the wood it had seemed later but it had still been morning when they had come out on the drive. White moths had fluttered over the dazzling lawn. She had stopped at the edge of the gravel, quiet and at last rebuttoning her blouse. Finally he had looked back. 'Tomorrow, if you like, we shall talk,' he had said. 'Now there are things I must see to. And this evening I must go into the village.'

He had avoided the endless turning of the drive and had led her straight out among the larches and rhododendrons to a place where the ground rose to the top of a knoll. She had made him stop.

'He made a very strange sailor,' she had said, not certain yet, although he was standing close to her, that he was listening. 'For one thing he always carried a bag full of books. Even when we walked in the streets, with the people staring, he read aloud to me. But I didn't care. Sometimes he told me strange things about myself. Foolish things. The first time he saw me he said that I would marry him. He had been to Africa and Marseilles. He was an engineer on a ship named *Anna*. He told me how he sat down with his engines, drinking gin and water and reading through the gales. He had never, he said, looked at a girl until he looked at me.' She stared down at her feet. 'He does not share the blame. It was a cold, little town by the edge of the sea.'

She hesitated.

'Truly, it was a wonderful gift,' she had said. 'But I will never go again to Bodø.'

'One day you may have need of it.'

She had told him then how she had slept in the wood and, meeting Plum, the thing she had given her to mail back to the steamship agent.

He had taken her arm.

The house stood above the great sweep of the lawn. Seeing it for the first time, she had held her breath. But he had been with her and she had not dared, had not wanted to loosen the touch of his hand. He had moved her up the steps, past the tangle of junipers and the thorns, into darkness. When he had closed the wide doors, she had stood perfectly still. She had made herself smile because her hopes had been so much greater than the worst of her dread.

The house was enormous. For a few hours she had been alone in it with him. From the start she had been aware of the quiet. She had gone carefully from room to room, knowing that whenever she heard a board creak or a door pull to, it had been Wykeham. He had said no other word to her and when he had gone into the village, she had simply waited.

The room he had given her had a close, sweetish smell. Nora guessed it had been ages since anyone had slept there. Steeling herself, she poked into corners and knocked on the plaster. There were only cobwebs and silences. But there was slut's wool under the bed and grime on the windows. She had let in the air. A little breeze (here there was always a breeze, she had noticed, either blowing or just about to) made the dusty shutters creak. She discovered bed linen folded on one of the shelves in the closet. In a trunk there were blankets. Nonetheless she did not set to work. Instead she stood at the open window. The trees along the drive obscured the approach to the house. Yet, if she stood there, he would be able to see her when he came up from the gate. The window would shine like a beacon. She need show no sign of her presence. The lamps lit her face. In the light her skin had a gentle radiance. Although she was tired, she held her head proudly. Turned to the proper angle, the line of her neck, she knew, was inviting. That much had not changed.

She felt a strange giddiness. She thought of the long, glowing evenings when she had strolled through the streets of her village. After the bleakness of winter the world then had seemed unbelievably light. The brightness had touched the golden hairs on her neck. Boldly, she had walked under the eyes of the sailors. 'Let us come with you,' they had called to her. But though her heart pounded, she had looked ahead steadily. When they are old men, she had thought joyfully, and I myself am an old woman, they will remember this moment. Yet, when she had come to the end of the pier, she had realized that her beauty must vanish if flushed and out of breath she were forced to climb the street again past them. Gravely she had loosened her dress from her shoulders. When she leapt, it must have appeared to the sailors that she had plunged to her death in the sea.

While they had searched for her, she had scrambled up on the rocks. She had tied a kerchief over her hair and, when the last of the men had gone, had returned by another village to her mother's house. Seeing her, the quiet old woman, abandoned herself by a sailor, had said nothing. When Nora slept she would mend the tears where the dress had caught and torn on the rocks.

Her mother had clear dark eyes, like her own. Once a year, on her birthday, a man from the town would ride out to deliver a letter. Nora would stand by her chair as the old woman tried to decide whether she would open it. The letters from other years lay sealed on a table beside her cot. But always her mother would shake her head. For the briefest moment her eyes would flash with defiance. 'No, child,' she would say this time as she had said the last, 'you are gift enough.'

A door slammed. But there was no tread on the stair. Just the wind.

Nora gathered the bedding. When she had finished, because he had still not come, she climbed up and propped her elbows on the pillow. Staring down at herself, she saw how ludicrously little there was of her and, even beyond the kick of her feet, how much bed. I am as small as this beside him, she thought as if she were the child, passing lightly over the fact that while he had money to give away steamship tickets, he was a boy really and still in school. To her mind he simply did not seem so. He was taller, for one thing, than any man she had known; the directness of his look matched his bearing. Abruptly, without a young man's shyness, presuming an intimacy as though by right, he had reached out his hand to her.

Toward midnight she woke.

She had wriggled out of her skirt. Having no other clothing, she had not switched on the lamp but had found the stair to the upper story by tracing her fingers carefully along the wall. The air was cool on her skin. Somewhere other windows must have been open. She took the steps two at a time. She was excited by the prospect of his finding her, this time deliberately, naked. More immediately, she thought of his bed. She would be warm there, warm, safe and high under the eaves of his house. It was surely the best place to wait for him, the one place he was certain to come. She wondered whether he would be tired or if tramping about in the night would leave him restless. Either would be agreeable, provided he slipped in beside her. She could content herself with touching his hand or, should it please him . . . Nora smiled at the darkness. The door to his room opened with a reassuring sigh.

Wykeham cut across the dark meadow. He took the shortest path, passing quickly among the caretakers' sheds. The roofs had fallen. Vines and tendrils obscured the stones just as thick tufts of grass now grew in the best garden beds. Wykeham grunted without truly noticing. Long ago the roses had turned into lawn. Unconcerned, he vaulted over a wall. There was an open stretch for a hundred yards and then more trees. He ducked under the branches. At last, against the blackness of the hill, he saw the stables. He remembered he had not met the hostler Longford had hired. He knew he ought to check on the mare. He did not permit himself another glance at the house. She would be waiting in any case. He entered the tackroom hurriedly and took a brush from the shelf, disturbed that there was so little time now that he had need of it.

It did not matter that he had other lives. In each he seldom had the use of more than a dozen years. Too soon friends with whom he had no hope of lingering began to notice the remarkable preservation of his changeless face. Sometimes, unwilling to renounce affection, he had stayed. But there is no welcome for an ageless man among grown children and enfeebled wives. Now and then he had invented his own death. More often he had simply turned his back. The longest voyages, to Maui and around the Horn, even under sail, were short to him. Afterward there were other years on land, at Heidelberg, at Oxford twice, at Yale, nights in the crowded libraries and peaceful mornings in the empty lecture halls, brief years among young men who themselves were swiftly gone to other lives. He was well aware such moments were a dream, crammed with the kind of promise which came, by rights, to nothing. He turned aside advice, declined – kindly when he could – offers from old men who, startled by his learning, saw him as the heir to labors that had cost them, without conclusion, half their lives. He knew he was no scholar. He had merely read the books before. Under their tutelage he had begun a thousand things and finished little. When he came back to the old university towns, those men were dead. He went back less often. But the shallow trough of the Housetenuc drew him. Now, after barely fifty years away, still haunted by its miles of squalid woods and low gray hills, he had reentered the valley. I must get on to Devon, he had thought when he had finally set foot again in the harbor. And although for the better part of three years, kept to his studies, he had not gone, it had been the reason he had settled on the college. From his rooms, looking out over the court, there had been a perfect view of the river. Certainly, there had been other reasons. Callaghan, for one, had been getting old and would need to be replaced. Duties had lain ahead of him, as they had each time he moved the trust from one hand to the next. Yet he had waited for this moment, indeed had welcomed it and in much the same way he had welcomed the sight of the unkempt and empty house. It was not a matter of choice. Houseman was dead. Longford, though a fool, was proving less a fool than he should have been. His wife was dangerous. Charon Hunt, despite its evident impossibility, was killing Indians. Wykeham let out a puzzled sigh. He gave a perfunctory pat to the mare's dry rump and wondered, this time, how he would manage.

He closed the door on the stalls and set the latch. Tomorrow he must introduce himself to the hostler. Then too, the roof of John Chance's cottage needed patching. That at least was no great trouble. In the morning he would send George Tennison down with fresh pitch and shingles, a reward for keeping Nora from the wood while Hunt was in it. Wykeham smiled speculatively. He wondered what the old lame bachelor thought of her. It had not been something he would have asked with Nora standing, half unclothed, between them. In his own kitchen he had asked the crow. But he had got no useful answer. He hoped she was pretty. It made no difference that he found her so. His own tastes had been set too long ago. In the markets of Maracaibo or in the streets of Lyme he had too often turned back to stare at women whom the men walking with him, captains of her Majesty's ships and London merchants, found common or, at the very least, unworthy of the effort of looking back. It had helped, of course, that he had seen that face before. In profile there had been no mistaking it. He had not been more than a few moments in her husband's shop when he recognized the tilt of the head, the exquisite line of the neck. He had had no need to ask why she was so far from home. His idea of justice was clear and literal: given sufficient opportunity, all things returned. Life especially came back, even across cold tides and oceans.

He had come up onto the porch and through the massive front doors. It was late; the house was quiet. On the first landing he looked in at Nora's room. The breeze, still pouring in through the small window, had driven off some of the dust and dampness. Even in the shadows he saw that the bed was made and that she had gone from it. He unbuttoned his coat. Knowing more or less what to expect, he climbed the last stairs to his room. She was asleep on his pillow, the edge of her tangled hair curled around her throat. He tried to imagine how she had looked at fifteen or twenty. It did not matter. He was not disappointed.

For a moment he stood silently, unwilling to wake her. Her face had turned toward him, dreaming. Her dark eyes were open. He supposed there was sadness in those eyes but, although there was every right to be, there was no despair. Nora moved suddenly, driving her mouth against the pillow. He knew she could only add to his troubles, now when he had troubles enough. Yet he was comforted. He would protect her if he could.

When she had quieted, he retraced his steps. Reluctantly, the hour pressing him, with too many matters demanding his attention and too little time, Wykeham closed the door nöiselessly, letting his daughter sleep.

PART III

Faces in the Earth

CHAPTER ONE

Dr. Holmes spread the photographs along the examination table in his surgery. The emulsion was still wet and he handled each print with a pair of small forceps. He had drawn up the lamp as he had when he had examined the corpse. Not that he saw much improvement. In the print's glossy surface he could make out little more than his own disappointed reflection. At one corner of the print, caught at the edge, there was a slender filament. Because of the magnification it might have been an eyelash or no more than the grain in the negative. There was honestly no way of knowing. He lay aside his pipe. Smoke no longer curled from the bowl. Muttering, he pushed another photograph under the lamp.

He had had such hopes. When he had set up his camera, Houseman's body had only just begun to stiffen. Such opportunities were in fact rare. He had attended a hundred deaths during the course of his practice. But nearly always there had been family. He had seen to the living. At such times they could not be expected to view his investigations with the detachment of science. Normally, hours later, he had had to prop open the taut lids in the narrow back rooms of morticians' chambers, had to focus his lenses on pupils that had already hardened. By then the image of whatever had held the sight at life's last moments had gone. But there had been no one to mourn Houseman, merely his employer, who, although he had shown a delicate interest, had not interrupted his journey. Peering crossly over his spectacles, Dr. Holmes edged the lamp nearer.

He was the same Dr. Holmes who wrote verses and sketches for *The Atlantic*, the same whimsical sketches and doggerel which in a universe not too far distant had earned him a minor but respected place in American letters. But here (having been born merely a decade, not a century, before the Great War) his writings seemed only quaint, the easy Latinity of his prose an impediment to popular acceptance. Instead he had made his mark as a physician and would be longer remembered as an anatomist.

Nonetheless, the outline of his early life was here not substantially altered. He had been born on the outskirts of Boston and had spent the first years of his manhood on Montgomery Place. After a dozen years of marriage, he removed to Bristol and the house inherited from his maternal great-grandfather. He knew Cornelius Mathews and James T. Fields but not Melville or Hawthorne, although assuredly their places were taken by others. (For in one form or another both are indispensable. A New World cannot be made without them.) Only his later years pulled atom by atom away from his other existence. In this world he would not die in his own bed and his oldest son, with whom he shared his name and many of his sympathies, would never become a supreme court justice. I will not judge which life better suited the man. In either world there had always been some who suspected that beneath the gentle satire of the poems, the strained didacticism of the novels, there was a pure vein of venom. It is certain that here that same bitterness had quietly deepened, had given him an added astringency and, when at last it was required of him, a sterner, more courageous imagination. Whatever the cause, something was changed in him. Perhaps there is no defense against doubt. At least it is not as unusual as it may seem that a man who felt himself nourished by the regard of an intelligent woman, buoyed and uplifted by the affection of able, caring children, devoted his private hours to the study of the possibility that all life, his own included, was without meaning. In any event, he did not dismiss the next photograph although at first glance it appeared much the same as the rest.

He was sitting still, deep in thought. After a while, with a weary swipe of his hand, he pulled the lamp nearer.

There was the same maddening configuration of light and shadow, blots more than squares. Yet the blots, by some as yet unfathomable arrangement, turned in rapid stages into squares. He shook his head. As easily it could have been the other way round, the pattern shifting, turning peevishly, automatically ungeometric. Either interpretation was possible. Between his lips his tobacco-blackened tongue flickered impatiently.

Behind him, from the cramped room that adjoined the surgery, he could hear his wife turning down the covers of the cot. He kept a small bed there, fitted snugly under the shelves of medicines. He could hear his wife humming to herself under the phials of laudanum, the tinctures of nightshade, and frowned. It was a rich practice. There were maids for such work. For that matter he would have done it himself. But Amelia's sense of duty required such small attentions to his comfort. She did not look in. He waited until the door squealed. Amelia's footsteps retreated into the hallway, turning back toward the main house where already the servants were in bed and the children slept. He shrugged his thin shoulders. He was thinking of death.

Taking the matches from his trouser pocket, he relit his pipe. The match flared above the photograph.

For that moment, enhanced by the spurt of flame, it seemed he was staring into a glowing blankness. Patches of light, jarred subtly, seemed suddenly to come loose. Unfixed, they began to squirm. He smiled slightly, fascinated by their curious mobility and yet knowing it could be no more than the temporary effect of the matchhead, that, or, because he was mortally tired, the crackling of the ragged circuitry within his own head. The match burned out and he blinked.

The brightness persisted. He moved and the brightness moved with him. He sat rigid, holding his breath. The brightness continued to fall into place. Squibs of light, turning cunningly among the blots he saw were bluffs and hills, joined link by link. The perception was so clear and definite that he moaned. The air rushed past. Beneath him, suddenly from a great height, he recognized the fiery line of the river.

Its brightness came down from the mountains.

Tipped as from a cauldron, it burned between hills.

He opened his eyes very wide and saw the distant towns, lurid and burning where the river itself was choked with flames. Some instinct made him wish to turn away. But the river blazed ahead of him. Lightly, luringly, at the bridge at Ohomowauke, where the river bent, it broadened, spreading in a widening crack as it reached the levels and wandered south.

He gazed over the earth. Across the southernmost horizon he saw the dismembered channels sunken into hissing silence on the coast. He bit his lip.

And, surprisingly, there was no river. Instead, the brightness suddenly reversed. A darkness – added as the light was added, link by link – changed over to blackness. Blots and shadows fused, became twisted limbs and climbed. He looked down into the maw of branches. Black leaves rushed about his head.

And yet, at the very same instant, he was certain it was still the river. He saw it then even more clearly. The only difference was in how he looked. His sallow cheeks reddened.

It was outrageous. He muttered something to himself. The words were familiar but it was not until he heard his own voice that he remembered where he had heard them.

*　　*　　*

He went in his bare feet to the closet. Old man's legs and old man's feet, he thought, feeling the prickly numbness of his flesh, the chill of the cold floor under his feet. Silence flowed back into the room behind him. Methodically he began to arrange his coat on its hanger. He knew he ought to have slept in the surgery. Yet by the time he had returned Amelia had switched on the lamp.

'I did not mean to imply – ' she started in once more. She was used to him and had no need to listen to guess that he had wasted his time. And yet, seeing him, his bare legs sticking out from under his robe, she added more quietly, 'I fear, Oliver, I do not explain myself well.'

He laid his spectacles on the bureau. Because of the light in the room he could not look out into the garden.

'Forgive me,' she said.

'I have.' He spoke with absolute definiteness. 'I have understood perfectly.'

Once again there was silence.

'You will let me see it?' she asked.

'In the morning.'

He climbed in next to her, bringing the cold in with him.

As calmly as she was able she reached out, taking his hand, waiting for the moment he would grasp her own.

'It is a photograph of the river,' he said. 'Only it is more than the river.'

Deliberately she tightened her hold on his fingers.

'Oliver?'

He went on implacably. 'But it was what the woman said that startled me. That convinced me that at last –'

Her breast rose. 'A woman?'

'On the train.' Then finally he had to look at her.

All at once she understood that something had happened. Until that moment she had not honestly noticed.

She watched him carefully. 'She told you something.'

'It was the dead man really. She was simply repeating it.' Suddenly he pulled away. Both his hands were free and he thrust them alongside his temples and into his hair.

She had made her voice soft. 'Can it matter?' she asked.

The house was silent.

But now, when he opened his hands and she could look again into his eyes, she was frightened.

*   *   *

However inimical, the pattern had to be the same. He understood this, even though he was quite as certain he was dreaming. The blackness of the trunk, which even in his sleep was wholly separate, wholly distinguishable from the river, existed, nonetheless, because the river existed. Seeing one meant the other was not, not simply faded, but gone. Yet they shared the same space. They were, or at the very least must be thought to be, contemporaneous. It was this that troubled him.

He had not chosen which he would see. Had he been given a choice, he would have dreamed of the oak. Its leafy vaults were elegiac and sad, matching his thoughts. Their darkness consoled him. In an earlier age such a dream would have been called a prefigurement of death. The strength of his youth was behind him. The yearnings of his early manhood, which had once filled him with impossible anguish, were over. Now, although he slept with a woman beside him, it was many years since he had found her naked in his arms.

It was not his will or even his intention that determined which, for a moment, prevailed. In fact he had dreamt of the great sprawling branches and continued to dream of them, intermittently. But where he had expected their pattern to hold he found instead its odd symmetry broken.

His numbed feet paddled through the bright water.

Holmes pressed his nose into the pillow.

Because it was a dream it hardly seemed he was climbing. Slowly he made his way forward. Down the river went and then up again, its queer shining current spilling outward over the steep valley wall. The heavy branch swayed. Increasingly it became difficult to hold his balance. Caught between wind and water, struck by the real possibility of falling, he no longer looked down.

The river forked.

Rather like a passage in a book he had read twice without, until the end, noticing, he realized that he had made this same passage before. To the left the river tumbled into more vivid life. Its brightness reflected up into brambles, lighted the meadows won long ago from the wood. But if he blinked? He made no decision. He did not dismiss one or embrace the other. There lay behind him years of speculation and doubt. They made no difference. There were endless worlds, each with its own composition and laws, each waiting invisibly for summoning. And it was chance that called them forth. Chance only that mattered. His child-sized hands pressed blindly into the bedclothes. For the briefest moment his exhausted eyes flickered. . . .

Against his cold fingers he felt the harsh, scored bark. The great oak coiled away under him.

He awoke with an erection.

Except for the blood in his loins, there was yet no warmth. Dawn merely edged the bricks on the back garden wall. He lay chilled and motionless. To his nostrils came unmistakably the scent of horses. He moved his neck. Someone was knocking.

'Yes?' he called out. His voice seemed unusually distant. What was it he had been thinking?

'Yes?' he answered once more, uncertain whether whoever it was could have heard him.

His daughter did not enter the room. 'Father,' she called softly. 'There is someone waiting down in the surgery.'

He struggled into his robe. This at least was a world he knew. He looked down at the sleeping form of his wife. Her tiny fishlike mouth opened and closed noiselessly.

'I shall be down in a moment,' he whispered.

His daughter went on before him. He had gone himself, more slowly, into the hall and had just finished buttoning his fly when she crept back. She looked at him hesitantly, her normally proud features suddenly perplexed. Somehow she had been found wanting. Not by himself certainly. Beginning to wonder, Holmes straightened his collar.

He padded in his slippers to the bottom of the stairs. He took a shortcut through the kitchen and, because he had gained a moment, paused, snatching a hopeful glance at the garden. The sky had not yet taken on enough color to allow him to see more than the roughest outline of the hedge. The barberry seemed pale and ordinary and failed to cheer him. In his mind he kept smelling the damnable scent of horses. He trotted down the corridor.

The man had been standing at the far side of the room facing the street.

He unfolded his manicured fingers. 'Please forgive the inconvenience,' he said.

Holmes took hold of the presented hand. The grip was firm and yet along the cool fingers he felt the slightest twinge of anxiety. His own small hand stiffened. Nearly at once Holmes placed the name that went under the large, well-proportioned head. 'Rather, it is an honor, Your Grace,' he said.

Without actually frowning the Duke conveyed the impression of a frown.

Holmes managed a look of absorbed seriousness. 'Perhaps you would care to tell me the nature of your complaint,' he suggested.

'I have been out driving,' the Duke said.

'Do have a seat.'

'Yes, of course.'

The Duke drew up a chair.

'I was out for a drive,' the Duke repeated. 'Out quite early.' He raised his eyes. His hands rested easily in his lap. He said: 'Generally I have my driver go north. I am fond of the river.' He looked to see if there were any reaction. Now that he had begun to speak, deliberately, in a low voice, he seemed utterly calm. Only his eyes were more intense. They moved across Holmes's face, watchful and yet deprecating.

'I believe that eventually I must have slept,' he said. 'When I woke I recognized the mills. It was at that point that I thought of you.'

Holmes waited.

The Duke put his hand into his pocket. 'I remembered that you had signed the death certificate.' He paused before drawing it forth. 'Since this arrived at the bank,' he said, 'I have carried it about with me.' He gave the paper to Holmes. 'You have a clear hand, doctor. The name is quite unmistakable.'

Holmes did not bother to examine the paper. 'But something isn't,' he said.

The Duke was staring at him.

'I needed to talk with you,' he began. 'I have already spoken with the police.'

Holmes remembered the two young policemen on the train. 'I imagine they were of no help,' he offered.

'He had never been sick,' the Duke said bluntly. 'Not even as a child. I spoke with the mother. In the family there is no history of illness. Even his grandparents are still alive.'

'You came by accident?' Holmes asked dryly. 'You were out driving, being driven –'

His Grace might have smiled then but did not. 'The hour at least was chance,' he said. 'I was already in Bristol. In any case I should have insisted on seeing you.' He drew himself forward. 'Forgive me,' he said. 'I confess to impatience. I might at least have waited until you had had your breakfast.'

Holmes shook his head. 'It is a doctor's life.'

'But in this instance the patient is already buried.'

Holmes noticed how for a moment the Duke's fingers dug into the arms of the chair. Holmes waited. 'There was literally nothing to be done,' he said. 'The young man had been dead for some minutes when I was called to him.'

447

'I have implied no impropriety.'

'Then why have you come?'

In the hall outside the surgery there was a step. The door opened. His daughter Amelia (named after her mother as Oliver, his oldest, was named for himself) pushed in with a tray bearing two white cups and a steaming china pot. She came and stood by her father, meeting his reproachful glare with her prettiest smile. He saw how trimly she had dressed herself, her mobile, flirtatious face clothed with impertinent cheerfulness. Rather as if in revenge, he thought. Somehow His Grace had offended her, probably by taking no notice. The man after all was at least as old as himself and, Duke or not, unless he seriously misjudged him, not the sort to have his head turned by a pink complexion and a new spring dress.

Holmes gave her a second provoking look.

'I listened,' Amelia said, setting the tray down disobediently. 'You were only talking. It isn't as if . . .'

His Grace had got to his feet when she entered. Standing himself, Holmes was struck, possibly for the first time, by the Duke's stature. The Duke made a vague gesture and Amelia extended her hand.

'My daughter, Your Grace,' Holmes said.

'Your Grace,' she repeated.

Oddly, that seemed enough. Having won or at least drawn even in a contest which remained to Holmes essentially mysterious, she poured quickly and with scarcely another look curtsied. As the door closed Holmes found His Grace staring after her.

'Undoubtedly,' Holmes said, faintly embarrassed, 'you have children of your own.'

As if to banish some foreboding, the Duke laughed. 'I am just an old bachelor,' he conceded.

'Confirmed?' The question slipped out without intention.

It surprised them both when for a moment the Duke did not answer.

CHAPTER TWO

When Wykeham stepped onto the platform of Bristol station it was exactly dawn. He was freshly shaved; the air felt agreeably mild on his cheek. His head turned expectantly. It was one of those suddenly bright spring mornings, mimicking summer, which give the solid practical earth the appearance of a dream. Like all real places met in sleep, the city below him seemed at once larger and more intimate. Wykeham smiled to himself. He went down the steps and onto the pavement.

He was dressed with more than usual care in a light gray suit which, although out of fashion, was on this occasion not conspicuously so. Earlier, soon after rising, his chin lathered, he had examined his face in the mirror. He had understood this was foolishness. After fifty years she was probably dead. At best she had gone off, as old unmarried women often did, to live precariously and barely tolerated with her younger relations. She did have sisters. He remembered he had met them, once, in the dining room of the King's Porter Hotel. He had taken her down to the little seaside town on their last holiday. How pale and injured she had looked then, her short black hair tousled. Only moments before they had come from their rooms. He had told her he was leaving her. As he remembered, a tiny wave of sadness washed back over him. Her elegant sisters, there by chance, looked up from their table. Their husbands, being men and more tolerant of scandal, commandeered the necessary chairs. But her sisters sat coldly. They had seldom approved of what their older sister did, certainly not her work for wages at a second-rate preparatory school for girls of the middle class. They had approved even less of Joseph Wykeham, although until this point he was known to them only by rumor. It was not that he was beneath their station (as to that the rumors were both extravagant and reassuring) but even wealth could not bargain away the distinctions of time. Had the situation been the reverse, had Wykeham instead been indisputably twice her age, the sisters might have learned to ignore the difference. A husband, even a dull old one, would have provided at least the outward show of propriety. But it was their Willa, regrettably, who was thirty-seven, nearly old enough, it had swiftly come back to them, to be taken for young Wykeham's mother. After the introductions, the younger women maintained a grim silence. It was one of the husbands, turning to look at her more closely, who first realized that she had been jilted. Motioning to the waiter, he ordered her wine.

The scene had all the elements of farce. Even now as he went through the sunwashed streets toward the school, Wykeham recalled with a pang of regret her look of incomprehension, then fear as, easing the chair from the table, he stood. Beyond the windows of the dining room the sea had been bright; white gulls cried overhead. 'Come walk with me,' he had said, knowing that she would not. He had not looked back. He need not have worried. This last time she had not disappointed him.

In the park the trees were in bloom. Their fragrance drifted across to him. For the better part of an hour he walked past the deserted shops, through empty squares, until, as the first men came into the streets, he approached the few last substantial white Federal houses and, simultaneously, the foot of the one great hill at the city's northwest edge. Here on its renovated foundations Bristol Academy perched overlooking the valley. The school was a fine puzzling mixture of wood and stone, the amalgam of architectual pretension and the plain common sense of its carpenters and masons. Before the turn of the new century it had been the estate of a brewer who, as the clockworks failed, slid toward ruin. The main building at the top of the drive had been converted into a dormitory, the untended gardens and the west meadow into playing fields. Other buildings, either rehabilitated or put up through subscription, lay clustered about the slope. Wykeham looked up, his eyes coming to rest on one little window, tucked high up under the dark roof of the main house. There, winter and summer, Willa had had her rooms. There, she had once told him, she had often stayed up, all the lights of the school but her own extinguished, writing him letters.

She was a born letter writer and for many weeks had continued to fatten envelopes with sheet after sheet of grief and news even after she had learned that he had been married all the while he had courted her. She wrote with quiet gravity of her students and, surprisingly, without malice, of her sisters' lives. He had told her, as unlikely as it sounded, that he had a son, an infant, whose name, Sebastian, he had invented as cavalierly as he had invented child and mother, merely to insure the orderly progress of generations required for inheritance. But thereafter, as much like a fond aunt as a lover, in letter after letter she had inquired after the boy. She made him toys. She was something of a sculptress, and from her affectionate fingers came dwarfs and winged rabbits, mischievous goats molded cunningly from clay, and shy, smiling giants, long-armed and heavy-shouldered, carved from pitch pine. Only at the end of her letters did she speak of her loneliness. There had been one long last letter waiting on the table in the front room at Greenchurch on the day it was reported that Joseph Wykeham had vanished. He had picked it up twice. For a time it had even rested in his breast pocket. But the letter remained in the house when he left.

For another long moment Wykeham stared at the window. After a while he walked on and began to climb the hill.

In the old days, of course, he had driven, in a shining green roadster, not unlike the magnificent automobiles George Tennison had watched in quiet despair. It made Wykeham smile to think, now, how quaint and old-fashioned that car must seem to any but his own eyes. He stood in the middle of the drive, halfway up, remembering. He would, he decided, have to talk with Charon Hunt about getting at least one of the cars back into service. He had already postponed their meeting longer than was wise. Tomorrow, he thought; but his smile faltered and he shook his head irritably.

Down the steps from the main house a half dozen young women, dressed in short gym skirts and sweaters and carrying sticks, hurtled breathlessly into the morning. One was pudding-faced, the rest audaciously thin. From across the courtyard Wykeham caught sight of dancing patches of blonde and auburn hair and acknowledged, without actually banishing Charon Hunt from his mind, that the world's irritations were not altogether without compensation. Wykeham found himself hurrying; but when he reached the embankment, they had gone out of sight. He pressed on.

In his will Joseph Wykeham had presented a rather remarkable sum to the school. The endowment, ignoring delicacy, had been in Willa's name, with her as executrix. The gossips had been left to think what they liked. The trustees would have found, he had expected, some way of accepting the gift. He wished frankly to see what she had done with his money. But he had scarcely taken another step when he saw a new figure moving against the broad classroom windows. She strode briskly toward him, her dark head thrown back, intent on the stout branches of a high-crowned elm growing up at the side of the court. She had not, even at the last moment, been paying the least attention to what lay in her path.

'Oh . . . sorry,' she said in a flat, puzzled voice. 'I was watching . . .'

She looked up, to see Wykeham smiling.

'Really, I am sorry,' she exclaimed, dismayed, realizing that he was no one she knew. 'There was a crow,' she said helplessly. Then, as though imagining how it sounded, she laughed. 'An immense crow.' She studied him for a moment. 'As black as a man's trousers.'

It stuck Wykeham, irrelevantly, that her eyes were blacker. He saw as well that his first impression had been mistaken. She was no more than a girl, perhaps fifteen or sixteen. Her figure, while tall as a boy's, was yet mostly leg. Above her narrow waist her torso was only just beginning to emerge from the compactness of childhood. Only her eyes and her mouth bore full witness that childhood was past. Yet, unaware of any discord, she stepped back, now quite willfully, to get a clearer look at him.

'Are you anyone important?' she asked.

'I like to hope.'

She gave him an appreciative grin. 'I mean you're not a new teacher or somebody's brother?'

'No.'

There was a fluttering in the branches. With a startling cough, the crow launched itself above the court.

'There it is!' she shouted. He turned but she was not at all sure what it was he was watching. The crow sailed away over the treetops. Spots of sunlight winked through the branches. On the still air they could both hear the faint cheering floating down from the playing fields. It was excuse enough if she wanted it. She might have gone. For a minute neither of them spoke.

A man emerged from between the buildings carrying buckets of ash. Ignoring them, he went down the path. If there were faces behind the windows of the main house, they chose not to look out.

She had grown up at the school. Her father, whom she adored, traveled most of the year. It had fallen to her teachers more or less by default to instruct her to be careful of strangers. They had advised her as strictly as was needed in a world which, except for the odd-job man, consisted solely of women. Once, unaccountably, there had been a male Latin teacher, an unhappy young man with cigarette-stained fingers and an untried degree in the classics, who, after less than a month, had fled back to his university.

She stood quite still. The expression on Wykeham's face, although well-intentioned, nevertheless had an extraordinary effect on her. She gazed at him frankly. Surely, someone would come to call her if she were at fault.

'It was perched on my windowsill,' she said, remembering the cold eyes that had peered in at her as she awoke in her bed. 'It was in the yard again after breakfast.' Her voice, which had sunk to a whisper, communicated a delighted sense of alarm, as if it had been no ordinary crow but a creature she had, with a quiet, amused determination, summoned.

'Perhaps it is an omen,' he suggested.

'Oh, do you think so?'

The sunlight was warm on her neck. She fancied she could feel it running between her shoulder blades, buoying her, covering and uncovering her like the waters of a bath. For no particular reason, she stretched herself and yawned. One of them, it was impossible to tell which, took the first step.

'What is your name?' he asked.

'Jane.'

'Only that?'

They walked slowly, each seemingly afraid to outpace the other. 'Jane Hawleyville,' she said, looking down. 'And your own?'

'Wykeham.'

She stared at him over her shoulder. 'Like the hall?' she said softly, thinking that she had found him out. Her smile darkened. But when Wykeham looked innocently confused, she pointed.

'Wykeham Hall,' she repeated. But something was wrong with his understanding and she pointed again at a building at the far side of the court.

'We have our science lessons there,' she added. 'They have frogs and intestines in bottles.' She made a face. 'We have to cut open cats.' She had turned her back on the hall and was watching him.

'I should like to go in,' he said.

Jane shook her head.

'You needn't cut anything open.'

'It isn't that.'

He could hear for the first time a nervous tremor in her voice.

'No one likes to go there,' she admitted. 'Not unless . . .' She wanted to say something more but found she could not. Instead she put her hand on his arm.

He was conscious of her touch, half curious and half cross with her for her insistence.

'Why not?'

His indignation took her by surprise.

'There was a woman,' she said haltingly. 'Years and years ago. She was a teacher and had the hall built.' She stopped.

A procession of pictures marched through her head, pictures she had made up herself because it had all happened long before she had arrived. Yet, from stories traded from one girl to the next, retold late at night when the wind blew dead leaves on the roof and, looking out in the moonlight and frightened, she could see the hall among the dark branches, she knew, knew exactly the awfulness.

'One day,' she said, her mouth dry before she had half completed a sentence, 'right after the hall was finished, the woman went to the top of the stairs. And before anyone had time to think or could reach her, she hanged herself. And so, sometimes –'

She saw how quickly he looked away.

She had made some terrible blunder.

All at once the excitement that had grown wonderfully inside of her was threatened. She pulled at his arm.

But his head was averted.

'You won't laugh,' she pleaded.

But he was merely staring across at the hall.

The sun breaking above the tops of the trees began to blaze on the windows. Amid the faded ivy stitched to the walls there were a few sprigs of green. The stone itself, inert, darkened by the door and blackened under the windows, took on a warmer tinge in the sunlight.

Wykeham turned.

'Then you must show me the playing fields.' His tone implied a command. Yet, before he had quite broken off, she realized that he had never let her hand go. Pressed against her palm she could feel the rough wool of his jacket and the arm beneath, tensed and leaning into her.

'Will you?' he asked.

For an instant, looking up into the strong sunlight she was blinded.

The same sunlight lay across the table in Dr. Holmes' kitchen. Holmes squinted. The day was already warm but neither man was as yet comfortable enough with the other to remove his coat. The cook, deprived of her kitchen, sat alone in the dining room, where, if her employer had had the least sense, he would have ushered His Grace. With a great affronted swelling of her bosom she drank herself the last of the coffee from a proper china cup. The little pinched-faced maid, intruding on the cook's misery, backed through the door. The maid's frail arms were laden with dishes she had been unwilling to set in the sink in front of His

Grace. It did not occur to either woman that the kitchen provided the only uninterrupted view of the garden or that Holmes, having discovered that the world was far stranger than he had expected, needed urgently to look at a hedge. But when he turned back, the Duke was still sitting across from him. Holmes put aside his napkin. As if to show he was not hurried, he folded it twice. The death certificate rested on the table before him. Face down beside it was the photograph he had taken at the last moment from the surgery. He had meant to slip it quietly into his pocket.

'Of course the body had been washed,' the Duke had been saying, describing the funeral. 'The mistake, clearly, was in putting him back into his suit. It was likely his best suit.' His mouth turned down at the edge. 'I am afraid it may have been his only one.' Remembering the room in the cheap lodging house where they had set the bare casket, the Duke paused. He thought of the wealth that had come into his own hands, that as easily would have come into Houseman's. In a month, even in a few days, he thought and as quickly cursed himself for thinking it. 'The suit he had worn on the train was in any case all they had. He was a fastidious man. They had no reason to suspect. Although almost certainly, I imagine, they had taken a brush to the sleeves and gone through his pockets. So it is even more difficult to believe that they missed it.'

'I'm sorry,' Holmes interrupted, 'but I don't –'

'The young man stank,' the Duke finished with brutal simplicity, 'like a hostler, as though not five minutes before he had been mucking a stable.'

Holmes shifted his head.

The Duke glanced up. He did not initially suppose it was important. It was just one more thing which for the moment he did not understand but for which, like Houseman, he shouldered unquestioned responsibility.

Holmes was again staring out of the window.

'Perhaps,' the Duke suggested, 'when you examined him –'

Holmes shook his head. 'It would have been fairly obvious. And it wasn't.'

The words left a silence behind them. Without being able to say how, the Duke saw that Holmes was lying; not lying outright, perhaps. He had seen, he believed, the doctor's essential honesty. If anything, Holmes had been forthright and, given the hour, remarkably unresentful. Presented with a direct question, he could not imagine that Holmes would be other than equally direct. The distortion, the Duke decided, had to have been in the question he had asked.

'Yet you did notice,' he persisted.

Holmes turned, as he had turned in his bed, his mind as well as his body seeking a new position. Nonetheless he found himself again staring over his spectacles into the garden. Disgusted, he drove a quantity of air through his nostrils.

'Not then,' he said, 'not at first.'

While he had kept his eyes on the hedge, he saw, reflected in the window glass, the startling image of his own sharp features. Was it his own face? Holmes wondered, the face of a man who was frightened? Because he was frightened. And for no reason. Because he had taken a photograph of blots and shadows. But, of course, he had not looked at it in the morning. His hand trembled.

A moment passed.

Holmes looked away from the window.

'Your Grace,' he said, 'I should like you to examine something.'

Without looking down he found it.

The Duke took the photograph into his left hand, turning it at once another way. With the other he half reached into his pocket, then he stopped.

'A horse,' he said confidently.

But he held the photograph again at arm's length as if to be certain. He continued to stare.

'Yes,' he said after a moment. 'See, here is a leg. In fact.' He counted four legs. But before he had finished he had counted four more. The Duke shook his head. 'A rather peculiar horse, I admit,' he said, 'but a horse indisputably.'

CHAPTER THREE

Olivia Tennison, who for the better part of a fortnight had been assistant housekeeper, half-scullion and full-time drudge, scuttered into Nora's bedroom without knocking. It was the end of the week, for there was washing. Her little wren's face was darkly flushed. Her eyes had been glaring. She advanced in fearless little hops like a bird on a wire. She had already stripped the master's bed, having removed a heap of books, a tablet of writing paper, pens and a hunting cap. His sheets, which were muddled and would cause no end of trouble, she had bundled into a pillowcase, which, with an air of injured dignity, she had placed by the door. By now she was accustomed to his thoughtlessness. More than once she had found his trousers, with most of a swamp still clinging to the cuffs, under the covers, where – weary, she supposed, after half a night's wandering with her Georgie through fields and ditches – he had kicked them. He threw his clothes every which way, more than likely still talking, his head swimming with plans, with innumerable tasks, changing every minute, which her Georgie, staggering after him from one place to the next and even up the old back stairs to his bedroom, must somehow see to as best he could. Olivia brooded. As if there wasn't enough to do, she thought, and only a few women for the inside work. She would have her Georgie speak with him. After all, they were thick, those two. Her face went completely blank. She had left the door open.

Nora sat at the end of the bed. Bars of dusty light fell across her bare legs. Because she still had only the clothes she had come with, she was dressed, as she had slept, in one of his shirts. She stretched her arms and yawned. The shirt hitched up on her thighs. Olivia's pale eyes hardened. She stood before the bed, staring at rather more of Nora's rounded legs than she approved of seeing.

'I'll trouble you for the sheets, Miss Barnacle,' Olivia said.

Nora reached for a brush and began on her hair. 'He doesn't call me that,' she said evenly.

'Oh, I've heard him, miss. Like a barnacle he says to Cook. Like those little things that attached themselves to ships . . . and no one knows how they got there . . . and they don't come off.'

From where she sat Nora could see out the window onto the drive. She became aware of a figure, standing in the gravel, looking up at the house. As the face turned toward her window, she saw it was the stableboy.

'He wouldn't,' she said.

'You'll suit yourself, I'm sure.' Olivia began to tug at the sheets. 'Though it isn't for my own good that I mention it.'

Nora climbed down from the bed. For a moment her fingers lingered on the carved pattern of the walnut post. He hadn't, she was certain, even if he had said it, meant anything of the sort. Nobody could tell her what he thought. She had listened. More and more she was convinced that he spoke in a language which was only incidentally directed to those around him.

There was no sound in the room, only the crunch of the stableboy's boots from outside the window. Nora reached across to the chair. She took the skirt and, stepping into it, drew the heavy woolen over her legs.

'I hold my own here,' she said coolly, sweeping out of her the last particle of doubt. 'I work as much as anyone.' To keep her long yellow hair from her eyes she had bound it back with a scarf. 'But I get up when I want.' She walked to the closet and began rummaging. But after a moment she turned back empty-handed. They were both looking down at her feet.

'You haven't by any chance . . .'

'No, miss.'

On an impulse Nora went out into the hall. Her shoes, tipped on their sides, were in plain sight on the carpet. She slipped them on, knowing all the while that she had not put them there. Finished within, Olivia, a new bundle in her arms, came through the door.

'You've found them, miss,' she said with pretended surprise.

'He is thoughtful, don't you think?' Nora answered steadily. They could think as they liked. The truth was he was innocent. Often enough she had waited in his bed; but he had on those occasions slept elsewhere or, for all she knew, slept nowhere at all. And what she had left of her presence, shoes or a scarf, the hairbrush (she had so little), he returned without comment.

Nora stood in the hall until Olivia trotted along down the stairs. Then she followed. Below a door opened. There was a faint sound of women's voices from the back of the house. She could hear the cook, old Norfolk's wife, complaining as she did regularly when, the men already come and gone, the last pan scrubbed, Nora came late to breakfast. 'I see how it is,' she announced in the abused tone she saved for those moments she had an audience. Yet Wykeham could come in without warning, in midmorning from wherever it was his jaunts had taken him, and Lizzy Norfolk, her heavy jowled face bent over the silver, was up in a moment and the kettle began singing.

'I can readily imagine . . .' The voice drawled on with accustomed resentfulness.

Nora took a small breath and went out onto the porch.

The stableboy was waiting. He turned on her with a brief bitter smile.

'He is gone,' she told him. 'I don't know where.'

The boy's eyes fell. His demeanor was intense, almost desperate; yet it seemed to her that he had no one to blame but himself. It was the fourth time he had come seeking Wykeham. She had watched him for as many days, in the morning, pacing up and down in the gravel, looking uncertain, uncomfortable out in the open before the house. He had never come up the steps, never knocked on the door. It was as if he waited for her instead, waited to be told over and over that Wykeham had gone.

'I shall come tomorrow,' he said.

She gave him an oblique look. 'You might try after dinner.' The boy stared back sullenly. She felt a sharp redness come into her cheeks. She had meant to be helpful but it seemed instead that a distance had opened between them. His grave small features were watching her. She realized suddenly how hard it was to look at him.

She had an impression of dark, haunted eyes, a plain lean face. Spikes of black hair fell in several directions across his forehead. But if she averted her eyes, what was left of her memory of him? She started to turn away.

He threw her a tortured look.

'Tell him,' he said quickly, 'that it is time he spoke with me.'

As if he perceived as well some danger of vanishing, he thrust his thin shoulders forward.

'If I see him,' she said. Nora hesitated. 'If I do, I will ask him to come to the stables.' Something else occurred to her and she turned, staring at the roofs, now partially mended, of the workmen's cottages. 'You will be there? You do live here somewhere?'

His eyes had run past her. He was looking instead at the house, at the wide uneven porch where she waited. The old railings were threaded with thorns and buttressed with vines, just now beginning to flower.

'He can find me,' he said.

There was a long moment. Then he went back down the drive, heading, it seemed to her, nowhere in particular. Later in the day she saw him again, shuffling idly along the edge of the hill. It was one of the last days of April; the sky was extraordinarily distant. He was standing out in the open without even the shadow of a cloud to cover him. She watched him as, unconscious of any immodesty, he relieved himself in the grass. It struck her then that probably he was ignorant of indoor plumbing. Looking out from the house, which now she seldom left, she found herself wondering where he had come from. Not from this place. He is like me, she concluded, feeling the tender stirring of sympathy.

There was a movement in the room behind her. Her heart rose to her throat.

The crow hopped onto the carpet. Shamed by her disappointment, she met its stare.

'Pretty girl, pretty girl,' the crow rasped consolingly.

The voice, however, because it was the first time she had heard it, only made matters worse.

In the darkness, looking across the valley, George Tennison rubbed his right hand, acknowledging with a sense of good fortune and prodigality the thickness of his calluses. There was a little mound of folded pound notes in his pocket and more coming at the end of each week as long as the work lasted. And the work, he assured himself with a private wink, was sure to last longer than he did. He grinned. The shine of many twinkling stars winked gaily back at him.

He went across the field and through the gate. Over the black hill he recognized – or might have, he thought, had he not been brought up in the smoke of the mills – the striking array of fixed stars. They were pictures, he had heard, of men and beasts, of impossible deeds. A strange excitement filled him. With the pleasure of Adam, because there had never been anyone to teach him, he named them for himself. Cunningly, among the splendid luminaries, he distinguished the labors of which he was now master: George Tennison (those three bright stars were his arm, the fourth was a hammer) restoring breached walls; George Tennison, just to the left of the moon, climbing over slick acres of slate to repoint the chimneys. Deep in reverie, he leaned back his head.

Floating in front of him were innumerable stars, great stars for the great labors while his back was still strong, lesser stars, their configurations as yet remote, for the lesser tasks awaiting his old age. He patted the lump of folded notes in his pocket. His men would be waiting in the village, drinking away their salaries in the front room of the Royal Charles. It was only sociable that he go and have a beer with them – his fine bunch of Bristol stragglers, laid-off clocksmiths, men like himself, craftsmen made over into common muckers and gardeners and lucky, he knew, for the chance. Once or twice before he made up his mind to join them, but Wykeham had always needed something looked into and needed it right then. Indeed, this was the first evening in over a week George Tennison had had his liberty.

He shambled out of the margins of South Wood. The Royal Charles was still a good few minutes' tramp down the road. He walked stiffly. There was a bit of arthritis in his leg, which he had got, he suspected, from wading most of the afternoon in an ornamental fish pond, trying to unstop the drain. Nevertheless, passing along the dark shut-in corridor of branches, he found himself quietly whistling, glad of the work and glad, at least for an hour or two, to be free of it.

A light burned steadily in the bedroom of the parsonage. George Tennison turned down the cracked walk under the trees, passing within a dozen yards of the house without noticing. He did not know these houses yet; they were simply houses. He recognized the feed store because he had been sent there once and Hunt's garage because it was a garage and because Fred Norfolk, with whom he had spent a day shingling the roof of a cottage in Black Wood, had kept muttering and laughing to himself about Charon Hunt without ever once quite coming to the point. It had merely strengthened George Tennison's conviction that Devon folk were an odd sort, not actually a mystery but crackbrained and out of touch. Like their church, he thought, coming abreast of it in the darkness. It was an ordinary church, with doors and a steeple like any church, except, of course, they had painted it green. Painted it once, and every fifty years or so it looked, kept repainting it, not out of some prankish habit, not because they liked it, but because (it had been Wykeham himself who had told him!) they believed a green church would never be burned by Indians. It just makes you wonder, he thought. But, in truth, he did not. Instead he mounted the two broad stone steps of the Royal Charles.

'George!' someone called out.

'Mister Tennison,' Adam France added loudly, because, after all, George was foreman now.

'Ten-thirty,' Jakey shouted, examining his watch. 'Well, you have a bit of catching up to do.'

'A beer,' George Tennison said, passing the counter. He stopped and, reaching into his pocket, uncurled a pound note and laid it out on the dark, polished wood of the bar. 'And a whisky.'

With a glass in each hand he wandered back among the chairs and tables where men he had never seen sat quietly absorbed in their glasses. He glanced abstractedly from one to the next, taking little notice until Fred Norfolk stood up.

'Come in at last, have you?' Norfolk said. He looked as though he wanted to shake hands, which, unless George Tennison put down a drink (and he had no mind to do that) was impossible. Comrades, nevertheless, Norfolk's lopsided grin seemed to announce, men of common understanding, both working up at the great house, their wives too, for that matter.

George Tennison looked for a way around him.

Norfolk saw it but did not move away. He whispered:

'You come along with old Fred.'

He seemed to realize the Bristol men were watching him. He winked conspiratorily. 'Later,' he said none too softly. 'Been waitin' a million years. Been waitin' forever.' He winked again, the model of patience. ' 'Keep till you've had a wee drop with your friends.'

Norfolk sat, or rather his big legs folded, compelling the rest of him to follow. Seated, although undoubtedly the world wheeled ever faster about him, he held himself still, his huge elbows propped up on the table. His bleary eyes, undeterred by the chairs and tables circling past him, tracked George Tennison until he sat far back in the corner and brought a glass to his lips.

Jakey moved over. He still had his watch cradled importantly in his palm. It was too big and expensive a watch for a man like Jakey, but then, he had made half the innards himself. It gave him exquisite pleasure just to hold it.

'Things aren't what they were,' he said mildly, not exactly sad but slightly perplexed.

'And what is?' asked Adam France. He lifted his glass.

'It's the bankers,' someone said.

Jakey smiled down in a fatherly way at the watchface and nodded. 'Bloodsucking capitalists,' he muttered. 'Squeezing out the last penny. One mill closing after the next.'

'Yet,' George Tennison said, the whisky warming his belly, 'well, you know, this is something too.'

462

And they nodded, for his sake if not for their own. Jakey examined his watch ruminatively and sighed.

When George Tennison came back from the toilet, where he had stopped perhaps a moment longer than he had intended, the table at which he had so comfortably passed two hours was empty. I'll be goddamned, he thought, disappointed but without hostility. They had their work and morning came early.

In any event, if he hurried, he would probably catch up with them. He considered the last little bit of whisky in his glass but, pricked by a barb of conscience, left it regretfully.

In his pounding head there was still a small cold corner of sobriety, enough so that he recognized the hulking shape of Fred Norfolk climbing unsteadily to his feet from among the confusion of tables. Regretted it later – although he explained carefully to Olivia that he had been too far gone to remember. In fact, however far he had got, it was not quite far enough since, afterward, he remembered a great deal more than he liked.

Preemptively, with an apelike arm, Norfolk covered his shoulder. 'You see who your f-friends are, G-Georgie,' Norfolk announced. His grin was more lopsided than it had been before; his large smug face was whiter. 'You c-come along with ol' F-Fred.'

Somehow George Tennison eluded him. He made his way erratically to the front of the bar, through the door whose latch, incomprehendibly, was either too high or too low but which, found, submitted at last with a groan. Only out in the street Norfolk was again beside him, looming suddenly out of the darkness, dark himself and swaying without the benefit of a wind. Once more Norfolk's arm secured its place on his shoulder.

'J-Just across the green,' Norfolk whispered.

There were no eyes to follow them. The dogs that might have howled had already been whistled for and lay curled indoors on their carpets in the houses of the Browns and the Underwoods. The Reverend Mr. Longford, his sermon – by his own lights – finished, dropped his head to his pillow and was instantly asleep. Slipped in beside him, Plum clutched his broad arm contentedly, reviewing the few minor changes she would make in the morning before he woke. In the pocket of the apron hung over a chair in the kitchen was an envelope, barely remembered, addressed to Nora but delivered to the parsonage. The first of the week would be soon enough to run it up to her. She had meant to pay her a call, poor child, to see how things stood. But there was time for that. Her hand found Tim's elbow. Nothing to worry over. With half the village coming and going from the place, working inside and out, she would have heard anything worth listening to. She smiled at the darkness. With amusement and an ecstasy she knew was foolish but never minded, Plum listened to her husband's rough snores.

George Tennison was listening as well. But all he heard were silences. 'No one home,' he said timidly.

'Don't matter,' Norfolk said, pushing in with his shoulder.

'Up them stairs,' he said, unmindful of any difficulty. 'Him and me t-together in this. W-were from the s-start.' His loud slurred voice trailed off into a snigger. ''Cept, of c-course, hiss s-start was a little before yours t-truly.'

George Tennison grunted. He tried to make his legs follow one after another. The stairs wound off into darkness. Unable to negotiate the steps and exasperated beyond measure, he began to swear.

'Y-you'll d-do al-rright,' Norfolk called back encouragingly.

At the top of the staircase was an even darker hallway. At the end of it, when Norfolk had managed to discover the light, there was a door. Norfolk pressed his disordered face next to George Tennison's. 'H-here we are!' he whispered. With a constricting hug he drew him back under his arm. With his free hand he pawed at the latch.

All at once Norfolk's vigorous grin faded. He shook his big head slowly.

'Y-you ain't f-frit?' he demanded.

George Tennison made a rueful noise. But to Norfolk one answer was as good as another. He pawed again at the door until it opened.

The light flooded in from the hall, illuminating a spare but otherwise ordinary bedroom. Charon Hunt was sitting beside the bed, a length of rabbit wire between his brown fingers. He was a large man, even larger than Norfolk. He was dressed in a blacksmith's burned and patched trousers. Despite the warmth of the room, a great coat covered his shoulders. The coat, like his face and hair, was red. Indeed, the man and his clothing gave out a ruddy glow. Even his great fingers, which were patiently tightening the snare, seemed to shine with an odd radiance. But however extraordinary, Hunt was a man, or nearly that. The other was not a man so clearly. George Tennison's mouth, soured by whisky, fell stupidly open.

On the bed, what might have been a large quilt made of feathers shifted suddenly. In the glare from the hall the feathers, which might once have been vivid, even defiant with color, appeared lifeless, a dull brown muddied here and there to a dark sepia. Moving under them, a lump of a head opened its mouth and screamed. It was not a sound a man would have made, although a boy, bitter, unrepentant, even in the face of an inescapable destiny, might have.

'Not even his death keeps him quiet,' Hunt said glumly. He let the clawed fingers, now skillfully rebound, fall from his lap.

Once again the young Indian bellowed.

'I care nothing for your bellowing,' Hunt bellowed back. 'Burn what you will when the High King comes. But until then, by Duinn, you shall damn well wait like the rest!'

George Tennison stood gawking. Because there was nothing else he dared look at, his stare fastened desperately on Norfolk.

When Hunt rose, it was like a hill rising. His shoulders got in the way of the light.

'Whose soldier is this?' he asked coldly. 'Whose side will he fight on?'

Norfolk went right on grinning.

'H-he is s-solid behind us,' Norfolk answered. 'W-works at the h-house, w-works for W-Wykeham.'

Hunt moved. He placed himself firmly in front of George Tennison and stared hard at him.

'Whose side?' he said.

His voice was louder and colder and yet, in an odd way, it was sadder as well. George Tennison stumbled backward. If his mouth would have worked, he would have uttered a cry.

It was Norfolk who answered.

'W-Wykeham's,' he said unhesitantly, without a twitch of concern or apology.

From the bed, as if that as well were an answer, there came a high-pitched wail.

Hunt's lips curled at the edge.

'What makes you think,' he asked, 'that this time, after so long, Wyck has chosen?' His voice, now softer, was colder still. 'Tell me,' he said, 'is the Sea-Road open? Have the Stone Kings put aside their sorrow?'

Hunt dropped his head.

The questions were addressed to no one in particular.

When George Tennison staggered alone into the street, he couldn't remember if anyone had answered. But he knew the green was in front of him. In the whirling space between the trees he could see the great burning stars, now greater and brighter because of drink. Disgusted, he turned away from them.

He wasn't altogether certain what he had heard or seen, but he had heard and seen quite enough. Like the stars, they were somebody else's business. He pitched himself forward. At the very least he knew the dark street climbed toward Greenchurch, that the hard grunting breath, very close at hand, was his own.

His head was swimming.

On the margins of South Wood, he failed to notice the clop of too many hooves, never felt the thick hands that lifted him onto the broad white back. Yet the wind did seem to sail more swiftly through the fringe of his hair. Under him too many haunches and shoulders rose and fell.

'How many legs?' he asked, despite himself. But it was a foolish question. Wykeham only laughed.

CHAPTER FOUR

There were really two kitchens at Greenchurch. The grand kitchen, with its five stoves and too many copper-sheathed tables, Lizzy Norfolk, although she did most of the cooking there, thought of as the men's kitchen. It was where the men sat for breakfast and dinner, pulling their bread with fingers that were never sufficiently scrubbed. Invariably they left their plates and their cups on the tables. Lizzy much preferred the smaller kitchen in the back with its one frugal stove and its single oak table. There, the men gone, she could sit with Olivia and, on rare occasions, with Nora. There she could keep a good lookout on the yard, on tradesmen, and, most particularly, on Fred Norfolk, who had a habit of slipping off. And there, having from the side door window an unhampered view, she presided over the house, over its routines and its schedules. Without regard for her failures with her own husband and with something less than the formal support of Wykeham, she had gathered about her not unsubstantial shoulders the sober cloak of authority; and, like an empress surrounded by savages, she felt it her given duty to chasten and instruct.

'It's a pity,' Lizzy said that morning before Nora, carrying her own cup, had quite found her seat by the stove.

Nora detected a guilty look in Olivia's eyes.

'What is?' Nora asked blandly.

'Why, George has missed his breakfast.'

'It's his leg, miss,' said Olivia.

Lizzy folded her fat arms. 'Funny things, legs,' she said.

'Your Fred –'

Lizzy smiled triumphantly. 'My Fred had his breakfast!'

Olivia examined the narrow front of her dress.

'Well, it was Mr. Wykeham,' she announced, 'he came home with.'

Nora's head turned up suddenly.

But it was Lizzy who saw the face at the door, or rather the chest and the hairy arms first, and the face a moment later pulled down uncomfortably to the window and peering. It was an alarming face, ruddy and thickened like the sun just poking over the ridge.

'That man!' Lizzy exclaimed. 'Now what can he want?'

But although she went to the door, she opened it no more than a crack. Nora could see one leg and one great shoulder and the grotesque half of a face, grinning. Nora examined the face with a curious stare. Something was missing. It was, she thought, as if another face, balancing the first, a face darker and less ridiculous, lay just out of sight. Nora put down her cup. She could hear the rumbling of the man's voice but she could not make out what he said. Lizzy shook her old head.

'No, Mr. Wykeham isn't here. Went away this morning. Down to Bristol, I think. Couldn't say why.' Her voice had grown petulant. She wanted to be done with him.

'No,' she repeated, taking a deeper breath, 'I wouldn't know which car he wanted worked on.' She was about to shut the door.

'It would be the Pope-Hartford,' said Nora.

Lizzy turned.

Looking straight back at her, Nora repeated it. The astonishing thing was that her tone carried an unqualified air of conviction. Lizzy screwed up her own broad face.

'The Pope-Hartford,' Lizzy said to the man at the door.

Charon Hunt grunted. His footsteps went away. In a few moments they could each see him lifting his long toolbox from the back of his truck. When he disappeared into the barn, Lizzy moved again to the table. But at the back of her mind a new and startling thought was forming. She was all too aware of Nora's talent for woolgathering. Right or wrong, she realized, it would be said it was at her direction, not Nora's, that the work had been started.

'That is what he wanted?' she snapped.

'Yes.'

'He told you directly. You weren't by any chance,' she improvised, 'listening to little blue birds or –'

Nora smiled composedly. 'Not little or blue,' she answered.

Her confidant, in fact, had been neither. That it had been feathered, she imagined, was nobody's business but her own.

The May weather was sultry and electric, filled with the delayed promise of thunder, and got on his nerves. Grown desperate, George Harwood went one last time through his lecture notes, finding among the scraps of paper and torn index cards the Duke's letter. It was to be today, he realized, shocked with himself for having forgotten. Not two days before, on the very morning he had received the letter, he had sent a message back to His Grace, agreeing (I shall be honored, he had written) to meet with him. On just what matters the Duke had been vague. Something, in any event, to do with Will Wykeham. His memory jogged, Harwood unfolded the paper. But he put it aside on the desk. The lecture first, he thought and felt a mounting sense of alarm.

What he sought, what, in fact, he had spent three quarters of an hour unsuccessfully seeking was the source of a quote and, if possible, the precise language, describing the moment of synthesizing imagination when the ordinary tangle of human thought converged dramatically on a single compelling abstraction. It was to be the climax of the term's last lecture. In the fall, in another course altogether and relying strictly on memory, he had used it. Unaccountably his students had cheered him. In a dozen years such a thing had not happened. He still basked in the glory.

Only, of course, he had misplaced it.

Harwood fussed with his shirt. He was perspiring. Nonetheless, fearing rain, he took the greatcoat under his arm and switched off the light. On the stairs he turned, went back to the door and locked it.

Halfway up the street he remembered.

For a moment the coat, which had grown heavier and more awkward than it had ever been in April, no longer troubled him. His strides became longer.

'Imagine a table,' Harwood commanded. The crowd of young men, bearing sluggishly along, took neither notice nor offense. Scores of backs, all of them coatless and damp, milled in front of him. With gentle but well-directed prods he steered past them. Just as the rain began to splash on the sidewalks, he went through the doors of the lecture hall and climbed to the podium.

He was early. Except for a pocket of stragglers from another class, the room was empty. A smaller group stood gossiping in the corridor. Yet slowly, driven in by the weather, the young men began to fill the hall. Their sleeves rolled up like laborers', they drifted down the aisles. A few anxious scholars, their notebooks already open, sat in front. But they would have sat as anxiously and as still and would, when he started, have begun to write with much the same ferocity and panic had he lectured on the *Encyclopaedia Britannica*. The windows along the sloping sides of the hall were opaque and emitted an uncertain light. I might as well lecture in a cave, Harwood thought; yet, in a way, it was almost pleasant, the air grown heavy and quiet. The world was shut out. Harwood felt a little flutter in himself.

'Shall we begin?' he asked. His voice, like the voice in a cave, surprised him. He opened a book and then for several minutes did not look at it.

'Even the smallest details are conserved,' he said, now in earnest. 'However minor and distracting, I shall expect you to remember. I have prepared a list . . .'

There was a groan.

'. . . of birthmarks and certain articles of clothing, birds seen at midnight, objects as simple and as serviceable as china, isolated in aspect. And yet, gentlemen, reiterated. Infinitely recombined. Characteristic, I should think, of the obsessive nature of literary imagination.' His voice became louder. He had forgotten his usual embarrassment. 'But today,' he announced, 'I shall ask you to take a broader view. I shall ask you to stand back and to see, if you can, the beauty of the underlying pattern. . . .'

The Duke, who had come in before the lecture had started, sat in the back. On the wall directly above his head was a painting of a clergyman, most probably one of the Mathers, giving a Bible into the hand of a muscular Indian. The plaque beneath it read *Ansantawae, by the Grace of God, Receives the Book.* The clergyman, his features hardened into a look of moral belligerence, is imbued nevertheless with a kind of wooden glory. But it is the Indian who is bathed in light. He stands under it as unnaturally as under a lamp.

It is the light that gives the painting its essential falseness. Its anemic shining reduces the ragged hills to a few cultivated fields, the bend of the intruding river to the ordinary flatness of an English pond. Harwood, who each morning faced it squarely, had often wondered what purposes were served in presenting a Pequod chief with a Christian testament. 'They could not speak together,' he had once told his students. 'Ansantawae understood only Algonquin.' In fact, in this detail alone, the painting preserved the delicate relic of truth.

It had been commissioned by Benjamin Church, who at the head of a militia of farmer soldiers had driven to their deaths the last remnant of the Pequod nation. Captain Church himself had supervised the final slaughter in the Fairfield swamps. He had shot three young men trapped between the water and the wood. Because of the cumbersomeness and delay in reloading, he had continued the killing with the stock of his gun. The corpses were muddied. It had been difficult to tell them apart. Nevertheless it had been the general opinion that Ansantawae was among them. It was this victory that the painting commemorated. The artist had been given a free hand. The captain, being well acquainted with John Bunyan, saw nothing amiss when a purposeful Mather was depicted in his place. In the darkening pigment of three centuries, his only contribution is now scarcely legible. Yet it is the one detail based on observation rather than religious bigotry.

Almost from the first, Captain Church had felt a deep affinity with the Indians. The entries in his diary describe how, before he turned to murder them, he had lived in their villages and made expeditions with their young men into the Dutch territories across the Hudson. He had admired their bravery and their wisdom. 'They know this Dark Land better than we ever shall,' he had written. As sympathetically as any of the English he had learned their ways and he had insisted, although now one must stand up very close to see it, that the Bible, its pages folded back to a passage in Genesis and given from the hand of a clergyman who clearly had not been there into the hand of an Indian who only may have been, be written in Welsh.

The Duke leaned into his seat. His head pounded. The outside world was hushed. The windows were whitened by rain.

'Reality –' Harwood was explaining when he stopped. His tongue, as though waiting inspiration, pressed on the edge of his teeth. It was, he felt, his most potent effect. It gave the illusion of spontaneity, the impression of a mind poised on a knife-edge and conjuring with darkness. Harwood smiled with excitement. '– Is a Protean fog –' he continued, '– into which we read –' He paused. '– Not so much what is but what we have been led to expect.' He waited.

'Consider, if you will,' he said, 'the pre-Copernican universe: the earth at its center. Devils beneath.'

There came into his mind's eyes a picture of angular little creatures with drooling mouths and leather wings.

'Very real devils, it would seem,' he went on, 'for they had a very real place – the vast basement of the universe – and could and therefore did tempt us to perdition. Only Nicolaus Copernicus –' He seized the book he had put down, from which in a moment, although it had nothing to do with Copernicus, he intended to read a long passage. 'One man,' he said, 'one man learning to look some other way, feeling, though none before him had felt it, the apparently fixed and solid earth, our oldest foundations, begin to slip, to slide beneath his feet, to –'

Someone coughed.

Harwood could feel his words creeping cold and friendless over the hall. No more than a handful were still listening.

The lines deepened on the Duke's forehead.

'Truth, gentlemen, particularly literary truth,' Harwood persisted, 'must be encountered suddenly.' He opened the book.

There was only the ignorant murmur of rain on the windows. The Duke tapped his long fingers. He considered the old woman buried on the grounds of the school in Bristol, the young man dead in New Awanux.

'Imagine a table,' George Harwood was saying.

The Duke rose quickly and went to wait in the corridor.

There was a moment's hush and then the clap of spring seats snapping shut. The young men pushed past him. The Duke scowled. Harwood gathered up his books and his coat and came up the aisle. Until he saw the coat the Duke had not truly recognized him. His clerk had made certain inquiries of the Dean. In the space of a few hours the Duke had learned that Harwood had been Wykeham's advisor, the one man at the college with whom, if it could be said of anyone, Wykeham had been intimate. The Duke had written straight off requesting a meeting. He had not troubled himself to think who the man was. He had cared only to discover what Harwood knew, what, if anything, he could explain about Wykeham's behavior. He had not stopped to wonder what effect Wykeham might have had on him. The Duke had only half listened to the lecture. Perhaps it had been clever. He was no judge. Certainly there was little else to recommend him. Harwood's figure was stout, his face without delicacy. Ordinarily, having learned what he could, the Duke would have left him abruptly in the emptied corridor. It was surprising, and even foreign to his nature, that instead His Grace had taken the man by the shoulders.

'I shall need two hours of your time,' he had said. 'If you can spare it. Afterward, my driver will drop you wherever you like.'

He felt the perspiration on the man's heavy shoulder.

'I hope I can drag you away,' he continued, though now he had not the least doubt. He had seen the expensive coat Harwood carried. He remembered the little lighted windows of the train into which Wykeham had vanished, leaving them both on the platform, both stranded and, for a moment, unable to walk away.

The street was mobbed with students running to get out of the rain. It was several minutes before the college towers slipped grudgingly behind. For the better part of a mile they crawled beside the long snaking wall of the First Settlers Cemetery, past the statues of Protestant saints, centuries old, crumbling back toward the shapelessness of the original stone. It was not until East Bridge, after they had emerged from under the railroad trestle, that they were able to pick up speed again. By then the unfamiliar street had narrowed. Between the poor row houses they caught a glimpse now and then of the river. Backed up by the wind, the estuary had swollen and was flooding the weirs. The traffic had thinned. The wipers thudded dully on the windscreen.

'He told you something of his travels?' The Duke asked finally.

Uneasy in the Duke's presence, Harwood rearranged his coat. 'Very little,' he acknowledged. 'I gather he had seen much of the empire. Certainly wherever there were any number of English.' Looking out at the river, Harwood was reminded, unhappily, of all the places he had never been. 'Though who can say,' he added deprecatingly, 'what exactly he remembers. He was, I believe, Your Grace, quite young.'

The Duke watched Harwood carefully.

'He isn't,' he said.

Harwood turned.

'Isn't English,' the Duke said.

This one point, at least, although he had been slow himself to see it, was indisputable. The ledgers, of course, had been in the vault. He had devoted his life to them, to records which in themselves were a kind of history, repeating not only Wykeham's existence but, in a sense, his own. Yet strangely, until the past evening, he had not brought them all, not one after another, to his desk. And even then, knowing them too well, he had not known where to start and at first he had looked in all the wrong places. He felt his heart sink.

'It is, I should have thought,' Harwood protested, 'the most English of names.'

'Yes. Yes, of course.' The Duke nodded. Somehow the topic had gotten away from him. His head still ached. He had been thinking of women.

It was not the first time. More than once he had found himself worrying over a mere few hundred invested yearly in a Norwegian bank. But the amounts had been so trivial he had let them pass. Nevertheless, he had gone on his own to visit the young women's academy. He had been a young man himself when he had walked over the lawn, stopping at the edge of the open pit where the new building would go up. The woman had trailed behind him from the house. He had not conversed with her. At the time he had not even been troubled. Surely there would be women. He had expected that. The trust could well afford the expense. His own habits were regular. He was not himself much given to foolishness.

It all seemed so long ago.

In the morning he had awakened at his desk. The ledgers had been scattered in front of him. On the borders of sleep he had seen her, a dark-haired woman in a blue dress, sweeping across the green lawn. She had almost stumbled. The brightness had been in his eyes. Until she was quite close to him he had not noticed that she wept.

His head still pounded.

'You shared, one would imagine,' he said quietly, 'certain confidences.' He tried to calm his mind, to remember that the dead woman, however he felt bound to her, was Wykeham's. 'You were his teacher,' he said.

'Yes.'

'And you talked?'

'We traded books.' Harwood smiled. He meant to be honest. 'I may have given him one or two,' he said. 'He gave me dozens. Late in the evenings he would come to my rooms and we would talk.'

'Of?'

Harwood thought he had been clear. 'About books,' he said. He was puzzled. The Duke was watching him strangely.

'He may have mentioned acquaintances.'

'Your Grace?' Watching him in return, Harwood realized that the Duke was drunk. Not alarmingly so. But there was a gauntness about the Duke's eyes, behind his deliberateness, the clear possibility of panic.

Harwood frowned.

'Did you gather –' the Duke continued. 'Forgive me, these questions are necessary.' His large, veined hands shifted uncomfortably in his lap. 'There were women,' he said. 'I know for a fact there were several. Not that I find that astonishing. But afterward.'

For a moment he was unnaturally conscious of the sound of the rain. He waited until his head had stopped buzzing. He said: 'There had always to be something new, don't you think? To distract him. Something to worry over.' His eyes shone. 'Something,' he said, 'to stir up all the wells of thought and feeling at once –'

His head tilted awkwardly. A strand of his dark, parted hair fell abruptly over his forehead.

The Duke sank again into his seat. He was tired. Since he had seen the photograph, he had barely slept. He had been drawn up short, suddenly, without reason. He knew that much. It was no help. Reason, he had decided, was of no help.

'May I ask,' His Grace began once more. He stopped. It was all too long ago. When Wykeham had abandoned Willa Brelling, Harwood had yet to be born. 'There were others,' he said. 'Probably more than I know. You are quite certain he never –'

'Your Grace?'

'Women,' the Duke said, a bit sharply.

'No,' Harwood answered. 'Not to me.'

On the outskirts of New Anwanux there was more open land. Grimly, the Duke stared at the patchwork of meadows. Harwood kept his gaze resolutely forward. Still His Grace was not without hope.

'Would you remember,' he asked, 'if Wykeham ever spoke to you of horses?'

Harwood shook his head dismally.

Crossing the trackbed, the car jerked twice. The driver cut the wheel sharply. A cluster of blurry shapes appeared out of the rain. At the end of the lane there were five rectangles of gray stone. Two of the mossed roofs had already fallen. The house itself was set back and to the left, its few small windows broken, its side porches rotted. The Duke felt an immediate twinge of displeasure. It was no longer a working farm. That it had been preserved at all was due to the rent he paid one year to the next, at Wykeham's direction, for the use of the barn.

Beyond the rusted front gate the car halted. The rain went on clinking on the hood. The sky, which until that moment had held a slight glow, had darkened. Harwood could see little but the two phosphorescent circles the headlamps cut in the fog and, even less perfectly, in snatches, the track that went up to the doors of the barn and, seemingly, under them. He rubbed at the glass.

The barn was unusually large, perhaps three stories. Its high eaves appeared and disappeared in the mists. Harwood peered up at it doubtfully.

'Is this what you wished me to see?' he asked.

The Duke did not answer. Without a word, he swung the door open. Suspicious and yet not wanting to be left behind, Harwood followed.

The yard, blocked up against the foundation, spread before him like a deepening pool. Harwood ran. But by the time he had reached the old, closed doors his shirt and trousers were soaked. Sheets of water rolled down his face. The Duke grunted. He was trying, unsuccessfully, a set of large keys in a padlock. For what seemed a very long time Harwood stared at his back. The air was much cooler. The rain was so heavy that neither heard the splash of the tires on the stones.

The cab ran onto the gravel and stopped. The small man who climbed out unfolded his umbrella. He looked up at the barn. After a moment, quite likely by accident, something brushed Harwood's arm.

'Your Grace,' the man said.

The Duke looked around silently. There had been no introduction.

The little man returned the pipe to his teeth and, maneuvering his umbrella, lifted a small dry hand toward Harwood.

'Holmes,' the man said.

Mistrustfully, Harwood held out his own. 'George Harwood.'

'So His Grace wrote me.' There was a slight movement behind the man's eyes. 'Professor of – ' he started.

'Assistant professor,' Harwood admitted, 'of Awanux.'

Holmes looked at him oddly. 'You realize, I hope, that you couldn't –'

'No.' This time, overcome by dejection, the Duke had not bothered to turn. 'He doesn't. And I haven't told him.'

No one, in fact, had told Harwood anything. 'Some one had better,' he sputtered. Just then the Duke gave a heave to the door.

A wedge of murky light was cast suddenly into the distant rafters. His Grace gave a second great push. The door rumbled and he stepped over the track.

Harwood walked ahead stiffly. The barn was quiet. At the far end, past the stalls where the track ended, he could make out the barest suggestion of another door. He lifted his head. It was Holmes who saw the indignation in his face.

'For the love of Christ,' Holmes whispered, 'hadn't it ever occurred to you that you should be? That you are,' Holmes corrected himself.

Harwood glanced down resentfully. 'I fail to see.'

'Details,' the Duke couldn't help saying.

'What?'

'English,' the Duke said, more bitterly than he had intended. 'Shouldn't you be a professor of English?'

Harwood only looked blank.

The Duke scowled with vexation. It was obvious once he started to look. The problem was to see it in the first place. Without Holmes, he knew, without seeing the photograph, he would have been just as stupid. Nonetheless he was nettled.

'We live,' the Duke said with patronizing coolness. 'We live, I am afraid, Mr. Harwood, at a very peculiar moment in history.'

By then Holmes had left them and was scuffling alone through the hay.

A channel for removing urine and excrement ran at his feet. He found a stick. Leaning sideways, he thrust it into the channel. But the stick encountered only dry stone. Unsatisfied, he wandered among the stalls. He rubbed his hands on the posts and, becoming less squeamish, poked into barrels. The walls were hung with straps and bridles. Advancing, he took each one and examined it. At a loss, he looked back. 'There is nothing,' he shouted. Under the rafters his small reedy voice echoed queerly.

Away from the door, in the brownish haze swarming with motes and the dust of hay, it had become increasingly difficult for Harwood to see anything clearly.

'What details?' he repeated uncomfortably.

'Names.'

'Which –'

The Duke compressed his lips. Yet there was nothing to do but go forward. 'Which are not,' he said bluntly. 'Although they should be. And were before the world started changing.'

It scarcely mattered that he had struggled with it himself.

'Names,' he continued, 'like Awanux, which are but should never have been. Since they are logically quite impossible. Like New Awanux particularly. The first English would never have called it that. They would have called it New Holborn.'

At the far end of the barn Holmes was opening the door.

The Duke felt his voice stiffen. 'Or New Kingston more probably,' he said. 'Or New Thames.'

They had both stopped.

The barn was filled again with the urgent beating of the rain. Holmes stood up ahead against the sky's blackness. He was straining into the wind.

'You had better have a look at this,' he called back.

The Duke stayed where he was. 'Are you certain there is nothing inside?'

The little man turned. 'It is not like that. All those years . . . Someone was certain to have looked.' But there was a sparkling flash. The barn was suddenly rocked by thunder. 'Not in here,' Holmes cried, trying to be heard. But the thunder blunted his words and the wind blew them back in his teeth. 'Just to be loaded,' he shouted. 'Only that.'

'What?'

'Not inside!'

The Duke cupped his ears. Hearing only a buzz, he lurched forward. As his right leg pitched in front of him, Holmes caught his arm.

Beyond the door the yard vanished. At his feet an immense pit opened. Its sides were a nest of roots, thick as a man but blasted. On the bottom the slippery wood was cracked, torn through as though something of astonishing girth had been wrenched from the ground.

The Duke knew what he saw but his mind rejected it. 'It was a horse,' he said obstinately.

Holmes shook his head. 'When you looked. And apparently when Houseman did. What I saw was an oak.'

But it was Harwood who, no longer caring to look, saw their peril. He was tired of their gibberish and wanted merely to return to the college. He looked over the rim without interest. He saw the tangle of wood. There were stones as well, he noticed, halfway down, boulders really, gripped between the gross fingers of the wood as though by pincers. He did not examine them closely. The pit was black and the boulders merely outlines. But at the same moment there was a searing light. For an instant, as starkly as in the woodcut that hung in his study, he saw against the bands of wood the perfect whiteness of the stone. It was enough. Before the darkness closed again and there came the hideous boom of thunder, he saw the chance that what was stone might also be a thing that watched him. Shadows became eyes, cracks reproving mouths. Legs, that seemed too thick to move, bent their ponderous knees and climbed. Five tall figures rose, cast before them the carnage of the tree, and clambered up. Beneath, three others were advancing.

He saw their crowns, fire-gold and gleaming. But as he saw them Harwood blinked. And then they were no longer kings but eight bare stones. Black clouds rolled overhead. Halted on the brink of the chasm, the huge blank stones, now silent, were slathered by rain.

CHAPTER FIVE

'But when we came down upon the carcasses,' the crow said, 'Duinn drove us away.'

'The dead are his.'

The crow fluttered down beside Wykeham's shoulder.

'Ah, but what I wished, lord, was so little,' the crow rasped. 'I might have been satisfied to pick at a bone.'

Wykeham stared into space. He was accustomed to the crow's bitterness. 'You will find no comfort,' he said. 'You are always hungry.'

'One small knuckle,' it said. 'Where is there harm? In Black Wood there are dead enough.'

Wykeham frowned. 'They are Duinn's.'

'To the least strand of hair?'

'Yes.'

'And the nails?'

'Even nails.'

'And memory?'

He was being drawn into the old argument, and on the wrong side. 'All that was given,' Wykeham said softly, mouthing the words he had ceased to believe.

They had crossed the boggy meadow into the wood. The storm that had come up from the sea in the evening had gone before dawn. Despite briars and the dampness, he was dressed in one of his better suits. But though she was the cause of this attention, for the time being, he put Janie Hawleyville out of his mind. He thought instead of the Pope-Hartford.

Through the trees he could still see the roof of the old stable where the car waited. Wykeham grinned. He imagined himself hurtling down steep roads into the morning. He could almost hear the roar of the engine, almost feel the roughness of the rain-washed air prickling into his eyes.

He thought, it is the nature of crows to grumble.

Looking back over the yard, Wykeham felt his heart lifted. He was in love, now, after nearly half a century.

No, he would not listen to the crow.

His house and his grounds, the green meadows and the deep woods of Greenchurch, lay all around him. Changed but unchanging, they provided the background before which, one life to the next, he moved. They would pass. One after another they would vanish. Everything vanished. But something always sprang up in its place. Under the trees the dark air flickered. Spots of sunlight seeped through the foliage.

Wykeham smiled.

Always there was something new to touch, something new to see and feel. He thought, not even an ageless man can hope to live long enough.

On the spur of the moment he decided to take Nora with him.

He owed her that much. Twice already he had promised to take her to Bristol. It would not greatly matter if she went along to the school. Her presence, although it meant the dress shop first and alterations done on the spot, might even reassure the headmistress.

He had been to a shop. He was trying to remember just where among the streets and alleys he had found it, when he saw the loose, weedy slabs of stone, tumbled down from the tower.

Wykeham looked around uncomfortably.

He had not intended to go into Black Wood. Yet he had only himself to blame for that. Out of habit, he went to bed late and rose too early.

While it was still dark he had washed and dressed. He had polished his own boots in the empty kitchen. Finding his solitude unnerving, he had gone to his desk and begun a letter to the Duke of West Redding. Ostensibly the letter was about the cost of ladders and scaffolding, a request for advice on a fair price for roofing the rotted patch over the library. In fact, he had written at the beginning of the month, a more necessary letter, which after rather longer than was customary the Duke had somehow not as yet answered. It had seemed untidy. Perhaps His Grace was simply getting older. Nevertheless, it paid to be certain.

The last drops of rain had skiddered across the window pane. At the edge of the world the bold light had risen. Light flooded into the valley, drowning the hills and farms.

His mind had been restless and he had found himself staring idly at the paper, daydreaming about the girl. He had put the unfinished letter aside and had gone onto the porch and then down the steps into the yard. In his mind he had been rehearsing his speech to the headmistress.

Fortunately, Janie's father was to be detained for some weeks by his business. He had already advised the school that his daughter would need to stay on at the academy for part of the summer. He should not, therefore, provided the headmistress agreed, prove overly difficult.

Wykeham had entered the meadow. The crow had come down to him and, together, they had drifted into the wood.

With an almost palpable sense of regret, Wykeham realized that he was not where he wanted to be.

He was less than a mile from the house. Yet when he came under the trees, the little path shriveled. The oak boughs, meeting overhead, thickened, turning the underwood moldy and dark. He was not surprised. The darkness had been deliberate. He had planted the grove himself, back in the sixteen hundreds, on the folded slope of the hill to conceal the huge stones. Even then the shoulder of the hill had closed around the base of the tower. Only the last heap of stones had risen above the ridge. Now, in less than four hundred years, whole new sections had fallen.

Wykeham went up to it. What was left of the tower leaned drunkenly. Unhappily, he lifted his neck.

Once there had been rooms without number, chambers and high vaulted halls, cocklofts and armories. The passages twisting between them had run out onto the walls. On the walls themselves there had been heralds and, under the open sky, yards filled with horsemen.

He had been a boy then, eager and dissatisfied by turns, frightened and waiting for something to happen. Like a child's, his eyes had flashed open with wonder.

Once the fair land undersea had been shining.

When he had ridden into the city, Lord Duinn beside him, all the colors of the harbor had danced on the stone. But the whiteness of the Great Horse Duinn rode had been more dazzling. Stunned, he had turned his head. He had looked very hard at the walls and the towers. He had looked everywhere except at the Stallion. Still his boy's fingers had ached to touch the white mane. In his heart he had already been a thief.

Out of a long pale face Duinn's deep sea-black eyes had watched him cunningly. He knew, Wykeham thought, even then.

It had been another time. Except for the scattered islands, all the West had been ocean.

Wykeham surveyed the rock. The great door, high above the ground, and the many shuttered windows were now no more than a few ragged holes. The flights of broad stairs, after years beyond counting, were merely a jumble of stones.

The old griefs boiled up in him. He waited for the crow to speak, knowing it must and not wishing to listen.

'And the Horse?' the crow said.

Turning aside, Wykeham began to climb up on the tower. He struggled over the boulders, for the handholds were gone. Blackness gave way to grayness. He grunted. The crow flew up to him easily. Wykeham pushed on through the branches and dug between thorns. At last he came out of the shadow and stood on the head stone, looking over the drive. The house and the stables were below him. In the distance, obscured by the green of the wood and the green of the meadow, there were two other towers, two more of the nine. But their rough mounds were broken, their stones carted off by farmers for back steps and cellars, remade into foundations and dry walls.

The crow settled down beside him and tilted its head.

'Since the world began changing, I have kept it,' Wykeham said with conviction.

From where he stood he watched the women come out onto the porch. It was his porch. He had set the posts. He had planted the hawthorn whose branches wound into the railings.

'Well, perhaps nothing will happen for a while,' the crow said.

Wykeham considered all that he had made and done. Now more than ever he did not wish to part with it.

'I am going to marry,' he said.

'Do you not fear him, lord?' the crow whispered.

'Always.'

'He will come for her.'

For a little while Wykeham was silent. 'There are other worlds,' he said.

The crow laughed. 'And he has gone into all of them.'

Wykeham stood in the sunlight and thought. Before him, in the lines of the walls, the squares of the meadows, he saw the spare ordered beauty of his own hand. The wide, windless landscape, the large country house at its center, was a picture he had fashioned, had marked with his longing and fixed with his thought. What had been before, what was Duinn's, eroded, was now nearly lost. It did not matter he had come to the tower. It was passing; all that had been, the ancient, violent warring world, would vanish.

Wykeham looked out, almost seeing the world that would be.

'With each day I grow stronger,' he said. 'Soon there will be a new land, a land which he never entered.'

The crow looked at him.

'Indeed, lord,' it asked quietly, 'how will that be?'

Wykeham reached down and scratched it under the beak and along the left side by its ear. 'I shall see it,' he said, smiling, staring over the valley.

The stone moved beneath him.

Wykeham turned, too swiftly perhaps to have noticed.

Pressed by its own enormous weight, the stone never felt the weight of the man. There was nothing to be felt. (It was not as yet aware of the difference between one thing and another, certainly not between a man coming into the wood and a man, after a time, leaving it.)

It seemed only a moment.

Old R'gnir reeled back, rising from the unspeakable darkness, from the choking stench of his blood. . . .

It had seemed like forever.

Stupid with fatigue, he had pulled himself up the rough tower stairs, away from the battle. He had expected the pain. In his heart he had known he was dying, was perhaps already dead. He pushed the monstrous thought from him.

In the end he had only been crawling. Yet it had been too much to crawl and to think, too much to listen to the pounding of boots gaining behind him. It had been enough to know that he must not die trapped in the rock, in the darkness.

At the top, before the high windows, he looked at the waste of the city, at the world that was gone.

The blow had come at his back. . . .

R'gnir moved his thick neck. The live, bitter fragrance of oak-flowers filled his nostrils.

He looked up at the blue shining sky. He looked down. At his feet there was a solid mass of trees and beyond it the green shut-in valley. Loping across the field a dark-haired young man lifted his arm. A crow fluttered out of the sunlight.

R'gnir blinked. It did not matter that everything shifted. There was a white bird now and a black field. It was all much the same.

The young man, his hair pale as the ghostly blankness of a photographic negative, continued to raise his long arm.

Nora drew back the thick curtain, on the chance of getting one last look at the diminishing figure, in a print dress, striding heavily away from the house. Instead she saw the stableboy digging his boot in the gravel in the shade of the drive. Wykeham had come into the room. He stood silently just inside the door.

Nora pulled her hand back.

Her face, she was convinced, was scarlet.

Deliberately his eyes did not rest there. Rather he looked where she was staring. A single branch, growing close to the ground, swung idly in the breathless air. Deer perhaps. Even in daylight, the deer, wandering among the bracken and the May-bushes, often came quite near the house. But the hearts of the deer were gentle. The least gesture caused them alarm. Wykeham held his head still.

Whatever had been there had gone.

'Is there some trouble in the village?' he asked.

Before she turned to him she had tucked the letter in the waist of her skirt. 'Only women's talk,' she said mildly, certain that this would not interest him. She ran her delicate fingers along her neck.

He would not let her see he was smiling.

'Put on your shoes,' he said. He did not have to explain they were going to Bristol.

Her breasts jiggled.

The Pope-Hartford, which was higher and grander than she had first imagined, gave a second alarming bounce. Nora held herself tightly. The river winked in and out between the dark trees. The car swerved, pulling her away from him.

She had been caught off her guard. Somehow the letter had slipped down under her skirt.

She gave a wriggle, trying to draw it back. The letter, unmoved, felt satisfyingly thick against her.

It was an immense sum, nearly three hundred pounds. Undoubtedly the steamship agent had sent a cheque. Somehow Plum had managed to cash it. Not that Nora had exactly asked her; under the circumstances, ignorance had seemed perhaps safest. But, however it had been accomplished, Nora was genuinely glad.

She was free, or could be, if she wanted.

Now, in the streets of Bristol, or, passing speculatively along the aisles of a shop, she could, if she dared, walk away from him. He would miss her then. Nora smiled. He would be in a panic. But when he returned to the house, she would already be stepping out of a taxi she had hired herself, wearing a dress that was already bought and paid for. She teased herself with the thought. It was as lovely as the feel of the letter, sharp-cornered and snug, pressed into her thighs.

Only it made her blush more deeply.

'I should like a blue dress,' she said all at once.

The sides of the car, like the sides of a carriage, were open and her hair blew all over her face.

Almost tenderly he drew a strand away from her mouth. 'A half dozen blue dresses,' he said. 'But there will only be time for one fitting.'

'Are we in a hurry?' Her voice sounded odd because she had been holding her breath.

For an instant his eyes left her. 'I have been thinking,' he said. 'It is a big house. You and Olivia can scarcely be expected to keep up with all of it.'

For a moment he seemed not quite to know what he wanted to say.

'I have engaged a maid,' he said quickly. 'Or nearly that.'

'Is it so difficult?'

He touched her arm.

'Is that difficult?'

He gave a little bark of a laugh. 'Not so that it matters.' He held his head still. He said: 'Yet, in one or two things you might be of help.'

She tried not to look at him. She did not want to know what was expected. It was only because the sky was so bright, she thought, so huge and so empty, that the tears came, squeezed out almost invisibly from under the lids.

The dressmaker fussed about her with pins. The woman was old and bent. Her own dress brushed the floor, covering all but the tips of her slippers. Nora shifted. In the glass she caught the woman's shrewd eyes watching her.

'You must hurry,' Nora insisted.

'Don't you worry, dear,' the dressmaker said. 'He knows well enough how long this takes.'

In the hall outside the fitting room a chair creaked. Nora was silent a moment. 'How would he know that?' she asked.

The dressmaker said nothing. Her crooked fingers stirred lightly on Nora's back, straightening a seam. She felt the quick movement of the younger woman's breath.

'You look lovely,' she said reassuringly.

Nora watched her reflection in the glass. Her eyes were gray black, hard and shining, like the eyes of a crow.

'What is she like?' Nora asked her.

'Who, dear?' the dressmaker said.

Nora moved. Her image moved with her. Faced with the inexplicable, Nora smiled shyly. I am a country woman still, she thought. The dressmaker lifted her shears.

'Myself I have a shop,' Nora told her. 'In New Awanux.' Her voice was strained. Without knowing why she began to cry again.

CHAPTER SIX

At first Willa Brelling behaved as though nothing had happened. Her deepest instincts told her that this was wrong, that some explanation was due her. But it was no good wishing for one. She was dead. It was impossible to question that. She remembered the details too clearly. She had been wholly resolved on suicide when she climbed the stairs. She had loved him. Because she loved him still, she was not revengeful. He had deserted her but he was also dead.

Had there been no bequest, no money, she would have followed him more quickly – with a knife over the thin bones of her wrist or a pistol at the forehead. (She had never been squeamish. It was not her own blood she feared.) Sometimes she wondered if the money were not a form of blackmail. It was as though, awkwardly and as unprepared as any of her girls, she had carried his child.

Nightly, the money swelling within her, she would turn away in the darkness. But he was stubborn and would come to her in her sleep.

You must care for this for me, he would say, softly, drawing the covers over his shoulders.

Tortured by longing, she would put her mouth clumsily against his and feel, instead, the dry woolliness of the blanket. She knew he was only pointing out to her the gulf between the dead and the living.

She did not wish to listen.

'I shall find you,' she would say.

He would lie in the darkness of the bed, still shaking. He would be so cold he would hunch forward, hugging his chest with his arms. He had a real child and a wife.

'Let me come to you,' she would plead with him.

No, he would whisper, your task is not yet over. The words were hard. She had given him everything. He had no right to claim more.

She would press her face into the pillow. Closing her ears to him, lulled by his silence, she would sink deeper into sleep. But long after, when he had left her bed, she would hear his footsteps by the window. She knew he was waiting.

'Yes,' she said, once, quietly, unreconciled.

She lived on. She built the hall.

She hired the architects herself. She visited a dozen firms in Bristol and New Awanux, interviewing not only the principals but the plain draftsmen before she made her choice. Afterward she sat on the lawn among the confusion of carpenters with the plans rolled out before her. She was interested in everything; details great and small kept her awake at night. During the day she plied the workmen with questions. She mounted the scaffolding and stood up so close when the men were lifting the stones for the chimneys that at last they had to make rules about where she could stand and when she could shout to them. It was beyond their comprehension that a woman could spend day after day contentedly watching. Yet at the close of each day, as the warm dusk was deepening and she rose to return to her rooms, out of respect they stood themselves. They waited until she had departed before they left the hill.

'Well, that is settled at last,' she said on the day the hall was finished. She put on a white dress and a veil. She shut the door behind her carefully and carried the rope to the top of the stairs. She did not cry out. The immensity of her love made her shy. 'You see I am here,' she told him and very quietly she broke her neck.

The moment should have passed.

Instead she felt the stone and the wood of the hall entering into her. She was astonished. Day after day through the huge arched doorways passed books and laboratory tables, jars of specimens pickled in formaldehyde and brine, glass retorts and Bunsen burners, until, finally, the last room was filled and ready and the first girls marched up the stairs. In the beginning she was silent. She simply hadn't thought of death in these terms. Impatient with the living, she could hardly bear to hear the lessons going on inside her. Hungrily, she waited for evening. The long autumn nights were velvety and cool. The rain trickled soothingly on the tiles of her roof. She listened to the sounds of the school. The hall was at the farthest edge of the court and quiet. An acre of lawn separated it from the main buildings. After evening chapel when the girls returned to their dorms and the last sounds ebbed into silence she waited for sleep, waited to extend to him, however desperately (and if only in dreams), all her unused emotions of love and longing. But she never slept, and now that she was dead, never dreamed, and the severe young man who, once, when she was needing love, had sworn it, never came.

Was he not also dead?

They had told her that.

There had been lawyers and bankers and papers to sign. There had been no casket, no grave. She had a sense of a cavernous ocean beating silently beneath the thin crust of the earth. His death had burst through it. But it was she who was going to drown.

Now, when the sun rose or was setting, the hall would be pervaded by a cold miasmic dampness, by the cool smell of oceans. Darkness lapped in the corners, sunlight danced on the ceiling, intermittently, unhurried. But now always the rooms were full of the slow, mournful sound of the sea. The sound settled on her, came in with long and sharp whispers, possessing her. Her throat, which had been closed by wonder, by longing and fear, suddenly opened. It was then that she had begun to scream.

She was only wood, only stone, only a blurred mist by the stairs. No no one heard her exactly or saw, beyond question, her presence. No ropes were found miraculously dangling from the banister. The beakers boiling in the laboratory never darkened vulgarly with blood. After a decent interval the whole affair lay generally forgotten. Within the year the headmistress, because it was the newest building, removed her office to the second floor of the hall, not a dozen feet from the stairwell. When in a span of years she retired, the new headmistress kept the same office. The death, like so many deaths, was put aside. The girls who had been taught by Willa Brelling turned wives or scholars and went their ways. It was the new girls, daughters, then granddaughters, young women born decades afterward, for whom Willa Brelling was merely a figure in a perplexing tale, who in fearing the hall preserved her memory.

Somewhere over the playing fields a crow sounded its harsh, mocking call.

The Pope-Hartford stopped at the side of the court. She saw him at once. Out of twenty windows simultaneously she watched him climb down. She did not move, for she could not. Though she was burdened and numb, her ardor reached out to him. He was still distant, yet she felt herself spinning. Overcome with amazement, she began to weep.

Please God, she cried, let him come.

He walked to the other side of the car, walked as she remembered, moving casually in a world of his own interests. He was not a phantom. He was so much like himself she knew at once he was not dead, could never have been.

The woman tilted her neck. Willa saw her, a plain, rather unremarkable woman in a blue dress.

She watched him lay his hands on her waist, watched him lift her, solicitously, as one might an invalid. The woman appeared to be trembling. His hands still supported her. He spoke to her quietly. But the woman was frightened. Murmuring softly, he looked toward the hall. For the first time her upturned face fixed on him. There was a question in her eyes. Nonetheless, when he turned away from her, she followed.

Willa was not prepared for the touch of his hand on the door. Across the doorposts and along the beams of the ceiling there was the faintest twinge of alarm. Suddenly he was inside her, could be felt walking, one direct step at a time, along the polished boards of the floor.

There was an odd, joyful smile on his face. The woman, hurrying next to him, weighed the look. 'Must I really say I am your sister?' she asked.

The smile had not faded. 'It would be helpful.'

'It would be a lie.'

'Perhaps not so much of one.'

'I do not understand,' she said simply.

'We live in one house,' he told her, 'chastely, like brother and sister.'

He began to climb the long stairs. Willa found the sound of his footsteps confusing. It should not have been so. In death she was so much larger. Truly, he was no different now from the other small creatures that invaded her rooms in daylight and went away in the evening. Except that he was himself. Should that matter? She had known him but four or five months. In all the years of her life that was so little time. In the years of her death it was less.

He moved quickly to the top of the stairs, to the place where even now some part of her, entrapped, was still lost. He paused, staring blankly. His hand, the hard blunt fingers, clutched Nora's arm. It was scarcely an instant. His attention turned.

'Yes,' she told him, speaking swiftly so that she would not change her mind.

He was about to answer.

'If you wish,' she whispered, unwilling to be interrupted. 'But I shall remain in the house.'

He watched her for a moment.

She waited as he opened the door of the headmistress's office.

Wykeham smiled, at her perhaps, or at the florid woman looking up from a book at the receptionist's desk.

'Mr. Wykeham?' the woman asked.

Wykeham nodded.

*   *   *

The headmistress came away from her desk and gave him her hand and shook his vigorously. She made a scrupulous effort to avoid noticing his youth.

'I am pleased you could see me,' Wykeham said. 'My sister,' he continued.

'Miss Wykeham,' the headmistress said charmingly, steadying her gaze on her. She was a woman of forty, athletic and handsome. Her hair was cut close to her forehead. She wore a white blouse, a purple scarf, tweed skirt and great brown riding boots. She took Nora's hand firmly. Pressing it, she ushered them both to a set of black chairs arranged starkly around a small table. A very elegant little table, Nora noticed, on which there rested a vase and a lamp. Nora looked around silently. The office was large and well proportioned, with two fine long windows looking out on the court. Yet somehow she got the impression of darkness. There was a strange smell, stale and disturbing. Nora found it vaguely menacing and she caught her breath. Perhaps she was not, even now, quite accustomed to expensive things. She turned a little. The woman was watching her.

'What a wonderful room,' she said suddenly.

The headmistress smiled. 'Of course we have your family to thank,' she said evenly.

Wykeham's eyes darted toward Nora.

'You are kind,' Nora answered. But her face was glowing. She took a seat quickly at the end of the table.

The headmistress selected a chair across from her. 'Not kind at all,' she said crisply, 'simply honest. It was a most generous gift.'

Wykeham frowned. 'It was long ago,' he said.

For the first time the headmistress looked at him directly. She became aware of his solidity and his quiet and was puzzled. She knew well enough what she thought of old money; she was less certain what she thought of young men. Although men, the trustees had the good sense to absent themselves from daily affairs. Having more pressing concerns, they hurried through the accounts and passed on, thankfully, to the brandy. After a few tedious hours, they were gone. Wykeham, on the other hand, had been seen lingering on the grounds of the school on six separate occasions.

On each he had spoken with the Hawleyville girl. He had spoken as well to several of the teachers. They had the impression that he was a student of provincial architecture. In any event he had asked a good many questions about the hall. It had come out eventually that he was a

490

descendant of the school's great benefactor, that he had, in a sense, a proprietary interest. Word of his presence had come to her. If by the third visit she had detected a delicate situation, the headmistress allowed herself the benefit of a doubt. A renewed acquaintance with the Wykeham fortune would be advantageous. She had not acquiesced yet she waited.

His letter had arrived in a fortnight. If she had hoped to prove to herself that the situation was not really delicate, the letter put an end to it.

She let Wykeham see her look when she glanced down at the letter she had carried away from the desk when they entered.

'It was good of you to come and explain,' she said.

'It is naturally a concern of yours,' Wykeham answered.

The headmistress smiled. 'I took,' she said, 'the precaution of writing myself.'

'To the father?'

Her smile lingered a second or two. 'He has concerns himself,' she said coolly. 'Regrettably, his business keeps him away. So it has been left, as with matters of her welfare generally, in the hands of the academy.'

'She will be disappointed,' Wykeham said.

'Do you think so?'

'Not to see him,' Wykeham added, 'now with the term ending and the summer ahead of her.' He looked across at Nora. 'It is with that in mind,' he said, 'that my sister and I have proposed an alternative.'

'You are not actually acquainted with the family, I believe,' the headmistress said.

'No.'

'You, in fact, only just met her.'

'Only recently, here at the school. I had come to look at the hall.'

He was not looking at her but at Nora. He continued to stare, frowning slightly. She stared back at him, uneasy, knowing more was expected but too uncertain and too nervous to venture anything. She knew she should leave this place, leave him as well almost certainly. Only there were moments, few and rare enough, but moments, like the instant on the stairs when he had taken her arm, which she saw as proof of his feeling for her. It could not be, must not be, without reason. Did she not, sometimes, fill his thoughts? He had taken her in. He had kept her since. She was conscious, by the steadiness of his gaze, that she filled his thoughts now.

She lowered her eyes. She had no doubt that she disgraced herself. But the whole morning, coming in from Greenchurch to Bristol, had been shameful. She had not meant to weep. Though she had told herself over and over she understood him far better than anyone, she realized that she had entirely misread him. Even the old woman in the shop had seen him more clearly. How often had he gone there? she wondered. With how many women?

So as not to cry out she stopped herself from thinking.

The headmistress reached out her hand. 'Miss Wykeham?' she inquired.

Nora moved away from her. The envelope, tucked up where it should have been safe, fell at her feet.

Nora froze in her place.

Unhesitantly, Wykeham leaned forward. Between his fingers he could feel the envelope's thickness, could see along the torn edge as he lifted it the large bundle of pale green notes. Without a change in expression he placed the letter in front of her. She did not move to reclaim it. He saw that she was strange and ill. 'Nora,' he whispered.

The sunlight, pouring in through the windows, lit her face.

She counted her heartbeats, waiting for the woman to turn on her. The envelope lay face up and accusatory on the table, the name typed in clear bold letters by the steamship agent: NORA BRELLING C/O LONGFORD . . .

Not Wykeham, she wanted to scream. Not his sister, not even his lover, only a harmless lonely woman in a blue dress, a stranger with no right to be here and no claim on him.

'Nora,' he said.

She struggled helplessly, trapped by all the things she was not.

The woman sitting across from her did not appear to notice. Yet her keen blue eyes watched Nora thoughtfully, looked down at the letter and looked back. Again the woman's gaze met hers, swiftly, but without incrimination.

'I am tired,' Nora admitted. But she realized, her thoughts unfolding violently, that it could only be the room's dimness that made them so stupid and blind. In the court beyond, the trees caught the day's pale illumination in their branches; their long shadows, cast into the room, fell wrinkled, light and dark, on the table.

'If only you could see!' she exclaimed. She reached across for the lamp.

But just as the light increased, she was distracted. For a breath's space she stared, seeing not the letter but the table under it, its plain surface glowing suddenly as a thousand tiny scratches caught the light.

She saw the hair first, saw in the nest of serrations the flat tongues of hair licked down and touching the face. The head itself was floating. Nora turned. The face turned and she thought with relief, It is my reflection. For an instant she wanted to throw back her head, wanted to look at them boldly.

It is nothing, after all, she thought thankfully.

Then the eyes opened. With a shock of alarm they caught sight of her own startled eyes staring into them.

'Oh, my God,' Nora murmured.

He slipped his arm around her. Both of his hands were touching her; he was searching her face.

She continued to stare at the head.

'I'm all right,' she told him, nodding, watching the head nod.

But her eyes were unfocused, as though she were not in the room but somewhere close by, looking back.

'It is a big house,' Nora said all at once, a mere whisper. 'Day after day, I am alone in it.' For a long moment she was silent.

She could see the head clearly, its poor haunted eyes straining to look up, to be sure she was there. Such sad eyes, lonely and watching. Its lips moved.

'My brother,' she said. Her voice stopped.

She looked up and found the headmistress's baffled face watching her.

'My brother,' she went on quietly, 'is often gone. It would be a comfort to have someone. Someone . . .' She extended her hand toward the envelope.

It was a moment more before they understood that she did not mean to take it, that she was only pointing.

'I would be grateful,' she said, speaking so softly she could scarcely be heard. 'The family would be grateful. Would be generous.'

They sat motionless.

A soft rustle came from the outer office and then the sound of a knock at the door. It was the girl. Nora was certain of that. Still she did not move. She did not wish to see her, not before it was over, not before it was paid for.

'Please take it,' she whispered, her gray black eyes watching them imploringly. It had never occurred to her that it would not be accepted. The head wanted it done; she wanted it herself. Even her mother, she remembered . . .

'It is not a gift,' she said distinctly; 'it is owed.'

PART IV

Indians

CHAPTER ONE

The letter lay for a moment on the desk where the Duke had tossed it. At last it was dawn. The sun, rising out of the harbor, cast a ruddy glow on the paper. Even the faces of two of the men, His Grace and Harwood, their defiant voices carrying into the bank's deserted corridors, were tinged with red.

The Duke shifted his weight in the chair. He adjusted his spectacles. The river, to which he had turned to avoid looking at Harwood, winked between smokestacks and steeples. Holmes's face alone was without color. He had kept his back to the windows, watching both men. Wearily, he took up the letter His Grace had discarded.

'He wrote something,' Holmes said. 'We accept that.'

'As you might,' the Duke muttered. He was drinking, had already drunk too much to be quite certain of the use of his reasoning. Yet surely some things were beyond question. 'I have had a hundred letters,' he said. 'Since he was . . .'

'A boy?' Holmes asked ironically.

The Duke scowled, recognizing that this was, in fact, just what he had meant. He had already told them of his discovery.

For a moment he recalled Wykeham's face as it had looked on the train, the same face that had greeted him here in this room nearly forty years before.

He had explained it all carefully, how he had walked out onto the platform of Water Street station, how in the window of the passenger car he had seen the young man, who, after four decades, was as he had been, exactly.

But it was the face of a boy that was set in his mind, a lad of seven who had written the very first letter that had come, signed with William's name, from Egypt. For two months he had known it was a lie. But it mattered.

The Duke sat very still. He looked down at his own blunt fingers.

He said, 'It is in his own hand. Isn't that enough? Do you question that?'

Harwood moved to the windows. 'It's not that it isn't,' he said too loudly. 'The point is that it needn't be. Not any more than at the pit . . .'

He did not continue. Each man knew what the other had seen. Hours afterward they still felt the thick hands reaching up from the roots and the gravel, still saw the grotesque legs, bending what should not have bent, begin to climb.

It all had lasted through the space of counted heartbeats.

Then they had heard the gale scream once more, felt the rain beating down.

Harwood turned again, wandering. 'It's just that it might have changed,' he said. 'It needn't be, word by word, what he sent.' He walked out into the middle of the room. 'I know it's crazy,' he whispered. 'My God,' he said helplessly, 'I thought you were both crazy.'

The Duke poured another whisky into his glass.

Harwood glared at him. 'It was you,' he said doggedly. 'You brought me out there. All the way out you kept badgering me, kept asking me questions, telling me how everything I thought I knew was changed.' Harwood shook his head ruefully. 'Well, I believe you now. Every damn thing's changed. Or could change. Anything might.'

'Almost anything,' the Duke said.

'Is that it?' Holmes asked, surprised.

'Is that what?' Harwood wanted to know.

Holmes stared again at the letter.

'Anything,' he said calmly.

The Duke set his glass on the desk.

'Something has to be fixed,' he said.

'And that one thing . . .'

The Duke nodded, relieved, and at the same time not caring. He alone knew the immensity of Wykeham's strength and his cunning. Knew more, at least, than Holmes, who, although he had gone to the train and examined the body, could not have spoken more than a dozen words to Wykeham.

It was now morning. All night they had sat together in this room, talking, trying to think through the puzzle they were caught in.

The Duke glanced blearily at Holmes. He was aware of the small man's good intentions. 'Since he was a boy,' the Duke said, 'he wrote me letters.'

'He was not a child,' Holmes reminded him.

'I know.'

'It was you who explained it,' Harwood said.

Harwood's insistent voice interfered with the progress of the Duke's thought. He lifted the glass.

They were not responsible. Holmes was merely the doctor called by chance to the death. Harwood, although he had known Wykeham longer, nonetheless shared no common act with him, no offense.

The Duke sighed.

Wykeham's life, he was certain, must have touched without consequence a thousand such men. He was not himself so weak and neutral. He had taken hold of what was given him, coldly perhaps, he knew that, and half in ignorance. But no matter what he did not know, a man was dead because of him.

'It was not an accident,' the Duke said. 'I will not accept that it was an accident.'

'Men die,' Holmes said.

Harwood's eyes moved from face to face. It had been his argument, but he had lost control of it. 'What are you talking about?' he asked tensely.

The Duke dug his hands into his lap. For a long while he was quiet.

At last he said slowly, 'Two months ago a man died on a train. He was a young man who worked in this bank. I had put him in charge of the Wykeham Trusts.'

The Duke looked down at his fingers. 'He was a man like myself,' he said quietly. 'No better, perhaps, yet no worse, not above doing what had to be done. He was supposed to meet Wykeham only once. Only talk to him once. It is written right into the Will, was written, over three hundred years ago. Surely that never changed. But Houseman . . . Did I say the young man's name was Houseman?'

Harwood shook his head.

The Duke studied his fingers. 'Well, it was Houseman,' he said.

'There was a young man,' Harwood repeated. 'And he took a train.'

'And he should not have.'

Harwood's eyes clouded over. 'Does that matter?' he asked.

'Wykeham was on the train,' Holmes said evenly.

'And there was a prohibition against that,' said the Duke.

Harwood threw up his hands.

'The man died,' Holmes said.

'He was murdered,' the Duke added quietly.

Holmes's eyes darted up. 'We don't know that. We cannot be certain.'

'You might as well be,' said the Duke. 'You took the photograph.

One of us, at least, should admit it. And you told me about the woman. I never saw her. Never heard what she said.'

'What woman?' Harwood demanded.

Holmes turned to look at him. 'There was a woman on the train,' Holmes explained, 'with the body.' He waited, but Harwood only stood staring miserably. Holmes rested back on his arms. 'A wretched, stupid woman, I think. She believed, quite inconceivably, that Houseman was drunk.'

The Duke watched Holmes carefully. 'It was what she said.'

'What Houseman said really,' Holmes corrected him. 'She was simply repeating it. Saying it over and over. As he did.'

'Which was?' the Duke insisted.

'The world's coming apart,' Holmes said, each word measured and spare, but the meaning fell heavily.

The Duke nodded, content. 'That was the first instance.'

'Of what?'

Almost in spite of himself, as if enjoying Harwood's confusion, the Duke grinned. 'Of anyone noticing. Seeing the world pulled two ways at once, literally ripping apart. Everything he knew and he trusted dividing inside of him. And not stopping. Never stopping.'

The Duke tilted his head. He squinted at Harwood's round face. 'You saw it yourself,' he said, 'for an instant, outside the barn.'

Harwood would not look at either of them; he was trying to think. But all he saw or could think of was Wykeham. 'Maybe he was a little stranger,' he said, 'a bit quieter. But he was kind.'

Harwood felt his mouth tighten.

'He would smile, I remember. Never much of a smile, as if things he knew amused him. But he never spoke of them. Three years and I barely knew him. Then one day he brought me a letter.'

Harwood paused. He seemed to be listening to an inner voice. 'The next day he was going. I went down to the train.'

He heard his own rough sounds of grief and looked away.

From the windows he saw across the green the bleak college towers jutting into the morning.

All his adult life he had spent cloistered in private rooms with the Dutchman, with Austen and James, believing each word added wisdom. And it was nothing. In a wink it could be replaced.

'There was a crowd,' he said. 'I never . . .' He lowered his head.

Holmes returned the letter to the desk.

The four sheets of white paper lay in front of Harwood.

In that instant he knew.

It made no difference. He had abandoned any plan of action. What action is possible? he wondered. Yet it was abundantly clear. He had already read the letter. Not this letter, of course. But he had sat, with Wykeham beside him, at his own desk with such a letter, staring into the morning.

Harwood looked across at the desk. The events of his life, all of which he had thought chaotic, whose scattered moments he had always found bewildering, fitted, he realized, row on row, in a line of cunning duplicates. He did not look ahead. The world was behind him.

He reached back and unfolded the sheets of paper.

'My dear Martin,' he said, reading. He looked up. 'That is your name, Your Grace? Your Christian name.'

Martin Callaghan, the Duke of West Redding, moved in his chair. 'Yes.'

Harwood nodded, returned to the paper. 'My dear Martin,' he repeated, his voice clear and precise and a little too loud as it always was when he was excited. The sun had lifted well above the harbor; the room, although it had been garish, was filled with an easeful light.

'In a little while it will be night again,' he read. 'I have done what I could yet the war is near. I have a daughter. Before too much longer you must come for her. . . .'

Michael Morag was having trouble adjusting his eyes. The breasts for one thing, though they were certainly breasts, seemed to bulge and lean without a normal regard to the stresses and strains of flesh, without respect for the sensible laws of gravity. For another, they hung so near to his face, were each so amply capable of filling his sight, that from one moment to the next he could not decide which to stare at.

He moved his head sideways. The breasts swayed, tugged asymmetrically, as if he watched them in a distorting mirror.

I'm afraid this won't do, the Reverend Michael Morag thought. Reluctantly, he allowed them to vanish.

The world became gray again.

He had a sense, at least, of grayness, of a place somehow betwixt and between. There was a light but he was outside the range of its radiance. The shadows lay at a discreet distance, drab as a monk's habit and as unremarkable. He took no notice.

What was needed, he imagined, was something plumb, with corners at right angles. Something boxlike and square, he thought, like the cottage in Black Wood. For an instant the thought was so sharp, so familiar that it made him homesick. But a cottage, he rather suspected, could be tricky. After all this was new to him. He might as easily arrive under the porch steps with old John rocking senselessly above him, too deaf and, as likely as not, too impaired by his whisky to heed. And he had no desire to be stuck under the joists, a fool of a dead man, hollering, banging up at the boards. So in the end he resisted the temptation.

Nonetheless he was by nature much too cheerful to be subdued by mere inexperience. It must be, he became suddenly convinced, that one begins more modestly. Perhaps with a table, he thought, encouraged.

He happened to glance up.

Plum was staring across the dinner plates at him. Her generous bosom, which had become agitated, bounced up and down with alarm.

The old minister mopped his bald head. 'Ah me,' he sighed appreciatively. He smiled at her. Altogether too broadly, he recognized, but death, he hoped, had its prerogatives.

He tilted his head and was astonished and more than a little pleased to discover he was sitting, in fact, in his own parsonage. He looked around at the heavy plates and thick glasses, at the starched white linen, relieved that they were not much changed.

'I hope you don't mind,' he said, aware that, as far as he knew, he was now quite powerless to undo his existence. 'I imagine this is distressing.'

'Who's this?' Longford asked, coming in at just that moment from the kitchen.

Plum breathed again.

'He was simply there,' she whispered. But she had almost said nothing. Morag bestowed a slight gracious bow and a provocative grin.

'Dear, dear,' he said. 'The husband, of course. I might have thought of that.'

Longford stared. He fancied an unaccustomed pink now suffused Plum's cheeks, but her head turned from him.

'Who are you?' Longford asked. 'How did you get here?' He was agitated himself and, although both questions had been directed at Morag, he continued to look at his wife.

'Name's Morag,' the other man answered. 'Though I've always thought just plain Michael sounded friendlier.' He spread his hands across his stomach and clasped his thumbs. 'I know I haven't been asked,' he said thoughtfully, 'but there are a few bottles of porter down in the cellar. Boxes actually. I laid them in myself. And if it wouldn't be too much trouble . . .'

'You're Morag,' Longford murmured, his voice grave.

The old minister clasped his thumbs tighter; his kindly face wore an expression of honest bewilderment. 'Didn't I just say so?' His large bald forehead wrinkled. 'Yes, I'm quite certain.'

'The Reverend Mr. Morag,' Longford told him.

Morag stared at an empty glass. 'Michael,' he said.

An odd flicker passed across Plum's face. 'The Reverend . . .' she started.

Old as he was, Morag's dark eyes filled with laughter. 'No longer, I think,' he chuckled. 'Not much use. Even less opportunity.'

He unlaced his brown fingers and reached for the glass. 'Of course it comes as something of a shock,' he went on, patting the crystal. 'Thirty years in His service. But they don't let you know beforehand.' He gave a good-natured shrug. 'I don't know. Maybe it's not what it seems. Perhaps He is somewhere.'

Morag was suddenly quiet, wrinkling his forehead and staring at the glass as if he saw two conflicting shapes in the reflection and was not quite decided which was wanted.

'Though hereabouts,' he declared, 'for the most part it's Indians.'

Almost as soon as her head touched the pillow Plum was asleep. Longford, still dressed in his shirt and his trousers, lay beside her. From the moment he had succeeded in getting her off to their bedroom he had wanted to talk. But she had gone about her preparations with unaccustomed privacy. While she undressed, he had caught her watching herself in the mirror, the very lifting of her head, the smallest turning of her mouth as she smiled, excluding him. It had seemed to him then that she was half a stranger; indeed it had seemed so all evening. She had filled a plate for Morag with her own portion and, with a maternal absorption, watched the old man devour everything greedily. Later, on her own, she had disappeared into the cellar, thumping back up the stairs shortly with four dusty bottles of porter tucked under her arms.

'They're his, after all,' she had whispered, passing her husband and seeing his frown.

Morag had poured out two glasses for himself. The glass he had poured for Plum she accepted readily. Longford's, untasted, remained in the middle of the table. In a few minutes Morag had reached for it. He had smacked his lips happily.

'It's a pity, don't you think,' he had said, 'to have wasted so much life wondering if there were delight both in the world and out of it?'

Longford had turned. He had expected to be frightened by the old face. He would have been, he realized, had Plum but showed the least alarm. There was a dead man at his table. For twenty years he had preached the certainty of resurrection, but he was not, lacking her, prepared to meet its confirmation without panic. Lazarus rose and so did Christ. He believed in miracles, but only in a far-off time, or in the world to come.

In their bed, watching Plum sleep, he understood how thoroughly he depended on her being near him. Every now and then her breast rose and there came from her lips a faint and barely perceptible moan, the sound distant and yet profound, as if something far beyond his reach had shaken her.

Unable to calm himself, Longford went down stairs. Morag was sitting where they had left him. The old man had brought up four more bottles from the cellar. Already two of these were empty.

'Don't you sleep?' Longford asked impatiently.

'Perhaps a little,' Morag answered. 'Though just from habit. No point in it.'

Longford stared at him foolishly. He had wanted to rail at something. Death had entered his house. Yet there had been no outcry, no horror. He desperately wanted to be driven against something else, something more clearly appalling and obscene. He wanted, at any cost, to save his wife. But the ordinariness of the old man had robbed him of the usefulness of his anger.

Longford looked down at his feet. He had forgotten his shoes.

'You might join me,' Morag said amiably.

'How are you here?' Longford shouted.

Morag raised his glass. 'Because,' he said, 'I find it difficult to imagine women.' He held the glass out at arm's length and gazed at it thoughtfully. 'Have you ever noticed how difficult it is,' he asked, 'to call their faces to mind? Or any part of them? Not the general idea. That comes easily. But the specifics. The precise turn of shoulders and noses. The exact shade of their skin.'

Morag's large splotched face looked a bit sad in the gleam that came from the lamp in the parlor.

'Of course geography's easier,' he said. 'The hills above the old towns stand out sharply. And the river certainly. From high up, coming in from the moon, you can see . . .'

Longford gasped. 'F-from the moon?' he stammered. He was struck by a sudden vivid image of the river, not as he had mapped it, not even as he had imagined it would be from the hill above Greenchurch, but from an airy distance away from the earth. For an intolerable moment he saw it, a ribbon of cold-blooded light, turning among the hills and the towers, imprisoned, wriggling back on itself.

Their eyes met.

'Like a serpent,' he whispered, 'its tail in its mouth.'

The old man smiled at his innocence. 'Like the living,' Morag corrected him. 'Like the dead.'

CHAPTER TWO

Jane spread her long legs, enjoying their nakedness. Though he was gone, the pillow still smelled of him. More than likely she smelled of him herself. You wicked girl, she thought, gazing contentedly at the tumbled sheets. Her new dress lay over a chair on the other side of the room. She remembered that she had been faintly surprised when looking down from his bed she had seen it there, without her. They had not, she knew, exactly agreed on any of this.

They had gone directly into the great room after dinner. For a quarter of an hour she had sat beside him under the odd old-fashioned woodcuts of horses, on her best behavior. Through the half-closed door there had come a sort of listening silence. The cook had been introduced at the table. But the old woman waited with the others gathered now in the hallway, anticipating a more formal introduction, at the head of the line.

'You'll do fine,' Nora had told her. Yet the hand which had reached toward her was trembling.

Jane thought at first that his sister meant simply to give her a pat, the fingers unheeding and as perfunctory as the questions about her schooling. But the hand which dropped into her palm was cold and, when Nora straightened, Jane felt the small weight of the ring she had left there.

His sister glanced at her slyly.

'Heaven knows he will not have thought of that,' she whispered.

Wykeham, paying no attention, was watching the door. He was dressed for riding in a suit of brown corduroy and long black boots. An old cloak hung from a peg on the mantel behind him. Its clasps were bronze; its hem, if once stitched with care, now was torn. Somewhere a window was open. Assailed by a gust of air, the ancient fabric turned restlessly, first one way, then another. Wykeham lifted his head.

'Is Mrs. Norfolk here?' he asked.

As if on cue Lizzy appeared in the doorway. She had washed her hands and abandoned her apron. Her heavy gray hair had been pushed into a bun.

'Lizzy,' he said, 'this is Miss Hawleyville.'

Jane felt in that instant somehow different. Wykeham, his mind elsewhere, scarcely looked at her. Yet she knew unmistakably that the situation which should have been awkward would not be and that, curiously, he was the cause of it. She had been conscious of this oddity from their first meeting. Nothing directly happened and yet always something was set in motion: slowly, with an almost casual inevitability, everything she expected, all that she had been taught to expect, changed.

The mountainous old woman bent one huge knee, curtsied.

'I hope you will be pleased with us,' she said. Though she did her best to smile, her eyes, Jane thought, were more suited to fierceness. Yet a charm seemed to hang on them. They jerked to Wykeham's face, suddenly, fondly, and then back again. The woman took a step forward. There was something knotted in her hand.

'It is but a token, miss,' she said.

'Oh I couldn't,' Jane protested, not even seeing what it was.

Wykeham laughed. 'Then you must say no to all of them.' His voice had become a deep chuckle. 'And to me as well.'

She had thrown back her head to look at him, when he kissed her. It was the first time they had openly kissed, there in the great room, in front of the women. He was still holding her, his hand pressed quite deliberately under her breast, when a second figure edged the door open and came into the room. She had not even a moment to collect herself or to savor her feeling of wonder.

The man was tall and stoop-shouldered, his large horse-teeth stained. But his wild hair had been combed and he had been fitted out in a jacket that looked as if it had been borrowed.

'My lord,' he said softly. He moistened his lips.

'Say what you have come to say,' said Wykeham.

Fred Norfolk pulled his big hands from his pockets. He turned what he had brought over in his fingers.

'Lady,' he said slowly, seeking courage, 'it is well you have come. A woman is a prop for a man in times of great trouble. In such times . . . In these times . . .' He moved a little, uneasily. Because he had come into the light she could see his face struggling and guessed that he had rehearsed the words. Norfolk took a great breath. 'Lady, it is well,' he began again.

Without looking she knew that Wykeham was smiling. It gave her a mysterious pleasure to feel how easily she had come to read his moods. The man had grown pale. He loomed over her, clearly trembling, his practiced words tumbling over each other. With a part of her mind she listened, trying to discover why he stood there and what he wanted. But

507

the other part, detached and unpuzzled, felt Wykeham's hands pressed hard above her waist.

'On this night of all nights,' Norfolk went on solemnly, 'I am honored to greet you . . . our little sister . . . our mother . . .'

Lizzy hissed at him.

Norfolk turned red. Quickly he gave what he held into Jane's hand and drew back.

The room became quiet. The only sounds were the one the little breeze made and the rustling of the cloak. Jane's eyes moved between them, uncomprehending.

'L-lord, I never,' Norfolk stammered.

'There is no harm,' Wykeham answered, 'only eagerness. How could I fault eagerness?' Wykeham smiled at him. 'On this night of all nights?'

Jane was sitting up stiffly. 'What is he saying?' she asked.

'Hush,' Lizzy told her.

Once again the door opened.

One by one they entered now, making their way in from the dark hallway. For a moment they hesitated before her, watching her, lingering as long as they dared: George Tennison first, then Olivi? Adam France and Jakey pressed in close behind. Then suddenly the room was filled with a great cheerful company, nudging and laughing. There was a line coming in from the kitchen, small farmers and their wives who now and again did a job or two at Greenchurch and a man who had walked the ten miles from Ohomowauke, though the moon that night was only a sliver. By ones and twos they came forward and presented their gifts. But along the wall a woman, afraid her child would cry, kept back timidly until Wykeham saw her and called her out. Beaming, he took the child and let him crawl in his lap while the woman approached, curtsied, and pressed a small parcel into Jane's hand.

Jane was left staring blankly.

'I was hoping you didn't mind,' the woman told her.

The child was quiet, respectful. His little face peered at Wykeham, then at Jane. He grabbed at her hair.

'Ah, lady,' the woman whispered, 'I just couldn't keep myself away.'

Jane was trying to listen, but the words seemed irrelevant. Without giving up the child, Wykeham had slipped his hand down and was loosening her dress. Then once more he kissed her. In the merest fraction of a second, before she could make up her mind what she thought, two dozen voices laughed and cheered.

* * *

She rolled over on his bare shoulder. It was not quite morning. They had not slept. She was certain that she had not, not that she remembered precisely all that had happened from the moment he caught her up in his arms. She had opened the door to his room because he could not have. His hands had been filled with her and the small, unopened presents she had borne away in the folds of her dress, presents which with his fumbling and fiddling had seemed ever in danger of spilling. And they had spilled, finally, onto the bed, falling all around her as she fell, drawing him after.

The cool morning air played about them. It swept behind her and snatched one end of the coverlet. With feigned modesty she tugged back and, by chance, touched the edge of one of the little parcels. Inexplicably, it had not been scattered by their lovemaking. She moved her fingers over the tightly wrapped paper and into the loops of the ribbon.

'What are they?' she asked.

She could not see his face, but she believed he was watching her.

'What is usually given,' he said.

She let her fingers rest and snuggled into his shoulder.

'It's customary then?' she said, grinning to herself. 'A poor girl's deflowering?'

'It's been done before.'

'Not to me.' It was but a small demonstration of her independence. But the old memory awoke in him and he caught himself staring at her, looking at her as if for the first time, as if, even now in his bed, in his heart as well, she were a stranger. She was a child, after all. The feel of a man inside her was new to her. He drew his finger along her thigh. There were so many things she did not understand, too many things he had not told her. And he must, despite the enormous difficulty of explaining. And he would. He was determined that this time it would be different. Listening to her breath, he remembered how, on a thousand other nights, he had been haunted by the terrible knowledge that the arms he held, that held him, would soon wither and grow old. The round flesh that bound him and would be bound by him gladly, would swell and rot. No, he thought, no longer.

He lay back in the darkness.

'They are wiser, love,' he said. 'They knew what was expected. They brought what must always be given.'

He felt her head turn.

'What must be given,' he repeated, 'for a child to become a woman. Whatever there is to be wished for: beauty by one, the second virtue, the third cleverness . . .'

He stopped because she had squirmed.

The grayness grew a little, widened, and he could see the small line of her breasts.

'You treat me like a child,' she said.

'No,' Wykeham said.

'It is a story for children.'

She was shivering now. This time, when she hunched over, he did not touch her.

'Tell me,' she whispered, her face set, only her mouth working. 'One day do I climb the attic stairs to a door? Do I say "Good morning, mother" to the old woman waiting inside with her spindle?'

Agony was filling her.

'Do I prick my finger?' she asked.

He let her go on. Because she was beyond comfort, he did not try to comfort her. She had grabbed at the bedclothes. He knew that it was his body that she knotted and twisted. Her tears, when they came, were heavy and splashed down on his arm. He did not hurry her.

The window, as it would be winter and summer, was open. The air was thick again with the smells of morning, hawthorn on the wet porch railing, damp hay, mist from the river. Morning always came so, he knew, the earth raw and dripping, as it first rose, from the sea. In the new light he cast a long strange shadow over her.

So Duinn first saw himself whole, he thought, recognizing the man-shape – in the world before mirrors – in darkness.

He began to speak, so quietly that she had to lean forward. Thus, in spite of her hurt, she was again drawn to him and felt, next to his ribs, his heart beat, unexpectedly.

'What if it were a story for children?' he asked. 'Would it matter?'

'Yes.'

'They are all children.'

'I am not.' Her eyes were wide open now, staring.

'Everyone . . .'

'Once,' she insisted. 'But it changes.' She had put out her hand, not to him, but he had clutched it. What she had reached for was not there. For a moment she had not even thought of him.

Her mother was dead. Her father, who when his knees were stiff and his legs unsteady she would help up the stairs in the drab little hotels where she had been taken on holidays, whose visits she nonetheless cherished, had been kept away, the headmistress had said, by his business. She was his only daughter. Without shame, ignoring the smell of his whisky, she had cheered him and had comforted him in his loneliness.

For a vivid moment, in her mind's eye, she saw his stooped shoulders, his sad grizzled head.

'You don't see,' she cried suddenly. 'But it changes. We start off. We have parents. We are their children. But it stops.'

'And if it did not?'

He had pulled aside the coverlet and she could see almost all of him. Except for his face and his arms, which were deep-tanned, the rest, the lean muscled back and the long hard legs, although equally dark, were, in a way she could not quite place, unblemished. Unused, she remembered thinking afterward, protected, like the smooth inner wood under bark.

The sunlight flooded in through the window. He was sitting up in it.

'What if there were a man,' he said, 'in the very beginning of the world –'

The light, and the words as well, because they had the sound of another story in them, annoyed her. 'Like Adam?' she said suspiciously.

'No,' he said. 'Just a man.' He leaned back and seemed to take a long look at her. 'Not even a man,' he said. 'Not at first. A boy. But he grew. He turned into a man and, like other men, he met a woman. And, after a time, there were children and the children grew, as children always have. But one day the woman, because finally she was an old woman, died. The man mourned her. He waited to be dead himself. But he was not. For something had happened to him. He did not die. In fact, he had scarcely changed. He was still the young man he was when he stopped being a boy. But he was alone, mourning the woman. So in time he found another woman. Perhaps as beautiful and as kind. Perhaps not. As before, there were children. But this woman also grew old and, like the other, also died. And the children, though themselves parents, also died. But the man still was.'

She was listening but she was not looking at him. She was watching, as the light turned more gold, the faint variations in the shabby plaster on the bedroom wall, the blistered paint on the door. In the rooms below there had been new paint and fresh plaster. She had seen that when he had brought her into the house. On the ground floor there had been hammering and men in overalls. The workmen, in fact, had been everywhere. At intervals, through the first afternoon, she had counted over a dozen. But she had lost count altogether, when after dinner they had trooped into the great room. It was like a small private army. Coming into the room, she remembered, they had bowed to him.

'They called you lord,' she said in astonishment.

When he was up and gone, she went to the door and looked out. Sunlight dappled the landing but the top of the house was empty. Sounds drifted up from the kitchen. She closed the door, and, because she was still naked, locked it.

'What if a man kept on having children?' he had asked her. 'Not only for a lifetime but for a hundred lifetimes? For a hundred times a hundred lifetimes? For longer?' He had paused.

It had seemed to her like one of those unsolvable problems they gave you in school. If Adam had two sons and each, in turn, had two sons . . . But that hadn't been right either. Not Adam. He had denied that. But some man having children.

She lay again on the bed. Absurdly, feeling where he had been, she uncrossed her legs. They had argued. But her recollection of the argument was muted, was mixed with the slow warmth of the sunlight and the touch of his arm on her neck, his hand on her thigh. Now that it was done, she was much less frightened than she had expected. He had wanted it but all the while she had known she might have stopped him and in the darkness it had been she, though he had been everywhere, who had found him. 'I have never been happier,' she thought. 'Nor has anyone,' she thought more grandly. Perhaps it was that that made her remember the argument.

How many people were there in the world? she wondered.

'If one man, the same man, kept having children,' she had asked, incredulous, 'for a hundred lifetimes?' She had given a little gasp.

'Longer,' he had said. 'From the beginning.'

'Then . . .' The word had almost the sound of a conclusion but he had interrupted her.

'Everyone,' he had said, 'or nearly that, given time.'

His eyes were black, his hair blacker, like her own. She could smell the scent of his skin. 'No,' she had said furiously.

Long after she could hear the sharp hooves of the stallion on the gravel below. She was hardly listening; instead she had pressed her nose into the pillow. By the time she had gone to the window he was already halfway across the lawn. He was walking the stallion, its legs and its shoulders deep in the hay.

Clouds had come up but there was still a patch of blue sky over the top of the hill toward the wood. On the nearer slope, before he turned and went from sight, she saw him stop and unbutton his trousers. The pressure of her bare flesh on the windowsill awakened a hint of delighted wickedness in her body. With a tinge of surprise she watched him relieve himself in the grass.

512

She had been raised chiefly by women. 'He is a boy after all,' she thought, smiling. As she went on smiling, her face lost the least trace of wickedness and she went back, for a moment, to being a child herself. She turned quickly and with the unconscious morality of children, knowing herself naked, began to put on her dress.

CHAPTER THREE

In the books they had read together, books which for the most part Wykeham had given him, the women were pushed off until the end, a reward presumably. But here, Harwood thought, they were, his wife and his daughter, inconveniently in the middle. The Duke, of course, could come and go as he pleased. Holmes was married. All the same, Harwood did not think it greatly impeded him. Doctors' wives, he was certain, were accustomed to having their husbands called away unaccountably.

Harwood thumbed through his wallet, counting the few notes, and threw them all down on the table. 'Twenty pounds,' he said unhappily, realizing that His Grace would have to pick up his share of expenses.

'We can look after ourselves,' his wife said with dignity. The girl, playing on the floor before the woman's feet, had not lifted her eyes to look at him.

'Just a few days,' he said in despair.

The woman let herself be kissed. Behind her the little kitchen was hung with laundry. She had washed his one good shirt, straight from his back, when he had come home that morning. It lay starched and expertly folded in the bottom of his suitcase. She had packed it herself with his underwear and his second pair of trousers.

'I would like to wear it again,' he explained and she nodded, distracted. Through the open window, hours before, when he had only just arrived, she had caught a glimpse of the old gentleman climbing into the limousine. If he were anyone important, her husband had not mentioned it.

'I cannot say what will come of this,' he had told her. He lifted out the shirt she had folded carefully, put his thick arms into it. 'But the details have to be the same, I think. Or nearly so.'

He was taking the overcoat.

'What do you want with that?' she asked.

She had the uneasy feeling that he was already gone. 'It's summer,' she put in scornfully.

Harwood looked past her.

'That first night I had it,' he said.

It had also been April – or March. He had forgotten which and wondered now if it mattered.

'I must be going,' he said, gently, and stepped out the door.

She watched him go down the walk. She did not know how long she stood by the curtain. It was not until she had turned back that she saw the suitcase open on the table.

Harwood went along the High Street and through the park, as he had come before, without luggage. As he crossed the intersection, cars with stone-faced chauffeurs hooted imperiously. Let out from shops and offices, men and women pressed into buses or, retracing familiar routes, melted anonymously into pubs and houses. Harwood trudged on doggedly. His Grace had been prepared to drive them all, Holmes included, out by the river road to Greenchurch, but Harwood had protested.

'You and I must start at the station,' he had told him. 'Please understand.'

But he had not. 'And Holmes?' he had asked.

'I must get on at Bristol, Your Grace.'

The Duke had sat with his back to them, overlooking the city. During the night it had seemed clearer; but now, the whisky deserting him, he had not been able to think.

'How will you get there?' he had asked.

In fact, Holmes had taken a taxi.

'It seems a foolish expense,' the Duke said, meeting Harwood by the information booth. Under the great dome of the waiting room his voice did not sound angry but humiliated. But he was not thinking of the money or, indeed, of Holmes. A daughter, he thought. It seemed impossible that Wykeham had not told him.

Except for the one secret, he had been told everything. He had earned that trust. He had worked indefatigably. It was he who had always been summoned to deal with lawyers, with loose ends, with death. But the one thing that counted, a child, the passing on of the inheritance, had, until the very end, been kept from him. It wrung him to think of it.

He walked stiffly beside Harwood. Because the evening was mild, the doors to the platform had been left open. They could both see the train.

As they neared the gate, Harwood stopped, shocked by the clarity of his recollection. His eye crept along the line of car windows.

'There ought to be a woman,' he said.

The crowd of passengers, already boarding, were finding their seats. No face peered down at him.

He had not wanted to look this far ahead, to visualize anything too completely, as if all their lives had been plotted. But at bottom he had kept a list; he was checking against it.

'She was staring out of the train,' he said, almost desperately.

For the first time the Duke noticed that Harwood was carrying the overcoat.

'There were two women,' he reminded him. But Harwood had forgotten the other.

It depended, the Duke realized, on who had been watching.

And three men, he thought. Four, if he counted himself. But he did not think he should be added; there had been nobody watching him. Harwood, he remembered, had walked ahead but he had stayed where he was. There had been no part for him. The Trust, even his office in the bank, had been given to Houseman.

The Duke was looking up at the train.

The sky, because it was summer, was tranquil; its lingering brightness glowed a soft reddish gold. In the cars the lights had been turned on. The faces of the passengers, illuminated in equal measures by the sky and the lamps, shied first one way, then another, nervously.

The engine expelled a cloud of white steam. From behind it came the bark of horns, the sound, almost lost under them, of ships' bells in the harbor. In the first car, by the window, a man took his seat.

Harwood looked and saw nothing. He glanced sharply around.

'Perhaps I was wrong after all,' he admitted. 'We could just as well have driven.' He paused, looking back at the station. 'I thought that if we could just repeat everything, one thing after another, as it happened, something would change. But it hasn't.' Dejected, he walked away. 'Are you coming, Your Grace?' he asked.

The Duke's eyes were fixed beyond him.

The face staring from the car window was printed indelibly on his mind: the thatch of dark hair and the high forehead, the deep hard eyes watching.

The man was looking out at the evening.

'At the light that was fading,' the Duke told Harwood afterward. 'Regarding it contemplatively,' he said later, 'as if it were something important, to be gravely considered.'

It had only been for a moment; the head turned.

'We must hurry,' the Duke said. Taking hold of Harwood's arm by the elbow, he pressed forward.

*   *   *

516

The train crawled past shipyards, past the tight-packed roofs of the slums, following the river. The Duke sat up in his seat. It was his second night without sleep but he was no longer tired. 'He did not see us,' he said in a rapid, low voice, his eyes shining. 'He was not looking for anyone. He would not have expected anyone.' His own face beamed. 'But he was seen.'

The sun's rays had disappeared. The plain of the river had become a cavernous darkness. Harwood did not care to look at it.

'Why should you be the one?' he grumbled.

The conductor had come through, collecting the tickets. The Duke paid both fares.

'Compensation,' he said cheerfully. 'You must admit I was owed something. It was my decision which sent him to his death. I felt the pain of it. It comes down to that, I think. Payment for sorrow.'

Harwood frowned. The dead man, sitting no more than a dozen rows ahead, did not look very dead. Yet from the back it was difficult to make judgments.

'I could walk up front,' Harwood suggested, 'to the lavatory.'

'What would you see?' the Duke objected. 'He was no one you knew.'

'I could see if he looks like a man.'

'He does,' the Duke said flatly.

'I could see for myself.'

'Isn't it enough that I told you?'

'You!' Harwood nearly shouted. 'Why you?'

Beyond everything it was this which had troubled him. If the world had changed, if this was an instance of its changing, why had he been excluded?

He looked around miserably. 'Why should it be you who noticed?' he asked.

But His Grace had already given his answer. 'Perhaps it only happens in pieces,' he added sympathetically.

'What?'

'Just a bit at a time,' the Duke said. 'Only changing things that he thought should be different.'

'That who thought?'

The Duke looked at him doubtfully. 'Wykeham,' he said.

Harwood shook his head. It was the same argument they had had in the bank; he was still adamant.

'Not Wykeham. Not pieces either,' he said.

He was remembering the woodcut that hung over his desk. The pattern, he recalled, once altered, changed incrementally from one tessellation to the next. Yet, looking back, he had never been able to tell just where the change in the pattern had started. A hundred times he had tried to find the place but always there were shadows, glimmerings, a place farther off for every place he looked.

'No,' he said fiercely. For an instant he looked straight at the Duke.

'There are differences,' he said. 'But they had always to have been there. Or to seem so, afterward.' In his excitement, he leaned forward.

A lock of his ginger hair had fallen into his eyes. He pushed it back with his fingers. He said, 'What changes one thing, I'm afraid, Your Grace, changes everything.'

'But it was William,' the Duke persisted. 'Or at least it was Joseph.'

'What makes you think,' Harwood asked, 'that only he could be the cause of it?'

'Cupheag,' the conductor called sharply, announcing the station.

'Metichanwon,' he said later.

But when he should have shouted out Bristol, he did not.

The train slowed. The conductor came into the car and then left it. Three or four times the Duke noticed him in the passage between the car and the engine, speaking to someone up front. Each time he came back into the car he was frowning. The Duke wished the man would stay in one place. The movement along the aisle was annoying and he was trying to think.

'Your pardon,' he said the next time the man passed him.

'There's been a delay,' the conductor replied curtly.

'How long?'

The man shrugged.

It grew late. The Duke let his forehead rest on the window. The sound of the wheels came softly through the floor, a faint, even throbbing that made the sound almost tender. He glanced up. Houseman, to his relief, was still there.

For a moment he felt safe again.

He had listened to Harwood, had tried to think honestly what the younger man had meant. He knew that something had gone terribly wrong and equally that it had been put right again. A man was dead. Over and over he had tried to grapple with the shifting tides of that responsibility but he had felt himself being pulled under. Now Wykeham had changed it. 'There is a place to stand again,' he might have said. He had been beginning to drown.

'Christ Almighty!' exclaimed Harwood.

The Duke dragged himself up.

The passengers rumbled awake, their sleep-slackened faces jolted into alarm.

The river was burning. Across the water-meadows and the marshes on the outskirts of Bristol they saw the bright sheet of flame: a thousand tongues of light, not upon the water but within it, gleaming balefully. It grew bigger and brighter. But it was itself without height. Without heat. Without sound.

'Like a reflection,' Harwood whispered.

He looked up. Even in the glare of the burning, his face grew pale.

'It's the city,' he gasped.

'But who – ?'

His Grace was staring.

The train crossed a small bridge. After a few hundred yards there was another. The sound of the wheels, rocking, echoed softly. Then the track, following the long curve of the bank, straightened. Suddenly the station was ahead of them. In the bright distance behind it the roofs of Bristol were engulfed in flame.

At the front of the car the door opened. The conductor walked through. He closed the door, locked it. The stricken faces of the passengers watched, unmoving.

'You must stay in your seats,' he said evenly. 'We will take only as many as we can. There is no need for panic. There are police on the platform. Everything has been arranged.'

'What has happened?' someone cried.

'Fires,' he said stiffly and went down the aisle and through the next door into the car behind.

The Duke did not watch him.

All around him was the confusion of the yard. Acres of track were sliding by him; odd little sheds and old carbarns flickered past. Usually untidy and blackened, they were now curiously enlivened. Touched with fire-gold and copper, they bloomed. The engine gave a small moan. The car bumped. Along the narrow platform, marshaled behind gates and high railings, crowds of people gathered by tens and by hundreds. The Duke did not feel their stares. His body did not seem to belong to him but to be floating above them, as the car passed, slowly, out of darkness, into light, again into darkness . . .

In the car the lamps were switched on once more.

He did not feel the blast of heated air as the outer doors opened. All but unnoticed, Dr. Holmes, pushing his way through the men scrambling down the aisle, threw himself, exhausted, into the seat beside His Grace.

'I had fallen asleep,' the Duke said afterward, as if that justified it.

But now he was strangely awake. His eyes ran down the rows of new passengers. More than a score had to stand, awkwardly, holding on to whatever they could find. He could not see Houseman. But he was there. The Duke was certain of that. The car was noisy with questions; he pushed his face next to Holmes's.

'Your wife?' he asked, almost shouting.

'I got her away this morning,' Holmes answered. 'With the children. Off to Cambridge.' He was very nearly shouting himself. Yet some dread that had been in him relaxed a little. Still, his eyes did not soften. He said, 'As far as anyone can tell, it is only this valley.'

'It's only here, isn't it?' Harwood said. 'Surely not in New Awanux.' He had just remembered his wife and his daughter.

Holmes shook his head. 'There were rumors this morning,' he said. 'When I came into the house, everyone was talking. We had time.'

'We heard nothing.'

'Then perhaps in the south there was nothing.'

Harwood had to hunch forward to hear. 'We were in New Awanux until evening,' he cried. 'No one said . . .'

Holmes's voice, raised above the voices nearest him, had at least the sound of honesty. 'No one knew. There were only rumors at first. It was hours before anyone saw them and then they were so few. We just looked at them. Everyone went out into the streets. We all stood around on the steps of the houses, looking up.'

His color was high, but it seemed less anger or resentment than a kind of sad embarrassment, as if he had seen what should have been hidden. He turned, not meeting their stares.

'They fell so quietly,' he said. 'Here and there we saw one, on the ground, standing alone by the bridge that crosses to Redding, walking undisturbed in the conservatory garden. They were waiting as we were. But we did not know that they were waiting until there were more of them.

'All we dared do was watch. We did not speak to them. Yet I cannot help but wonder what I might have asked, what answers they might have given me.

'The odd part was they seemed to have nothing to do with us.

Perhaps they were just watching. I counted seven on the lawn at Saint Stephen's before I went in to have my lunch. The house was empty, the bedroom empty. The shutters in my daughter's room were open. She had washed her hair, had been drying it in the sun before she left. I have tried to think if I shall ever see her.

'But I suppose I shall not,' he said after a moment. 'It would appear they are only men.'

Harwood stared. 'They?' he asked at long last.

'Indians,' the Duke explained irritably.

Holmes looked away. 'When there were too many to count,' he said, 'they began burning the churches.'

CHAPTER FOUR

'Flukes and flames!' the man cried, not yet seeing her. ' "The Pequod . . ." '

He leaned unsteadily against the counter and waved the book in the air.

' "Freighted with savages and laden with fire!" ' he shouted. ' "Burning a corpse and plunging into that blackness of darkness . . ." ' The voice ended in a strangled yelp.

A moment later the book sailed by her head. Landing in the gutter outside the shop on Abbey Street, it joined dozens of volumes, their torn, stained pages fluttering in the breeze that prowled the late afternoon. The headmistress, thinking the man had simply been drunk, realized that he had been reading.

She stood in the doorway, clutching the envelope she had carried with her from the academy. It had taken her two whole days to trace the name.

'You are, I trust, finished throwing things,' she said, fixing him with her fiercest, most reproving stare, the one she reserved for recalcitrant students and, more rarely, for their parents. 'It is safe to enter.'

He held on to the counter. By his elbow there was a mound of books. On the floor hundreds lay scattered. It looked as though there had been an explosion.

'Finished?' he asked severely. 'Not till I'm rid of the lot of them.'

'It is your business, I believe,' she said calmly. 'I am quite certain of that.' She marched into the shop. 'I had it investigated.'

'No more it is,' he announced, loudly. 'I've stopped for good. Stopped forever.' He picked up a book, spread the pages at random.

' "Give not thyself up, then, to fire," ' he read, ' "lest it invert thee." '

All at once his thin shoulders heaved; tears rolled down his cheeks.

'There, you see,' he said helplessly. 'It's all like that.'

'Like what?'

'Like that. All opera and savages . . . howling infinites and poetry. Every bloody word of it.'

He pressed the book between his small fingers.

'It was a book about finches,' he said, trembling. 'A very nice little book about the different shapes of their bills. But it isn't now. None of them are. They're all changed.'

'I wouldn't know about that,' she said.

'Almost no one knows,' he said with terrible seriousness. His eyes were red. He looked ill. He stood up and staggered out into the room. 'But I read them,' he said savagely. 'Hardly anyone did. Did you know that? But I did and I remember.' He went to the shelves and began pulling books down. 'Not these!' he cried, kicking them as they fell. 'When I was at sea, sitting by myself with the engines, I was in the habit of reading: Darwin and Homer, Shakespeare and the Evangelists. I remember what was in them. Even now I haven't forgotten.'

He put his head in his hands.

'You have a wife,' she said.

He looked up. 'I am not referring to that,' he said.

'You have a wife,' she repeated indomitably.

'No.'

'And sisters,' she said. 'The oldest was an instructress at Bristol Academy. That was nearly fifty years ago. You were the youngest, the black sheep, if you will forgive me for saying so. I have had it all carefully researched. You drank, I am told. You were years at sea. When you came back, you brought a young woman.' The headmistress was holding out the envelope upon which the name was written. 'I have met her,' she said.

Carl Brelling's face, as much of it as was visible between his grizzled beard and his sailor's cap, was red.

'Lies,' he said. 'Damn bloody lies.'

He seemed so vehement that at first she hesitated, uncertain whether she ought to go on. She had devoted two days to calculating the new and wider scope for powers which, by the chance of a name on an envelope, had been opened to her. She would not let it pass. It now seemed that she had spent all her life preparing for just such an opportunity. Admittedly, it had sometimes not seemed much of a life: the headmistress of a second-rate private school, not even in New Awanux, but in a city of no particular importance. And little as it had been, she had had to struggle for it, without allies, by the sheer force of her will. The vagueness and obscurity of those years, the smug and yet indifferent faces of the trustees especially, stirred old bitternesses. But all the while something had been leading her. Forces she had not imagined or guessed had been tugging her into place. She had failed to notice. Then out of the blue Wykeham had come to the academy, bringing a woman. And suddenly the world that had so often seemed elusive and disappointing revealed itself to be, to have always been, her own.

'Your wife came to see me,' the headmistress said, watching him closely, 'in the company of a young man.'

She could see his face more sharply now. She saw as well the poverty of the shop, knew he had never made much of a living at it, that now he would make none at all.

'Mr. Brelling,' she said, 'I am going to be of some help to you.'

He was on his guard. 'What kind?' he asked uncertainly.

'You are not a wealthy man,' she said. They looked at one another. 'I quite understand. For longer than I should like I have myself been lacking proper resources. There are many, however, who are not similarly troubled.' For a moment she let him ponder that.

'Is there any good reason,' she asked, 'that either of us should continue . . . as we have been, when there is one young man for instance, who never had to give a thought to how he would manage?'

He seemed not to be listening.

His head was sunk on his chest, his eyes vacant. She was casting about for words to draw him to her, to fit him, a small, unhappy but very necessary piece, into the great cunning pattern she saw opening before her when he said: 'She was only a child when I met her, no more than a girl with a head full of dreams.'

Speech left him and he began to sway. He looked down at himself with contempt.

'I was old enough to know better,' he said. 'Yet, you know, in a way she warmed my heart. She wanted to marry a sailor.' He shrugged his thin shoulders. 'It seemed wrong to let her find out what dreams usually come to.'

He shook his old head.

'Do you know,' he said, 'I was remembering her and I thought: suppose I had never gone to Bodø, never saw her striding down toward the sea, would I think of her? Would I still wonder if something were missing?'

He had gone beyond her, into his memory, but she knew she must not press him with questions. He was drunk and bad-tempered and, because he was feeling sorry for himself, likely to do anything. Yet she needed him. 'There is a plan,' she said carefully. 'A definite pattern.'

He lifted his eyebrows.

'The most insignificant parts,' she said, 'have a use and a purpose.'

'What good is that?' he asked truculently.

'It helps,' she said.

'How?'

'If you know a little, you can predict the rest.'

He looked at her uncomprehendingly. 'Why should that matter?'

The headmistress smiled.

'Though you had never met,' she said evenly, 'you would have missed her.'

But again he did not seem to be paying attention.

He looked around at the shop, at its ruin. The air of the shop smelled of whisky. At last his eyes met her face.

'But she is gone,' he said lamely.

'Then you must go and get her back.'

'I couldn't . . .'

'That is why I have come,' she said. 'To take you.' She turned on her heels.

He was not certain, even afterward, why he followed. But a moment later he was in the street, trotting behind her. He coughed and muttered but she would not hear. She was in a hurry, walking briskly. He trailed after unhappily.

Old as he was, it seemed to him that he had always been at the mercy of women. He had never intended it. Though they seemed always in a jumble, he had had dreams of his own; but then suddenly a woman would turn her eyes on him. He was not a big man, but he always felt himself getting smaller.

His fingers found the opening in his coat. Cleverly, he brought out the flask.

'It was not what I wanted,' he grunted.

He put the flask to his lips. 'It is not as it should be.'

He could hear the gurgle of the whisky going down. His teeth chattered.

But it's the way it is, he thought bitterly, feeling himself in fact growing smaller. He had been sucking at the flask like an infant for a good half minute and was now very near the end. Soon, he knew, he would not be able to walk. Abruptly, he threw back his head. But suddenly, his attention distracted, he began to grin.

'Stand straight,' she told him.

But he was leaning into her, his head lolling.

'Why's the sky red?' he asked, leering foolishly, as though asking a riddle. His hand, no bigger than a child's, was outstretched and pointing.

Her head turned.

From the High Street, looking out across the wide commons, she saw the great steeple of the old center church rising in a pillar of flame.

'Aye, we know something about that,' he said darkly.

For the first time she seemed undecided. 'What do you know?' she asked.

He cocked a bleary eye at the heavens.

'Savages,' he said, disgusted. 'Damn bloody savages and poetry.'

CHAPTER FIVE

'What I cannot seem to discover,' Harwood repeated in a temper, 'is how you knew.'

The Duke pulled at his chin. 'Knew what?' he asked innocently.

Harwood blanched. His voice rose. 'That they would be Indians,' he said too loudly.

In the Royal Charles there were no more than a score of small tables, each packed closely with men. At the last and the smallest the Duke examined his glass. Harwood was watching him narrowly.

Half an hour before, they had followed Houseman onto the platform. They had seen him bobbling in front of them among the few dozen passengers who dared leave the train so near to Bristol. But when they had gone into the yard, he was gone, swallowed up by the darkness. No one had suggested they go straight off to Greenchurch. 'We must have a plan,' Harwood had said, and they had straggled along at a distance behind a pair of elegant young men who, having borne away with them nothing but their expensive suits and black fedoras, announced bitterly to the evening the fate of any Indians who, by mischance, might manifest themselves out of the air.

There had been workmen and laborers behind them, put off in Devon because they had been short of the fare. Staring as Holmes had been staring, they had looked up at the closed doors of the houses, seeking some sign of welcome. But the long street remained silent. The gardens, full of old-fashioned flowers, peonies and sweet william, hollyhocks and roses, were as empty of dogs as of men. At the bottom of the green, a small boy, peeking from a second floor window, was gathered in quietly, the shades pulled quickly after him, the last porch lamps extinguished.

But the lights of the Royal Charles shone like a beacon. On the step by the broad, open door a man was singing noisily, with equal enthusiasm and disregard for the tune. In his hands he had held a portion of a quilt which, rid of its feathers, he was shredding for bandages. Seeing them, his solemn face broke slowly into a grin.

'New recruits,' he observed and, smiling gravely, waved them on.

The Duke stared but Harwood moved past him.

With its low ceiling and one small window, the bar seemed half a cottage, half a shed. Harwood stepped down into the room. The other two followed, picking their way slowly among the chairs and the tables. By the time they had settled, the man on the step had gone back to his song. '. . . Nine on the hills,' he was singing.

Holmes sat very quietly, his elbows on the table, his small hands cupping a match. Quantities of blue smoke filled the air about his head. Listening intently, he pulled on his pipe. 'One met him face to face,' the man sang,

'one man alone
bore himself bravely
seated in his saddle . . .'

Holmes waited silently. The man at the door went on with his song. 'When the stallion stood,' he sang,

'there dropped from the mane
dews into the deep dales,
hails in the high wood,
whence Duinn his harvest . . .'

Holmes remained motionless. His eyes had faint lines at their sides.

'Perhaps I just drew it out of the air,' His Grace was saying. His voice was cold. This wasn't what mattered. There were more important things to attend to. He looked across at Holmes, as though for confirmation, but Holmes only glowered.

'By Christ,' the Duke added, 'it was merely something I said.'

'But you were right,' Harwood told him.

'I didn't know it.'

'You knew something,' Harwood said tensely.

'He has a daughter,' the Duke said. 'I know that.' He felt around in his coat, touching the letter but leaving it. Nothing showed in his face. 'I have come out to find her.'

All at once Holmes dropped his small hands to the table. 'She may not be there,' he said softly. Both men looked at him but again he lapsed into silence. In itself that was not surprising. For two days he had been the quiet one, the one who watched and who listened. Now, for several minutes some deeper quietness had seemed to move at the back of his eyes.

For a long moment he looked about the room. 'There is at least the possibility, Your Grace,' he said quietly, 'that she may not be anywhere.'

The Duke lifted his head. 'You disappoint me, doctor.' He spoke as if it were a challenge. 'I was sent for. I am here for the purpose of finding her.'

Again there was silence.

'I never questioned that,' Holmes said at last, his face and even his voice expressionless. 'In a way we have all been sent for. That was never at issue. The question, from the start, I think, is not what we are to do but what has got hold of us.' He stopped for a moment. 'Before we even knew there was anything,' he said, 'before we had even started to notice, what already would not let us go.' His little gray eyes stared without blinking. 'Each of us,' he said carefully, 'not just the two of you.'

The Duke frowned stubbornly. He was about to speak.

'No,' Holmes said, gathering his thoughts together, calmly. 'You knew him.' He nodded toward Harwood. 'You both knew him. I did not.'

He drew again on his pipe. 'It cannot be Wykeham,' he said, stopping, pulling the fumes from the pipe deeply inside him, 'however remarkable he is. Rather, if you are both right, if somehow he has been given the gift, or the curse perhaps, of living forever, then really he is the very last thing it could be.' He stopped, puffing once more. 'Indeed, he could only be the enemy of what has taken hold, of what –'

The Duke turned on him. 'It is not the dead man,' he said angrily.

Holmes paused. 'Not the dead at all,' he said. 'But the thing, Your Grace, whatever it is, that sees to the killing.'

'I don't see –' Harwood began, interrupting.

'Or you never read,' Holmes put in quickly. 'It comes down, I am almost certain now, to a sort of biblical question. Though, of course, it's in Milton. Everything's in Milton.'

Harwood's voice was like something tearing. 'What is?' he asked.

'Angels,' Holmes said. 'Devils, too, for that matter. I haven't been able to decide which. They both can have wings. But they are all, every one of them, men. You have only to look.'

'Look where?'

'In the Bible,' Holmes said. 'From Michael to Gabriel. Lucifer to Beelzebub.' He paused once more to consider His Grace. 'Or on the platform,' he said simply, 'or the train. Even here, in this place.'

The Duke was staring out at the room.

'Have you thought . . .?' began Harwood, but Holmes cut him short.

'I have tried not to,' Holmes conceded. 'Not even to remember.' His clear, open gaze was without emotion. They had not, even then, begun to suspect what that had cost him. 'I have a daughter,' he said, 'had a daughter . . . a wife.'

He was looking at the backs and the faces of the men crowded under the rafters.

'Though by now,' he said quietly, 'like all the rest, I suppose, they are gone.'

At the front of the room a man stepped silently over the threshold. For an instant, blocking the light, his huge shoulders threw a grotesque shadow over the floor.

They were aware, at first, only of red hair sweeping out like the halo of a furnace, a long red face as ferocious and unsympathetic as flame.

At the center of the room the tall old man halted. Wearily, he began removing his coat, freeing from the large shapeless garment first one arm, then the next. He unfolded the third and the fourth from where they were strapped to his chest. His mouth turning, as from some trivial discomfort, he withdrew the last pair from his back.

The arms were long, their flesh mottled with bruises and covered with fresh welts and scratches. Skillfully, with three of six great hands, winding with each the little ragged strips of the quilting, he began to bind his wounds.

'Someone fought you, then?' the barman asked.

'Some will,' Charon Hunt said defensively. Stung by the implied criticism of his work, he turned away, looking instead at the room full of men. His own large face was plain, his grim frown dogged as an old hill farmer's.

'Yet they must come with me,' he said with a harsh pride. 'For how shall they cross,' he asked no one in particular, 'unless I carry them?'

The world fell silent, the men behind him gone. But whether they found some hole to hide in was their own business. Houseman was not curious about them. He had no great interest in his fellow men. His duty, as he saw it, was simply to find his own way. If now in the plain, shuttered houses along the dark street there were no signs of habitation, it did not trouble him. Though he was dead, he was not remorseful. He was surprised, however, that he was clothed in a good black suit and a white shirt with a firm, starched collar.

In the drawings of the damned, which he had carried out of childhood, the damned had been aggressively naked. The drawings had stayed in his mind and, although he had never been able to remember where he had found the book, he recalled ever afterward the massive torsos and ponderous legs of large, scornful men falling shamelessly into darkness.

He looked himself over carefully. I will need shoes, of course, he thought, only half wondering why that one item had been neglected.

Yet he could walk. The soles of his feet had somehow hardened and he went quickly over the pavement. His lungs, though they filled gently, scarcely needed the air: he might just as easily, he imagined, have been sucking in the enormous emptiness of the space between worlds. What little light there was left on the hill was the light of worlds, distant and receding. When he had entered under the interlocking boughs of the wood, the stars were not even a memory.

Thereafter, in spite of the darkness, he had gone swiftly for what may have been hours, except that it was not a matter of time. It was not, he supposed, exactly a matter of space either.

It was more like a jigsaw puzzle. The vague gray shape of the hill, the snaking contour of a wall, even the wood's feral darkness, while useful as points of reference, were only phantoms. There was a deeper order, an arrangement in which hills, walls and woods, the clearness or mistiness of the evening were merely decorative. Underneath their momentary divisions, deeper and more permanent, there were lines. He had thought of them as lines at least, although he suspected they plumbed the depths and rose up, virtually without limit, through the heavens. They could not be seen, could not, either with hands or by the shiver of the flesh, be felt, but he had known when he crossed them. Having seen and experienced nothing, he had been forced nonetheless to acknowledge that he had passed from one sphere of reality to the next.

He had recognized it first on the train. He had awakened into the light, coming back to awareness on an old, damp seat, staring out at the smoky yellow light of the evening.

He had counted three worlds then: the one he had been born into and in which he had toiled unceasingly, year by year, at the bank for a reward that, when fate had granted it, death had taken; death itself, which although it was dark and empty, he was certain was also a place; and the world after, which was not empty and not, he was equally certain, either world he had left. For one thing, it was summer.

He had watched the huge evening sun falling past the vast roof of Water Street station. Feeling the light sweeping through him, he had smiled, a slight yet cunning smile filled with purpose, as if, by daring and perseverance, he had outwitted an ancient enemy.

He had crossed the fourth line at Bristol. From the train window he had stared straight ahead at the fires, smiling his brief triumphant smile at the glowing ruins of houses. He had licked his lips greedily, watching the bright bands of flame.

But under the eaves of the wood it was dark again. The village was long behind him. As he pushed his way in through heavy brakes and sharp brambles, there was nothing to be seen. The hill had vanished, even the grim old trees were invisible and, conscious only of darkness, he was left with a feeling of inescapable dread. At the back of his mind he could hear now and then a distant crow complaining somewhere in the branches. But the sound seemed to come from everywhere at once. Perhaps direction itself, he thought apprehensively, is immaterial. And yet he felt more and more certain he was advancing toward the fifth line. At all events, it did not matter which way he came at it, it was now Wykeham land.

His jaw had fallen open and he was drooling as he lumbered on blindly. Twigs cracked under him and he nearly slipped on the path.

He must burn, Houseman thought, angrily, imagining the purifying breath of flame that alone could free him, that would free them all, he hoped, from the damned white-faced English. But it was the rustle of the bare soles of his feet over straw that convinced him that he was outside the barn.

He stopped and, for a time, stood staring wildly into the darkness. At last, grown impatient, ignoring the one clear order Wykeham had given him, he gave a heave to the door so that the car, riding the double line of the track, could enter. He had, he knew, really no alternative: a door will not open by itself. His long clawed fingers clung for a moment to the latch.

The stench as of some old heavy animal in its lair was overpowering. He coughed and clamped his mouth shut.

The sound of men running, when it came to him, was slow and unnatural. The roar of the gun itself was deafening. Something crossed in the air. With a jolt he felt it enter him, felt the wall of his chest ripping open. And yet it was not until he had been lifted by what seemed too many hands onto the back of the ancient Ford pickup that he noticed the odd treacly smell of his blood. He lay groaning. Bitterly, with the shattered fragment of a wing, the young dead man covered his head.

Nora put her hand on his bed, passing her fingers caressingly over the sheets. In the warm summer darkness she felt more than saw that he was gone. She had expected that. He rose early. But he has been here, she thought, and so sooner or later, would be there again. Everything returned. In all her life she had not known it to be otherwise. But all the same she had wished for one last meeting. During the night she had dreamed of him; now with the sight of his bed she remembered her longing. 'Ah, men!' she whispered but, knowing only too well her own inadequacies, she sighed. Kneeling down, she gazed without jealousy into the sleeping face of the girl. Jane was quite naked, her wide, ungirlish mouth open. Her bare arms were stretched lazily above her head.

'It is time,' Nora said.

The girl's breathing went on quietly.

Without another word Nora began to undress. When she had taken off everything, she went to stand by the window. A small, hot breath drifted over the sill. Her nostrils twitched curiously. There was something uncertain in the air. But the yard below looked as it always did, the gray meadow quiet and still, the gardens harboring darkness. In the dawn the tops of the tallest elms seemed to sputter. Nora drew herself up. Around her the room was gradually brightening. But for a long moment she stood undecided, examining herself in front of the window.

Even now her body was slim and white. Her knees and the tips of her breasts were likewise pale. She lifted her arms. Only there was there darkness, prickly and damp, in two spots, and a third, in the crease where her belly ended.

Nora shook out her hair. Her head filled with memory, she tried to recall the bodies of the girls in the faraway village and found, surprisingly, that she was ignorant of what had lain under their shifts. She had not, although they had shared but a single room, seen even her own mother naked. Finally, she turned. The girl, the sheet drawn away from her, was, she had to acknowledge, the limit of her experience.

Watching her, a brief smile passed over Nora's lips.

Deliberately, her hand no longer trembling, she reached down, touching herself. In the crease between her legs the feathers were not as yet thick, just soft black quills.

Jane did not speak but Nora saw she was watching.

'I cut them,' Nora said. 'In the pocket of my apron I carry a pair of sharpened scissors.' She gave a short laugh. 'There is always the chance a man may wish to sleep with me. And being men they are easily frightened.'

She managed a grin. 'But always they grow again,' she said.

Jane's fingers moved restlessly down her leg. 'I don't think he noticed.'

'Not in the dark,' Nora said. 'Never the first time when they are filled with impatience.' She no longer looked at the girl. Where on earth had she ever learned such things? she wondered.

Her husband, of course, had been frightened. Yet his misfortunes he had brought on himself. He had not touched her. In the ignorant way of men who have learned what they know of honor out of books, he had never taken her to his bed until they had married. What is done is done, he had said afterward; but in the small bedroom over the shop his eyes were swollen with sleeplessness.

'Why did you never tell me?' he had asked her once, abandoning all caution.

'It has always been so,' she had told him.

Jane dropped her feet to the floor.

'You go out and I'll dress,' she said.

Nora's smile lingered. 'What is the need?' she asked. 'They are gone.'

In the kitchen Lizzy and Olivia were already naked. Lizzy was packing away the last of the dishes. Olivia lowered her eyes rather than look at them. 'Who will take care of the house?' she asked. 'Who's going to make breakfast?'

'They will have to manage without,' Nora said evenly.

They went onto the porch and down the back steps. But they did not start out. They were waiting. In the east the immense sky shone like a mirror. Even under the elms there was a blink of watery sunshine. But in the wood under the hill there was darkness. The wind that only brushed at their ankles seemed to blow harder there. The old, dark trees seemed to beckon. They tried not to look. Instead for a time they stood quietly, sunk in memories of the house and of the men they were leaving.

At last they heard the sound of Plum's heavy feet on the gravel. She came around the corner of the house, the crow on her shoulder. Its wings were spread, its weight gently balancing on the air, so the murderous claws would not tear her pink flesh.

'Well, it's begun,' Plum said. Her large round face was haggard. In their black sockets her eyes had an expression Nora had never seen in them.

Jane lifted her head. She was the youngest and her face conveyed her confusion. 'It's women and children first, isn't it?' she asked.

'The children have already gone,' Lizzy told her.

'There was a boy,' Nora said all at once, remembering. But it was much too late. Under the eaves of Black Wood the village women were gathering.

PART V

October Wars

CHAPTER ONE

The letters that morning, because the postman had punctured two of his fingers with the toasting fork, were smeared with blood. 'Daughters of Belial!' the postman muttered, thrusting both fingers into his mouth. Standing in the middle of his kitchen he glared at the window and wondered why it was not yet light. He had half expected to see his old wife spreading strawberry nets in the garden; but the garden, like their bed, was empty. 'And I was ever kind to her,' he announced to the rooms from which she had gone empty-handed. The postman shook his gray head. Lifting his bag onto his shoulder, he stepped out onto the porch.

Above the long village street the stars were still shining.

In Black Wood John Chance rocked contentedly, taking no notice. In the summits of the trees a high wind was blowing. The old man never lifted his head. He was remembering the starry evening Okanuck had come out of the darkness to sit with him, remembering the woman who had arrived the next morning, slept in his cottage and gone. To his mind they both seemed to stand at a beginning. He remembered them because they had brought on a feeling of profound anticipation and because they had shared, with only a difference of hours, the moment of Wykeham's return. After fifty years something was about to happen.

He had no desire to join in their lives; he only wished to see for himself what they did. His own life, he had come to believe, had taught him almost nothing. Not that this mattered. It only meant that one life was never enough. What was needed, he suspected, was not a few decades but centuries, time to feel and smell the grain of existence and uncover its possibilities.

'Young Wykeham's home again,' he repeated to himself, only slightly puzzled by the swirl of dry leaves that came tumbling from trees that had been old when Adam, barred by the angel, walked away from the wood.

Hearing the postman, the Reverend Mr. Longford rushed out onto the dark porch in his socks.

The postman stared at the minister's feet. 'You in a hurry, Tim?' he asked.

'It's the shoes,' Longford answered. His voice was strained, his eyes wandered. 'Three pairs,' he said thickly. His gaze turned abruptly to the host of small stars that by now should have faded. 'Tried each one,' he said softly. 'But they all seem to have shrunk.'

'You might have Plum stretch them.'

Longford looked away.

'She's gone then, is she?' said the postman.

Longford did not answer.

To cover the moment's awkwardness the postman dug into his bag. When he had fished out the letter, he thrust it into Longford's fingers.

The minister looked down distrustfully.

'There is something wrong . . .' he began.

'Cut myself,' said the postman.

Longford brought the letter closer to his face. 'Where did you get this?' he asked.

'At the station.'

'It's from here in the village.'

The postman nodded. 'Her Majesty's Mail,' he said glumly. 'Everything goes first to Bristol.'

'But it's only down from the hill.'

'Sent two days ago,' the postman admitted.

'You are certain?'

'Mr. Wykeham gave it to me himself.'

Longford screwed up his eyes. In the shadows and without the aid of his spectacles, it was difficult to read. In order to see at all he had brought the letter up so close he could smell the ink and the paper.

'October, I think,' he said irritably.

The postman looked puzzled.

'The postmark,' said Longford. Out on the lawn something fluttered. He looked up.

From the gray hills a sharp exhalation flowed down into the village. The dawn wind, ruffling the grass, filled the yard with the cool, unmistakable breath of autumn.

An hour later, on the grimy steps of Hunt's garage the postman was shivering.

'. . . and the sun was late,' he muttered, adding to his list of complaints.

Hunt took no interest. With two of his hands, he was sharpening a scythe. The leaves that came spinning through the air dropped noiselessly at his feet. The only sound was the monotonous grinding of stone on metal.

'The birds are gone,' the postman went on sadly, remembering how in the hedges there had been sparrows. Each morning when he passed the cemetery there had been a crow on the gate. This morning the gate had been empty.

'It's the women who take them,' Hunt said.

'I expect they fly south.'

Hunt smiled. With a free hand he rubbed the blood on his trousers. 'Believe me,' he said, 'it's the women.'

He tore open his letter.

The postman waited. In his own hands he was shuffling a pair of letters, stamped UNDELIVERABLE, that had come back to the village. Dr. Oliver Holmes, the postman read, turning over one envelope then the next, Professor Harwood. Hunt tucked the letter away in his pocket. Like the others it was an invitation to Greenchurch.

'You plan to go up there?' the postman asked.

'It's not a matter of choice.'

The postman stared vaguely into the street. At the far end of the green a team of horses was hauling a well-laden wagon toward the hill that climbed to the House. 'Do you think there will be women?' he asked.

Hunt shrugged one of his shoulders.

'I was kind to her,' said the postman. 'I was sober.'

'Perhaps you've a hard heart,' Hunt told him.

The postman sighed. 'I've thought of that,' he said miserably. 'Or maybe no heart at all.' He looked down at the blood still oozing from his fingers. 'Do you think they can tell?' he asked.

Hunt only frowned. He went back to the scythe, his powerful, broad hands moving rhythmically. With his great strength he could mow an acre of barley in less than an hour. Nonetheless he was impatient. He drew the stone roughly over the metal. Men, he thought thankfully, were much shorter work.

The wheels clattered on the pavement. On the high front seat, the butcher was singing. His bass voice rolled over the green. Undiminished, it echoed among the houses. It was fortunate perhaps that Longford had gone in for his breakfast. It was a foolish song, but, with his theological turn of mind, it would have hurt Longford deeply. Yet it was the song's simple foolishness which most pleased the caroler, the plain fact that the song had nothing to do with the boxes of oysters or the fine pickled salmon soaking in claret, nothing whatever to do with the six wheels of Midland Stilton cheese, the rib roasts or the four Banbury cakes wrapped in paper, all of which and a great deal more he had carried, at Wykeham's request and starting well before midnight, up the river road from Bristol. The butcher threw back his head.

'Shoes,' he roared cheerfully,

> 'I got shoes,
> You got shoes,
> All God's chillun got shoes . . .'

Holmes lay slumped on the ground, sleeping off his whisky in the alley behind the Royal Charles. The song drifted into his mind and then out again. The sunlight was cool on his face but did not wake him. Finally, hearing odd gulping sounds, he stirred. Harwood was sitting up beside him. He had wrapped himself in his greatcoat.

'How did you manage to sleep?' he asked bleakly.

'It seemed more sensible than staying awake,' Holmes answered. For the first time the doctor looked about him. 'It must have been hours,' he said, looking into the morning.

Harwood sniffled. 'It was longer,' he whispered. In his voice was the same weariness that showed in his face.

Propped wide awake by the wall while the others had slept, Harwood had watched the bright stars swing through the heavens. Hour by hour he had watched them, the warm summer stars sliding westward, withdrawing, the fall stars climbing colder and fainter up from the east. Alone in the darkness he had felt the world turning. With an almost infinite slowness, his muscles beginning to stiffen, he had felt himself turning as well; and it had come upon him with sudden sickening horror that he would surely die.

'How cold the wind is,' he said with a shudder. He was shivering but his forehead was damp with sweat.

At the bottom of the alley the Duke slammed the door of the privy. Grasping his trousers with one hand, he clambered across the alley. With the other he was holding a letter.

'We can go there,' he cried out excitedly.

Holmes tried not to grimace. 'Just walk up to the house,' he said dryly, unable to stop himself, 'and inquire whether he is a murderer?'

'If you like.' There was a pleased look in the Duke's eyes. 'The point is he expects us.'

'We knew that,' Holmes said. 'You are to save the daughter.'

'Yes, of course.' His Grace was smiling. The daughter was a matter beyond question.

'You could have gone before,' Holmes persisted. 'Probably any time you wanted.'

'Not until seven,' the Duke said. He dropped the invitation into Holmes's lap.

'When did you get this?'

The Duke went on smiling. 'On the morning he went away, I'm afraid.' He put his hands into his pockets. 'Yet I seem to have carried it about with me since.'

Straining to look at the paper, Holmes was baffled. 'But this is not until . . .'

'– till hell freezes,' Harwood said hoarsely.

On the front step, in the clothes they had slept in, they waited for the public house to open. Out in the street the procession of wagons continued. One after another they thundered up the hill and, in under an hour, came rumbling back empty. Swinging wildly without their ballast, they disappeared around the edge of the green.

Holmes listened to the last hurried shouts of the drivers. 'I wonder how many are invited?' he asked.

'An army,' Harwood whispered. They both looked at him, but Harwood had slipped into silence.

Damn him, the Duke thought, annoyed with the man's bitterness. Certainly there were worse things than spending the night in an alley. The Duke himself had slept soundly. Slept at once, he remembered, falling away into a stillness so deep that, had he listened, the movement of the stars might have seemed audible. In fact, he had heard nothing. The intent dark eyes that in the deepest moment of his sleep had turned as though from other, pressing thoughts to gaze at him had watched him silently.

He was too old, too confident of his powers to be lured away by a memory that on his waking paled. He had not let his thoughts dwell on it. He wondered instead what Wykeham was doing and what would come of their meeting. But there is nothing so small that it is unimportant, even the flushed red cheeks of a woman, met and all but unremembered in the stillness of sleep.

The air now was cooler, sharper. The patch of blue sky visible between the trees was shining. The Duke stood over Harwood. Somewhere within him a longing he thought he had put away quickened.

'It is time we were about our business here,' he said roughly. Without quite knowing why, when Harwood did not move at once, His Grace kicked him.

'Your manners seem to have got lost altogether,' Morag said. His conscience pricked him a little to say it. A man with his wife just run off was bound to be short on charity. Doubtless, he must try to be a bit more understanding. But Longford was being insufferable.

Morag stared enviously at the racks of clothes hanging in the minister's closet. 'It is only the loan of a dinner jacket,' he said.

'You're not invited,' Longford replied wearily. He had climbed up on the bed with his last pair of shoes and was attempting, without noticeable success, to enlarge them by making holes with a knife.

'I was his guardian,' Morag reminded him. He looked once more at the closet. His own jackets had hung there until someone, packing away the things of the dead, had disposed of them. For all he knew it might have been Longford himself. Still, it seemed mean-spirited to mention it. 'I am expected,' Morag said civilly. 'There have to be nine at the table.' He looked shrewdly at Longford. 'I can assure you I am one of them.'

Longford worked on without speaking.

Morag rested his small, plump hand on the windowsill. In the yard the light was already failing.

'We are to be his generals,' Morag said. 'His commanders in the field.'

The shoes were a hopeless mess and Longford abandoned them. 'You are not coming,' he repeated.

'Who's Wykeham to find on such short notice?' Morag asked. 'Nine are expected.' His splotched forehead wrinkled. 'Eight just wouldn't do. It would be the ruin of everything.'

'It would be a blessing,' Longford retorted, wishing to have a few hours free of the old man's company.

'Do you think so?' Morag turned. 'This particular world in ashes?'

Longford looked at him oddly. He had been feeling that he must put his foot down once and for all; only, it occurred to him suddenly, he had no idea what Morag was talking about.

'The world . . .?' he began.

'There wouldn't be,' Morag answered. 'In any event not this one. And not the world he intended.' Morag shook his old head. 'Though I suppose there would have to be something. But what's the good of a world if you're no longer in it? And you wouldn't be. You can be quite certain of that.' He took out his handkerchief and blew his red nose.

'So it has to be nine,' he continued. 'Just as there were the time before. As there will be now, if I may have the loan of a dinner jacket.'

A final spasm of annoyance came over Longford. 'You can't talk to me!' he shouted. 'You're . . . why, you're . . .'

Morag nodded. 'Quite right, of course. Here in this room, if you'll pardon me saying so.'

Longford's face flashed with despair.

'But then,' Morag went on, 'as far as I can determine, they were most always dead.'

There was a long silence. Morag saw that Longford had understood nothing.

'We are less distractable,' he explained. 'That is why, I imagine, it is generally old dead men. We remember the shape of our lives. That's the real point. To have seen it before. To know enough not always to be expecting new faces, new anything. Though, of course, Wykeham would challenge that.'

Longford made a movement of irritation.

'You said nine,' Longford whispered. Because the rest had seemed gibberish, he had gone back to that.

There were nine towers in the village. He had discovered them, one after another in the hills, on his tramps during his first weeks in Devon. Uncertain of their meaning, he had suspected nevertheless that they were bound up with the river, with its changing, and had recorded their positions on his map.

Longford took a deep breath.

'Why are there nine?' he asked quickly.

'I told you.'

'Tell me again.'

Morag sighed. 'Because there were before.'

Longford stared at him uncomprehendingly.

'Before what?'

'Before this!' Morag said, raising his voice. 'In the world before now. In the last world Wykeham fled, making this in its place. Though it made no difference. But he wouldn't learn. He never did learn and so can't learn now, that's what I think. Because he never ended, never had to stop, and so thinks somehow he can just keep on, world after world. And yet you and I will help him, though it won't change anything. We will make a world again.'

The words poured forth in one breath.

Longford lowered his head, understanding none of them.

'But why nine?' he persisted.

'That never mattered.'

'Give me a reason.'

'They all come to the same.'

'I don't care.'

Morag looked out the window.

'Because he fell,' Morag said quietly.

Longford stared at him.

'Him,' Morag whispered, 'the Almighty Power hurl'd headlong . . .'

Morag frowned. '. . . Nine times,' he continued, his voice flat, reciting, 'the space that measures day and night.'

Across the green the postman had dragged a chair out onto his porch. The old minister's eyes remained fixed on him.

'Because it is three times the Trinity and holy.'

The postman climbed onto the chair.

Morag grew still.

'Because for eight days,' he said softly, 'Hobbamocko labored. But when each hill was piled up, when the oakwoods were thick and the great, holy river ran between Greylock and the sea, then on the ninth day Hobbamocko rested.'

Longford was about to protest.

'Because,' Morag went on obdurately, 'once at the beginning of another world there were nine great kings whose hearts . . .' Helplessly, he watched the old postman swing his stiff, arthritic legs into the air.

Morag closed his eyes tightly.

'Not that it mightn't have been thirteen . . . or seven' – his voice faltered – 'not that it would have made any difference if it had been. But once . . . and so ever afterward . . .' He trembled. 'Oh dear,' he said. 'Poor man.'

Longford had never once looked out the window. No longer quite listening, he found himself staring at Morag's feet.

'About that jacket,' he said. 'I don't guess. I mean, if I were to let you borrow one, you wouldn't . . .'

'It is just one more instance,' Morag said, interrupting him, 'just a bit of something to cover one's nakedness.'

A shadow had gathered in his face.

'It began with a cloak,' Morag said. 'Did you know that? A wondrous cloak probably, beyond cost, stitched with silver and embroidered with gold. Yet to Duinn it was nothing. It is said at least that the grave Lord gave it lightly, seeing only that the boy was cold. With his cares, it is perhaps not so unlikely. But Wykeham, we must imagine, never forgot. And though on one world after another he might have taken a stand, might at last have stood and faced him, out of pity, remembering that one kindness, he . . .'

His old eyes found Longford's and, though the other did not want to look, held them.

'I wonder if Wykeham ever knew,' Morag said, 'how many worlds would come to ruin because of that?'

CHAPTER TWO

In the men's kitchen George Tennison worried the joint with too small a knife. Norfolk took up a cleaver.

'Here, let me do that,' he cried impatiently and gave two quick whacks. The blood splattered. Fortunately they were both wearing aprons; only George Tennison felt more foolish. Flushed with embarrassment, he turned and began taking down the dessert plates, setting them aside for the end. Through the door he could hear the voices of the men finding their seats at the table. He gave a final stir to something in a pot, poked at it tentatively, hoping that, whatever it was, it was now cooked, and dumped the unknown contents into a serving dish. The steam rose in his face. The smell and the dampness made him dizzy; opening the door with his shoulder, he scowled. He was hungry as well as exhausted. It seemed unfair that in order to have his dinner he should have to make it.

'Give way,' Norfolk said, pushing a cart at his heels.

They came into the room almost at the same moment. As if waiting, the other guests remained standing. In the light of the hearth their faces seemed darkened and out of date, like the faces in old photographs. Did people really look like that, George Tennison wondered, trying to remember the old men of his childhood, men in shirts without collars, their oiled hair oddly parted. If the truth were known, he felt rather old and out of place himself. He put the platter down beside Wykeham.

The young master smiled at him.

'Your seats, gentlemen,' he said.

There was a scuffling of chairs, the clink of crystal as one of the heavier men bumped the table leg. Norfolk, the cart unloaded, was the last to find his seat. From the bottom of the table he grinned up at Wykeham.

Wykeham nodded. Behind him the tall windows reddened.

All through the day the village men had been gathering, coming on foot or on horseback and building fires on the lawn. In the middle of the afternoon Norfolk had opened the larder and just before dark he had rolled a half dozen barrels down the wide steps and then out under the trees. Seeing him, the men wandered up. 'But when we start,' Norfolk had warned them, 'when the last comes up onto the porch, then you must be silent.'

The men laughed. Already one of the barrels had been hauled onto a makeshift table. Licking his lips, the sexton removed a broach from his pocket. 'And how shall we tell,' he asked mildly, 'when the last have come?'

'You might count,' Norfolk suggested.

The old sexton smiled. He looked back at the house. 'Quite right,' he said. 'It was never our business to meddle.' He rolled the broach over in his fingers. 'Only, if you'll pardon me asking, how are we to know, what with all that coming and going, who is worthy of being counted?'

'It is not a matter of being worthy,' Norfolk answered.

'Of what, then?' The sexton's smile broadened. 'Just as a matter of clarification, if you see what I mean.'

The others had drawn nearer. Norfolk stared at them grimly. 'You'll have to ask Mr. Wykeham himself,' he said.

'Aye, there's the rub,' the sexton mused slyly. 'He's inside and we ain't.'

'Six more,' said Norfolk.

He turned quickly. But partway across the lawn Norfolk slowed to a walk. They were his mates. He tried to remember that. It ill suited a man, raised though he had been above them, to seem too eager to leave them forever behind.

'I wouldn't have taken Fred for one of them,' muttered Izzy Franklin, who for forty of his sixty years had run the feedstore on the far side of the green. He put down his tankard. 'Fred Norfolk,' he said petulantly, 'Lord of Creation.'

'So much the worse for the world,' said the sexton. He fingered his rifle. 'Still, it takes all kinds, I should think.'

The storekeeper gazed at the drive. 'But what possible use could Fred be?' he asked.

The sexton shrugged. 'Must be that a drunken man remembers something worth keeping.'

By now the wind, which was always about somewhere, had begun to tickle his neck. He looked across the lawn. Dusk was falling over the gardens. Except for the fires, the hill itself was fading. Which of us, he thought, will still be here come morning? But it was not a question which submitted to an answer. He sat quietly, waiting. It was becoming so dark he could scarcely see the Ford pickup making the last turn of the drive; but the sound, echoing harshly against the barns, he heard plainly.

'That will be the first,' he said.

The old engine sputtered. The ancient doors rattled. When Hunt switched off the ignition, the whole frame seemed to tremble. Hunt gave a slam to the hood.

'You be quiet as well,' he said, looking across at the Indian bound in the back. But the words went unheeded. Arthur Houseman stared with narrowed eyes at the fires.

Borne up by the wind, the sparks were carried into the darkness. In the upper air they grew smaller and more distant. Yet they were not consumed. Houseman leaned into the corner of the truck and worked at the ropes.

Something had come into the world. Or something had left it. He did not concern himself with which.

It burns, he thought joyfully.

'And the wood fires blinking on a winter's night,' Wykeham said, gazing one by one into their faces. 'The Royal Charles with Fred Norfolk sprawled on the counter.'

His shadow, amplified by the firelight, ascended the opposite wall. He alone had remained standing. His glossy black hair had been parted in the middle. Brushed behind his ears, it had given his head an unexpected dignity.

Like the head of a bishop, Longford would recall afterward.

The Duke's tired eyes rested on the large open features. Like a tyrant, he thought, casting about in his mind for an image. In spite of the years it had been the longest he had looked at him.

On the lawn the men of the village had turned silent. Wykeham had himself stopped a moment. He smiled.

'The church draped for Christmas,' he continued, 'and Morag up in his pulpit, his congregation asleep, all the bored, bundled children staring out at the snow.' He rubbed his chin. 'And pigeons,' he said, almost gaily, 'crowds of wild pigeons in South Wood with spring coming . . . But the river first. The river before everything.'

'The land?' Longford asked uncomfortably.

'This valley,' said Wykeham. 'Since I plan to keep what I like.'

'What you must,' Morag told him.

Wykeham made a vague gesture. 'I had never intended to start from nothing, Michael.'

'Could not,' Morag told him.

Hunt shifted the mass of his arms. He got up and walked to the sideboard. Finding a fresh decanter, he brought it back. One way or another this business had to be settled and he was obliged to play his part in it. But until this moment, eased by a sense of familiarity, by the firelight and darkness, he had held his contempt in check. It was the terrible paralyzing emptiness that must be safeguarded against. Nothing else mattered. But death came, he knew, always, reasserting the pattern. Everything that had happened or that was likely to happen returned to that single and compassionate end. Whatever he attempted, Wykeham could not alter that.

Hunt laughed but now there was relief in his laughter.

'It is late,' he said. 'What is coming is already on its way.'

'Not yet,' Wykeham answered.

'A little while, surely.'

'Time enough,' Wykeham said. 'Until morning.' He had smiled again, his odd, quiet smile.

'You were only the instrument,' he said. 'Long ago I had given up hating you.'

Hunt frowned.

'There was a river before you were here.'

'I have not denied it.'

'You have taken credit . . .'

'For what pleases me,' Wykeham said. 'From the start I took whatever attracted me. What otherwise would have been forgotten. And now it is stamped with my thought.' He drew himself up. It was his house and his table. Smoke rose from the hearth, curled from Holmes's pipe. 'And not only the fields and the miles of walls,' Wykeham went on confidentially. 'Certain conventions, some of the institutions of men. Did you suspect that?'

Longford looked at him uncertainly.

'What, for example?' he asked.

'Ministers.'

Longford stiffened.

'Married priests,' Wykeham said, explaining. 'The just living by faith.' All at once Wykeham grinned. 'In the latrine at Wittenberg, in the rotted old tower I squatted down beside the young friar. I whispered in his ear.'

Hunt turned in his chair. 'He never did,' he said and laughed again. 'He never did much of anything. Not that lasted.'

Holmes stared in dismay.

The musculature was wrong. The bones were impossible.

'He murdered a man,' Holmes said quietly.

'Cured him,' Hunt said. 'And, of course, made him worse.'

'Stopped him,' Wykeham added. 'But then I had run out of choices. I had given him only a single rule. Had he kept it, the world, for the time that was left, would have become infinitely wider. He would have walked this valley freely . . . as in a garden. And there, to make him happy, I would have sent him a woman – a daughter of my own flesh.'

The Duke looked up.

'I have not forgotten,' Wykeham said. 'From the first you were to come with me. Still, what I gave you, you have by default.'

His hands, long and hardened by a work only Hunt knew, clutched the table. For an instant he turned to the windows. There was only candlelight and hearthlight to see by, only the red gilding of the lawn from the bonfires.

'It is out of ignorance,' Wykeham said, 'you would have me be merciful. But the law in itself is the supreme mercy.'

The Duke's eyes searched his, uncomprehending, seeking a motive.

'Ignorance is forgivable, Your Grace,' Morag warned him.

'Only ignorance,' the Duke said.

Wykeham's jaw hardened. 'We do not, perhaps, quite understand one another,' he said.

'I understand a little.'

'Not enough.'

'A man is dead,' said the Duke.

'What you question is justice.' Wykeham paused. 'There was a law, Martin.'

'– And I broke it,' the Duke said angrily. 'I went myself to the station. Though I had sworn I would not, I watched . . .'

With a swift, sullen movement Wykeham turned away so that the Duke would not see his face. His Grace remained staring.

Somehow the sky seemed to darken. It was as if a wall had come to stand between the house and the lawn.

For a moment the Duke thought he heard a rustling out on the porch. He turned but saw only shadows. Yet there was something. It had almost a smell, as of twigs and branches, the deep renewing recesses of leaves.

Wykeham was watching the darkness.

'That was merely for the Will,' he said slowly, carefully. 'It was of no consequence. I have told you there was but one law.'

'Then I do not know it,' the Duke admitted.

Wykeham was silent.

The men looked at one another but Morag was staring at Longford. He said nothing, only stared at him, waiting for understanding to come.

All at once Longford lowered his head. His lips grew white. 'Dear Lord,' he said softly.

One last time Wykeham smiled at them. It had been first of laws but it was broken.

'There is a Tree,' he said, 'One of many planted in darkness, drawing strength from the ground. Of these I had given you freely. But the One you may not see, may not touch. . . .'

By then the hedge had reached the second story. Norfolk, who had been sent to make certain, edged down the stairs carrying a broken section of a branch. He had torn it off as it had coiled in through a bedroom window. The gray brown stem continued to grow in his hand. He set it down gingerly in the midst of the table.

The doors had already been tried. Like the windows they were impassable. With all his strength George Tennison had given a kick to the mass of thick stems spreading over the sill. A tremor had run through the wood. As though with pain, the queer dark leaves seemed to hiss at him and he had drawn back, afraid. All about him there had come scrapings and creakings, the muffled slither of limbs reaching furtively into the shingles. When he looked out, he was no longer able to make out the end of the porch. Soon, he thought, the roofs and the chimneys will be covered. He had gone back to the table. They had all gone back, from the west wing and the attic, from the little-used and out-of-the-way rooms that, since his return, Wykeham himself had not often visited.

They found their chairs silently.

Harwood disentangled himself from the twigs, which somehow had caught hold in his pocket.

'There are roots in the basement,' he said. 'Already they have broken in through the walls.' A trickle of blood ran down the side of his nose. He blotted it with a napkin. 'Thick as a man,' he said, looking around at the circle of faces.

'I don't suppose we have an ax?' Holmes asked. He was nursing a cut on his forehead. Burrowing his way out of the kitchen he had snagged his coat and scratched his face horribly.

'Not much use if we had,' Morag answered.

The old dead man kept his eyes averted. Even the nearer hallways were choked with limbs. He had just been able to clear a path through.

Nearly gasping, he slumped over his plate. He was too old for this. For the first time in a long while he felt resentment for the thinness of his legs and the immensity of his stomach. He had always feared the physical world a little. But once his size and his clumsiness had protected him. He saw no reason now for Wykeham to call on what, before, no one had thought to ask of him.

'You have made your point too well, William,' he said sadly.

'What point?' Holmes wanted to know.

Hunt's teeth showed between his lips. 'That we are safe,' he said.

Harwood swore. 'You mean that we are hopelessly trapped.'

'That may be,' allowed Hunt; yet his voice, which seemed flat, had anger lurking under it. 'Still, what is out there won't get in. Or at least not at first. So there may well be time. That is it, is it not?' His eyes stopped at Wykeham. 'As though a hedge . . .' he began, grinding his teeth.

'What is out there?' the Duke demanded.

Hunt did not bother to answer.

'Living men, I hope,' Harwood said in his place. 'But beyond them an army of the dead. And beyond them again –'

'Duinn,' Hunt said coldly and felt Wykeham's stare.

He looked again into the unmarked face and, watching, thought how, because Duinn had willed it, he had carried him, a boy, his eyes grown large with fear, across the holy river into the lands of the dead. And let him come back. Because that too had been Duinn's will. Or his pride, Hunt thought, or that vanity called pride.

Wearily he reached out. He took a drink from his goblet, unhurried, enough to last him.

'You are lord of this world,' he said. 'Yet he will not let you stay in it.' He raised a pair of his arms, impatiently. In his lap his fingers twisted. He said, 'It was never life he gave you. Surely, you must know that. Even he has not that power. It was only death he kept from you.'

For a breath's space there was silence. Wykeham lifted his head. He smiled into his eyes. 'Forever,' he whispered.

'For as long as you do not tire of it,' Hunt reminded him. 'No longer.'

'I do not tire.'

Hunt put down the goblet. It was blood they drank. There was no other truth. Though a man yearned only for pleasure or searched for understanding, to the end of his days he would learn nothing more. 'All that live must tire,' Hunt said.

Wykeham's deep eyes in which the memory of a million deaths were drowned looked him steadfastly in the face. 'Whatever must come,' he said, 'I shall be here.'

'Protected by a few miles of wall?'

'And these few hills and a wood. And this house looking over them.'

'And a hedge?' said Hunt. He scowled. 'Like some damn story for children?'

'It was always for children.'

'Where are the women, then?' Hunt asked him.

CHAPTER THREE

'In Black Wood,' Chance said, the wind of memory blowing through him.

He was silent a moment. 'Still, I did not die of it,' he said in a voice that quivered unexpectedly. He looked away into the fretwork of branches.

In the breeze the trees parried, drifted apart, only to return, limb by limb, to where they had been.

'The trees were mostly blackthorn then,' he went on more quietly. 'The only barn still standing Alf Jenkins's. And him only lately put underground and myself no more than a lad and feeling, the moment we entered the loft, a sinister dread on his behalf.' He looked again into the evening. The cold had withdrawn a little. Emboldened, he said: 'She was not yet sixteen. Still, it seemed a great difference.' He managed a trace of a smile. 'Before I had even touched her, she took off her dress.'

'And you have thought of her since?'

Chance lowered his head. 'Chiefly about other matters,' he said. 'But I have thought of her.' He reached for the bottle, as the other had done, so that at a distance it seemed that the two figures sitting in the starlight were respectfully toasting one another. Once more Chance brought the bottle to his lips. The whisky was strong and smelled of rainstorms and oak. He smelled other things; they floated out of his memory, the smell of fire, of earth, the old puzzling smell of dying. He looked around. When he recalled the scent of her hair, his eyes filled with tears.

She had had wonderful hair, brazen and red as flame. When she had looked up from under it there had been something touching about her glance, and something shameless too. She had not minded what the village women said of her. If things had come differently to him, he thought, if she had not been older, in his youth when a few years, it seemed, had been everything . . .

'I was seventeen when she married,' he murmured. 'She was twenty.'

'Her young man died.'

The breeze stirred and a shadow crawled onto the porch.

'Soon after,' Chance said. 'He is buried at Greenchurch.'

'Then, had you wished?'

Chance half closed his eyes. 'I was roaming,' he said, 'down to Bristol. Later to the docks at New Awanux.' He seemed to shake his old head. 'It was ten years before I was home again.'

The boy sat with his legs dangling in the grass. He was looking into the darkness. The spikes of his black hair fell over his collar. He took up the bottle.

Chance tried to speak casually:

'There's no hurry, I suppose?'

'There are many I won't even sit with,' the boy said.

'When that business up at the house is done,' Chance said obstinately. 'I've earned something, damn you, sitting in this place, keeping company with them who no one else would listen to.'

'Have you had supper?' the boy asked.

'Don't eat.'

The boy nodded. Unsmiling, he set the bottle down next to him.

'I've a paper,' Chance said. 'Sixty – seventy years I've had it.'

He had thought he would be frightened but he was more angry than frightened. He hadn't planned when it should be but that it should be now, before he saw whether Wykeham, with all his years, had made any difference, was senseless. It was cruel. Bitterly he dropped his eyes to the floor. He could see his legs, stuck out straight and stiff, and tried to pull them back. It worked its way into his consciousness very slowly that he could not.

'Fifty years,' the boy said.

'No matter,' Chance answered, brushing those years aside, although at the end they were all that was left to him. 'Time enough,' he said hoarsely. He started to draw a new breath. He could hear his chest begin to suck clumsily. It made him angrier.

'And nothing of him changed,' he whispered. 'While to me . . .'

The boy turned his head. The darkness had rubbed the expression out of his face. His eyes were now murky holes, his mouth a vague tear. Chance shut his sight fast against them. Do not feel, he thought.

After a little while he heard him get up.

'When I took her,' Duinn said, 'she was waiting alone at her window.' His footsteps came nearer. 'Waiting as she had night after night, hoping for another look at a red, naked man who, long after she had forgotten you, once waved at her from the midst of the air.'

Presently Duinn put his hand on the weeping man's shoulder.

'Shall I tell you what I did?' Duinn asked.

The man did not answer.

'In fact, it is a little thing,' Duinn said, almost diffidently. 'Like killing a hare.'

CHAPTER FOUR

It was late, too late, Willa Brelling was afraid, when she began her journey; but then, until the fires, she hadn't understood that it was within her power to go. It had not even been in her mind – a stone only watches, wood only waits – and with every nerve rigid, she had watched endlessly, waited endlessly, while the nights had piled up about her. In her innermost self she still felt the hands that long ago had pulled her down on the cot, still felt even now, in the darkness of classrooms and corridors, how he had covered her with himself. But she had no happiness out of the memory and though he had come again, he had gone. She could not follow. It was only because she was often at the windows that she had watched the fires.

For hours, becoming one substance with the glass, she had observed the Indians gathering. They had floated down from the sky, effortlessly, never touching the ground. All afternoon they had lingered in the air. The frost had turned the elms into torches of fire. It did not seem strange to her that the flesh of men should likewise burn. Like herself, the Indians seemed intent on no other business but waiting. It was not until evening that they came down onto the roof of the chapel. Dancing upon it and jeering at those within, they blew the sparks from their mouths onto the shingles. She saw the building begin to glow dully. From the main house a dozen figures rushed onto the lawn. When the chapel exploded, the odd-job man was still dragging up buckets of water. The fires that twisted on his back rose abruptly as he ran. Coming over the hill he looked like a shooting star. Her star. Rushing toward her.

The body dropped and lay still. She drew a part of herself into the front step and waited. Smoke escaped from the rags of its clothes but the life that had been there had gone. Yet something of its warmth remained. She did not mind that its chin was covered with bristles or that, in its agony, it had fouled itself. She was frightened, however, that someone might take it from her. She could hear the women drawing nearer and knew that she must conceal it from them.

All that was necessary, she thought, was to inhabit its legs. She could

557

do such a thing. Every board and timber of the hall was filled with her. A body was much smaller.

She entered its feet through the soles, hastily, eager only to be done. But there was more room inside than she had imagined. She had a feeling of terrible vastness. In order to fill it, she was forced to draw herself down from the roofpeaks and out of the walls. Yet life can only be filled with life and, although she had pushed all she was into it, the sense of emptiness was appalling. Nonetheless she could make it stand. She could open its eyes.

She looked toward the road on the side of the hill. The road led toward the river and the trains. It led, she did not doubt, to Greenchurch and the house to which he always returned.

If she wished to, she felt, she could follow him.

She made the legs bend. They carried her down the hill. In her heart there was a sudden, overwhelming nostalgia for movement. Ignoring the sluggishness of its gait, she crossed the first poor square, passing into the narrow street beyond with an air of giddy anticipation.

The fires were not yet general. The few men stood about idly, unnoticing, or sat in groups on the steps of the houses, talking in the lateness of the evening. But already the women were leaving. Each alone, with eyes shrewdly vacant, they strolled out onto the avenues. Yet they seemed without purpose and, if a man they knew caught sight of them, they smiled and went on without speaking. In the darkness their footsteps were soon gone beyond hearing. Unless one followed down the dim, shifting streets that led to the trains, one would never have guessed their numbers.

Bristol station slanted upward into the blackness. Out on the platform the women assembled. Their stares, which at first had been impersonal and questioning, warmed as they met the stares of others. Very little was said. They knew and, assured of the reasons, had no cause for concern. Some of the women had owls, others jays or wrens, in little wire cages or free on their shoulders. Unmindful of the soft twittering, the women looked across at the river. Their eyes had become clearer, the lines at the sides of their mouths more deeply satisfied.

'Go home, father,' said the matron who was the first to see the old man climbing the stairs from the street. Her voice was kind but it was firm. 'Get along home,' she repeated.

Willa did not try to speak. It was the body of the man the woman was talking to. And the body was not interested. It was stiffening. Willa let it lean on the rail. The woman continued to speak to it.

'We – needn't – take – care – of – you,' the woman said, spacing the words and giving them a certain triumph. 'We needn't bathe you, though you need it. Needn't clean up after you. Not ever again. And there is no use in following.' Pausing, she saw its face and mistaking what she saw there, said more gently but as earnestly: 'You will just have to get by as best you can.'

The body waited, unmoving.

To Willa, who was alone in it, the corpse seemed larger than it perhaps was, but it seemed even emptier as well. At last, robbed of any argument, the woman wandered away. Women hurried by, pushing past her. Willa watched the crowd of absorbed faces indifferently. The mouth of the corpse hung open. Its muscles and tendons were beginning to feel like iron. Soon, Willa thought, it will not move at all. But when the train pulled into the station, she dragged its halting feet over the platform, made its legs mount, heavily, one by one, the black metal steps into the car. With every step the corpse looked older and more vile. But, within, under the glare of the lanterns, the women recognized the dazed and temporary nature of its life. There was nothing to do, they decided, nothing worth the trouble of taking charge of, and so they did not protest. It only sat with its ropy hands hung between its knees, staring rudely at the many colored birds that shared the car, listening wearily to the unmerciful joy of their voices.

The young woman, her chin lowered and her hands in her lap, did not wake until the train started. It was the wrong place to sleep but her body was exhausted by the life stretching and pulling inside her and any respite had been welcome, forgetfulness most welcome of all. She twisted awake. Startled at finding the old man sitting next to her, she moaned.

'They have made you sit here,' she said unhappily. 'To punish me. Because I am already pregnant.'

Its stench sickened her; still the woman did not move. She accepted the punishment as she had accepted the life growing in her, because she felt or wished to feel the presence of the man. The women, of course, had done this. She was certain of that. They had sent the old man, his head like a skull, to remind her of the mortality of earthly affection: the man, they as much as said, will become as this man.

She had known all the while they were leaving, going off to a much better world. Nonetheless when the man had come to her she had put that knowledge aside. Afterward, in the large rented room of the King's

Hotel, although they had talked on for hours, they had never discussed the possibility of a child. When he had gone away, the man had gone away unknowing.

Carolyn let her head fall back on the seat.

In the darkness of the river she could see the darkness of his eyes. It was odd, she thought, to think of him that way, not eyes black as the darkness but the darkness as black as his eyes. But she knew it was fitting.

The women in the library had been kind. They had tried to be comforting; yet, she had seen the disdain in their faces. Poor nasty fat thing, they had said, without speaking a word. Poor thing, they had whispered, watching her waddle between the rows of books, lugging the life about with her like something in a sack.

'In the new world,' Carolyn told the old man, 'they will always be thin.' She kept hold of her smile, partially out of bitterness but as well from embarrassment. It was much the same smile that had lingered in Wykeham's mind when on the night he was leaving he had written her his last letter. 'How can I explain?' he had written, saying the words a second time, to himself.

'And when they bear,' Carolyn went on softly, 'the child becomes as the woman, the one repeating the other. Without pain.' She looked at the old man carefully and said, 'So they have explained it to me. But I will never know for certain. Not with a life already inside me. Because of it, when the time comes, I shall not be permitted to cross.'

She settled farther back in the seat. The darkness had not changed but now in the blackness of the river she could make out a succession of shadows. Moment to moment, they seemed to resemble a tree, a galloping stallion, a ship. She folded her hands on her stomach.

'Sometimes I am afraid,' she whispered, wanting none but the old man to hear. 'Suppose,' she said, 'it is something fit only for circuses.' She pressed her plain fingers into the lap of her dress. 'Something for Barnum, with stubs of wings or too many legs.'

She discovered the old man watching her. Its chest moved.

'It's done in darkness,' it croaked.

'Loaded in darkness,' it insisted, its breath a dry hiss.

Not understanding, Carolyn merely continued to stare.

The corpse set its teeth. 'Life,' it said sharply. The body felt heavy and terribly cold. It had been dead only a few hours. But in fifty years, Willa knew, she had not learned to be ready.

'You can't see,' the corpse said, her voice in its voice, its cold breath touching her own dead heart with awe. 'You can't ever see. You must simply wait.'

An army, the stationmaster thought in his sleep, listening to the tramp of feet on the platform. He had been no more than a boy during the Great War; but the trains, coming down from the north, had passed through quite often. Now and again, because of delays on the line, the troop cars had stopped at the village. The men, spilling onto the street, had had time for a smoke or, if they were daring, just time enough to run the quarter mile across to the Royal Charles – though, of course, it had been the Royal Edward then.

The night breeze blew stiffly through the office window, stirring the stationmaster's memory. It was the same sound, he decided without waking. Though, in truth, it wasn't the rumble of boots he heard but the shared sense of purpose and hurry that was missing from the scramble of ordinary passengers. The sound was continuous and, for the space of several minutes, deafening. Yet by the time he had struggled out of his sleep, it was gone. He stuck his head out into the cold night air.

Except for the very pregnant young woman leading an old man across to the stairs, the platform was empty. He watched them go down slowly into the street. He looked at his watch. It was not quite two-thirty. The train, he decided, was late.

'I am slowing you,' the corpse said. It was not an apology.

Carolyn was silent. She did not say that her own careful slowness was as much a matter of her sickness and pain. Left alone she would never have been able to keep pace with the scurrying feet of the women.

Far ahead the last had already vanished under the trees. A ridge of cloud was creeping up from the south and it had become very dark. Had it not been for the birds screeching about the entrance to the path, she would have missed it entirely. Carolyn's eyes flickered up at the branches. She was frightened.

'There are Indians,' she whispered.

'I have seen them.'

'Perhaps you should not,' she said pointedly. She kept looking over her shoulder.

It was the first time in her life she had stirred from New Awanux, the first time, apart from Wykeham, she had dared much of anything. But it had done no good. In the damp chill of the wood she saw nothing that had any meaning, only half-things that were constantly changing. She walked more painfully. For a moment even the lame old man was in danger of drawing ahead of her.

The air smelled different. They were among the stones. She could feel their vague huge shapes looming over her.

'It is strange to think,' she said, 'that it is all a mistake.' She stopped and rubbed her hands on her dress. With the back of her wrist she pushed her hair away from her eyes.

'We will come to water soon,' she said. 'There he who will carry them across will be waiting.'

Her hands which had been seeking something to hold, something to touch, fell helplessly.

'Someone has blundered,' she said.

The old man looked blank.

'A Redd Man,' she whispered. 'Can't you see that? The fetcher, the stalker by streams.'

She peered desperately into the eyes of the corpse.

'Red as the old cock salmon,' she whispered, 'red as blood.'

Her hands, which at last found some purpose, now hid her face.

'A Redd Man,' she cried out, a sob breaking through the mask of her fingers. 'A Redd Man,' she wailed. 'Never Indians.'

CHAPTER FIVE

Deep into the evening a tender little breeze moved through the hedge. It stirred the tall curtains, shaking, ever so faintly, the cloak which hung by the hearth.

The Reverend Timothy Longford watched the rotted old fabric as though transfixed. The firelight had touched its veins of gold with a bright rime of flame, its threads of fine silver with radiance. He tried to moisten his lips.

'Dear Christ,' he whispered.

In his mind the flickering vision of God and His angels still lingered. He felt a mortifying guilt. For twenty years, as rich and as holy a mystery, the woman, forsaking all others, had clung to him. In sickness and in health, he said, not aloud, but his lips moved reciting the service. He looked again at the cloak. How could he have been so mistaken?

'Dear sweet Christ,' he repeated. But it was the woman who was gone.

At the table the discussion went around him.

The Duke refolded the paper. Returning it to his pocket, he became aware of a swift flutter of pain. Still, it was no more than a gentle pressure on his chest, and he hunched his thick shoulders, ignoring it.

'You wrote me a letter from Egypt once,' he said. 'I was at the bank, William, when I opened it, in the chair I was to give to Houseman.'

Wykeham was looking away.

'Thirteen years ago,' the Duke reminded him. 'It was about women. Their bowing and nodding, you wrote, reminded you of birds.'

His Grace shook his head.

'I would have thought they would have been herons,' he said. 'Or whatever white birds there are in Egypt. They were blonde after all. They were English women.'

He waited and then cleared his throat. 'But they were like crows, you said. Their eyes soulless like the eyes of crows.'

'Not crows,' Hunt offered ruefully.

With two large hands Hunt hitched up his trousers; with another he took up his cup and looked over it. 'But all the same,' he said, 'like a flight of birds turning.' His old red face glowered. 'One creature,' he said, 'thinking one thought and turning –'

'But where?' Longford asked desperately.

Holmes was not listening. He was watching Hunt's arms. Yet, until he struck the match and saw the bright flame twisting above the bowl of the pipe, he had not remembered the photograph.

At once his head tilted up.

'What if,' he asked, surprised, 'from the very beginning we have had it wrong?'

It was only then that Wykeham looked at him.

'What then?' he asked.

'Suppose there were two Creations.'

Wykeham frowned.

'Or twenty,' Holmes said.

'Or hundreds,' Harwood added disagreeably. It was the first time in a long while he had spoken. 'Like beads on a string,' he said, his voice too loud because he thought they were ignoring him.

'Only here, I think,' Holmes said quietly. He was concentrating. 'Only sharing this place,' he said softly. 'Only using this place and, though struggling, never able to get free of it.'

There were endless worlds.

In this one there was water.

Carl Brelling edged to within a few feet of it.

He had tried to move carefully, avoiding the mounds of dead sticks and the briars, but scrambling over the maze of bleak walls in the heart of the wood he had fallen. Although he had managed not to cry out, his elbows were bruised and his trousers in shreds. But because he was sober he began to feel the cold. He stood in the reedy grass at the water's edge, cursing the darkness and shivering.

It was like coming to the end of the world.

It was just that, he thought, the world's end. The shame was he was alone at it.

The woman who had marched into the shop and whom, half in a daze, he had followed, was gone. She had driven him, he thought, along the river. He remembered the car at least. He had got into the corner of the back seat and had paid no attention while she had gone on about Nora and the young man. It was not that he was uninterested; he could no longer make out the meaning of the simplest words.

What was love? he wondered.

What, damn them, were women?

He did not pretend these were original questions but, despairing of answers, he dug his small boots into the dirt of the bank. The night wind had come and chilled him. It had been hours, he thought. Perhaps longer.

For a long time he had looked out the car window.

At the beginning, on the plain, the fires had been everywhere. Like the swift streak of a line-squall fires exploded over the roofs of New Awanux. They erupted from chimneys and doorways, fell hissing out of the low sky. He sat and stared without speaking.

Bristol, when they came to it, was already in ruins. The flames formed a ring halfway across the horizon.

The woman peered out through the windscreen.

'It is still dark up ahead,' she said gravely.

The houses of the village had come up on the left. All at once at the crown of the hill there were women. The street and the sidewalks had been filled with them. By hundreds, they tramped through the bare gardens and over the lawns.

The headmistress stopped the car at the top of the green and climbed out.

'Where are you going?' he asked, but she moved away with the others. When he opened the door of the car, no one stopped to look back.

His poor eyes squinted into the darkness.

On the side of the green there was a garage, its doors closed and its dark windows shuttered. The field beside it was wild and overgrown. Unmindful, the women poured into it. At a distance he watched them.

The path they made twisted; it wound among the rough stands of burdock and thistle. Conscious only that he had been left behind, Carl Brelling started after them. He went toward the far edge where the ground fell steeply. He ran. Inside his chest he was suffocating. Just once, out of the corner of his eye, he still saw them. But as the trees at the margin of the wood came up at him, he stopped, gasping, dragging the cold air back into his lungs and found only their clothing.

He closed his eyes tightly. But it was not the nakedness of the women he was imagining but the hallway in his mother's house, long ago in New Awanux. He had been the youngest, a boy in a house of women. His big, grown-up sister had left her stockings curled at the foot of the stairs, her skirts on the railing.

Trudging up to the landing, catching up one thing then another as she went, his mother had thrown each one back to him. The mound of his sister's clothing had grown in his arms.

'She has no sense of decency,' his mother said. She stopped outside Willa's room and glared in.

'And this is the way you treat me,' his mother said bitterly to the girl on the bed.

He had peered around his mother's waist.

'Like a servant,' his mother said.

Frightened, he had pressed his face into the loose jumble of garments. But the smell of them, damp and faintly sour, rising like a guilty transmission, cut through him.

Willa's long bare legs dropped to the floor. She had not looked at him, perhaps had not even know he was there. But he fled.

At the head of the stairs where the light poured in through the window he tripped over a pair of worn pumps, which, after her slip, were the last things she had abandoned.

Carl Brelling had scarcely taken a half dozen steps when the sensation of water brought him back to himself.

The light began on the far bank. At first it seemed no more than a small ragged tear. But in a moment it was several yards wide. He stood and stared, praying that it would stop. Instead the light grew. Presently, in its brightness, he could see the many shapes of their arms, the endless variation of their breasts and their legs.

A thousand women were crossing the clearing, on their way up the great, fissured slope of a hill. Not a hill exactly. It kept rising, and a hill, he was certain, would not. He drew his hand to his brow, shielding his eyes from the light.

Far up, above the highest tops of the water oaks, he saw the first branches. They were distinguishable only because his eyes were still fixed on them. But as long as he looked they were everywhere – straining outward with immense sweeping arms. The wind stirred them and was itself stirred, was filled with fluttering leaves. He forced his head higher.

It was in that instant he saw her, saw only her.

'Nora!' he called.

The harsh slit of her mouth opened. It vomited flame.

Turning frantically, Carl Brelling bumped into a man.

He tried to run, but the man had got hold of him.

Ducking, scrambling on hands and knees, he tried to crawl. Suddenly there was another in his way. Reaching out when already he knew he should have stopped, he felt the prickly wool of her dress. The distended sack of her belly jutted over him.

The woman stared down at him in horror. He was not old and he was thrusting his small wet hands in her dress.

'Get away from me!' she screamed.

Whatever was there in truth was perhaps no great matter. The eyes Willa looked through saw the face clearly. She remembered his lies. She had taken her own life to be with him.

The corpse shivered. Its tongue went stiff in its mouth.

'You were not dead!' it cried. 'You were never –'

It was not a man's voice, or a woman's. But it was old and terrible and made desperate by longing.

Carl Brelling turned his head.

The arms grasped him tightly and twisted. At that same moment something came loose in his memory. The name came to him without his seeking it. It did not matter whose name. There was a woman, and a man. There was water and darkness, a child about to be born and a man dying.

It did not matter whose death.

He could feel his breath squeezing out.

'Is that you?' he asked, whispering soundlessly, because now he had no breath at all.

The hands that held him dug into his neck.

'Please,' he said meekly.

Their dark shapes, though scarcely bigger than himself, loomed over him. They were cradling his head and pulling it. He felt the vertebra crack, heard it splitting. He smelled the quick, sour exhalation of air rushing under him and, for one last moment, looked back on the red, pumping stalk of his neck.

It was fine. The breeze had dropped. Its cold breath was gone from her breasts and her legs. The branches stretched invitingly toward the pale windless dawn. Smiling, she hurried along them, mounting from starlight to shadow and back into light. About her the tree was thick with singing birds, with blackbirds and sparrows. Above her the crows shook out their splendid wings. The women, walking close beside her, were fair. The world would always be as it had been in her childhood, when the dreams had gone with the morning, and the man, who, like the God who had made her, was not even a memory. She would no longer dream of him. She would no longer grieve for what, now unremembered, was lost.

On the cold bank below something lifted its head.

She did not mean to look but it called to her.

Nora stiffened.

'Woman!' it cried.

There was something moving under the tree. She saw the tender crown of his forehead. His tousled hair made him appear younger than he was. Yet she knew him. Surely she had always known. His skin was pale; his eyes, watching her nakedness, much too innocent. Uncertain, she made herself laugh.

'Nora,' he whispered, finding her name.

'He is not here,' she called back.

The boy's small face darkened, as though he felt she was deceiving him.

She did not need to ask the reason why he had come, but she did ask.

'Why,' she whispered, 'should he be where I am?'

His eyes looked up.

'You followed him.'

She laughed again, more bitterly. 'With little hope,' she said, 'and no more chance than you of finding him.' There was a touch of defiance in her voice but her mind raced, trying to think of a way to flee from him and yet terrified that he would hear her thoughts.

Indeed, her thoughts lay before him, as the thoughts of all living things came to him. Even then he would have wept for pity of her. He took no joy in the killing. In the gray twilight he had made, he gathered the dead. In the halls of blackened stone, he kept them. It was the Redd Man who did the slaughter. But Wyck had brought his fearful servant to the Great House, ringed by its walls and a wood, and set him there within a hedge beyond his reach. Thwarted, Duinn's face was weary but his jaw was set.

He lifted his head.

Then at last, in the shadow of his cheek, she saw the cheerless, grizzled color of his hair and the long hands partly hidden in his cloak; and where the cloak was parted, she saw the ax.

'There was a man,' he said, 'who would have loved you.'

There was a silence.

'In the house,' he said. His grimness softened, for a moment he looked a boy again.

'What do you need of me?' she asked.

'I would have you bring me where he is,' he said.

Her perch in the tree was high above him. Still, she shrank back. She said: 'Lord, I have come too far.'

The sky was even higher than she was. But she wondered if even that were high enough. With stubborn terror her mind sought a place more distant.

It was almost morning. The setting moon had dropped within the maze of limbs; slipped in between the branches, a blade of its wan light, touching her fingers, made them visible. The feathers sprouted from her nails. Feathers grew without pause from her wrists and arms. With one wild push, she brought them up. In the first silver chill of morning their hard, bright edges caught the air.

'Lady,' he murmured.

But in that vast place the light was empty. Even the tree that from the beginning in countless worlds had rooted at his will was gone; only the man was left.

An icy wind blew cold against the bank. Lodged between the stones, the white body of a crow, grim with frost, lay frozen stiff.

For a moment Duinn gazed at it. But if there had been pity in those eyes, when he turned them toward Greenchurch, it was gone.

In the final hour, in that gentle darkness which comes before dawn, there was a stillness. Wykeham watched the men before him. The table was cleared, the bottles emptied and returned to the shelf. Grumbling, the Duke examined his watch. Morag mopped his damp forehead. But nothing was said. In the hearth the last live coal glowed once faintly, then went out.

When the stillness was deepest, Longford's tired blue eyes filled with tears.

Wykeham laid a hand on his arm.

'It is the worst time,' Wykeham said. 'The hour when death seems most welcome.'

The minister's face twisted. 'It is not for myself,' he said. 'I would not care for myself, if I were certain. If I knew –'

'Then let him tell you,' Hunt said.

Longford's head came up in astonishment.

'Tell me what?'

Wykeham looked at him. No muscle in his long face changed but he avoided the question.

'At dawn there will be a wind,' he said.

Fred Norfolk groaned. He had kept out one last glass for himself and now he drank it. 'By Christ,' he said loudly, 'there is always a wind. A queer wind, blowing up mischief.' He put his glass back down on the table and stared at it. 'But it wasn't a wind that I looked for,' he complained. 'It was a war, I thought.' He waved his hand toward the window. 'It was what they thought, those men on the lawn. Staying up all night, waiting just like we were waiting.' He grunted. For a long moment he studied Wykeham in silence. 'God damn it all,' he said at last, bitterly, 'a man can't fight wind.'

'It will be a great wind,' Hunt said, 'with the dead riding it.'

'Which dead?'

No one looked to see who had spoken, for each had had the same thought. Each sat very still, remembering, peering into nothingness and trying to think of a way to keep, for good or ill, what had been.

Amelia, Holmes whispered.

Nora!

Olivia!

Plum!

Wykeham had shut his eyes, but not against them. He could feel the fierceness of their longing. Before him, even with his lids clamped shut, he saw the lonely tangle of their separate lives; saw Longford in his bed, with Plum beside him; saw the little room of Harwood's study and the arching rosemary barberry that twisted beyond the kitchen door in Cambridge when Holmes was six. Fondly, through Morag's keen, unfaded eyes, he saw all the wonders of women and porter the old minister had left, too soon, behind. He saw the dusty yards and barns and the high sun over the hills where Norfolk had wandered. Reaching with long, scarred hands, he touched with Martin Callaghan's fingers, not his own, a son, a boy with jet-black hair who never was.

He moaned.

A branching labyrinth had opened before him. Beyond the ragged sounds of his own breath he heard the great surging hiss of their memories filling the channels, coursing through them, heaving the weight of their dreams to break and form again, like waves against a shore. Beneath that avalanche the long hill shook, the house shook on its old stone, and the earth and sky for an interminable instant tore.

It seemed only a moment. But in that moment he bound them, rejoining what they most remembered, gathering all that elsewhere had been quickly lost, the laughter and the vital nerve of longing, the snow-mired streets, the sure, swift hazards of sun and wind. All that had been his hope and theirs he took and forged, until, clear in its common shape, it moved before him. A world moved, a substance of shadows, a substance of rivers and mountains and unbroken light.

Wykeham threw back his head. His black eyes flashed open.

It was George Tennison who stood. Angrily, seeing no vision, the old workman pushed his way through the hedge. But now, when he touched them, the rough, gray limbs fell. He stood stock-still among the wreckage.

The lawn was empty; only the cold, useless stumps of the fires remained. It was not quite day. A bare light shone on his face.

Harwood had come out beside him. One by one, parting the hedge, the men followed. Wykeham stood nearby, his face watchful.

Harwood opened his mouth, but there was no sound.

The men looked at one another. They looked over the trampled grass and gardens but there was nothing to be seen. From the depths of the wood there came a cold silence.

The wind began with the dawn.

'Look there!' Norfolk shouted.

At the very edge of the wood the wind sprang. Out of the wrack of branches a turbulent black stream came tumbling. A thousand dark shapes filled the air. Some solitary, others in knots and wheels, pitching out of the shadows, they leapt and soared. There were none the same. Shooting out over the wide brown meadow, their black wings churned a booming thunder from the air. They rose. Then, all at once, almost cloud high, they turned and, swept on by the gale, came direct as an arrow toward the house. Shapes that had become dim specks grew breasts and arms. Eyes, where they had been only unheeding shadows, peered out from under strands of streaming hair and smiled again.

Norfolk rushed out on the lawn. Yet even as he ran it seemed to him that the sound of the wind had changed. That it beat against the earth with antic wildness. It tugged at his sleeves and tore the buttons from his shirt. He placed his hands on his hips and laughed. Morag had run out after him; Longford followed.

'Listen,' Norfolk cried. 'Listen!'

Morag craned his neck and simply gasped.

He did not know how Wykeham had managed it.

He himself, he hoped, had never wronged them. Yet, whatever rage was felt against the race of men, whatever insult had been kept and harbored, by whatever cause, no longer mattered.

The wind whisked through his fringe of hair. It would never be still, he knew, could never be held to one thing without turning. His eyes by now had a curious dreaming look.

All about him, over the wide bright lawn, the women were floating down.

Morag flung out his arms.

Plum loomed above him. The white of her breasts, the white of her neck and shoulders were suffused with a deepening blush, her cheeks the color of red petticoats. They watched each other's eyes. Conscious that they were drawing nearer, both chuckled. Each leaning forward, they swayed, almost touching, until one final gust blew them together and they fell in a quivering jumble on the grass. Plum squeaked. Morag giggled and nuzzled her ear.

Longford could not bear to look. There had been but one woman he had loved. He stumbled out into the middle of the lawn. 'Plum,' he wailed. 'Oh, Plum!'

Hearing him, the stout, gray-haired woman, the bald head of the old gentleman supported like a baby in her lap, looked over her shoulder. As though it gave her exquisite pleasure just to look at him, she smiled.

All the while Norfolk was pulling little Welsh girls by their pigtails down from the wind. There were three already clinging to his knees, grinning merrily. But he was not able to pull them down quickly enough. He had been thinking of seven but had only got five when he caught sight of Lizzy bearing down on him. He gave a mild shrug. With one last backward wink and more courage than he had thought himself capable of, he accepted Lizzy bravely into his arms.

One after another the women were caught and brought down. The men who had spent the night on the lawn, hiding themselves, now got up quickly. The sexton, hoping to get the best pick, had climbed onto a barrel, where, waving his thick arms, he barked in a voice of thunder: 'She is mine! She is mine!'

Nobody challenged him. There were only a few dozen men and the women, it seemed, were without number.

Holmes came down from the porch, staring around guiltily for his wife. He walked into the noisy yard, his hands held behind him. Leaves and thistledown were blown over the edge of the lawn. There for a moment he saw her, drifting toward the barn, the stationmaster trotting along under her. Her small, fishlike mouth parted happily. She waved to him but her thoughts were occupied. Holmes turned away. He scarcely saw the young woman in the air before him.

'Good sir,' she called out to him, 'why are you filled with sorrow?'

He did not want to look but courtesy made him answer.

'I do not know,' he said. He thought of the woman who had shared his bed. 'I had a wife,' he said, 'yet even then I grieved for something.'

The young woman smiled. 'I was a wife to someone,' she answered, 'but I have been blown about by the wind today and I do not think, even if I found him, I would take him back.'

For the first time he truly looked and saw the plain, brown, eager face. He was almost relieved she was not beautiful.

'What will come of this?' he asked.

'Like you,' she said, 'I do not know.'

'That much is certain,' he answered, but with a brief, grave smile he drew her down.

The gale had tipped a wagon on its side and sent a line of haystacks blundering toward the fence. Half of the new shingles George Tennison had hammered onto the roof had broken off and lay scattered across a hundred yards of lawn. 'There will be work again,' Olivia told him. George Tennison nodded.

'We can put it to rights,' he said confidently. Slyly, pretending to survey the damage, he drew a hand around her waist.

Something, however, had to be done about the women who remained in the air. A few too many men, finding much delight in the women they had landed, had already begun to slip off with them, leaving their less fortunate sisters stranded and just beyond reach. The neglected women rolled about helplessly, bumping and generally getting in each other's way. 'Bitches! Husband-stealers!' they cried out to the women on the ground. The village policeman, reinforced by a thin, dark-haired lad from over the line in West Redding, came back from the stables with a pair of painters' ladders and were kept busy for hours, untangling and drawing them down.

Martin Callaghan took his hands from his pockets. Two or three times he had been about to go down, but he had held back, not frightened, but watchful. On the hillside the bodies of men and women moved over one another in the grass. From the porch he could hear their soft voices. He stepped back. For no clear reason he trembled. Around by the sheds Harwood was speaking quietly to a young woman. He was touching her neck. In front of them a small blonde girl was playing. Even Hunt had not gone off alone. His face strangely resolute, he sat out under the elms, squeezing the pink nipple of a plump, white-faced woman between the blunt fingers of his huge, blood-red hands.

Martin Callaghan turned his head irritably. 'Is this the world, then?' he asked in a low voice.

'Part of it,' Wykeham told him.

'And the rest?'

But Wykeham was still watching the wood. Once it had been spring there, then summer. Now even the last warmth of autumn was leaving the air. As he watched, what he took for a flock of wild gulls came swirling over the lawn.

Wykeham shut his eyes and still saw them. The sky was turning white with their wings. They beat against the blank screen of his eyelids, falling, settling down on the earth.

When he looked again, they were standing in front of him.

Nora was first, before them all on the steps. But Willa was mounting behind her.

'I have come,' she said simply.

'As I promised,' Jane said.

'As you dreamed,' said another, coming nearer. Synchronously, a spirit of laughter touching their brains, the multitude smiled on him.

PART VI

Winterking

He waited as a man waits in a cell. The gray, silent hills, drawn away from him, seemed to rise like the walls of a prison. This also will be a place of darkness, he thought, dismayed. He had a sense, again, of terrible emptiness, as if the valley itself, in spite of cities and towns, in spite of hedgerows and the hundred million boughs of the wood, was, in fact, the pitch-dark corridor of a hideous dungeon. Wykeham gave a second jerk to the reins. But as quickly as the impression came it passed.

It was a dream, he was certain. Like any dream it was a jumble of pieces, each seeming to make the others impossible.

For one thing the long, twisting drive seemed to wind toward the sea. A little breeze had sprung up, carrying the wet flavor of salt. To his ears it carried as well the hurrying sound of waves. Turning his back to it, he gave a kick to the ribs of the stallion so that the animal broke into a lumbering trot. When he made the last turn of the drive, he could see Martin Callaghan waiting. Watching the intent, dark face in the dusk, Wykeham forgot he was dreaming.

'Where in the name of God have you been, William?' Martin shouted.

Wykeham dropped down by the front door, giving the reins into the hands of the stableboy.

'How is she?' he asked.

Martin made no reply.

Together they mounted the steps. But inside he knew it was a dream again; he was in an unreal house that only existed when he entered it. Still, it pleased him immeasurably to see the house spring to life around him. Women, hearing his boots on the carpet, peered out of hallways, looking up tenderly as he passed. He could smell potatoes and ham from the kitchen and knew that Lizzy would have a huge dinner waiting when he came down.

The room was on the third story, at the end of a passage that ran along by the side of the house. A dim light showed under the door.

When he went in, Morag was reading the service. Holmes was

drawing the sheet over the head. The head made one mound, the breasts two large others. Wykeham knelt down, pressed his hands along the sheet. He was surprised, full of wonder.

'What did you expect?' Morag asked him.

'I'm the father, you son of a bitch.'

'It could not be helped,' Morag told him. 'There was a storm. She was caught in it.'

In the silence that followed, they could hear the wash of the sea below the house. Wykeham tried to move away but could not.

'God help me,' he whispered.

The dream Callaghan stood behind him, watching quietly.

'It is the way the world is now,' he said, unconcerned. He might have stopped but did not.

He said: 'Tell me just what it was you wanted.'

'Nothing.'

The dream Callaghan shrugged. 'As you please,' he said. But Wykeham cried out:

'Nothing more than I had.'

A frown settled heavily on Martin Callaghan's face.

'Very well,' he said patiently, 'but when?'

That, of course, Wykeham realized, had been the first error. But, in a way, he had half expected it, for he was always remembering a little more than he intended. Nonetheless, there were worse fates than too many women. If that was all that had gone wrong, he would live with it. He looked directly at Nora's slender corpse, aware that outside the dream he had saved her, that when he woke she would be whole again.

Beyond the window the gulls went on crying. In the darkness he could hear the cold waves crashing on the beach. He knew the sound. It was the same beach which, world after world, he had walked with Duinn. Still, it is a dream, he thought, reassured.

Wykeham lifted his neck.

When he reached out his arm, it was morning. Beside him there was a warm patch in the bed where Jane had been. The sea was gone. By the gentle vagueness of the light he knew it was snowing.

The women were up early. When Jane came in from the hallway, the kitchen was glowing with warmth. The kettle steamed and puffs of drowsy smoke escaped from a crack in the chimney. As though by right, Nora and Lizzy had the best seats, with Olivia, on the edge of the bench, squeezed in next to them. Mrs. Harwood, however, had to watch from the corner, her hands resting protectively on her daughter's small shoulders. Between mouthfuls of jam, the child was trying to count all the women. But the room was crowded and in the confusion her eyes kept coming back to the Welsh girls. Entwined in each other's arms, they sat on the floor by the wall exchanging glances and whispering about Fred Norfolk. Braving the snow before daylight, he had already gone twice to the shed where they had set up their housekeeping, to look in, he said, and see how they were doing. Lizzy went to rinse her cup in the sink. She had a word or two to say about Fred Norfolk and didn't care much who else heard. But as she stretched herself up there was a thump on the porch.

A few too many thumps, Nora thought, who had been expecting only Plum.

But when the door opened, it was Plum in fact, standing on the threshold with half a hillside of snow on her shoulders.

'Found her,' she said, panting, pulling in a bedraggled young woman, an even greater shawl of snow covering her.

The young woman blinked. Her skin, what they saw of it, was blue and she was shivering. By the way she held herself it seemed she feared something inside her would break.

The women sat her in a chair. They rubbed her all over, toweling her long legs and thin arms until the skin was red again and her hair a nest of limp, black curls.

Plum dried herself.

'Like you,' she told Nora when Nora brought her a cup. Plum drank it down.

'By the edge of the drive,' she said, 'as you were.'

'Not like that I wasn't,' Nora laughed.

'Mama,' the little girl said, 'the lady –'

Mrs. Harwood ushered the child from the room.

'Let's try not to think of it,' said Olivia.

But the young woman by the stove was already asleep and the talk left her even before it had started.

There were to be a great many women. The change wouldn't treat them all just the same. A few, perhaps, would remain as they had been. Nonetheless, it was a new world and the women had expected everything to be a bit strange and were astonished when they remembered even the smallest things exactly.

'This cup has a chip,' Lizzy said, 'here on the bottom. Now how would he know that?'

'Perhaps Fred – ' Olivia suggested.

'Don't talk to me of Fred,' Lizzy snapped at her furiously. But in a moment, on her own, she had launched into a long, bitter complaint against the Welsh in general and Welsh girls in particular.

'And what does Mr. Longford think of Mr. Morag?' said Nora, speaking to Plum before Lizzy had run out of curses.

'God have mercy!' Plum exclaimed loudly and grinned. 'It's an odd life I'm in for.' She edged her way through the crush toward the kettle. 'Like a bag full of cats and myself in between.'

Jane looked around nervously.

'Like my William,' she said.

'You mean Joseph,' said Willa, entering the conversation for the first time. 'Only it's all of us in the bag with him.' Willa sighed.

She was a tall, handsome woman of about fifty. Her short black hair was obviously dyed but that was the way she remembered herself, a woman whose white skin had begun to pucker under the eyes, that instead of the dazzling beauty a dozen years younger whom Wykeham had transported to seaside hotels on holidays. If she thought about it at all, she would have said that now she was simply more comfortable. But it was clear enough, Willa thought without wavering, what Joseph saw in the girl.

'You're the very image of myself,' she told Jane. 'Although I don't suppose it was only that he saw in you.' Her tone was hushed. It troubled Jane more than if she had blubbered.

Jane said reproachfully:

'He can have who he wants.'

'Lord knows,' Willa said softly. 'But, if we are any measure, child, what he wants is always the same.'

Several new women had come in from the hall.

Jane looked around at them, staring. 'He will marry me,' she announced.

In the chair by the stove the very pregnant young woman started screaming.

He was on the stairs when His Grace noticed Nora. Strands of her long yellow hair, shaken loose by exertion, stuck to her neck. She was hurrying. In her arms were towels and blankets, which she was carrying up to the third story, to Wykeham's room. There were plenty of bedrooms but in most the men lingered. Wykeham, however, had quit his room just as the house began bustling. His bed, Nora had told them, was the biggest, and when it had become available, with three or four to help, they had brought the young woman and laid her down in it.

Nora moved toward the railing to let His Grace pass.

He held out a hand to stop her. 'Have I seen you?' he asked, watching her curiously.

'Forgive me,' she said. 'There is a young woman.'

His hand had not left her elbow.

Nora's eyes darted to the top of the landing. 'You were on the porch,' she said quickly, 'when we came. You were standing with William.'

He nodded but it was not what he meant. His eyes took in the curve of her neck, the flamboyant blush that began at her throat. Surprised by her vehemence, he smiled.

'Sir, I must,' she said firmly.

He watched her expression change from impatience to anger.

'Go on, then,' he said.

But at the top of the stairs she looked back.

'There is a doctor,' she called to him. 'Please, if you could find him –'

In the middle of the stairs Martin Callaghan turned.

Off the second floor landing were a half dozen rooms. In the first two, when he knocked, he found strangers. 'Holmes,' he cried at the third and, without pausing, walked in.

Holmes was sitting up in the bed. The woman was mostly dressed. She was putting on stockings. Looking His Grace over hastily, she grinned.

'You're up early, Your Grace,' said Holmes.

'It's habit. I'm sorry.'

Holmes began to search for his trousers.

'There's a patient,' His Grace told him.

By now the young woman was sitting down at the mirror, combing her hair. Just for a moment, when he had got his trousers onto both legs and half buttoned his shirt, Holmes's eyes shifted back to her.

'Which of us, do you think, is responsible?' he asked Callaghan.

His Grace did not see what was meant.

'I'll be quick, my girl,' Holmes said fondly, 'if I can.' He went into the hall.

'There were nine of us,' Holmes continued, trying to be perfectly clear. 'But which of us,' he asked very seriously, 'thought of her?'

The young woman weighed down the bed. Her mountainous belly, spread over the sheet, frightened Martin Callaghan unreasonably. He sat at the far end, in the corner, giving everyone room. He was not wanted but he had come in with the doctor. He had climbed the stairs after him, holding the railing. He had been compelled to go slowly so that Holmes, who was hurrying, had been forced to look back. His Grace waved him on.

There was a chair, thankfully. The Duke thrust his heavy shoulders against the wood. But it was not his eyes, he thought, but the snow falling that made the room dim. The wind, sweeping across the roofs, made whines and moans as real as the whispers of women. The woman he had met on the stairs was busily filling the lamp. He consoled himself by watching her back. Once she turned sideways to look at him and then swiftly, her pale blue eyes still angry, looked away.

'She seems very near,' Plum said flatly.

'She's in labor already,' Holmes said. But his eyes seemed uncertain. He guessed that the woman was trying to estimate the extent of his knowledge and so mustered an air of confidence.

'An hour, perhaps,' he said. But honesty got the best of him. 'Perhaps longer.'

The women were looking from one to another.

'I'll need a bowl of water,' Holmes said. 'To wash my hands. And a fire. Do you think we can get a fire? It's cold as death up here.' He finished buttoning his shirt. 'There were other rooms, I suppose,' he said. 'Something nearer the kitchen. So why in the first place –'

He broke off when he saw the young woman staring up at him.

Her eyes wide and amused, she lay very still, watching.

Nora, not realizing his confusion, answered simply.

'Because it's William's bed,' she said. 'So it's fitting. The baby will be William's certainly.'

Plum was squinting at her.

Nora laughed.

'By the looks of us,' Nora told her, 'there'll soon be a great many babies. But here's this one already, though the world's not a day old.' Nora ran her fingers into her dress.

'It's his,' she said carefully. 'Either something he wanted or, if he didn't, that came anyway.' She laughed again. 'It's the one thing he never could stop, things coming back to him.'

While Nora spoke, it seemed that Holmes scarcely breathed. The young woman in the bed was smiling at him. She was lying in the middle of the mattress, her large dark eyes attentive and critical, yet smiling as well.

'You needn't worry,' Carolyn told him.

His hands moved quickly, bringing the lamp nearer, holding it up next to her, to be certain she had spoken.

'You don't have to think about it,' she repeated. 'Needn't concern yourself.' She settled back on the pillows. 'It's already done. I have seen him.'

He waited for her to continue.

Carolyn smiled at his slowness. 'Out there,' she said.

She tried to turn but some heaviness restrained her. She must have them move the bed, she thought, so she might look with no need of turning and could watch and study him when he came again to the window. It was such a relief to see how tall and strong he had already become. He must be very strong indeed to climb so high, with great hands to hold onto the roof and large shoulders to ward off the wind. But he would be hungry, she knew, his hard, clever mouth seeking her. Feverishly, thinking of his hunger, she drew her hands up under her breasts, pushing them, as his huge dark face would push, to start the flow of milk. He would be hungry and lonely and cold. Such a cold morning to come into the world, she thought. Once more she attempted to look at the window.

'Do you see him?' she asked.

Holmes could see the sharp points of her breasts just under the sheet, see them lift and fall with the fierce, failing struggle of breath.

Nora bent down beside her. In the lamp's glare, watching both faces, Martin Callaghan found himself filled, first with irritation and then with what he recognized was jealousy. 'My God,' he said suddenly, realizing they were the same women he had seen on the platform following William out to the train.

'What is she saying?' Plum asked.

Holmes shook his head. Not even hearing, he reached forward, touching the vein of the neck.

Though he was tired and sick at heart, the Duke stood. He went to the bed and, prying the lamp from Holmes's fingers, carried it to the window ledge. Just for an instant, looking out, he saw the deep drifted snow on the roof. The shoeless prints came up to the window and stopped. He turned his back on them, not knowing yet what they meant. But of one thing he was certain.

'He has one more death,' he said grimly.

Nora glared at him. She could feel her whole body shake with rage against him, against all men who, finding a death, admitted no more than a single loss, one cruel absence, when it was worlds that went.

'The child,' she said desperately. 'And the child that might have come from that child and from that.'

She was looking hard at him, seeing the dark molding of his flesh against the vague, snow-filled window. Her face was scarlet. For one awful moment each understood that she had meant herself.

'Hush now,' he said softly; then quietly, as a father might take a child and yet not that exactly, though it was no less kind, he extended his arms and drew her to himself.

Wykeham sat without moving, the ragged cloak draped over his shoulders. The chairs, as the men had left them, were turned about in disorder. The women scratched at the door but he sent them away. Jane had come, incautiously, calling him. But when he did not answer, she had slipped away again to the kitchen.

His Grace listened to her footsteps retreating. 'Which one is she?' he asked bitterly.

Wykeham did not try to look up. 'From the school,' he said.

'As before?'

'Yes.'

'It was a girl's voice.'

Wykeham turned his eyes on him. They were young man's eyes and it hurt His Grace to look at them. Wykeham rested his hands on the table.

'We tried to walk to New Awanux once,' he said. 'I don't suppose I wrote you that? One evening I drove to the school. It was late and I stood under her window in darkness, throwing stones at the glass. When she came down, she was yawning and only half in her dress. It was too far, of course.' He looked down at his hands, thoughtfully, as though measuring himself against an obstacle. 'We only made Bristol.' He paused. 'Before it was light, I found a cab to take her back.' He stopped once more. 'I do not think, Martin, there was a time when I was happier.'

His Grace waited until he was certain Wykeham was finished.

'It was a risk,' the Duke said.

Wykeham shifted; his face did not change.

'There were always risks. But none to myself. You must remember that. There was never a moment when I could not as simply have walked away. One more Wykeham vanished. Lost overboard, presumed drowned. Even now I could go out that door and in an hour I would be on a train. There are ships in New Awanux. I made certain I remembered ships. One would be waiting.'

The words slowly took hold. 'This house?' His Grace said.

Wykeham almost smiled. 'I have told you.'

'This room?' His Grace persisted. He looked around uneasily beginning to understand all that had been done. 'Chairs?'

'Even chairs.'

His Grace shuddered. 'And in your bed?' There were tears in his voice suddenly.

'No!' Wykeham shouted. 'No, I never –'

Just at that moment Longford burst through the doors. He tore the cap from his head, flinging cold drops from it. He stomped his boots on the carpet. Morag came after him, pawing his nose with his wool-gloved hands. But the stench clung to him, was mired in his clothes and his skin. Even the tramp through the fields, stumbling against the storm's icy fury, had not rid him of it.

'Burned,' Longford said.

Morag closed the doors tightly. He did not want the women to come in.

'It is the one thing that was not supposed to happen,' he said. 'It was painted. I had seen to it.' He looked briefly at His Grace, who was glaring uncomprehendingly.

'Greenchurch,' Morag whispered, his face wretched. 'Green as oaks, as a hedge. Not an English church.' His old desperate eyes fixed on Wykeham.

Wykeham turned to the window, watching the storm.

'But white,' he said softly, 'when snow covered it.'

Martin Callaghan moaned. He threw himself into a chair. 'One of us had to think of that,' he said, grumbling.

Suddenly they were all very still.

Wykeham studied them. 'You will each deny it. I deny it myself.'

For a while longer no one spoke.

'All the same it wouldn't matter,' he went on, 'if that were everything. If it stopped. But it won't.' He was still watching them, his eyes settling on each face for a moment, considering. 'How many are missing?' he asked.

'Five,' Morag said at once.

Wykeham rose from his chair. 'Then we had better find them,' he said.

•

George Tennison came from the cellar, from making both coffins. His fingers were stiff from the cold and he was covered with sawdust. Fearful of a new catastrophe, he edged back the doors. Holmes, who had just come himself, pulled a chair to the table. 'Where is Harwood?' he asked, glancing swiftly about the room. In fact, Harwood was sitting alone by the window, keeping watch on the hill. His face was unshaven and his head hung morosely to one side. In front of him the heavy wind washed streaks of ice across the panes.

Snow was everywhere. One of the great elms had toppled under the weight. It lay sprawled across the yard, its limbs fattened and nested until the shape was nearly unrecognizable.

Harwood stared, spellbound.

He had not heard the tree fall but it had fallen, he was certain, sometime during the night. The snow, he imagined, had muffled the sound. Still, he should have felt something. A tree crashing. A young woman dead. Each hour of the night he had lain awake, listening to the woman beside him, the child at the end of the bed. Outside the endless snow was filling the darkness. The world was being purified, was being remade. He had only felt cold.

He still was. He was shivering when, tilting his head, he caught sight of the sleigh. It was only a speck at the bottom of the hill. But the speck grew and, when it made the next turn, there were four horses galloping into the yard, sending up waves of white snow. For a terrible moment Harwood had the impression that the horses were coming onto the porch. Then he had a glimpse of red hair. A flurry of arms, jacketless, immune to the cold, jerked at the reins. When the snow settled, it was Hunt who climbed down. He handed the reins to the stableboy. Fred Norfolk followed after him. It was not more than a minute later they were both in the house.

'Greenchurch is burned,' Morag told them.

'An Indian,' Longford said.

'Though I had it painted,' Morag added.

'But we never thought of the snow,' Longford said bleakly.

Hunt moved across the room, passing slowly among the chairs. They watched his heavy shoulders and thick arms from which the snow had already melted, and thought how little it must interest him whether there were fires or blizzards or the earth itself opened. His dark quiet eyes looked around the circle of faces.

'And one of us must have thought of it?' he asked dryly, not bothering to look at one any more than another, not caring.

'Someone had to,' Martin Callaghan said.

'And you will find him?'

The Duke nodded.

'And when he is found?'

The Duke stopped. He had been answering, not thinking where the answers led.

'There are women here,' he said angrily. 'A world just beginning.' He turned abruptly, staring at Wykeham. 'Lives' – he began.

'Against one life?' Hunt asked. 'Where is the worth in that? What is saved in the end? You all die.'

His Grace stood mute.

Quite unexpectedly he found himself remembering the young woman he had held in his arms. It was unreasonable. He had held her only a moment. How odd and old-fashioned he must have seemed to her, patting her shoulders, running his stiff, old hands along the side of her neck. Yet, although he admitted as much, he couldn't bring himself to feel ashamed.

'It matters,' he said. 'Although I never thought to stop its coming, it matters when.'

'No longer,' Hunt said.

The Duke had raised his head, to debate with him, when the house shook.

Suddenly George Harwood, who had been staring without point or purpose, began to scream.

For a moment there was no other sound, only his high, choking sobs and the creaking floorboards as the men rushed to the window. Then the house shook again. The flames in the hearth shuddered and in a dozen rooms the pictures of horses and cities fell from the walls.

The men stood before the glass.

On the windward side of the hill, where the whirling snow poured into the cuts and breaks between the trees, the nine advanced. Their shapes were tall and black against the frozen wood. Their ancient faces, carved and pitted in the rock, were sad and still. But when they moved, the earth groaned under them. And they went on moving, their heavy footfalls, slow, unturning, across the cold white lawn.

Harwood braced himself against the chair.

'What do we do?' he asked.

'Ah, Jesus,' Longford moaned. 'Jesus.' He had closed his eyes.

But Wykeham bore the sight a few seconds more. It was the end, he knew. The world would be broken now, its last foundations pulled apart and scattered. He had imagined such a day as this. But it had always been far off. There seemed so little cause for it to happen. And yet it was not without justice. He had lived years beyond counting and his wrongs were many. He felt their weight, each like a stone, upon him. But the worst were these: he had abused love and he had murdered. But he thought: 'Those I have left were dying and I could not die. And by taking life there were lives I kept.' Still, he had found no peace.

He would have died once long ago, died well or badly, but died in fact had not Duinn, without cause or reason, spared him. He did not wonder now where Duinn was. He was near. At the end, when the hills were gone and the sky rolled up, he would step out on the empty shore. Would he pity then the dead he made? When the last were not even memories, when there were no more lives to grieve and dream, would the silence, empty of windstorms and faces, set him making worlds again?

In his mind Wykeham tried to imagine other worlds. It was then he smiled. Himself, he had made them. There was a meadow running down to the bluffs above Ohonowauke which was his indisputably. There was a line of workmen's cottages, slant-roofed and always falling down, worn by the use of men whom, one generation to the next, he had set to scratch and toil on the land. And the house itself, with its hallways and kitchens, its rooms of horsehair beds and wooden chairs, its black scalding stoves and cool cupboards of white china. Each he had set and ordered. And in their places, deliberately, the pattern clear before its start, men and women, ministers and a minister's wife, the honorable Callaghan, Norfolk and Lizzy, Harwood with his silent wife and sullen child, his all too visible sorrow and his attacks of melancholia, Willa and Jane, both Tennisons, and Hunt who from the first of worlds had followed him. One by one he drew them forth to look at them and smiled, contented. They were his and, although at any moment he might have changed his mind, he did not wish them other than they were. Their lives still filled him. Why then did everything end in death?

He had grasped his cloak, his long, blunt fingers worrying the cloth. It was no longer Duinn he thought of but Jane. 'Who has done this?' he thought, his mind wrestling with the fabric of all he had made, seeking the flaw in it that it might be mended or, willingly, if every weave proved false, to tear it whole, to cast to the last and final darkness all that by the force of his will, his love and longing he had shaped and fashioned, if only she were saved.

What thread was lost? What one thing unremembered?

His mind flew back to Harwood's study, to the train. He thought of the tree, its endless branches spreading high and wide across the earth, and of the rout of withered leaves that blew through Black Wood. He remembered the hill at the edge of Bristol; and Jane, her figure dark against the windows of the hall, walking briskly, not paying the least attention, even at the last instant when she stopped: 'Sorry, I was watching –'

He looked up, to see the massive shoulders of the stone. For a moment he was unnaturally conscious of the sound of the wind.

'It should have been an old Ford truck,' George Tennison said. Scowling, rubbing his trembling hands on the glass, he peered down at the sleigh and the horses. 'There has been a mistake,' he said.

No one was listening.

'I see him!' someone cried. The others, staring, could not be certain whether it was one more shadow or a man that moved below them.

It was His Grace who realized that it was Houseman. The face was changed, the gaze colder and more insolent. The jaw, which was left open, seemed incapable of laughter or crying or any other human attitude save hate and fear. But even dead, the Duke knew him. He looked more real than ever he had in life. His voice cried out more desperately, remembering all he had lost, the bitter darkness he had been given in its place. He unfolded his wings. He lifted up his huge square hands, the torches in them red with flame.

But it was Harwood who saw the woman, not dressed for cold weather, running from the house. Her bright yellow hair streamed from her head. She was running very fast. Caught by surprise, he wondered, as he had once before, not who she was but where she was going.

The wind howled. But Nora had no time for that. Too many things had happened all at once. Even as she ran she watched the vast cold shapes, their solemn figures moving roughly into the yard. She had seen them in the wood and knew there must be nine; and, although they had not begun in her memory, she had called them forth. What need he had of them she did not know. Perhaps, if she abandoned them, they would pass from his mind as well. Surely they were the ghosts of something that had happened long ago. Yet it had seemed a sort of unfaithfulness to let them fade. Well, he had seen them now and he could make of them what he wished. For herself, she could not think of what to do with them.

For one brief moment she had considered Indians. Might they not sweep down from the valley's rim, an ancient host, reclaiming with fire and thunder the world they too had lost? But the rock was here before they came and death, she knew, could never take again what already it had stripped and robbed. Still, it had its use.

She had made his bed a place of death. Once, without watching, at least without knowing that she watched, she had seen the other woman at the train. Alone in his bed, wondering how many women had loved him, how many he had loved, it was this face, not the dark-haired child's, that stirred her memory. In the darkness of that bed, in the gulf between what is and what may never be, she called to her. And the woman came.

She was not surprised when death came after. It was fate, Nora thought, still recklessly, still not certain it was so. Yet it pleased her to see the ease with which she had repositioned all their lives.

She was well across the yard, nearly under the ragged elms, when, for a moment, she found herself wondering about His Grace. His arms, she remembered, had been warm and gentle about her waist. His dark eyes, looking down, had filled her with anxious tenderness. She knew she was frightened by those eyes and with her fear there came a desperate urgency, a sense of the quickly passing years. She ran.

In the torchlight even the stones' huge shadows glittered red. The snow was red about his feet.

'You keep out of this!' Houseman cried.

But she never could. She only hoped she had not forgotten anything.

It was only a little distance from the porch to the patch of broken ground where Nora stood by herself, watching Martin Callaghan opening the door. He blinked, trying to adjust to the cold and the wind. She was amazed how frail he looked. He came down the porch steps slowly, casting glances back at the house and then toward the wood. She saw his face darken as he noticed the man and the girl. They had stopped just short of the trees. Wykeham had been leading a horse by its bridle. Now they were both standing still, looking back at the house. Then carefully, showing her the stirrup, he lifted the girl onto the stallion's wide back. When he had climbed up beside her, he gave a flick to the reins.

The Duke never saw the stableboy. It was Nora who watched him standing alone in the open door of the barn, quietly folding the rag of a cloak.

Nora made no move at all.

The Duke stopped.

'I don't understand,' he said resentfully, realizing suddenly he knew a great deal more than he thought.

The snow was still falling. Without answering, she took hold of his arm. He limped a little as they walked together toward the house. She saw the pain in his face and knew that he was dying. Not all at once, but by inches, as men always died. Still, there will be a few years more, she thought. Time enough, when the world was her own.

At the top of the hill, because the trees were bare, she caught sight of the river. The hill was not of sufficient height to see the whole pattern but the river's jagged line, black against the snow-mired banks, described, she was certain, a nearly perfect figure.

'N' for Nora, she thought, smiling, remembering as well the little curving lake in Black Wood. 'C' for Callaghan, she thought and went on smiling. From a distance both figures would appear to join, a piece of common mischief, shining out against the coming darkness, as if someone on the dwindling continent had left a message for a god.

EGRESS

Bridgeport – Ridgefield
March 1982 – September 1984

NAMES

Like burrs old names get stuck to each other and to anyone who walks among them. I have not tried to change that. Nine tenths of the names I used I borrowed. But then, the old names never lived one life and died. Remembered and reborn, they have entered other tales. While it is impossible to explain quickly matters that were a thousand years in the telling, in each name some vital part has kept its life. Their strength is their own. But because some readers may have forgotten them and because now and then I have gone my own way, I have listed a few which may require identification.

Agravaine	an early name of Finn
Anu	the Great Mother, goddess of fertility and fire
Ar Elon	the last of the seal-lords, High King of the land between the seas
Badb	the crow of Anu who stole Finn's eye
Cerridwen	the hag of Tywy, mistress of the quern of time
Dagda	the High King of the gods
Duinn	Death's Lord, lord of the sea and the darkness
Eachanhagen	a captain of the sealmen
Finn	Ar Elon's heir, the son of Yllvere
Fir Dhearga	an early name of Mug Dafad
Géar	Finn's twin sister, daughter of Yllvere and Ar Elon, the mother of Llugh
Géar Finn	the two-horned mountain above Morrigan
Glas Awyddn	Lord of Tir na Trí Oileán, given armor by Géar
Grieve	Finn's youngest sister, the daughter of Yllvere and Urien
Gwen Gildrun	the god-tree, sometimes found in Anu's wood and sometimes not
Hren	the island where Finn murdered Ar Elon, the gateway to the Other World

Hwawl	a village along the river Undain
Kell	the race of witch women who once mated with the sealmen
Llugh	the Shining One, the son of Finn and Géar
Morrigan	the house where Finn grew to manhood
Mug Dafad	the 'Servant of Sheep'
Mughain	title of the queen of Tywy
Njal	Finn's youngest son
Ormkill	the great hall that Ar Elon built on the hills above the river Undain
Penandrun	the nine lords of undersea
Redd Man	he is named elsewhere
Ryth	one of Finn's sisters, daughter of Yllvere and Urien
Sanngion	one of Finn's sisters, daughter of Yllvere and Urien
Tabak ap Ewyn	one of the many names of Ar Elon
Tech Duinn	the House of Duinn
Thigg	Ar Elon's steward who ruled in his place at Ormkill
Tir fo Thuinn	the 'Land under the Waves'
Tywy	the women's holding on the coast across from Hren
Unn	Finn's queen
Urien	Yllvere's old husband, Finn's foster father
Vydd	Yllvere's older sister, Finn's aunt
Wyck	Glas Awyddn's dog boy
Yllvere	the mother of Finn

A STAR IS BORN . . . AND A DREAM IS FULFILLED

DEBORAH FOWLER

Propelled into the spotlights when the leading lady fell ill, Anna Wetherby soon learned that there was a price to pay for her new-found fame.

It wasn't just that her co-star in *Sometime . . . Never*, one of the greatest actors of his generation, turned out to be a cynical, self-pitying drunk. There were all kinds of problems . . .

The audiences who flocked to the West End to see this rising young star could scarcely have guessed at the gossiping intrigue backstage. Because there were suggestions that Anna was ruthlessly exploiting the situation to further her own career, particularly when a handsome Broadway producer appeared on the scene with a lucrative contract in his hand . . .

0 7221 3699 4   CONTEMPORARY ROMANCE   £2.50

The classic Amber series continues

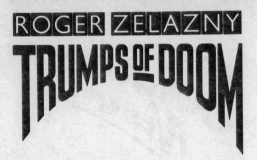

ROGER ZELAZNY
TRUMPS OF DOOM

RETURN TO AMBER – The irresistible powers of the kingdom beyond imagination draw Merlin, son of Corwin, back to the magical realm . . .

Merlin is content to bide the time when he will activate his superhuman strength and genius and claim his birthright.

But that time arrives all too soon when the terrible forces of evil drive him mercilessly from Earth, and upon reaching Amber, he finds the domain in awesome, bloody contention.

And in every strange darkness of his fantastic crusade, there stalks a figure determined to destroy Merlin and wipe out the wondrous world of Amber . . .

SCIENCE FICTION   0 7221 9410 2   £2.50

Also by Roger Zelazny in Sphere Science Fiction:

DAMNATION ALLEY
MY NAME IS LEGION
EYE OF CAT

In the Amber series
NINE PRINCES IN AMBER
THE COURTS OF CHAOS
SIGN OF THE UNICORN
THE GUNS OF AVALON
THE HAND OF OBERON